# HARD STUFF: A COLLECTION

---

## HARD CODE, HARD WARE, & HARD BYTE

### MISHA BELL

♠ MOZAIKA PUBLICATIONS ♠

Published by Mozaika Publications, an imprint of Mozaika LLC.
www.mozaikallc.com

Cover by Najla Qamber Designs
www.najlaqamberdesigns.com

ISBN: 978-1-63142-726-8
Print ISBN: 978-1-63142-727-5

# HARD CODE

ONE

"YOU HIRED a hooker to test a bunch of sex toys?"

"Use your inside voice!" I hiss at Ava, my face burning as I scan the other Starbucks patrons waiting in line with us. Most have headphones plugged into their ears and are lost inside their phones, but still. What if someone overhears?

She grins mischievously and lowers her voice to the closest thing to a whisper she's capable of. "Only if you spill all the gory details."

"Fine. First and foremost, Dominika is *not* a hooker. She's a showgirl."

"Wait." Ava's amber eyes glint impishly. "Is this the 'showgirl' from the strip club Voldemort dragged you to in Prague? The one who violated the nuns on stage?"

"She was playing the role of a succubus. They weren't real nuns."

Her reminder of He Who Must Not Be Named—a.k.a. my ex— only increases my discomfort. I went to that club to prove to Bob that I wasn't a prude, but he broke up with me anyway.

Ava knows me well, which is why she launches into something guaranteed to distract me. Raising her voice an octave, she says, "I'm surprised the Rockettes aren't putting on a show like that for Christ-

3

mas. One of them could penetrate a faux nun with a strap-on, another with a fist—"

"Hush!" My cheeks are hot enough to make an omelet on them. "I needed someone with experience using sex toys, so I hired her, okay?"

"Uh-huh." Ava steps forward as the line moves. "For your new QA project."

I cast another furtive glance around us. "Like I said, I'm testing an app for a teledildonics company."

"Teledildonics," she repeats, savoring the word. "The prefix *tele* refers to long distance; the suffix *onics* means pertaining to, and the root is *dildo*... as in the thing I've been convincing you to try." Her voice grows louder. "Are we talking about long-distance dildos?"

As I cringe, I make a mental vow: I will get her back for this. She will rue this day.

"Precisely." I'm proud of how even my voice is. "The app I'll be testing lets one user control a device being utilized by another user over the internet."

"Sure. Sure." She makes her face look serious. "To put that in layman's terms: a dildo will go into Dominika in Prague, and you will make her come with the app from New York."

At this point, it's not just my treacherous cheeks that are red—my ears are too. "It's called end-to-end testing. It needs to be as close to the way the product is going to be used in the real world as possible."

"Or rear-end testing." She waggles her eyebrows suggestively. When I pointedly turn my back to her, she laughs and says, "Isn't that basically having sex with Dominika? After paying her? How is she not a hooker then?"

The reality is actually worse. Dominika and *her boyfriend* will be participating in the testing, but I'm not telling Ava this now. Or maybe ever. "Fine. She's not just a showgirl. Happy now?"

"Hey." She finally lowers her voice. "I have nothing against the world's oldest profession. If I hadn't already wasted years on medical school, and if all the johns were hot and STDs didn't exist, I'd sign up. At least if it paid well and I wasn't dating anyone. Especially if I was as orgasm-deprived as you. Come to think of it—"

Thankfully, it's our turn to order now. She gets enough caffeine to send a rhino bouncing off the walls, and I request my venti chamomile tea in the hopes of calming down before the meeting I've been dreading.

We step aside to wait for our drinks, and Ava grins like the Grinch. "So, back to teledildonics."

Before I can shush her again, *he* comes in.

I forget what I was about to say. I forget to *breathe.*

Carved features that remind me equally of Greek gods and angels, eyes the deep blue hue of a lapis lazuli stone, framed by stylish horn-rimmed glasses. Lips that beg to be kissed. Shaggy jet-black hair, with a stray strand that falls in the middle of his face and just begs me to walk over and brush it back—which I'd have to reach high to do because he's at least a foot taller than me. Despite the warm weather, he's dressed in a black trench coat with a black shirt underneath, an outfit that accentuates the powerful breadth of his shoulders and—

"Earth to Fanny." Ava's voice intrudes into my oxytocin-addled brain.

I spin around before she realizes I was checking out Hottie McDark. Knowing her, she'd push me at him, or nag me into starting a conversation, or do a million other things that would embarrass me straight into a panic attack.

Someone like me and a guy that hot do not mix.

Before she can resume pestering me about teledildonics within possible earshot of Hottie McDark, I preemptively jam my hand into my pocket and pull out one of my most treasured possessions—my phone, a.k.a. Precious. "You have to see the app I created," I tell Ava and steal a glance behind me.

Did Hottie McDark's eyebrows lift at the mention of an app?

Nah. Nor, despite appearances, is he looking at me right now. He's probably studying the menu board directly behind me.

"Okay..." Ava sounds as enthusiastic as I do when she shares a horribly gross story about her residency in the ER. "It lets you cartoon yourself, right?"

"Nope." I bring up the app and stare proudly at the crisp user interface that I toiled over for months. "It tells you which cartoon character you most resemble."

"Potato potahto. But I'll bite. Who do *I* look like?"

Feeling a little naughty, I position her just right and snap an image with the app. Except I aim the camera at Hottie McDark instead of Ava—and the app promptly brings up a cartoon character: Clark Kent from *Superman,* the animated series.

I can see that. That strand of hair, the glasses, and the chiseled features do match. The evil genius of this move is that the app also stores the original photo, so I could, should I wish, backward search from the image to, say, his social media profile.

Assuming I wanted to become a stalker, that is.

Before Ava catches on, I aim the camera at her and snap another pic.

"You're Belle." I show her the doe-eyed, brown-haired image on the phone. "From *Beauty and the Beast.*"

"Tale as old as time," she singsongs. "I guess that's a compliment. Can I do you?"

"Be our guest." I thrust the phone into her hands, mostly because I want to see if she can figure out how to use the app without my help.

To my great relief, she figures it out on the fly. This isn't as good as a grandmother test, but close. I had to teach Ava how to program her universal remote control.

When the app gives her the result, she chuckles. "Snow White. Is it always a Disney Princess?"

"Not always."

"I bet it's your easy-to-blush pale cheeks." She examines me closely. "Or the round face."

I sneak another peek at Hottie McDark. "I'm just glad it's not one of the seven dwarves."

"Oh yeah, put a beard on you, and you'd be a dead ringer for Bashful."

I cringe. Her voice is the loudest it's been yet; the guy would have to be deaf not to notice us at this point. "Please keep it down."

"Sorry." She hands me my phone back. "Are you going to make any money on this app?"

I glance at the time to make sure I'm not running late before I pocket Precious. "The app is free. I even made it opensource, so anyone can take and use my code however they wish."

"Is it for that promotion you want, then?"

I shrug. "Not a promotion, a lateral move. The app was to prove to myself that I have what it takes to be a developer. Now I just need to make the people at work believe in me too, or at least value me enough to give me a chance to switch departments."

In the corner of my eye, I see Hottie McDark placing his order, which means if we don't get our drinks soon, he'll be standing close enough for me to smell him.

Or touch.

Or—

"And this smart sex toys project will help?" Ava asks, again speaking too loudly for my comfort.

"Our company owner himself wrote the app. That makes the testing as high profile as it gets." I strain to hear what the guy is ordering but only make out the word *tea*—and it's nice to know there's another sucker out there willing to pay a huge premium for a bag of dried leaves.

"And said owner is the infamous Vlad the Impaler, right?" She says the name with relish.

"That's what the rumor mill at the office calls him. I'm sure he's Mr. Vladimir Chortsky to his face."

"Or Master," she says in her best Renfield voice. "And you're meeting him today? Shouldn't there be garlic around your neck, or a cross inside your panties?"

I chuckle nervously. "They do say he never sleeps. Or at least he answers emails at any time, day or night."

Ava makes a swoony face. "Does he glitter?"

"I'll find out today." Hottie McDark is now walking our way, so it takes everything I have to keep my cool. "I checked out his code for this app, and it was very elegant and inventive—appropriate for a centuries-old creature of the night. My boss, Sandra, also told me that when he writes something, he doesn't work with the development team, yet the resulting apps never have any bugs—"

"How not thrilling." Ava exaggeratingly yawns. "What I want to know is: Has he impaled any female employees?"

Sensual notes of tangerine and bergamot waft into my nostrils.

Someone's tea or Hottie McDark's cologne? He's now right next to me, so close that I don't dare look at him lest I melt into a puddle. My heart hammers unevenly, and I can feel a new wave of hot color washing into my cheeks.

"Fanny. Ava." The barista slams our drinks on the counter.

Perfect. Before Ava can further embarrass me in front of Hottie McDark, I snatch my drink, thrust hers into her hand, and drag her out of the Starbucks by her elbow.

"I have to go to work," I say when we get outside. Right away, the deafening honking of taxis fills my ears. We're across the street from Battery Park, with the Statue of Liberty visible in the distance.

Ava pecks me on the cheek. "Good luck. And if the Impaler turns you into a vampire, you must do the same to me as soon as you can. I can steal us blood bags from the hospital."

I sneak a final longing glance at Hottie McDark through the

tinted glass. "You better be on your best behavior, or I'll just make you my blood whore instead."

She laughs as she walks away, and I sprint to the nearby skyscraper and ride the elevator to my company's floor.

Exiting, I survey my surroundings. *Binary Birch*, the plaque on the wall states in a very serious-looking font. The cold utilitarian nature of the modern décor hasn't changed since I was here for my in-person interviews a few months back. No game rooms or sleeping nooks like they might have at other, hipper software companies—not with the Impaler at the helm.

The people around me are mostly strangers. The company policy is that everyone has the option of working remotely if they wish, so I've been working from home and communicating with the office via email, instant messenger, and occasionally, a teleconferencing app.

I pull out Precious and check the time. Ten minutes until I have to brave the Impaler's office.

Sipping my tea, I jump on the Wi-Fi and check my messages.

Sandra, the QA manager and my direct boss, wants to see me if I have the time.

I head into the maze of cubicles. Since she's one of the few people I know by sight, I locate her quickly and knock on the glass wall of her cube.

"Hi, Sandra," I say when she tears her gaze from her screen.

"Oh, hey, Fanny. There you are." With a prim smile, she stands up and leads us to a small meeting room.

"So," she says, not meeting my gaze as we sit down across from each other. "I just wanted to double check... You're okay with the eccentric testing project you're about to undertake, right?"

"I am," I state as confidently as I can fake it.

I know why she keeps asking. The last thing the company wants is for me to file a sexual harassment suit over this, or for me to say that I'm not cool with it when I speak to the Impaler, thus making her, my manager, look like an idiot.

"I'm glad," she says, and we quickly go over the project I've just finished testing, an app that works with a wristband fitness tracker.

She smiles when I tell her that I even lost a few pounds thanks to all the walking to test the pedometer functionality.

Then it's time for the meeting I've been dreading, and Sandra leads me to the only non-glass-walled office on the floor.

According to some jokes, the Impaler doesn't like the light, and according to others, he needs the privacy to make his kills in peace.

"Want me to take that?" Sandra asks, worriedly eyeing my almost empty cup.

"No drinks allowed in there?" I ask.

She darts a nervous glance at the door. "I better take it."

As I hand her the cup, my previously steady hand begins to tremble.

How scary can our glorious leader be?

"Keep me in the loop." Sandra opens the door for me.

Feeling like a lamb going to the proverbial slaughter, I shuffle into the Impaler's lair—and before I can catch sight of the man himself, my manager helpfully closes the door behind me, like a vampire's minion springing a trap.

Soft music is vibrating the airwaves in here. *In the Hall of the Mountain King* by Edvard Grieg—a fitting melody to get exsanguinated to.

I catch a whiff of tangerine and bergamot, and my stomach drops.

Can't be.

I turn around.

Illuminated by the bluish light of a large monitor is the gorgeous face of the stranger I was just drooling over at Starbucks.

Even his tea is here, on his spotlessly clean desk.

"Hello, Ms. Pack," Vlad the Impaler says with a slight Transylvanian accent. "Good to finally meet you."

# TWO

THE ACCENT IS ACTUALLY RUSSIAN—EVERYONE knows that much about our reclusive CEO. And his place of birth might be why he addressed me so formally; I've read that in Russia, they often use the plural *you* and patronymics, both as a sign of respect and to separate close friends from strangers.

Ms. Pack is a decent English equivalent, except that it makes me sound like Ms. Pac-Man: round and starving for doughnut holes. And sidebar—shouldn't that game have been called Pac-Woman, or Ms. Pac? Actually, thank god it wasn't Ms. Pac; that's too close to home and I was teased enough being Fanny Pack as it is.

Then blood leaves my face.

He could've overheard me and Ava. What was the last—

I realize he's suddenly looming over me, hand outstretched, like Nosferatu.

Must've used his preternatural vampire speed to leap out from behind his desk and dash toward me before my brain could process it.

Crap. How long have I been standing here, ignoring that hand? And how the hell did this happen? How is Vlad the Impaler Hottie

McDark? All the rumors about this man skipped a critical detail: how mouthwateringly attractive he is.

"Are you okay?" the Impaler asks, his accent thickening.

Ugh, now I'm ogling him. And still ignoring that hand. Gathering my courage, I stick out my arm and clasp his much, much bigger palm.

Holy estrogen.

My heart rate spikes, and a jolt of orgasmic energy spreads through my body, electrocuting a nest of angry butterflies in my stomach before settling somewhere low in my core.

How many hours is it socially appropriate to hold a hand like this?

Reluctantly, I peel my fingers away from his.

He looks down at me, his expression completely unreadable. He's either an amazing poker player or this handshake didn't affect him at all.

"Take a seat." He gestures at the chair in front of his desk, and by the time I plop into it, he's already in his. It's Embody by Herman Miller, the very chair I have at home, only mine is blue while his is black.

He lowers the music volume with a small remote. "You have a great reputation at Binary Birch, Ms. Pack."

I do? That's news. Even if that were true, how would he know that?

I don't dare ask as that might be as suicidal as reciprocating by telling him his reputation *isn't* so stellar.

"Thank you," I stammer before the silence veers into uncomfortable territory. "I love working here." And by *love*, I mean *tolerate*. But what's a little white lie between a monster and his prey?

He stares at me, and I feel like I might drown in the lapis depths of his eyes. "The project I'm trusting you with is extremely important."

I bob my head up and down so vigorously, I nearly give myself whiplash.

"The client—Belka—will get a chance to demonstrate the final product to the editors of *Cosmopolitan* magazine in two weeks." He peers at me as though to verify that I know what *Cosmo* is, so I blush and nod, just in case. "That is a huge opportunity." His dark eyebrows furrow minutely as he finishes with, "We can't let Belka down."

"Yes, sir." I give him a crisp military salute.

Wait, what? Why did I do that?

There's no hint of amusement on his face. He must be used to such gestures from back when he participated in Napoleonic wars and what-not.

He steeples his fingers. "I realize you must have the most thorough testing plan in mind."

Actually, I have the desire to suck on those long, masculine fingers in mind at the moment, but I keep that to myself.

"I hope you will let me enrich your plan with some extra test cases—which may already overlap with yours." He reaches into his desk and takes out a couple of stapled sheets of paper.

Only now do I realize that he's basically telling me how to do my job—which would be like me teaching him how to properly drink blood. Control freak much?

As I snatch the papers, our fingers brush for a second, sending another dozen joules of electricity into my lower regions.

Flushing, I glance at what I'm holding.

Hmm. Pink paper. A faint smell of perfume. Pretty cursive with hearts dotting the occasional "i." A woman must've put this together for him, and not Sandra, whose scent is more evocative of boiled cabbage. Besides, Sandra is obsessed with electronic communication, judging by all the constant "Save a Tree" propaganda in her email signature.

The pang of jealously I suddenly experience is as inappriate as it is insane.

To avoid dwelling on it, I skim the content of the paper—and as I do, I feel the flush spread to my ears and chest, turning them beet red.

There are items like "was orgasm achieved?" and "how many times?"

I have the former in my testing plan already, but not the latter—which, of course, isn't the source of my discombobulation.

It's just that reading the word *orgasm* in his presence feels wrong.

And dirty.

And somehow hot all at the same time.

I better get out of here with what passes for my remaining dignity.

"I will make sure to, um… utilize this"—I fan myself with the papers—"in my testing."

He reaches under the desk, yanks something out, and places it on the desk between us.

I gape at it.

Strictly speaking, it's a carry-on suitcase—but only in the same sense as a disco ball is a globe. It's covered in frilly polka dots and bejeweled with so many differently colored stones, you'd think a rainbow-farting unicorn had ejaculated on it.

As I look closer, I realize most of the designs are not polka dots but tiny multicolored penises and vaginas that someone painstakingly drew by hand.

At least I hope it was by hand.

My cheeks veer off the red end of the visible spectrum, radiating as much infrared as a welding torch.

Annoyingly, Vlad's face only shows the neutral professionalism he's been displaying throughout this whole encounter. Maybe he's one of Anne Rice's vampires—her older ones become as if made of stone over time.

"The hardware is inside," he says.

A hybrid between a hiccup and a giggle escapes my throat.

He just called a collection of dildos *hardware,* and probably not as a joke.

"Got it." I leap to my feet and reach for the suitcase just as he slides it forward.

Our fingers brush, generating enough of that electric jolt to power the toys for a week. I swallow and yank the suitcase off the desk.

It's heavy. There must be more than a few dildos, and who knows what else.

I hope Dominika's vagina can handle it all. Not to mention, shipping this "hardware" to the Czech Republic will cost a small fortune. I really hope no one at the DHL office asks me what's inside. For that matter, I pray no one here at the office asks me "What's with the suitcase?" as I sprint to the elevator.

"It was good to meet you," I tell Vlad and prepare to make the sprint.

"Will I see you at the monthly meeting in five minutes?" he asks.

I nearly drop my genital-inscribed luggage.

In theory, everyone is supposed to attend the monthly meeting. Its purpose is for us to have an idea of what the rest of Binary Birch is working on, find opportunities for synergy, and other corporate speak gobbledygook. In practice, since I've been working from home, I typically dial into this meeting on the phone, then promptly tune most of it out as I do my actual job of testing.

I do know one thing: the Impaler is famous for never joining this meeting in person either—and he doesn't have the work-from-home excuse. He just dials in and never says a word, though people claim to get emails about some things discussed at the meeting, hinting that he actually listens—which is why everyone is always on their best behavior during it.

Yet he said "see you," not "hear you," so tradition is about to be broken for some reason.

Of course, now I have to attend the meeting.

With this suitcase.

Shoot me now.

"Affirmative," I reply belatedly and fight another urge to salute. "See you soon."

Gracelessly, I spin around and head for the door, eager to escape the lair and its vampiric occupant.

His voice stops me as I'm reaching for the door handle. "By the way, Ms. Pack..." he says to my back, and for the first time, I detect a hint of emotion in his tone. "You should know something. I don't impale my employees."

# THREE

SUITCASE IN HAND, I shoot out of the Impaler's office to the bathroom as if the hounds of hell were on my heels. A single thought spins through my mind like a broken vinyl record.

He heard us at Starbucks.

At least the part about him impaling female employees.

What else did he hear?

How screwed am I?

"What the bejesus is that?" asks an attractive black-haired woman as I come out of my stall.

I dart an awkward glance at the suitcase I left by one of the sinks. "My niece's school bag."

I don't have a niece, but if I did, and this *were* her school bag, she'd need serious therapy.

The stranger looks at me like I'm some exotic cricket in a terrarium. "I'm Britney Archibald."

This day is getting worse and worse. Though I've never seen her in person or on video, we know each other—at least over instant messenger and email.

She's one of the five women working in the development department, and I recently tested some code she wrote.

Unfortunately, unlike the rest of her department, she's not a very good programmer—or at least, she's a careless one—because I found a plethora of bugs in her app, much more than usual. She turned out to have a paper-thin skin when it came to my findings, and her correspondence with me took an adversarial turn. I've tried to patch things up, especially since I'm angling to be in her department, but she's rebuffed my attempts to jump on a video call and clear the air.

The only reason I haven't escalated this to our managers is that I'm not a snitch. Plus, rumor has it that Britney is a much better hacker than she is a developer. Apparently, after she broke up with one guy in the sales department, she hacked into his social media accounts and made his profile images a photo of him during some sort of pony play.

Just my luck to bump into her, of all people, with the genitalia-decorated atrocity in my possession.

I call forth all of my professionalism and extend my hand. "I'm Fanny Pack."

She glares at my palm in disgust.

Oh, shit. I haven't washed my hands yet—and I doubt she'll accept "urine is sterile" as an excuse.

I also see her eyes narrow as she recalls why my name is familiar.

"Good to put a face to a name," I blurt, and grabbing the suitcase, I sprint for the door. Over my shoulder, I add, "See you at the monthly meeting."

I think she replies with something catty, but I don't catch what it is.

I rush to the pantry and wash my hands in the sink there. Then I down a glass of water and sneak into the large conference room where the monthly meeting is going to take place.

Great.

I'm the first one here.

I take the chair in the farthest corner and stash the suitcase under the table.

There. No one should see it now, and the comfort of my knees is a small price to pay.

As I wait for the rest of the employees to file in, I get Precious off the company's Wi-Fi and search the internet for information about the Impaler.

It's eerie how little I find.

He's obscenely rich—but I already knew that. He owns a successful software company—I work there, so duh.

There are no pictures of him online. Not on the Binary Birch website, nor in the newspapers, nor anywhere else I look. If I hadn't snapped his pic with my app, I would've been sure he's the type of vampire that doesn't reflect in mirrors or appear in photos.

He also doesn't have a social media profile of any kind, not even a professional one, like LinkedIn. My Starbucks idea to backward search him via that photo would've failed.

Of course, I don't need to do that now. I know who he is, and any sort of romance is out of the question. He's my boss's boss—or boss squared—not to mention a notorious workaholic who doesn't have time for anything else in his life.

Besides, I'm sure he wouldn't be interested in someone who works for him—as that would involve impaling that someone, and he said he doesn't do that to employees. And even if impaling were on the table, I'm sure he wouldn't want to do it to me.

I shouldn't even be thinking in this direction, not at such a pivotal moment in my career.

And yet, I create a Google alert for his name. This way, if something about him does show up online, I'll be the first to know.

A door slams, making my head jerk up.

As I stash Precious in my pocket, I realize the room is now packed —and the man I was just cyberstalking is standing at the head of the table, his rich blue eyes gleaming intensely behind his glasses.

I gulp.

Usually, one of the project managers chairs this meeting, but right now, their whole team is cowering in the corner.

At least the men. The women in this room appear to be spontaneously ovulating.

Britney is practically choking on her drool, and even Sandra—who must be at least thirty years his senior—is nearly as red as I am.

"For the last few months, I've been working on Project Belka," the Impaler says without so much as a "howdy y'all." "It's now in the testing stage." He glances at me for a heartbeat, and Britney's eyes turn my way, then narrow into slits.

I sink lower in my seat and do my best tortoise impersonation. For the love of C++, please don't tell them about the suitcase full of sex toys. Pretty please, with a gallon of the juiciest blood on top.

He doesn't.

Instead, he moves his gaze to where the accountants are sitting. "If the QA team files any expense reports tagged *Belka*, the paperwork is to be expedited. If you have *any* questions about the whys of the reports, direct those to me."

The expressions on the faces of the accounting team imply there will be no questions. Ever.

This is actually great. I really wanted to expense the exuberant shipping costs I'm about to accrue, but without his executive order, I wouldn't have bothered. The accounting team gave me a runaround when I ordered myself an ergonomic keyboard, and that's as work-related as any expense can get.

But how did he know? Is he a precognitive vampire, a la Alice in *Twilight?*

"This goes for everything else." His gaze sweeps the room, lingering on me for a second. "Project Belka is a priority."

Wow.

No pressure or anything.

Did Sandra just sneak a guilty glance at me? She *was* the one who assigned me to this project, but then again, given how important this thing is turning out to be, she'd kind of paid me the compliment of "let's throw the most likely to survive under that bus."

Britney raises her hand with the excitement of a grade-schooler who knows the answer to something for the first time in her life.

Ignoring her, the Impaler turns on his heel and strides out of the room.

"Do you need any help?" Britney shouts at his back. "I can code review if—"

The door slams behind him.

The room takes a collective relieved breath—everyone except Britney, that is. She looks like someone has just shaved her beloved pet tarantula.

The conference bridge phone beeps, notifying us that the Impaler has just rejoined the meeting as his usual ghostly presence.

One of the project managers takes over the meeting, but I can't follow what he or anyone says due to all the adrenaline coursing through my system.

This project is mega important.

I can't mess it up.

To soothe myself, I take out Precious.

Pretending like I'm glancing at an important memo, I bring up my app and use it on my coworkers.

Sandra's cartoon doppelgänger turns out to be Dory from *Finding Nemo*. Britney gets Maleficent—no surprise there. Someone in sales reminds the app of Sylvester J. Pussycat, a woman in accounting is Pepe Le Pew, while two guys from the development department match Beavis and Butt-Head.

Seeing most of my fellow employees like this makes me realize something: The ratio of women to men in the development department, and the company overall, is much higher than for the software industry at large. This is especially interesting in light of said ratio in the educational system. When I was taking computer science courses at Brooklyn College, I was often the only female in my class.

Is the Impaler behind this, or the HR department? If it's the Impaler, color me impressed—with his vampiric lifespan, he might've grown up when the glass ceiling was two inches above the floor.

Well, whoever's behind it, it's one less thing to worry about when it comes to moving to the dev department.

Speaking of which, I feel more determined to do that now than ever. In fact, I think I should make my request ASAP. At first, I was waiting for the completion of the Belka project, but thanks to this meeting, I've earned some visibility and there probably won't be a better time.

For the rest of the meeting, I play out different versions of my "move" pitch in my mind.

When it's over, I wait for everyone to leave before I deal with the suitcase again.

Sylvester J. Pussycat and Pepe Le Pew are among the last to leave, with Beavis and Butt-Head on their tails.

Only Sandra is left now, and she's clearly stayed back on purpose.

Whatever her reason, I decide to seize the moment before I chicken out. "Hi, Sandra. There's something important I wanted to talk to you about."

She pales. I bet she thinks I'm about to flake on the testing project.

Before she can have a heart attack, I hit her with my real agenda, and as she listens, some color returns to her cheeks.

"Do you have any experience coding?" she asks when I'm done making my case. "This is the first thing they'll ask me when I bring this up."

I tell her about my app and offer to share a link to the source control database, so she can pass it on to whoever wants to see what I'm capable of.

"Please," she says. "I'll get that over to everyone on the development team, along with a glowing recommendation from me."

I beam at her. "I'm sorry to leave your team. Testing isn't—"

She waves this off. "It will be a shame to lose you, but you have to think about your career first and foremost." She darts a furtive glance at the door and unplugs the conference room phone. "I wanted to talk to you about something as well. I know you always do a great job, but please do your best when it comes to the Belka project. I'm worried that if something were to go wrong, both our jobs would be on the line."

Great.

I'll either get the position I want, or lose my job altogether.

"I got it," I say with a confidence I wish I felt. "Leave it to me."

Sandra plugs the phone back in. "Let me know if there's anything I can do to help."

"I'll do that." I smile and hope she'll leave.

She stands there.

"Bye," I say.

She frowns. "You're not leaving yet?"

"Have to check on an email," I lie.

Though she's in the loop on the sex toy testing, I still don't want her to see the suitcase.

"Good luck," she says and finally leaves.

I wait another minute for everyone to disperse to their cubicles, then snatch the sex toy carry-on from under the table and sprint out of the meeting room—and nearly tackle Britney, who's lurking in the corridor on the way to the elevators.

"Fanny." Her voice is laced with poisoned honey. "I'm glad I bumped into you."

She is? Is hell experiencing climate change?

"I wanted to ask you about the Belka project," she says.

Ah. There it is.

"Please direct all your inquiries to Mr. Chortsky," I say politely.

I can see she's unhappy with that answer, so I clutch the suitcase and step forward, hoping to quickly get past her.

She doesn't move.

"Excuse me," I mutter. "I'm late for a meeting." With that, I forcefully squeeze myself between her and the wall and rush into the elevator as if I were being chased by an evil fairy.

Once outside the building, I speed-walk all the way to the DHL office on Church Street.

Wiping the sweat from my brow—it really is warm outside—I scan the paperwork involved.

This day gets better and better. The customs form has an item list on it.

This should be fun.

I locate the nearest bathroom, lock myself in a stall, and open the suitcase.

Fuck me. This is a lot of toys.

A dildo in a clear plastic box. Something that looks like a buttplug. A cock ring. A vibrator. And lots of items I don't even recognize.

Luckily, there is a type of menu here, written by the same female hand as the auxiliary testing cases sheet. In fact, the inside of the suitcase also smells like that same perfume.

I wonder if she's the Impaler's lover. That might explain why he's giving this such a high priority.

*Kill her,* the green monster of jealousy shouts inside my head.

*I don't know who she is,* I reply. *You've got to chill.*

*Find out and rip her hair out.*

*You're nuts.*

*I'm you.*

Silencing the green monster, I pocket the list, close the suitcase, and get back into the main DHL office.

Has anyone blushed this much filling out a customs form before? My face is so hot I worry my hair will catch on fire.

When the form is done, I get into the line and wait.

And wait.

Growing bored, I take out my phone.

Hmm. An email from Dominika.

When I read the subject, my heart rate speeds up.

*I'm sorry.*

No.

Can't be.

I open the email, scan it, and nearly drop Precious.

It's my worst nightmare come true.

Dominika won't be my tester.

# FOUR

THE CAR RIDE home happens in a confused haze.

Dominika's email almost seems like a cruel joke.

Apparently, she's joining a convent tomorrow. She, the woman who pretended to seduce—and then creatively violate—all the orifices of "nuns" at a strip club.

I fire off an email asking her if she's kidding, only to get an instant autoreply reiterating her plans to become a nun.

If I tell Ava, she'll die of laughter at my expense. Dominika the Nun will have a forked tongue and will be covered from head to toe in tattoos, some of which depict sexual acts prohibited by the sacred texts.

Entering my apartment, I feed Monkey, my guinea pig. Originally, she was a gift to my ex, but he didn't want her, so I ended up with her in the reverse of a custody battle.

"What do I do now?" I ask her when she's done with her chow.

The little rodent hops up and down as though she's dancing.

"You're no help," I say, then refresh her water and pace the apartment as I ponder my situation.

I thought I'd gotten a lucky break with Dominika. She's an expert with toys, lives impressively far away, and was willing. I guess the far away part isn't a big deal—I can use a proxy server to simulate that with someone local if I want. But the willingness to shove toys into holes is harder to find.

I meet Monkey's pink eyes. "Do you think I should hire a prostitute?"

She scurries into the little house she usually sleeps in.

Judgmental much?

I resume my pacing and think further about prostitution.

The biggest problem is that it's illegal in New York. More importantly, I have no clue where to find one. Or a pimp. Do they still use pimps?

Either way, I doubt you can just place an ad for a hooker on a freelancer site.

Damn Giuliani—or whoever it was that cleaned up 42nd Street. Back in the day, you could hire a sex worker *there*.

Maybe I could put an ad on Craigslist?

A quick search later, I learn that they got rid of the relevant section of the site, and some other similar services, like Backpage, got shut down completely.

As I read up on the topic, I realize that by hiring a sex worker, I could inadvertently end up supporting the evil that is human trafficking.

So that's a no-go.

Would women working in a local strip club be interested in this? Or some escort service, perhaps?

Are traffickers involved with *that*?

Unlikely, but not sure I want to risk it. With hindsight, even Dominika could've been a victim of exploitation. Maybe it's for the best that she backed out.

So where does that leave me?

A silly idea crosses my mind.

Sandra said to let her know if there's anything she can do to help.

I picture myself approaching my boss for this and preemptively die of mortified laughter. Apart from the obvious, what if she has a weak heart and dies on me? I'd be infamous as the weirdest murderer in the history of crime.

But asking a woman I know *is* a promising direction.

Would Ava help?

She swears by her vibrator.

Obviously, she'd never let me live this down, but at least I'd keep my job.

The phone rings.

Speak of the devil.

"Hi, Ava," I say, snatching up Precious. "Are you having a slow day at the hospital?"

"How did your meeting go?" she asks. "Any impaling I should be aware of?"

I tell her everything but tone down my reactions to my boss's boss because... well, because.

Sure enough, she's choking on laughter when I get to the part where I lost my sex toy tester to a convent.

"So," I say at the end, "there's a pretty big favor I want to ask you."

"Noooo," she squeezes out in between hysterical giggles. "I'm not having cybersex with you."

"That wasn't the favor," I lie. "I was wondering if—"

"Dude," Ava says. "You don't have a problem."

"I don't?"

"You should test it on yourself," she says with a giggle. "It'll be fun, and you haven't had an orgasm since what's-his-name before Bob."

"But—"

"Wouldn't it be nice to loosen up a little?"

I squeeze Precious tighter, the mention of my ex and the phrase "loosen up" tempting me to say something very unkind to my bestie.

The reason He Who Shouldn't Have Been Named broke up with me was that I wasn't "adventurous enough, sexually."

Those words sting to this very day, especially because there might've been a kernel of truth in them. Not that Bob was any kind of wizard in bed... not even a Hufflepuff.

Ava's tone turns serious. "I didn't mean that, I'm sorry. I just stuck my big foot in my mouth."

"More like your whole butt." The grumpiness in my voice is only partially faked.

"Look," she says with a sigh. "If you really insist, I'll think about being your tester."

"No, it's okay." I pinch the bridge of my nose. "You might have a point. I shouldn't ask you to do something I'm not willing to do myself. The problem is, even if I do it, I still need a guy for the male toys."

She snorts. "I wouldn't worry about that. Crook your finger at the first male you see, preferably of legal age, and he'll test whatever you want."

"Uh-huh. It might work like that for *you*."

"It would work like that for pretty much anyone with a uterus. But let's say it doesn't. You can still get on Tinder or something like that. Tell the guys who match with you that you want cybersex before your dates and see how enthused they'll get."

That actually does sound more plausible, though when I try to picture it, I feel deeply uneasy. Also, for some reason, the only image that forms in my mind is of lapis lazuli eyes and—

"Ooh, sorry," Ava says. "They're paging me."

"Wait, I—"

The phone goes dead.

Paging. Still. Leave it to the medical profession to live in the Stone Age. I wonder if they also have dialup modems at the hospital, or cassette tapes.

Hey, at least they no longer use leeches, so that's progress.

Unless they still do?

A quick search on Precious later, I learn that they do indeed still utilize the little blood-sucking monsters, and that the FDA somehow managed to classify leeches as a "living medical device to clear localized blood clots."

The article mentions that maggots are used too, and I stop reading there, because gross.

Monkey peeks out of her cage and squeaks.

I give her half of a grape. "I know, I'm procrastinating."

Snatching the grape, Monkey hides in her little house.

Fine. I can figure this out on my own.

Jumping on my laptop, I open a fresh spreadsheet, name it "testing on myself," and fill out two columns: pro and con.

Under "con" are things like: "might be hard to face my coworkers afterward, especially the Impaler" and "it's a less realistic test than if there were a second person involved."

In the "pro" column are tidbits such as: "keep my job," "Ava might be right and this could be fun," and "prove ex wrong."

Since the pro column ends up longer, I reluctantly accept the inevitable.

"I'll be my own guinea pig," I say out loud. "No offense, Monkey."

Precious pings.

It's a text from Ava.

*So? You doing it?*

I reply with the okay sign.

*I'd wax if I were you. Makes one feel sexy.*

*Seriously?* I text back.

*Like a heart attack. Now stop beating around the bush and get rid of your bush.* Emojis of lips, cat face, cherries, flower, peace sign, wishbone, hot spot, and peach are followed by a razor.

I didn't even know there was a razor emoji.

Silencing the phone, I dart a glance at the suitcase.

Nope.

Not ready yet.

Maybe Ava is right. Would I be more eager if I made myself prettier down under?

Since the jungle that is my legs is on my to-do list anyway, I'll just do that and some ladyscaping at the same time. The breakup with my ex made me experiment a little in this area. I've tried styling my pubes geometrically with upside-down and regular triangles, aeronautically with a landing strip, and—briefly—what could best be described as a dictator's mustache.

Speaking of, what's with all the dictators sporting a 'stache? I bet one started the trend, and the dictator-sheep copycatted. Come to think of it, their inspiration might've been the original Vlad the Impaler. The painting of him had a mustache so big and bushy, he probably had a pet name for it, like Pufos—which means fluffy in Romanian.

Thank the hipster gods "my" Impaler doesn't have such a crime against nature above his kissable lips. He only has a little bit of sexy stubble up there—just the way I like it.

In any case, nowadays I'm sporting a retro bush of epic proportions, with cobwebs and tumbleweeds down there, and "No Trespassing" signs. This isn't a feminist statement, unfortunately, just a sign of self-neglect.

Well, even if feeling sexy weren't a goal, getting that hair under control could make locating my bits a little easier for the testing—so off it shall go.

I dart into the closet where I keep my disposable gloves and N95 mask, then take it all to the bathroom, fully aware of how much I look like I'm planning a naughty game of doctor.

There's a fly in my bathroom.

Gross.

I try to evict him, but the clever beastie sneers at my futile attempts, buzzing around tauntingly.

"Fine," I tell him. "This place is about to smell like hair removal cream. If you get wing cancer, don't come crying to me."

Of course, I didn't get the cream to ward off insects. I just happen to hate the stubbly feel of my legs after shaving, and I've never felt masochistic enough to wax.

Stripping down to the buff, I trim the affected area as much as is possible without garden shears. Next, I prepare a wet washcloth by the tub and put on the mask to avoid fumes.

As soon as I strap on the gloves and squeeze out a handful of cream, I feel an itch on the top of my head.

Then my nose itches under the mask.

Then my eye.

Ignoring it all, I get into the tub and slather the cream on my legs.

I glance at my pubes.

Am I really doing this?

I guess I am. I get more cream and go to town in the vaginal region. That done, I awkwardly place one foot on the edge of the tub and upgrade the experience to a full Brazilian—I saw a butt plug in that suitcase, so this might help.

I then wait for the cream to break down my hair's protein structure. Bored, I wonder how the Seven Dwarves would've reacted if they'd walked in on Snow White doing something like this.

Especially Bashful.

The fly lands on my mask.

"Shoo." I swat at him.

He buzzes angrily and scurries over to my forehead.

"Get out!" I swat at him once more. "Perv."

The fly's buzzing sounds indignant as he zooms through the room and slams into the closed window.

Serves him right.

In the next moment, I forget all about the fly because my most private area begins to burn.

Ouch. It's *really* burning—like an STD they punish rapists with in the seventh circle of hell.

I shoot a glance at the clock. It's not the full five minutes yet, plus my legs are fine.

This must be because I switched brands, and some ingredient in this formulation doesn't agree with my bikini area. Which is ironic, given that this brand markets itself as being "for sensitive skin." In defense of the manufacturer, most such creams warn you about using this stuff in the exact area that currently burns. It's just never been a problem for me before, else I would have done a patch test on a small part of my privates instead of going all in.

Grabbing the warm cloth, I rub myself hard enough to start a fire.

There.

No more cream on my vag.

Now my butt burns, so I take care of that next.

Which is when my legs start to itch.

With a growl, I wipe all the melted-looking hair from my legs and wash myself all over with a thoroughness an OCD sufferer would be proud of.

Soon, no sign of the cream remains.

I look down.

Things are angrily red, like I'm some animal in heat.

There goes feeling sexy.

Also, there's a strange sensation on the side of my forehead.

More specifically, the right eyebrow region.

A *burning* sensation.

No. Can't be.

Toweling off in a rush, I leap for the mirror.

Crap! There's a glob of hair removal cream on my right eyebrow.

Did I scratch an itch there without realizing? Or did the cream splatter when I battled the fly?

Either way, I frantically wipe the cream off—and most of my eyebrow goes with it.

I wash my face thoroughly and make sure there's no cream lurking somewhere else—like my scalp or my eyelashes.

Nope. Just lost the pubes, leg hair, and an eyebrow.

In the mirror, my remaining eyebrow makes my expression seem equal parts curious, suspicious, and skeptical despite the fact that I'm feeling none of those things, just shame.

Getting my makeup kit, I try drawing the eyebrow back.

The result is acceptable enough for a teleconference, but if I want to see people face to face, I might have to sacrifice the other eyebrow and draw both.

I'm too traumatized to test anything now, so I spend the rest of the day integrating the handwritten test cases into my electronic list, then expanding the document to accommodate all the diverse contents of the suitcase. I also make sure the resulting document will automatically back up to the cloud. The last thing I want is to go through the testing, only to lose the documentation thanks to a busted hard drive and have to start over again.

It's happened to me once, and it was the worst feeling imaginable.

By the time I head to bed, the redness from the hair removal debacle has subsided, and as my head hits the pillow, I feel a stirring of excitement for the day ahead.

I never thought I'd have such concrete plans to play with myself or that I'd get paid for it, but here we are.

The thought of work brings to mind X-rated images featuring a certain someone's intense blue eyes and stern mouth.

I fight the sudden urge to reach down and explore the newly bare skin near my clit. My orgasms belong to the project at the moment.

With a sigh, I hug my pillow and drift off to sleep.

## FIVE

IN THE MORNING, I feed Monkey and check my work email as I eat an omelet.

"You better be good." I jokingly frown at my guinea pig as I collect my work laptop, work phone, and the suitcase. "I'm about to spank the monkey."

She looks at me with a blank expression.

"What, you think *monkey* is supposed to represent a cock in that phrase?" I ask her.

No reaction.

"I know, right? Why are so many animals used as a euphemism for genitals in the first place? Cat, rooster, monkey—does humanity have a subconscious bestiality streak?"

She turns on her heel and scurries into her house again—clearly not interested in dignifying my words with a response.

I carry the work phone, the laptop, the suitcase, and Precious into the bedroom, then light a few candles around the bed and play Leonard Cohen on my Echo to set the mood.

Opening the suitcase, I take out the vibrator, the toy I've been most curious about—mostly because Ava has been singing praises of hers so much I suspect she gets a commission from the manufacturer.

This specific vibrator is made of some squishy Space Age material that feels like a jelly made out of slugs—but sexy pink, so I guess it's okay.

I already have my first quality complaint: the vibrator box doesn't have any instructions on it, nor is there a little paper manual inside. There's only one short note on the box: *Get the Belka app for your phone.*

I make a note of this in my testing document. It's feasible the Belka peeps omitted more instructions because these are prototypes, but unlikely. The packaging is too polished for that, so this might well be an oversight.

Hopefully, my Bachelor of Science degree will help me figure out how to use a vibrator, even a smart one.

I get the app onto Precious and choose "Vibrator" from the screen with the different toy options. The app informs me that it's connected to the vibrator via Bluetooth, and that the vibrator's battery is full—a great start.

I click on the "Connect with Partner" icon and learn that you can do so via email, text, or even social media.

I opt to test the text version for now and put in the number of my work phone.

To make it seem like I'm testing the toys over the internet, I set up my work phone to connect through a proxy server located in Tajikistan—the farther, the better. Then I click on the text and am directed to download the Belka app. Once the app is ready to go, it opens up a small videoconference window—with options to see/hear your partner or not.

I document all this.

The setup was pretty effortless. Then again, it might be good to have someone less tech-savvy play with all this just in case—perhaps someone's adventurous granny?

In any case, the work phone version of the app is now in "Giver" mode, while Precious is the "Receiver."

I leave only the work phone in my hands because I need the controls on it. They consist of a start button and the knob for intensity.

First things first. I apply the vibrator to my forearm and press start.

Wow.

It's not just vibrating. The strange material makes it ripple, for lack of a better term. It feels... interesting. I play with the intensity until I find one that I suspect will feel good on my clit, then stop the vibrator.

Hiking up the skirt of my dress, I pull down my panties. Just for shits and giggles, I'm wearing the gag pair Ava got me after my breakup. They boldly state "Open for Business."

Carefully, I press the vibrator to myself. It feels tickly and a little cold.

Here we go. Time to start my workday.

I open the timer app for the "Duration" section of the testing document and reach for the start button.

Precious pings, stopping me.

Swapping the work phone for personal, I see that I just got a text from Ava.

Figures. Is it considered cockblocking when someone prevents you from using a vibrator?

*When you get around to the toys, think of being impaled by the Impaler*, her text states.

How did she sniff out what I'm about to do? She must've used her own vibrator so much she's gained a psychic superpower. Or maybe she was bitten by her vibrator—by its Bluetooth, perhaps?

Precious pings again. This time, it's the eggplant emoji.

*I'm busy*, I reply and silence Precious before grabbing the work phone once more.

As my finger hovers over the start button, I do my best to thwart Ava by not thinking of the Impaler.

Riiight. As everyone who's ever tried *not* to think of something knows, the more you try, the more you end up thinking of the forbidden object.

And that's doubly so for when said object is as hot as the one I have in my mind's eye.

Fine. Whatever. I might feel better if I picture yummy lips touching my clit instead of slug jelly.

The image of hypnotic lapis lazuli eyes firmly in my head, I set a timer and press the start button.

Bzzz.

I drop both the phone and the vibrator as a powerful orgasm unleashes a wave of endorphins into my system. A full-on, toe-curling orgasm—as amazing as it was unexpected.

As the last spasms ripple through my body, I stare at the toy dumbfounded.

Did that just happen?

Is this a military grade vibrator, or did I just develop the female counterpart to premature ejaculation?

Chewing on my lip, I open the laptop and look at the testing document.

"Was orgasm achieved?" You can say that again.

"How many times?" Once so far.

"Session duration?" No clue. I put down a microsecond.

What now? Maybe I do the same test one more time? After all, whoever put the handwritten notes together implied there would be multiple sessions.

When I attempt it, I grunt in pain instead of pleasure. My clit is super-sensitive from the last go.

I might have to give it a little break.

With some trepidation, I snatch the dildo from the suitcase and open the packaging.

Again no instructions, just a small packet of lube and the thing itself—huge and made of the same squishy material as the vibrator, only avocado-green instead of pink.

I don't mention this in my work report, but this thing reminds me of an alien tentacle. I mentally dub it Glurp.

Taking Glurp in my hand, I uncharitably compare him to my exes' equipment.

Yup, Glurp is a big boy, almost frighteningly so.

Opening the lube, I nearly drown Glurp in the viscous liquid and bring up the mental image of the Impaler as I slide the tip into my opening.

Hmm.

It fits and feels kind of nice already. The prior orgasm must've gotten me ready for this.

I push Glurp deeper and pick up the work phone to bring the tentacle to life.

Bzzz.

I don't instantly come this time, but the vibration or whatever it's doing feels amazing. My inner muscles tighten, and I feel like I'm on the verge of something truly intense.

A few interesting options show up on the app, like A-spot and G-spot stimulation.

I'll have to test them all, but for now, I decide on the G-spot because it's the one I've actually heard about.

I jab my finger at the G-spot button.

Glurp begins to lightly twist inside me, as if zooming in on a target.

*Bing-bing.*

The videoconferencing app on my work phone hides part of the Belka app screen.

Crap. It's Sandra, my boss.

What the hell does she want? There's micromanaging, and then there's interrupting your loyal employee from finding Nemo.

I stab the screen to reject the call.

The videoconferencing app expands to full screen.

Oh, shit.

I must've fat-fingered it.

"Hi, Fanny." Sandra's eyes widen. "Am I interrupting something?"

I redden like a boiled crab and swiftly disable the video.

Did she see anything? Can't be—the camera was aimed at my face, not at Glurp.

At least I hope it was.

But then why the question? Maybe she figured something was up by the blissed-out look on my face?

"I just wanted to make sure Project Belka is on track," Sandra says apologetically, and I realize I haven't responded to her still.

"Don't worry about a thing," I half say, half squeal. "It's in good hands."

I have no idea if she hears or responds because at that moment, Glurp finally gives my G-spot a knockout.

I bite my cheek to prevent a moan from escaping as my eyes roll back in my head.

"Thanks," Sandra says. "Email an update when you get the chance."

"Yes!"

She hangs up.

I extricate Glurp from myself and rush into the bathroom to splash some icy water on my overheated face. Leaving Glurp behind to be cleaned, I get back and record this session in the document.

They better allow me to move departments. After today, I can never work for Sandra again, or look her in the eye.

Also, can one develop a fetish this way? Next thing I know, I'll need Sandra to call me every time I get hot and heavy.

Looking into the suitcase, I debate what to test next.

The buttplug catches my attention.

It's small enough not to be intimidating—a good thing for me, a butt play virgin.

I take the package out and read the title.

*Anal Belka.*

Does Belka mean something besides the name of this project?

A quick search reveals that Belka is actually a common word in various Slavic languages. It means *beam* in Polish (ouch), *egg white* in Macedonian (weird), and *squirrel* in Russian (hmm, okay). Given Vlad's country of birth, I have to assume the title of both the toy and the project means the latter.

In which case... an anal squirrel? Sounds like a rodent obsessed with keeping his park nice and tidy. Who decided that was a good name for this thing?

Then again, Ava told me about the time they had a guy come to the ER with a hamster stuck in his butt—so rodents in butts must be something people are interested in doing. Why not a squirrel, too?

I can never tell Monkey about this. As a rodent herself, she'll be scarred for life. At least in the case of this Belka, no animals need to be harmed.

Placing the work phone on the bed, I lie on my stomach and squirt the lube that came with the squirrel toy into my butt.

The things I do for science.

Or quality assurance.

Or a paycheck.

Feeling naughty, I place the tip of the toy at my opening and push lightly to see how much resistance my body provides. There's some, but not as much as I expected.

Well, okay, the squirrel *is* small.

I get bolder and increase the pressure.

There's a small hint of discomfort, and then, like a baster into a turkey, the squirrel dives right in.

# SIX

WHOA. That feels strange. But also kind of good, maybe? I can't decide.

I set the timer on the phone and load "Anal Belka" as the toy on the app.

A few new controls appear on the screen that weren't available in the case of the vibrator and Glurp. For example, there's a button named "Out" and one named "Deeper."

I'm not ready for deeper just yet, and out is premature.

I press "On."

The squirrel begins to vibrate.

The feeling is odd, but not unpleasant. As I adjust, I feel ready to brave more, and a button that says "P-spot stimulation" catches my gaze.

I've never heard of a P-spot. Then again, I've never heard of the A-spot either. To be honest, I didn't even know there were "spots" in the backdoor area, but I guess there must be since so many women like butt play.

I hesitantly press on the P-spot button.

The squirrel stops vibrating and gently burrows deeper into me.

42

Weird.

It keeps moving.

Wait a second.

It stops. I feel it whirling around as if looking for something, then it starts moving again.

What the hell? I jab the stop button.

Nothing happens. The squirrel continues on its merry way.

I frantically press the out button.

The squirrel stops.

Whew.

Wait a second. The squirrel is whirling around again, as if rooting for something inside me. Not finding whatever it is, it burrows even deeper.

What the fuck? Does "P" stand for pancreas? I think that's an organ in the digestive system, but there's no way that's a fun spot.

I scan the screen in panic.

There's a help button here, plus a few more that don't look promising.

I punch all the non-help buttons at once.

The squirrel keeps going deeper.

I'm beginning to freak out. What if "P" stands for the pituitary gland in the brain?

The squirrel stops. An error pops up on the screen, stating, "Prostate not found."

Prostate? Oh, no. Women don't have one—at least not in the butt area. There's something called Skene's glands on the front side of the vagina that are sometimes referred to as "the female prostate," but that's clearly not what the squirrel was looking for.

Through my panic, I begin to parse out what happened. The squirrel must be from the batch meant for the male sex. When the Impaler wrote the app, he forgot to account for a situation where someone who wants P-spot stimulation lacks a prostate to stimulate.

It's not a surprising bug, but it *is* a major pain in my ass—and that expression has never been this literal.

I swipe angrily at the error message until it disappears from the screen. Then I pound the out button.

The error comes back, and nothing else happens.

Out of options, I click the help button again.

A sound resembling a dial tone emanates from the phone.

That's not good. I bet that's meant to dial customer service when Belka toys get into the hands of real customers. This early, I doubt anyone's going to answer that call. Not that I'd know what to tell them if they did.

Frantic, I drop the work phone on the bed and grab Precious to dial Ava.

"I'm a little busy," she says in lieu of a hello.

"This is a medical emergency! Code red. I'm not joking, this is—"

"Whoa, slow down, slow down. What happened?"

"I have a squirrel stuck in my rectum. Or maybe my colon. Somewhere up there."

A moment of silence, then: "Is this a joke?"

"I wish! I was testing the toys and—"

Ava sounds like she's got something stuck in her throat. "So the squirrel is a toy?"

"No, I mean a real fucking animal."

"Hey, you never know. I've heard of lots of things stuck in there. Fruits, vegetables, keys, candles, coffee and peanut butter jars, lightbulbs, deodorant, smartphones, bottles of body spray, Buzz Lightyear—"

"That's not making me feel any better." I squeeze the phone tighter. "What should I do?"

"Go to the ER," she says.

"How about something less drastic," I say, picturing how embarrassing such a trip would be—especially since my name is Fanny.

For the rest of their lives, the nurses would tell everyone, "The patient's name was Fanny, and she had a toy stuck in her fanny."

Ava takes an audible breath. "Do you have any abdominal pain?"

"No."

"How about bleeding?"

All blood drains from my face. "This just happened. You think there could be bleeding?"

"Unlikely, if there's no pain. Just make sure not to reach in there with tongs or anything that could cut or bruise the area. That includes your nails."

I squeeze my eyes shut. "I'm not an idiot. At least not more of an idiot."

"Okay, but just keep in mind: There are cases where tongs have gotten stuck along with the original object."

"No tongs," I say firmly. "What can I do, though?"

"Other than going to the ER? You can try to poop it out."

I feel a pang of hope. "You think that would work?"

"If it's small enough, it should come out the way it came in."

I look at the empty box from the toy. "How small is small enough?"

"I have no idea. Did it go in easy?"

My face reddens. "Kind of."

"Then maybe it'll be a case of easy come, easy go."

Ugh. "This isn't funny!"

"Look, I've really got to run. Keep me posted. If you decide to go to the ER, come here, to Presbyterian."

I grimace. "I'm trying the poop method first."

"Eat some fiber," she says. "Better yet, a laxative."

With that useful advice, she hangs up.

As I place Precious back on the bed, I see something on the work phone that chills my bones.

The help call looks to have connected somewhere.

"Hello?" I squeak into the receiver. "Is someone there?"

"Ms. Pack," says a familiar, Russian-accented voice. "I strongly disagree with your plans and am on my way to take you to the ER immediately."

# SEVEN

"NO, don't! I'll call 911. Don't come here!"

No reply. He hung up.

Growling in frustration, I click the help button again.

A sound resembling a dial tone emanates from the phone once more, but when I wait and wait, it doesn't connect anywhere.

Maybe I can call him directly?

Sure. Just as soon as I magically figure out what his cell phone number is. Unless... maybe Sandra knows?

Ugh, no. I don't want her involved. She'll either have a heart attack from thinking the project has gone awry, or from laughter when she learns what's happened.

How does the Impaler even know where I live? Did the app access the work phone GPS, or did he simply take a look at my employee file?

Anyway, the how is not important. The fact that he's going to be here is. It's bad enough he overheard the whole "squirrel in my butt" conversation with Ava—a fact that makes me want to crawl into a ditch and die. If he comes here and needs to rescue my ass—literally —I might just melt from mortification.

There's only one thing to do.

I must poop out the squirrel.

Having a clear-cut goal feels good, so I cautiously stand up.

Still no abdominal pain, so that's good. Unfortunately, the squirrel doesn't start moving down with the pull of gravity—on some level, I was hoping it might.

Fine.

I shuffle to the bathroom with a stiff gait. So this is why they call this style of locomotion "having something stuck up the butt."

I get on the toilet and wait.

Nothing happens.

I strain.

Nada.

After a few minutes of pointless waiting, I recall Ava talking about fiber. Getting up, I stiffly shuffle into the kitchen and grab an apple.

Crunching it, I return to my white throne.

Nope.

Oh, who am I kidding? I know fiber needs more than minutes to do its thing.

Getting up, I try pacing the apartment.

Doesn't help.

I roll out my yoga mat and do a Standing Forward Bend.

Not even a little stomach cramp.

Doing other poses doesn't work either—neither the Downward-Facing Dog, nor the Triangle, nor the Seated and Supine Twists.

Monkey watches me do all this with an unreadable expression.

"Don't judge," I tell her and prepare for the big guns: the Wind-Removing Pose, where you're on your back and your knees touch your chest.

Even this mighty yoga weapon doesn't work.

Okay. I need to be ready for the eventuality of seeing the Impaler —and I'm a mess in ways beyond foreign objects in my rear end.

I quickly change my drab casual dress for a prettier one, grab my makeup kit and a mirror, and perch on the toilet (hope springs eternal) to make myself look semi-human.

Lipstick is easy. Lashes too. But no matter how hard I work on the missing eyebrow, I fail to make it look like the sister of the other—barely a second cousin is the best I can do.

Maybe I should get rid of the remaining one right now? Problem is, I don't own a razor, and I don't dare play with the hair removal cream under the current circumstances. The last thing I want is to end up with bald spots on my head or hair removal cream in my butt. Or worse.

The eyebrow situation adds to my frustration.

Who does he think he is, coming here like this?

Well, I guess he thinks he's my boss squared. Probably realizes that having the power to fire me allows him to do what he wants. Probably doesn't like the sound of the lawsuit my parents would file if I somehow died because of the squirrel. Still—

The doorbell rings, sending my pulse through the stratosphere.

He's here!

Even the prospect of the upcoming humiliation doesn't loosen anything up—so much for stories of people soiling themselves out of fear. Then again, there's also a conflicting "anus clenching in fear"—so maybe that's what's happening here?

My work phone rings. Then Precious joins in.

Feeling like I'm about to die, I answer.

"How are you feeling?" the Impaler asks.

I gulp. Is that genuine concern in his voice? "Never better. You didn't need to come. I got this—"

"We're going to the ER." The statement is a command with no room for negotiation. "Do you need help coming out?"

Am I hearing a threat in that question? Will he break my door down if I answer the wrong thing?

Nah. His kind need to be officially invited to enter someone's home.

I rub my burning cheeks. "I can walk."

"See you soon then." He hangs up.

I text Ava an update, grab both phones, shuffle over to the door, and put on a pair of sneakers.

Here goes nothing.

I open the door.

He's here, in all his mouthwatering glory.

He meets my gaze, and something—probably shame—makes my knees go weak.

His strong hand grasps my elbow.

Electricity shoots up my arm from his touch, and I nearly stumble.

His expression changes, a scowl appearing on his face. He yells something in Russian, and a burly middle-aged dude is suddenly holding my other elbow with sausage-like fingers that are hairier than those of a sasquatch.

He came with a minion?

"Step carefully," the Impaler instructs.

When I put one foot in front of the other without faceplanting, he grunts approvingly.

Reluctantly accepting their help, I let them lead me to a limo that's waiting at the curb.

They open the door and deposit me inside. The Impaler climbs in to sit next to me. I catch a faint whiff of his yummy bergamot and citrus scent, and my breathing turns fast and shallow.

I hope I don't faint. Who knows what could come out of me if I do?

The minion gets behind the wheel and slams the door behind himself.

I clear my suddenly dry throat. "So, you have a chauffeur?"

The Impaler leans over and secures me with a seatbelt—nearly causing my brain to melt in the process. "Ivan is more what you'd call a personal assistant."

Really? Ivan looks more like a bodyguard, or that mobster guy who wanted to chop the yellow M&M into little bits and sprinkle them on ice cream in that Super Bowl ad.

Ivan's expression is grim as he turns the key in the ignition.

Could he be *the* Ivan, as in The Terrible? I can picture it now: The Impaler was feeling lonely, found a man with a name almost as grandiose as his own, turned him, and began a beautiful friendship.

With a squeal of tires, the car torpedoes forward.

"We're going to Presbyterian, right?" I ask when I swallow my heart back into my chest.

The Impaler closes the partition, separating us from Ivan. "Your friend sounded like she knew what she was talking about."

As I recall the conversation he's referring to, a wave of tingling heat hits my face.

Without paying much attention to me, he picks up a laptop from the neighboring seat and pops it open to a page filled with stylish lines of code.

His eyes narrow on the screen, and those lickable fingers dance over the keyboard with the grace of a pianist.

"Give me the phone that's in Giver mode," he says without looking up.

As I hand him my work phone, I get an inkling of what he's doing, and fleetingly debate jumping out of the car.

After a few minutes of typing, he attaches the phone to his laptop's USB and drums his fingers on the trackpad as he waits for something—my guess is for the app to update.

"Say something if you feel anything," he says and clicks a button on the screen, confirming my suspicion.

Somewhere inside me, the squirrel comes to life.

"Something!" I redden to boiled lobster levels.

He nods approvingly and clicks something else, putting the

squirrel back to sleep.

"You fixed the bug I found," I say, voicing my earlier theory.

"It was a good find." He looks right at me as he says this. "Great job."

My heart flutters pleasantly in my chest. If I were always complimented on my testing like this, I might not want to switch to the development department.

Reddening more, I reach for the phone in his hand. "Let's stop at the nearest bathroom, and I'll take care of the rest."

"No." He yanks the device out of my reach. "I've done some research. You need an X-ray and a doctor's supervision."

He did research on things to do when your employee has an object stuck in her fanny?

Someone shoot me. It would be a mercy killing.

The car comes to a jerky stop.

"We're here," he says, leaning in to unbuckle my seatbelt.

My hormones go into overdrive.

*Stop it. He's your boss squared.*

*But he smells so yummy.*

*Now you sound like a cannibal. Get a grip. He—*

"Are you okay?" he asks.

"Peachy." Was that concern again? More importantly, how long was I talking to myself?

"Let's go." He guides me out. Then he and his personal assistant grab an elbow each and lead me into the ER entrance like an invalid.

Hey, it could've been worse. He could've wheeled over a wheelchair. Or a gurney.

Leaving me in the waiting room, my boss squared sends Ivan back to the car and goes to get forms from the check-in desk—which gives me a moment to shoot a text to Ava to let her know that I'm here.

*I'll come see you,* she replies. *Wait there.*

*Sure. I was so going to prance away before, but now I'll wait.*

Coming back with the forms, the Impaler helps me fill them out —as though my fingers are damaged. Midway, we have an argument: Instead of letting me use insurance, the very same one his company provides me with, he wants to pay for everything himself.

"I made you come here," he says over my objections. "It's the least I can do."

Fine. He did drag me here. Let him pay—and I'm sure the bill will be huge enough to teach him a lesson about people's free will.

"Fanny!" Ava is wearing her scrubs and grinning like a loon. Her eyes dart between me and my boss squared.

"I'm going to hand in the forms," the Impaler says after I introduce them.

Ava waits until he's (hopefully) out of earshot before she jumps up and down and claps her hands like a preschooler. "You didn't tell me the Impaler looked like *that*. And he brought you here? Did the two of you—"

"Is there a private room where you can hide me?" I glance over to see how far away the Impaler is—and it's a good thing I do, because he's coming back.

"Not officially, but yeah," Ava says. "First, I'll take you for an X-ray."

Catching the end of that sentence, the Impaler nods approvingly.

Ava quirks an eyebrow. "Mr. Chortsky, would you like to wait here, go to Fanny's room, or come with us for the X-ray?"

I glare at her. I don't want him anywhere near my room. Or my X-ray.

He grabs my elbow again—sending another wave of tingles through me. "I'm going with."

Ava winks at me before she helps him lead me to the service elevator, which she opens with her hospital ID.

A corridor later, she ushers me into the room where a technician awaits. I cast a worried glance at her and the Impaler, who hang back together in the hallway.

I have a bad feeling about this, and not just because it makes me jealous. Ava doesn't have much of a filter when she speaks, so who knows what damage she might do?

Since I don't have a choice, I do my best to make the X-ray process as fast as possible, and when I sprint out of the room, Ava and the Impaler stop mid-word.

Does she look guilty?

Before I can confront anyone, I'm led to a nearby nurse's station where Ava turns a screen our way.

On the screen is an X-ray that shows what one would expect: an image of a classically beautiful pelvis with a ghostly outline of the squirrel toy below a nicely shaped coccyx bone.

No wonder my parents always said I'm beautiful on the inside.

I catch the Impaler peering at the image with a deep frown, and I'm not sure how I should feel. On the one hand, he's seeing inside me—which is another level of embarrassing. On the other hand, there's definitely concern on his face, and even if it's due to fear of liability, it's still a sign that he kind of cares.

Still, I do wish he'd bought me a few dinners before I showed him my sacrum like this.

*What are you saying? He can't get you dinners. Boss squared, remember?*

"In light of this, your plan should work," Ava says to the Impaler.

I glare at her. "What plan?"

"The app." He waves the phone. "I can guide the—"

My glare moves to him. "You're not doing anything. If anyone's using that app, it's me."

Face unreadable, he hands me the phone. Our fingers brush again, and I feel a jolt of sensation that goes straight down to my core, reminding me of the orgasms I experienced just a short while ago.

Ava clears her throat. "Let's take you to your room."

I grumble as they lead me there, but nobody listens to me. When we arrive, Ava tells me to go in first so I can put on a robe.

I lock eyes with the Impaler. "You're staying out here—and that's final."

He inclines his head. "As you wish."

With an eye roll, I go inside and change.

Ava comes in a few seconds later and gestures for me to lie down on the bed.

When I'm horizontal, she hands me a bedpan. "Good call asking him to wait outside," she says, grinning hugely.

Muttering unintelligible curses, I put the bedpan under my rear end.

With a wink, Ava nods at the nearby defibrillator. "You think you're going to make it?"

Ignoring her, I click the out button on the app and hold my breath.

The squirrel comes to life once more and slowly, almost anticlimactically, begins to back out of its hiding spot.

It doesn't hurt at all, and if it weren't for the indignity of it all, I might even find the associated sensations a little interesting.

There's a moment of discomfort as the squirrel clears my opening, followed by a loud clang as the darn thing lands in the bedpan.

Giggling, Ava puts on a pair of latex gloves, snatches the bedpan, and dumps its contents into a biohazard bag.

"Seriously?" I ask.

She ceremoniously extends the bag to me. "When we remove bullets, we let people keep those too."

I jump off the bed and take a few steps.

"Feeling spry?" she asks.

I grab the bag, toss it into a garbage disposal labeled "Biohazard," and begin to change in sullen silence.

Ava refuses to leave it alone. "Do you want me to at least email you the X-ray? Or send it to him perhaps?"

I round on her. "Do that, and I'll smother you in your sleep."

Her eyes gleam with mischief. "So you like him a lot."

"Hush!" I hiss, cutting my eyes toward the door. "What if he's eavesdropping?"

She dramatically fans herself. "What a scandal."

I finish dressing and come toward her. Leaning in, I whisper, "Did he say anything about me when I was getting that X-ray?"

"Depends what you mean. He basically outlined the app solution and asked if that's safer than what a doctor would've done. No declarations of undying love, though."

"Well, good," I say, hiding my disappointment. "Let's go."

I stride out of the room, Ava on my heels.

The Impaler's deep blue eyes zero in on my face. "Did it work?"

The redness that had managed to leave my cheeks during the squirrel removal procedure returns with a vengeance. "All good. The hardware is toast, though. I hope the Belka people can provide another."

"Don't worry about any of that." He adjusts his horn-rimmed glasses—a theoretically unsexy gesture that his fingers somehow turn erotic. "How do you feel?"

"Like getting *Exit Only* tattooed on my left butt cheek," I blurt, then redden painfully.

His expression is unreadable, his demeanor as aloof as ever. Ava, however, looks positively gleeful. "Make that a tramp stamp."

I glare at her.

"Actually, that might not work as intended," the Impaler says, his tone utterly serious. "Some may take it as a challenge."

Oh. My. God. Does he realize what he just said?

Ava makes a choking sound as I hustle to the elevator, determined to hide my flaming face.

We ride down in silence, and as I stare at the Impaler's implacable face, a new worry invades my mind.

What happens now that the squirrel is out of me, and the emergency is over?

Am I about to lose my job?

# EIGHT

I TRY to parse that indecipherable expression of his.

Is he angry about what happened? Is that why he told me not to worry about any of it? Are my days of testing toys—or anything —over?

It's possible. I doubt any other employee has interrupted his day like this, and made him drive them to the hospital.

Then again, my snafu did help locate a possible bug in his code, so that's something. Unless he's like Britney—touchy about the flaws in his app.

Oh, well. Even if he does want to fire me, I bet he wouldn't do that right after I've been rushed to a hospital—it wouldn't look so good if I decided to sue.

Which I wouldn't, but he doesn't know that.

The elevator doors slide open.

"See you," Ava says to me when we exit. Turning to the Impaler, she adds, "Thanks for taking care of her. Nice to have met you."

He inclines his head, and she sprints away.

We check out of the hospital and leave the building.

Ivan is waiting inside the car.

The Impaler opens a door for me in a gentlemanly fashion, and I climb in, making sure to plop on the seat opposite to where his laptop is. I don't think it's wise for me to sit next to him after all of this.

I might expire from blushing.

Before he decides to buckle me in again, I do that myself—same reason.

He takes a seat next to his laptop, as I hoped he would, but for some reason, I feel a pang of disappointment.

Ivan floors the gas pedal.

The Impaler raises the partition between us and his minion, and glances at his laptop before pinning me with an intent stare.

Crap. I'm probably interrupting him from something important.

"So…" I shift in my seat uncomfortably. "What now?"

He cocks his head. "We're taking you home, of course."

Since it's been whole minutes since I last blushed, I do so now. "I meant, testing-wise." Or put another way, do I still have a job?

"You need to rest."

He's really good at making statements that sound like military orders. At least I don't salute or yes-sir him this time.

"How about after I rest?" I dare to ask.

"You're not going to worry about that right now."

That again. Should I just ask him straight out if I still have a job? Or will that just put the idea in his head?

"You went to Brooklyn College, right?" he asks out of nowhere.

"I did." Wait. How does he know? Did he notice it in my file when he looked for my address?

"Great computer science program," he says. "Soothing campus."

I blink at him. "How do you know? Are you a fellow alum?"

"Guilty." Something almost like a smile touches the corners of his eyes. "I graduated eight years before you, so our paths never crossed."

Huh. So he did look up my file, even down to the date of my graduation.

I wonder what it would've been like if we'd met in school and he weren't my boss squared.

*Are you crazy? Who says he's even attracted to you? He's just giving you a ride home, followed by a possible job termination.*

I moisten my dry lips. "Did you also major in comp sci?"

Did his gaze just fall to my mouth?

"What else?" he asks, the corners of his lips tilting slightly—a definite smile, and a panty-wetting one at that.

"History," I blurt—and thank goodness don't add, "That would be easy for you, since you lived it."

His lips stretch into a full-blown smile. "No, I've been into programming forever. My older brother got me into it." He tilts his head. "How about you? Why did you choose that as your major?"

"It was an act of rebellion at first," I admit. "My parents are hippie-artsy types. They hoped I'd major in something like music, photography, or film—nothing practical, like computer science."

He arches an eyebrow. "There are other practical disciplines out there."

"Sure. I took a bunch of introductory STEM courses first, but something about programming appealed to me. Also, an asshole in that class didn't think I, a girl, could do it—which spurred me on."

At the mention of the asshole, the Impaler frowns deeply. Maybe it wasn't HR behind the women-to-men ratio, after all?

"The irony is," I continue, "writing code feels like that creative process that my parents yammer about all the time."

The frown relaxes. "Programming can be as much art as science."

I smile. "Just don't tell my parents that."

"I wouldn't dream of it," he says with mock seriousness. "Let them suffer knowing their daughter got herself a degree that will virtually guarantee she's always got a well-paying job, and one that will likely intellectually stimulate her as well. The horror."

My smile widens. "What did *you* like about computer science when you tried it?"

He adjusts his glasses again. "I liked the logic and certainty of it. In other sciences, there are a lot of theories which may or may not be the ultimate truth. In ours, most theories have proofs, like in math. I also like the feeling of control when I code. With computers being as prevalent as they are, not knowing how to program, or at least how it all works, is a little like not knowing how to read and—"

His phone rings, distracting us both, and I realize I was listening openmouthed—in part because I got drawn in by the passion in his voice. If being a super-rich company owner ever gets boring, he can always do inspirational speaking on the side.

He glances at the screen of his phone but doesn't pick up. "Where was I?"

Crap. Did he just ignore something important because of me? "It's fine," I say. "You should take that."

He pockets the phone. "You said your parents are into art. What do they do for a living?"

His phone rings again.

He ignores it, his gaze trained expectantly on me.

Would it be rude if I insist that he pick that up and therefore ignore the question?

Sensing my reluctance, he takes out the phone and pointedly silences it.

"Mom is an opera singer," I say after the phone disappears into his pocket again. "Dad's a painter."

He looks fascinated. "Does she perform somewhere, and does he have exhibits?"

"Mom mostly teaches others, but Dad did finally get famous enough to be able to sell his works. That happened just as I was graduating from college. When I was growing up, our income was pretty low—full-ride financial aid for college kind of low."

"I also got that," he says to my surprise. "When we arrived in this country, we didn't have an income at all."

Ah, yes, of course. Immigrant background. "Your parents must be proud of what you've accomplished."

"Take it for granted, more like." He frowns again. "I think they feel like they gave up their lives back in Russia for their kids, so their standards for what's considered a worthy accomplishment are out of control."

"Well, at least they didn't name you Fanny when your last name is Pack," I say, eager to rid him of that frown. "As you can imagine, I was the butt of a lot of jokes. Pun intended."

My evil plan works. Another smile touches the corners of his eyes. "I think I would prefer parents with a sense of humor—even if it meant I'd end up named after an accessory."

"That's because you don't know my parents. You know how teens are embarrassed by their parents? I've felt that way my whole life. They're completely inappropriate. For example, they had 'the birds and the bees' talk with me when I was five—with diagrams and everything."

Another real smile graces his lips. "Better than never—as was the case with mine."

I want to trace the curve of those sexy lips with my finger. *No, stop it, perv. Boss squared, remember?* With effort, I return my focus to the conversation at hand. "Still, you've never been to middle school with my name," I say.

He's unfazed. "My last name, Chortsky, means 'from a chort'— which is Russian for 'demon.' Chort is also a popular curse word, kind of like 'damn.'"

Huh. So it's official, he *is* evil. Still, poor guy. I picture a little boy with that name, being teased unmercifully. "At least your parents didn't choose that name," I say. "They suffered with it too."

He shrugs. "They could've changed it."

"Fine, you win—if it's a win to have parents worse than mine." I cock my head. "What do they do?"

"Right now, they own a restaurant on Brighton Beach. In Russia, though, my father was a surgeon and my mother an architect."

Before I can ask anything else, the limo comes to a stop.

I glance out the window.

Wow. I didn't even notice the ride home.

"Go rest," he says, his commanding tone returning and the earlier smile gone without a trace.

I fight the urge to ask about testing again. Something tells me it wouldn't be welcome at this juncture.

"Bye," I say as I open the limo door.

"Until later, Ms. Pack." He pauses, then adds gently, "By the way... you might want to check on your eyebrow."

# NINE

I BURST into my bathroom and stare in the mirror.

Of course. The eyebrow I drew earlier is barely a shadow of itself, and that mixture of curious, suspicious, and skeptical expressions is on my face in full force.

Ugh. Could this day have gone any worse?

The entire time I was talking to him, he must've been staring at that eyebrow. No wonder there were some smiles. He must've been dying of laughter inside.

I take out Precious and order an indelible eyebrow pencil, eyebrow powder, and temporary eyebrow tattoos. I even splurge on stick-on human hair eyebrow wigs in the hopes that one of these things will let me look human again.

When my mortification subsides a little, I check my work email.

Empty inbox.

I've never had zero email before. Even on my first day with Binary Birch, a welcome message was waiting for me, as well as something from HR and Sandra.

Speaking of Sandra, I dial her up.

"You're supposed to be resting," she says instead of a hello.

"I am?" Did she say that sternly?

"I just got off the phone with Mr. Chortsky. He made his feelings clear."

I feel like I'm about to fall through the floor. "Did he explain why?"

"Mr. Chortsky, explaining himself to me?"

This time, I definitely detect a note of annoyance—hopefully at the Impaler and not me. "Look, Sandra, about the testing I was—"

"That's another thing." Her tone is clipped. "We're not to speak about Project Belka or any sort of work until you've rested—and once you have, he wants our interactions to happen face to face."

Weirder and weirder... unless they plan to fire me, that is. I think firing someone face to face is how it's usually done.

"Is there anything else I can help with? Some other projects I can work on?" I ask in desperation. "Being bored won't help me rest."

Sandra sighs. "What about your app? You can always work on that. The cleaner that code, the higher the chance it will impress people."

Is that a hint? Do I need to prepare a resume and use that app as my portfolio?

"Did you send a link to my code to the development department?" I ask, fishing for more hints on my fate.

"As soon as I got it," she says.

"And?"

"I haven't heard back from anyone yet. I'm sure the dev team will review it in due course."

Unless I'm fired. "Okay, thanks, Sandra. How about I swing by the office tomorrow, after I've rested for the remainder of today?"

"Is that what you and Mr. Chortsky discussed?"

"He didn't exactly define the word 'rest' for me, if that's what you mean."

She heaves another sigh. "Fine. As long as you've rested by then, I'm free at eleven tomorrow. Would that work for you?"

"Yep. See you then," I say and hang up before she can change her mind.

———

AFTER I EAT lunch and feed Monkey, I decide to do what Sandra said—check on my app source control repository.

A surprise is waiting for me there.

For the first time ever, someone is collaborating on the project with me.

The first message is about a bug report.

Actually, it's more than that. It's an unwelcome critique of the app as a whole—dripping with cattiness.

*Quaint app. Not bad for someone who's never coded a day in her life. For your information, if you aim the app at an image of a cartoon character's face, the returned lookalike isn't the same character. So, for example, I used it on Daffy Duck, and your app decided he looks most like Donald Duck. If you think about it logically, Daffy looks most like Daffy.*

Hmm. I bring up a picture of Daffy on my work phone and use Precious to aim my app at him. The app indeed says he looks like Donald instead of himself.

So this is a legit bug—especially if one forgets for a second that the app was made for people to use, not cartoon characters. At least a duck looks like a duck. If the app claimed Donald Duck looked like Bugs Bunny, that would be worse.

I check out the helpful user—screen name CrazyOops. No profile image, but the screen name itself is enough for me to guess who this is. First half must refer to (*You Drive Me*) *Crazy* and second half to *Oops!...I Did It Again*, both songs by Britney Spears.

I'd bet Monkey's liver this user is another Britney. As in, Britney Archibald. She must've been dying to find a bug in my code to retaliate for the numerous flaws I found in hers.

Hey, at least it means the development department got Sandra's email, and some of them are looking at my code. Maybe the others are less biased. In fact, I see a couple of other messages already.

First, though, I record CrazyOops's IP address. If she's made other accounts in order to further diss the app, I'll know it's her.

Surprisingly, the next message is not a bug report. Instead, someone located the reason the app was doing what Britney bitched about and fixed it.

Holy binary. Who is this mysterious do-gooder?

The screen name is Phantom, and the profile picture is of the half-masked face of the Phantom of the Opera.

That's not a lot to go by. Maybe she or he is someone who likes the classics—but that can be lots of people.

Putting aside the mystery of the identity of this person, I check out the next message from them.

It's not a bug report or a fix this time, just a direct message. A long one at that. In it, Phantom suggests a whole range of interesting and fun features for the app and includes references to open source projects and libraries that I can use to implement said features with relative ease.

Also, Phantom suggests a number of improvements that would "make the app ready for wide use." The issue that stands out to them is that my database of user pictures is public at the moment, which will cause privacy concerns with the more paranoid users. Here, too, Phantom suggests references that I can use to make this job easier.

I double-check the IP. Not the same as Britney's, but I could've guessed that based on the supportive tone and because she'd never end a message to me the way Phantom has:

*Your code is elegant. I think you have a talent for this. Don't give up, and you'll go far.*

Even though I have no idea who Phantom is, it's got to be someone on the dev team, which makes me swell with pride.

Also, I get the screen name now. Whoever this is, they're acting like a mentor, which the Opera Phantom was to Christine.

I just hope this Phantom isn't hideous, or harboring a dark obsession with me. Note to self: Don't call the Phantom an Angel of Software and keep an eye out for a mannequin that looks like me in a wedding dress.

Grinning, I write a thank-you message to the Phantom of the Code and spend the rest of the day familiarizing myself with all the sources they've provided me with.

As I work, I actually feel myself becoming a better programmer—or at least a cockier one.

When my eyes get tired, I log off and feed myself and my grumpy guinea pig some dinner. After that, I put on the gloves and the N95 mask again so I can rid myself of the one remaining eyebrow. I manage to do this without getting the toxic substance in my eyes, mouth, ears, or any other orifices.

Eyebrowless, I survey my pale face in the mirror. I look like I've gone through chemo, yet still better than when there was just one eyebrow.

Belatedly, I realize my big eyebrow-related shopping won't arrive in time for my meeting with Sandra. Oh well, I'll just draw them on and make sure to redraw as needed.

Thus determined, I finish my evening routine and go to sleep.

---

WHEN I ARRIVE in the office the next morning, Sandra and I grab the meeting room nearest her cube. She looks uncomfortable, exactly as I imagine she would if she were about to fire me.

Crap. Is this it?

"So," she says, steepling her fingers.

I brace myself. "Yes?"

"How are you?"

"Ready to work on something," I say, doing my best not to sound insubordinate.

She shifts in her seat. "The order from the top is that you're only to work on Project Belka."

I raise the patch of skin where I drew one of the eyebrows. "So I can just resume that?"

Sandra clears her throat. "Not until you've been deemed rested."

"Do I not look rested?" I take out a mirror and make sure that I don't have bags under my eyes—and that the eyebrows are still in place.

She glances furtively in the vague direction of the Impaler's office. "I'm not the one who has to decide."

"I see." I drum my fingers on the desk. "So let me get this straight: I can't work on anything but the project that's on hold until I'm miraculously rested. And to top it off, if we want to talk about said project, it has to be face to face?"

She nods. "Sorry you ended up coming here for nothing. I was actually hoping you'd have an update for me."

Ah. She might be a little sore that I ended up interacting with her boss directly. She doesn't realize that was by accident.

I sigh. "I didn't mean to criticize *you*."

She gives me a slight smile. "I know. I'm sorry again that I got you into this mess in the first place. He wanted my best person on the project and—"

"Oh, don't worry. And thanks for passing along my code. I already got some feedback."

"That's great," she says. "From who?"

"They used screen names. But maybe you know... Is there anyone in the office who likes the Phantom of the Opera a little too much?"

She rubs her chin. "Rose, in accounting?"

Rose is pushing ninety, so if it's her, more power to her.

"My guess is that this is someone in the development department," I tell Sandra.

She frowns. "No one comes to mind."

"Okay, thanks." I stand up. "If that's all, I'm going to get some tea and head home."

"Good idea," she says. "My official directive to you is to rest."

"Got it." I give her the same crisp military salute I gave the Impaler, but this time as a joke.

She grins, and as we leave the room, she says, "My unofficial advice is to keep improving your coding skills."

Is that another hint about my fate? I almost ask outright, but I don't want to put her on the spot.

When I get to the pantry, I grab a chamomile packet and pour hot water into a cup.

Before I can dunk the tea bag into the water, I feel a presence enter the small room, creating a disturbance in the Force that gets my Spidey senses tingling.

As I look up, a pair of lapis lazuli eyes capture my gaze, making my stomach flutter.

"Ms. Pack," the Impaler says, his accent stronger than usual. "I hope I didn't startle you."

"Hi." The syllable comes out as a husky whisper that should be in an HR rulebook, filed under "inappropriate for the corporate environment."

"How do you feel?" He pours himself a cup of water.

I finally drop my chamomile packet into the water and pray that something about teabagging isn't about to escape my lips. "I feel ready for work again." There. I can be appropriate when I focus very, very hard.

Speaking of, I shouldn't say the word *hard* either.

"Ready for work?"

It must be a Russian superpower to imbue such a short question with that much skepticism.

"Ready as a tropical storm." I lift my chin. "Isn't Project Belka urgent? You said that—"

"Not here." He frowns at the pantry entrance.

Sure enough, Britney is standing there, her eyes narrowed.

Was she a ninja in her past life?

"I understand," I say.

"Did you eat lunch yet?" he asks me.

I shake my head, struck mute by the question.

"In that case, it's my treat."

Taking my affirmative reply for granted, he strides toward Britney, whose eyes are catlike slits at this point.

For a second, I wonder if he'll be forced to tackle her.

But no. She moves out of the way.

As I hurry past her, I can feel a cloud of malevolence emanating from her, like poisonous mercury fumes. I don't have a chance to analyze it, though, because I'm overwhelmed by the realization that I'm going to lunch with the Impaler.

Me.

And him.

Eating together.

Like on a date?

No, that's stupid. This isn't a date. It's a work lunch, one that might be a ploy to fire me outside the office so I don't cause a scene.

Still. I feel giddy, like I'm going to prom—and I never actually went to prom.

Now I wish I were better dressed and had those premium human hair eyebrows glued on.

The Impaler stops by the elevator, and I'm so preoccupied with my thoughts that I slam into his back.

Holy cow. I just felt some seriously hard muscle.

Waving away my mumbling apology, he jabs the elevator button.

I stand there *not* thinking about licking his finger.

Nope.

Not me.

When the elevator doors open, he gestures for me to go first, so I do.

Realizing I'm still holding my tea, I gulp it down, the heat burning my insides. He mirrors me by downing his water in one go. His Adam's apple bobs up and down, and I want to lick it.

*Stop fantasizing about licking random body parts.*

His phone rings.

"Excuse me," he says and checks the screen.

Frowning at whatever message he's just received, he types out a reply with the speed a teenage girl would be proud of.

"Everything okay?" I ask when he looks up.

"Yes, but I only have fifty minutes for lunch. Is that okay?"

Even if it weren't okay, which it is, it's not like I'd tell him so. "You're a busy man. I understand."

We exit the building and cross the road, his long legs taking such wide strides I have to speed-walk to keep up.

Before I get sweaty, he stops next to a place I've never been to—because it's one of the best restaurants in New York City, and maybe the world. Or if not the best, then certainly the most expensive.

The Impaler pulls open the ornamental glass door. "After you."

Swallowing my awed disbelief, I step inside. As soon as the host sees the Impaler, he fawns over us as though we were royalty, leading us to a well-positioned table by the window—no doubt next to C-level executives of all the major corporations in the downtown area.

Boss squared must be a regular here.

Before I can say "nice to be in the top point-one percent," our glasses are filled with wine that no doubt costs more than I make in a year.

"Where's the menu?" I whisper, not wanting to sound like a rube to the nearby CEOs.

"I usually order the chef's choice," he replies, matching my lowered tone. "Want to risk it with me?"

Nodding, I take a sip of the amazing wine and check out the impeccable tablecloth in front of me.

This place is fancy. Too fancy to take someone if you wanted to fire them. Or just talk to them about testing sex toys, for that matter.

But then—

Can it be? Am I on a date?

# TEN

NO. This can't be a date.

This is just a place he likes—and why not, if he can afford it? Since his parents own a restaurant, he's probably a major foodie and a snob for tablecloths and such.

Yeah. That must be it.

He scans my face. "Are you sure you're fine? You seem a little shell-shocked."

"It's this place, not the... umm... incident from yesterday," I reply, my cheeks instantly burning.

He looks around as if seeing the restaurant for the first time. "We could go somewhere else."

"No, this is fine. You've only got fifty minutes as is. I want to get down to business."

He arches his perfectly real eyebrow.

"Project Belka," I say. "I wanted—"

The waiter appears as if out of thin air and inquires if we've decided what to order.

"Chef's choice," we say in unison.

The waiter bows and scurries away.

"Back to the matter at hand." I take a sip of the wine, for bravery. "The testing for Project Belka—"

"Is not something we want to discuss in such a public venue." He glances at the swanky people nearby. "Wouldn't you agree?"

I put my wine glass down with a little too much force. "Isn't that why we're here?"

He gestures at the ice statues and the other décor. "We're here because we need to eat."

My cheeks flush, but with anger instead of embarrassment for a change. "I don't like having something like this hanging over me."

His sensuous lips flatten. "It doesn't have to."

Is that a threat? "So you're firing me over—"

"Firing you?" He looks genuinely perplexed. "Given the circumstances, I just assumed you'd want to give up the project."

I get it now. He doesn't think I can handle it. Like my asshole ex, he probably thinks I'm too much of a prude goody two-shoes for sex toys.

I'm so sick of this. Just because I have a round baby face that's prone to blushing, everyone makes these sweeping assumptions about me.

Fuck that.

"I'm not giving anything up. You'd have to pry the project from me. Is that clear?"

"Crystal." Amusement touches his eyes, but also something else —admiration maybe?

"I get that we can't talk details here," I say, switching to a tone that's much more appropriate when addressing my boss's boss. "Please pick a time and place that suits you. I'd really like to proceed with the project."

"Deal." He pulls out his phone and fires off a text. "How about this? If you come with me to my next engagement, we can talk in the limo on the way."

Next engagement? Before I can ask him for more details, the

waiter arrives, carrying a small plate with something that looks like a crepe with caviar on it.

"De Jaeger," the waiter says. "And *kuznechik blinis*. The chef sends his regards to your father for the recipe."

So, my theory about his parents' restaurant having something to do with this lunch was correct.

This isn't a date.

Too bad. I was warming up to the idea.

"Care to explain what this is to this gourmet dummy?" I ask as soon as the waiter hurries away.

"Taste it first," he suggests.

I do, and an explosion of umami flavor tantalizes my taste buds. "Subtle nuttiness," I say in my best imitation of a posh food critic, "with the slightest hint of sweet, savory, and a note of woodiness."

"That's not a bad description," he says, tasting his portion.

"And what is it?"

He points at the white eggs. "That's snail caviar. And blinis are a type of Russian crepe, only instead of traditional buckwheat, these are made with cricket flour, which provides that nutty flavor."

Blood drains from my face.

To fight my gag reflex, I stay so silent you can hear crickets.

No. Must. Not. Think. Of. Crickets.

Or snails. Or slugs. Or the Blob. Or sentient snot. Or—

"This food is perfectly safe." The Impaler gives me a worried look. "You liked the way it tasted, didn't you?"

Well, yeah, but that was before I knew what abomination I was eating.

He waves at the waiter, who rushes over right away.

"The lady will have the chef's sampling of the children's menu," my boss squared declares.

The children's menu? So now he thinks that I'm not just unadventurous sexually, but also when it comes to food.

"No," I snap. "The lady will stick with the chef's choice."

The corners of the Impaler's mouth tilt up slightly as he asks the waiter, "What's coming next?"

"Balut Benedict," the waiter replies.

I nervously sip my wine. "That doesn't sound so bad."

"*Balut* is a duck egg in which the fetus has gotten a chance to develop into a little bird," the Impaler explains. "That Hollandaise sauce is usually made with duck eggs too."

"Fermented," the waiter adds helpfully.

Fermented.

Of course.

I didn't think my face could get any whiter, but there it is.

"I'm still sticking with it," I shock myself by saying. "What comes after the eggs?"

"Huitlacoche chowder," the waiter says, and I think he's beginning to enjoy himself at my expense.

The Impaler full-on smiles. "Huitlacoche is also known as corn smut—a fungus that used to destroy corn crops but nowadays is a delicacy."

"Seriously?" I look at the waiter.

He nods.

"I feel like I'm on the hidden camera version of Fear Factor," I say.

"You know what, I'll take the children's menu," the Impaler tells the waiter. His eyes gleam behind the lenses of his glasses as he asks me, "Want to join me?"

I sigh in defeat. "You don't need to do that."

"I insist. I've never tried the kids' menu, so I'm going to do it today."

"Fine." I take a small sip of my water, mostly to keep the crickets and the snail eggs down. "I'll have the children's menu too."

The waiter leaves.

The Impaler rightfully assumes the rest of the crepes are all his, so he finishes them as I sit there, trying to think of how I can save face after all that.

Or at the very least, start some kind of a conversation.

My phone buzzes.

It's a text from Ava.

*Impaled yet?* This is followed by a syringe emoji and an eggplant.

It's like she sniffed out this maybe-date.

A burst of irritation at the world at large crystalizes into something more specific—namely, annoyance at Ava. I blurt out loud, "Who do you think would win in a fight: Snow White or Belle from *Beauty and the Beast?*"

There. It's more civilized than asking him if he thinks I'd succeed in pummeling Ava into the ground.

The Impaler swallows the last bite of his dubious appetizer, his forehead furrowing in thought. "Would this be a random encounter in a neutral location?"

"Why not?" I sip my wine, fighting the urge to push back that unruly lock of hair that keeps falling over his forehead.

It really, really wouldn't be appropriate.

The furrow underneath the lock of hair deepens. "We're talking standard versions of those characters?"

"There are versions?"

"Sure. The original story of *Beauty and the Beast* was French, but there's also a Russian one, which even has a cartoon that's much better than the Disney one—at least in my opinion. On the other hand, *Snow White* was originally a story by Brothers Grimm. It also has a Russian version. She goes by Snowdrop and lives with seven *bogatyrs* instead of dwarves."

I lower my voice. "Is bogatyrs something disgusting they serve at this restaurant?"

He adjusts his glasses. "A bogatyr is a warrior from Russian legends."

I cock my head. "So this Russian Snow White lives with seven warrior dudes?"

He nods.

"That sounds like a reverse harem romance."

Amusement glimmers in the blue depths of his eyes. "I think she stays pure for her prince—who's not one of the 'dudes.' Also, the Disney version could be seen as reverse harem also, if your mind is dirty enough."

As someone whose mind is never far out of the gutter, I redden as I picture Sneezy, Grumpy, Dopey, and Sleepy in a gang bang with Snow White.

"How about we stick with Disney versions?" I say.

"In that case, Belle would win." He sounds as serious as if we were talking about the quarterly reports. "Of those two, Belle is more adventurous. She fought for the Beast at the end and had more depth when it came to her reasons for falling in love. In contrast, Snow White is a stereotypical damsel in distress who'd probably ask Prince Charming to fight Belle in her stead."

Damn it, he's right. I couldn't win even in this allegorical battle—and what's worse, he just called my allegorical doppelgänger unadventurous.

The waiter comes back, carrying a tray filled with plates.

Everything looks safe enough, but I wait for him to explain what it is.

"Mixed yuca and yam fries in bechamel sauce," he says, pointing at the relevant plate. "Bluefin tuna fish sticks. Quail nuggets. Beaufort D'Été quesadillas."

I beam at the waiter in relief. "It all sounds delicious."

When he leaves, I lean toward the Impaler. "That's the kid's menu? Do they even allow children in this place?"

Another hint of a smile. "I've never seen one—and I'm a regular."

Figures.

I reach for one of the fries, and he must've had the same idea because our fingers touch.

I suddenly feel a hunger that has nothing to do with food.

"After you." He gestures at the fries.

I snatch a couple and stuff them into my mouth.

Wow.

Not sure if I got a yuca or a yam, but it's yum. The fish stick I try next is the best I've ever tasted, the nugget is pretty amazing as well, and when I bite into the quesadilla, I almost moan in pleasure.

Then I notice something. He's using a fork and a knife for the items I've just eaten with my fingers, like a cavewoman.

I spear the next nugget with a fork. "This is much better than snail eggs."

"I'm glad, Ms. Pack. I wouldn't want you to regret my choice of this restaurant."

I chew the nugget, debating if I should ask him this or not. Finally, I decide to just go for it. "Look, after the hospital thing and this lunch, would you mind calling me Fanny?"

That way, I'll be able to stop thinking of round, hungry things and, more importantly, might forget for a moment that I'm lusting after my boss's boss.

His sexy lips quirk. "Fanny," he murmurs, and hearing my name with that accent makes me like it for the first time in my life. "Call me Vlad, then."

My heartbeat speeds up. "Vlad," I repeat obediently.

Wait, did that sound too husky? Because I really like the sound of his name on my lips. No more boss squared or the Impaler business for me. I'm calling him Vlad every chance I get.

Another smile curves his lips. "But no diminutives, okay?"

I blink at him. "Isn't Vlad already a diminutive form of Vladimir?"

He looks impressed. "I'd call it the short form, but that's pretty good for a non-Russian."

A warm glow spreads through me at his praise. "I picked up a few things in Brooklyn College. A high percentage of the computer science students shared your background. One guy called me Fan'ka, so I looked into this."

A dark gleam appears in his eyes—that or my imagination is running wild. "Fan'ka sounds like something you'd call a naughty child. The affectionate version would be Fannychka."

Fannychka. I like it. Fannychka Pack doesn't sound like a waist bag anymore.

Nor does Fanny Chortsky for that matter.

He narrows his eyes. "That mischievous smile... If you were thinking about calling me something like Vovochka, don't. It happens to be a character that's the butt of a lot of Russian jokes."

Huh. I had no intention of doing so, but that's interesting. And thank God he's not an actual vampire and can't read minds. "Deal," I say. "But you have to tell me one of those jokes."

He frowns. "They don't translate well."

"That's fine. I still want to hear one."

"Okay. Bear in mind that Vovochka is usually a misbehaving child. Think Dennis the Menace. Also, Russian humor can get pretty dark."

"Now I really want to hear one." I pick up my wine glass.

"Here goes: One sunny Sunday morning, Vovochka runs to his mother: 'Mom, hurry, Dad hung himself in the living room!'. The mother nearly has a heart attack as she rushes to the living room—just to find it empty. 'April Fools', Mom!' Vovochka says. 'Dad's hanging in the bathroom.'"

I nearly choke on my wine.

Vlad's phone dings with a text.

He glances down, then looks at me apologetically. "The limo is outside. I have to go soon. Are you coming?"

I wipe under my nose and sneak a peek—no wine. "Is it far?"

"No, just a short drive away."

I'm about to ask more, but he loads a heaping portion of nuggets onto my plate. "Let's finish this quick. We don't have much time."

We attack the food as if we were in a hot-dog-eating contest, which doesn't prevent me from having a couple of foodgasms. Sadly, his phone begins beeping all too soon, so we leave some delicious stuff uneaten and get up.

He leaves a fortune in cash on the table and leads me to the car. As he opens the door for me, I catch a glimpse of Britney across the street. She's standing there, staring at us.

Stalker much?

Ignoring her, I climb in and sit next to where he left his laptop in hopes that he'll sit next to me.

I'm a Machiavellian genius.

Vlad takes a seat right next to me, and his lapis lazuli eyes meet mine.

My breath catches in my throat at the dark heat in his gaze. The air in the car suddenly feels charged with so much electricity I all but smell ozone.

His eyes fall to my lips, and as if pulled by a magnet, he slowly leans toward me.

Holy Kobe Cow.

Is Vlad about to kiss me?

# ELEVEN

MY HEART DRUMS a battle hymn in my chest, and my skin feels like it's burning all over. All I can see are his lips, so beautifully shaped, so soft-looking. All I can think is leaning forward and closing that small remaining distance so that—

The car rips forward, jerking us both out of the moment.

"Buckle up," Vlad says, his voice hoarse as he scoots a few inches away.

Moving like a zombie, I buckle up while he barks something at Ivan in Russian.

The car slows down.

Vlad raises the partition and turns to face me. "So, you wanted to talk."

I take in a deep breath and gather my courage. "As I said earlier, I'm doing the testing, and you can't stop me."

The amusement that touched his eyes the last time I made this ultimatum is there again. "Didn't you have someone else lined up for this testing originally? Sandra mentioned something along those lines."

I shake my head. "She flaked." There's no way I'm going into the whole succubus-turned-nun debacle with him.

He sighs. "Fine then. Test it yourself if it means so much to you."

I peer at him to make sure he's not kidding. "That's it? You're just okay with it?"

He folds his arms across his broad chest. "You'll have to convince me you can do it safely, of course."

My cheeks burn. "I can be safe. That squirrel thing was an honest mistake. Going forward, I'll do more due diligence and learn about the... err... hardware before using it. My plan is to break it all up into male and female batches, and obviously, I'll make sure to test only the female toys from now on."

He cocks his head. "Who will be testing the male batch? Or did he flake too?"

"It was the female's boyfriend, so yeah, I lost him when I lost her. My new plan is to either create an ad on Craigslist or a Tinder—"

"Absolutely not." The thunderous expression on his face must be what gave someone the idea of calling this man the Impaler.

My heart skips a beat, but at the same time, I feel my hackles rising. "No?"

The car halts.

"We're here," Vlad says through his teeth. "Do you want to wait for me in the car, or would you like to see the offices of a video game company?"

"The latter," I say, mostly to show I wasn't cowed.

In sullen silence, he holds the limo door for me, then leads me into a high-rise building, past security (where I learn he's a consultant for the video game company we're about to visit), and into the elevator.

"Look." His tone turns conciliatory as the elevator starts moving. "Getting a random guy off the street is extremely dangerous. I don't want you washing up in the New York Harbor because of this job."

He might have a point.

Before I can reply, the doors slide open and he gestures for me to come out.

"To be continued," I say and exit.

He gets us in with his ID, and I stare at the décor around us with unabashed curiosity.

The plaque on the wall is in a fun font reminiscent of comic books. It proudly states: *1000 Devils.*

That sounds vaguely familiar. I think I've played a game they made, maybe even two.

In contrast to the rather sinister company name, there are bright colors all over, and the distant laughter makes it feel like a children's playground.

This is a corporation? It almost seems like someone tried to design the exact opposite of the oppressively boring grays of our own silent-as-a-tomb office.

"First things first." Vlad leads me into a walk-in closet to the side. "Gear up."

Huh?

There are no clothes here, just Nerf guns.

Lots of Nerf guns.

Alrighty then. War it is.

Vlad grabs two rifle-shaped ones, then opens his trench coat and stuffs a handgun-shaped toy into the belt of his pants.

Lucky gun.

Shrugging, I pick out a two-handed white-and-orange blaster that reminds me of the Tommy Gun they show in old gangster movies.

"Stay back to back with me," Vlad says, no hint of a smile on his face.

I do as he says, though when our backs touch, my hormones go haywire.

I bet there's a drooling grin on my face.

We walk like that onto the main floor, like a pair of cops storming a mobster hideout.

Suddenly, an orange projectile smashes into my fake eyebrow.

"Hey!" I rub the spot before I recall that I have to be careful not to smear the drawing. "Not the face."

"Sorry," someone says.

I spot the assailant—a forty-something redheaded dude with a beer belly—and squeeze the trigger to unleash a cloud of darts into his chest.

Someone leaps out of the corner.

Vlad lunges in front of me and takes the next dart in the chest.

This time, the shooter is a lady a little older than Sandra, but I don't let that stop me from unloading the rest of my darts into her torso.

Two more attackers join the fray.

Vlad is out of darts, and so am I.

Dropping his weapons, Vlad ushers me against the wall, so that the swarm of projectiles that are meant for me smash into his back.

Wow.

He's right up against me, and it's intoxicating. I can smell the sensual notes of bergamot and citrus and feel the warmth coming off his big body.

He looks down, and our eyes meet. His pupils are dilated, his high cheekbones edged with a hint of a flush. Slowly, he bends his head and—

"Leave my brother alone," a voice booms over the sounds of the Nerf guns firing. "He's here to help."

# TWELVE



BROTHER?

My hormone-addled brain recalls a mention of a sibling who inspired Vlad to go into computer science.

Vlad steps away from me, rounding on the newcomer with a string of Russian.

Now that there are no delectable muscles blocking my view, I scan the speaker.

Yep. Has to be a brother. They look so alike they could pass for the same person—except the older sibling is a scruffy, laidback-looking version of the two.

"This is Fanny," Vlad says, switching back to English. "We work together at Binary Birch."

Work together—that's a nice euphemism. He could've said "works under me." No, wait, that would make me sound like a hooker.

The brother extends his hand. "Alex."

No Mr. Chortsky here, interesting. Oh, and I get the 1000 Devils reference now—Alex owns his last name, it seems.

"Nice to meet you," I say as I give his hand a professional shake.

"Step into the war room," Alex says and leads me and Vlad into a large conference room with a view of Central Park.

A bunch of people are already here, and unlike the exuberant gun-toting colleagues we left outside, they look subdued, even haggard.

"We have a problem with Squirrel Simulator," Alex says, but he makes it sound like there's a double "w" where the double "r" should be in Squirrel, and a "w" instead of "r" at the end of simulator.

Weird. He said war room without doing that, so it can't be a speech impediment.

"Again?" Vlad frowns and explains to me, "1000 Devils just released a fix for a major glitch in that game."

So, Squirrel Simulator is a game. I should've guessed that.

"Is it like Goat Simulator, but with a squirrel?" I ask.

"Much more fun." Alex's chest expands with pride. "A squirrel is smaller, so it can get into places a goat can't even dream of."

Vlad darts me a quick glance, then asks, "Did the glitch not get fixed?"

I redden. Was that glance in reference to the "squirrel can get anywhere" comment? It might be, since in my case, a type of squirrel was up my butt—and that wasn't really fun. At least not for me.

"The last glitch is gone, but I think the big update with the fix introduced this new problem." Alex picks up a remote, and YouTube shows up on the screen in front of us.

A video starts playing with a cute squirrel scurrying under a park bench. Suddenly, the furry creature expels smoke out of its mouth, which turns it pixelated—making the squirrel look like a demon from the deepest circles of hell.

Vlad frowns. "This reminds me of that glitch in the Sims, the one that made babies look like monsters."

"It's eerie," I say, looking at the distortions in the image that look like claws and tentacles. "Almost like you did it on purpose to scare people."

"Exactly." Alex opens a laptop on the conference table and looks at his brother. "Can you check if we've been hacked?"

Vlad takes a seat in front of the laptop and starts typing away.

"Did you know cybersecurity was yet another one of my little brother's talents?" Alex asks me with a wide grin.

"Nope." I shoot a hungry glance at Vlad. Realizing the brother might catch on, I clear my throat and ask, "Have you ever been hacked before?"

"Never—and for the same reason. Vlad set up the security."

"Have you already found the bug in the code?" I ask.

"No. The development team are on it, but it's hard so far because we've been having trouble replicating the problem here in the office. The only reason I know that video isn't a hoax are the one-star reviews from angry parents whose children couldn't sleep after seeing this glitch."

"Mind if I check out the game?" I ask. "What platform is it on?"

"It's available everywhere," Alex says. "Phones, PCs, consoles—you name it."

Nodding, I pull out Precious and search the app store for Squirrel Simulator made by 1000 Devils.

I don't find it, but I do see Squiwwel Simulatow.

Alrighty then. It's *really* for kids. This explains why Alex pronounced the name that way.

I kick off a download of the game, and as I wait, I ask, "What was the glitch you just fixed?"

Wincing, Alex pulls up another YouTube video. In it, the still-super-cute version of the squirrel approaches a bully-looking kid who's holding a baseball bat.

The squirrel halts.

The kid smashes the bat into the furry creature.

The squirrel takes flight, and flies and flies until the cityscape under him is barely visible.

Then the plummet begins.

"I take it that wasn't supposed to happen?" I ask.

"Bug in the physics engine," Alex says, sounding defensive. "We're not the first to have something like this happen. The giants in Skyrim send people flying into the sky to this day."

"Which is why we should've left it alone," Vlad chimes in, his fingers still dancing away on his keyboard.

Alex shrugs. "We were getting hundreds of bad reviews for that, not to mention the emails from upset parents."

Noticing that my download is done, I bring up the game.

Cute. I get to pick what I look like. I choose orange fur, maximum tail length, and white belly—mainly because that's how the demon squirrel from the video looked before the horrific transformation began.

The game starts with a tutorial. I learn important facts, like that my teeth never stop growing and therefore I have to gnaw on things constantly to stay healthy. It also teaches me how to zigzag when escaping dogs and other enemies, how to bury nuts so that a fellow squirrel won't steal them—sometimes even faking the burying process to mess with AI squirrel minds—and how to use my tail for balance and as a parachute during a fall or an umbrella on snowy days.

At least the realism isn't one hundred percent. I'm sure the complaining parents wouldn't like their kids to know that there's a type of squirrel that has giant genitalia—at least for a squirrel. My ex told me about them. Their shlongs are forty percent of the length of their body, and the family jewels are about half that. My ex was clearly envious, especially of the other factoid: During masturbation, these squirrels can bend over and stick their penis in their own mouth. Also, most female squirrels have multiple male partners when they're in heat—I've seen such an orgy a few times in the park.

When the tutorial is completed, I direct my furry self to scurry over to the nearby park, one that looks like the setting of the YouTube video. I figure that with my QA experience, I have as good of a chance of replicating this bug as the next corporate drone.

I climb every tree in the vicinity, eat some nuts, seeds, and a few eggs from an unattended bird nest—but look cute and cuddly throughout.

Hiding nuts doesn't help, nor does hiding inappropriate things, like the lollipop I steal from a toddler.

I'm about to give up when I spot something that strictly speaking shouldn't even be in this game—a cigarette butt under one of the benches.

I get that these are everywhere in reality, but this is a children's game.

I also recall something I read once: Squirrels are addicted to nicotine from eating leftover butts, and also caffeine from licking discarded Starbucks cups.

Would the game let me eat a cigarette butt?

Hopping over to it, I grab it in my furry paws.

Before I can put the disgusting thing in my mouth, Vlad's voice pulls me out of the game.

"It's hard to prove a negative," he says. "But as far as I can tell, you haven't been hacked."

Ignoring Alex's reply, I put the cigarette butt into my mouth as if it were a juicy acorn.

Eureka.

Instead of eating the thing, the game cuts to smoke expelling out of my mouth—which, in hindsight, was a clue—and I become demonic, just like in the video.

"I reproduced," I say.

Everyone snickers.

Vlad rolls his eyes. "Children."

"As I was trying to say, I was able to reproduce the problem." I show the screen.

Vlad stands up and comes over, invading my personal space. "How?"

Though it's difficult to think like this, I explain about the cigarette butt.

His eyebrows furrow. Then he hurries back to the seat and bangs away on the laptop again.

Alex and I watch over his shoulder.

C++ covers the screen, and Vlad mutters something as he skims the code.

"Aha," he says and minimizes the code window. He plays around in the source control repository until he has a code submission on the screen. One that, presumably, introduced the problem.

"This did it," he says, confirming my suspicion. "Talk to Johnny Kove. If he did it intentionally—which seems to be the case—fire him."

Does he own this company also? He sure sounds like he does.

Alex looks upset. "He's one of my best developers."

"You're one of your best developers," Vlad retorts. He explains to me, "Alex originally wrote this game, as well as a few other mega hits."

"He's being too modest," Alex says. "We wrote it together, but now that he's so busy with Binary Birch projects, I work on it with my dev team."

"Well, it's your call," Vlad says, but his tone doesn't match his words. "Keep in mind, though, if the guy does something like this again, I won't come to the rescue."

Alex says something in Russian. It sounds conciliatory, but it could be my imagination.

Vlad replies sternly, and they go back and forth like that for a bit. Something tells me the topic has shifted from games to something more personal.

"Thank you both," Alex says when the sibling bickering comes to an end. "I'll walk you out."

That saves us from the Nerf gun attack. When the elevator opens, Alex glances at his brother with a mischievous expression, then faces me. "Fanny, we're having a big 1000 Devils anniversary party at my parents' restaurant next week. Could I ask you to please drag Vlad over there? It would mean the world to the family."

"You don't have to dignify that with a reply," Vlad growls.

Since Vlad ultimately pays my salary, I take that as a hint to stay silent.

The elevator doors slide shut, and Vlad jabs the button for the lobby. "Back to our earlier conversation," he says as we descend. "Did you think of a safe way to test the male batch of the hardware?"

I did, in fact, do just that. Running around as a squirrel is very conducive to plotting evil deeds, as well as testing procedures. The problem is, I don't know if I have enough proverbial balls to voice my insane idea out loud.

"Look," he says softly. "If you want to quit the project, I understand."

This again? He thinks I've chickened out? That my prudish nature has won?

I straighten my spine. "Actually, I have the perfect male in mind for the testing. Someone you'll think is safe, guaranteed."

His lips thin into an angry line. "Who?"

I take in a deep breath and call forth all of my courage. "You."

# THIRTEEN

"ME?" Eyes widening, he steps back.

I'm committed now, so I barrel ahead. "It makes sense. I presume you trust yourself not to toss me into the Harbor. The privacy of the project isn't compromised. And, well"—I blush horribly—"you have the right parts for it."

Unbidden, my eyes drop to said parts, then I quickly look up.

The elevator doors open.

"Let's continue this in the car," he says, his expression turning unreadable.

Crap, crap, crap. Is he hating the idea? Hating me for even suggesting it? Ugh, how awkward is it going to be if he says no?

Am I about to get fired for coming on to my boss's boss?

We get into the limo again, sitting opposite each other this time.

He makes the partition go up. "Just to clarify: I test the male batch, acting as both giver and receiver, right? I actually already tested one of the pieces on myself after I wrote the app, so I could in theory do the same with the rest of them."

Yes! He's actually considering it. I want to jump up and down, even as the blush that had slightly receded on the walk from the elevator returns in all its glory. "That wouldn't be good end-to-end testing, and you know it. You wrote the code; that makes you biased."

His nostrils flare. "Then how?"

Even my feet are blushing at this point. "You just act as the receiver. I act as the giver, and record the testing data. It's the proper way these things are done."

His eyebrows lift. "That's stretching the definition of the word 'proper' way outside its comfort zone."

"Look." I try to mime his accent as best I can. "If you want to quit, I understand."

A slow, sensuous smile curves his lips. "I don't shy away from a challenge."

Can my panties really melt, or is that just a saying? Doing my best to play it cool, I quirk my fake eyebrow. "That's a yes, right?"

"Yes. How do you see this working, logistically?"

Holy guacamole. He's in. I got him to commit.

But what now?

On some level, I didn't expect him to actually agree to this madness, and now that he has, I'm faced with the logistics of using sex toys on my boss's boss. Logistics that will include getting him off —and recording how fast in a spreadsheet.

Or worse, recording that I *couldn't* get him off.

C++ help me, there are worse logistics than that. For example, don't most guy toys require an erect penis to go into some of the toys? How do I make sure his is ready for testing... logistically?

"You don't have to decide all this now," he says, once again seemingly reading my mind.

"Right." I clear my throat and reach for my inner QA analyst. "Off the top of my head, it would be best to use the app as close to how it was intended as possible. Meaning remotely." As in, I don't want to be next to him for the "getting the penis ready" part of these logistics.

Unless, maybe I do?

No. Must at least pretend to be professional. Or what passes for professional under the circumstances.

"Yes, doing this remotely makes sense." Is that disappointment hidden behind the indecipherable expression on his face? "When do you want to start?"

"I'm free tonight," I blurt.

Crap. That wasn't smooth. Do I look like a loser who has no life?

Recalling the scent of perfume on the testing sheet and inside the suitcase, I quickly add, "Assuming you don't have a Friday night date, that is."

He pulls out his phone and sends a few rapid-fire texts. "My evening schedule is now cleared. This is very important."

"Why is it so important?" I ask.

What I really want to know is if it has something to do with someone who uses a little too much perfume.

He frowns. "I thought I explained this earlier. There's a chance to demo the final product to the editors of *Cosmo* in two weeks."

That's why it's important to the Belka company, but not why it's important *to him*. Oh, well. I guess he doesn't want to tell me the real reason—which might mean it has something to do with the perfumed mystery lady (or possibly gentleman—why not keep an open mind?).

If I needed another reason to keep things professional between us, here it is: Vlad might already be taken.

*Who is she?* the green monster of jealousy demands.

*How would I know?*

*Find out, then tell her you humped her man with a sex toy.*

*Belka is probably the company she works for, so she might not care.*

*Plan B: kill her.*

The car comes to a full stop, and with a mixture of relief and disappointment, I realize I'm home.

"So... see you tonight?" I unbuckle my seatbelt.

He exits the car and holds the door open for me. "Unless you change your mind—which would be totally fine."

Unless I chicken out, he means.

Nope. Not happening.

Hopefully.

"Get home safe," I blurt.

Is he staring at my lips?

Am I staring at his?

A faint smile touches those lips. "You too."

"Thanks." I make a concentrated effort not to trip over something as I sprint for my door.

As I get into my building, I catch a glimpse of him still standing there by the limo, watching me.

Dashing inside my apartment, I lean with my back to the door, fanning myself.

Monkey peeks out of her little house.

"I know, right?" I say. "What did I just get myself into?"

---

AFTER MONKEY and I get our bellies full, I find creative ways to keep myself from worrying about the upcoming testing—and what works best is looking at my code.

I implement some of the easier ideas the Phantom had suggested, then check to see if he's written to me again.

He has—along with making a change in my code.

*I hope you don't take offense, but I renamed all the counter variables to use the word "count," which is the Binary Birch standard. While I understand that your variation—Chocula—was a joke, it detracted gravitas from your otherwise elegant code. You can, of course, revert this change.*

Huh. I, too, get the urge to change code I dislike when I see it. Especially when I spot the kind of atrocities I saw in Britney's work.

Since Phantom has a decent point there, I don't revert the change. As much as I like Count Chocula—and I go coo-coo for the stuff—the last thing I want is for the development team to think that I don't take coding seriously. For that matter, it's not good to publicize my cereal addiction so widely, especially now that I have a new delicious vampire in my life—Vlad.

Speaking of the devil, it's almost time for the testing.

As I redraw my eyebrows and in general make myself more presentable, I contemplate if the testing should take place in my bedroom or the living room. Since living room seems a tad more professional, I tidy it up, then rush to the bedroom to get the suitcase with toys. Returning, I park it next to my couch.

What should we test?

I open the suitcase, examine the male-oriented toys, and choose the one that seems the least intimidating. Still, I go on Precious and research how to use the thing—no more toy-related hospital trips, thank you very much.

The toy is a type of sleeve, and its use is usually pretty straightforward: lube it up, then stick a shlong into it. From here, the user would usually slide it up and down by hand, but the Belka model is high tech and will do the sliding up and down by itself. It'll also vibrate if that's desired.

Determined to be ready for any eventuality, I lube up mine and put a finger in.

Then two.

Interesting.

I've never put fingers inside another female—only myself—but this is eerily similar, except it feels cold. So more like a dead female, I guess.

How stretchy is this thing?

I put another finger in.

No problem.

I put in a fourth.

Still no problem.

I make a tight fist, and it slides in.

Great, I'm fisting the poor jellyfish/dead woman's vagina.

Going back to two fingers, I bring up the app with my other hand to see the options I'll need to use later.

The major buttons are "Stroke" and "Vibrate."

I click Stroke, and the sleeve tries to swallow my fingers like a hungry jellyfish.

Wow. How did they get it to move like that?

I press Vibrate next—and now it feels like that jellyfish is trying to swallow my fingers during an earthquake.

Throughout this exercise, I do my best not to think about Vlad.

Or his cock.

Or—

Precious pings with a text.

Crap. It's time.

I sprint to the kitchen, toss the sleeve into the sink, and wipe the lube from my fingers with a paper towel.

Returning to the couch, I check my phone.

Right. It's the text that will link my app with Vlad's.

As soon as I set that up, the videoconferencing part of the app comes to life.

Picking up the call, I try to be cool and not blush. This is work related. No reason to panic.

Then I see his lapis lazuli eyes gleaming behind his lenses, and all professionalism goes down the drain.

My cheeks burn as if stung by that same hungry jellyfish.

"Hi, Fanny," he says, his accent thicker than usual.

"Hi, sir." I fight the urge to salute him.

The corners of his lips twitch. "You can call me Vlad, remember?"

"Right. Vlad. I picked out the toy for today. The sleeve. It's the—"

"I know the one." He disappears from camera view, and I hear him rummaging in what I assume is his own suitcase.

When he reappears, he's holding the toy in question.

Impossibly, my blush deepens. "Yeah, that one."

"Good choice." He brushes the tip of his finger around the toy entrance—making my lady bits insanely jealous. "This is the same one I used for my own testing."

"Great." It takes effort to hold the phone steady. "So... I guess you put yourself into it?"

Echoes of my earlier logistical thoughts buzz around my head.

He needs to be hard for this. Is that my problem? Surely not.

"Do you need a minute?" I nervously lick my lips. "To watch an adult video or—"

"I'm ready." His gaze seems to be on my mouth. "Where do you want me to point the camera? I'd prefer it to be my face, but if—"

"Your face is good." The words come out like the pained croak of a toad that's been run over by an ice cream truck.

I mean I'm only human, so I really, really would like the camera pointed down, but there's no QA reason for it that I can think of, not unless I'd made the sleeve and wanted to make sure it fits snugly on his—

"I'm in," he murmurs.

Alrighty then.

That means it's my turn... to get him off.

# FOURTEEN

<br>

STAY PROFESSIONAL.

Clinical.

Somehow.

"I'm going to test the Stroke button first," I say, and pray I don't have a stroke as I do.

He nods.

I press the Stroke button.

His pupils dilate.

An intensity dial pops up on my screen.

"I'm going to scale up the speed." Did my voice come out husky? Got to quit that.

He bites his lip and nods.

I slowly get him to fifty-percent intensity.

His jaw muscles tense and his pupils dilate even more as his eyes roam my face with the hunger of a predator.

I like it. A bit too much. I cough nervously into my fist. "Tell me if it gets to be too much."

"This is good." His breathing is clearly ragged.

Damn, this is hot.

Way, way too hot to be professional.

I never would've guessed how much I'd enjoy this. I have to constantly fight the urge to sneak my hand down so I can join him in the fun.

"I'm adding in the vibration. Okay?"

I take the grunt of his response as a yes, and click the button.

He groans, and his neck muscles tense. Then he exhales loudly, relaxing.

As I watch his O-face on my screen, I nearly have that stroke.

It's official.

I brought my boss's boss to orgasm.

Yep. That happened.

At least, I think he orgasmed.

Better check.

"Did you finish?" I ask, my voice barely above a whisper. "I need to know for the documentation."

There. That sounds semi-professional—especially if I were a courtesan.

"Yes. It was intense." His voice is raspier than usual. "When I used the same toy on myself, it felt much less so."

"Huh," is all I can say at first. "Must be like tickling yourself. I wonder if my testing earlier wasn't valid since I also did it on myself."

What am I saying? Why did I go there?

Probably because I want him to get me off more than anything in the world.

He tilts his head, eyes fixed on me intently. "If you want to retest, I can help."

"Right," I hear myself saying as if from a distance. My heart pounds in my chest. "Good idea."

*What?* a part of me shouts. *Are you so horny your brain has stopped working?*

"I better hang up now," he says. "Have to clean up."

Clean up. Right. Because I made him come. My face burns bright again, even as disappointment snakes through me.

I'm not ready for this to end.

"When should we resume?" I ask, trying to keep my tone even. Professional, as befits an interaction between an employee and her boss's boss. "Tomorrow?"

His eyes gleam. "I appreciate your enthusiasm, but I wouldn't want to make you work on the weekend."

Ah, right.

It's Friday night.

I forgot that—along with my name.

"Weekend is no problem," I manage to say. "I did all that resting. This isn't going to eat up my whole day anyway. We'll just do one more piece of hardware. You said this was important."

Do I sound overeager?

Am I overeager?

"How does eight p.m. tomorrow sound?" he asks. "Unless you have plans?"

So, he and the perfume lady aren't meeting on Saturday night either. That raises the chances there isn't anything going on between them—unless whatever is going on doesn't require formal dates, that is.

I take in a deep breath. "I'll clear my evening schedule."

"See you then," he says and hangs up.

I make sure he really hung up, then grab a female toy at random and finish myself off to regain a semblance of sanity.

Giddy with relief, I document today's testing, finish my daily routine, and go to sleep.

THE NEXT DAY goes by in a haze.

I code more of Phantom's suggestions, play with Monkey, and in general try to keep my mind off the big event that's happening at eight.

A package from UPS comes in the afternoon, filled with eyebrow paraphernalia. It takes me a while to try out the indelible eyebrow pencil, eyebrow powder, and the temporary tattoos, but the winning look turns out to be the stick-on human hair eyebrow wigs, proving once again you get what you pay for.

Doing my best not to think about where that human hair actually came from, I go about my day until I get a call from Ava.

"Have you been avoiding me?" she asks instead of a hello.

"No," I say.

She huffs. "You didn't reply to any of my texts."

"Fine, maybe. I just had a lot going on."

There's a prolonged silence on her end of the line. "Is it Impaler related?"

"Yes." I tell her what happened.

"OMG," she squeals when I'm done. "You're such a hussy. I love it!"

"Am not. We're keeping things strictly professional."

"Uh-huh. Denial is not just a river in Egypt."

I roll my eyes. "He might have someone. We work together. I—"

"For tonight's testing, choose that prostate toy," she says, and I can almost hear her grinning. "Guys can be touchy about their butts, so if he lets you shove something in there, he's into you, for sure."

My face burns like the surface of the sun. "We're testing remotely, so any shoving will be of his own doing."

"Tomato, tomahto. End result: toy in butt."

"Well, he agreed to test all the boy toys." I fight the urge to scratch my human hair stick-ons. "I assume he realized the squirrel was on that list."

"Trust me. He might not have connected the dots all the way up his rectum. If he doesn't back out when you bring this up, it means something. At the very least, serious dedication to work, but more likely proof he's really into you."

I scratch the eyebrow after all. "I guess. I don't see how it will hurt."

"It might hurt him," she says with a giggle. "Make sure to use lots of lube and take it nice and slow. When I do that sort of thing, I like to start with a little bit of—"

"TMI," I shout and begin singing Happy Birthday as loudly as I can.

"Fine," she says. "I better go check on my patient anyway."

I feel a pang of guilt. I haven't even asked her where she was. "They're having you work yet another weekend?"

"I'm used to it," she says. "Keep me in the loop. Byeee."

"Bye." I hang up.

For the rest of the day, I research every toy in the suitcase and ponder an important question: Which toy should I let him retest on me?

After a long deliberation, I settle on the clit vibrator. My own session with it was super quick, which might be good for the first time with Vlad.

First time.

There will be a second. And a third.

My heartbeat skyrockets, and I begin to hyperventilate—but then the videoconferencing part of the app comes to life, so I take in a deep breath and accept his call.

Damn. I almost forgot how hot he is, with those sculpted features and dangerously kissable lips. And that lock of hair is at it again, taunting me, making my fingers itch to touch it.

"Hi," I say, trying not to drown in his intensely blue gaze.

"How's your weekend so far?" he murmurs.

"Keeping busy," I say on autopilot. "How about you? Do something different?"

He seems to seriously consider the question—like someone who's never made small talk before. "I took Oracle to a rodent specialist," he finally says. "That doesn't happen often."

I blink at that nonsensical sentence, then grin as I decipher its meaning. "I assume Oracle is a rodent? Otherwise the specialist would be pretty confused."

He returns my smile. "Oracle is my sea piglet."

I arch a human hair stick-on. "What's a sea piglet? Not those horrific-looking sea cucumber creatures with seven legs that lurk in the ocean depths, I hope? Those are not rodents. More like miniature Lovecraftian monsters."

His smile widens. "Sorry, it's the one English word I often mess up. I meant *guinea pig*. *Sea piglet* is a literal translation of the Russian term. The 'guinea' part of their name never made sense to me. The animals are from the Andes mountains of Peru, so—"

"Wait, you have a guinea pig?" I squeal the question, almost like a regular pig.

"Yeah. Why?"

"I have one also," I say proudly. "Her name is Monkey."

"Seriously?" The smile is a full-on grin now. "Show me."

"I'll show you mine if you show me yours," I say—and blush instantly as I realize how that came out.

The camera blurs as he gets up. I catch a glimpse of a room the size of my living room but filled with ramps, toys, hay, and other guinea pig goodness. In the middle of it all is a fluffy orange creature with fur that goes down to its feet.

"That's Oracle," he says. "She's a Coronet."

Huh. Now I feel like a bad piggy mom. I don't even know what variety of guinea pig Monkey is. Nor have I ever taken her to a rodent specialist. I thought a regular vet would suffice.

Hey, at least I didn't call her Oracle, which I presume is a refer-ence to the database company.

It could've been worse.

He could've named her Microsoft.

Realizing we're at the "I show him mine" stage of the proceedings, I grab a seedless grape to lure Monkey out and point a camera at her when she starts munching on it.

"So cute," he says. "Looks like an American breed."

"Don't worry, yours is almost as cute," I say.

It's a lie. His is actually cuter, but I can't say that in front of Monkey. She'll never forgive me.

He goes back to where he was sitting earlier. "We should organize a playdate. Oracle doesn't display any signs of loneliness, but I sometimes worry about her. And I've heard two females might get along well."

"A playdate?" I look at Monkey for feedback but don't get any. "Is Oracle sick, though? You said you took her to a specialist—"

"No, that was prophylactic. She got a clean bill of health."

Should I take Monkey to a vet prophylactically? In my defense, I don't even go for annual checkups myself.

"Monkey might enjoy a playdate," I concede. "How would that work logistically?"

His face smooths out, assuming his signature unreadable expression. "Let me look at my schedule after we're done. I'll text you the details."

*After we're done.*

I almost forgot what we're here to do.

My pulse picking up, I return to my place on the couch. "Back to business?"

He nods. "What's on the agenda today?"

"Umm. I've chosen the hardware but haven't decided who should go first."

His eyes gleam behind the lenses of his glasses. "How about ladies first? Or should age go before beauty?"

In his case, age doesn't stop him from having more beauty, but I keep my mouth shut. I don't want him to think I'm flirting. "I'll go first, and I'm keeping the camera on my face, like you did."

"Of course," he says. "Which toy are you about to use?"

Blushing, I rummage in the suitcase at my feet and pull out the clit vibrator.

His nostrils widen.

He totally just pictured me using that.

"Tell me when you're ready." His words sound strained.

"Give me a second." Eyes locked with his, I slide down my panties with my free hand.

Now his eyes widen.

I bet he knows what I just did outside his view.

My cheeks burn horribly, but something about the scenario is more arousing than embarrassing, which is embarrassing in itself.

Underwear off, I press the toy to my clit.

# FIFTEEN

"READY," I whisper. "But go easy with the intensity."

His finger grows big on my screen as he presses the "On" button.

The most minute vibration begins.

Wow.

I'm already on the verge.

His eyes roam my face.

The vibration intensifies.

Heat spreads through my core.

Must. Not. Moan.

The speed slows.

What the hell? The orgasm that was almost there begins to slip away.

Is he teasing me?

The speed increases again.

Then slows.

Then speeds up.

"Don't stop," my mouth says without my conscious permission.

Is that a satisfied smile? My vision blurs because the speed skyrockets.

I can't help but moan. And moan again.

The speed increases once more and takes me fully over the edge, which is when I cry out in pleasure.

Hey, at least I didn't scream out his name.

Feeling melty aftershocks, I move the toy away and try to catch my breath. "That was definitely more intense than when I was doing the driving."

"Told you," he murmurs, looking a little smug. "Now, do you want to be done for the day?"

"Nice try. Your turn now."

He arches an eyebrow—a real one, which makes me jealous. "Which toy?"

Until now, I wasn't sure if I'd do what Ava suggested, but because he played with the speeds, making me moan like a porn star, I decide to go for it. "Since we're in retesting mode, I was thinking the squirrel."

The hint of smugness disappears from his face, replaced with his usual indecipherable expression. He rummages somewhere and holds up the butt toy to the camera.

My sphincter nervously squeezes. It might have PTSD. "Yes, that." Wait, was I trying to sound sultry? "Unless you want to officially chicken out?"

"Why would I chicken out?" he asks calmly. If he minds this, he hides it well.

"No reason. Tell me when you're ready."

As he lubes up the toy, I do my best to keep a poker face.

One of his hands disappears from my view, and I fight the urge to giggle.

I can't believe he's really doing it.

He's putting—

He winces slightly. "Ready."

Does he look hesitant? Do I care?

A professional wouldn't care.

This is just testing, after all.

The familiar "P-spot stimulation" button appears on my side of the app. Feeling disproportionally naughty considering I'm just pressing my phone's screen, I launch the squirrel.

He looks thoughtful as the toy looks for his prostate.

I hold my breath.

If there's still a bug in his code, the toy might miss the prostate, and we'll have another hospital visit on our hands.

Nope.

The screen informs me that the squirrel has reached the promised land that is Vlad's prostate.

I clear my throat. "Last chance to back out."

"I'm good." The words don't match his expression, but I take them at face value and jab the "On" button.

An intensity control panel shows up. Feeling merciful, I set the vibration to its minimal level.

His eyes widen.

Is that a good sign? I've never played with this stuff before, so it's hard to tell.

Cautiously, I up the speed a smidge.

His breathing becomes ragged, and the veins on his neck pop out.

He's enjoying it, right? Did we need a safe word for this?

Figuring he'd say stop if needed, I up the speed a little bit more.

"Fanny!" he grunts.

Fanny, speed up or stop? I keep the speed the same.

He grunts again, this time clearly in pleasure, but the O-face is different today... almost as confused as it is blissed out.

I stop the vibration.

He sits there, breathing heavily.

"It happened, right?" I fight the urge to add, "Was it good for you?"

"Oh, it happened." His voice is hoarse. "It was very different, though. I've heard about orgasms without penile stimulation, but—"

He stops talking, no doubt realizing the questionable profession-alism of "penile."

Blowing out a breath I didn't realize I was holding, I order the squirrel to get out of him.

"You okay?" I ask when I see him wince again.

"All good," he says. "But I have to go now."

I bite my lip. "We'll get in touch tomorrow?"

"I'll text you," he says and hangs up.

I stare at the blank phone.

Well, that just happened. I violated my boss squared. Gave him a sexual experience he's never had before—a new type of orgasm, in fact.

But was his willingness to do that proof that he's into me, as Ava suggested?

Nah. I bet he just said yes because he's that dedicated to this project and/or open-minded. Which makes me wonder if he'd let me—

No. Stop that.

I get up, clean myself up, have a snack, and stumble into bed.

For the entire night, my sleep is restless and dreams are of the wet variety.

# SIXTEEN

A TEXT from Vlad is waiting on my phone first thing in the morning:

*Sorry if the end of testing was a little abrupt last night.*

Huh. I didn't even think about that. Now that he's pointed it out, it's understandable. If I were the one with a toy in my butt, I'd have hung up even faster than he did.

*No problem,* I reply and even add a smiley emoji.

A new text arrives instantly:

*What's Monkey's schedule like? I figured I'd introduce her to Oracle today, and if they like each other, we can set up that playdate.*

Introduce guinea pigs? What would it look like if they did or didn't like each other?

Given that I find the playdate idea adorable, I reply with:

*Monkey is wide open today.*

Wait, did I just make Monkey sound like a slut?

*How does eleven sound?* he asks.

I check the clock. There're a few hours left, so I agree with this too, a little more hesitantly this time. The logistics of the introductions are a little fuzzy in my head. Are we doing it over video conferencing or—

*Great. Oracle and I will be over at eleven.*

Over? As in, to my place? I knew something about this introduction business was dodgy.

Well, it's too late to back out of it now. Plus, a part of me loves the idea of seeing Vlad in person.

*See you at eleven,* I text him and launch into a cleaning frenzy.

By ten fifty-five, my place is cleaner than it's ever been, and I'm wearing my nicest casual dress, plus the premium eyebrows.

"You're about to make a friend," I tell Monkey.

The door rings.

My heart leaps into my throat. He's a little early. I sprint over to the door and open it.

Vlad is frowning on the other side. "You don't have a peep hole, yet you didn't ask who's there."

I just stare at him.

He's got his usual black trench coat on, but the blue shirt underneath is more casual than the dark, crisply starched ones he wears in the office—though not by much.

"What if I were some criminal?" The deep blue eyes are glaring at me disapprovingly, and I finally realize what he said.

"You told me you'd be over at eleven." I try not to sound defensive. "What are the chances a criminal would come to kill me at that exact time?"

"Still, I—"

"Is that Oracle?" I point at the creature in the carrier he's holding. "She's even cuter in person."

His stern expression warms as he follows my gaze. "I hope this works. It'll be fun to see her play with a peer."

"Well, come in and let's do this," I say, gesturing toward the living room.

He takes off his shoes—probably a Russian thing—then walks into the living room and over to where Monkey lurks.

As he passes by me, I detect a faint hint of that same woman's perfume I smelled earlier.

Shit. Was he with her, whoever she is?

Asking would be extremely inappropriate; we're supposed to be acting like colleagues, not jealous lovers.

*Smash something,* the green monster demands.

*Now you sound like the Hulk.*

*Smash her head.*

*Correction, you sound like a homicidal maniac.*

"Hi, Monkey," Vlad says in a tone that sounds suspiciously like baby-talk.

Monkey watches him with unusual interest.

He places his carrier next to Monkey's home and waits.

"What's happening?" I ask, putting the question of perfume out of my mind for now.

I'm not giving in to the green monster. I refuse to.

"This is so that they can see and smell each other, but not touch," he explains.

Monkey scurries closer to edge of her cage, and when she spots Oracle, she squeaks.

I'm not a huge expert, but it sounds like a happy squeak.

Oracle's reply squeak is similar, and she's also at the edge of her carrier. Their noses are now only a few inches apart.

"That's cute," I say as they begin sniffing each other—which kind of looks like an air kiss.

Suddenly, Monkey jumps into the air, the way I've seen her do when I think she's happy.

Oracle does the same.

"That's called popcorning," Vlad says, his gaze not leaving the pets. "Very positive sign—and unexpected so soon."

"Interesting. What's next?"

"Not sure. My research says to keep them separate for a while, but given this reaction, we could risk putting them together right away—assuming you're up for it.

"Let's go for it."

He takes out his phone and sends someone a text.

The green monster stirs. Did he just ping the wearer of the perfume?

A few seconds later, the doorbell rings.

"That's Ivan," Vlad says. "But do ask who it is before you open it."

"Yes, Mom," I say and hurry to the door, Vlad on my heels.

"Who is it?" I enunciate.

"Ivan," says a heavily accented voice.

"Can I open now?" I ask Vlad.

He nods. "Now it's safe."

When I open the door, Ivan is standing there with a huge aquarium in his meaty hands. The floor of the enclosure is scattered with toys, veggies, and other things Monkey would go gaga for.

"All new stuff," Vlad says, noticing my confusion.

"Why?"

He smiles. "Gives their first meeting a neutral space. Less chance someone will feel territorial."

"All right." I gesture for Ivan to come in.

The big man also takes off his shoes, then deposits the aquarium near Monkey's house. When she sees him, she bares her teeth at him, the way she always did with my ex.

"Monkey, you pig, don't be mean to Ivan," I say sternly.

"It's fine." Vlad glares at Ivan as though the big man had provoked the teeth-baring somehow. "Ivan was just leaving."

With a huff, Ivan stomps out of the apartment.

"Oracle doesn't like him either." Vlad takes his guinea pig out of the carrier and holds her to his face. "Do you, girl?"

Wow. His guinea pig rubs noses with him. Monkey never does that with me.

Vlad deposits his pet on the floor of the aquarium. "Do you mind if I put Monkey in there too?" he asks. "How does she feel about strangers?"

"She didn't bare her teeth at you," I say. "So go for it."

He gently reaches into Monkey's home. To my surprise, she leaps into his hands. Crazier still, when he raises Monkey to his face, the treacherous creature rubs noses with him too.

I feel doubly jealous. That should be me rubbing noses with him, or at least it should be me that my pet rubs noses with.

"You're a guinea pig whisperer," I mutter as he gently puts Monkey into the aquarium.

It's either that, or he does have those vampiric powers after all, the ones that allow him to make animals his bitches.

"Monkey probably just smelled Oracle on me," he says. "They're clearly soulmates."

Aww. He's right. The two pigs begin running around like a couple of happy toddlers, squealing excitedly, rubbing noses, sniffing all the toys, and eating all the veggies. Not once do they hide in the little houses available in the corners of the enclosure.

"You know, that looks like a guinea pig mating dance," I say, watching their antics. "I've seen it on YouTube. Are you certain Oracle is a girl?"

He turns my way. "Are you sure Monkey is a girl?"

I grin widely. "All I'm saying is, Monkey's not on the pill."

He feigns seriousness. "If there are piglets, I'll take them."

"If there are piglets, you'll pay child support," I deadpan.

The pigs stop the dance, plop down, and begin grooming each other.

Double aww. "Adorable."

He looks up from the pigs and scans my face, eyes gleaming. "Adorable indeed."

# SEVENTEEN

FOR THE FIRST time since he's come over, I fully process the fact that I have him here, in my home.

He looks good here.

Like he belongs.

Wish I could keep him.

"How long should this introduction be?" My question comes out a bit breathless.

His lapis lazuli eyes capture my gaze. "The introduction is pretty much over, and is a resounding success. We're all set for a playdate. When are you and Monkey free in the near future?"

I smile. "My work schedule has been pretty chill, so any day should work."

"Speaking of work..." He steps toward me. "Are you up for more testing tonight?"

Tonight? I'm ready for some right now. The mother of all blushes adorns my cheeks as I nod.

"How about eight p.m.?"

I nod again.

He takes another step toward me. We're now close enough for me to smell his warm, sensual scent, but also that slight undertone of perfume.

He stares at my lips.

Fuck it. I'm going to ask him about the perfume.

Any second now.

Just need to make words, that's all.

The doorbell rings.

He draws back. "Are you expecting anyone?"

Still mute, I shake my head.

"Who could it be?" he asks. "Your parents? Ava?"

I force my vocal cords to function. "Ava's at the hospital. Parents have the keys to this place and, sadly, just barge right in."

He takes out his phone and sends a text.

"Could it be Ivan?" I ask.

His phone pings. "Not Ivan. Some guy. Blond, thin, with—"

I furrow the human-hair eyebrow wigs. "That sounds like my ex."

Vlad's real eyebrows snap together. "Ex-boyfriend?"

"He's been finding excuses to visit from time to time." I'm unsure why there's so much defensiveness in my voice. "A month ago, he 'realized' he forgot an Xbox game. Two months prior to that, it was a hoodie."

"He just comes unannounced like that?"

The doorbell rings again.

"Let me see if it's actually him." I head over to the door.

Vlad follows, and I feel a little giddy at the prospect of Bob seeing a guy this hot in my apartment—and reaching conclusions.

"Who is it?" I shout at the door.

"Fanny, this is Bob," the person says in the voice of the One Who Shouldn't Be Named.

I open the door.

Bob grins at me—a grin that peters out when he spots Vlad. "I was... err... in the neighborhood," he stammers. "Realized I forgot my copy of *GEB* at your house. Any chance you can give it back to me?"

I glance over my shoulder at Vlad. "*GEB* is *Gödel, Escher, Bach.*"

Vlad's face is vampire cold. Maybe even liquid-nitrogen cold. "Right. The book by Douglas Hofstadter. I've read it. It's great."

That makes sense; lots of people in our industry like that book.

"You're Bob, right?" Vlad says in a voice colder than a vampire after his daily liquid-nitrogen bath.

With a noticeable gulp, Bob nods.

"I want you to think really hard about any other object you may have forgotten here," Vlad says, practically oozing menace. "This is your last chance to get it."

Was that a threat? Bob's face definitely looks like he's taken it as such.

What should I do?

"I j-just came to get t-the book," Bob says with a stutter he never had while we dated. "I can't t-think of anything else."

Vlad lays a possessive hand on my shoulder. "Fanny, do you know where the book is?"

"Sure." I make my voice breezy, mostly to cut the tension down to about-to-explode-balloon levels. "I'll go get it."

As I leave the two men behind, I wonder if there will be only Vlad by the time I get back, plus an exsanguinated husk.

Locating the book, I rush back.

Bob looks whiter than a brand-new porcelain toilet, while Vlad's eyes are like icicles as he stares my ex down.

"Here." I thrust *GEB* into Bob's noticeably shaking hands.

"Thanks," he mumbles.

"Did you think of anything else you will ever need?" Vlad's tone could cut through glass. "I mean it. This is your last chance."

"N-no. I will never come here again." The words come out as a stuttered oath. Then Bob turns on his heel and dashes away as if a thousand devils were chasing him.

It's official. My ex just got impaled by the Impaler.

"What did you say to him while I was gone?" I ask, closing the door.

"Nothing much," Vlad says calmly. "Now I've got a lunch meeting."

Before I can ask for details, he strides back into the living room, gently picks up Oracle from the aquarium, and puts her into the carrier.

"You can keep the neutral play space here," I say. "This way, it'll be ready for the play date."

Assuming the play date is still on. He looks stormy enough to cancel it.

"You sure it wouldn't be in the way?" he asks, his expression warming by a degree or two.

I wave my hand dismissively. "Leave it."

"Thanks," he says. "But it might be best to put Monkey back into her own habitat before the play date."

"I get it," I say with a chuckle. "The famous guinea pig territorialness." It's almost as bad as that of a company owner over his testing minion.

His answering smile doesn't touch his eyes.

I usher him to the door and hold Oracle's carrier as he puts his shoes back on. Handing him the carrier, I ask, "We're still on for eight, right?"

His eyes narrow. "Why not?"

"No reason," I lie. "See you then."

He heads toward Ivan's car, and I close the door, exhaling the breath that seemed to have been in my lungs from the start of the Bob debacle.

What the hell was that about? Was Vlad jealous?

No. Can't be. Bob must've inadvertently broken some Russian custom—something like "never come over unannounced." That or Vlad gets particularly hangry around lunch time.

Yeah. One of those must be it. Someone who has a perfumed sidepiece doesn't get to be jealous.

I make my way to the aquarium, pick up Monkey, and hold her near my face.

Nope. No rubbing noses for me. Clearly, that's only something she'll do with Vlad.

Figures.

I gently put the little traitor back into her home, give her a snack, and go make myself busy until eight o'clock rolls around.

# EIGHTEEN

I EXAMINE the toys I've chosen for the big testing session.

If tonight had a theme, it would be suction: The toy for him is something called a penis pump, while mine is its tiny cousin—a clit suction device.

According to my research, both of these toys are meant to work as appetizers of sorts. They draw blood to the target area, heightening sensitivity. The Belka models seem to take this a step further by incorporating vibration and who knows what else.

Since there's time, I take the pump that's a duplicate of the one Vlad will use later and stick my fingers into it.

The material is soft but not all the way jellyfish.

I turn it on.

Wow. It's like having my fingers inside a vacuum cleaner. Is this really going to feel good for him?

I turn on the vibration.

Still feels like a vacuum cleaner, just a louder one.

Turning off the pump, I take the clit sucker and slip the tip of my index finger into it before turning it on.

This feels like the device is trying to give my finger a hickey.

With vibration, it feels like it might want to keep the tip of the finger forever.

Hmm. I wonder how this will feel once it's used as directed?

Maybe I should choose a safer toy?

The videoconference feature of the app rings, and I pick up.

"Hi." Vlad smiles, his earlier grumpiness seemingly gone. "How did the rest of your day go?"

I shrug. "Caught up on some chores. How about you? Did you and Oracle get home okay?"

"I was much too busy for a Sunday," he says. "Oracle is good but acting subdued. I think she might be missing Monkey already."

Come to think of it, Monkey was a little glum after they left. Is she also missing her new piggy friend? Or maybe Vlad?

"We'll have to set up that play date soon," I say.

He nods. "You said your schedule is open, so maybe we make it a work day, sometime early in the week?"

"It's a piggy date," I say. "Now, should we get to work?"

Did those blue eyes just turn hungry behind the horn-rimmed glasses?

"Are we doing ladies first again?" he asks.

Nodding, I show him the toys I have in mind.

He unbuttons the top button on his shirt. "Let me know when you're ready."

I'm wearing a dress without any underwear, so it's a matter of a single moment to put the suction thingy next to my clit. "Ready."

His eyes darken. Has he just figured out my commando situation?

The toy comes to life and latches onto my clit like an FDA-approved leech.

Wow. The finger test didn't properly prepare me for this.

I sneak a glance under my skirt. Damn. Things are engorged. It looks as though I'm about to sprout a penis. I'm glad he can't see that situation. My heart hammers, waves of heat washing over my body as the sensations intensify.

As if from a distance, I hear him ask, "Should I up the suction?"

"No," I pant. "Let's give vibration a try."

As soon as the vibration begins, I have the most intense—borderline painful—orgasm of my life.

Something between a moan and a scream is wrenched from my lips.

Then the device turns off—releasing the vacuum but also causing another orgasm.

This is when I realize that in the throngs of passion, I dropped the phone onto the couch.

Reddening to record levels, I grab it.

His face on the screen is unreadable again.

I belatedly cross my legs. "Did you see anything?"

A hint of a smile. "A gentleman never looks and tells."

That's a yes! How much did he see? And why did it all need to be red and swollen from the suction thing?

What am I saying? I'd be just as mortified if everything were nice and pink down there. Now if my old bush was still there...

Crap, I'm making this worse by staying silent. "It's your turn," I say, my brain kicking into high gear. "According to my research, you don't need to be, umm... ready for that one. The suction of the gizmo will take care of that step."

His hand disappears from view for a few moments. Then he says, "Ready."

As a testing perfectionist, I want to ask if he's starting this out fully erect or not, so I can document that fact. My mouth doesn't form those words, however, so the testing documentation will be less than perfect.

Not that it really matters. As I told him, the device makes it so he'd be hard pretty quickly—a version of the same pump is even used on ED patients.

I press the "On" button.

I can hear the motor whirling on his end of the call.

It sounds strained or something.

His eyes widen.

"I'll up the suction, okay?"

He nods.

I twiddle with the intensity controls.

He sucks in a breath.

If he wasn't hard earlier, I'd bet big money he is now—and that knowledge sends tingles into my oversensitive lower regions.

Suddenly, there's a strange sound. Vlad grunts, but in pain rather than pleasure.

I gape at his face.

It's not his O-face. I know what that looks like now.

This looks more like an uh-oh face.

I halt the suction. "Did something happen?"

He looks down and shakes his head in disbelief. "The pump broke."

"Broke?" I look at my own version of the pump for any breakable parts and don't see anything of the sort.

"It appears to be a sizing issue." This is said almost shyly, and certainly without any hint of superiority or ego.

My eyes bug out.

A sizing issue? As in, the pump got him so big he broke the freaking thing?

How big is he?

I look at my version of the device again.

To break it, he'd need to be as large as Glurp.

Poor little pump. It couldn't take the impaling.

Shit.

Could I?

"Do you think this test was a failure?" Vlad's voice intrudes into my insane thoughts, and I realize I've been silent all this time.

I force myself to smile. "No test is a failure. We've learned something that needs to be addressed, and that's good for Belka. In this case, it's more of a hardware rather than a software problem."

He nods seriously. "You're right. I'll pass this information along to the people at Belka."

Huh. That should be a fun conversation. "How about we wrap up the testing for today?"

Because that monster cock needs to rest.

"Sure," he says. "Same time tomorrow?"

"Works for me," I say and hang up so that I can finally spring over to my utility drawer and get my measuring tape.

The pump is eight inches in length and seven in circumference.

That gives me the lower bounds of what Vlad must be packing—and it's big enough to require its own name.

I don't have to think hard to come up with one.

*Dracula.*

# NINETEEN

MY SLEEP IS EVEN MORE restless than the night before.

In the morning, I find an email from Sandra in my inbox. She wants to meet for an update.

I tell her I can be down at the office by 11:30 a.m.—time chosen because I, not so secretly, hope to bump into Vlad and have another lunch together.

Sandra thanks me and says that time works, so I dress in my favorite pencil skirt and blouse to look extra professional, put on my good eyebrows, and commute to the office.

As I'm about to step into our building, a classically beautiful woman catches my gaze. She's model tall, has pouty lips, shampoo-commercial jet-black hair, and striking blue eyes.

When she passes by me, I understand what's caught my attention.

It's not her looks but her scent.

I recognize it.

It's the perfume that was on Vlad the other day. It's all over her, as if she took a bath in it.

*Attack,* the green monster commands. *Kill first, figure out if it's her later.*

*No.*

*I get it. Too many witnesses. Stalk her into a dark alley.*

*I have a meeting with Sandra.*

*Puny weakling.*

*Shut up.*

*Don't tell me to shut up. I'll kill you too.*

A security guard looks at me suspiciously, so I get my ID out and finally enter the building.

As I step into the elevator, a guy stops the doors from closing and follows me in.

He looks familiar, but I draw a blank for a second. Then I recall that I saw him at the monthly meeting the other day. My app had decided he looks like Butt-Head; it's just harder to place him without Beavis.

"You're Fanny, right?" Butt-Head asks. "Fanny Pack?"

"That's me." I extend my hand. "And you're..."

"Mike," he says. "Mike Ventura."

I press the button for our floor. "You work in the development department, right?"

I've tested his work, so I know this to be the case, but it seems polite to ask.

"Yeah, I do," he says. "I hear you plan to join us from QA. Saw your code. Pretty elegant."

*Elegant.*

*Phantom keeps saying that about my code.*

*Could Mike be Phantom? Would it be weird to just out and ask?*

The elevator doors open.

He gestures for me to leave first. "If you'd like, we can get together, talk about code and whatnot."

"Sure," I say, figuring that might also be a good time to learn if he's Phantom without being late to see my manager. "Shoot me an email. It's *fpack* at Binary Birch."

There, work email.

Keeping things profesh.

"Sounds like a plan," Mike says with a wide grin. "See ya."

Waving goodbye, I sprint over to Sandra's cube.

"Things are progressing ahead of schedule," I tell her once we grab a meeting room and settle in our chairs. "Nothing to worry about."

She exhales a breath of relief. "Thank you. I'll have to give an update to Mr. Chortsky this afternoon, so this really helps."

I redden. He already knows how things are going, but I obviously can't give Sandra a heart attack by letting her know who my male tester is.

"Anything else?" I ask, eager to run to the pantry to see if he's lurking there.

She smiles. "I heard from my equivalent in the development department."

That catches my interest. "And?"

"She says they don't have an opening right now, but that your code impressed everyone, so when they do get one, you're going to be the first person they interview." Sandra lowers her voice to a conspiratorial whisper. "The feeling I got is that the interview would be a mere formality at that point."

Yay! They like me. "Do you know how often they have openings?"

She shrugs. "Can't be more than a few months. Company's growing."

My excitement dwindles a bit. That's forever away. I should've asked for the move sooner; the countdown could've begun then.

Then again, I didn't have the app to impress everyone with.

Sandra stands up. "Thanks again. Please keep me posted on further progress."

"I will."

I wait for her to leave, then beeline for the pantry.

My heart sinks.

Vlad isn't here.

How wrong would it be if I just popped into his office?

If by "wrong" I mean "inappropriate," then very.

Daydreaming about his eyes, I pour myself some hot water. As I'm putting in the tea bag, the cup slips off the edge of the counter, the water spilling everywhere.

Crap. At least I didn't get burned.

Grabbing some napkins, I bend over and begin to dab at the liquid. My skirt makes a strange creaking noise—it might be too tight for this maneuver—and I feel it rolling up my thighs.

Crap. Is that air I'm feeling on my thong-clad—or rather, un-clad—butt?

I smell citrusy bergamot just as someone clears his throat.

I straighten so fast I nearly give my spine whiplash.

Of course.

It's Vlad.

It wasn't enough that he saw my vag last night; now he's seen my butt too.

Does he at least like it?

I discreetly check his pants to see if Dracula is showing.

Yep. There's a bulge. A nice, big one.

"My eyes are up here," Vlad says.

Oh shit. Now he's caught me staring at his crotch.

At work.

Jerking my head up, I catch my reflection in his glasses.

Surprise, surprise. My burning cheeks are redder than a rhesus monkey's butt.

Like a case of déjà vu, Britney walks into the pantry at that very moment, her eyes jumping between me and Vlad.

"Lunch?" he asks me as soon as he spots her.

I nod, toss the wet towels into the garbage, and sprint out of there as if Britney has sprouted boils.

An elevator ride and a short walk later, I find myself in the same restaurant as the last time—except now I'm wiser and order the children's menu right off the bat.

"The kids' menu for me too," Vlad tells the waiter.

"You don't have to always get the same thing I get," I say, still flushed and flustered from the tea bag incident. "Why should you miss out on tuna eyes, or cobra heart, or whatever else the chef has decided to cook up today?"

"We do have the sesos tacos you like," the waiter chimes in.

My Spanish is so-so, but I'm pretty sure *sesos* is brains. Can someone say *mad cow disease*? At least I hope we're talking cow and not, say, honey badger brains.

Vlad looks intrigued by the brains. I guess vampirism has gotten tiresome, and he's ready to try being a zombie instead.

"Seriously, have the chef's choice," I say. "Otherwise I'll feel bad."

Vlad smiles. "If you're sure."

"I insist," I say and mean it. The other alternative would be for me to get the special with him, and my stomach isn't strong enough for that.

Vlad looks up at the waiter. "Since the lady insists, I'll have the chef's choice after all."

"Of course." The waiter pours us some wine and makes himself scarce.

Vlad raises his glass. "To your health."

Do I look unwell? "Same to you." I raise my wine ceremonially and take a dainty sip.

He puts down his glass.

I do the same, and get distracted by his fingers again—specifically, the urge to lick them.

"Can I ask a personal question?" he asks, snapping me out of my inappropriate reverie.

I quirk my left human-hair eyebrow wig. "Only if I can ask you two in return."

His eyes glimmer with amusement. "Traditionally, these things go quid pro quo."

"I scorn tradition," I say with mock seriousness. "One personal question for the price of two, final offer."

"But you will answer anything I ask," he says. "Truth or Dare rules apply."

"Deal," I say and can't help but feel I might regret it.

"Why did you break up with the book picker-upper?" he asks, his blue eyes narrowing like some truth detection machine.

I was right. I already regret the deal we made. "You mean Bob?"

"If that's his name," he says with noticeable distaste. "The person who couldn't just get himself a new copy of *Gödel, Escher, Bach*."

I take a bigger sip of my wine. "I didn't break up with him. He broke up with me."

Vlad's eyes widen—which flashes me back to the other day when he was enjoying himself under my control. "Why would he ever do that?"

The way he puts that question makes me feel warm and fuzzy inside. Except I don't want to answer that. Not even a little.

He pushes his glasses higher up his nose with one of those lickable fingers. "You want to back out of our quid pro quo?"

I lift my chin. "I already answered your question, so you owe me two answers."

"You know what I meant to ask." He picks up his water. "Do you really want to weasel out on a technicality?"

I take yet another sip of wine for bravery. "He thought I was unadventurous."

Vlad chokes on his water. "Bullshit. You? You're one of the most daring people I know."

Whoa. I gape at him. "I am?"

"I've seen you do something daring each time we've done our testing—and what is that if not adventurous?"

"I guess." I dubiously survey the nearby tables. "But I haven't tried the food here." Or asked him about the perfumed lady.

He waves his hand dismissively. "I bet you could eat it if you wanted to. But why? Food is meant to be enjoyed. If the picker-upper asked you to do something you didn't feel like doing, that doesn't make you unadventurous. His labeling you that makes him an asshole, though."

The waiter brings the food, sparing me from needing to comment on what he said.

He's not wrong, though. Bob *is* an asshole. In hindsight, I should've broken up with *him*. But I was busy with my new job at Binary Birch, and I simply didn't have the mental bandwidth to analyze my relationship. I just kind of went with the flow, even though the sex was at best meh—a situation Bob tried to fix by pushing for ever-more-exotic bedroom acts that I just didn't feel like doing with him. The final straw was after we came back from Prague, where we'd gone to the succubus show at the strip club—which I'd greatly enjoyed, by the way, due to high production values, topnotch costumes, and great acting. In any case, Bob decided that since I was down for seeing showgirls fist each other on stage, I might be cool with golden showers—and that was a hard no for me. And my hard no pissed off Bob—pun intended—who promptly broke up with me. Though sometimes it seems like he wants me back, because he keeps stopping by my place every once in a while to pick up the few items he left there.

Feeling myself getting riled up all over again—normally, I don't even like thinking of Bob's name—I focus on the food in front of me.

It's the same as last time: yuca and yam fries in bechamel sauce, bluefin tuna fish sticks, quail nuggets, and the fancy cheese quesadillas.

I don't look too much into Vlad's selection. As long as it doesn't crawl from his plate onto mine, I'm happy. In any case, my mind is still churning with unwelcome thoughts of my ex—and more annoyingly, of the mystery perfumed lady.

I really need to do something about the latter before the green monster drives me mad.

"So," I say when I finish a fish stick and a nugget. "My turn to ask a question."

Vlad slurps down something I can't—and don't want to—identify. "Shoot."

"Why did your last relationship end?" I ask, pinning him with an intent stare. "Unless... you're still in it."

# TWENTY

THERE. Not very subtle, but hey.

He bites into what must be the brain-based taco, and I half expect his eyes to glaze over, zombie style.

"My last relationship was a couple of years ago," he says after he swallows. "She broke up with me because we didn't have much in common—her words, not mine."

Not enough in common? That's better than "couldn't handle Dracula."

"Since that breakup, I haven't dated much," he continues. "Not because I'm heartbroken or anything. I've just gotten very busy with my company and helping Alex with his."

So not currently dating?

Must suppress glee.

This also means the perfume lady is, at most, a casual hookup—way better than a steady girlfriend, though still not ideal.

But, wait, is he still too busy for dating someone worthy... someone who might look like Snow White?

How obvious will it be if my second question is about that?

Transparent.

One corner of his mouth lifts in a devilish smile. "You have one more question. I'm curious to hear it."

Here's proof I'm not as daring as he thinks. Instead of asking if he's ready to date now, specifically me, I blurt, "How come there's no information about you online?"

The smile disappears. "Because I'm an extremely private person."

I heap some fries onto my plate. "That's not really an answer. *Why* are you so private?"

"Why is everyone else not *more* private?"

I grin. "Is that another question?"

He shakes his head. "Do you have any idea how many people didn't get a job at my or my brother's company based solely on the things they've posted on Facebook and Twitter? And that's a benign example. A government can do something much worse than not hire you. They can put you in jail, or place you on some list, or who knows what else. To me, the fact that millions of people share their most private moments with the world of their own free will is completely nuts. An ego trip gone horribly wrong."

"Wow. Tell me how you *really* feel," I say, mentally cataloguing what I've posted on my social media. Some of it I should probably take down posthaste.

He bites into a questionable morsel that proceeds to ooze something green and sticky. "As the saying goes: knowledge is power. I don't like giving up my power."

I reach to scratch my eyebrow, then recall its precarious nature and scratch my forehead instead. "I get what you're saying. To me, though, it sounds a little paranoid."

This time, I'm pretty sure it's a piece of blood sausage that he puts into his mouth. Hopefully made with pig's blood, but you never know.

"How about a thought experiment?" he says after the sausage is a goner. "I give you a scenario, and you tell me how it makes you feel."

"Sure." I bite into a fry.

"You met with Sandra today." This is said as a statement, not a question.

"Yeah, I did. So what?"

He leans forward. "How about if I told you that I witnessed your whole conversation through the security camera in the meeting room?"

I frown. "I'd say that was a little creepy, but hey, it's your company. Now if you said you peep into the bathrooms, that would be a different story."

"I'm not a perv." As though to contradict his statement, he sticks his fork into something fermented—with a sticky, slimy texture that no food should ever have. "But now you're beginning to get what I'm saying. That feeling you'd have if someone did put a camera into your bathroom is what I'm talking about." Face tightening, he adds, "It's particularly developed with me, and for a good reason."

I freeze, another fry halfway to my mouth. "What do you mean? Did something happen?"

He puts down his fork. "My grandfather was executed based on a political joke a neighbor overheard."

Holy shit. I was not expecting that.

"That's terrible," I say when I find my tongue. "I'm so sorry."

"Thanks. This was before I was even born, so I'm okay."

Whew. I thought I'd stepped on a major landmine. "That wouldn't happen here and now," I say. "What you're talking about was Soviet Russia—a totalitarian regime."

He spears another morsel from his collection—something that looks like two jumbo shrimp glued together. "You never know who'll get power and what they'll do with it."

"I guess. But you don't even have your picture on the company website. Or a bio. That's another level of caution altogether."

He devours the shrimp-looking thing so appetizingly I almost want to try it too. Putting down his fork, he says, "A while back, a local paper wrote an article about my parents' restaurant. It helped the business, at first. Then, one day, racketeering mob types walked into the place, recognized my mom, and forced her to empty the safe at gunpoint. It was thanks to that article that they knew what she looked like, and that the restaurant was doing well." As he says this, his eyes get flinty, hinting at how he got his Impaler moniker.

The bite I was chewing feels stuck in my throat. I think I'm beginning to understand his obsession with privacy. If that had happened to my family, I'd be paranoid also.

"That must've been terrifying for your mom," I say, fighting the urge to put my hand over his. "Did the police catch the bastards?"

His mouth tightens. "Not exactly."

"They got away?"

"Not exactly."

I stare at him expectantly.

He sighs and sweeps his gaze over the nearby tables, as if checking for eavesdroppers. Then, in a lowered voice, he says, "Someone traced the criminals to their Russian social media accounts. Like the rest of the public, the gangsters weren't big on privacy, so they openly discussed criminal activity in their messages. The FBI got the translated transcripts of that communication through an anonymous tip. Just as the mobsters were taken into custody, their offshore bank account got mysteriously wiped out."

Whoa. Is he saying he robbed the robbers? If so, that's pretty badass. I want to pry into it deeper, but he doesn't look inclined to elaborate. If anything, he seems like he regrets saying what he did.

Not wanting him to worry, I raise my hands theatrically. "You win. I almost feel like shutting down my Facebook and Instagram. But if I do, how will I stay up to speed on the health of everyone's cats?"

His expression warms by a few degrees, and he stabs his fork into another morsel on his plate. "You own a guinea pig. Cats are the enemy."

"True, true." I watch as he eats it with even greater gusto. Finally, I can't help myself. "Okay, I think you've inspired me to be daring and try something from the chef's selection. Assuming you don't mind sharing?"

He smiles and gestures at his spread. "Be my guest."

As I scan it all, my burst of enthusiasm begins to wane. "What would you recommend?"

"That." He points at the glued jumbo-shrimp thing. "They're divine today."

Right. That was the item he seemed to savor the most.

I narrow my eyes at the thing but draw a blank. "What is it? Or is it better if I don't know?"

He pushes the plate toward me. "It would be more daring if you *did* know and ate it anyway."

I spear one of the things with my fork. "Fine. Hit me. What is it?"

"Frog legs," he says. "French style—fried with parsley and garlic sauce."

Right. Now that he's said it, I can see it.

Not giving myself much time to deliberate, I stick the two legs dangling off the fork into my mouth.

The explosion of yummy flavor almost makes me moan in pleasure. It's like someone took the best qualities of chicken and fish and mixed them together.

He watches me intently.

"It's good," I say as soon as I can speak again. "I never exactly liked frogs, face to face that is, and wouldn't pet one, but I guess I *can* eat them."

And they're not as gross as snail eggs, that's for sure.

He nods. "I wouldn't pet a sea urchin, but they are delicious."

"Makes sense. Next time, I might just get an order of these."

"You should. Also, if you like French-inspired cuisine, you might enjoy the fare at my parents' restaurant. Speaking of..." He rubs the stubble on his chin. "Remember that party my brother invited you to?"

"The 1000 Devils' anniversary?"

"That's the one. It's tonight, and my family has been pestering me to go."

I blink. "So go. They're your family."

His gaze is intent on my face. "Would you join me? My brother did want you there, remember?"

"I think he wanted me to bring *you*, not the other way around." I sneak a worried glance at the more dubious items on his plate.

"The food will be much less exotic than here," he says, discerning my concern. "The most unusual thing on my parents' menu is probably caviar. Regular black caviar, that is—and you don't have to eat it."

Is he asking me out on a date?

No. His brother invited me first.

Still. This sounds fancy. And it's Vlad who's now pushing me to go.

His lips curve into another wicked smile. "How about we make another deal? I will go only if you go with me."

"Hey. That's not fair. That's like some weird emotional blackmail."

He cocks his head. "You're not the only one who can play hardball."

"But... tonight?" I frantically glance down at my work outfit. "I don't have anything fancy to wear."

"How about I get you something?"

"I'm not sure—"

"If you don't like the clothes, you can opt not to go."

I squeeze the bridge of my nose. "You're pushy."

His eyes gleam. "I go for what I want."

My throat suddenly feels dry, so I sip my water.

"Come on," he says. "Yes or no?"

"Maybe," I say, figuring I can always flake because of the outfit. "Now, can we please talk about something else?"

He looks satisfied, smug even. I guess he's decided I'm going. "Well... there was an interesting computational problem today. Want to hear about it?"

Huh. Does he know about my interest in transferring to the development department? Could be. I wouldn't be surprised if he's on the same mailing list as the rest of them—and could've seen Sandra's email about my ambitions.

"Sure," I say. "What was it?"

"Have you ever heard of the Scunthorpe problem?"

I shake my head.

"Scunthorpe is the name of a town in England, and citizens of that town couldn't create accounts with AOL back in the day because the name contains the substring 'cunt,' which activated AOL's profanity filters."

I grin, which spurs him on to provide a bunch more examples of the same issue, such as when someone couldn't register a domain called *shitakemushrooms.com* because of the first four letters—never mind that the proper spelling of that particular mushroom has an extra "i" that would've fixed the problem. Or when a doctor by the last name of *Libshitz* was not able to register an email. My favorite is how the Montreal Urban Community website was blocked by web filtering software because their French name was *Communauté urbaine de Montréal*, which meant their acronym and therefore website address was "cum."

"And today's problem was almost the same," Vlad says with a grin. "Our HR spam filters were blocking resumes of magna *cum* laude graduates."

As I laugh at this, his phone beeps.

"Sorry," he says after checking on it. "I have to get back to the office."

"Of course," I say.

He throws wads of cash on the table, and we hurry out of the restaurant.

"I'm going to run," he says. "See you tonight."

Before I can clarify that he *might* see me tonight, he's already crossing the street.

Crap. The clothes he gets me would have to be truly hideous for me to be able to flake without looking like an asshole. And if I do, I'll genuinely feel bad if he ditches his family as a result, even if I rationally know it would be on him, not me.

He *is* evil. But that's not news.

As I trek home, I ponder an important question: Did he invite me on a date?

We *have* been spending a lot of time together, and the testing has been hot and heavy, so I could see why he might.

But is it something I want?

Obviously, yes, at least I would if he weren't my boss squared. As is, I can't help but worry how this would look to the rest of Binary Birch. Not to mention, if we dated and broke up, would I lose my job?

Also a factor is the perfumed mystery woman. He saw her as recently as this morning—which doesn't mesh well with my fantasy of this invite being a date.

These thoughts loop in my head throughout the entire commute and when I get home. Then I start wondering when the dress is supposed to arrive and what time the party actually is.

He really didn't tell me anything.

At four p.m., my doorbell rings.

"Who's there?" I ask.

"Delivery," a distant voice says.

I open the door and see two boxes sitting on the welcome mat.

I guess that answers one of my questions.

Bringing it all inside, I open the bigger box.

There's a folded dress with a note inside:

*I will pick you up at seven.*

Okay, another question answered.

I unroll the dress.

It's a gorgeous little black number that might've been inspired by Audrey Hepburn's iconic look in *Breakfast at Tiffany's*.

It looks suspiciously close to my size.

I put it on.

The thing fits me down to a millimeter. Almost as if someone took a cast of my body and designed the dress around it.

Did Vlad hack some online purchase I made? Or did he look at me so closely that he could guess my measurements this precisely?

Befuddled, I open the second box.

A pair of shoegasmic Christian Louboutin pumps is inside—and they fit me as perfectly as the dress.

What is happening?

I check myself out in the mirror and can't help but wolf-whistle.

It's official. There's no way I could say this isn't a great outfit without sounding like a dirty liar.

Taking a selfie, I text it to Ava.

The reply is instant:

*Hot! What's the occasion?*

When I tell her it's to go to a Russian restaurant with Vlad, Precious rings right away.

"Tell me everything," Ava demands as soon as I pick up.

I bring her up to speed, concluding with my doubts about this being a date.

"Oh, it's a date. The guy is majorly into you. He used the squirrel toy, for fuck's sake."

I squeeze the phone harder. "What about the other woman?"

"Ask him about her," she says. "Maybe ply him with a few drinks first."

"I guess..."

"No guessing needed. Do it. Also, have you done your makeup and hair yet?"

"No." I look at myself in the mirror. "My makeup isn't bad. I just got back from work."

"I'm hanging up, and you're dolling yourself up. Do you want me to send you some useful YouTube videos?"

I roll my eyes, though she can't see it. "I can use the internet all on my own. Bye."

I dive into my makeover and end up with an updo and enough makeup to make a naked mole rat look presentable. I even trim the eyebrow wigs a little and gel them up to keep the bushiness under control.

Just as I'm finishing up, the doorbell rings.

Crap. He's here.

Diving into the shoes, I click-clack over to the door.

"Who's there?" I say pointedly, so I don't get chastised for opening the door for criminals with impeccable timing.

"Vlad," he says.

I open the door.

Oh my.

Dressed in a bespoke black suit that hugs his every muscle, a crisply starched white shirt, and a black tie, he's a sight to behold.

"You look amazing," he murmurs, his eyes greedily scanning me from head to toe.

Ignoring the heat in my cheeks and other regions, I twirl coquettishly. "It's the dress you got me."

His voice roughens. "No. It's you." Before I can respond, he gestures at the limo. "Come, we're already late."

Drunk on his words, I get to the limo on autopilot.

He holds the door open for me.

With a goofy grin, I slide inside and sit by his trusty laptop—the last time, this had made it so he'd sit next to me.

Yep. He slides over, his presence making me tingly and giddy.

"Is it hot in here?" He plays with the air conditioning controls.

*So hot. So take off all your clothes...* "I'm okay," I lie, the words of the song playing through my head.

He gives me a warm smile and tells Ivan, "*Poyehali.*" He then raises the partition.

The car torpedoes forward, and we sit there, staring into each other eyes like a couple of staring-contest champions.

"What's the name of the restaurant?" I force myself to ask.

His lips twitch. "On Yelp, it's listed as the New Hut."

"Any relation to Pizza Hut or Jabba the Hut?"

"The latter has two Ts in his name," he says with a smile.

I fight the urge to grab him by the tie and lick that smile. "Well, the word 'hut' doesn't make it sound as fancy as I imagined."

He adjusts his glasses. "It's fancy. The hut bit is a leftover from its longer name—The Hut on Hen's Legs."

I blink, taken aback. "That's a horrible name—no offense."

"I don't disagree. It's a reference to Russian fairy tales. A hut like that was the home of the infamous Baba Yaga. If you've seen the John Wick movies, he was for some reason compared to her constantly."

I lift a well-groomed eyebrow wig. "I've heard of her. She's a cannibalistic witch, right? Ate little children. Great association for a restaurant."

He grins. "That's what I told my parents too. They kept the name anyway. At least everyone's switched to calling it the New Hut, so less cannibalism associations."

"But why is it new?"

"Because the old one burned down, and my parents got the empty space on the cheap. They kept the name because it already had some recognition among the Brighton Beach community."

The limo comes to a full stop, and I spot a green street sign that informs me we're already on the famed Brighton Beach Avenue—or Little Odessa, as it's sometimes called.

Just to confirm this, a train makes thunderous noises on the aboveground subway tracks nearby.

Getting out, I smile at the storefronts with names written in Cyrillic and at people who look like extras in a movie about Soviet Russia.

Vlad leads me to what must be the restaurant—a giant, multi-story wooden hut with, not surprisingly, chicken legs where most other buildings would have columns.

As we walk up the creaky wooden stairs, I brush my fingers along one of the "legs."

It feels as though it's made from real chicken skin.

Raw chicken, that is.

A nice touch. Always have people think *salmonella* before a dining experience.

Inside, the place couldn't look more different from its rustic external vibe if it tried. Marble and crystal are everywhere, evoking Grand Central station and the Metropolitan Opera at the same time.

The party is in full swing, with people shaking booties on a huge dance floor.

There's also a full-on stage here, with a pudgy bearded dude wearing an outfit that shines brighter than a disco ball. In his hairy sausage-like fingers, he's holding a microphone and singing his lungs out.

So, this place isn't just a restaurant. It's also a club and a theater, it seems.

The music is played on a keyboard and sounds vaguely familiar, but it takes me a moment to parse what the bearded guy is actually singing; his thick Russian accent and this context throws me off.

The song is *Single Ladies (Put a Ring on It)*.

Seriously? Beyoncé would die laughing if she heard this butchery of an interpretation.

Vlad leans in, his breath warm on my ear. "They do a lot of

covers at this place. With the American audience, expect a lot of this."

I try to ignore the pleasurable goosebumps spreading down my arm. "Can't wait."

As we proceed further, I notice that most of the patrons are software engineer types—clearly 1000 Devils' staff.

"There." Vlad touches my shoulder and points at a table to the side of the dance floor. "Come meet my family."

# TWENTY-ONE

I RECOGNIZE Alex right away and guess that the older couple sitting at the table must be the parents.

The mother's makeup makes me think of burlesque dancers and drag queens, and her exposed cleavage is so big it probably has a name. Helga, maybe? She's wearing a skintight purple cocktail dress with a confidence I hope to emulate when I'm her age.

The father sports a heavy mustache and in general resembles the singer on stage—hairy and pudgy but with a unibrow that the singer must've plucked.

I again feel a slight stab of eyebrow envy. I'll never take forehead facial hair for granted again.

Neither of the parents have many features in common with the two brothers, but they both remind me of someone. I just can't say who.

"Mom, Dad, this is the woman I was telling you about," Alex says as we approach. "She saved my company the other day, and, as I hoped, has dragged Vlad over here today."

Each of the parents gives me a grateful nod.

"Oh, I can't take the credit." I smile nervously. "Vlad had to convince me, not the other way around, trust me. Nice to meet you both."

Another set of approving nods. If my goal is to get these people to like me, Alex has clearly given me a head start.

"Mother, Father, this is Fanny," Vlad says, his expression surprisingly cool.

They both get up. She's ridiculously tall—a good head taller than her husband. Must be where the brothers got their height from.

"Nice to meet you, Mr. and Mrs. Chortsky," I say, extending my hand.

The father ignores my hand in favor of giving me a scratchy kiss on the cheek.

The wife smacks him on the back. "She's an American. They don't kiss strangers, you old pervert."

"Call me Boris." The father grins so widely the edges of his mustache touch his temples.

The mother smacks his back again, then shakes my hand with a genuine smile and drags me closer. Thankfully, her kiss is of the air variety. "Forgive my bear husband, dear," she whispers conspiratorially. "Call me Natasha."

As I pull back, I do my best to keep a poker face.

Boris and Natasha? That's exactly who they remind me of—the two villains from that old cartoon show with the moose and the squirrel. They even share their names.

I bet if I used my app on them, it would confirm this too. Even their heavy Russian accents are nearly identical.

"Please, sit." Boris pulls out a chair for me—and gets another smack from his wife for his troubles.

"Thanks." I sit down, and Vlad sits next to me.

The table is teeming with plates covered by cloth napkins. No one has begun eating yet, it seems.

"Service the lady," Natasha says to Vlad sternly, gesturing at the covered food.

Service me? Maybe if he got under the table or something, but even then, it would be hella awkward.

Vlad's face is stormy as he gazes at his mother. "Shouldn't we wait for *everyone* to gather first?"

This isn't everyone?

Natasha scoffs. "Latecomers do not get to eat."

"Or drink." Boris grabs a giant bottle of Stoli and pours me a shot without asking if I want one.

He then does the same for Vlad, Alex, and his wife. For himself, he pours the vodka into a wine glass.

Natasha stares daggers at Boris. "You will have shots, like a normal person."

Boris waves for a waiter to come over and says something to him in Russian.

The waiter sprints away and returns with a handful of shot glasses that he pours Boris's vodka into.

"How about a compromise?" Boris says to Vlad and uncovers one plate. "We'll have some pickles and a drink for now, as an appetizer."

"Whatever," Vlad mutters, then spears a pickle and deposits it on my plate.

Boris puts a pickle on his wife's plate, then his own, and Alex "services" himself.

"I claim the first toast." Natasha raises her shot glass and looks around as if daring anyone to contradict her.

Did Vlad just roll his eyes?

Natasha doesn't seem to notice. Looking at me, she says, "Only alcoholics drink by themselves, without a cause, and without a toast."

Wise. I'm not sure any of that is part of the twelve-step program, but I keep my mouth shut, opting to drink some water instead.

"As a woman in her middle years, I can be forgiven if I think about my family legacy," Natasha continues, for some reason narrowing her eyes at Alex before looking approvingly at Vlad.

Looking directly at me, Natasha raises her glass even higher. "To the health of my unborn grandchildren."

I choke on my water and begin coughing.

Boris leaps out of his chair and smacks me five times on the back.

The water comes out of my nose, and eventually, I resume breathing.

"Sorry about that," I say when I can speak. "Didn't mean to mess up your toast."

"It's fine, dear." Natasha sounds comically magnanimous. "I wasn't finished anyway."

"Go on, pookie," Boris says, greedily eyeing his shot glasses.

She nods solemnly. "May my unborn grandchildren be wealthy and joyous. May their mother stay the color of spring and roses. A source of sweet dreams to the man in her life. His attraction and inspiration. May she stay simple yet regal. A princess. The muse to an opera of love. May her days last forever and beyond. To this, we shall drink until we see the bottom of our glasses."

Amen? I feel like someone should give me an Oscar for keeping a straight face.

With a theatrical gesture, Natasha downs her shot in one gulp, then sniffs her pickle before violently biting into it.

Vlad and Alex follow their mother's example, while Boris downs one shot, then another, then a third, then a fourth, and so on until they're all empty.

Not being suicidal, I take the smallest sip from mine that I can.

Fire explodes in my mouth, then spreads through my chest and into my stomach.

Gasping, I try sniffing the pickle like everyone else did.

Nope. That makes it worse.

I bite into it.

Okay, so now I have a salty taste in my mouth on top of the burn.

"So, Fannychka, do you have any Russian in you?" Natasha asks.

If I say no, will she say "do you want some?" and point at Vlad?

After that toast, it wouldn't surprise me.

"I have no clue." I cautiously put down the pickle I was still clutching. "My parents call themselves pure-bred American mutts. I've been planning to take a DNA ancestry test, but haven't yet. But you never know."

My answer seems to please her. At least she looks approvingly at me, then at Vlad.

Boris refills everyone's shot glasses, including the half dozen of his. When he sees that mine is almost full, he frowns but doesn't say anything.

Instead, he dramatically rises to his feet and raises a glass. "The time between the first drink and the second ought to be short."

"Shouldn't we eat something more substantial than a pickle first?" Natasha hisses.

Before her husband can answer, a familiar scent reaches my nostrils.

Perfume.

*The* perfume.

I glance behind me.

Yep.

The modelesque woman I saw by our work building is striding toward our table on five-inch heels. Her makeup looks like war paint —perhaps due to the furious expression on her face.

What the fuck?

Did Vlad invite his side piece to a family event?

# TWENTY-TWO

"AH, if it isn't the fashionably late," Natasha says snidely to the woman.

She was also expecting her?

"Parents." The newcomer's voice is icy. "Bros." The voice is a tiny bit warmer now. "Couldn't wait even a minute, huh?"

Bros?

Whew.

She's Vlad's sister, not his lover.

Unless there's some *Game of Thrones* crap going on, which I doubt.

Vlad stands up and pulls out a chair for her. "I tried to make them wait."

As she sits, I sneak a glance. Now that I know she's Vlad's sibling, I can see the resemblance: the jet-black hair, the blue eyes, and even the ability to put on that chilly expression.

"Bella, meet Fanny." Alex sounds placating. "Vlad's friend."

The ice queen expression melts as the heavily mascaraed blue eyes swing toward me. "Oh, you're Fanny? Nice to put a face to a name."

Face to a name? She's heard about me?

I guess Vlad could've mentioned me when she came to see him this morning. Or Sunday—he did come over smelling like her.

I give her my warmest grin. "Nice to meet you, Bella. You look amazing."

Her return smile is radiant. "You don't need to flatter me. I'm already your biggest fan. Your help on—"

"No business at the table," Vlad says sternly.

Business?

Hold up. What help does she mean? Surely not the testing we—

"Your brother is so right," Natasha says, wrinkling her nose. "No reason to talk about your work in polite company."

Huh? Is she a prostitute or something?

Vlad gives his mother a slitted stare. "Bella's company is the best in its field. They're about to get a writeup in *Cosmopolitan* magazine."

I blink a few times.

Her company.

The *Cosmo* writeup.

She owns Belka?

If so, I was right a moment ago. She was about to compliment me on my help with the testing.

As in, Vlad told his sister about what we've been doing.

I nearly choke again. The snafu with the pump—he was going to tell the folks at Belka they need to get more generous with sizing.

That must've been a fun thing to tell his *sister*.

"Bella shames the family." Boris's usually warm demeanor is gone.

"Bullshit." Bella glares at her father. "*You* shame the family, with your drinking and—"

"Belka, stop it," Natasha hisses. "We have a guest."

Oh, boy. Sucks to be in the middle of a family squabble.

At least I've learned something. Besides meaning "squirrel," *Belka* also appears to be the diminutive of *Bella.*

"Can we eat now?" Alex asks, and before anyone answers, he removes the cover from the plate nearest him.

"Good idea." Vlad does the same to another plate.

"I'm starving," I lie and join them in uncovering the food.

The parents and sister join us more reluctantly. They still look upset. I make a mental note to steer the conversation somewhere safe if I get the chance.

For now, I examine the food.

Vlad didn't lie. It's less weird than the chef's choice from the restaurant—not that the bar was set all that high.

"Is that a Jell-O made out of meat?" I point at the item standing next to Vlad.

Natasha smiles patronizingly. "That's *holodetz.* Try some with *gorchitza* and *hren.*"

"She means *mustard* and *horseradish sauce.*" Vlad puts some of the holo-whatever on my plate and garnishes it with the two items. "Try it."

I do it gingerly.

The thing tastes like a really meaty chicken soup but has that jelly texture, which somehow works.

"Yum," I tell the expectant Chortskys, and as a reward (or maybe punishment), they begin educating me about the rest of the dishes.

The main thing I learn: Russians like to pickle things I wouldn't even dream of pickling, such as watermelon, apples, grapes, and herring.

Also, there are at least four more shots of vodka and long toasts throughout the lesson. Not wanting to get too drunk, I keep sipping on my one shot glass.

My favorite dish turns out to be Oliver or something that sounds like it—I mentally call it "the kitchen sink salad." It has chopped potatoes, meat, carrots, pickles, eggs, green peas, and enough mayo to keep Hellmann's in business for a month.

"She doesn't want caviar," Vlad says when his father tries to put a crêpe and some black stuff on my plate.

I smile sheepishly. "I only dislike snail eggs and cricket flour blinis. If this is buckwheat and sturgeon roe, I'll try some."

Boris laughs. "I can't believe they made my joke suggestion at that restaurant."

"It was pretty good, actually," Vlad says with a grin.

I try the famous delicacy and enjoy it.

"That's nothing as exotic as what we had in Ecuador." Natasha looks at Vlad challengingly. "Did I tell you about *cuy asado*?"

"Fanny won't like that story," Vlad says sternly. Touching my hand, he explains, "*Cuy asado* is grilled guinea pig. Mother likes to tell that story because she doesn't like Oracle."

What? That's horrible. Monkey shall never hear of this dish—she already acts like I might eat her.

Natasha wrinkles her nose. "A rat is a rat."

Wow. So many minefields with this family.

Deciding to save the day, I ask, "Can you tell me some Vovochka jokes?"

The parents exchange an approving glance. It must look like I'm more versed in the Russian culture than I actually am.

"I'll start." Boris puts down his shish kebab. "In biology class, the teacher draws a cucumber on the blackboard and asks, 'Can someone tell me what this is?' Vovochka raises his hand. 'It's a cock.' The teacher storms off. The principal rushes into the classroom. 'Who upset the teacher, and more importantly, who the hell drew that cock on the blackboard?'"

Chuckles all around.

"I know one too," Natasha says. "The teacher says, 'Vovochka, I hope I don't catch you cheating off your neighbor on the next test. 'I hope so too,' Vovochka replies."

More chuckles.

"My turn," Bella says. "Vovochka says to his Mom, 'Where do babies comes from?' Without hesitation, she says, 'The stork brings them.' 'I know it's the stork,' Vovochka replies. 'But who fucks the stork?'"

Even though his joke was also dirty, Boris gives Bella a disapproving glare.

"Can I go?" Alex asks, and before anyone replies, he says, "Vovochka puts on rubber boots. 'Vovochka, there's no dirt outside,' his mom says. 'Don't worry, Mom, I'll find it,' Vovochka replies.'"

Again chuckles.

"That one sounds just like Vlad when he was little," Natasha says to me conspiratorially.

"That's true," Bella says with a grin.

Vlad elbows his brother. "This one wasn't much better."

"We should have another drink before the show starts," Boris says and pours everyone another round.

The show? Is that what the stage is for?

Everyone downs their vodka. Upon seeing how easily Bella does it, I knock back a full shot glass.

It must be the function of the buzz I have going already, but the vodka doesn't burn as badly going down as it did before.

The lights dim.

What I presume to be Russian music begins to play, though to me it sounds a lot like K-Pop.

A bunch of scantily clad girls run out onto the stage. They're wearing masks from that pre-orgy scene in *Eyes Wide Shut*, but their dancing reminds me more of The Rockettes.

After they raise their legs for the umpteenth time, the masked dancers depart, and the music changes to that of *Swan Lake*.

A ballerina steps onto the stage.

At least, she's a ballerina on the bottom. On the top, she's wearing horrible makeup that makes her look like a witch—with wrinkles on her forehead so large they're sprouting their own wrinkles.

Must be a Baba Yaga impersonation. Didn't know the old witch was a dancer.

The one on stage sure is. She performs some truly acrobatic ballet moves—that is, until the pudgy singer from earlier rushes onto the stage, dressed like a child.

Yep.

That's Baba Yaga, for sure. Why else would she pantomime eating the dude?

When she's done pretending to eat him, the bearded child grabs the mic, and the music changes again.

"My milkshake brings all the boys to the yard," he sings with a thick Russian accent.

The Rockettes ladies rush back, also wearing Baba Yaga makeup. Each of them holds a toy that reminds me of the killer Chucky doll—and these dolls are missing random limbs.

Did the Baba Yagas get peckish off stage?

Instead of kicking up their legs like before, the Rockettes/Baba Yagas launch into the famous Russian Cossack dance—the one with lots of squats and leg thrusts.

For elderly witches, they're incredibly athletic.

From here, the show gets even weirder. There are Cirque du Soleil-style acrobats dressed like Teletubbies, jugglers pretending to be bears, a clown straight out of Stephen King's worst nightmares, and a Baba Yaga on a unicycle for the finale.

When it's done, everyone begins to clap, and I join in.

"Ladies and Germs," the singer dude says after the ovation, sweat beading on his brow. "I want to see you on the dance floor." And just like that, he starts butchering Madonna's *Like a Virgin*.

"What did you think of the show?" Natasha asks me, beaming with pride.

Did she choreograph it? "It was... very interesting."

"I am glad to hear it," she says. "We had to simplify it for the American audience."

Simplify? The original must've been the equivalent of an LSD overdose.

"Ask the lady to dance." Bella gives Vlad an exasperated glare. "You're making the family look bad."

"Yeah, bro," Alex says. "Dance."

Smiling with his eyes, Vlad stands up and extends a hand to me, Prince Charming style. "May I have this dance?"

I leap to my feet before my brain can even think about vetoing this questionable idea.

With a knowing smirk, Bella rushes to the stage and yells something to the singer dude in Russian.

He nods.

The music changes once more to a slower song I don't recognize.

Vlad takes my hands like a professional ballroom dancer.

Heat spreads through my whole body from his touch—as though I have vodka for blood.

He pulls me closer.

I swallow my heart back into my chest.

We start to slowly sway to the music.

Can you have a heart attack from being too turned on?

"Bésame," the pudgy dude sings, and for the first time, I feel like he's in his element. "Bésame mucho."

Why, oh why, did I ever learn Spanish? That's "kiss me a lot"— which is exactly what I want Vlad to do to me.

Around us, some of the 1000 Devils' staff get the same idea. People are making out left and right. Hopefully, they're each other's significant others, and not, like in our case, bosses and their subordinates once removed.

Vlad leans down.

I shouldn't kiss him.

But I really want to.

But I mustn't.

He locks eyes with me.

Not fair. It's harder to control myself when looking into those hypnotic blue depths.

And what if he kisses me?

I think he might. And if he does, I won't be able to resist. I'm only human.

He pulls me even closer, and our lower bodies touch.

Holy phallic symbols.

Is that the proverbial flashlight in his pocket, or is Dracula very happy to see me?

I should step back, but I can't.

My legs refuse to move away—not even when Vlad slowly lowers his head, as if his mouth is drawn to mine by a puppeteer's string.

Got to do something. Now.

"We should test today," I blurt, stopping him an inch from my lips.

Eyes gleaming, he lifts his head. "Should we?"

"At your place." Wait, what? How is that better than kissing? This is clearly the hormones and the vodka talking.

His nostrils flare. "Now?"

"It *is* a school night." School night? Did that pop into my head because this is so much like the fantasy of a prom I never had?

"Let's go." He guides me through the slow-dancing throngs of software engineers.

Before I can blink, we're in the limo again.

"What about your family?" I say as Ivan floors the gas pedal.

Vlad takes out his phone and sends a few rapid-fire texts.

A bunch of replies arrive immediately.

He rolls his eyes. "To sum up, everyone liked you. A lot."

Why do I have the feeling the actual texts mentioned unborn grandchildren or worse?

"Good to know." The words come out too breathless for my liking.

"First things first." He reaches into a drawer on the side and takes out something resembling an asthma inhaler. Changing the mouth piece, he thrusts the gizmo in my face. "Blow."

My cheeks burn. Apparently, they pictured my lips around Dracula's shaft, not this device.

"What is that?" I ask, though I can guess.

"A breathalyzer. I want to make sure you're not intoxicated."

Huh, okay. Shrugging, I blow into the thing. I took a drug test before I started working for Binary Birch; this is not that different, I guess.

He frowns. "Point-zero-five percent. I think we're going to take you home."

Is he calling me a lightweight? I lift my chin. "Below eight is safe to drive in NYC."

His frown deepens. "Do you have a car?"

"No."

"Good. Don't even think about driving in this condition."

If the idea was to ruin my buzz, he's definitely succeeding. "Why do you have a breathalyzer here?"

He nods at the driver's section. "I do random checks, especially around the holidays. Russians make fun of drink-and-drive regulations. Ivan isn't allowed to have any alcohol when on duty."

Suddenly feeling mischievous, I lick my lips as seductively as I can. "You sure you want to take me home? The testing is oh-so important."

His jaw flexes. "Fine. Let's go to my place. I better keep an eye on you."

Wow.

His place.

This is really happening.

I sober up some more. Suddenly feeling shy, I voice something that bothered me in the restaurant. "Do you not get along with your parents?"

He shakes his head. "When I visit them one-on-one or with Alex, we get along just fine. I just don't like bigger gatherings because of how they treat Bella. She's a great sister and an amazing daughter—not to mention, an MIT grad—but they don't appreciate her."

I frown. "Because of her sex toy company?"

"No. It started much earlier. Bella was a tomboy as a kid, which our mother hated. In general, Bella has always been a free spirit, and I guess my folks didn't like it that she didn't fit the mold they had in mind for her. They always think the worst of her. Like they claim she does drugs—but she doesn't. They think she's promiscuous—but she isn't. It's infuriating."

"That sucks." I cover his hand with mine. "I know about not meeting parents' expectations. And the funny thing is, I think mine would love to swap me for Bella."

His expression warms. "Well, at least mine love you."

"Because they think I'm a prude goodie two shoes?" The question comes out more bitter than I hoped.

He leans in, the corners of his mouth tilting up. "If only they knew what you wanted to do at my place."

Even my blush blushes. "Too bad that's cancelled."

He pockets the breathalyzer. "Maybe not. Depends on your liver function."

Oh?

The car stops, and before I can respond, he opens the door for me.

His building is modern and pricey-looking. He waves at the security guy as he leads me to the elevator and presses the button for the penthouse.

Is this really happening?

I will my body to detox the alcohol as fast as it can.
The elevator opens into a large hallway.
Vlad holds the doors for me. "Welcome to my home."
I stumble out of the elevator.
This is surreal.
I've willingly come to the Impaler's lair.

# TWENTY-THREE

"KITCHEN IS THROUGH THIS CORRIDOR." He leads the way.

As we walk, I gawk at everything.

The place is huge, especially for New York. The décor reminds me of our office—cold, modern, spotless. But unlike at work, there are human touches here as well. Specifically, posters of *The Matrix* movie franchise. And I mean a lot of posters. In multiple languages. Of every character. There are even posters tangentially related to it, like the one that states, "In Soviet Russia, Bullet Dodges You."

We enter the kitchen.

"Sit." He presses a button on an espresso machine. "Milk, sugar?"

"Just black is fine." I plop on a chrome barstool. "So, let me guess. *The Matrix* is your favorite movie."

He cocks his head. "What gave me away? Was it the trench coat?"

I want to smack myself on the forehead. He loves that movie so much he even dresses like the characters.

How did I not pick up on that?

I grin. "Oracle. That's also a reference, isn't it?"

He pours two cups of coffee and puts one in front of me. "Tell me you like the first *Matrix*."

"I don't like it." I blow on my coffee. "I love it. I've been Trinity for every Halloween since I've seen it."

He gives me such an admiring look that, for the first time ever, I wonder if this could actually work between us.

Whatever *this* is.

We love the same movie.

We're into coding.

I find him attractive, and he clearly doesn't think me hideous.

If only I'd met him outside of work.

"Every programmer likes *The Matrix*, at least a little," he says. "How can we not? The hero is one of us."

I take a big sip. The coffee is good, smooth and only moderately bitter. "How psyched are you about the fourth one?"

He grins. "Since they confirmed its existence a few months back, I've been counting down the days."

Hmm. I wonder if he'd take me to the premiere.

"What's your favorite scene?" I ask.

He tells me, and I share what mine were. Then we talk about other movies we like, and here, too, our likes and dislikes fit together like pieces of a puzzle.

"Can I see Oracle's room?" I ask when the coffee is gone.

With a wide grin, he leads me there.

It's as big as it seemed on the screen. There are millions of people in NYC who have less square footage than this lucky pig.

"How are you feeling?" he asks. "Still drunk?"

This again? I glare up at him. "I wasn't drunk before. Even less so now."

He pulls out the breathalyzer. "If you're below point-zero-four, I'll clear you for testing."

Testing. Crap. I totally forgot about that. Do I want my alcohol to be low or high?

I blow into the gizmo.

"Good enough," he says. "We can test—if you're still up for it, that is."

My cheeks turn redder than the Soviet flag. Can I back out of the testing now, after dragging us from the party under this pretext?

He might've been right earlier. I was drunk. How else to explain that bold invite?

I take a step back, frantically trying to think of ways to minimize the insanity of what's about to happen. "We keep things professional."

He steps toward me. "I wouldn't have it any other way."

"I'll use the Kegel balls. This way, I keep my clothes on." I feel like I just might fall through the floor as I say it.

He loosens his tie. "Is there a guy equivalent to those balls?"

"No. I mean, there's the cock ring, but I imagine Dracula won't fit inside your pants if—"

He lifts an eyebrow. "Dracula?"

I didn't think I could redden more, but here we go.

Oh, well. Might as well fess up.

"I often nickname things." I glance down at my chest. "I dubbed the girls Pinky and the Brain, if that makes your ego feel any better."

He stares at Pinky and the Brain for a second too long, then raises his gaze back to my face. "You don't look at Dracula, and I don't look at you when you're using the balls." He takes off his glasses and puts them on a nearby table. "This way, I can't see much anyway."

I suppress a semi-hysterical giggle brought on by the phrase "using the balls." "Where do we do this?" I ask.

"Follow me." He leads me into his giant living room. "There." He points at a twin of my suitcase. "Get what we need."

I fish out the toys in question and hand him the cock ring, my face burning the entire time.

Must. Not. Think what Dracula would look like with that bling on.

As he takes the ring, our fingers brush, sending shivers down my body.

Perfect. Now I won't need any lube for the Kegel balls.

"Where's your bathroom?" Did that sound husky?

He points at a nearby door.

I lock myself in, take off my panties, and wash my hands and balls. The Kegel balls, that is. Thus far, no matter how ballsy I feel, I've never sprouted a pair, thank uterus.

Just in case, I lube up the balls and gently slide the first of the pair in, then the string that holds them together.

Feels pretty neutral so far.

Making sure to leave the removal loop out, I let the second ball join the first, and push them in as far as I'm comfortable with.

Hmm. This way, they feel tingly, and it's not a big effort to keep them in.

I could probably walk around like this all day—which, of course, would be a bad idea. Vlad could then activate the vibration at any time, even if I'm at the DMV or the fish market, or at a meeting with Sandra.

I pace from sink to tub.

Yep.

Thanks to my pelvic floor muscles, the balls stay put.

Still, walking like this is a little scary. This must be what it's like for guys to walk around worrying about their balls all the time.

I come back to the living room and find that he's dimmed the lights.

Is this to lower visibility or to set a sexy mood?

He darts a glance at my skirt, then quickly drags his gaze to my face. "All good?"

Is that hunger in his eyes? I squeeze my muscles around the balls for reassurance. "Peachy."

He runs his tongue over his lower lip. "Ladies first?"

I gulp in a breath. "How about together? You turn around and—"

"Sure." He spins on his heel, and I hear the loudest zipper opening in the history of sound.

Do cock rings require erections? If so, Dracula was clearly ready for action, because almost instantly, Vlad says, "I'm all set."

His phone lights up.

"No video." I pull out my own phone and launch the app.

He grunts his agreement and clicks something on his end.

Oh my. The balls begin vibrating inside me, and I nearly drop Precious.

Holy A-spot, this feels good.

Too good. Moaning in the same room with Vlad kind of good.

Must distract him.

Frantically, I activate the vibration on his toy.

Did the phone just shake in his hands?

The ball vibration increases.

I up his also.

He ups mine again.

Why didn't we sit? Or lie down?

My eyes begin to roll back, but I still manage to up his vibration one more notch.

When the orgasm smashes into me, I can't suppress a moan.

His back tenses.

My pelvic muscles spasm a few more times, then relax.

Oh, no. The Kegel balls slip out of me onto the living room floor and begin rolling.

Fuck. If he sees my slickness on those balls, I'll die.

"Close your eyes!" I shout. "And please don't ask why."

"Done." The word sounds like a grunt.

Good.

Without turning off his vibration, I stash Precious into my purse and sprint over to where the balls stopped—four feet in front of Vlad.

Giving him his privacy, I resist the strong urge to peek at Dracula as I bend to pick up the balls.

The darn things slip through my fingers and roll away.

Since it's hard to not look at his junk and chase them this way, I drop on all fours and chase after the toy like a predator hunting her prey.

Finally.

I grab the balls.

Nope.

They slip out of my grasp once more.

Did I have to lube them up so well?

Knees beginning to hurt, I crawl to where they stopped.

Yes! I snatch them and manage to keep a grip.

Then I see the legs in front of me.

I look up.

Yep.

I'm head to head with Dracula.

# TWENTY-FOUR

WOW.

I'm a tiny mouse in front of an anaconda.

This is how Mowgli must've felt when he first met Kaa.

Clutching onto my balls for dear life, I gulp down the gallon of saliva that my salivary glands suddenly spurt into my mouth.

Did I mention wow?

Dracula is beautiful in his engorged hugeness. Noticeably bigger than even Glurp, he might not fit in me, though it might be fun to try.

The ring squeezes and vibrates Dracula near the base, somehow accentuating the already-awesome sight.

Somewhere above me, Vlad grunts in pleasure.

Fuck. I forgot they're attached.

I start to back away—just as a white, creamy liquid shoots out of Dracula and lands on my cheek.

I blink in disbelief.

Did that just happen?

More gushes out.

I instinctively squeeze my eyes shut as the warm liquid lands on my forehead, the other cheek, nose, and chin.

A warm droplet lands on Pinky and two on the Brain.

Well, now I know what it's like for the porn stars in those bukkake videos. When Bob wanted to do this exact thing with me a while back, I refused, thinking it degrading. Now I'm not so sure. Maybe if—

"What are you doing there?" Vlad sounds like he's seen a ghost.

Crap. He must've finally opened his eyes.

Keeping my own blinkers shut lest my eyeballs get impregnated, I climb to my feet. My cheeks burn so hot I half expect the Dracula juices to sizzle, like egg whites on a skillet.

"Don't move." I hear him rush away.

Is he escaping? Taking a picture? Ordering takeout?

I hear him come back, and a strong hand cradles my head.

Well, that's nice.

"The water should be warm," he murmurs.

I dare not peek.

A paper towel touches my forehead.

Oh. He's cleaning me up. That's sweet, or as sweet as this can be, given the substance in question.

Speaking of the substance, is it too late for me to sneak a taste?

No. He'd see, and though most guys would find that hot, I'm not sure what the protocol is for when the guy in question is your boss squared.

"I'm sorry," he says when he's done with the area around my eyes. Despite his words, his voice is more than a little husky. "I'm not sure how this happened, but—"

"It wasn't your fault." I open my eyes and watch as he finishes wiping my cheeks and chin, then looks uncertainly at my cleavage.

"It's fine," I say, flushing impossibly hotter. "Go for it."

His pupils dilate as he dabs the few droplets from Pinky and the Brain.

I glance down.

He's zipped up Dracula, but there appears to be a new bulge there.

Useful, I guess, in case we decide to do more testing.

He balls up the dirty towel in his hand. "Just so you know, I'm clean. I got myself tested after the last relationship, and I haven't been with anyone since then, so—"

"I'm clean too," I blurt. "And on the pill."

His eyes gleam. "That's good to know, but the reason I told you about my medical history was so that you wouldn't worry about a herpes outbreak on your face. It wasn't quid pro quo."

Of course, that's what he meant. Stupid mouth. First it blurts TMI, now it wants to kiss him. Would he think it gross if I did kiss him? My mouth was spared the fountain of—

He dips his head and locks lips with me.

My heart goes supernova, and my knees threaten to buckle.

This is clearly a day of wows. His lips feel warm and soft and so good I nearly have another orgasm—and almost drop my balls. The room fades around me, and all my worries seem to evaporate. All my senses focus on the way his tongue gently strokes the inside of my mouth, the sweet, faintly minty warmth of his breath, the pounding of my pulse in my temples and—

He pulls away.

I'm breathing raggedly, and so is he.

"Why?" I ask breathlessly, staring up at him.

"We shouldn't." His voice is hoarse. "Still under the influence."

I draw back sharply. My arousal evaporates, replaced by an irrational surge of anger.

What the fuck is that supposed to mean? Is he saying he only kissed me because he had beer—or vodka—goggles on? Or does he think I can't make adult decisions with a mild buzz?

Before I can voice any of this, he has his phone out and is sending a text.

When the reply comes a millisecond later, he says, "Ivan will take you home. Come."

He herds me into the elevator, walks me down to the lobby, and holds open the limo door.

The ride home happens in a haze. A million questions loop through my mind, but two most of all: Why did he stop? And if a mere kiss was that amazing, how would it feel if we did more?

When I get home, I drop the balls into my sink and stare at myself in the mirror.

Ugh. My lopsided expression is a mix of curiosity, suspicion, and skepticism again. The glue on my left eyebrow wig must've given out at some point. At least I assume that's what happened. The thing is now missing, probably left in Vlad's towel.

No wonder he didn't want to do anything with me.

My first shower is scorching, the second one icy.

Jumping into my bed, I cover my head with a pillow and try to block out what happened.

# TWENTY-FIVE

THE FIRST THING I do in the morning is check Precious for messages from Vlad.

Nope. Radio silence.

I check my work email next and find a message from Sandra, requesting yet another update. I ask her if she's okay doing it tomorrow. Until I hear from Vlad, I can't honestly tell her everything is on track.

There's also an email from Mike Ventura in my inbox—a.k.a. Butt-Head and maybe-Phantom:

*Want to have that chat at 11:30 tomorrow?*

As I think about it, Sandra replies that she's fine with my suggestion.

I set up a meeting with her for eleven and tell Mike I'm game for eleven-thirty. This way, I'll kill two birds/coworkers with one commute stone.

Precious dings with a text.

My heart leaps.

It's from Vlad.

*Are you up yet?*

Hand shaking, I reply with: *Yes. And no hangover. You?*

He calls me instead of replying via text.

"Hi," I say.

"Hi yourself."

I clear my throat. "Look, about yesterday—"

"Can we do the pig playdate today?" he asks at almost the same time. "Oracle looks lonely this morning."

I hesitate for only a second. "Of course. What time did—"

"We're on our way," he says. "Have you had breakfast?"

"Not yet."

"What would you like?"

Feeling a little surreal, I tell him I won't say no to some blueberry muffins.

"Have a snack for now," he says. "We'll be there soon."

"Sure," I say, but he's already hung up.

Crap.

I have to make myself presentable, pronto. At least my place is still clean from his last visit.

Attacking my makeup kit, I recall the eyebrow debacle from last night. Was it why he stopped kissing me or not? Either way, I use the temporary eyebrow tattoos as the second-best solution, then order another pair of eyebrow wigs for later, in case my own eyebrows don't make a reappearance soon enough.

Just as I'm wriggling into a clean pair of jeans, I get a call on Precious. I nearly trip as I dash to pick it up.

It could be Vlad.

Nope.

It's Ava. She demands an update, so I give it to her.

"Unbelievable," she says when I'm done. "How could two people give each other that many orgasms yet only get to first base?"

I roll my eyes. "Aren't sex toys third base? And aren't facials some kind of a base too?"

She chuckles. "All I'm saying is that you should've gone all the way."

I sigh. "I don't think he wanted me. He might find me repugnant."

Ava scoffs. "Repugnant? You? Are you—"

The doorbell rings.

"Got to go," I shout into the phone and hang up.

"Who is it?" I ask pointedly, approaching the door.

"Vlad," he says, a note of approval in his tone.

I open up.

Damn. Why do I always feel surprised by his looks?

Breathlessly, I take in his shaggy black locks—including the unruly one that makes my fingers itch to touch it—and the beautifully shaped lines of his lips. His eyes are the deepest shade of blue behind his horn-rimmed glasses, and he's wearing his Matrix-inspired getup. In one hand, he's holding Oracle in a carrier, and in the other, a brown bag.

I swallow my drool. "Please come in." I gesture toward my living room.

He takes his shoes off again, hangs up the trench coat by the door, and brings the carrier over to Monkey's house.

"Here." He hands me a muffin. "Mind if I put them into the play area?"

"Please." I attack the muffin with fervor.

Yum. He either stopped by the best bakery in NYC, or I'm very hungry.

As I eat, I watch Oracle and Monkey rub noses together.

"I brought them snacks too." Vlad takes out a green vegetable I've never seen before. "You mind?"

"Not at all. What is that?"

"Hop shoots." He bites a piece of his. "They're washed. You want to try?"

With a shrug, I taste the veg. It reminds me of kale, with a faintly nutty aftertaste. "This is good. Why have I never seen these in the supermarket? Or restaurants? Is it a special guinea pig crop?"

And if so, why did we just eat it?

He places a long shoot into the aquarium. "The process to harvest this stuff is elaborate, so they're a little pricey for most people."

Seeing the shoot, Oracle grabs it and starts nibbling.

Monkey tastes it from the other side, and must love it because she begins pulling on the green stem pretty vigorously.

Almost violently.

In return, Oracle pulls on her end.

Monkey keeps pulling on hers.

It becomes a hilarious tug of war—at least hilarious for me.

Vlad actually frowns. "I forgot how much Oracle likes those things. I might've inadvertently created friction."

He's right.

After they rip the plant in half and finish eating it, Oracle begins to chase Monkey around—with squealing throughout.

When she finally corners Monkey, she mounts her and begins to hump.

Huh, okay. When Vlad mentioned friction a second ago, I didn't think it would be of the sexual kind. But why humping? They're both female, so wouldn't it make more sense if one went down on the other, or—and I'm not sure if their bodies are built for it—they could try something like scissoring.

"You said Oracle was a she," I say, suppressing a laugh as the humping intensifies. "Doesn't this require boy parts?"

"It's about dominance." He tosses two pieces of the veg in two different corners of the aquarium.

As if to confirm his words, Monkey sprints out from under Oracle, makes a loop, and begins trying to make her friend her bitch.

"Guinea pigs must be sexist," I say, grinning. "Why is the one who gets humped the less dominant one? And shouldn't that only apply in the bedroom anyway, not to who gets more snacks?"

He returns my grin. "And yet, how funny would it be if people tried this in boardrooms?"

We watch as the two guinea pigs eventually tire of trying to hump each other and just eat a hop shoot each.

"I think it's a truce," Vlad says. "Neither is trying to steal from the other."

"Where can I get that hop shoots stuff?" I ask. "Monkey clearly loves it."

"My dad has a hookup." Vlad drops more of the veg in front of the two piggies. "But as I said, it's a little pricey."

I eye the nondescript vegetable. "How much can it be?"

"With Dad's discount, four hundred per pound," he says with a straight face.

A *little* pricey?

I gape at the guinea pigs, then at him. "Seriously?"

He nods.

"And will they lay a golden egg now?"

He chuckles. "Not likely."

I shake my head. "That's like feeding a cat caviar."

A grin flashes across his face. "My mom did that with her cat, and only stopped because it apparently made the kitty litter too smelly."

Holy cow. "I must not be a good pet owner," I say. "I wouldn't dream of getting Monkey a vegetable that costs more than a pair of shoes."

He hands me another hop shoot. "Would you get it for yourself?"

I taste it again. "Nope. Not unless I was sick, and this was the only cure. Actually, in that case, I'd get it for Monkey too. As medicine."

"Well, don't worry." He dumps the remainder of the snack into the aquarium. "I'll bring more to all the play dates, so Monkey will continue to enjoy this."

Aww. He wants the girls to have more play dates. And, as a side effect, he's willing to spend more time with me.

This might be a great time to bring up yesterday.

"Listen," I say, proud that I'm actually going for it. "There's something I wanted to ask."

He gives me his full attention.

I blush.

The words don't come out.

I guess this is mission abort. I'm clearly chickening out.

"What is it?" he asks, now looking a little concerned.

"The testing," I blurt in desperation. "Since you're here, and we're now okay doing it face to face, I was wondering if you wanted to be productive."

Eek. I almost said "reproductive" there at the end.

He looks thoughtful.

Crapo. If he thinks I'm repulsive, he'll come up with an excuse not to do it.

"Of course," he says. "Let's."

I guess that's good, but this doesn't definitively prove anything. He might be just doing this for his sis.

A way to tell might be to watch him closely during the testing, see if he enjoys watching me.

My blush deepens. "Do you want to do it now?"

He glances at the guinea pigs. They're back to being best buds and are enthusiastically grooming each other. "Sure."

I run to my bedroom and come back with the genitalia-decorated suitcase. Opening it wide on the floor by the couch, I contemplate my choices.

His expression is guarded as he examines the suitcase with me.

Beginning to lose my nerve, I point at a large wand-type vibrator. "How about that one?" As I speak, my heart rate skyrockets, and I have to remind myself that I've just chosen the least naughty toy of the bunch. They sell these things at Target under the guise of "massager."

Hell, my mom got me one like this once. She called it the Vibronator.

"Sounds good." His gaze lifts from the suitcase to my face. "Should I be looking away, like yesterday?"

It would be hard to tempt him if he turns, but I don't have the balls to undress either, so I say, "How about I use it over my jeans? It should be powerful enough to work that way."

Looking unsure, he gets the device out.

Is he wondering if he should be the one to hold the thing in place for me? Do I want him to?

"Here." He hands it to me, much to my disappointment. "I'll get the app ready."

As he plays with his phone, I lie back on the couch and spread my legs a little—just enough to be seductive yet still believable as the position necessary to get the vibration job done.

When he looks back at me, his breath seems to hitch.

Score.

I feel a sudden boost of courage.

"Here." I pat the couch next to me. "Things didn't go well the last time we did this standing."

He sits down next to me, the sensual notes of his cologne teasing my nostrils as he murmurs, "Let me know when Mina is ready."

"Mina?" Has he forgotten that I'm Fanny? And why am I in third person all of a sudden?

His sexy lips quirk. "Mina was Dracula's romantic interest. I figured since you named mine, I'd help you name yours."

Holy vampirism. He's beyond perfect. None of my exes ever played along, finding my penchant for nicknames silly.

Doing my best to hide my glee, I lift one of my temporary eyebrow tattoos. "You should leave all the nicknaming to me. Mina is a terrible one."

He lifts an eyebrow. "Go ahead then, rename it."

Hmm, a challenge.

I hope I can rise to it. Between having never named that part of myself and all the adrenaline, I'm drawing a blank. Then it comes to me. "How about Gizmo?"

He shoots a glance at my crotch. "Like an electronic device one wants to play with?"

I grin. "No. Like the cute creature from the Gremlins. You know... dangerous if wet."

He groans, and we both burst out laughing.

When we stop, he shows me his ready-to-go screen. "Shall I?"

Still high from all the laughter, I feel extra bold. "I was wondering if you could hold the wand for me."

His smile disappears. "You sure?"

My face is on fire, but I nod. "Please." I hand the wand to him.

He activates it through the app, and it roars like a chainsaw in my palm before he snatches it away.

I gulp in a deep breath.

It's happening.

Holy wandness, it's happening.

He puts down his phone, then leans in and slowly presses the loudly vibrating toy against my jeans.

The air whooshes out of my lungs. Even through the layers, the vibration is insane—and brings me to an orgasm almost instantly, dragging a loud moan out of me.

His pupils dilate, and I see he's about to pull the wand away, so I clasp his wrist to keep it there. I'm greedy for another orgasm, which I can already feel building. The tension is coiling low in my core, my skin tingling as my nipples harden in the confines of my bra.

His face is a mask of purely male satisfaction, even as his eyes are heavy-lidded with arousal.

The orgasm crashes over me, making me cry out. It's shameless, bold, but I don't care. I like how this is affecting him. There's a huge bulge in his pants, mere inches away from me.

Should I unzip him and unleash Dracula?

Not yet.

For now, I grab his other hand and place it over Pinky, bucking my hips against the wand to intensify the sensations that are mercilessly building again.

His eyes darken, and he squeezes my flesh appreciatively, just as another orgasm rocks me, making me scrunch my eyes shut and moan yet again.

As the aftershocks fade, I open my eyes—and stare right into my parents' faces.

# TWENTY-SIX

DO ORGASMS MAKE YOU HALLUCINATE?

Wait, no, they appear to be real.

Holy fuck.

Mom and Dad have barged into my apartment yet again.

Stiffening, Vlad yanks the vibrator away from my crotch area as I gape at my grinning parental units, painfully aware of the open suitcase of toys at my feet and the orgasm they must've just witnessed.

"That is simply fabulous, my dear!" Mom sounds positively giddy. "I knew the Vibronator would come in handy."

I leap to my feet, and so does Vlad. Swiftly deactivating the wand, he tosses it into the suitcase and closes the thing shut.

I debate whether to die on the spot or not. Pretty sure people have fallen on a sword for much less dishonor.

At least my orgasm-flushed face can't get any redder.

Somehow, I recover my tongue. "Mom, Dad, this is Vlad." I'm proud of the steadiness of my voice. "Vlad, these are my parents. They've clearly never learned about boundaries."

Coolly composed now, Vlad extends a hand to Mom. "Nice to meet you, Mrs. Pack."

Mom looks on the verge of drooling. "Please call me Venus."

"Of course, Venus," Vlad says and extends a hand in greeting to my dad. "Mr. Pack, it's great to meet you as well."

"Call me Wolf," Dad says, and it's clear he's also impressed by Vlad, though unlike Mom, he doesn't look like he's about to jump him, cougar style.

My embarrassment eases slightly.

Time for payback.

"You heard that right," I tell Vlad. "He's a one-man Wolf Pack, like that guy in *The Hangover*. Grandparents named him that as a prank, and these two played an even worse prank on me."

"Great to meet you, Wolf," Vlad says, showing no sign that he heard what I said.

In general, he's handling this much, much better than I would've if his parents had barged in on us.

Mom beams at Vlad. "We came to drag Fanny to lunch. Would you like to join us?"

"I'd love to," Vlad says without hesitation.

Wait, what is this now? Lunch with my parents *and* Vlad? We're not at the "meeting the parents" stage.

We're still in the limbo stage.

Then again, I kind of met his too.

Could we do this any more backward?

"What kind of food do you like?" Dad asks Vlad.

"I'm not picky," he replies.

Dad proposes a laundry list of cuisines, and he and Mom debate where they want to go as though Vlad and I are not even in the room. As they go on, I sneak a glance at Vlad's poker face.

I have no idea what he's thinking about the two intruders.

Mom and Dad were the first people I tested my app on. My code determined that Mom looks like Princess Fiona from Shrek, but, spoiler alert, after she turns permanently into an ogre. Dad matched with Garfield—and that might be why Monkey is absolutely terrified of him.

"What do you think of sushi?" Mom asks Vlad.

He places a hand on my shoulder. "I go where Fanny goes."

Spying the hand, Mom exchanges a knowing glance with Dad. "The food Fanny likes is too plain."

"Hey, I eat sushi," I say, trying and failing not to sound indignant.

Mom chuckles. "In Japan, they serve California rolls in the American food restaurants, along with burgers."

I narrow my eyes. "I get other stuff too. How about we go, and I'll let you order for me?"

Mom claps her hands in excitement, and I herd everyone out of the apartment.

My phone pings.

I sneak a peek at it.

It's a text from Vlad:

*Want to take the limo, or walk to a great little place nearby?*

Did he type that in his pocket?

"Mom, Dad, Vlad knows a great little sushi place nearby," I say. "What do you think?"

They gladly agree to a walk, and we set out on our journey, with Mom and Dad quizzing us about how we met and how long we've been dating.

"We work together," Vlad replies, unflappable as always. "How about the two of you? How long have you been married?"

The diversion works. Mom launches into the story I wish I'd never heard, and especially not the dozens of times she's told it in my presence. Apparently, she replied to an ad in the newspaper and posed nude for Dad's painting, he found her irresistible, and one thing led to another, by which I mean that they covered each other in paint and had wild sex on a giant canvas. The resulting work of art actually hangs in their living room to this day.

If I ever get therapy, I'm sure I'll bring it up. A lot.

Vlad listens to this inappropriate story as calmly as if she'd told him they'd met on eHarmony.

Then another text from him arrives:

*Do you want me to have Ivan buy you a keychain lock for the door?*

Is he afraid the next time they'll barge in, they'll start making art at my place?

Grinning, I reply in the affirmative.

*How about one of those smart video doorbells? I know a brand that's extra safe, privacy-wise.*

As I agree to this too, we reach the restaurant and walk in.

"Konnichiwa," the restaurant staff yells at us in unison.

Vlad replies in kind, his pronunciation sounding flawless to me.

I catch Mom and Dad exchanging an approving glance.

We get seated, and Mom orders me a sushi deluxe, then gets the same for herself and Dad. Vlad orders his sushi à la carte, naming the pieces by their Japanese names like a pro.

"So, Venus, I heard you sing opera," Vlad says when the waitress leaves. He pulls out his phone. "Would I be able to find a performance by you online?"

She bobs her head enthusiastically. "Search my name, but ignore all the packs of razors and razor blades that pop up early on in the search."

Two seconds later, Mom's mezzo-soprano emanates from Vlad's phone's speakers.

"Ah," Vlad says after barely two beats of music. "*The Habanera* from *Carmen*."

"Marry him," Mom says in a very loud whisper.

My face matches the red top of the full-sodium soy sauce.

Facing Vlad, Mom asks, "What is that wonderful accent I detect in your speech?"

"Russian," Vlad says. "Speaking of, have you been in anything by Tchaikovsky? *The Queen of Spades* is my favorite of his."

The food comes as they launch into an animated discussion of Russian opera, and one thing becomes clear to me: no matter what happens between us, Mom will never, ever, stop talking about Vlad.

"Wolf, you're a painter, right?" Vlad asks when Mom's mouth becomes busy with a piece of fatty tuna.

And just like that, Dad and Vlad are soon dropping names like *Repin* and *Malevich* as they talk Russian art.

I eat my sushi and enjoy most of it. However, there are two pieces of something brown I've never had before, and they look particularly unappetizing.

"That's *uni*," Vlad says, noticing where my chopsticks are hovering. "It's sea urchin gonads."

Of course it is. Still, that's a better name than what I had in my head: poopy sushi.

I'm determined to be adventurous, though.

I eat a piece of pickled ginger to cleanse my palate, then dip the tip of my chopstick into the brown substance and lick it gingerly.

It's creamy in a gross way and much too briny for my taste.

There's no way I'm eating it.

Grr. Now Mom will get to say, "I told you so." Which is unfair, because I ate all the other stuff, raw fish included.

"You know, that's my favorite," Vlad says, noticing my grimace. "Can we please trade?"

I squeeze his knee gratefully and put the uni on his plate, grabbing a piece of his salmon and yellow fish in exchange.

"Uni is considered an aphrodisiac in Japan," Mom whispers to Vlad conspiratorially.

If that's true, given the way she flirts with Vlad, she must've eaten a whole ocean of urchin gonads for breakfast.

"Have you been to Japan?" she asks Vlad.

Here we go. When I was in college, my parents started to travel, and now they never shut up about it—and about the fact that other than my one and only trip to Prague, I haven't been anywhere outside the US.

It's another dig at my unadventurousness. Which is unfair. I simply haven't had the time or the funds to travel at this stage of my career.

I would totally go lots of places if I could.

Probably.

I hope.

Vlad nods. "Kyoto was my favorite city, but I've been all over the country."

Mom grins. "Us too. Everything was matcha-flavored in Kyoto. Did you go to the Monkey Park?"

They bond over Japan for a while before switching focus to Russia, which they quiz Vlad about. It's a destination they haven't crossed off their bucket list. I listen as he gladly answers their questions, telling them all about his hometown of Murmansk and how one can see the Northern Lights there in the winter.

I have to admit, I would kill to see those.

The aurora borealis phenomenon is definitely on *my* bucket list.

We finish off the meal with fried green tea ice cream that, according to Mom, "isn't as good as the ones you can get in Kyoto."

When the check comes, Vlad grabs it and hands his card to the waiter before my dad can so much as open his mouth about splitting the bill.

"Thank you," Mom tells him as we walk out of the restaurant and head back to my place.

The Russian quiz continues during our walk home. As we reach my building, Vlad stops and smiles warmly at my parents.

"It was very nice to meet you both," he says. "Would you like a ride home?"

They look confused until he gestures at the limo.

Mom gives him her cougariest onceover of the day. "Yes, please. Thank you."

We walk over to the limo, where Vlad takes a large backpack from Ivan and says something in Russian, nodding at my folks.

Ivan dips his head in agreement and holds the door for Mom and Dad as they scooch in.

"Bye," I say with a wave. "Call before you come over next time."

The limo pulls away, and I let out a sigh. "They won't call."

Vlad unzips the backpack. "This should help."

Inside the bag is a drill, a keychain, and a box with, presumably, the video doorbell.

When we get to my door, I watch Vlad install it all in a matter of minutes—an unexpected display of handyman abilities that's a stronger aphrodisiac than urchin gonads.

Once the doorbell is set up and I have the prerequisite app running on Precious, Vlad says, "Let's test it."

I go inside and flip on the new keychain, leaving him on the doorstep.

He rings the doorbell.

Precious shows me his gorgeous face.

"Yep. It works." I open the lock but not the keychain.

He tries to open the door, but the keychain thwarts him.

"Great." I let him in for real, my heartbeat speeding up as I prepare to be bold once again. Looking him in the eyes, I say as steadily as I can manage, "Now we should probably resume the *other* kind of testing."

His face goes taut. "You sure?"

Instead of an answer, I lead him into the living room and open the suitcase again.

Like one of Pavlov's dogs, I'm already salivating at the promise of more orgasms.

"I almost forgot." Vlad takes out a small bundle of lacy cloth from his pocket. "You left this in my bathroom."

Holy crap. I forgot my underwear at his house and didn't even realize it.

Cheeks going nuclear, I snatch the panties out of his hand. "Sorry about that. Had to leave in a rush and all."

"About that." He steps closer, his eyes impossibly blue behind the lenses of his glasses. "I hope you're okay."

Okay? What is he—oh. All the warm fuzzies leave me as I recall last night and the way he so abruptly pulled away.

"Was it because I looked like a freak?" I blurt.

His brow furrows. "What are you talking about?"

"We kissed. You pulled away. You thought I looked like a freak, right?" I gesture at my fake eyebrows.

His expression shifts from confusion to unmistakable desire, his lids lowering as his eyes sweep hungrily over my body. Stepping up to me, he cradles my face in his broad palms. "Fannychka..." His voice is rough velvet. "You'd be beautiful without a single hair on your head."

Oh. My. God. If I were a computer, system error messages would be blaring through my speakers. As is, my heart hammers, and every hair on my body stands on end, as if an electric current is running under my skin.

I. Am. So. Turned. On.

"You had vodka in your system," he continues without letting me go. "And I—" He takes a deep breath. "I want your mind clear when you beg me to fuck you."

Wow. Now the computer would explode.

I was not expecting to hear those words come out of his mouth—and now that they have, the images dancing in my mind are beyond X-rated.

And hot.

So scorching hot that I seem to have lost my tongue.

"Beg?" I finally manage to squeeze out.

A cocky grin tugs at his sensual lips. "I guess you can also just ask. Nicely."

"Nicely?"

"Good enough," he murmurs and dips his head, slanting his lips across mine.

Holy overactive ovaries. Now I feel like someone has taken the little bits of the exploded computer and began putting the pieces back together, paying special attention to the erogenous zones.

The kiss is hungrier than the one last night.

More primal.

My knees start to feel weak.

He must notice. Still kissing me, he backs me toward the couch, and as I plop backward onto it, he leans over me, lips brushing my ear as he murmurs roughly, "I wanted to bend you over the table at Starbucks when I first saw you."

*Error. Error. Hormone overload. Speaking functions compromised. Reboot required.*

Losing my head completely, I ball his shirt in my fist and drag him on top of me.

The coiled muscles press firmly against my body.

We resume kissing.

My hand slides through his thick, silky hair.

He nibbles on my lip.

I suck on his tongue.

Steam collects between my skin and clothes. I want them off, so I begin to unbutton my shirt.

He leans slightly back, pupils dilating impossibly wide.

I slip out of my top.

He rips his shirt clean off, sending buttons flying like bullets across the room. Left in a white t-shirt, he strips that off too.

*Video buffer overrun. Graphics card overclocked.*

Vlad must spend serious time at the gym. That or his body was sculpted in ancient Greece. The hard-quilted muscles gleam with beads of sweat, and I want to lick them all off.

He unbuttons my bra, releasing Pinky and the Brain from their prison.

"Beautiful." He cups Pinky, and my nipple practically stabs his palm.

Can you go crazy from lust? I need him inside me so much I think I might scream.

Kissing his neck, I slide my tongue over his pecs, down the washboard abs and lower, toward the landing strip of hair below his navel. At the same time, I unzip his pants.

Holy hell.

Dracula is almost bursting out of his underwear.

Vlad kicks off his pants, then peels my jeans off.

"You okay?" he asks, eyes hooded.

I pull down my panties in my reply.

After this, I dare anyone to call me unadventurous.

"Beautiful." His voice comes out guttural, caveman-like.

He straddles me, his naked skin rubbing over mine.

I can't believe this is happening.

He kisses my neck, then sucks on my nipple before languidly dragging his tongue over my belly and lower. And lower still, with mind-numbing, teasing slowness.

After what feels like forever, I feel his warm breath on my sex.

*Division by zero. File not found.*

He gives it a probing lick.

I cry out.

Belka's squishy Space Age material has nothing on his swirling, clever tongue. So clever, it should get an honorary PhD from Harvard.

The pressure builds.

I knead my hands in his hair, arching up as the pressure grows unbearable, intensifying with each passing second.

With a loud moan, I blast apart.

He looks up, primal male satisfaction written all over his beautiful face. "More?"

"Lie down." My words come out boldly, almost like a command. There's no room for shyness in the desire gripping me.

He gladly obeys.

I pull down his underwear, unleashing Dracula.

*Input device driver error. Allocate more space.*

Cautiously, I give his shaft an ice cream lick.

He twitches in response, urging me on.

I slide all of him into my mouth, jaws stretching to the limit.

"Fuck," Vlad grunts above me.

Taking that as encouragement, I make a circle with my tongue.

And another.

After a third, he pulls away. "I don't want to finish like that." His voice is hoarse, his breathing uneven. "I want to be inside you. Assuming you're ready for that."

Ready?

If I don't get him in me, I might die.

There's just one problem.

"I don't have a condom." I glance around the living room as though looking for the latex fairy.

His eyes roam ravenously over my body. "Me neither. This whole development is a little unexpected."

I dart a glance at his erection. "You said you're clean."

His breath hitches, voice roughening further. "You did too. And you're on the pill."

"So are you. I mean, I *am* on the pill. The only one on the pill."

Ugh, why am I babbling? And flushing again?

Instead of responding, he lifts me up and manhandles me until we switch places, with me sprawled on the couch and him on top, Dracula against my belly.

His lips slant over mine once more, and as I return the kiss, I feel his wicked fingers enter me.

Whoa.

I gasp into his mouth as he locates my G-spot with a precision Glurp would be jealous of, then gives it a light rub.

I come undone with a scream.

Eyes heavy-lidded, he brings his fingers to his mouth and licks them clean. "Delicious."

His fingers leave a gnawing emptiness that needs to be filled.

Time to take my daring to the ultimate level.

I wrap my hand around Dracula and slowly guide him into me.

*Input device connected. Error. Reboot imminent.*

Vlad's face looks strained as I take him in by small increments, letting my muscles adjust.

Okay. I *can* take him. I was worried for a second.

"You okay?" he grunts when Dracula is rooted as deeply as he can go.

I manage a small nod.

He begins to thrust, lightly at first.

I moan.

He speeds up.

My nails dig into his back.

The thrusts intensify, yet it's not enough.

I crave more.

Harder.

Deeper.

Sliding my hands to his glutes, I arch up, impaling myself as I tip over the edge.

My toes curl as I scream his name.

As my pelvic muscles tremble around Dracula, Vlad grunts in pleasure. I feel him harden, and then there's the warm sensation of his release—which brings me to yet another climax.

"Fuck." He hugs me tight, his chest heaving against mine. "That was remarkable." Realizing he might smother me, he pushes up on one elbow.

Smiling into his face, I rub my nose against his, channeling my inner guinea pig. "Merely remarkable?"

"Amazing. Mind-blowing." He grins. "Better?"

"A good start." I wriggle out from under him and jump to my feet. "Keep talking as you join me in the shower."

Giggling, I run into the bathroom, and as he chases me, he peppers me with enough positive adjectives to fill a thesaurus.

Once inside, I set the shower water to a comfy temperature and get under the stream.

He looks me over hungrily, then steps in, taking up all the freaking space.

Before I can object, he begins to lather me sensuously.

Okay, I guess all is forgiven.

Once I'm squeaky clean, I return the favor, covering every one of his copious muscles with soap.

"You know," I say as I lather his washboard abs. "If I wanted to be mean to *my* kid, I'd call her or him Six."

He grins. "Six Pack. That *is* pretty wicked."

When the shower is done, we wrap ourselves in towels and return to the living room.

"Your shirt is toast." I kick the buttonless mess with a bare foot.

He shrugs. "I can wear the t-shirt."

He'll actually look casual for a change? The universe just might implode.

Seeing him with that towel turns me on again, and my newfound boldness shows no signs of abating.

"What should we do now?" I ask, glancing at the suitcase.

Did Dracula just stir under that towel?

Vlad smirks. "What did you have in mind?"

"There are toys we haven't tested yet." I fake innocence by batting my eyelashes at him. "I, for one, think that's an oversight that needs fixing."

He unwraps his towel to reveal Dracula ready for action.

Insatiable much?

I love it.

Giddily, I choose a toy to use on him—and bring him to another climax. Then he returns the favor many times over since there are more female-oriented toys.

Countless orgasms later, we run out of toys, and my stomach growls.

"How unladylike." I spank my belly before wriggling into my underwear and jeans.

"We better feed the beast." He takes out his phone. "What are you in the mood for?"

"Pizza?"

He nods approvingly. "One of the best places in the country is just a few blocks away."

---

THE THIN CRUST pizza is out of this world, and we devour it over beers and a good conversation. Among other things, we learn each other's ages—he's thirty-two to my twenty-four—and when each other's birthday is, a topic that leads into a discussion about our mutual skepticism regarding Zodiac signs.

When our dinner is done, we feed the other beasts—Oracle and Monkey.

Once our pets are happy pigs, Vlad and I cuddle on the couch and watch *The Matrix*. As the movie plays, I try not to think about the implications of what's just happened and just enjoy the moment. Because if I do think about it, I will freak out.

Because I just slept with Vlad.

With my boss's boss.

The computer will definitely crash if I go there.

Instead, I focus on the movie. We say our favorite lines together with the characters and, in some rare cases, complain about something we think could've been done better.

For example, why did the machines use humans as batteries when guinea pigs would've required a much simpler virtual reality prison to keep them content?

"I think the original reason the machines needed humans was as a computational substrate," Vlad says. "That seemed too complex of an idea for the general public, so it was dumbed down to batteries. Or maybe it was just product placement."

I grin at him. "I bet you're right."

"This always bugged me," he says when Trinity quips the classic "Dodge this" line and shoots the agent in the head. "Given how fast the agents can move, she wouldn't have had the time to finish the words before he'd have thwarted her."

I vehemently shake my head. "When a line is that cool, you need to just relax and not overthink it."

He laughs and we finish the rest of the movie without comments. Then we stream the sequels, complaining more often as we do.

"I should head out," he says when the credits on the last of the trilogy roll on the screen.

Still on my bravery high, I say, "If you want, you can stay here."

Turns out, he very much likes the idea of staying, so we make our way to the bedroom, where I promptly end up on all fours.

"That was even better than before," he murmurs huskily when we're both just limp noodles on my bed.

My oversexed grin is goofy. "You know, if we were guinea pigs, you'd officially be the dominant one after that."

His chuckle morphs into a yawn.

"Spoon me." It comes out bossier than I planned, but he grins and does it.

Before I know it, I fall asleep like that.

Cuddled securely in his arms.

# TWENTY-SEVEN

I FEEL warm and cozy and only partially awake.

Sometimes sleep is like a computer reboot for my brain, and this morning, this is truer than ever—I'm certainly having thoughts that have hidden in my subconscious until now.

It's insane how close I feel to Vlad.

Also—and maybe this is me being delusional—I feel like I know him. Know the real him, not the Impaler mask everyone at the office fears.

In fact, in barely no time at all, I've begun to feel that the two of us fit together like a set of nesting matryoshka dolls.

I grin as I think back on us cuddling on my couch. It was the best evening I can recall having. And the sex was the most mind-blowing of my life.

In fact, I might've had more orgasms yesterday than the entire year prior.

Most importantly, I've never felt this kind of connection with a guy. My longest relationship was Bob, and in the year we dated, I don't think I knew him this well, or felt like we fit this well, or enjoyed the intimacy, or—

Shit.

Could I be falling for Vlad?

A jolt of adrenaline banishes the remnants of drowsiness.

Falling for him could be a disaster. He might not feel the same—and he's my boss squared.

Crap.

I actually slept with the head of the company.

If anyone found out, they'd accuse me of sleeping my way to the top—or into the development department. And what if I do get moved or promoted for a reason other than merit?

Ugh. These would've been good things to consider before taking off my panties. In my defense, he had his shirt off by that point, and I'm only flesh and blood.

I open my eyes.

Vlad isn't in bed with me.

Forget the boss angle. My fear now is that last night meant nothing to him.

The scent of something fried and delicious reaches my nostrils.

I jackknife to my feet.

Maybe Vlad isn't gone after all?

I sprint to the bathroom to make myself presentable.

Interesting. I have a five-o-clock shadow. In the eyebrow area—not my cheeks. The temporary tattoos are holding on too, but given this growth spurt, I won't need them in a few days.

Teeth brushed and makeup applied, I put on some clothes and rush into the kitchen.

It *is* Vlad.

His back is to me, and he's only wearing pants.

Those back muscles make him look like a rower or a swimmer.

Drool forms in my mouth, only in part due to the smells of the fried goodness he's working on.

He should cook completely naked next time.

Wait, no. That could expose Dracula to hot oil burns.

I loudly clear my throat.

He turns around. "Ah. The sleepy kitten has risen. When I got up, I accidentally made a lot of noise, yet you didn't even twitch."

I grin. "I'm not a light sleeper."

He nods at the pan. "I hope you like your eggs over easy."

Over easy?

Is that subliminal messaging? Is he saying we're over or I'm easy?

He quirks an eyebrow. "A frown at my egg choice? How about I take this batch, and you tell me how you want yours done?"

Did I frown? Crapo. "Scrambled, please."

"Very American. Sit." He gestures at the table.

I obediently plop down next to a chair that has a man's shirt draped over it—a shirt with buttons that are attached, meaning it's not the one from yesterday.

"Where did you get a change of clothes?" I ask.

"Ivan brought it, along with the groceries." He turns back to the stove. "There were cobwebs in your fridge."

Great, Ivan knows Vlad stayed here.

Actually, Ivan, being his driver, would know either way.

Still, my cheeks warm. Though I've never done the walk of shame, I bet it feels a little like this.

He makes small talk as I drum my fingers on the table, debating if I should just flat-out ask him what he thinks is going on between us.

I should.

And will.

Any moment now.

His back is turned. That makes it easier, doesn't it?

Nope.

Not happening.

I must've used up all my boldness and bravery yesterday.

Mouth watering beyond reason, I watch as Vlad slaps the contents of the skillet on a plate, then cracks another egg, puts a little bit of milk in, and stirs.

Damn. Who would've thought such domestic minutiae could be this hot? I feel my brain scrambling along with that egg.

How weird would it be if I played with myself here at the breakfast table?

Or if I got a toy?

"Here." He scrapes the skillet onto another plate and brings the yumminess to the table, along with a bottle of ketchup.

I attack my food. After the exertions of last night, my appetite is through the roof.

"It's eight forty-five," I say when the worst of my hunger is satiated. "You're legendary for being in your office at the crack of dawn. What gives?"

He shrugs. "The beauty of not having a boss is that I get up when I want."

"I bet that's nice." I shovel more egg into my mouth. "How did you end up owning your own company in the first place?"

He smiles. "After college, I worked for Bloomberg for a bit. Since I lived with parents, I was able to save a little money. When I realized that I needed to run things myself if I didn't want to go mad, I asked my parents for a loan to help me start Binary Birch. The rest is history."

"Impressive," I say, attacking the rest of my eggs. And I mean it, too. To own a successful software company at thirty-two years of age is no small feat.

"What are your plans for the day?" he asks.

I swallow the eggs in my mouth. "Write up Belka testing results. Meet with Sandra to give her the good news—and hopefully get new work. After that, I have a meeting with Mike Ventura."

He frowns. "Ventura? Why?"

Is that jealousy I hear in his voice?

"Code chat," I say.

"I see," he says, the frown going away. "You know, if you have any programming questions, you can talk to me. I might know a thing or two Ventura doesn't."

"I'll take you up on that now that I know." I grin impishly at him. "Would you like me to cancel the meeting with Mike?"

He spears the last of his food. "It's fine. Ventura is a decent coder. I doubt his advice can do much harm."

I take our empty plates and carry them to the sink. "What about you? Big plans for the day?"

To my deep disappointment, he begins putting on his shirt. "Meetings. Krav Maga training. Lunch with you, assuming you're willing."

Huh. Is Krav Maga how he got so in shape?

"I think I *might* be available for lunch." My eager grin makes it difficult to play coy.

"Good. Mind if I leave Oracle here?" He gestures at the aquarium. "After I fed them, she and Monkey had a blast playing."

"Of course she can stay."

Especially since that guarantees you have to come get her.

And maybe stay over again.

And—

"Come lock the door behind me," he says.

I follow him there.

He puts on his shoes.

I suddenly feel shy. "Bye?"

"No." He leans down and gives me the hottest goodbye kiss of my life. When he straightens, there's a purely male smirk on his lips. "Now it's a bye."

Closing the door, I fan myself.

That man will turn me into a sex addict.

My steps are light as I prance back to the living room. Opening my laptop, I finalize the testing documentation—reddening at my recollection as I type.

When I'm done, I check on the pigs. They're grooming each other, happy as clams at a vegan restaurant.

Since my meeting with Sandra is getting closer, I set out on my commute to the office.

# TWENTY-EIGHT

AS WE SETTLE in the meeting room, Sandra doesn't meet my gaze. Weird.

Does she think I'm about to disappoint her?

"I have good news," I say, and tell her the testing is completed.

"That's great," she says, still not meeting my eyes. "I'm sure Mr. Chortsky will be pleased."

Did she wince at the last bit?

What the hell is this about?

"I'm ready for other projects now," I say. "Do you have anything interesting for me to test?"

She finally looks at me. "This is a little sudden. Let me have a think, and I'll get back to you."

Okay. I guess I did ambush her with being done with this project so quickly. Still, I can't help but feel she's behaving oddly.

"How are things with you in general?" I ask.

Maybe something is up with her health?

She stands up. "Everything's great. I have another meeting, though, so I better run."

Okay, whatever.

I wait for her to leave and check the time.

Still a few minutes before my meeting with Mike.

Going to the pantry, I make tea, wondering the entire time if Vlad is going to catch me here again.

Or rather, hoping he does.

Nope. Tea finished, with no Vlad in sight.

I get to the meeting room early and sip another cup of tea as I check for new messages from Phantom. If Mike turns out to be my mystery mentor, it would be polite to be up to speed on his wisdom.

Turns out Phantom was too busy to write.

Oh, well. Maybe like me, he had a busy Monday.

I pull out the work phone to check my email, but before I do, the meeting room door opens, and Butt-Head—I mean, Mike—waltzes in.

With a wide grin, he passes by a dozen chairs before plopping into the one right next to me.

Is everyone acting weird today, or is something up with me?

"Where's your laptop?" I put my phone down on the table. "I didn't bring mine."

"Laptop?" He gapes at me like I've sprouted a pink mohawk.

I eye him in confusion. "Don't we need a screen to look at code?"

He slides the chair closer to me. "Actually, I have a confession to make. It wasn't code I wanted to talk to you about."

Why do I have a bad feeling about this?

I shift my chair away. "What then?"

He leans in, and I can smell stale coffee and even staler garlic on his breath. "Rumor has it, you're using the guys around the office to test sex toys—and I want to throw my name in the hat."

# TWENTY-NINE

MY EYES all but pop out of their sockets. "What?"

He frowns. "I thought we had a moment there, in the elevator. Or do you only invite people who can help your career?"

I jackknife to my feet, my face burning as if from a slap. "This conversation is over."

He jumps up and grabs my elbow. "Hey. I'm in dev. You want to move over there. I'm sure I could help."

I give him a scathing glare. "Let me go."

"Come on. Don't be like that." His grip tightens. "I just—"

"Let. Go. Of. Her."

The voice is pure Impaler.

Mike loosens his grip instantly.

Vlad is in the doorway, his gaze trained on my assailant.

If looks could kill, Mike's body would be a bloodless husk.

Paling, Mike looks from me to Vlad. "I was just—"

Before I can even blink, Vlad is between me and Mike. "Get out."

Mike takes a shuffling step back. "I just wanted to be a tester, like you."

Vlad takes a menacing step toward his employee. "You're fired. Effective immediately."

For a second, Mike looks shell-shocked—as though the concept of getting fired for harassing a female coworker is rocket science to him. In the next moment, anger replaces the shock on his face. "How convenient. A spot opens on the dev team just as your mistress wants it."

"You're trespassing." Vlad's voice is guttural and frightening. "One more word, and you will be forcefully removed from the premises." His powerful fists clench and unclench at his sides.

Mike pales further, his bravado deflating. Turning on his heel, he scurries out of the room.

Vlad strides over to the phone in the middle of the table and orders security to make sure he leaves the building and never comes back.

As he does that, I finally recover from shock enough to start putting the pieces together.

*A rumor. About my testing.*

Was that why Sandra had acted so weird? Had she also heard about said rumor?

And what a strange one it is. Me testing with a bunch of men? Why would I do that? I only needed the one.

And Vlad coming to my rescue. How did he get here in such a timely fashion?

Then I remember him talking about hypothetically watching my meeting with Sandra through the cameras.

I guess that wasn't hypothetical. He really does watch what happens here, at least when he's jealous.

Hanging up, Vlad turns his ferocious stare my way. "I knew something was off about this meeting."

I take a step back. "I thought he was Phantom. How was I—"

"Phantom?" He pronounces the word with a strong Russian accent. "He isn't. I am."

"You?"

I feel like a dope.

Of course it's him. That long conversation with my mom about opera. Elegant code. Concern about the privacy of my photo database.

Who else could it have been?

"Why didn't you just say so?" I ask dazedly.

My emotions are all over the place. I have no idea what to think about any of this.

He scrubs a hand over his face. "I wanted the freedom to mentor you without complicating our already-complex relationship. More importantly, it simply didn't come up."

Complex relationship.

That's an understatement of the century.

"How did they find out about the testing?" I sneak a peek at the office floor through the glass walls. "Sandra?"

His jaw muscles tense. "She wouldn't. I think you revealed it. Inadvertently."

"Me?" The question is the closest I can get to a growl. "What are you talking about?"

"You don't take privacy seriously." The words come out clipped— an accusation if there ever was one. "I guessed the password on your source control repository effortlessly. Chocula2019, right?"

I stagger back. "How?"

"The whimsical variable name you overused, plus the current year. Not rocket science. And I bet you use the same exact password to log into the cloud server where you keep the testing documentation. Tell me I'm wrong."

He's not wrong, but he also couldn't make me feel stupider if he tried.

I start to see red. "You hacked me?"

He gives me one of his Impaler glares. "Someone else hacked

you. I cleaned up that counter variable, remember? I was looking out for you."

What bullshit. "If you knew my password wasn't secure, why didn't you tell me?"

"I didn't get a chance. Besides, I didn't want you to think I was invading your privacy."

"Right, okay. And now my reputation is in shambles." A situation made infinitely worse by the fact that it's all my fault.

I couldn't feel more embarrassed if I tried.

He sighs and adjusts his glasses. He looks infinitely less angry now. "I'll have to look into that rumor business. For now, you should change your passwords everywhere you can think of. Better late than never. Instead of using the letters in your favorite word, you can swap them for numbers that correspond to the position of those letters in the alphabet. Or just use—"

"Don't patronize me!" Rationally, I know I'm not being entirely fair, but I can't take this anymore. The cauldron of anger and embarrassment in my chest has reached its boiling point. "I aced a class in cryptography in the same school as you."

His eyebrows snap together. "I wasn't—"

"I'm leaving." I circle around him and head for the door.

"What about the lunch?" he calls to my back.

"I lost my appetite." I sprint for the elevators.

I'm not running away from him so much as this office, with its toxic rumors.

To my relief, no one crosses my path on the way. As soon as an elevator door opens, I jump inside and jab the lobby button.

As the doors are closing, I spot Vlad stalking toward me, his expression night dark.

He's chasing me?

Doesn't matter.

The elevator doors slide shut before he can jam his hand in.

IN THE CAB on the way home, I replay what just happened in my head.

Over and over.

No matter which angle I look from, what used to be my great reputation at Binary Birch is now history.

Though people don't know that I went full cliché and actually slept with the company owner, they do think I used toys on him and on other dudes—the latter being a hurtful lie. No matter what happens now, the specter of preferential treatment will taint my career, which sucks because I work hard at my job. In fact, I got into this mess *because* I was such a good tester. Not that anyone will care anymore. Now they'll assume I'm using sex to get what I want, be it a transfer into the development department or a promotion.

The worst part is, if I do get that transfer now, I myself won't be sure it happened for the right reasons.

As the cab enters Brooklyn, my thoughts turn to Vlad, and my embarrassment and anger give way to a mix of guilt and regret.

I shouldn't have stormed out on him the way I did. What happened wasn't his fault.

I mean, could he—Mr. Privacy—have handled the password situation better?

Probably.

Did he owe me the Phantom info?

Not exactly.

In fact, Phantom's praise had actually felt nicer, more deserved *before* I knew Vlad was behind it.

We stop next to my place.

I pay and rush to my door.

A package is waiting for me there.

Inside the box is a fanny pack—though it calls itself "a waist bag." It's Chanel, stylish as hell, and contains a note signed by Vlad:

*Own it.*

I don't know how I should feel about this. The bag must cost thousands of dollars.

The shipping date is from the day before yesterday, so he didn't know about today's mess when he sent it. Or that we'd sleep together.

Is it a sign that he likes me or a thank-you for a testing job well done?

I know I'm not thinking clearly right now, so I take out Precious and call Ava.

She doesn't pick up.

I leave her a voicemail to call me back ASAP, and even send her an SOS text.

No reply.

Maybe I should email her for good measure? Sometimes she checks her inbox from her work computer when her phone is dead.

I launch my email, and something in my inbox catches my eye.

It's that Google alert I'd created to monitor for news mentioning Vlad's name.

Curious, I click on the alert and open the article in question.

It's on *Cosmopolitan*'s website. The tagline states:

*Belka sex toys so addictive, reclusive CEO Vlad Chortsky couldn't help but test on himself.*

# THIRTY

PRECIOUS SLIPS out of my fingers, hitting the floor with a thud.

Hands shaking, I pick up my poor phone.

The screen is cracked, but the article is still visible and I'm able to read the rest of it.

According to a source, Vlad and a female QA tester couldn't help themselves and used the toys to reach multiple orgasms. The article even goes as far as to list the number of orgasms he and I had, and every type of toy used.

What's worse, they have a picture of Vlad, and I recognize it. It's the very same one I snapped at Starbucks when I first saw him, the one used by my app.

This proves it.

Vlad was right when he said that it was me and not Sandra who's responsible for this info getting out. Someone snooped around that public photo database my app uses—the very same one that Phantom/Vlad had suggested I make more private. The leaker dug out that photo and guessed my password to get my testing results from my documentation. They then handed all this to *Cosmo*, along with the gossip about Vlad, whose name wasn't in my write-up.

Since the *Cosmo* folks were going to write a story about Belka toys anyway, they jumped at the chance to make it juicier.

This would be bad even if Vlad weren't obsessed with privacy. As is, I can't even fathom how pissed he'll be when he learns about this.

Fuck.

Between my storming out earlier and this, I doubt I'll ever hear from him again.

Feeling masochistic, I text him the link to the article, asking, *Have you seen this?*

No reply.

I begin to pace my apartment.

With every second he doesn't text me back, I get more anxious.

He could at the very least say *something*, even if it's "You're fired" or "I never want to see you again."

To calm myself down, I grab some treats and go to feed Monkey.

She's not alone.

Of course.

Vlad left Oracle here.

That's just great. Every time a guy dumps my ass, I get another guinea pig.

Soon, I'll have a whole pigsty.

Since this isn't Oracle's fault, I feed both of them as they squeak and run around, popcorning in joy.

Their cute antics actually make me feel a little better. That is, until I get angry—but this time, not at Vlad.

It's the hacker.

The person who actually contacted *Cosmo*, and no doubt spread those rumors around the office as well.

Whoever it is, I hate them, and it's always good to know who you hate.

Jumping on my laptop, I navigate my way to my cloud storage account and check access history for the testing document.

It doesn't take long to locate what I'm looking for.

Someone who lives in Queens—as in, not me—has regularly accessed the file in the last couple of days.

I grit my teeth. The IP of the scum looks familiar.

I bring up the IP of that CrazyOops user who'd said catty things about my app.

Yep.

It's a match.

Which means there's a very good chance it was Britney behind all this.

Not a huge surprise. She's known as a hacker, she hates my guts, and she's been sniffing around this project from the start. She'd even stalked our lunches.

Vlad being rude to her at the monthly meeting probably didn't help matters.

Fuming, I go down the rabbit hole of internet searches to find out if what she did is legal.

Nope. Unauthorized access to computer systems is a crime.

Speaking of crimes, smothering Britney would also not be legal, no matter how good it would feel.

I resume my pacing.

It's been hours now, and nothing from Vlad.

I might as well admit it.

He's ghosting me—and I can't blame him.

His privacy is kaput, all because of my negligence, and his sister didn't get the write-up she'd hoped for.

Well, screw him. By not talking to me, he's missing the Britney info.

This might actually be for the best. I was beginning to fall for that bastard, and if he's like this, I'd rather learn early.

Yeah. I should thank him for not texting.

This is like ripping off a Band-Aid.

That's always a good idea, right?

*Maybe not if the Band-Aid is covering a festering wound.*

I stop pacing and force myself to eat.

Everything tastes like cardboard. Montages of my lunches with Vlad play out in my treacherous brain, followed by recollections of us cuddling last night.

And the orgasms he gave me.

Okay, need major distraction.

I immerse myself in video games—something I haven't done in a while. It helps a bit. Beheading zombies isn't as satisfying as scalping Britney would be, but at least it's more socially acceptable.

Maybe this is what I should've done with my computer science degree: made games that let people forget the crap in their lives, at least for a while.

By midnight, any hope I had for a reply from Vlad is gone, so I stumble into bed and cry myself to sleep.

---

I WAKE up to the chime of a doorbell.

Leaping off the bed, I rush to the bathroom and make myself semi-presentable before sprinting for the door.

"Who is it?" I ask, then belatedly recall that I can now look at the video app on my phone.

"Ava."

Crap. I've never been so disappointed to hear my friend's voice.

I open the door.

She looks furious. "Who texts SOS and then ignores her friend's calls?"

I blink at her. "I didn't ignore you."

She pushes her way in. "I texted and called a hundred times. Literally."

"Hold up." I stumble into the living room and pick up Precious. "Nothing from you."

She scoffs. "I called and texted. Repeatedly."

A sinking feeling builds in my stomach—but also a flutter of hope.

I check Precious more thoroughly.

Damn it. It's not just the screen that's cracked. When I dropped it, it also lost the ability to receive calls and messages.

Which means Vlad might not have ghosted me.

I was too out of it yesterday to realize that Ava had also disappeared on me. If I were in my right mind, that would've raised all sorts of red flags.

Ava puts her hands on her hips. "You need to spill whatever it is. Now."

I make us two bowls of chocolatey cereal, and we gobble it down as I give her the whole awful story.

"I bet he thinks you ghosted *him*," Ava says. "You stormed out and all that."

I put down my spoon. "That's what I'm afraid of."

She slurps the last of her milk. "So what now?"

"Give me your phone."

She does. I pull up Vlad's number on my mostly dead Precious and call Vlad from Ava's phone.

He doesn't answer.

Maybe he's screening numbers he doesn't know?

I look for my work phone but can't find it.

Did I forget it at his place, just like my panties?

No. It must've been that meeting room.

I remember putting it down on the table, but I have zero recollection of picking it up.

Fuck it.

I jump to my feet. "I'm going to go to him."

Ava wrinkles her nose. "You might want to make yourself look like a human first."

"Right." I drop our bowls into the sink. "I'm sorry you came all this way just to watch me leave."

She grins. "Don't worry about me. It might be fun to help you get ready."

I rush into my closet and look for something to wear that screams "grand romantic gesture."

It doesn't take me long to pick out the perfect thing.

It's my Halloween costume of many years in a row.

Donning the black vinyl, I return to the living room.

"What do you know?" Ava says, scanning me from head to toe. "Yet another rich guy into BDSM."

I roll my eyes. "I'm supposed to be Trinity from *The Matrix*, and you know it."

She grins. "Let me help you with makeup."

"How about you do it on the way?"

She agrees, and I get her to order us an Uber.

While we wait for the car, I check my work email, just in case.

As I suspected, there are countless messages from Vlad, proving without a shadow of doubt that he didn't ghost me.

*You're not answering your phone*, one says. *Can we talk?*

Next one: *I understand why you're upset. Can you call me?*

I scroll down to the fifteenth email.

*Just found your work phone. Did you lose your personal one as well?*

Before I read any more, Ava's phone informs us that the driver is outside. We run out and jump into the car, where Ava makes me look borderline goth—a makeup style that works nicely with my dark hair and pale skin tone.

"Go get him," she says when the car stops next to my work building. "You look amazeballs."

"Thanks." I jump out and put on my Matrix-inspired sunshades before rushing into the building.

Exiting the elevator on the Binary Birch floor, I bump right into a bunch of people with coffees in their hands. They're exiting the other elevator.

Ugh. They're from the dev team, and thanks to Murphy's law, Britney is among them.

I suppress the urge to go for her throat. Murder is wrong, and downright dumb when you're surrounded by so many witnesses.

Clearly unaware of the danger she's in, Britney looks me over with an eye roll. "Is it time to test the nipple clamps already?"

The people around us shift their gazes between us, looking uncomfortable.

I take off my shades so I can properly glare at her. "Your jokes are as crap as your coding skills."

A few bystander eyebrows shoot up.

She narrows her eyes at me. "What could you possibly know about coding, you hack?"

Red mist veils my vision. I've been waiting for this for so, so long. "More than you, that's for sure. You don't use consistent indentation, you leave zero comments, and you misspell the words in variable names half the time. And I don't think you even know the meaning of 'modularization.' Do I need to keep going? Because I can."

To my shock, several of her teammates nod approvingly. Someone even mutters something like, "Mad burn."

Britney squeezes her coffee so hard it spills over. "At least I didn't let the Impaler poke me with a dildo."

My glare can melt lead at this point. "He wouldn't poke *you* with a ten-foot pole, that's for sure."

She bristles, advancing on me. "How dare you?"

Fine. No more Ms. Nice Fanny. "I know it was you," I grit through my teeth.

Blanching, she stops in her tracks. "I don't know what you're talking about."

I rattle out her IP address. "Does that sound familiar? Because I called your ISP, and they confirmed that's yours."

I did no such thing, but the bluff clearly works. She whitens to ghost levels and takes a step back.

Time for the kill—unfortunately metaphorical. "If I see your face or IP address ever again, I'm going to give the info to the Impaler. Given how crazy he is about privacy, and how rich, he'll probably make sure you rot in jail."

She's so green I'm tempted to give her Dramamine. "It was just a joke."

I put my sunglasses back on. "Like I said, your jokes are as crap as your code."

# THIRTY-ONE

NOT WAITING to see the dev team's reaction, I hurry down the hallway and barge into Vlad's office.

He's not here.

Damn it.

Where is he?

I look for a calendar, but of course, this isn't 1989 or whenever it was when everyone stopped using paper.

Bolstered by my outfit and the encounter with Britney, I circle around Vlad's desk and wake up his computer.

It's locked.

Of course. Standard company policy—which sucks, because if I could sneak a peek at his digital calendar, I'd figure out where he is.

If only I could guess his pin code...

I bite my lip, considering it.

Our pin codes are six digits, so there are a million different random combinations.

So guessing at random is out.

I have to try to think of what he might actually use.

I look up, and sure enough, there's a security camera in the corner of his office.

Is that in case someone tries what I'm about to do?

Well, hopefully he won't be too mad at me.

I wave at the camera. "This is what you get for stalking me in your meeting rooms."

Just in case he watches the tape later.

For now, I try 123456 for the pin code.

Nope. That would've been too easy.

I try 654321.

Still no.

I try different permutations of his birth date.

None work.

The beginning and end digits of his phone number don't work either.

If I keep this up, the computer will lock me out for too many failed attempts.

Then I recall something he'd said right before I stormed out of that meeting room, about how you can use numbers to represent the letters of the alphabet in a favorite word.

Could it be that simple?

I convert what I think might be his favorite word—Neo—to 140515.

Score!

The computer unlocks, and the first thing that stares me in the face is an email Vlad must've been drafting before he locked his screen.

Its subject line states: "Britney Archibald's Termination."

Unable to help myself, I skim the message.

Of course.

Vlad figured out she was the leak and the one spreading the rumors. Attached are transcripts of instant messenger conversations where she told Mike how I was testing sex toys with multiple men at

Binary Birch, including the guy in HR whose name happens to be in the "To" of Vlad's email.

She is so screwed.

Somehow, Vlad even managed to dig up proof that Britney had hacked the social media accounts of her ex from the sales department—something that was only rumored until now.

It's official.

Britney bit off more than she could chew when she gave Vlad's name to *Cosmo*.

Minimizing the email, I check Vlad's calendar to see where he is.

Huh.

He's at 1000 Devils, and where the agenda should be is my name.

Is he asking his brother for some relationship advice?

That doesn't track. Vlad has attached my resume to this meeting, as well as links to my app's code. I'd hope those aren't critical for any relationship we might or might not have.

Then it hits me.

*He's getting me a job.*

Leaping out of his chair, I sprint out of the building and jump into a cab.

Time to face 1000 Devils.

# THIRTY-TWO

I STEP out of the elevator furtively.

Nope.

No one shoots me.

At least not yet.

Sprinting for the Nerf gun armory, I get myself a proper arsenal: two handguns that I stuff into my waistband and a two-handed machine-gun contraption.

If I'm going to work at this place—and I don't know if I am—I'll have to fit in with their quirky culture.

If that means shooting my way to Vlad, so be it.

Clutching my Nerf machine gun, I exit the room and creep onto the main floor.

An orange projectile is hurtling at my face, but I sidestep and it whooshes by my ear.

"Nice one," someone says.

I spin around and put a bullet in the chest of a redhead with a beer belly. I vaguely remember him from my last visit.

Someone jumps out of the cube on the right.

I dodge her shot, then shoot her in the boob.

Another person leaps out of a cube.

I lunge behind a column, avoiding the projectile.

Peeking out to take aim, I kneecap the last assailant.

A bunch of darts hits the column.

I stick my head out, spot an older lady unloading her gun in my direction, and shoot her in the arm.

Another round of darts misses me.

I peek once more.

A guy with a buzzcut is reloading.

I shoot his neck, then sprint for the column near the large meeting room.

Through the glass, I see Vlad and Alex speaking animatedly, but they don't notice me.

Which is fine.

I don't need backup anyway.

Taking in a deep breath, I sprint out of my hiding spot.

The next few moments happen like a slow-motion effect in *The Matrix*.

I dodge a dart, then hit its source in the shoulder.

Leaping over a low-flying projectile, I drop my empty machine gun to the floor and pull out two handguns while still in the air.

*Bang. Bang.*

Two handed, I hit two people in my path to the meeting room and grab the door handle.

A whole cloud of Nerf darts is now flying my way, but I'm already behind the glass door.

The darts hit the glass and drop futilely to the floor.

Victory!

"Fanny?" Vlad is staring at me with a mixture of confusion and approval. "What are you doing here? How did you get here?"

I take off my sunglasses. "Guessed your pin code and took a peek at your calendar. Sorry about before. My phone was broken. I wasn't ignoring you. Because of the article, I thought—"

I stop, catching the fascinated expression on Alex's face. "Never mind."

A slow smile spreads over Vlad's face. "It's good that you came. We were just talking about you."

Alex stands up. "Hey there, Fanny. Good to see you again." He shakes my hand. "I was going to get my HR folks to reach out to you first, but since you're here, I want to formally extend you an offer for a developer position here at 1000 Devils."

So, my guess was correct.

Vlad is getting me another job.

And not just any job.

Software development, exactly what I want to do.

My excitement battles with embarrassment. Before this goes any further, I have to ask Alex something important. "Is this because I slept with your brother?"

Eyes widening, Alex darts Vlad a questioning glance. "You did? I guess... good for you guys?"

If I hoped that recent events had desensitized my cheeks from burning, no such luck. They heat up with an almost sadistic enthusiasm as I sneak a peek at Vlad.

Did I just blurt something I shouldn't have?

Will he be even madder at me now?

His face is unreadable, though one corner of his mouth appears to be twitching in either amusement or anger.

Alex scratches the back of his head. "Actually, Fanny, I wanted to hire you after you found that glitch in our game, but Vlad and I have a no-poaching policy, so I figured it wasn't meant to be. When he told me you're looking for something more fun and challenging, but in the coding area instead of testing, I got intrigued. And since he just showed me your recent work, I have no doubt you'd be an asset here. We're currently working on an RPG where we want to match user's images to a database of pre-prepared character faces that look like them. Does that sound familiar?"

My excitement grows with each word he speaks, and by the time he's done, I can't help but bob my head repeatedly. "That's basically what my app does." My voice all but bursts with eagerness. "Just replace cartoon characters with game ones."

Alex smiles. "Exactly. You'll be able to hit the ground running. Assuming you're interested?" His expression turns more serious. "Before you decide, I can tell you here and now: Whatever happens between you and my brother will never have any bearing on your job. I can put that in legalese if you want me to."

I grin so widely I can feel it in my ears. "In that case, yes."

I extend my hand, and we shake on it.

Vlad rises to his feet. "She actually means 'maybe.' To get a yes, you need to wow her with things like salary and benefits."

I almost smack myself on the forehead. "Vlad's right. My talents don't come cheap."

Alex grins. "I'm sure we can work something out. It's Binary Birch we're competing with, after all." He gives Vlad a good-natured wink. "For example, our dress code is less restrictive—Matrix attire being purely optional."

I beam at him. "Thank you. This is very exciting. I'll be on the lookout for a formal offer. Now if you don't mind, I need to talk to Vlad." I give my-soon-to-be former employer a hesitant smile. "Assuming you *want* to talk to me?"

Vlad cocks his head. "We can talk... provided you let me cook you a lunch of my choice."

I resist the urge to jump up and down like a kid. "It's a deal."

As Alex walks us out of the 1000 Devils building, I make the easiest decision of my life.

Unless it's a huge pay cut—and I doubt that very much—I'll take the 1000 Devils' job. Making video games is something every gamer thinks about as soon as they start their introductory programming classes, and a company like this seems particularly cool. The culture at 1000 Devils is quirky, with the guns and all—but that just seems like a fun adventure, not a drawback.

In fact, even if I'm given the option to work from home, I'll work here at the office.

"I missed you," Vlad says when the elevator doors close.

I snap to attention, all thoughts of the job offer forgotten. "I missed you too," I say, proud of how steady my voice is. "I'm sorry about—"

"No." He takes my hand, his fingers strong and warm around mine. "I'm the one who should be sorry. I should've fired Britney after she hacked that guy in sales. You heard about that, right?"

Oops. I guess hacking is on his list of no-nos. "Did you hear me earlier? I got into your computer. And when I did, I saw the email you were writing about her. I'm sorry about invading your privacy like that."

He squeezes my hand reassuringly. "I guessed your password, and you guessed my pin. I'd say we're even."

I want to kiss him, but the elevator opens and people look at us expectantly, so we get out.

The walk to the limo happens in a flash, with me feeling like I'm waltzing on air the whole time. Climbing in, we sit next to each other, and he buckles my safety belt as though that's a normal thing to do— and I love it.

"How did your sister take the whole article debacle?" I ask when the car rushes forward.

He smiles. "Her phone is off the hook. She thinks the hint of scandal in the article actually helped. She might be right. The original would've sounded more like an infomercial."

Whew. "So she's going to be okay?"

His smile widens. "Yep."

I bite my lip. "How about you?"

"All good as well. I contacted *Cosmo* with a correction to the article, and they fixed it." He pulls out his phone and shows me the screen.

I skim the article. His name is still there, but I'm no longer referred to as a QA person.

According to this article, I'm Vlad's girlfriend.

Girlfriend.

Me.

I want to jump out of the car and dance a jig in the middle of Times Square.

"That's okay, right?" he asks, his dark brows furrowing. "I figured that—"

"It's more than okay." The words come out breathlessly. "But why didn't you make them remove your name from the article while you were at it?"

He shrugs. "Didn't want to risk it. What if the correction reduces the exposure for Bella?"

I nod solemnly. "Very noble. Sacrificing your privacy for your sister."

A corner of his mouth twists wryly. "That, or I don't have that much leverage over the folks at *Cosmo*."

The limo stops, and he opens the door for me.

As we get into his building, he tells me about a guinea pig herd he discovered upstate—a place where owners can let their pets play with large numbers of other piggies.

"Monkey and Oracle looked like they enjoyed being together," he explains as we ride the elevator. "So I started to wonder whether they wouldn't want even more socialization."

"Sure," I say as the elevator opens into his place. "I like the idea of this herd. We'll take them there one day."

The part I like the most is that he's making plans that involve me.

First, I'm his girlfriend, and now this.

The only way I'd feel happier is if he got naked.

Hmm. Maybe this can also be arranged?

"So..." I take off my boots. "You never gave me a tour of your place."

He hands me a pair of slippers that happen to be exactly my size—making me feel like Cinderella.

"I'm going to fix that oversight immediately." He opens the door down the hall. "This is my bedroom."

Check and mate. Bedroom is the destination I needed for my evil plan.

Once we're inside, I close the door loudly to get his attention. Then, as he watches, I unzip my top.

Dracula displays immediate interest—as does Vlad.

His eyes gleam predatorially behind his lenses as he closes the distance between us. "That outfit has been driving me insane."

I reach over to unbutton his shirt collar. "Right back at ya."

"Wait." He catches my wrists. "There's something you should know."

"Oh?" A kaleidoscope of butterflies flaps their wings together, starting a whirlwind in my belly.

He takes a breath, his expression uncertain for the first time since I've known him. Softly, he says, "It's going to sound crazy, but I've never experienced this kind of connection with anyone before. The way we are together is like the most elegant, bug-free code that works perfectly as soon as you finish writing it. Fannychka..." His voice roughens. "I know it's only been a few days since we met, but—"

"You love me," I blurt—and flush immediately.

I have no idea where this bold statement came from, but I'm absurdly certain I'm right.

He lets go of my wrists, amusement glinting in his eyes. "Is it some American custom to interrupt such things?"

My already-prodigious blush deepens. "I'm so sorry. You were saying?"

He takes my face into his hands, the way he did the other day when he told me he'd like me even without any facial hair. His eyes are the purest, deepest blue as they peer into mine. "Fanny Pack," he says solemnly. "I love you."

The storm in my belly morphs into a full-fledged tornado, one that spins higher up my chest, encasing my heart with the warmest, sweetest glow. "And I love you," I breathe.

He leans in, claiming my lips in the deepest, most passionate kiss. Lips locked and tongues dancing, we stumble to the bed, our clothes falling off as if by magic, and what happens next can only be described by one word.

Lovemaking.

Hours later, as we lie there utterly spent, I secretly pinch myself to make sure this is really happening.

It is.

It's real.

I've gotten the vampire of my dreams, Vlad the Impaler himself.

Who could've guessed?

And just to think... it all started with a suitcase full of sex toys.

# EPILOGUE
## VLAD

**_Six months later, Iceland_**

ON OUR TABLE is a plate of peculiar Icelandic delicacies, including fermented shark and soured ram testicles.

I'm not surprised that Fannychka has bravely tried a bite of every single thing here and liked it, even the poor ram's nads—a dish I personally skipped. Out of, as she teasingly put it, "male solidarity."

In the last six months, she's become a connoisseur of delicacies from all around the globe—at least, the ones you can get in NYC, which is many.

She's also a connoisseur of sexual acts, positions, and toys, much to my delight. If she ever gets tired of being a game developer, I bet she could write the next Kama Sutra.

This is our first official vacation, and she's loved it thus far—though more thanks to the geothermal pools and the alien-planet landscapes rather than the Icelandic cuisine.

I keep my face neutral as I watch her drink her apple cider, though the sight of those scrumptious pink lips wrapped around the bottle drives me insane, as usual.

Does she have any clue what I'm about to do?

Maybe. Maybe not. You never know with this one. She can be deviously clever.

I scan our surroundings for clues.

The glass roof and walls of the restaurant create an uber-romantic ambience that could give me away. You can see city lights down the mountain, as well as the night sky above.

Also, we're the only ones here, so she might rightfully deduce this is my doing and not the restaurant suffering from a lack of patrons.

Hopefully, the not-so-romantic food selection was a good-enough misdirection.

Now I just need the weather to cooperate. The forecast was good, but if not, there's always tomorrow.

I want her to remember this forever.

So, I carry on a conversation as we eat, but I also wait for my moment.

As par for the course on such auspicious occasions, I can't help but think back on some of the highlights of our time together.

When I saw her at that Starbucks, with her pale skin and black hair, she'd looked like she stepped out of the *Underworld* movies—ironic, considering all the vampire jokes she still makes at my expense.

I knew then and there that I wanted her, and I took a picture of her surreptitiously—another bit of irony considering she did the same to me with her app.

When she stepped into my office mere minutes later, she looked like I might eat her—cannibalistically—while the truth was that I wanted to devour her in a very different way, completely inappropriate for the office.

I tried to stay professional—not an easy task given the project on her plate—but then she contacted me with that toy emergency, and all my good intentions went out the window. I was shocked at the protective emotions she stirred up. A part of me knew most people would find her situation humorous, but I was way too worried about her getting hurt.

Things began to spiral even more when I took her to our first lunch and started to learn how much we had in common. By the time she told me she wanted to test the toys on some random guy, I wanted to rip him into shreds.

Then the testing started.

Dracula gets rock hard every time I think about that—including now. It's a good thing I don't need to get up anytime soon, else—

"Look, babe, the Northern Lights!" Fanny is gesturing at the glass roof, her blue eyes shining in excitement.

Spoke too soon. I do have to move, erection or not.

This is the moment I've been waiting for.

Fanny has been dying to see this wonder, and I can't blame her. As a kid, I couldn't get enough of watching these things back in Murmansk.

It's a perfect distraction, so I ignore the bulge in my pants along with the gorgeous aurora borealis in the sky.

By the time she looks back at me, I'm in position.

On one knee, a diamond ring in hand.

A ring my sister and Ava helped me choose—before I swore them to secrecy, of course.

"Fuck. Me." Fanny gapes down at me, her pupils the size of a dime. "When did you get down there?"

Seems like she didn't expect this.

Good.

Ignoring the question, I launch into my spiel. "Fanny Pack, I first want to thank you for all the joy you've brought into my life." I know that sounds like one of my parents' toasts, but the words are coming from my heart, and the bright glitter of her eyes seems to indicate that they resonate. "You have been the most important thing in my world for the last six months. I love you, and you love me. Will you—"

"Marry you?" she breathes.

I grin. It's become a tradition of sorts for her to interrupt me during moments like this; she did it even when I asked her to move in together.

I lovingly clasp her small hand. "I was actually going to say: Will you make me the happiest vampire in history by letting me finally turn you, so we can spend an eternity together?"

She spreads the fingers on her free hand. "Yes. Please. I've always wanted to sparkle in the sunlight."

Heart thudding heavily in my chest, I slide the ring on her finger, making it official.

Our big adventure together is about to begin.

# HARD WARE

# ONE

IS THAT A *BEAR*?

The Kegel balls feel like they're on the verge of escaping my vagina. I squeeze my well-trained muscles to keep the toy inside. The pair of balls are of my own design, so I know if I squeeze them one more time, the vibration feature will activate, and this isn't a good time for that.

The leash jerks in my hand.

"Bonaparte, behave." The sternness in my voice is futile. My Chihuahua keeps tugging, his gaze glued to the bear and his tail wagging so rapidly I half expect him to helicopter into the air like a drone.

To my relief, the bear merely sniffs the fire hydrant, oblivious to the delicious four-pound appetizer a mere leap away.

Digging in my heels, I pull back on the leash. "Seriously, Boner. Do you *want* to get eaten?"

The pulling stops, and my dog looks up at me, a mixture of sadness and indignation in his green eyes. As usual, I can imagine what he'd say if I were a dog whisperer:

"*Ma chérie*, that dog is ignoring me. *Moi!* Unthinkable."

I toss him a biscuit. "That bear clearly has no manners. In its defense, though, would *you* be able to resist sniffing that hydrant? We're next to Central Park. Millions of dogs have peed there. The smell must be heavenly."

With a leap, Boner catches the treat, swallows it without chewing, and returns his attention to his gargantuan quarry.

My own gaze shifts to the man holding the beast's leash, and my jaw drops as my inner muscles involuntarily squeeze the Kegel balls.

The vibration activates, but I ignore it, my eyes hungrily roaming over the tall, athletically built male specimen in front of me.

The bear's owner is hot.

Scorching, panty-melting, uterus-exploding hot.

The kind of hot that I'm going to end up masturbating to.

Wait. Strictly speaking, I *am* masturbating to him—the vibration inside my vagina is building my climax with every passing second. Thankfully, he's not looking at me, so I can gobble him up without shame.

The man checks all my boxes, even ones I didn't know I had.

Thick, silky-looking hair the color of mink's fur. Short, neatly trimmed dark beard that emphasizes his regal nose and carved features. Broad shoulders padded with just the right amount of muscle and a chest to die for, all tapering down to a lean waist and narrow hips. He's even wearing a turtleneck, for fuck's sake—and everyone knows that's the guy equivalent of a sexy black dress.

Oh, and his lips. I want to make a mold of those lips and turn that mold into a sex toy.

Speaking of sex toys, the balls are getting me ever closer to the edge. Though I've been accused of being blasé about such things, even I recognize that coming here and now, in front of a stranger, isn't the most socially acceptable move on my part.

I've got to disable the balls, which can be done if I squeeze them three more times. The problem is, each squeeze also changes the vibration speed, so my situation will get worse before it gets better.

No helping that, I suppose.

I squeeze.

The vibration intensifies.

Twice more to go and—

Boner barks.

The bear's massive snout unpeels from the hydrant, and giant brown eyes zero in on the dog-shaped hors d'oeuvre at my feet.

Finally getting the attention he craves, Boner rapidly wags his tail and tries to sprint to his doom.

I squeeze the balls again, involuntarily. One more time, and they're off. Except the vibration is now on full speed, and it feels amazing. So, so amazing...

Crap. What am I doing?

Have to squeeze one last time.

Except the prerequisite muscles have turned to jelly, and I'm having trouble squeezing.

Is this it?

Am I going to have an orgasm just as my dog gets eaten—all in front of the insanely hot stranger?

Fleetingly, I wonder if I should let the bear eat my best friend to distract from my imminent combustion—and maybe so that the bear's owner will sleep with me later as recompense for my loss.

No, that's madness.

I tug on the leash, stopping Boner's noble sacrifice in its tracks.

Except now he's on the bear's radar.

The beast lunges—and the swift jerk of its leash catches the hot stranger off guard. By the time he realizes what's what and digs in his heels, the bear's maw is mere inches away from Boner's tennis-ball-sized head.

Clutching my handbag, I back away, pulling my overexcited friend with me. Not that I'm not overexcited myself. My heart is pounding, and I'm sweating from the effort of holding back the orgasm as the balls continue to vibrate on max.

Squeezing isn't working. Maybe I just ride it out, keeping a poker face?

The stranger says something to the bear in a language I don't recognize, though the guttural quality makes it sound like a distant relative of Russian. Then his eyes narrow on Boner, and still without looking at me, he growls in perfectly unaccented English, "Keep that rat away from my dog."

His voice is deep and as ridiculously sexy as the rest of him, but thankfully, his words make me angry enough that the impending orgasm recedes.

Such a shame. All these gifts wasted on a man who's clearly an asshat.

I tighten my grip on Boner's leash and narrow my own eyes at the stranger. "I'll keep my *dog* away from your *bear*."

There. Not a bad comeback considering my situation.

He finally deigns to look at me—and I'm once again struck dumb.

Those eyes, set beneath a pair of thick, dark eyebrows, are the most beautiful color I've ever seen, a mercurial sort of hazel that seems to shift between dark green and amber-tinted brown.

Said eyes widen as they travel over my body, lingering for a moment on my short skirt and bare legs, but then his gorgeous face takes on an imperious expression. "Oh, please. She's more of a dog than yours will ever be."

His rich, deep voice conspires with the balls inside me to get me even closer to a place I don't want to be.

Maybe I could do what guys do in this situation—think unsexy thoughts.

*Goop from the eyes. Ear wax. Squeezing a whitehead. Smelly armpits. Flaky scalps. Gray stuff dug out of belly buttons. Nail fungus.*

Nope. None of those are working.

*Mother?*

That seems to do the trick.

Speaking of her, I channel what she derisively calls my "Snow

Queen demeanor" and finally find the words to reply to the stranger. "Dogness isn't about quantity; it's about quality."

His thick eyebrows lift just a smidge. He's clearly never had anyone talk back to him before. "Why is that yappy little thing out of your purse in the first place?"

Ugh. Definitely an asshat. At least the annoyance is keeping the orgasm at bay. I hate that Chihuahua stereotype. Despite having been named after Napoleon, Boner doesn't actually have the complex that so many of his brethren do and isn't yappy in the least. He's been to doggy school, so he's well behaved. Mostly. He *is* a dog.

Fine. Ms. Nice Bella gloves are officially off.

I level a cold glare at the crotch of the stranger's jeans, then look back at his face, one eyebrow arched villainously. "Let me guess. The big dog is there to compensate for something?"

Whew. Where's my Oscar? I doubt even Angelina Jolie can tell someone off while holding back an orgasm.

The bastard just smirks. Those mercurial eyes gleaming, he drawls, "Want to bet?"

Oh, no.

With the picture of a gargantuan cock in my mind, I finally lose the fight against my balls and come.

# TWO

IT'S a miracle that I'm able to suppress my moan—a miracle that deserves yet another Oscar. All the women who fake orgasms should try the reverse. It's harder than I would've imagined.

The big question is: did he see it on my face?

The last spasm deactivates the balls, so at least I'm spared a repeat performance.

A loud bark rings out somewhere in the park.

Both of us glance down at our charges—I guess on the off chance they've learned to project their voices long distance, a feat that even I, a skilled ventriloquist, am not capable of.

Boner's nose is pointed in the direction of the distant bark, tail wagging with excited curiosity. "*Ma chérie*, I think that dog barked because there's a squirrel there, in Béchamel sauce. Can we please, please go there? Please!"

In contrast to Boner, the bear is cowering pitifully, giant fluffy ears drooping and three-hundred-pound body shaking like a furry brown leaf.

Crap. Now I feel sorry for the bear, but also vindicated.

Who's the bigger dog now?

The stranger croons something soothing in his language, patting the bear's head, and the beast snaps out of her panic.

With a small wag of her tail, she turns her snout toward Boner and takes a big sniff.

Forgetting the other dog, Boner looks up at the bear and also sniffs the air.

With a huff, the stranger says something in that Russianesque language again and drags the bear away without giving me the chance to mock his "real dog's" cowardliness.

Boner longingly eyes the bear's rear end. "*Ma chérie*, that is a lot of butt to sniff. What a *tragédie*."

"I feel your pain," I whisper, my eyes roaming the tight, muscular tush outlined by the jeans of the irksome stranger—a tush that looks extra tempting in the orgasm afterglow. "I'm not sure if I want to sniff it, per se, but I think having that butt attached to that brain is a loss for womankind."

We resume our walk, and every time Boner stops to sniff something, I sneak a glance at the annoying stranger and make sure not to accidentally squeeze the Kegel balls again.

He's taking the bear to Boner's favorite spot, a doggy playground —though on occasion, I've seen human toddlers on those ramps as well.

Great. Now we can't go there.

Unless we should?

No. Forget that guy.

Unfortunately, as we continue on our walk, I find that forgetting him is hard work, especially in light of the warmth still pulsing in my core.

Why does the universe have to be so unfair? I so rarely come across guys I'm attracted to, and when I finally find one, he turns out to be an ass. Then again, given my past relationships, the mere fact that I'm attracted to someone might be a red flag. According to my friend Xenia, I'm an asshole magnet. Case in point: my most recent ex.

There's a reason I prefer my sex toys to real men.

A sixth sense pulls me out of my daydreaming just in time to spot Boner sniffing a snail on the ground.

"No!" I shout just as he—unsurprisingly—shoves the snail right into his maw.

"Spit that out."

He looks up at me with a guileless expression. "Why? It's *escargot.*"

I channel the alpha in our little relationship. "Spit it. You could get the French heartworm."

Looking contrite, Boner spits the creature out and watches it crawl away, unbothered by dog drool. "French heartworm sounds like my kind of heartworm."

I toss him another treat. "Good boy. I bet that bear isn't nearly as well trained. She would get a parasite in a heartbeat, but not you."

"*Touché.*" He resumes his walk, ears drooping.

Poor guy. First he couldn't sniff a bear; now he's not allowed to eat a snail. I can relate. I was denied premium man candy myself.

Guiding Boner toward a fire hydrant, I watch him forget all his worries as he hikes up his leg impossibly high and pees at a level only a big dog should be able to reach.

If only my key to happiness were so simple—I'd hike up my leg in a heartbeat. Well, not right this moment—my balls would fall out.

Happy with his urinary work, Boner resumes his trot.

Not for the first time, I wonder why he has such ambitions when it comes to his pee. Is it part of a delusion where he thinks he's a much, much bigger dog? Or could it be that all dogs want to shoot for the stars, and being small and limber helps Boner not tip over as he hikes his leg higher than his head?

Boner stops and looks wistfully in the direction of the playground.

Since the bear is still there, I say, "How about we feed John first?"

At John's name, Boner approvingly wags his tail. John either doesn't have a home or has some other reason why he never bathes—which makes him a fun human to smell, for a dog.

Halfway to John's bench, a black cat crosses our path. Since the cat is bigger than Boner, he pretends not to see it. I, on the other hand, halt in my tracks and nearly squeeze the balls too hard once again.

Thank goodness my brothers aren't here to mock me. A black cat crossing the road is a major Russian superstition that I find difficult to ignore. The MIT-trained engineer in me can't fathom how the bad luck from the cat would even work, yet I keep standing there, hoping someone crosses the cat's path and therefore takes the bad juju onto them.

With the business venture I'm launching, I can't chance any bad luck.

A squirrel suddenly dashes right over the tainted path. Since it's not bigger than him, Boner tries to give it a chase, but I hold him back just in time.

Whew. The squirrel will now get the bad luck instead of me or some nice old lady.

As we resume the walk, a king poodle walks toward us.

I grin. With that lion haircut, this dog looks a lot more French than mine—not that Boner has anything French in him besides his name and his soul. He actually looks like he could be in those "¡Yo quiero Taco Bell!" commercials, and with his Mexican ancestry, it's anyone's guess why he doesn't have a Hispanic accent when I picture him speaking to me.

Boner tries to be friendly with the poodle.

The bigger dog shows its teeth and growls.

Boner halts in his tracks and looks at me. "How *impoli!*"

I give the lady owner a dirty look.

She shrugs at me guiltily and hurries past us.

The rest of the way to John is uneventful, and when we get to the bench, he's there as usual, just staring blankly into the distance.

Tucking Boner's leash under my armpit, I take out the sandwich I made for John from my handbag. "Hi."

"Great. The commie is back," John grumbles before bending down to fluff Boner's fur.

I thrust the sandwich at him. "I was born after the Soviet Union had already collapsed, and I came to this country when I was five years old, so I'm much more of an American capitalist pig than a commie."

John frowns at the sandwich. "Once a commie, always a commie."

I guess that's fair. From what little I know of John's story, he's a Vietnam vet and is thus justified in his opinions on commies.

He's also too proud to accept charity, so I tread carefully, as usual. "This is from my parents' restaurant," I say, nodding at the sandwich. "They brought me too much food again, and in Russian culture, it's considered bad luck to throw out bread."

That last bit is actually true, which is why I only buy the frozen variety.

Mumbling something about dumb commie superstitions, John snatches the sandwich and begins wolfing it down.

There. Over time, I've learned how to make this transaction go pretty smoothly. When I first met him, John was unhealthily thin, but now he's—

The leash escapes from under my armpit as Boner suddenly torpedoes forward.

Crap.

"Later, John," I shout over my shoulder as I launch into a run. "I've got to catch him!"

I don't hear what John says, but I do see where Boner is headed.

The playground.

"Boner, stop!" I yell.

He doesn't. So much for that doggie school.

As I pick up speed, I curse myself for my constant desire to multi-task. Though I've taught myself to leave my phone at home to avoid getting distracted by work emails, I just had to test out the Kegel balls on this walk.

Squeezing my pelvic muscles for all I'm worth, I speed up some more. Juggling balls has nothing on trying to keep them inside one's privates while sprinting.

Boner vaults up the ramp right next to the bear.

No. He can't mean to—

But he does.

Using the height advantage of the ramp as an assist, my Chihuahua mounts the bear and begins to hump.

# THREE



"BONER, STOP, I SAY!"

That doggy school owes me a serious refund—this scenario should've been a part of their curriculum.

Oblivious to the world, my Chihuahua thrusts his tiny butt at the bear's gargantuan behind. From a distance, Boner looks like a bird hitching a ride on a hippopotamus.

Damn it. Silly dog. Why would you even attempt to have sex with something a hundred times bigger than you?

The thrusting accelerates.

My lungs burn as I pick up speed despite the obstacle of my tight skirt. At least I'm wearing my cute new sneaks instead of my usual high-heeled boots—those would make this impromptu track session impossible.

"Boner, stop it!" I pant.

He does the opposite. His humping grows frantic, making it look like he's having a sex seizure.

I further pick up the pace and my thong shifts, creating an unpleasant draft on my lady parts.

Why is the bear not eating him for this? Not that I'm complaining. Maybe Boner's tiny wiener isn't even in that cavernous vagina. I have no doubt that if a beast that big felt assaulted, Boner would be a dead dog.

Crap. Is this an assault? Is my little buddy a rapist?

But no. The bear's fluffy tail is up, providing Boner with easier entry. That has to be her way of consenting to this—along with the fact that she's not crushing him with her massive jaws. For all I know, they came to an agreement when they sniffed each other.

He must've seduced her with his mighty Chihuahua pheromones.

Of course, none of this will save Boner from the bear's annoyingly hot asshat of an owner. When he sees what's happening, he'll undoubtedly turn murderous. Luckily, his attention is on the guy he's currently talking to—or, more accurately, gesticulating and shouting at. The guy is holding a camera, which I hope he won't use to take a picture of Boner's misdemeanor.

My leg muscles burn as I sprint faster. I'm now only twenty feet away.

The camera guy loses whatever the argument was, and slinks away.

This is it.

The stranger turns and his gorgeous eyes widen as he registers the bear's situation.

Leaping for the ramp, I finally grab Boner's leash. Before I can drag him away, he disconnects of his own free will and looks up at me, tail wagging with masculine satisfaction.

As expected, the stranger's jaw turns to stone, his regal nostrils flaring.

With effort, I restrain myself from yelling "bad dog" at Boner. I don't want to give my little friend a sex complex, the kind my mother gave me when she caught me masturbating in my early teens.

Dogs deserve to be sexual beings just like humans do.

The bear owner's flinty gaze shifts from Boner to me. "Did your rat just—"

"My *dog* is sorry about what he did." It requires tremendous restraint to sound placating. "As am I. I got distracted, and he escaped."

Boner looks at me uncomprehendingly. "Why apologize, *ma chérie?* This is *le grand amour.*"

The stranger regards me with a withering stare. "Let me guess. You got lost in your phone?" Under his breath, he mutters something about Americans with their incessant posts and tweets.

My hackles officially rise, and it's an effort to keep myself from squeezing balls—his and the ones inside me. "Let *me* guess. You like to judge people without a shred of evidence? As it so happens, I don't bring my phone on my dog walks. Nor am I an American in the strictest sense of the word. Nor do I use social media, for that matter."

Curiosity replaces some of the anger on his face. "Then how did you let him escape?"

I give him my signature icy glare. "I don't have to explain myself to you."

I might've been too intense there. The bear's ears droop, and she hides behind the stranger.

His eyes narrow again. "Your dog violated mine. The least you can do is be civil."

Like me, Boner doesn't like his tone. Putting himself between us, he growls at the stranger.

"Easy, boy," I mutter, then take a deep breath to calm myself. Sometimes you win by taking the high road. "I do want to apologize."

"I don't need your apology. I need to know if your dog has any STDs."

Somehow, I still keep my cool. "This is the first time he's had real sex, so I highly doubt it."

Immediately, I want to smack myself for emphasizing the "real" bit; the last thing I want to get into is how I've built my dog a sex toy.

The stranger looks a bit calmer now, as does the bear behind him. "That's good. Still, semen can harbor a wide range of viruses. How do we know your dog isn't infected with something?"

I shrug. "He hasn't been sick? Besides, we don't know if he actually penetrated her—or if there was any semen."

Dog semen. Now that's a subject I didn't think would come up when I started my day.

"That's not good enough," the guy says. "I'd like you to take him to a vet and do a thorough checkup." He pats his pockets and comes out with a wallet. "I'll pay."

How does he get under my skin so easily? "I can pay for my own vet. Thanks."

"If you insist." The wallet disappears.

I straighten my spine. "I insist."

He gives me a more thorough once-over, his gaze once again lingering on my legs. "And you'll let me know the vet results?" His voice is a shade huskier as his hazel eyes return to my face.

My treacherous heart skips a beat. "I'll need to put my number into your phone. As I said, I don't have mine."

Is that a hint of a smile quirking his sexy lips?

"That would be great, except I also don't bring my phone on my dog walks," he says. Wryly, he adds, "Nor do I use social media. Nor am I an American."

That last bit I could've guessed, but no social media? I thought my paranoid brothers and I were the only ones abstaining in this day and age. And no phone on a walk? Even said brothers make fun of me for doing *that*.

"Do you have a business card?" I ask, ignoring the temptation to tally up our similarities. Just because we're having a civil conversation doesn't mean he's not still an asshat.

I'd offer him my own business card, but for some reason, I don't want him to know I own a sex toy company. There's something about him—maybe the understated yet obviously expensive cut of his clothes, or the imperious angle of his jaw—that makes me think of Fortune 500 boardrooms and ten-course dinners under crystal chandeliers. Men like this tend to look down on nontraditional entrepreneurs like me—though why I care what he thinks is a mystery.

Typically, I'm out and proud about what I do.

He reaches into his pocket and pulls out a pen. "I don't have a card." He looks around and spots a couple of coffee cups some litterer left on a nearby bench. Grabbing the cleaner-looking one, he writes something on it and hands it to me.

*Dragomir*, it says in a bold, masculine scrawl, alongside a phone number with a Manhattan area code.

Dragomir? Is that Drago for short? Sounds like a Harry Potter villain.

"I'm Bella." Setting down the cup, I politely extend my hand.

His eyes gleam as he accepts the greeting, his much larger palm engulfing mine—and my breath catches at the electrifying warmth of his skin.

It's a wonder it doesn't activate the balls inside me.

"Dragomir." He pronounces the name with a Russian-sounding accent.

I reluctantly reclaim my hand. "Where are you from, originally?"

"Ruskovia," he says, again with that same pronunciation.

Hmm. I've heard of that place. If I remember right, it's smaller than any of the New York boroughs, and kind of backward, at least insofar as they still have a ruling monarchy. I have no clue where it is on the map, what their customs are, or whether it was the inspiration for Sokovia in *The Avengers*.

What I do know is that if this guy is anything to go by, Ruskovia might be the best-looking nation in the world.

I must be looking kind of blank because he says with a slight eye roll, "Ruskovia is a country in Eastern Europe—in case your knowledge of geography is that of a typical American."

My brothers always say my geography could be better, but who is this Dragomir to criticize me or the American educational system?

"I know where Ruskovia is," I say, only slightly fibbing. "I was born in Russia myself. That's also in Eastern Europe—in case *your* knowledge of geography is subpar."

His eyes tighten at the word *Russia*, and I belatedly recall that a lot of Eastern European countries don't like my motherland thanks to the efforts of the Soviets back in the day to bring communism to them, usually at gunpoint.

"I was little when I moved here," I add, before I can ask myself why I'm trying to get on his good side.

He cocks his head. "That *would* explain your perfect English."

Was that a compliment? It sure feels like it.

"How about you?" I ask, deciding to take it at face value. "How come you don't have an accent?"

"I had great teachers," he says and glances down with a frown.

I follow his gaze and suppress a snort. While we were talking, Boner and his bear got together, and she's just given him a lick—a big, slobbering lick.

Boner seems like the happiest dog in the world.

Dragomir says something to the bear in what must be Ruskovian. The only words I can make out are *Winnie* and something like *Pooh*.

Or was it lower-case "poo?"

Sheepishly, the bear scoots away from Boner.

My good humor evaporates. "Did you just insult my dog again?"

"No. I told Winnifred not to lick him. Don't Russians use the command 'fu' as well?"

*Fu.* Not *poo*. And yes, my parents always yell "fu" at Boner when they see him doing things they don't like. To me, it always seems like they're trying to teach him martial arts, à la *Kung Fu Panda*.

Then something clicks. "Your dog's name is Winnifred? As in, Winnie, for short?"

He nods.

"You realize that's a bear's name, right? As in, Winnie the P—"

"I wasn't the one to name her. What's the name of yours?"

Who doesn't name their own dog? "Bonaparte."

He arches his eyebrows. "You don't think that's a little too ambitious for a dog with a brain the size of a pea?"

I cross my arms over my chest. "Chihuahuas have the biggest brain-to-body ratio of any breed."

"Still." He looks Boner over with skepticism. "Winnie's brain might just be the size of his whole body."

"Or it might be puny if she has a very thick skull," I say, adding under my breath, "like you."

He gives me his imperious stare. "Winnie is of the misha breed. They've rid Ruskovia of wolves and bears and are the smartest dogs in the world."

"This breed is actually called *misha?*" I suppress the urge to ask how exactly Winnie would be able to hunt wolves when she was scared of some random dog's bark.

He sighs. "They are called that. So what?"

"Misha is associated with bears in Russia. You know, like Olympic Misha... the bear?"

"Well, in Ruskovia, misha is only associated with majestic, highly intelligent dogs."

"I bet you Boner is more intelligent than Winnie." As soon as I say it, I picture a lecture from my mother. When I was little, she tried to convince me that men don't like to be challenged and wouldn't want to go near a competitive girl like me.

Not that Dragomir wants to go near me in any case. Given the way this encounter has gone so far, my competitiveness is unlikely to make the top of his cons list—assuming he has a list with any pros on it.

He looks at Boner, then at me. "Are you serious?"

I decide to double down. "As taxes. I know a decent intelligence test for a dog, and I'm confident Boner will ace it before Winnie."

The gleam of battle enters his eyes. "I, too, know a test. And Winnie will wipe the floor with your Napoleon wannabe."

"So, it's official." I rub my hands together. "We have ourselves a competition."

Is that a cocky smile on his lips? "What does the winner get?"

The Grinch would be envious of my answering grin as I think of the perfect thing. "If I win, I want you to get down on your knees and—"

I stop as his eyes widen. He glances at the hem of my skirt, a hungry expression appearing on his face.

Wow.

I know what he's thinking, but it's not what I had in mind—until this moment, that is.

# FOUR

HE STEPS CLOSE ENOUGH for me to detect the cinnamon notes in his sensual cologne. "Get on my knees and do what?"

My own knees feel oddly weak. I clear my throat, but my voice still comes out huskier than is wise. "Get down on your knees, face Boner, and tell him he's the smartest being you've ever met."

Is that disappointment on his face?

Is there some on mine?

He shrugs. "As unpleasant as that outcome would be, I don't need to worry about it because Winnie will win."

"Well then, on the off chance she does, what would you want *me* to do?"

He rubs the short, dark hair of his beard. It's more of an over-grown stubble, really—something he might've grown in a week or two, I realize as I peer at it closer. His hair is just so thick and luscious that it looks like there's more of it than there really is.

Wait, why am I obsessing over his hair? I just asked him an important question, and he's taking his sweet time answering. Does that mean he's going to demand something indecent? I can almost hear his deep voice growling in reply, "Get down on your knees and unzip me, then take out my—"

"*When* I win," he says, interrupting my lewd imaginings, "we'll walk together until Winnie defecates, and then you'll clean it up."

He looks smug.

Damn. Those are big stakes. Literally.

Does he use ten-gallon garbage bags to contain all that poop? Will I need a shovel?

The one part of that scenario I like is that we'd walk together. And depending on Winnie's fiber consumption, we might get a chance to get to know each other. Maybe stop butting heads for a change. Maybe even—

"Are you chickening out?" The words carry a clear-cut challenge.

I glare at him. "No way. It's on. What's the test?"

He pets Winnie's head. "You put a towel on a dog's head and time how long it takes them to get out from under it."

I don't show my glee. I've done that with Boner once. He got free in less than thirty seconds, which was very good according to the article I was reading. "Where do we get towels?"

*Please say "your place."*

The stubble gets another rub. "Our clothes?"

Before I can reply, he grabs the hem of his turtleneck, exposing a flash of toned abs, and pulls it over his head.

Fuck. Me.

As in, *fuck me, please.*

I almost activate my balls once again.

Under the turtleneck, he's wearing my second favorite article of male clothing, albeit one with an unfortunate name: wifebeater. More importantly, he's ripped. His shoulders are perfectly round with muscle, his arms crazy buff, and his pecs are the kind that can dance.

I want to change my ask if I win to something inappropriate.

Also, would it be so bad if I activated the balls on purpose and had another orgasm right here and now?

"You don't have to take off your top," he says, misinterpreting my stunned expression. "Given your Chihuahua's size, my handkerchief will do."

A handkerchief? What is this, the eighteen-hundreds?

Thanking the fashion gods for my decision to wear a bralette under my shirt, I begin to unbutton.

As his eyes widen again, the light brown in them seems to turn into molten gold.

I'm not shy, but by the time I shrug my shirt off, I'm on the verge of blushing at what I'm seeing on his face.

"I don't want Boner to lose because he doesn't recognize the scent on your hankie." There. Voice unruffled. And my getting undressed has nothing to do with trying to, say, seduce anyone. Nope. Only a truly devious woman would do *that*.

He pulls out the aforementioned hankie and dabs his forehead. "Do you have a watch with a stop clock?"

"Why? We don't need it to see who gets free first."

"I want to record the time for posterity. Under thirty seconds is considered a very good result."

Does this mean he's also done this test on his dog?

I guess I should get ready to shovel giant doodoo.

I wave my empty wrist. "Sorry, no watch here."

"How about we use mine?" He tilts his muscular forearm so I can see the piece.

Under the pretext of seeing the watch better, I sidle up to him until I'm within kissing range. This close up, his scent is intoxicating, all warm male skin and rich, cinnamon-y spice. My mouth literally waters as X-rated images fill my brain again.

"Are those hand-drawn penises on your handbag?" he asks, forcing me to snap out of yet another lust-induced fantasy.

Why is everyone an art critic when it comes to this? Yes, I like decorating my possessions this way. Sue me.

"Do you have a problem with my drawings?" I angle my body so he can't see my bag. In the process, I accidentally step on his foot.

Damn it. Stepping on a foot is a bad omen. It means the person doing the stepping is going to have a conflict with the person whose foot was stepped on.

Or in this case, more conflict.

"No problem," he says—and it's unclear if he means the foot or the penis drawings.

I hesitate, then decide to just go for it. "Can you step on my foot?" According to Russian tradition, this annuls the bad juju.

He raises an eyebrow. "Russian superstition?"

I nod, flushing slightly.

"In Ruskovia, if a woman accidentally steps on a man's foot, it is said they will end up together. Of course, I don't believe in such nonsense myself."

Yet he gently steps on my foot, then shows me the watch again and smiles.

*That smile.* Would it be too obvious if I fanned myself? More importantly, would I be a perv if I activated the vibration now? I really want to. Not only does he smell all masculine and yummy, but at this distance, I can feel the heat radiating from him, as though he were a fire-breathing dragon.

Maybe that last bit is why he's named Dragomir?

Realizing I've completely forgotten about the watch, I give it an exaggerated once-over.

Wow. It's by Patek Philippe, the makers of the world's most expensive wristwatches. This particular masterpiece appears custom made, with Cyrillic-looking writing that must be Ruskovian and a strange design made out of diamonds.

No wonder I got the old money vibe from Dragomir. This thing must cost millions.

"So," he murmurs, causing my gaze to jerk up to his face. "Will you trust my watch?"

Some instinct is telling me not to trust anything about him, period. Still, without a rational comeback, I simply nod and rip myself away from the gravitational pull of those mercurial eyes.

"On my mark," he says, turning his attention to the watch.

I hold my top over Boner.

He tosses his turtleneck on Winnie's head. "Go."

# FIVE

AS I DROP my shirt on Boner, I realize this test isn't going to be fair. My Chihuahua is so tiny that my shirt is a much bigger obstacle for him than Dragomir's turtleneck is for Winnie.

I should've agreed to the handkerchief, after all.

Oh, well. If I bring this up now, Dragomir will accuse me of being a sore loser.

Let's just hope Boner is that much more intelligent—or good at this particular test.

Both dogs begin their struggle to get out.

The seconds tick by.

Realizing I'm holding my breath, I loosen my tightly bunched shoulders and gulp in some air.

Suddenly, a paw appears from under my shirt, then another, then Boner's head.

I point excitedly. "He's done!"

Boner wags his tail. "*Ma chérie*, did you have any doubts I would emerge *victorieux*? Not cool."

"Twenty-five seconds," Dragomir growls, his gaze on his turtleneck.

A few more seconds pass, yet Winnie is still not out.

Then a few more.

Suddenly, the turtleneck begins to shrink, though it's unclear how... at least at first.

"Is she eating it?" I ask.

He starts, then grabs the turtleneck and tugs on it.

Yep.

The bear has decided the best way to get out is by eating the obstacle.

A few tugs and a few soothing words in Ruskovian later, the turtleneck is in tatters, but at least none is in the dog's stomach.

For no reason at all, Dragomir gives *me* a glare.

Talk about a sore loser. The guy must be even more competitive than I am.

"At least she found a creative way to get out," I say, figuring an olive branch never hurt anyone.

His chilly gaze warms a few degrees. "You still won this round. What's *your* test?"

I walk over to the bench and pick up the two leftover cups, combining them with the one with his digits on it.

"This is meant to test their memory," I say.

A cocky smirk flashes across his face. "I think I know this test too."

Damn it. I was hoping to have an advantage here. But hey, at least I'm in the lead so far.

"First, we teach them that a treat will be under a cup." I demonstrate this by taking out a gourmet doggie cookie and sticking it under the cup to the left. "Boner, get it."

With a wag of his tail, he pushes the leftmost cup over with his nose and gobbles up the treat.

"Winnie can do that too," Dragomir says, then takes out a treat and sticks it under a cup.

Winnie cocks her head.

He says something in Ruskovian.

She points her giant snout at the cup.

Smiling warmly, he lifts the cup and lets the big girl eat the treat.

Something inside me squeezes. That smile looks good on him, but then again, pretty much everything does.

"So," I say, fighting the urge to activate the balls, "now that they know the protocol, we hide a treat so they can see the right cup, turn them around for thirty seconds, then test their memory by turning them back to see if they go for the right cup on the first try. Or the second. The more guesses, the worse the test performance."

He nods. "Ladies first."

"Dog or human?"

He grins. "Your team goes first."

I get another treat, put it under the middle cup, turn Boner around, and count thirty Mississippis.

"Thirty seconds," Dragomir says, reminding me about his watch.

Oops. I'm glad it's Boner's memory we're testing and not mine.

"Sweetie, get the treat," I say.

Without hesitation, Boner knocks over the middle cup and swallows the treat. "*Savoureux.*"

Yes! Who's a smart boy?

"Your turn," I tell Dragomir, unable to keep the smugness from my voice.

He puts his treat under the middle cup and turns Winnie away.

Another thirty Mississippis later, he turns her back.

She cocks her head again.

He gives the Ruskovian command.

She looks up at him, as if confused.

His next command sounds a little sharper.

She turns back toward the cups, seems to concentrate, then puts the rightmost cup in her mouth and begins to chew.

Wow. She really buckled under the pressure.

"Winnifred, fu!" Dragomir orders, his tone that of someone whose every command is obeyed without question.

Ears drooping, Winnie spits out the chewed-up cup, then points her nose at the middle one.

He lifts the correct cup so she can eat her treat.

I wait a few beats to make sure I don't sound like I'm gloating. "I guess we win."

"It was the smell of coffee on the cup." He sounds defensive. "She loves coffee."

I meet his gaze. "Are you welshing on our bet?"

He blows out a breath. "Let's get this over with."

Since he's about to kneel, I step away, else he might see up my skirt—a problem, especially since I haven't had the moment of privacy required to fix my thong.

Placing what's left of his turtleneck on the ground next to Boner, Dragomir gets on his knees, towering over my dog's tiny body.

"Pick him up so the two of you are eye to eye," I say, trying not to laugh. "Assuming he's okay with that."

This is also a test. Two actually.

First: Will Dragomir be an ass about it and refuse?

Second: Boner is a decent judge of character when it comes to letting people touch him. For instance, he growls at both of my parents when they try. So if Dragomir is evil on *that* level, this won't go smoothly.

To my shock, Dragomir croons something in Ruskovian and gently scratches Boner behind the ear.

Am I jealous of my own dog?

Boner wags his tail.

Operation Pick-Up is clearly a go as far as he's concerned.

Dragomir lifts him gently, looks him in the eyes, and with impressive sincerity says, "Napoleon Bonaparte, I'm sorry. You're the smartest dog—nay, being—I've ever met."

In reply, Boner licks Dragomir's face.

I start laughing, all the tension between us popping like an over-filled balloon.

Dragomir gently puts Boner back on the ground and grins at me.

I wasn't the only one who felt jealous, apparently. Winnie rushes to Dragomir and also licks his face—leaving a giant jellyfish worth of slobber on his chiseled features.

My laughter is now out of control. My eyes tear up, my nose runs, and then, to my horror, the muscles in my vagina suddenly fail at their job—and I feel the Kegel balls slipping out.

Crap. I was able to run and have an orgasm without losing the slippery things, just to be done in by laughter?

Boosted by adrenaline, I catch one of the balls by my knee. The second one, however, drops to the ground and rolls in Winnie's direction.

*No.*

*Please don't—*

Without a second of hesitation, Winnie snatches the ball with her mouth.

"Fu!" I yell.

The command doesn't work.

Winnie swallows the ball.

# SIX

DRAGOMIR LOOKS AT ME QUESTIONINGLY.

Of course. He's just heard me say "Fu."

How do I explain what happened? *Gee, your dog must like the taste of my girl juices because she just swallowed a sex toy I've been hiding in my vag.*

Do I even need to tell him?

Won't Winnie just poop the ball out?

Ugh, but what if there are some complications?

I can't not tell him.

"You're going to be mad," I say, frantically trying to come up with the least embarrassing way to deliver the news.

His thick eyebrows snap together. "What happened?"

I show him the ball I caught. "I was trying to relax using these... err... Chinese meditation balls, and one fell and Winnifred swallowed it."

There. Sounds believable.

Unfortunately, it doesn't take a linguist to know that the next thing Dragomir growls in Ruskovian is a curse. Squatting next to Winnie, he urges her to upchuck the ball—to no avail.

He mutters another curse under his breath and jumps to his feet. Darting a glance at his watch, he starts dragging her away without so much as a goodbye, his long legs eating the ground in furious strides.

Crap. "Is she going to be okay?" I call after them.

"How the fuck should I know?" The question is thrown over his shoulder with such intensity that both dogs flatten their ears. "That's why we're going to the vet."

I grab Boner and run after them. "Let me come with you. I feel terrible about this."

"You've done enough." He lengthens his strides.

I give up chasing him. "I'll call to check on her!" I yell to his back. "And I'll let you know if Boner has any STDs."

I might've yelled the word *STDs* a bit too loudly, because I get a bunch of strange looks from the passersby.

If Dragomir hears me, he doesn't show it.

"Well, that sucked." Going back, I grab the cup with the writing on it and lead Boner away.

WHEN I GET HOME, the first thing I do is locate my phone so I can enter Dragomir's number into my contacts.

Turning the cup over, I stare at it, dumbfounded.

There's no number or name on it.

Well, there is a name, but it's Barbara.

Grr. When I grabbed the stupid thing, I didn't double-check to make sure the writing on it was actually *his* writing.

"I'll be back," I tell Boner and run back to the park.

As I approach the spot where I first met Dragomir, I notice a garbage truck driving down the street, which gives me an unpleasant feeling in the pit of my stomach.

The feeling deepens as I get to the doggy playground.

The two cups I left behind are now missing.

As I feared, someone has cleaned them up.

Heading back home, I picture Dragomir waiting for my call, then assuming I'm a terrible person who doesn't give a crap about the fate of his dog—which couldn't be further from the truth.

By the time I enter my apartment, I'm so upset I need a mood boost, so I ask Alexa to play Boner's favorite song: "Who Let the Dogs Out."

As always when it comes on, Boner begins to howl-sing to the music and bark at the *woof* parts. Though I've seen lots of other Chihuahuas sing to music on YouTube, none seem as talented as mine. He's so good, in fact, I half expect him to compose a doggy opera one day—and call it *La Bonerhème*.

"You're a genius," I tell Boner when the song is over.

He wags his tail. "Tell me something I don't know, *ma chérie*."

With a grin, I go get his snack, and when I come back with it, I catch him licking his butthole.

"So much for genius," I mutter.

Seeing the treat in my hand, he darts over and eagerly gobbles it down. Afterward, as he often does, he rushes over to Remy, the sex toy I designed for him, and begins humping it.

Remy is a plush rat that looks a lot like a female Chihuahua, only with a tiny sleeve-style faux vagina built in. Bringing this product to market is on my to-do list, though for now, human sex needs are a bigger priority for my business.

"Dude, you just had sex in the park," I say gently, to avoid giving him that sex complex. "Minutes ago."

"This is what a healthy libido is like, *ma chérie*. Envy doesn't look good on *vous*."

Grinning, I go to my office to give him privacy.

That turns out to be a mistake. Now that I'm alone, thoughts of Dragomir resurface.

Jumping on my laptop, I look up Ruskovia and Dragomir.

Nope. Too many results, and none of the top ones point in his direction.

It's official: I don't have a way to get in touch. The best I can do is hope that we'll meet again in that section of the park, but Boner and I have always gone there and this was our first time running into Dragomir. He must not come there often—and after what happened, I wouldn't be surprised if he'd outright avoid that spot from now on.

With a sigh, I check my calendar.

Great. I almost forgot an important meeting with my brother later today.

I need to clear my head, pronto. But how?

One option is to masturbate while thinking about Dragomir. I have a whole suitcase of toys—all designed by me and produced by my company, Belka.

No, bad idea. That would only make me think of him more.

It's time for the big guns.

I turn on my TV and put on a movie that never fails to cheer me up: *Frozen*.

Ever since I was a little girl, I've been compared unfavorably to the Snow Queen, a villainous character from a Danish fairy tale that is popular in Russia. And then Disney came along and made that same character into a kickass princess, turning the whole thing on its head. I love it, and not just because I'd lived by the key lesson of *Frozen* even before I saw it—being yourself without apologizing for it.

Or in the words of my favorite song from the soundtrack: I don't care what they're going to say... about my sex toys.

As always, the movie lifts my spirits. Afterward, I get some food and coffee, then work on designing a new toy. I make great progress, getting as far as sending a prototype to my 3D printer.

When it's time, I grab a gift for my bro, put on my sharpest business suit and most kickass boots, and head to his office.

# SEVEN

STEPPING OUT OF THE ELEVATOR, I grin at the plaque that proudly proclaims, "1000 Devils."

This is my brother's way of owning our last name, Chortsky, which means "of the devil." He's made it so that "a thousand chorts" is no longer just a Russian curse, but also a cool video game development company.

I've done something similar myself. "Belka" is what our mother calls me when she's unhappy with me—which is all the time. So—in part because that word also means *squirrel*—I've decided to claim that name for my sex toy company.

Before I advance any deeper into the lobby, I take a sharp turn into the armory and choose a couple of my favorite guns. This office has a tradition of its employees shooting Nerf guns at visitors, and I like to dish out as good as I get.

Holding my weapons Lara Croft style, I dash onto the floor, eyes scanning for foes.

For some reason, the male employees here rarely, if ever, shoot at me. The female employees, on the other hand, are always out for my blood.

I have a big advantage, though. I was a tomboy growing up, and I have two brothers, one of whom created this shooting tradition in the first place. If there were a SEAL Team Six of Nerf assaults, I'd be on it.

The first woman to leap out at me is not even trying. She's got her gun in one hand and a coffee in the other.

Without aiming, she shoots.

I duck, then launch a dart at her collarbone. As I'd hoped, the projectile drops from her shirt and into her cup.

That should teach her.

The next lady is older, so I'm more respectful as I unload my gun into her, aiming for the legs.

The next two I get before they even get the chance to pull the trigger.

Suddenly, a dart smacks me between my shoulder blades.

So it's like that now? Hit me in the back?

Pivoting on the attacker, I shoot without aiming.

Oops.

I happen to know this lady's name is Karen, and she must've been about to yell a war cry or something because the dart is in her mouth now... or maybe her throat.

She's making gagging noises and flapping her arms like a headless chicken.

Dropping the guns, I rush over and prepare to do the Heimlich maneuver. Since my parents own a restaurant, everyone in my family has learned how to do this, just in case.

Karen doesn't seem to need the help, though. After a few more gagging sounds, she spits out the dart, clears her throat, and gives me a sheepish smile.

The incident puts a damper on the shootout, so no one bugs me as I collect my guns and make my way to the meeting room.

Alex, my oldest brother and the owner of 1000 Devils, gives me a warm hug as I walk in.

Pulling back, I grin at him. With his blue eyes, black hair, pale skin, and symmetrical facial features, he's like my gender-bending mirror—especially if you ignore the perpetual scruff on his face.

Sitting down, he shakes his head. "If Karen sues, you'll owe me."

I take a seat in front of him. "She shot me in the back. Mess with the bull, get the horns."

He grins. "Wouldn't you be a cow in that scenario?"

I pull his gift out of my bag. "Why is everything cattle-related so sexist? Why does *cowed* mean *submissive*? Why is it a bullish market instead of a cowish market? Bullshit instead of cowshit. Bull Terrier instead of Cow Terrier. Bull in a china shop instead of cow. Did you know that cows kill more people per year than sharks?"

He shrugs. "Hey, given how many get slaughtered for our pleasure, it's only fair they even out the odds sometimes."

"I've got a gift for you." I slide the box across the table.

Cringing, he peeks inside.

I put on my ventriloquist hat. "Like, hello." I make my voice low and creaky, throwing it so it seems to be coming from the box. "I'm, like, totally your new girlfriend. You seriously better use me or else."

He rakes his hand through his messy dark locks. "Another sex toy?"

My grin is evil—I get to make fun of both of my brothers in one go. "That's a sleeve made out of Belka's patented material. More importantly, it's Vlad's favorite."

Vlad, our middle sibling, recently got embroiled in testing my products—with his employee, no less. Now said employee, Fanny, is his girlfriend. So naturally, Alex and I will never stop teasing him about it.

Alex's chuckle is uncomfortable, to say the least. "Thanks. I think. Just know that the world at large can twist your good intentions to make us look like the Lannisters—or the Borgias."

"Couldn't care less about rumors," I say breezily.

"What if I told you I can get my own toys?" he says. "I can even buy them from your website."

Another evil grin. "I'll make you a deal. Get yourself a girlfriend, and the gifts might stop."

He rolls his eyes. "Double standard much? When will you start dating?"

I feel a pang of regret. If I hadn't lost that cup, maybe—

"Hey, sis, I'm sorry," Alex says, misinterpreting my expression. "I forgot that it's a sensitive topic."

He's talking about my last disastrous relationship. The ass turned out to be married—a lie by omission that left me devastated.

"I'm fine," I say, shrugging off the unpleasant memories. "How about we get down to business?"

"Right." He stashes my gift under the table. "This has something to do with the business venture you've been trying to launch? The sex suit that works with VR?"

"I prefer thinking of it as an immersive sexual experience, but yes. The idea is to democratize pleasure. To bring sex to people who have trouble getting it for whatever reason, or who don't want it with real people. Burn victims, people with disabilities, those with an extremely contagious sexually transmitted disease or crippling social anxiety—the list goes on and on. The same product can also help people in long-distance relationships, as well as astronauts and—"

"Dude, you don't need to sell me on it," he says. "I think the venture sounds really cool, and might make you the richest one in the family."

"You know I don't care about money—though having said that, money is kind of why I'm here."

In an eyeblink, he's got a checkbook in his hands. "How much do you need?"

I smile. "You don't have the kind of money I need. VR hardware is big leagues."

He whistles. "You plan to design a VR headset? I thought it was just the suit."

I shake my head. "Off-the-shelf VR companies are prudish when it comes to their app stores, and their headsets are not that friendly to people with smaller heads—like women. Besides, the best kind of suit would have the VR gear built in anyway. I found a promising company that makes adjustable headsets that's not doing so well. I want to buy it and integrate them into my venture."

He puts the checkbook away. "Wow. Buying a VR company? Didn't Facebook pay two billion for Oculus?"

"This won't be at the same level, but yeah. This is why I've been looking for investors."

"And?"

I sigh. "I've been at it for months, but no luck. I don't know if it's Belka's core business, or my gender, or my pitching abilities, but no one is biting."

He steeples his fingers. "How can I help?"

I dig a flash drive out of my bag and slide it over to him. "It's all there. To sum up, I want to start a joint venture with you that might sound more appealing to potential investors than one that's solely mine. The sex stuff doesn't need to be overly prominent in our presentation."

He pockets the flash drive. "A bait-and-switch strategy?"

"Kind of. What we'll tell them is the truth: I'll build the hardware, and you'll head the team that writes the software. The project will still be labeled as adult entertainment."

He scratches his scruffy chin. "So what will the software do, officially?"

"Your call. I'm thinking casino, or life simulation à la Second Life or the Sims."

He grins. "And we just don't mention that the casino will have a strip club section, or that the most popular activity in this VR second life will be hooking up?"

"Yep. At least not if they don't explicitly ask about that."

In other words, it will be a lie. I have no illusions on this front. Not telling someone something important—like their marital status —*is* a lie.

Alex drums his fingers on the table. "That's a lot to think about."

I stand up. "Please review everything on that drive and let me know your decision. If you're not interested, I'll go to Vlad. It just sounds more like your cup of tea."

He also rises to his feet. "It does. I have experience making VR games already. They're PG, but still. Also, I have to say, this sounds very promising, both as a coding project and financially."

I give him a line from my current spiel for investors. "Porn is a hundred-billion-dollar industry. It's been shrinking because of piracy and free content, but that wouldn't be an issue for this venture because we're going to be selling special suits. Plus, VR apps and games are more challenging to pirate."

He walks to the meeting room door and opens it for me. "If the investors worry about piracy, I can tell them the steps we take for 1000 Devils games."

I give him a peck on the cheek as I leave. "I knew you'd be useful. Let me know as soon as you decide either way."

# EIGHT

"A STANDARD SHIPMENT OF ANAL BEADS?" I double-check with the rep on the phone.

"Yep. Also, we want to double our order of butt plugs," she says.

"I'll get my people on it."

"Thanks," she says and hangs up.

I sigh. I made a point to hire a person to deal with adult toy super-stores, yet I still occasionally have to field the calls myself, especially from the bigger clients.

Before I forget, I write an email to the person who should've gotten that call and copy the whole Belka logistics team for good measure. I use our item number codes in place of words like "anal beads" and "butt plugs," as this greatly cuts down on unnecessary giggles, especially among newer employees.

Since I'm already in business mode, I check on our Amazon sales, as well as our other major retailers.

Business is great, though the line of smart toys isn't yet selling as well as I want. Our bestsellers are still the Cucumbernator, the cucumber-shaped dildo I designed on a lark, and the Squidinator, a mollusk-shaped clit massager made from our patented material that actually makes it feel like a squid.

For the rest of the day and the two days that follow, I wait for Alex to make his decision and keep myself from thinking about Dragomir by designing new toys and working on the VR suit.

I also walk Boner in the same part of the park, but no luck. I have yet to come across the bear and her gorgeous owner again. I'll just have to hope Winnie pooped the ball out without any problems.

As I arrive home from the park the next morning, I receive a text from my best friend, Xenia. It's in Russian but written with English letters:

*Come have brunch with me. I found a place where they allow dogs.*

I haven't seen Xenia in a while, so I eagerly reply in the affirmative, pick out a gift for her, and rush out with Boner in tow.

---

THE DOG-FRIENDLY RESTAURANT turns out to also be kid-friendly—which isn't very friendly to Chihuahuas.

"*Ma chérie*, keep those giant *monstres* away," Boner's frightened eyes seem to say as I shoo a five-year-old boy and girl away from our table while cursing Xenia under my breath for being late.

Once the kid threat is averted, I resume doodling on the paper tablecloth. By the time Xenia finally arrives, our table is completely covered in small penises. Besides looking cute, they provide the added bonus of motivating most moms to keep their offspring away from my dog.

"Hi, honey," Xenia says in Russian and pecks me on both cheeks.

"Hey, babe," I reply in English.

A mix of English and Russian is how we always talk; this way, she can improve her English and I my Russian.

"Happy belated birthday." I thrust a box into her hands. "And don't worry, I won't ask how old you've turned. Only your current weight."

Somewhere in her mid-sixties, Xenia is my oldest friend—both in terms of her age and in how long we've known each other. In fact, we go all the way back to when she was a chef in my parents' restaurant. We stayed in touch after they fired her for "being vulgar" and "corrupting" me. Of course, the truth is just the opposite. Even as a teen, I was a much worse influence on her than she was on me.

"Thank you." She shakes the box skeptically and lowers her voice to a whisper. "Is it yet another dildo?"

"Open it to find out."

She does, after first looking around furtively. "It *is* a dildo."

"A custom-made one I printed just for you. I designed it a week before your birthday but waited until after to give it to you."

She nods approvingly. Even more superstitious than I am, Xenia knows that giving someone a birthday gift or congrats before the actual date is a huge no-no. In the Russian tradition, you can only do it on the day of or after.

"See that evil eye thingy at the tip?" I ask.

She pulls the dildo halfway out so she can examine its mushroom-like head.

Since Xenia is always worried about jinxes and evil eye curses, she wears a nazar amulet in the shape of an eye to ward off bad spirits and malevolent intentions. Now she also has a toy decorated with the same design.

As she examines it, her face flushes and her eyebrows pull together. "Do you think someone could cast an evil eye down there?" She glances down her body. "Only Boy Toy ever sees it. Well, and the doctor."

I shrug. "Better safe than sorry."

Xenia is a widow who was single for many years. But recently, she met a forty-five-year-old guy whom she's dubbed her "boy toy." According to her, he looks like Liam Neeson, Xenia's celebrity crush. Having met Boy Toy, I personally think that with his beer belly and bushy gray beard, he looks a lot more like Santa Claus, but I'll never mention this to Xenia since I highly approve of her dating.

"Mommy, what is that?" A little girl points at Xenia's gift, her eyes widening.

I deepen my voice and throw it so it appears to come out of the box my friend is holding. "I'm the nice lady's very special new best friend."

The kid goggles at the dildo until her mom drags her away, muttering something about crazy people.

Xenia laughs and stashes her gift away. "When are you going to find yourself a man instead of playing with these toys?"

Before I can reply, a waiter arrives and we both order mimosas and the Eggs Benedict.

When he leaves, I tell Xenia about Dragomir.

"Wow," she says. "You should, as they say in English, 'hatefuck the guy.'"

She looks up to find the waiter with a tray and blushes. He's clearly caught the last bit of her wisdom.

Once our food and drink are on the table and we have privacy again, I say, "I can't do anything with him. I lost his number."

She waves dismissively. "If it's meant to be, it's meant to be. Remember how you put that top on backward last month? I told you that meant you'd meet someone new."

Xenia knows some extra-obscure superstitions, many of which are clothing-related for some reason. Recently, I accidentally wore a T-shirt inside out, and she claimed I'd get beaten unless a friend punched me first. So she whacked me. Talk about a self-fulfilling prophecy.

"I'll keep walking Boner in that section of the park. Maybe he'll show up." I toss my little friend a treat, and he gratefully wags his tail.

Smacking herself on the forehead, Xenia rummages in her bag

and takes out a plastic bag. "It's for the little devil," she says with a grin.

Xenia's new business is gourmet dog food, so I know Boner will appreciate the contents of the bag.

Since we have company, I throw Boner's voice under the table for Xenia's pleasure. "*Ma chérie*, let me sample the goods before you hide them."

I toss him one of Xenia's creations.

"Ah, Xenia. You're a *génie culinaire*."

"Merci," Xenia says to Boner, then looks up at me. "Do you think this Dragomir could be the one?"

She doesn't mean one true love. At least I don't think so. She's one of the few people who knows about a problem I've developed since my last bad relationship: I can't seem to achieve an orgasm with a guy. So, when Xenia says "the one," she usually means "the one who can make you come without the aid of sex toys."

I shrug. "He could've been. I *did* already have an orgasm next to him."

Her eyes widen, and I tell her about the Kegel balls.

"You're not wearing those things here and now, right?" she asks with a slight wrinkling of her nose.

"No, but you probably should be. Boy Toy would appreciate the results."

"I've found them to be too tickly," she says. "Now, how about you tell me some more about this guy."

"Like what?"

"Well, with a name like Dragomir, is he Russian?"

"Nope. Ruskovian."

Xenia's eyes widen. "Ruskovian, huh? They have a reputation."

"For being rude?"

She looks around. "For being well-endowed."

I nearly choke on my mimosa.

"Don't move." She narrows her eyes on my face, then reaches in and grabs something from my cheek.

"An eyelash." She shows it to me. "Make a wish."

I blow the eyelash away as the superstition dictates. As I do, I wish to run into Dragomir again, so I can check if Xenia's statement holds true for him—purely for science, of course.

Hold up. I should've used up the wish on the new venture instead. Oh, well. Hopefully, I'll shed another eyelash someday soon.

For the rest of the brunch, we give each other updates on our work lives. As I'm about to leave, Xenia stops me from using lip balm by saying, "If your lips are dry enough, they'll itch, which means you'll be kissing someone soon."

Hmm. I wonder if purposely drying your lips annuls that. Just in case, though, I don't apply the lip balm.

"Keep me posted on Dragomir," Xenia says as we hug goodbye.

I sigh, stepping back. "I doubt there will be updates, but sure."

---

BEFORE GETTING HOME, I take Boner into the park on the off chance the eyelash magic actually happens.

Nope.

When we get home, I check for messages from Alex.

Aha. He wants to talk, so I call him up.

"Hi, sis."

"Hey. Did you decide?"

"It's a go. We should talk details."

A cab ride and a shootout later, I'm back in his office, where we discuss the logistics of the venture and the fundraising for the rest of the day. Since his company is the respectable one, and he's the one with the penis, we decide that he'll be the first to meet with the investors, then pull me in as needed.

We also divvy up some tasks. I'm to continue working on the suit, and he's going to put together two demos of the software: sexy and vanilla.

---

ALEX'S first meeting with the investors takes place the next week, and our strategy works. We get our first backers. Unfortunately, they only commit a modest sum.

Still, when I get home that evening, I feel like I should celebrate, so I pour myself a glass of wine and put on a movie that never fails to turn me on: Michael Fassbender playing Steve Jobs.

It's not that I like either of these men. I just love a guy in a turtleneck.

Pulling out my favorite vibrator from my suitcase of toys, I get myself off, though instead of the movie, it's a mental image of Dragomir in a turtleneck that I actually orgasm to.

Thank fuck for toys. As a teen, I nearly got carpal tunnel from masturbating to the album cover of *With the Beatles*—the one where the whole band wears turtlenecks. I also used to do it to the very old *Cosmos* show, in which the host, Carl Sagan, always wore a turtleneck.

The latter might also be how I developed a passion for science, which later led to an obsession with engineering, and then, naturally, the designing of high-tech sex toys.

To quote *The Lion King*, it's the circle of life.

# NINE

"WHICH SOUNDS BETTER: a dildo attachment for a drill, a clit stimulator attachment for an electric toothbrush, or a saddle that goes on top of a washing machine?" I ask my focus group over Zoom. "Or none of the above?"

The toothbrush attachment turns out to be the winner, so I design a few that can work with the most popular electric toothbrush brands.

As I'm eating lunch after my design-fest, I get a videocall from my brother Vlad.

"Your new venture," he says as soon as I see his face, one nearly identical to Alex's, only way less scruffy and with glasses. "I want in on it."

I grin into the camera. "And hello to you too."

"Sorry. Hi, sis. I was just a little annoyed to be kept out of the loop."

"Oh, sorry. I just didn't want to put you in an uncomfortable position. We both know that if I'd asked for money, you would've wanted to say yes regardless of what it was for."

His stern expression softens. "I didn't think of that."

My grin widens. "After all the testing you've done for Belka, I figured it was time I imposed on Alex instead."

He rolls his eyes. "Well, Alex told me about your project, and I want to invest. Let's talk details."

So we do, and in the process, he agrees to help me and Alex with cybersecurity—his specialty. He also comes up with a cool name for the venture—Project Morpheus—and last but not least, he commits a cool mil, bringing me a little closer to my goal.

FOR THE NEXT WEEK, we attempt to hunt down more investors without much to show for it. Nor do I bump into Dragomir in the park—a double bummer.

I do get hiccups on Thursday, though, which means someone is remembering me. I hope it's him.

The week after that is the same: no new funding and no Dragomir. Though on Wednesday, my ears do feel hot, which means someone is thinking of me—again, hopefully him.

Thursday night, Xenia comes over to my house for a Liam Neeson marathon. Turns out, he and many other hot male actors wear turtlenecks in *Love Actually*—info that goes into my ever-growing turtleneck-related spank bank.

The last movie we watch is *Star Wars*, and something about her favorite actor with long hair and Jedi powers must really do it for Xenia, because she fans herself every single time his character is on the screen.

When the credits roll, I attempt to get her to try VR games—one of my favorite leisure activities.

"You'd like *Beat Saber*," I say, holding out the VR headset. "It's a game where you hold two lightsabers, just like Liam did in *Star Wars*, and swing them at notes to the beat of a song you like."

She reluctantly agrees, so I put the headset on her head and thrust the game controllers into her hands.

Boner steps aside—he clearly remembers how I'd nearly trampled him during my last VR session.

As soon as the game starts, Xenia screams bloody murder in Russian and flaps her arms so wildly that one of the remotes flies out of her hand and smashes into my boob.

Massaging the injury, I help my friend escape the evil headset.

"I guess VR isn't for you," I say as she glares at me.

Too bad. Until now, Xenia was on my short list of beta testers for the Project Morpheus VR sex suit.

Is that amusement in Boner's eyes?

"*Ma chérie*, I'm suddenly craving some chicken, ideally with the head cut off."

<hr>

ON FRIDAY of the following week, Alex tells me he's found a "whale"—a venture capital firm with deep pockets that might commit all the money we need in one fell swoop. They liked what he had to say, and now they want to meet with me to get all the technical details about the hardware.

I'm so excited I give myself three orgasms using my best toys, then stay up all night ironing out my presentation. By morning, I'm a little bleary-eyed but bushy-tailed and prepped to the max.

I put on my most conservative business suit, slip my feet into my favorite stilettos, slather on some war-paint-quality makeup, and take a cab downtown.

All the dough to fund my dream, here I come.

# TEN

EVERYTHING about this company screams swanky, from the gleaming glass-and-steel building to the immaculate marble floors and the giant, testosterone-filled meeting room I step into.

Alex winks at me, then addresses the room of eight other men with a serious expression. "Gentlemen, this is Bella Chortsky, my partner and the hardware expert we've been waiting for."

The guy who seems to be the leader had been eyeing me like a piece of candy. Now his look shifts to undisguised disappointment. "She's going to explain the hardware?" he asks, with way too much emphasis on *she*. His accent sounds Eastern European, and his face looks vaguely familiar for some reason, though I'm sure I've never met him before.

I reward the asshole with my Snow Queen glare.

Alex's hands bunch at his sides. "Indeed. She *is* the expert. An MIT graduate, mind you, with—"

"I didn't mean anything." The guy takes a step back from my brother, who despite his general laidback-ness, can be pretty frightening when angry. "Why don't we go over the technical specs of the suit as we wait for Mr. Lamian?"

Alex's expression goes back to congenial. "Sure. I cede the floor to Bella, my sister and the co-owner of Project Morpheus."

The guy extends his clammy hand to me, and I shake it with a fake smile.

"I'm Marco Fluroff," he says. "Please, call me Marco."

"And you can call me Bella," I say, extracting my hand and resisting the urge to wipe his sweat off my palm.

Wait. Marco? *That's* who he reminds me of. The villain from *Taken*, the movie I re-watched with Xenia during our Liam Neeson marathon. Even the name of the human trafficker from that film was the same: Marco.

Taking over the big screen, I open my presentation and launch into my carefully rehearsed spiel about the hardware. As I go through all the technical details, I can't help picturing myself delivering a paraphrased version of the ultimatum from *Taken* to this Marco:

"I have a very particular set of skills—skills making sex toys. I have acquired them over a very long career helping horny people. These skills make me a nightmare for people like you. If you commit the money now, that will be the end of it—I will not look for you, I will not pursue you... but if you don't, I will look for you, I will find you... and shove a giant dildo up your ass."

"Any questions?" I say with a bright smile when I've gone through all the salient points.

Shrugging, Marco glances at a dude in glasses. "Eugenius?"

The guy stands up. "Just to clarify, the haptic feedback you've designed into the suit will allow users to experience a touch as light as that of a feather?"

Feather, if you're into tickle play, or a lover's kiss, or a lick as well—but I don't say any of that. "That's right. As you can imagine, this will allow for extremely life-like sensations when wearing the suit."

"Interesting stuff," Eugenius says approvingly. "Is it customizable for sensitive users?"

"Definitely," I say, and he sits back down. I level a challenging stare at Marco. "How about you? Does everything I've explained make sense?"

Based on how his eyes had glazed over when I got technical, I highly doubt it.

He clears his throat. "I'm more of a financial guy, but it all seems clear to me. And I just got a text from Mr. Lamian. He's about to step into the—"

The doors open, and a tall, powerfully built man dressed in a dark suit strides in.

His piercing hazel eyes land on me—and immediately narrow into catlike slits.

Fucking fuck.

My heartbeat leaps into overdrive, and my entire body flushes.

This is Mr. Lamian?

I know him by a different name.

His first name.

*Dragomir*.

# ELEVEN

"YOU?" Dragomir growls, crossing the room toward me in long strides.

"You?" I exclaim almost at the same time.

Everyone looks at us with confused expressions.

I can't blame them. Dragomir looks like he's on the verge of spitting fire.

"I lost the cup with your number," I blurt before he has the chance to accuse me of something awful.

"A convenient excuse." He sweeps his gaze around the room and commands, "Leave us."

His company isn't run as a democracy, that's for sure. Marco and the rest leap to their feet and scatter like hunted quail.

Only Alex stays. He puts himself between me and Dragomir, his face twisting into something scary. "Who are you, and what the fuck do you want with my sister?"

"It's okay," I say in Russian. "I've met him before. He's got a reason to be upset. A misunderstanding. I'll clear it up."

If my ovaries don't explode, that is. Dragomir looks so damn good in that suit—maybe even better than in a turtleneck. No, that's blasphemy. But maybe a suit over a turtleneck? Yeah, that would be—

Wait, what am I thinking here? I have to focus. My dream project is at stake.

"I don't give a fuck what his reason is," Alex growls back at me in Russian. "If he so much as—"

"I just want to talk," Dragomir says in accented Russian. "I'd never harm her. What kind of a savage do you take me for?"

He's trilingual? I guess I shouldn't be surprised. A lot of folks in Eastern Europe learn Russian as a second language. English too, for that matter.

"Just talk?" Alex's fierce expression eases slightly. I think he's recalled that I'm not a preteen, and that this is a corporate environment, not a playground riddled with bullies. Not that I needed my brothers to handle bullies for me, much to my mother's chagrin.

"Probably a short chat at that," Dragomir says, switching to English. "Can we please have some privacy?"

Alex reluctantly heads toward the door. Before exiting, he turns and gives Dragomir another glare, just in case. "If you hurt my sister in any way, it won't end well for you."

He sounds so convincing that I have to remind myself he's a software engineer and not a mafia enforcer from *Eastern Promises*.

"Is Winnie okay?" I ask as soon as Alex closes the door. "Did the ball come out?"

Dragomir nods. "Everything got resolved that same day." He studies me intently, his mercurial eyes seeming to fluctuate between green and gold-flecked brown. "Have you tested Bonaparte for STDs?"

Crap. I'm tempted to lie, but that wouldn't be cool. I opt for the truth. "I'm sorry. I didn't have your contact info, so I didn't think it was necessary."

Now that I think about it, I should've done it anyway—and I would have, if things hadn't gotten so busy with all the fundraising.

Dragomir's lips twist. "Like I said, a convenient excuse."

I step toward him, trying not to think about how sexy those lips seem even now. "Listen to me, please. I know how this looks. If I were you, I'd probably be skeptical too, but I swear this was a mix-up. I took a cup that had writing on it, but it turned out to say 'Barbara.' I ran back immediately, but they'd just cleaned the park and picked up the trash. I went back every day after that, trying to find you and Winnie so I could make it right."

And so I could see him again, but I don't tell him that. It's way too soon. Also, getting closer to him was a strategic miscalculation—at least as far as keeping my thinking clear. With that subtle hint of cinnamon tickling my nostrils, all I want is to jump into his arms and—

Wait, did his hard expression just soften?

Score!

Maybe he's remembered seeing the name *Barbara* on one of the cups.

I press my advantage. "Now that we've reconnected, I will of course test Boner for anything you want and as soon as possible."

He tilts his head. "Is that so?"

"Of course."

"How about now?"

I blink at him. "As in, right now?"

"You said as soon as possible."

"Fine, let's do it now," I say, belatedly realizing how big of a bust this investment meeting is—which really sucks, as I was hoping to be done with the fundraising part of the venture so I can get to the fun bits, like actually building the suit.

He steps over to the door and opens it for me.

As we walk out, everyone looks at us questioningly, especially Alex.

"The meeting is adjourned," Dragomir says in that uncompromising, boss-of-the-world manner of his.

"We have a private matter we need to attend to," I whisper to Alex in Russian. "Don't worry. He's not a threat to me."

At least not to my physical wellbeing. To my hormones, Dragomir is kryptonite, but that isn't something my brother needs to be worried about.

"Text me whenever your matter is concluded," Alex says, and it's clear I'll have to tell him the whole story, sans the balls in my vagina.

"Deal," I say, and we all ride the elevator down in the most uncomfortable silence I've ever participated in.

Marco is the first to escape the elevator at the lobby, with Alex and the rest of the investment crew filing out after him. Dragomir and I stay to ride down to the parking lot.

"This is us." Dragomir gestures at a strange vehicle already waiting by the curb.

I gape at the thing.

If a bus, an RV, and a limo blew up, and the parts randomly got reassembled into a single hybrid car, it might look like this.

"Is this even allowed on the streets of New York?" I ask. "It looks like a mobile home... for an eco-tech billionaire."

His mouth quirks. "It's legal. Parking can be a challenge, but thanks to Fyodor, I don't have to worry about that."

A door opens and a ladder descends. A man wearing a tuxedo jacket with tailcoats greets us in a deep, British-accented voice. "Please, come inside."

The RV has a butler?

"Thanks, Fyodor," Dragomir says and gestures for me to go first.

Impossibly, the vehicle looks bigger inside than outside—like the TARDIS from *Doctor Who*. I spot a treadmill large enough for a bear to run on—which is exactly what Dragomir's bear is currently doing —a sleek computer desk that's designed to alternate between sitting and standing positions, a plush leather couch bigger than the one in my living room, and a full-sized bar that appears to be stocked with every drink imaginable.

"There are studio apartments in Manhattan smaller than this," I say in awe as Dragomir joins me.

"Winnie gets lonely when I leave her at home," he explains with a shrug. "This way, I can take her with me on most trips."

And I thought my Boner was spoiled rotten. Turns out he doesn't know the meaning of the word.

"May I get you something to drink?" Fyodor asks.

"I'm good," I say.

"We're in a hurry," Dragomir says. "We're headed to Ms. Chortsky's home." He looks at me. "What's the address?"

I grimace. "Please don't call me Ms. Chortsky. That sounds too much like my mother."

"Shall I call you 'mistress' then?" Fyodor asks without a hint of humor.

"Unless you want me to spank you, please call me Bella," I say, and to halt any further discussion on this topic, I rattle out my address.

With a bow, Fyodor scurries away to take a seat at the wheel, and as soon as the vehicle gets moving, a partition between us and Fyodor goes up, blocking him from view.

The treadmill stops, and Winnie notices Dragomir.

A whoosh of fur, and she's on her hind legs, licking his face.

Lucky bitch. I'd like to do that myself.

As Dragomir deals with his bear's affections, I scan the room.

Besides all the comforts I've already noted, on the shelf near the treadmill is the latest and greatest VR headset—better even than the one I own, and I splurged.

This really sucks. Besides rolling in dough, Dragomir is into VR. He would've been the perfect investor for our venture if I hadn't screwed everything up. Now who knows how long it'll take to find another investor like him.

It'll probably be as difficult as finding another man I'd be this attracted to. Even with that slobber on his face, if he wanted to kiss me right now, I'd let him.

Finally freeing himself, he pulls out a pack of wet wipes, cleans his face, and mops up the residual moisture with his handkerchief.

Odd. The initials on the hanky are D.C. Shouldn't that be D.L. for Dragomir Lamian?

"Take a seat." He gestures at the couch.

I obey and he joins me—though, sadly, he ends up on the cushion farthest from me.

"Are you into VR?" I ask, waving in the direction of his headset.

He nods. "That's what had caught my attention about your venture. Headgear is almost mainstream now, and there are some special-purpose treadmills on the market too." He glances at the one Winnie was running on. "A whole-body VR suit is the logical next step."

"It is," I say enthusiastically. "And I plan to be the one to bring it to people."

His sexy lips curve in a smile. "You don't lack confidence, that's for sure."

Is that a compliment? I'll take it.

"What's your favorite VR game?" he asks before I can steer the conversation toward the possibility of him investing in Project Morpheus after all.

"*Beat Saber*," I reply with a grin. "You?"

His eyes seem to shift from light brown to green. "Same. What's your favorite song?"

"'Radioactive' by Imagine Dragons. You?"

"Again, same. Have you beaten it on Expert?"

"Of course." I examine my bright red nails. "I've also done it on Expert Plus."

He lifts his eyebrows. "You have?"

Trust issues much? Why would I lie about something like this? Since I want to stay on his good side, I say, "Definitely. My name is on the worldwide scoreboard in the top ten: BabushkaPwned. Check me out. Or better yet, I can demonstrate my skills."

He shakes his head. "In a moving car, that'd be dangerous."

Yeah, sure. The ride is buttery smooth. I bet he just wants to master Expert Plus when I'm not around. That's what I'd do if I learned that someone I know in real life is better than I am at my favorite song. Or any song. Or any game.

I guess I am a bit competitive.

Since I doubt that challenging him would incentivize him to invest, I change the topic. "How old were you when you moved to the US?"

"Twenty-four," he says. "How about you?"

Wow. Those teachers who taught him English must've been really good—or he has a knack for languages.

"I was five," I say. "I barely remember Russia."

He grimaces. "I remember Ruskovia just fine."

So, he doesn't like something back home. I guess that's normal for folks who left one place for somewhere else.

"How about your family?" I ask. "Did they all move with you?"

At the word *family*, his face turns cold and expressionless.

Interesting.

Before I can ask anything else, the car stops.

"Go get Boner," he says, his tone once again coolly imperious.

As I make the trip, I ponder his reaction, and an unsettling idea jumps into my head.

Could he be married and hiding it, like my asshole ex?

It's feasible. A guy that hot and rich would usually be with someone. The lack of a wedding band on his finger doesn't mean squat based on my painful experience, nor does the lack of family pictures around his RV.

Once in my apartment, I immediately go to my computer and type "Dragomir Lamian" into Google.

Nothing.

There's zero information on him.

That's bizarre. My brother Vlad is almost pathologically paranoid about his digital profile, and even *he* has more data out there, like a mention of him on his company's website.

Dragomir's venture capital fund doesn't say who's at the helm.

"Isn't that sketch?" I ask Boner as I ready him for the trip.

"*Oui.* He might have *une femme.*"

Crap. The possibility of a wife means I need to stop being attracted to him. Actually, even if it turns out he's not married, there are just too many other issues. It's obvious he's filthy rich and moves in high-society circles—he's got a butler, for fuck's sake—so he's probably going to look down his regal nose at my sex toy company. Also, if his firm does end up investing in our venture, as unlikely as that seems right now, business and romance don't mix.

I square my shoulders.

Decision made.

No matter how much I want to lick his face, bear style, I will not give in to that urge.

# TWELVE

BONER IN MY ARMS, I step back into the RV-limo.

Damn it.

Seeing Dragomir's chiseled features once more, I realize that merely telling myself not to be attracted to him is going to be tricky. If I'm really serious about this, I'll have to avoid him after the STD test.

Yeah. That'd be the smart thing to do.

When Boner and Winnie spot each other, their tails begin to wag, with his repeatedly smacking my chin and hers nearly tripping up Dragomir.

Unable to help myself, I throw my interpretation of Boner's voice a few inches down to where his head is.

"Ah, Winnie, *ma petite*. I haven't been able to get our last *rendezvous* out of my mind."

That's definitely a smile that dances in the corners of Dragomir's eyes.

In the worst example of ventriloquism in history, Dragomir makes Winnie's voice sound much too deep, as if it's coming from his crotch—and gives it a Russian accent for some reason.

"How dare you, Napoleon Carlovich? Take a woman's virtue and then no call, Facebook message, or even a tweet?"

I grin. "Carlovich?" Is he trying to give the dog a Russian-style patronymic? Unless... do they have those in Ruskovia too? Mine is Borisovna, as in *daughter of Boris*. Does that mean—

"Carlo Bonaparte was the famous general's father," Dragomir says, answering my unspoken question. "Speaking of history, if anyone should be called anything petite, it's your dog. One of the real Napoleon's many nicknames was *Le Petit Caporal*."

"I hate to tell you this," I say in a conspiratorial whisper, "but my dog isn't actually a reincarnation of the real Napoleon. I know it seems uncanny, given how intelligent he is and all."

The smile spreads to Dragomir's lips. "You have to admit, put a bicorne on his head and they'd be like twins."

I laugh. "Do you mind if I let him hang out with her?"

Dragomir's smile disappears. "Let's make sure he's clean first, then we'll see."

Both Boner and Winnie look miserable at not being allowed to interact, so we distract them with treats and belly rubs as much as we can.

Thankfully, the ride to Dragomir's vet is brief.

"Stay with Fyodor," Dragomir says to Winnie as soon as we park. "We'll be back soon."

Winnie makes a strange whining sound and looks at the door.

"Fyodor!" Dragomir shouts, then rattles out something in Ruskovian.

The butler appears and puts a leash on Winnie. After we all step out of the vehicle, Dragomir turns to me and says, "Hold your breath."

Huh?

Before I can clarify what he means, he looks at Winnie and issues a command in Ruskovian. It sounds like "Kraken"—though that word could be on my mind because of Liam Neeson/Zeus in *Clash of the Titans*.

*THPPTPHTPHPHHPH.*

The fart coming out of Winnie's rear end goes on for what feels like an hour.

Boner tenses in my arms, his eyes widening.

I'm so shocked I forget Dragomir's order to hold my breath and accidentally inhale.

Fuuuuuck. My eyes water, and I begin to gag.

To say that the bear's flatulence smells like rotten eggs would be a disservice to rotten eggs. If I'd eaten fermented cabbage infused with pure hydrogen sulfide all my life and held in a fart for a decade, the final product still wouldn't have approached this level of foulness.

Is this how this dog breed rid Ruskovia of wolves and bears?

Shaking his head, Dragomir holds a handkerchief to his nose, surgical mask style. "Sorry about this. As you can imagine, if she'd done this in the car, I would've had to get a new one."

A new car or a new dog?

He strides to the building, and Boner and I hurry after him.

When we're inside, I finally take a breath.

Impossibly, the stench has managed to follow us in, but at least it's now diluted and merely reminds me of the worst fart I'd previously had the displeasure of smelling.

Boner looks longingly at Winnie through the glass door. Knowing dogs, the Kraken incident might well have made his infatuation with Winnie that much stronger.

"*Ma petite,* cruel *destin* has ripped us *à part.*"

Hurrying to get farther away from the fart epicenter, we leap into the elevator.

By the time we enter the doctor's empty waiting room, the smell is finally gone.

"Why haven't you simply tested Winnie for STDs?" I ask Dragomir after I suck in a grateful breath of stale medical office air.

"I have. But what if Boner has something with a long incubation period?"

I barely resist rolling my eyes. "Like what?"

He shrugs his broad shoulders. "I don't want to take any chances. In fact, after Boner is done, I'll get Winnie tested one more time."

Before I can ask what the point of that is, the doctor—a bewhiskered man who looks vaguely like Einstein—comes out. Looking at Dragomir though a pair of glasses with the thickest lenses I've ever seen, he says something in Ruskovian.

"In English, please," Dragomir says.

"Large apologies," the doctor says with a thick accent. "Allow me decoding of my tongue. I asked, 'What's with bitch?'"

I narrow my eyes. "What did you just call me?"

"*Winnie* is with Fyodor," Dragomir says. "We're here for the other matter."

Ah. The good doctor was enquiring about his female dog patient. I guess he gets to live another day.

The doc reaches for Boner with a mad scientist's leer. "So, this was stud?"

"*Ma chérie*, I hereby decree everyone refer to me as 'stud' going forward."

I arch an eyebrow at Dragomir.

"I told Dr. Delomalov what happened in the park."

With a nod, I hand Boner to the doctor.

Boner looks at me pleadingly.

"*Ma chérie*, don't let them take my manhood, *s'il vous plaît*."

"It's just a test," I tell him.

"Dr. Delomalov has assured me the test will be completely painless," Dragomir chimes in.

The vet croons something in Ruskovian that seems to somewhat reassure Boner, but as soon as they disappear, I find myself anxiously pacing.

When I bump my shin on the table with the magazines, I stop

and whip out my phone so I can check if the vet was lying about the pain level of the test.

Weird.

My phone has no bars.

"It's like a Faraday Cage in this place," Dragomir says. "I usually bring a paper book if I know something will take a while."

Huffing with disappointment, I resume pacing.

"Don't worry," Dragomir says when I make the tenth back-and-forth. "Dr. Delomalov is the world's most renowned dog expert."

I force myself to sit.

He pulls out his phone. "How about we exchange our contact information? Properly this time."

My heart performs an excited backflip. I'm sure this is for our dogs and potential future business collaboration, but my hand still shakes slightly as I create a new contact and have him fill in his digits. He then does the same.

I pocket my phone, and my mind turns to said business collaboration. I consider the best way to approach it, then decide to just go for it. "If Boner is clean, would you consider investing in Morpheus?"

His thick eyebrows pull together. "I would consider it either way. Business is business."

I blow out a relieved breath. "I was worried that with everything that's happened—never mind."

He rubs the stubble on his chin. "There *is* a caveat."

Crap. Does he know about my sex toy company already?

"I'll need to recuse myself from the decision process," he says.

Whew.

"You'll be working with Marco instead of me."

Spoke too soon.

Dealing with Marco will be a terrible experience, I know. Based on our interactions thus far, I might have an easier time convincing Marco to kidnap the daughter of a man with a certain set of skills.

Naturally, telling any of this to Dragomir would be opening a can of worms, so I just ask, "Why are you recusing yourself?"

He studies me with those changeable hazel eyes. "I like to avoid making business decisions based on emotion."

I draw back, irrationally wounded. "You hate me for Winnie's mishap that much?"

He quirks a dark eyebrow. "Who said anything about hate?"

# THIRTEEN



I BLINK AT HIM.

If not hate, what emotion would mess up his business decisions?

Before I can ask, the doctor comes out holding a rather wild-eyed Boner.

"*Ma chérie,* it was *terrible, horrible.* Let's never come here again."

"Stud was champ." Dr. Delomalov hands me my dog.

"Will you let us both know the results?" Dragomir asks. "Assuming Bella doesn't mind?"

"I don't mind," I say, stroking Boner on the head to calm him down.

"Great," Dragomir says. "Now I'd like to take care of the payment."

Right. Payment. I totally forgot about that.

"I can pay my dog's bills myself," I say. My company might not be a fancy venture capital fund with offices in a swanky building—or any formal offices, really, as my employees and I work from home—but it's nicely profitable and growing fast, with this year's revenues already in the low seven figures.

Dragomir touches my wrist, sending shivery energy down my spine. "Bella, please, allow me. I dragged you here, after all."

I just stand there, rendered mute. It's possible I'd say yes to anything after that touch. Even some unspeakable things. *Especially* unspeakable things.

"I vote Dragomir pay," the doctor says.

I frown. Is he being sexist, or is my money no good here for some reason?

With a knowing smile, Dragomir takes out an honest-to-goodness golden coin from his pocket. I catch a glimpse of an older man's face on one side before Dr. Delomalov stashes the coin in his wallet.

What the hell was that about? Have I fallen asleep and ended up in a *John Wick* movie? The criminal underworld uses gold coins in that franchise.

Come to think of it, Dragomir has other things in common with John Wick. For example—spoiler alert—it's easy to picture him going on a revenge spree if someone were to kill *his* dog. In fact, he might be capable of murdering someone for simply looking at Winnie the wrong way.

"*Ma chérie,* by that *critères,* you're also John Wick."

"Almost forgot." The doctor hands me a form. "Need stud and your information."

"Right." I set Boner down and begin to fill out the form.

"I'm going to go downstairs to make sure Winnie is ready for her test," Dragomir says. "See you soon."

I rush to complete the form so we can ride down together, but he's gone by the time I finish.

"Thank you, doctor," I say, handing him the form. "Now if you'll excuse me..."

The doctor takes the form from me and then, to my shock, presses a light kiss to the back of my hand. "I had pleasure with Napoleon and you meeting. Such beauty and grace not often found in this country."

Yeah okay, whatever, dude. I barely prevent myself from rolling my eyes as I reclaim my hand. Older Ruskovians must be even worse than their generation's Russian counterparts, though my parents' friends are also prone to cringy OTT compliments.

Boner and I take the elevator down and run into Dragomir and Winnie in the lobby. Spotting her, Boner begins a drone impersonation with his tail.

"*Ma petite. Ma petite.* Has it been a year since I've last seen your *beau visage?*"

Winnie's tail smashes into Dragomir's thigh with such force I half expect the man to stumble. "*Da*, Napoleon Carlovich. I lost count of time, yearning for our encounter."

"Fyodor will take you home," Dragomir tells me. "No need for the two of you to wait as Winnie is tested."

So much for the doggies hanging out. Or the two of us.

Hiding my disappointment, I nod and exit the building.

Impossibly, it still smells like the bear's fart outside.

"*Le bouquet, ma chérie. Le bouquet exquis.*"

Holding Boner tight, I dash to the RV limo. Fyodor opens the door just as I reach it, then waits politely while I catch my breath inside.

"Ready to go, madam?" he asks.

I inhale blissfully fart-free air. "Take us home."

# FOURTEEN

AS SOON AS we're back at my place, I make a sandwich and take Boner for a walk.

After the trauma of the vet and separation from Winnie, he clearly needs his spirits lifted.

The walk is a success. Not only does Boner speedily do his business, but John accuses me of being a commie only once as I give him the sandwich—a new record.

When I get home, I find a message from Alex:

*Good news. They've rescheduled today's meeting. What was that between you and the owner?*

I videocall Alex and explain how I met Dragomir—skipping the Kegel balls part so as not to traumatize him.

"Sounds like you want to date this guy," Alex says when I'm done.

I grimace. "That would be a bad idea."

"You said he's recused himself. What's the problem?"

"So many things, but the main one is that I think he's hiding something."

Alex drums his fingers on his desk. "You should talk to our

snoopy sibling."

Now *that's* not a bad idea. Besides hiding his own private info from the world, Vlad is scary good at uncovering things other people want hidden. Stalin would've found him very useful.

"Wouldn't it be an invasion of Dragomir's privacy?" I ask, arguing with myself as much as with Alex. "I wouldn't like it if a guy *I* was dating did a deep dive on me."

He waves his hand dismissively. "As you said, you're not dating. More importantly, we're about to go into business together, which makes this fairly reasonable. I bet he's looking into us as well."

Great. That means he'll learn about my company and pull out. And not in a birth control way.

I sigh. "I guess I'll talk to Vlad."

"Make sure it's face to face." Alex smirks. "You know how he is."

Vlad prefers face to face in general because, as he puts it, "Why invite the NSA to the conversation?"

"Thanks," I tell Alex. "I'll set something up with him. Now—"

"Wait. Are you going to Mom's birthday?"

"How could I not? What am I, Vlad?"

He grins. "He's been much better about attending family shindigs. Fanny is a good influence."

"Agreed. See you at the party."

Alex hangs up and I text Vlad.

His reply is instant:

*Want to come visit me at Binary Birch tomorrow at 9?*

I grin as I think of a gift for him.

*Sure. See you then.*

---

EXITING the elevator on the floor of Vlad's company, I glance at the serious-looking plaque.

Sometimes I wonder if my brothers set out to make their companies look like complete opposites. Binary Birch has a modern art feel, in that cold, utilitarian way. There are no nerf guns in sight, nor game rooms, nor sleeping nooks.

In fact, it looks a bit like the offices of Dragomir's venture capital firm.

I check my phone. No calls or texts from Dragomir.

Bummer. A part of me was hoping he'd get in touch first thing.

There are also no calls or voicemails from the vet about Boner's STD tests—something that would give me an excuse to call Dragomir myself. Not that I need an excuse. If this were another guy, I'd probably call or text, but given all that's happened between us, I want to see if he wants to get in touch.

So for now, I wait. Or rather, since it's almost nine, I rush over to Vlad's office.

When his employees spot me, they scurry out of the way—though I'm not sure whose reputation scares them so much: mine or his.

"Hi, sis," Vlad says when I step into his office.

We hug, and I kiss his cheek before thrusting a plastic box into his hands. "A gift."

Without looking inside, Vlad drops it into a drawer and pointedly slides it shut.

"Hey, don't you want to know what's in there?"

My brother's expression is unchanged. "I can guess."

"Fine, I'll just tell you," I say, pouting in disappointment. "That is a penis pump. Replacement for the one you and Fanny broke."

He shakes his head. "She had nothing to do with it. I told you, it was a sizing issue."

"Sure. Sure." I keep my face exaggeratedly serious. "That's why this unit I got for you is double the size of the one you shattered. Hopefully, it will be able to accommodate someone with your prodigious... gift."

He sighs in exasperation. "I suspect you came here because you want something from me. Do you really think teasing is the way to go?"

I give him my best puppy-eyed look. "Come on, don't be like that. You know you can't say no to your little Belochka."

His lips twitch. "There is that. Still, say one more word about the size of my junk, and I'll find the willpower for that no."

"The favor has to do with the business you're now a part of," I say. "So you'll be helping yourself. And Alex."

"What's the favor?"

I explain the mystery of Dragomir's lack of online presence.

Vlad unlocks his computer. "Spell that name for me."

I do, then add, "Besides Dragomir, it might be worth checking what you can find on Marco Fluroff—he's the guy I'll be dealing with to get the funding."

Vlad nods. "I'll see what I can do."

"I assume I'm going to see you at Mom's birthday?"

He manages to make his nod reluctant, like I'm somehow forcing him to go.

I get up. "Later."

He leads me to the elevator, and this time, people dodge us even more thoroughly.

He must scare them more than I do.

---

AFTER I GET HOME and feed Boner, I check my phone again.

No calls.

Damn it.

I'm dying to learn what emotion Dragomir had alluded to before recusing himself. Also, it would be nice just to hear from him.

Oh, well. Instead of waiting by the phone, I'll keep myself busy— Belka day-to-day operations won't take care of themselves.

I dive into emails first.

A client wants an order of our vibrating rubber duckies with attached dildos, so I email the right team. Another client wants our camera-enabled butt plugs and dildos, so I take care of that too.

Someone in marketing suggests we extend our reach into food-flavored lube and further expand our catalogue of BDSM paraphernalia.

Hmm. Would edible lube require FDA approval? Also, what flavors would people want? Bacon? No, that's more up Boner's alley. Strawberries?

In any case, flavored lube sounds like a headache for another day, so I look at what's popular in the BDSM sections of the online retailers to see what we don't already make and what the market might be missing.

Interesting.

We could start a line of spanking paddles that leave funny red marks on people's butts—something like faces of celebs. Oh, yeah. That should sell nicely. We already produce butt plugs that are shaped like politicians that people love and hate, and those do extremely well.

Since I'm on a kink kick, I spend the rest of the workday finalizing my design for another toy—a shoe with a dildo that's meant to allow someone to penetrate their partner with their foot.

If I play my cards right, I'll be the person who redefines the expression "playing footsies."

***

NOTHING FROM DRAGOMIR the following morning.

I prep what I'll say to Marco tomorrow, then spend the rest of the day working on the suit for Project Morpheus.

Turns out, nipple stimulation is a real headscratcher. Vibration and air pressure that might work elsewhere on the body aren't enough in this case. I need to make sure the nipples can have the sensation of being caressed, touched roughly, pinched, licked, sucked —the list goes on and on.

Also, since we're branching into BDSM gear anyway, should the suit support something like nipple clamp play from the start?

As the day progresses, I have to whip out my nipples repeatedly and press them against different materials to see how well they approximate human touch.

No call from Dragomir when it's time to go to sleep.

Too bad.

Picturing him in a turtleneck, I use a range of toys to get myself nice and sleepy, then punch out for the day.

---

"LET'S TALK FINANCIALS," Marco says to Alex and rattles out a list of questions.

To say I'm annoyed with today's meeting would be an understatement. Not only was Dragomir completely missing from the room—a bummer in and of itself—but Marco hasn't asked me a single question today. I know he doesn't realize this venture is basically mine, but still, the whole thing chafes.

Since I want the funding, I stay cordial until the end.

"Thanks, Alex." Marco shakes my brother's hand. "We have a lot to think about. I'll reach out to you soon."

"We'll wait for your call," Alex says, emphasizing the *we*.

Marco looks at me as though he forgot I was there. "Of course. I meant the plural you."

Sure he did. Now that I think about it, only Alex got the new meeting request the other day.

Whatever.

Alex and I exit the conference room, leaving Marco and his team behind. When we come out of the elevator, I finally see him.

*Dragomir.*

He's waiting in the lobby—hopefully for me.

"I've got to run," Alex says with a wink, correctly assessing the situation.

I give him a hug and mumble something along the lines of, "See you later."

My heart is racing. Seeing Dragomir again is exciting. Maybe too exciting for my own good.

"Hi," I say when I reach him, unsure if I should give him a hug or a kiss as I would any other acquaintance.

He resolves my dilemma by extending his hand. I shake it—and receive a jolt of electricity that streaks right into my core.

He doesn't look unaffected either. His eyes are intent on my face, his lids lowering to a half-hooded position as he lets go of my hand with obvious reluctance.

"There's a very nice coffee shop next door," he says, his voice holding a hint of sexy roughness. "Or if you're hungry—"

"Coffee sounds great," I blurt.

Inside, I'm jumping up and down.

Is this a date?

I haven't been this psyched about a guy's attention since high school.

"Did you drive down here in your RV?" I ask as we exit the building.

"Sure did." He gestures at the street.

Yep. There it is, driving by slowly.

"Fyodor couldn't find parking, so he's making circles," Dragomir explains as we step into the coffee shop.

The place is empty, so it takes us mere moments to order what we want. As we step to the waiting area, Dragomir's phone beeps with a text, and he excuses himself to check it.

Recalling that I put my own phone on silent for the meeting, I unmute it and check my messages.

I have a voicemail from the vet notifying me that Boner is clean, and a text from Xenia.

*In the city. Want to grab sushi?*

Before I can shoot her a reply, I see Dragomir looming over me, looking apologetic.

"What's up?" I ask, my pulse leaping at his nearness.

"Something's come up, and I only have a half hour before I have to run to a business meeting."

"That's fine," I lie. "I'll be having sushi with a friend around the same time as your meeting."

As in, I will be *now*.

Is that disappointment in his eyes?

Hey, he was the one who turned out to be busy first.

Excusing himself one more time, Dragomir gets back on his phone, so I text Xenia that I can meet her at our favorite place in forty minutes.

She instantly replies with an excited affirmative.

The barista tells us our drinks are ready. Before I can grab mine, Dragomir picks up both cups and carries them over to a comfy table.

A gentleman. I like it.

Taking a seat across from him, I blow on my coffee in the most seductive way I can muster, but he seems oblivious to my subtle flirting.

Hmm. What's with such a serious expression? Not very date-like.

He puts down his cup. "We need to talk."

Damn. Now I know why guys dread those four words so much.

It's definitely a foreboding phrase.

"Sure." I set my own cup down. "What did you want to talk about?"

He captures my gaze, his hazel eyes mesmerizing in their intensity.

Whatever he's going to say is bad.

Really bad.

Has he already learned about my sex toy company? Or is it something even worse?

He takes in a breath. "We're pregnant."

# FIFTEEN

I STARE AT HIM BLANKLY. "Did you say 'pregnant?'"

He nods.

What. The. Fuck?

It seems to be the day of phrases guys dread. In fact, "we're pregnant" might often follow "we need to talk."

In any case, I thought I was supposed to be the one to say that to him—if we'd had sex and he'd knocked me up, that is.

"Remember how Winnie took the tests after Boner?" he says. "One of them was a pregnancy test."

Oh.

I want to smack myself on the forehead. Boner humped Winnie. That's why we've been testing them both for STDs. Humping can lead to babies—or puppies in this case.

I should've thought of this. The fact that I haven't might be an insult to Boner's virility, and I'm glad he isn't here to witness this exchange. He would be traumatized.

Oh, and when he learns about this, he'll want his name officially changed to Stud. After all, he's impregnated a freaking bear.

Dragomir puts his hand over mine. "I know it's a lot to take in, but say something."

The heat coming off his big, warm palm feels amazing, and more than a little distracting. With effort, I refocus on the topic at hand. "Are you sure it's his?"

He pulls his hand away. "How would you like it if you told a man he was the father of your baby and he questioned you?"

Good point. "I'm sorry. I'm just having trouble digesting this, that's all."

He nods, as gracious as a king granting pardon. "Winnie has only had sex once in her entire life, so Boner must be the father."

"Okay. Okay." So we're dealing with a near-virginal bear. I pinch the bridge of my nose. "Is she... err... keeping it?"

Crap. Why do I keep sounding like the guy who's just learned that his casual hookup is preggers?

Dragomir's eyes are now narrowed into slits. "If you're talking about an abortion, it's out of the question at this stage. And it's going to be a litter, so I'd say 'them,' not 'it.'"

I gulp down some scorching coffee. "I didn't mean it to sound like I *want* an abortion. I really don't. Boner having puppies sounds amazing. I just wasn't sure what Winnie's stance was on the whole pro-life versus pro-choice debate."

He regards me with a serious expression. "Winnie is a dog, remember? We can only guess at her stance, so the best I can do is assume she'd want to keep her pups."

"Sounds reasonable." I rub my temples. "This is pretty confusing."

He picks up his coffee. "I get it. When I first heard the news, I was a little taken aback. Bear in mind, even if Winnie magically learned to speak and said she wanted the abortion, it wouldn't be safe to do at this stage of her pregnancy. The doctor thinks the best option for her health is to proceed to the end. After the birth, once she's ready to part with them, we'll find a nice home for the pups. Or I'll keep them."

I picture what said pups might look like, and my mood rapidly improves. "I'll help you find the pups the best homes possible. Also, let me know if you need anything else at all. I can be there if there's an ultrasound. We can split the bills and—"

"Thank you." A genuine smile appears on his face, one so sexy that my panties all but dissolve under my skirt. "There was actually something along those lines I wanted to talk to you about."

"Oh?"

"A DNA test, for Bonaparte," he says. "I want to know if there's any genetic disease risk for the pups."

I cringe internally. "Another trip to the vet? He's still traumatized."

"It's just a saliva swab. I'll get Dr. Delomalov to teach me how to do it, and I'll come over to your place and perform it myself. Bonaparte won't even know he's being tested."

"Well, in that case, sure," I say.

Wait. He's just invited himself to my place. And I said yes!

He takes a sip of his coffee and regards me over the rim of the cup. "So, obviously, you haven't neutered your dog."

I grimace. "Yeah, sorry. I couldn't bring myself to do it. I have nothing against people who go through with it, but it's just a sensitive issue for me, personally. Boner is a sexual being, and he'd miss that if it were taken away."

Should I tell him I take this issue so seriously that I built Boner a hump toy?

Nah. Too close to the sex toy company topic that I want to avoid. Nor should I tell him why it's so personal. If it were socially acceptable, my parents would've spayed me when I was a teen. Not that I slept around or anything; any expression of sexuality on my part was taboo in their eyes.

"How about you?" I ask, pushing away the unpleasant memories. "Winnie was obviously not spayed."

It's his turn to grimace. "I couldn't bring myself to do it either. Also, there's the fact of Winnie's breed. She's of the purest misha bloodline—a part of Ruskovian history."

"Great. Boner has tainted a historical bloodline."

"That's not what I meant," he says. "Besides, he didn't really. Winnie can have purebred puppies later on. These ones can still find a loving home without being called 'mishas.'"

"Or we can start a mixed-breed trend. We'll call them Chishas. Or Mishuahuas."

He chuckles. "I kind of like the sound of Chishas."

I grin. "So, another pretty obvious question... You had no idea Winnie was in heat?"

He shrugs. "Maybe I'm not as comfortable as you when it comes to thinking of my dog as a sexual being. I've never looked into how any of that heat stuff works—figured I'd do so when there was a chance to continue the misha bloodline. Besides, now that I have read up on it, a lot of the signs are less noticeable due to how furry Winnie is." He looks slightly uncomfortable. "She was spotting around the time of the incident, but I mistakenly thought that meant she was less fertile as a result."

I keep a poker face. "Don't beat yourself up. That *is* how it works... for human females."

To his credit, he doesn't look grossed out at the mention of a human period. Instead, he leans back, draping his arm over a nearby chair in that king-of-the-world manner of his. "How about we talk about something other than our dogs?"

"Deal," I say. "But after this one last dog-related request."

He inclines his head. "Go ahead."

I watch his face as I say, "When you come over for the saliva swab, can you bring Winnie so she and Boner can spend a little time together?"

He frowns.

I knew it. He doesn't like the idea of them interacting. What a snob.

"Look," I say, getting angry on my canine friend's behalf. "Boner is clean of STDs. And it's not like he can make her any more preggers."

"Fine," he says, to my surprise. "It's a playdate."

A playdate?

Why does that sound so sexual?

I'm jealous of our dogs all of a sudden.

He smirks. "Now you owe me a topic of conversation that isn't dog related."

I match his smirk. "How about wolves? Is that too close to dogs?"

"No wolves, or bears, or rats," he says with a straight face.

"Are lions off the table too?"

"You can talk about lions if you wish," he says magnanimously.

"Finally. *Something* we can talk about."

His lips twitch. "That something being *lions*."

"Well, I've always found it weird how much fictional lions roar when they want to catch something. I think the real-world ones only roar to scare other lions away from their territory. During a hunt, I bet they're silent stalkers. I would be."

He nods seriously. "I think you're right. In Hollywood's defense, a roaring lion is more impressive."

"A lion with wings would be even more impressive, but they stick to reality on that front. Now that I think about it, this roaring thing happens with other fictional animals, too. Wasn't there a roaring barracuda in *Finding Nemo*?"

He shrugs.

"I think so. Forgetting the whole silent stalking bit, I doubt it's even possible to roar underwater."

"A submarine motor might roar," he says.

"Hmm." I consider it. "You might well be right."

He grins at me, and I'm about to say something else when I notice a man outside the shop, pointing a camera at us.

To my shock, I recognize him.

Dragomir was yelling at this very dude just as Boner was humping Winnie.

I didn't give it much thought before. I was too busy worrying about vaginas—as in, keeping the Kegel balls in mine and my dog's penis out of Winnie's. Now I realize this guy's behavior was pretty odd.

Dragomir must notice something on my face because he turns. Instantly, his powerful back tenses, his shoulders bunching tight.

Huh. I guess he and the guy are *really* not friendly.

Dragomir launches to his feet, but before he can step outside, the guy bolts, swiftly disappearing around the corner.

Dragomir looks as if he's debating giving chase.

Curiouser and curiouser. Who is that guy? What's with the camera?

A cold sensation settles at the bottom of my stomach. What if he's a private detective that Dragomir's wife hired because she suspects her husband of cheating?

That happened to my ex after I broke up with him—mostly thanks to Vlad's anonymous email to the wife suggesting that very thing.

Well, if there's a wife, I won't be the one the asshole will be cheating with.

Never again.

Apparently deciding against chasing down his enemy, Dragomir sits back down.

I'm all business now. I either get to the bottom of this marriage issue, or I can't see him ever again—no matter how hot he is. Or how cute the puppies might turn out.

"Who was that?" I ask, doing my best Snow Queen impersonation.

He shrugs. "I don't really know that creep. I've only seen him once before. I've told him to stay away, though."

Okay, that was too roundabout of a question. I need to just ask him point blank.

He looks at me intently.

I take in a big breath. "Dragomir, are you married?"

# SIXTEEN

HE APPEARS TAKEN ABACK by the question. "No."

Just as he says the word, he sneezes.

I feel a huge sense of relief.

In Russia, we believe that when someone sneezes after making a statement, it means they're telling the truth. But we also believe in "trust but verify," so I'm not going to be completely happy until Vlad tells me what he's dug up. Also, I need a better answer about that creepy guy who ran away—something tells me Dragomir has no intention of really explaining that.

Since we're on this topic anyway, I might as well probe deeper. "Do you have a girlfriend? Boyfriend? Lover? Mistress?"

His eyes gleam with amusement. "No. I'm single. I have to say, this is a lot more personal than the chat about lions."

Crap. He's right.

I got very personal. Too personal, considering he's a potential investor.

"How about you?" he asks before I can apologize. "Married?"

I blow out a relieved breath. "Nope."

"How about a boyfriend?" he asks, matching my earlier tone. "Girlfriend? Lover? Master?"

I shake my head. "I've been man-free for almost three years."

His gaze sweeps over me in a way that makes me wish I had those Kegel balls to squeeze. "That's very hard to believe," he murmurs when his eyes return to my distinctly warm face.

Being a twenty-six-year-old woman, I resist the urge to flip my hair like a teenage girl in front of her first crush. "Okay then, we're both single," I say briskly instead. "I wonder what else we have in common."

He regards me speculatively. "Well, an Eastern European heritage is one thing, for sure. Some Ruskovian traditions are nearly identical to Russian. Architecture, too."

"There you go," I say, downing the rest of my coffee. "And let's not forget that we're both crazy about our dogs." *And want to fuck each other's brains out*—is what I want to add but opt to keep it inside my head, and not just in case that part is one-sided.

"We're both into VR." He reaches for a refill of his coffee at the same time I reach for mine—and our fingers brush, sending another mini-lightning sparking through my nerve endings.

My breath turns unsteady. "We're both competitive," I say, refocusing on the conversation with effort. "Though, of course, I'm much more so than you are."

His nostrils widen. "No way. I'm much more competitive than you. By a wide margin."

"Oh, please. I'm so competitive there's a picture of me in the dictionary under that word."

He leans in, eyes narrowed. "I invented that word."

"Yet you still don't know its meaning. Which is *me*."

He tsk-tsks. "Just admit defeat already. Competitive is my official middle name."

"Hmm... Dragomir Competitive Lamian—your parents must be worse than mine."

His smile falters.

Crap. Have I just stepped into something? Are his parents even alive?

His phone beeps.

"I'm sorry," he says. "This is that business thing I mentioned earlier. It's in a few minutes."

I check my phone.

Yep. I also have to run to meet Xenia.

I guess time flies when you discuss dog pregnancy with the guy you're lusting after.

He stands up. "I hope we can get to know each other a little better when I come to take Bonaparte's DNA."

Speechless with glee, I nod a little too vigorously.

He picks up our empty cups. "Maybe the list of our similarities will grow?"

As he disposes of the cups, I wrestle with the urge to jump him right here and now, by the garbage can. It's not a good idea. He's still an investor. Still doesn't know about my sex toy company. More importantly, Vlad hasn't finished his snooping—meaning Dragomir could still be married, just outright lying about it. For all I know, he might be devious enough to have faked that sneeze at just the right moment.

Being Ruskovian, he could know all about truth and sneezing.

"Do you want a ride to the sushi restaurant?" he asks.

Given my thoughts a moment ago, a rational woman would say no, but I giddily bob my head. My agreeableness is rewarded when he puts his hand on the small of my back as he leads me out of the place.

I'd be game for him to lead me this way for a few hundred miles, but to my disappointment, the RV limo is already waiting.

Fyodor opens the door, and we climb inside.

Winnie stands on her hind legs and licks Dragomir's face again. Or rather, slobbers all over it.

As he's cleaning himself up, she transfers her attentions to me, perching her paws on my shoulders and going in for the kill with a huge, wet tongue.

I half laugh, half squeal—a mistake, as it gets slobber into my mouth.

The experience is equal parts gross and adorable. Plus, I think by some transitive property, I've just made out with Dragomir. Or at least exchanged some bodily fluids with him.

When I'm freed, he readies a hand wipe. "May I?"

He wants to touch my face?

"Yes, please." I hold my breath.

He rubs my face gently, and dog slobber or not, this is the most sensual experience of my life—and it goes on and on. He's really thorough, making sure he gets every last bit of drool off my skin. I give a brief thought to all the makeup coming off along with it, but it's worth it. Hopefully, he won't think I'm a troll without it. Or a goblin. Or an ogre. No, wait, Fiona from *Shrek* is an ogre, right? Yeah, ogres are cute.

Eventually, he stops the rubbing and ever so gently dries my face with his handkerchief. Judging by the heat glimmering in his hazel eyes, my troll-goblin concerns were overblown.

He steps back, and I exhale the breath I've been holding.

Does this RV have a shower? I could use a cold one right about now. Also, I know exactly what I'll be thinking about when I'm holding my vibrator tonight: his hands on my face.

"I'm sorry," he murmurs.

Sorry? For that? That's like Michelangelo apologizing for making his David statue. Unless he's sorry for ruining my makeup?

"She's never done that to anyone before," he continues.

Ah. He's apologizing on Winnie's behalf.

"It's fine," I say. "I hope it means she likes me."

He looks down at Winnie. She's now wagging her tail incessantly and gives us a doggy—or beary—grin. "To be honest, I always thought that greeting was a sign of love, not mere like."

"Well, what did you expect?" I say with a straight face. "Bitches love me."

Before he can reply, the car stops and the partition to Fyodor slides down.

"The sushi restaurant," the butler announces pompously.

"I'll walk Bella out," Dragomir tells Fyodor and opens the door for me.

As I step out of the vehicle, I feel light, like I'm floating. Dragomir walks me all the way to the sidewalk.

I stop, looking up at him. "That's the restaurant." I wave at the place. "My friend should be here any minute."

He steps close enough for me to detect the cinnamon notes of his cologne. His eyes gleam with warm amber undertones. "I had a great time hanging out with you."

"Me too," I say, my heart fluttering—just like it would after a date back in high school.

Maybe I've time-traveled without my knowledge.

"I'll get in touch about the playdate," he says softly.

I dampen my lips. "Looking forward to it."

His gaze falls to my mouth, and a peculiar tension seems to invade his body. Slowly, as if pulled by something, he bends his head.

My pulse skyrockets, and I rise on my tiptoes, swaying toward him. Our lips are just a breath apart now. If I just—

"Bella?" some evil person calls out in Xenia's voice. "Is that you?"

Dragomir pulls back.

I spin around and level an icy glare at the source of the noise.

Yep. The cockblocker is indeed someone I've always considered a friend.

"Dragomir," I say, my voice husky. "Meet Xenia."

Dragomir extends his hand. Xenia snatches it and shakes it like a wet towel, her eyes the size of tea saucers throughout.

"Nice to meet you," she finally manages in a thick accent.

"A pleasure," he says and looks down at the hand Xenia isn't letting go of.

"We should go," I tell her pointedly.

Xenia looks at me, then at her hand, then finally remembers that you eventually let people go when you do this sort of thing.

Dragomir's lips curve in a wry smile. "I'll be in touch," he tells me and disappears in his RV.

Xenia watches the RV's departure with a strange expression. Finally, she turns toward me. "It's against the rules of nature for a man to be that gorgeous."

For once, I agree with her—a woman who likes to say that a man needs to be only slightly better-looking than a gorilla.

# SEVENTEEN

"TELL ME EVERYTHING," Xenia demands as we take our seats and get two orders of Sushi Deluxe.

I fill her in on the whole dog pregnancy situation.

"His dog has the right idea," she says.

I pick up my glass of water and take a sip. "She does?"

"You should have that man's baby."

I nearly spew out the water in my mouth. "Baby?"

She nods sagely. "The two of you are the most beautiful people I've seen in real life. If you make a baby, it will be a movie star."

I use a napkin to wipe up the water droplets that went into my nose. "I'd expect this sort of thing from Mother, not you."

She gives me an insulted look. "You're comparing me to Natasha?"

"You're right. I'm sorry. That was too harsh."

The waiter brings out two boat-shaped plates, and we swap sushi pieces the way we always do: I give her all the boring things, like crab stick and cooked shrimp, and she gives me all the items she's too scared to eat, like uni, which is sea urchin gonads. Like the rest of my family, I'm an adventurous eater, while Xenia is noticeably less so—something that no doubt limits her as a chef.

For the rest of the meal, we chat about recent TV shows we've seen, and she gives me the latest scoop on her and Boy Toy, ending with her suspicion that he might pop the question soon.

"Will you say yes?" I ask, putting the last spoonful of my fried green tea ice cream into my mouth.

She shrugs. "I'm not a young chicken. This might be my last chance at this sort of thing."

I don't tell her that she once again sounds like my mother. Instead, I just say that she should only marry Boy Toy if she wants to, not to settle.

"I do want to. He's just so young..."

I roll my eyes. "He's forty-five and doesn't take good care of himself. Your life expectancy is probably the same—assuming that's what you're worried about when you talk about his age."

She sighs. "Who knows if he will even propose."

I strongly suspect that he will. Xenia is an amazing woman, and Santa—I mean, Boy Toy—doesn't strike me as a stupid man. Jolly, sure, but not stupid.

---

WHEN I GET HOME, Boner is extra excited to see me.

"Do you smell Winnie on me?" I ask him.

"*Oui.*"

"Can you tell from her scent that she's knocked up?"

"*Oui.* Call me Stud from now on."

I reapply the makeup I'd lost in my encounter with the bear, grab a sandwich for John, and take Boner out for a walk. When I return home, I get a message from Vlad requesting a meeting, so I make another trip to the Binary Birch offices.

"I COULDN'T FIND anything on Dragomir," Vlad says once we get the pleasantries out of the way.

"Nothing? That's suspicious in and of itself."

Vlad shrugs. "Who are we to say that? If he were to look into either of us, he wouldn't find much either."

I wince. "I actually *am* hiding something. My sex toy company."

My brother pushes his glasses higher up his nose. "Right, and they'd have to dig really, really deep to learn about that—we set you up with a New Mexico LLC and all that."

"Is there a way you could also 'dig deep?'"

He rubs his chin. "I'd need more info about him."

"Like what?"

"Names of people close to him, like siblings or parents. Maybe the name of his best friend. Anyone who might not be as paranoid as he is."

"I don't know any of that," I say. "But if I find out, I'll let you know."

"Just be subtle. If he's anything like me, he won't like it if he thinks you're snooping."

"Good point. Sucks that this has turned out to be so difficult."

Vlad nods sympathetically. "On the bright side, I found out something about that Marco guy."

I sit up straighter. "Is it juicy?"

"He's got two women," Vlad says. "Two families, in fact—one in Ruskovia and one here in the states."

Wow. Even my ex hadn't gone that far.

"Do you think they know about each other?" I ask. "Maybe it's a polyamorous relationship or something like that."

"Doubt it."

I shake my head in disgust. "What an asshole."

Vlad gives me a speculative look. "What do you plan to do with this?"

I blink at him uncomprehendingly. "What do you mean? I can't exactly confront him without letting Dragomir know that I'm snooping—and I don't think he'd like that."

"Well." Vlad glances at his office door and lowers his voice. "Someone unscrupulous might use this information to help themselves secure the funding they need."

"What? No! I'm not going to blackmail the guy. That's not my style."

Vlad gives me an approving half-smile. "I didn't think you would. Just throwing it out there. Alex tells me it's been hard securing more investors."

I clench my jaw. "Still not doing that."

Thankfully, Vlad drops the topic and asks me about the suit design—which I gladly tell him all about. I especially enjoy the way he squirms when I discuss nipple stimulation at length.

As I'm leaving, I can't help myself. "Once I have a working suit," I say ingeniously, "do you think you and Fanny could test it out for me, for old times' sake?"

# EIGHTEEN

THE NEXT MORNING, I get a text from Dragomir:

*Can we stop by at 11?*

Replying in the affirmative, I feel a jolt of excited energy far exceeding what's expected from my morning espresso.

In an hour, he's going to be here.

In my apartment.

Not far from my bedroom.

I even out my breath and attempt to keep my cool by making myself presentable. Once my hair is brushed and makeup is applied, I realize I have to clean up my place.

Right now, it looks like the lair of a sex-toy-obsessed hoarder serial killer.

Glancing at the clock every few minutes, I start the epic quest of hiding all the work-in-progress dildos, butt plugs, vibrators, anal beads, and other Belka paraphernalia. By five to eleven, seeing that I'm not making fast enough progress, I resort to desperate measures. Instead of neatly putting away the remaining items in drawers, I simply kick them under the couch and bed wherever they happen to be.

Everest—a particularly large dildo—ends up jammed under the TV stand.

It's eleven.

Whew. I think I made it.

I do a quick walkthrough and find a nipple clamp prototype being used as a clip for a bag of caramel popcorn.

Crap. What else have I missed?

The doorbell rings.

"Who is it?" I yell as I frantically toss the popcorn in the trash and stash the clamps in the freezer.

"Winnie and Dragomir."

"Coming," I yell and dash for the door, nearly tripping over Boner, who's already in the hallway, wagging his tail insistently.

Catching my breath, I open the door—and go back to hyperventilating.

I mean, come on. Who does this?

Dragomir is wearing a tight shirt that shows off his broad-shouldered, muscular frame in near-anatomical, panty-wetting detail.

The only way this could be worse is if he were wearing a turtleneck.

"Hi," he murmurs.

Before I can act on a wide variety of inappropriate urges that play out in my head, Winnie rushes past me like a bear tornado.

Dragomir says something sternly in Ruskovian but to no avail.

Ignoring him, she gives Boner a thorough sniff and licks him from head to toe, like a lollipop.

Boner seems to be in heaven—that is, until he decides he wants to sniff Winnie's butt but finds that it's much too high for his nose to reach.

Even when he leaps up, he gets only partway to where he wants to be, and then Winnie turns away before he can make another jump.

I voice Boner for Dragomir's pleasure:

"*Ma petite, destin* has us *ensemble* once again—but why did it put your *postérieure piquant* so, so far away?"

With a grin, Dragomir does Winnie's voice:

"It might be for the best, Napoleon Carlovich. I already bear the fruit of your loins."

I grin like a loon. "Call me Stud, *ma petite.* Call. Me. Stud."

Shaking his head, Dragomir pulls out a small box from the pocket of his jeans. "I have the test. Do you want to take care of that first?"

"Sure," I say. "While he's drooling at the sight of Winnie, that swab should yield a ton of saliva."

Dragomir and I work together on this. I hold Boner down, Dragomir offers him a treat to increase the drooling, and as soon as my little friend opens his maw, Dragomir uses the swab, then rewards him with the treat.

All in all, Boner doesn't seem to realize he's gotten a medical procedure.

If only they could all be like this.

Dragomir seals the swab in a plastic bag. "This should do it."

"Great. Why don't we go into the living room?"

He follows me, then stops and whistles, looking around. "Do you have a child?"

"Please don't whistle in the house," I say before I can stop myself.

He looks amused. "Another Russian superstition?"

"Whistling indoors means bad financial luck," I say. "And as you know, I'm seeking funding."

"I'll make sure not to whistle indoors from now on," he says, his lips curving in an agreeable smile. "But you never answered—do you have a kid?"

"No," I say defensively.

I think I know what this is about.

Sure enough, the next question is: "Are you into Disney?"

"Nope. I just like *Frozen.*"

He gestures at the large poster of Elsa on my wall, figurines of

Anna and the rest of her family on the bookshelf, and stuffed Olaf on the couch. "Clearly."

Great. Next time, besides hiding sex toys, I have to put away all the regular, kid-appropriate toys as well. You never know why someone will judge you.

Dragomir is now looking at the VR headset on the coffee table. "You've been practicing *Beat Saber*?"

I narrow my eyes at him. "Let me guess. You now can do 'Radioactive' on Expert Plus."

His grin is cocky. "Not only that—I bet I can beat your top score."

"You're on. It's a dance off. Or is it a sword fight?"

He shrugs. "Either way, I'll win."

I grab the headset and the controllers and hand everything to him. "Show me what you've got."

As he adjusts the headset for his much bigger head, I check on the dogs to make sure they don't end up under his feet—a tricky VR problem.

I catch Boner giving Winnie his biggest chew-ball, the one he can barely fit in his mouth.

"No." I snatch the ball away. Winnie was no doubt about to swallow the thing whole, which would mean yet another vet trip.

Boner rushes away and comes back with a bone he's been gnawing on for the last couple of days.

"That's better," I say, then check on Dragomir.

He's already got the headset on, and the controllers are in his hands.

Before I can ask if he's ready, "Radioactive" rings out of the headset speakers, and Dragomir begins to move to the rhythm.

Oh, my.

He wields the virtual swords with a regal grace, slicing and dicing the notes in a sleek, athletic mixture of martial arts and dance.

It's a good thing the headset blocks his vision. I'm drooling more than Boner did at the sight of the treat.

A part of me wonders if I could dig out one of my toys from where I've stashed it and use it before the song is through.

"Two hundred thousand points," Dragomir exclaims, breathing hard from excitement.

Wait a second. I don't think I had that many points by the "deep in my bones" line in the song—and that's a problem. I've been too busy salivating over the show he's put on to realize I could actually lose this competition.

Hell, no. I'll just dance and slice my butt off when it's my turn. Failure is not an option.

For now, I might as well enjoy the show—and enjoy it I do. That is, until he stops and announces his final score, which is higher than my record, but fortunately, by just a few points.

"Don't be so smug," I tell him as I readjust the headset to the size of a normal head. "I'm going to be beating your score in a moment."

He doubles down on the smug. "I'm sure you're going to try."

Grimly determined, I put on the headset and grip the two controllers—which in the game world look like two lightsabers, red and blue.

The music starts. The notes fly at me like bullets.

As I slash each one while ignoring bombs and dodging walls, I can't help but wonder what I look like to Dragomir outside VR.

Hopefully fierce like a ninja and graceful like a ballerina.

"I'm waking up to ash and dust," sings Dan Reynolds, and though this is the first line of the song, I'm already beginning to sweat—and I can't wipe my brow like in the song.

When I get to the first chorus and its signature "Radioactive, Radioactive," I'm sweating in earnest, but my score is the highest it's ever been at this point.

I could actually win.

Suddenly, I hear Dragomir shout in Ruskovian. All I can make out are two words: "Winnie" and "Fu!"

Shit.

The bear has breached my game space.

Before I can freeze in place, my right arm finishes slicing a set of notes—and my fist smashes into something hard.

I yelp in pain.

A man grunts.

Bear fur brushes against my leg.

I rip the headset off my head so I can see what disaster has befallen me.

It's worse than I thought.

Dragomir is patting Winnie with one hand, and with the other he's clutching his eye.

An eye that's already beginning to swell up.

# NINETEEN

"LET ME SEE THAT HAND," Dragomir orders in a voice so commanding I comply on autopilot, which is very unlike me.

Taking my hand, he examines it like a surgeon. "Can you move your fingers?"

I wiggle them, and he nods approvingly. "Do you have an ice pack or frozen peas?"

"One sec." Nearly tripping over Winnie, then Boner, I rush into the kitchen and check the freezer.

The nipple clamps are now nice and cold, but I don't think using them as a cold compress on anything but nipples would work all that well. Since I don't have any ice or peas, I grab a big slab of frozen chicken, slam the freezer door shut before anyone can see the clamps, and turn around—bumping right into Dragomir's chest.

We both stumble back, staring at each other. The heated energy that's just passed between us feels downright... radioactive.

"Use that on your hand," he says in the same commanding tone, glancing at the chicken in my hand.

"What, no? This is for your face."

"I'm fine. Just do as I say."

Was that a growl? And is it weird that I'm turned on by his bossiness?

"You're acting like I broke my hand," I say in exasperation.

He frowns. "Good point. Let's go get it x-rayed."

"Dude, I just banged it. Your face—"

"It's nothing. Start icing the hand."

I roll my eyes. "How about a compromise? I'll hold the chicken in my 'injured' hand next to your eye."

He sighs. "If that's what it takes."

I sit him down and hold the meat to his eye, all the while wondering just how unhygienic this is.

Can one get salmonella through the eye?

Soon, my fingers feel like they're about to get frostbite, but on the plus side, being so near him gives me a warm feeling in my chest.

After what feels like twenty minutes of nonstop tension, I say through chattering teeth, "I'm freezing and my hand is much better. Can you hold this in place?"

"I'm fine too." He takes the meat and heads over to the freezer.

"Let me do that." I snatch the chicken out of his hand and do my best to hide the freezer and the clamps inside it with my body as I put it away.

He doesn't say anything, so I must be successful.

Blowing out a relieved breath, I turn to face him and assess the damage.

Yep.

Icing or not, he's got a shiner—growing up with two brothers, I'm very familiar with the phenomenon.

"Let's go wash up." I walk over to the sink and use dish soap to make sure no chicken juices are left on my hand.

He washes his face as well, then uses one of his Winnie wet wipes and dries himself with his handkerchief.

Great. Now I can lick his face safely.

Wait, what?

I must be hungry. That has to be it. "You want to order some lunch?"

He nods, watching me with a hooded, amber-toned gaze.

Fuck, he's sexy. Even with a shiner.

Pushing the thought away before I jump him, I grab a few menus off the fridge, and we quickly settle on a pizza.

Order placed, I open and close my hand, feeling for any pain. All good there.

"I'm ready to restart the song," I announce.

"No." The word sounds like a royal decree.

I cross my arms over my chest. "No?"

"I don't want you hurt," he says in a much more diplomatic manner. "I forfeit the competition. You win."

"It doesn't work like that." I know I sound grumpy, but I can't help it.

I need to win. It's a compulsion.

"Please. Don't tax your poor hand anymore. Do it for me?" The beseeching look accompanying the words silences my next objections.

Crap. I hope he doesn't use that look for evil, like, say, seducing me right here and now.

It would work, too.

Alas, no seduction commences. Instead, he looks around the kitchen and frowns. "The dogs have been suspiciously quiet. We should check on them."

"Just to remind you, Winnie can't get any more pregnant," I say, but lead him to the living room anyway.

We get there just in time to witness an amazing display of super-Chihuahua strength.

"What the hell?" Dragomir mutters.

Oh, fuck. All that cleanup effort for nothing.

Boner has somehow managed to extract the Everest dildo from where I'd jammed it behind the TV, and is now dragging the thing toward Winnie—a feat doubly impressive because the silicone shlong in his mouth is almost the size of his whole body.

"It's not what it looks like," I blurt.

Dragomir gives me a look that seems to say, "Your dog is not about to gift a giant dildo to mine?"

I'm about to backpedal more, but then I realize that a) Dragomir looks more amused than judgmental and b) one dildo does not a sex toy company make.

Oh, well.

Let him think I'm into giant fake cocks.

It's not like I'm not.

Panting as though he's just finished a triathlon, Boner triumphantly drops the dildo at Winnie's feet.

Is there some phallic symbolism here or something? Or is this the dog equivalent of a marriage proposal?

Whatever it is, Winnie is happy. Her tail wags so hard it creates a noticeable draft in the room. Without pausing, she grabs the dildo in her maw and sprints into the kitchen.

"Well," I say sagely. "At least it's too big for her to swallow."

Dragomir is not listening. He chases after his dog—which she interprets to be a fun game because she dodges him and rushes back to the living room, dildo still clutched in her teeth.

"You know," I tell him when the two of them dash back into the room. "If you're trying to get Everest back for me, don't. She can keep it. I'll buy myself another one."

There. "Buy" implies I don't have a giant collection of these in a warehouse—and tells him I'm not a pearl-clutcher when it comes to these things. He might as well start getting to know the real me.

Victorian lady I'm not.

He shakes his head, again looking more amused than judgy. "She'll want to play fetch with it in the park."

He's got a point. Not everyone will be as understanding as he is.

To that end, I join the bear hunt, and after fifteen minutes of yelling and chasing, Dragomir finally catches Winnie and I help him extract the dildo from her.

She gives me a betrayed look and lifts her maw, letting out a wolf-like howl.

A slew of treats and a promise of a new toy later, Winnie calms down and walks over to give Boner's muzzle another slobbering lick.

He beams at her. "I have now made an honest bitch of you, *ma petite*."

Another tongue bath from her. "You're my stud forever, Napoleon Carlovich."

The doorbell rings, sending both dogs into a barking frenzy, and I leave Dragomir to calm them down as I go answer it.

It's our pizza.

I bring it in and set it on the kitchen table, then give Boner and Winnie some treats.

"Hungry?" I ask Dragomir as he sits down.

"Starving," he says, grabbing a slice. We chow down on the pizza for a couple of minutes, and then he says, "So, your brother mentioned that you went to MIT. That's impressive."

I shrug. "I was lucky. I set my sights on that school early on, so I kept my high school GPA a solid 4.0, took all the AP classes, aced the SATs, and did all the right extracurriculars. When I had my interview with them, I made sure to impress, and the rest is history."

He scoffs. "That's not being lucky. That's taking your fate into your own hands. Your parents must be very proud."

I sigh. "You don't know my parents." With a thick accent and my best impersonation of my mother's voice, I say, "Your father and I gave up everything to come to America. Going to a good college is the very least you can do."

Instead of being proud, my parents are disappointed with me—and only in part because of what I've chosen to do for a living.

"I'm sorry." His gaze holds genuine sympathy. "Parents can be tough."

My throat inexplicably closes up, and my next bite of pizza tastes like cardboard. With effort, I rein myself in and say lightly, "Mine are the toughest, that's for sure."

He grimaces. "You haven't met mine."

"Now that's a competition you'll never win," I say. "My parents are borderline evil—that is, to me. They treat my brothers just fine."

"Bullshit," he retorts, a little too harshly for my liking. Taking a deep breath, he continues in a calmer tone. "There's no possible way your parents could be worse than mine when it comes to preferring your siblings—or being disappointed, or anything else."

"Look," I say gently. This is clearly a sensitive topic for him as well. "This is not a competition I *want* to win, but I would."

He stubbornly shakes his head.

"How about a wager then?"

"I'd bet anything," he says promptly.

Anything? Pornographic images dance in front of my eyes, dispelling some of my funk.

"Problem is," he continues, "how would we decide?"

An evil idea occurs to me. "My mother's birthday is coming up. You can come as my plus-one and meet them. Once you admit defeat and run away screaming, I'll win the dubious honor of having the worst parents."

Wait. Did I just ask him to meet my parents?

"Deal," he says before I can backpedal.

Great. Now even if something does happen between us, it will be over after he meets my parental units in all their glory. Then again, maybe that would be for the best.

Nothing *should* happen between us.

"It's been ages since I've been to a Russian birthday celebration," he says.

I blow out a breath. "You're so going to regret this."

He looks unfazed. "What do your parents do?"

I grab another pizza slice. "Back in the motherland, my father was a surgeon and my mother an architect. They now own a restaurant on Brighton Beach—something they consider a downgrade. They never let my brothers and me forget about the noble sacrifice they made." I bite into the pizza and, still chewing, ask, "How about yours? What do they do?"

Dragomir's lips flatten. "They've never had anything resembling a job—unless intrigue counts."

Huh. That's weird. "They're still in Ruskovia?"

His eyes shift to the color of cold, hard jade. "They are, but they do come to New York on a regular basis."

Okay, maybe he does have bigger issues with his parents than I do.

"How many siblings do you have?" I ask, hoping to lighten the mood.

Nope. Judging by the way his shoulders tighten, I might've just made things worse. "There are ten of us," he says with distaste.

"Wow." I try to picture birthing ten babies and shudder at the gory images in my mind. His poor mom's vag—no wonder she's mean. "Is it a Ruskovian tradition to have such a large family?" I ask cautiously.

He shakes his head. "Just my family's. What about you? I've met Alex, of course. Is there anyone else?"

I smile. "Yep. Vlad."

"Is that short for Vladimir?"

"You guessed it."

"I hope you get along with him as well as with Alex."

"Oh, yeah," I say. "Both of my brothers adore me."

He looks wistful. "That must be nice."

I desperately search for another subject. "Where did you go to school?"

"A university in Ruskovia," he says. "I doubt you've heard of it."

I've barely heard of the country, so yeah. "When did you start your venture capital fund?"

There. That should be a nice, neutral topic.

"A few years after college graduation," he answers.

I quirk an eyebrow, impressed. "Don't you need capital to start something like that?"

His jaw tightens.

Oops. Apparently, I'm not out of the minefield of his past.

"Can you please do me a favor?" he says after a tense moment of silence.

I regard him warily over my pizza slice. "Depends on what it is."

"Don't ask me about my business."

I stuff the pizza into my mouth, channeling the Twix commercial.

Because if I'm not mistaken, that's the exact quote from *The Godfather*, and it plants an idea in my head that I don't like one bit.

Could Dragomir be in the mob?

# TWENTY

AS I CHEW, I realize it's not as crazy as it might sound.

He's Eastern European—neatly fitting into the more recent Hollywood stereotype of organized crime—and mysterious as fuck, not wanting to talk about either his business or his family.

Maybe his family is *the* family, in the mafia sense.

That would explain the gold coin he slipped to the veterinarian.

Wait a minute. Could the guy who I thought was a private investigator be an actual investigator—the kind that works for the police or the FBI? Am I going to get approached one day and asked to assist with a sting operation?

Is his venture capital firm a way to launder money?

It's an effort to finally swallow my food.

I wish I'd considered this possibility *before* I invited him to my mother's birthday. My parents had a run-in with Russian mobsters some years ago, and it wasn't fun. Luckily, Vlad was able to help them out.

Speaking of Vlad, he should be able to shed some light on this. If Dragomir is being investigated by any agency, that's a clue for my snoopy brother.

"Are you upset?" Dragomir asks, and I realize I've been quiet for a while. "If it's that important to you, I—"

"No," I say quickly. "I'm just trying to recall if I took Boner out for a walk in the morning."

At the mention of the word "walk" and his name, my dog begins a happy dance.

Dragomir smiles at Boner, then looks at the bear. "Winnie likes to walk in the afternoon. Want to go together?"

"Sure," I say.

Might not be the worst idea to get a possible criminal out of my apartment. The park is public, so Boner and I should be safe.

"I only have a half hour, though," I say. "I have a meeting with Vlad."

It's not exactly a lie—I'm totally going to drop in and see what my brother thinks about my crazy theory.

Dragomir nods, and we attack the rest of the pizza. Then we prep our charges and go to the park.

As we walk, I ask Dragomir to tell me something interesting about Ruskovia, figuring that's a safe topic under any circumstances.

"Like what?" he asks.

"I don't know. Interesting traditions, maybe?"

He scratches his chin. "We have a holiday where everyone throws ripe grapes at each other—a bit like La Tomatina in Spain, though they use tomatoes for some weird reason."

"Sure," I say with a smirk. "Grapes are logical projectiles, but tomatoes are crazy talk."

"Here's one thing you might find amusing," he says, shortening Winnie's leash before she sticks her nose into the horse poop left by one of the carriages that crisscross Central Park. "We have a bear festival, during which people set out food bears like and even dress like bears."

I grin. "You sure it's not a day dedicated to the misha breed?"

"Positive," he says and tells me about a few more traditions, like everyone's dislike of the color red, thanks to the Soviets, and how Ruskovians toss baby teeth on the roof instead of leaving them under a pillow. My favorite is their stories of Grandpa Krampus—a sort of demon anti-Santa who scares children into being nice.

When we accidentally let a tree come between us, I force Dragomir to circle back. "It's another Russian superstition," I explain. "Two people should not walk on different sides of a tree. Got to pick a side, or we might have a fight."

He touches his black eye. "I feel like the fight has already happened."

Wincing, I apologize for the eye again, and we walk until the doggies do their business.

"Do you have OCD?" he asks as we head back to my apartment.

"No. Why?"

He gestures at the pavement. "You never step on a crack."

"Oh. That's not OCD. Stepping on cracks is bad luck."

"Sure, sure," he says with a grin.

I watch myself walk the rest of the way to my building and realize how automatic my crack avoidance actually is.

Well, whatever. I need my luck to stay good—especially for the rest of this playdate.

When we finally cross the street and stand next to my building entrance, I demonstratively take out my phone and glance at the time. "I'd better go."

He steps closer to me. "This was fun."

My heartbeat speeds up at his proximity. "We should do it again sometime."

Hold up. What am I saying? Didn't I just theorize that he's a mobster? I should figure out a way to uninvite him to my family event, not—

He closes the distance between us.

The cinnamon yumminess of his warm male scent leaps into my flared nostrils and scrambles my brain.

His eyes shifting from light brown to green-flecked gold, he places his hands on my hips.

Fuck.

My hormones take over and I melt into him, eyes never leaving his.

He leans down.

I rise on tiptoe.

Our lips fuse.

# TWENTY-ONE

FUUUUUCK.

This. Is. Amazing.

My first ever mouthgasm. My skin pebbles, and as though acquiring a will of their own, my fingers splay over the sizable bulge in his jeans.

Very sizable bulge.

We're talking Everest levels.

Growling low in his throat, Dragomir deepens the kiss, and I feel like I might explode from arousal.

He might be "the one" indeed, because we're nowhere near sex toys and I'm almost ready to come.

My clothes start to chafe, and my fingers go to work on his zipper. Why isn't he naked already? Before I can free Everest from his pants, I feel Dragomir's entire body stiffen. Breathing hard, he lifts his head and steps back, eyes mirroring my frustration.

I gape stupidly at his kiss-swollen lips, then at his almost-undone pants.

Crap.

I forgot we were outside.

I also forgot that I never take a guy's pants off on the first date—not that today was even a clear-cut date.

Flushing, I gulp in some air and back away, out of his Jupiter-like gravitational pull.

Winnie cocks her head at me. "Tsk, tsk, Bella Borisovna. Making puppies in public?"

A slow smirk curves Dragomir's lips as those hazel eyes travel over my body from head to toe. "To be continued?" he asks huskily.

Oh, no. No, no, no. Potential criminal, remember?

"I've got to go," I mutter and pull Boner into the building, my gait unsteady.

I can feel Dragomir's burning gaze on my back.

Boner drags his feet all the way to the elevator. As the doors begin to close, he whimpers and gives Winnie a longing stare.

"I know how you feel, bud," I say hoarsely.

"Oh, *ma chérie*. The Lamians and Chortskys are a match made in *paradis*."

"Not if the Lamians are in the mob," I say and work on steadying my breathing for the rest of the elevator ride.

<hr>

AS I DROP BONER OFF, I debate digging up one of my toys, but decide that seeing Vlad is a higher priority than my misfiring libido.

I take a cab downtown and try not to think about what just happened. But my mind is stuck on that amazing kiss anyway, and all sorts of questions swirl through it.

How could I have kissed him mere minutes after thinking he might be a mobster?

Does this mean I'd be okay with becoming a mob wife?

No. No way. Not if it means he'd cheat on me the way Tony did on Carmela in *The Sopranos*. Not that I'd let him. If *I* caught my husband cheating, I'd have him whacked. But crap. I'd then have to run his criminal organization by myself, and that's on top of my sex toy company. No way would I be able to handle both. I'd burn out and resort to drugs. Like coke. I'd be a cokehead in no time, breaking the cardinal rule of not getting high off your own supply.

So, in conclusion, I shouldn't kiss him ever again.

But what if he wants to?

What if, having tasted me, he now wants me so much he's willing to kidnap me? Would I end up on some secluded compound in Ruskovia, where I'd develop the quickest case of Stockholm syndrome in history?

When the cab stops, I rush into Vlad's office like a whirlwind.

He tears his gaze away from his coding, a concerned expression on his face. "What's the matter?"

I plop down into the chair across from him and explain.

He shakes his head. "I've already checked to see if he's being investigated—and he isn't."

"You have?"

He smiles. "I had to pull some strings, but hey, how many favorite sisters do I have?"

I almost jump up and down from glee. "You don't think he's mafia?"

His smile deepens. "I honestly don't even think there's such a thing as a Ruskovian mob. Not in his home country and especially not in the US."

I begin to feel silly. "Why not?"

"Ruskovia has one of the lowest crime rates in the world. They don't have any jails—or databases of criminals that someone could hack into."

Is Vlad saying he'd be willing to hack into a foreign government's criminal database for me? If so, this might be the last time I ask him to snoop on someone. I wouldn't want to be the reason he gets into trouble.

I fight the urge to chastise. He's a big boy. Instead, I say, "Japan has a low crime rate, but they have the Yakuza."

"Good point. But there also aren't enough Ruskovians in the US to run a criminal organization. Oh, and unlike the Japanese, pretty much all Ruskovians are wealthy. Old money, too—so less motivation for the risks associated with crime."

I exhale in relief. "Okay, in that case, you're right. I guess a Ruskovian mob would be about as likely as one from Monaco."

"Exactly," he says.

"Well, I'm glad. I invited him to Mother's birthday and—"

"Just because he's not in the mob doesn't mean *that* was a good idea," Vlad says with a frown. "He's still an enigma, and that sounds like a date."

I sigh. He's right—and he doesn't even know about the kiss. "Maybe you can dig up something on him if you meet face to face?"

My brother eyes me quizzically. "How?"

I shrug. "Take a picture of him and reverse image search? Hack into his phone? I don't know, it's your area of expertise."

"Bad ideas, all. Unless you don't care if he finds out about my snooping."

"I definitely don't want him to find out."

"In that case, reverse image search is out. If he's anything like me, he has a page set up that will trigger an alert when searched that way. As to the phone, we'd have to steal it to get inside it. I'm not the NSA —I can't just do it remotely."

I get up. "Forget it. We'll stick with the old plan where I try to get you more info. Maybe he'll mention the name of one of his many siblings. Or his parents."

Vlad also stands up. "That's smart."

I give him a hug, remind him that he'd better be at the birthday, and head back home.

FOR THE REST of the day, I work on my product designs and grow more and more excited about the upcoming date with Dragomir. The next morning, Alex gives me an update: No word from Marco and team, and no other prospects.

Thanks, bro. A great way to put a damper on my excitement. Despite the fact that Dragomir has recused himself, going on a date with him is playing with fire as far as our funding is concerned.

Busying myself with work may not be the most mature way to deal with my Dragomir doubts, but that's the path I take, and by the end of the day, Belka has a new product: an anal plug with a fluffy squirrel tail sticking out of it, all made out of a dishwasher- and washing-machine-safe material for ease of cleaning.

Which reminds me: I've got to get my mother a birthday gift.

I ponder this for a while.

An overt sex toy would upset her, so that's a no go. But then again, she often complains about neck pain, so why don't I get her something that's allegedly for that?

It doesn't take me long to decide.

Mother will be getting Belka's stiff competition: The Hitachi Magic Wand.

Trademarked back in 1968, this "personal massager" was the vibrator of choice for women at a time when female pleasure—especially masturbation—was more taboo than today. Which means it'll fit perfectly into my parents' household.

And if Mother only uses it on her neck, that's her loss.

Gift chosen, I check my phone.

Score! A text from Dragomir.

He wants to know more details about the birthday.

I text him directions to my parents' restaurant and tell him to meet me there. This way, I can get there early and beg or bribe my family to be on their best behavior—which I realize is inconsistent with the whole "my parents are worse than yours" bet we've made.

I guess I don't want him to run away screaming and never think about me as a romantic possibility, which he is sure to do if he sees my parents uncensored.

Wait, what am I saying? I *should* let him run away screaming. That was the whole—

*Should I bring a gift?* His text rips me out of my ruminations.

*I've got one that can be from the both of us,* I reply. *You can bring flowers if you want. Just make sure it's an odd number. For Russians, an even number of flowers is for funerals.*

His reply is a smiley face, which bolsters my earlier excitement.

Next on my list is cheering up Boner. He keeps looking gloomy, likely because he misses Winnie. Luckily, I know just the thing. I put on *Ratatouille*, Boner's favorite animated movie, in the living room.

It works.

As usual, he perks up and begins to pace the room while sneaking glances at the screen that last as long as his doggy attention span allows.

It's a fun mystery as to why he enjoys this particular story. I like to think that he might have dreams of becoming a great French chef, like the rat hero, though a more pragmatic part of me knows the answer might be simpler. He may just think this movie is about a fellow Chihuahua.

Then again, both theories might be wrong. He doesn't like other movies with Chihuahuas, like *Legally Blonde*, nor the ones about French cooking, like *Julie & Julia*.

"*Ma chérie*, don't strain your pretty little brain about it. I'm just a mystery wrapped in an enigma... and bacon, okay?"

---

THE MORNING of my mother's birthday, I get a text from Xenia:

*Huge news. Can I come over?*

Even though I can guess what the news is, I pretend to be oblivious until she comes over and tells me exactly what I thought she would: Boy Toy has proposed.

"It was so romantic, too," she says when I'm done with all the expected jumping, hugging, and squealing. "Here."

She shows the ring, then a picture of a freezer with a row of four Stolichnaya vodka bottles, where Boy Toy replaced the usual labels with ones that form a phrase: "Will you marry me?"

"Aww, that *is* romantic," I say.

It's also a possible sign someone needs to look into the twelve-step program, but hey, it sure is original.

"I have the perfect gift for the two of you," I say and rush out of the room.

I come back with a tray that Xenia examines dubiously.

"Are these wedding bands of some kind? If so, most look way too big."

"These are cock rings," I say. "Vibrating cock rings."

Xenia looks at the tray, then at me, her expression still confused.

"It's for Boy Toy to wear on a special night," I explain. Then I grab a dildo from the nearby coffee table and show her where a cock ring would go and how to turn it on.

"And it vibrates?" She sounds intrigued.

"Yep. Just pick his size."

Xenia looks wistfully at the extra-extra-large, extra-large, and large. Then her gaze settles on one of the bigger mediums.

"Good for you," I say as she grabs that ring. "Let me know what you guys think."

GETTING out of the cab next to my parents' restaurant, I pray that I've beaten Dragomir here after all. Murphy's Law has made it so I'm late to yet another family gathering—and I left a half hour earlier than the last time.

Actually, it's likely that I have beaten him. Otherwise, there would be a text from him, and there isn't yet.

My parents' restaurant is called The Hut, which is short for The Hut on Hen's Legs. It's a reference to Baba Yaga, a cannibalistic witch from my childhood nightmares. You know, the perfect association for a restaurant.

Shaking my head, I run up the creaky wooden staircase and slip inside between the decorative hen "legs."

I think my folks are so prudish they're oblivious to the vaginal symbolism they've accidentally created here.

Inside the restaurant, the party is in full swing.

My father's namesake, Boris, is the singer today, and for some reason, he's belting out a song from his non-Russian repertoire: "Gangnam Style."

I don't speak Korean, but I can still tell Boris has a heavy Russian accent as he butchers the words of the song. On the plus side, thanks to his stocky build and the mirrored sunglasses he's sporting, he actually resembles the original singer—or would if Boris were to shave off that beard. Also, his horse-riding dance moves are spot on. Same goes for the backup dancers on the stage.

As I navigate the dance floor, I'm nearly trampled by elderly Russian people who are horse-riding to K-Pop without fear of heart attacks or broken hips. The party has just begun, but I bet the average blood alcohol level here is already in the DUI territory.

Some of these peeps are distant family, but most are my mother's friends and acquaintances. As one, they give me dirty looks, no doubt because I'm the reason the poor wretches have had to listen to her complaints about me over the years.

My family is gathered at the usual table, all of them, so I'm officially the latecomer again.

"Hi, all," I say in English, figuring that's the language we'll be speaking for most of the night, given Fanny's presence at the table.

My brothers smile at me, as does Fanny—but my parents scowl, as per usual.

Hey, at least they haven't started eating or drinking without me this time—a huge insult in the Russian culture.

"Fashionably late again?" Mother's makeup is so heavy today, a drag queen would be jealous. She's also showing enough cleavage to choke a horse.

Vlad darts her a narrow-eyed look, and Alex rolls his eyes.

I force a smile. "Happy birthday, Mom." I thrust the gift box into her hands. "May you be healthy and prosperous."

There. The high ground.

Let's see how long I can stay there.

Grabbing the box, Mother looks momentarily appeased. Then her features become disapproving once again as she asks, "Where's your date?"

"I told him the shindig starts a little later than it actually does," I say.

"Why?" Father asks. His mustache looks extra bushy today, as does his unibrow.

I take a deep breath. "He's a potential investor, so I want to ask you all not to embarrass me in front of him today."

In other words, I'm asking for a miracle.

"When have we ever embarrassed you?" Mother asks, her eyes flinty.

Is she serious right now?

Figuring a fight isn't going to help my cause, I say, "I'm not saying you have. Just don't do it today of all days."

"We'll be on our best behavior," Vlad says pointedly. At his side, Fanny solemnly nods, and Alex says, "We'll keep to the topics appropriate for polite company. No religion, politics, or money talk."

"We always avoid those topics too," Mother chimes in. "Besides, if anyone would shame the family, it would be Bella."

I try to think happy thoughts. She gave birth to me. It must've hurt. It's her birthday. I don't want Fanny to run away screaming if we get into one of our infamous rows.

Speaking of Fanny, Vlad leaps to his feet and folds his napkin as if he's planning to leave. Alex looks ready to bolt as well, and Fanny fidgets, extremely uncomfortable.

"Hold on," Mother squeals, seeing where things are headed. "No religion, politics, or money talk, I swear."

Is that an actual compromise from Mother? If so, is a unicorn about to fart a rainbow? If I had to guess why this is happening, I'd say she's trying to stay on Vlad's good side. Now that he's got Fanny, she thinks he's her most direct path to holding a grandchild—an obsession of hers that borders on insanity.

"I'm going to sit," I say and head for a chair farthest away from my parents.

"Don't sit there," Mother says. "It's the corner."

Of course. How could I have forgotten a superstition? Sitting at the corner of the table means you won't marry for seven years.

"Sit next to Fannychka," Vlad suggests.

I gladly comply. I've actually brought a little something for Fanny today, and this will allow me to stealthily gift it to her without getting on Mother's radar.

"Hi," Fanny whispers when I plop next to her. "Nice to see you again."

"Great to see you too," I say, and mean it.

I actually have a platonic crush on Vlad's girlfriend. She's one of the cutest creatures I've ever met—and that includes my dog. With her round, often-blushing face, she all but radiates sweetness and wholesomeness—yet I know she's got a secret wild side and plenty of spunk.

Looking at her and Vlad, I can see why Mother pines for a grandkid from them. With them both being pale, dark-haired, and blue-eyed, it's easy to picture what their potential offspring would look like: an adorable hybrid between a cherub and a vampire.

"I got this for you," I whisper into Fanny's ear conspiratorially.

She looks at me like the proverbial deer in the headlights.

I hand her the bag with my gift. "This is my latest creation."

Appearing even more hesitant, Fanny peeks inside the bag. As soon as she spots the butt plug with a squirrel tail, her eyes widen cartoonishly and her cheeks turn a shade of red I didn't think existed in nature.

"Thanks," she stammers, looking like she wants to sink through the floor.

"No sweat," I reply with a grin. "Vlad wanted a pony as a kid—so you might want to pretend that's a horse tail instead of a squirrel tail."

Vlad must overhear something because he narrows his eyes at me.

Before I can counter with an innocent puppy look, I spot Mother's eyes widening as she looks into the crowd. She then fans herself and bites her lip.

Well, that's weird.

I follow her gaze and immediately understand her reaction.

Dragomir is here, in all his mouthwatering, panty-melting glory.

# TWENTY-TWO

WEARING a bespoke suit that accentuates his muscular frame, he's holding a bouquet of flowers so massive someone must've chopped down an entire field of plants for it.

I stand up and wave him over.

Lips curving into a sexy grin, he approaches the table.

To my relief, his black eye is either gone or not visible in the current lighting.

Mother leaps to her feet with such vigor it's a miracle her ample bosom stays inside her dress.

"Everyone, this is Dragomir," I say. "Dragomir, this is—"

"Natasha," Mother says breathlessly.

"I was going to say 'everyone,'" I say with a slight eye roll.

"Hi, everyone and Natasha," he says.

"That's Fanny"—I point at her—"and Vlad." I gesture at my brother. "You already know Alex, and that"—I nod at Father—"is my dad, Boris."

I check Dragomir's face to see if he's noticed that my parents' names are Boris and Natasha—like from the *Rocky and Bullwinkle* cartoon. Most people instantly realize the connection because my parents actually look like that villainous duo and even have similar accents.

If Dragomir makes the connection, he doesn't show it.

"Happy birthday, Natasha," he says in nearly perfect Russian. "May you have health above all."

Mother looks swoony as she mutters her thanks.

Geesh.

With a regal bow, Dragomir hands her the flowers.

Mother clutches her pearls—literally—then waves over a waiter and hands him the bouquet. Freed, she all but jumps on Dragomir, kissing him on the right cheek, then the left, before hugging him as though she wants to smother him in her bosom.

Father stands up and strides toward Dragomir.

At first, I wonder if he's jealous of the attention his wife is paying to the man and will do or say something to embarrass the family.

Nope. As soon as Mother stops slobbering on my date, Father gives Dragomir the kissing of the cheeks treatment.

Hey, at least he didn't go for the hug. Pretty sure in another minute, Mother would've been copping a feel.

My brothers, being normal, simply shake Dragomir's hand, and Fanny shyly waves, blushes, and murmurs a hello.

Good job, Fanny. You get to live.

As Dragomir sits on the chair next to mine, the cinnamon notes of his cologne make me want to bite him.

Or lick him.

I'm ravenous, and not for the food.

I want to drag him to the dance floor and rub against him as soon as is socially acceptable—probably after at least a few toasts.

Father grabs the vodka bottle.

Fanny lifts her shot glass, but Vlad gently pushes her hand back down to the table—it's bad luck to fill a glass in the air.

"Now that everyone is here, let's begin." Father flashes a dirty look my way. He likes to drink, and I've made him wait an extra couple of minutes.

Without asking if everyone wants vodka, he pours a round of shots. In his defense, that's the Russian tradition.

"Remember, not too much for yourself," Mother tells him. "You promised."

With a sigh, he pours himself a shot instead of a full glass and says, "As the birthday girl's husband, it falls to me to say the first toast." He thinks very hard, then looks at Fanny apologetically. "Dear, do you mind if I say this first one in Russian?"

Fanny smiles and shakes her head.

"I'll translate afterward," Vlad says with a slight frown. "We don't want anyone to feel left out."

Father begins his toast.

I lean close enough to Dragomir to nibble on his ear and whisper, "Every shot will have a toast, and there will be a lot of shots."

Dragomir nods.

"If you don't want to look like a wimp, finish every shot you lift in one gulp," I continue. "In general, be careful. If you try to keep up with anyone in my family, you'll be under the table in no time."

What I don't add is: if he gets too drunk, we won't be able to dance.

Dragomir leans toward me, his breath warm on my ear. "This isn't my first Russian get-together. As to anyone going under the table —you'll be there long before me."

"Oh yeah?" I grin. "Challenge accepted."

"I have at least sixty pounds on you," he whispers. "You keep starting fights you can't win."

My grin widens. "Just match me drink for drink, and we'll see what happens."

He shakes his head in exasperation.

I tune back into Father's toast, which is long, even for him.

When the toast is finally over, everyone downs their shots and eats a pickle after—except Fanny. She only sips hers and skips the pickle completely, the former being a big no-no as far as Russian drinking superstitions go, but something we pretend not to notice. A little bad luck is better than losing her to alcohol poisoning.

Everyone serves themselves food, and Vlad translates the toast for Fanny, who's clearly doing her best to keep a poker face.

"Happy perfect day, angel-like being. She who still causes my heart to tremble like a leaf in the wind. She whom I want to caress with my love. The mother of my children. May you have eternal health and happiness..." And so on and so forth, in that vein.

I shake my head at Vlad's translation. Caress with my love? a) TMI and b) That's not exactly what Father said. It's more like "cuddle with my passion," which I guess is also TMI.

"Eat something," I whisper into Dragomir's ear. "Else drinking you under the table won't even be a challenge."

With an eye roll, he takes *sel'edka pod shuboy*—a dish that translates to something like "herring dressed in a fur coat."

"Please send my compliments to your chef," Dragomir says loudly after he tries it. "This is the best version of this dish I've ever tasted."

Both of my parents beam with pride. Though they don't cook the food themselves, they do participate in recipe creation.

I hear Vlad explain the herring dish to Fanny. "The fish is fermented," he's saying, "and it's served under a layer of shredded cooked beets and eggs, mixed with mayo."

Drowned in mayo, more like.

To her credit, Fanny accepts a small portion and tastes it without wrinkling her nose. The last time I saw her at this place, she was a much more cautious eater. My brother is clearly rubbing off on her— in more ways than one.

Still, she draws the line at *kholodetz*, a jellied meat dish that contains ingredients she finds unthinkable, such as pig snout and ears, chicken feet, and beef tails.

On my own plate is my favorite, *vinegret*—a salad with boiled beets, potatoes, pickles, carrots, onions, sauerkraut, and peas.

As soon as I'm done with my portion, Dragomir offers me more, and I let him put a serving on my plate.

Seeing this, Mother whispers approvingly to Father, "Her date is servicing her. A keeper."

Did she not catch the part where Dragomir speaks Russian?

With a nod at Mother, Father grabs the vodka bottle again. "The time between the first drink and the second ought to be short."

His toast is more concise this time—only long enough for everyone to start yawning—and then we drink.

I sneak a glance at the dance floor. Hopefully, we can be there soon.

The time between the second and the third shot also appears to be short, and I begin to feel a pleasant buzz. That is, until Mother stands up to make a toast, at which point the buzz is replaced with dread.

"I hope a woman of my years can be forgiven if I think about my family legacy, especially on my birthday," Mother says and narrows her eyes at Alex—probably because he's the only person at the table without a date. Then, glancing approvingly at Fanny and Dragomir, she says, "To the health of my unborn grandchildren."

Even though this is not the first time she's been through this, Fanny blushes.

I half expect Dragomir to choke on his food or at least blink, but he takes it in stride, as though she's toasted to the health of our dogs— which, hey, is not such a bad idea.

Maybe Ruskovians also lack any subtlety when it comes to these things?

We drink the shots.

Vlad refills everyone's glasses and makes a toast next.

Then Alex.

When it's my turn, instead of toasting to the health of our dogs, specifically, I say that we should drink to the health of everyone's pets, "whatever they happen to be."

Annoyingly, Dragomir doesn't seem drunk yet—that or I'm getting too woozy to spot it.

Now would be okay to dance, and I'm about to say so, but then the lights dim.

Crap.

How could I have forgotten about the show when there's one at every celebration? And when I was forced to perform at them as a kid?

Yeah, my ventriloquism wasn't exactly a hobby I picked up on my own, though it's a skill I'm now grateful to have.

These shows take place at every major celebration here, and they're choreographed by my unqualified-for-this mother. As such, they're a hodgepodge of things she likes, including but not limited to ballet, fairy tales, Cirque du Soleil, and the Rockettes.

True to form, showgirls dressed as trees kick up their legs on the stage until our host, Boris—now dressed as Baba Yaga—does his best to dance ballet among them, looking more like a hippo than a witch.

Fanny's eyes grow wider as the show goes on, but Dragomir acts like he sees mustachioed cannibal witches pirouetting around all the time.

From there, it's one of the more common Baba Yaga stories—which itself is very similar to *Hansel and Gretel*. Of course, in Mother's version, it's a ballet, and in my opinion, Hansel is too handsy when he tosses Gretel into the air. I'm just going to tell myself they're step-siblings in this adaptation.

Blissfully, the show ends with Baba Yaga getting burned in a stove represented by orange-clad showgirls.

"Ladies and gentlemen," Boris announces. "The dance floor is yours."

With that, he starts to sing "A Million Scarlet Roses," a Russian slow-dance classic.

This is it.

I want to dance.

In a display of true psychic powers, Dragomir smoothly rises to his feet and extends his hand to me in an unmistakable gesture.

In my peripheral vision, I see my parents nodding approvingly at this, and Mother gives Vlad a pointed glare before gesturing at Fanny.

"May I have this dance?" Dragomir murmurs.

Grabbing his hand, I leap to my feet, and my heart speeds up at the feel of his strong fingers surrounding mine.

He takes a ballroom dance stance.

I put my other hand in his as well.

Wow.

His touch ignites my every nerve ending, his proximity making it hard to breathe.

We begin to sway to the music.

Double wow.

His mercurial eyes are hypnotizing. Claiming.

Is the floor a little shaky today?

I feel a little faint.

Breathless.

Fluttery.

I press against him.

His hard parts press against my soft ones, and my breathing hitches.

If the slow dance is meant to be a seduction, mission accomplished. If it's meant to be foreplay, bring on the main course.

He pulls me closer.

I feel Everest pressing against my belly.

He leans down.

Thanks to my high heels, we're face to face, so it's only a matter of a heartbeat before our mouths engage.

Triple wow.

The room around us seems to disappear.

I'm pure sensation—aware only of his soft lips, his gliding tongue, his large, hard body.

Speaking of the latter, I sneak my hand down and feel Everest over his pants.

How many wows has it been now?

He tears his lips away and whispers huskily, "Not here."

Fuck.

I forgot where I was again. Or didn't care.

On some level, I still don't *really* care—I want him that badly.

Suddenly, the music changes. The slow melody is replaced by the cheerful notes of one of Mother's favorite dances: Lambada.

Based on a Bolivian folk song called "Llorando se fue," this melody has found its way into the repertoires of a bunch of singers over the years, and from the first line Boris belts out, I recognize Jennifer Lopez's "On the Floor."

With a cocky smirk, Dragomir slides his hand to my lower back and pulls me in close—the Lambada position.

Another wow.

Legs arching, we take fast steps from side to side, sometimes turning, sometimes swaying, and all the while moving our hips as much as possible.

Or in other words, dry humping in public.

They didn't call the original inspiration for this song "the forbidden dance" for shits and giggles. It *should* be forbidden—at least on the dance floor of your parents' restaurant.

Especially if said parents already think you're an oversexed nymphomaniac.

"If you go hard, you gotta get on the floor," Boris belts out in his best impersonation of JLo—which isn't very good at all.

However, Dragomir *is* hard. That's the problem. I can feel every inch rubbing against me, and an answering pressure builds in my core.

Wow number three thousand.

I'm about to come. No toys, not even actual touching.

Forget him being "the one." He's more like my personal orgasm trigger—because I'm about to have one right here and now, in the middle of Mother's party.

Dragomir's pupils dilate, his eyes darkening to a rich, deep amber. I think he knows.

"Grab somebody, drink a little more," Boris sings.

I ignore the lyrics and focus on my building orgasm.

It's almost there.

I just need a few more dry humps—I mean, sways to the music.

Just a little more.

Almost there.

Almost—

The song stops.

No!

Dragomir pulls away—and I can see why. We've done such a good job with the dancing, people are clapping.

Crap. Crap. Crap.

I catch Fanny's gaze. Blushing, she winks at me.

Fucking fuck.

The next song better give me an excuse to rub against Dragomir some more.

Nope. Not my day.

I recognize what the song is based on the first few notes. Everyone does. Boris is clearly on a Latin kick right now. In his thickest Russian accent yet, he sings, "When I dance they call me Macarena."

As one, Mother's friends and all my distant relatives extend their arms like a horde of zombies.

With a sigh, I do the same, as does Dragomir. Then we flip our palms up along with everyone else.

"They all want me." Boris seems to really enjoy that line, and hey, why *not* keep the hope alive?

Each person puts their right hand on their left shoulder, then repeats the action with their other hand.

My near orgasm is but a distant memory. This is as close as a dance can get to a cold shower.

We put our hands on the backs of our heads.

Shoot me now.

The hands go on our hips, and everyone starts to rotate said hips.

Okay, this is more interesting. With his hips moving that way, Dragomir manages the impossible: actually making the Macarena sexy.

Sadly, he soon joins everyone in a ninety-degree jump to the side, as do I.

Some people do a scuba dive move while others clap. Then the sequence repeats again. And again. And again.

When the song finally stops, I pull him toward me and whisper, "Let's go to your place."

His eyes widen, shifting to golden-green, and his face turns taut. "You mean right now?"

Ugh, he's right. We can't leave right this moment. The second course hasn't even been served. Mother would notice if we skedaddled, and would leap onto the stage, singing, "It's my party and I'll cry if I want to."

Fine.

We'll just keep dancing.

"Ladies and gentlemen," Boris says instead of launching into another song. "Now is the chance for you to grab this microphone and say a toast for our dear Natashen'ka."

Great. They're doing this bit? It's usually super boring.

We return to the table, and Father pours a round of shots.

My great-aunt recites a poem she's composed in Mother's honor.

After the poem is blissfully over, we drink.

The waiters bring out the shish kebab course, so we drink to that.

Someone from Mother's book club wishes her "sturdy offspring," and we drink to that too.

One of Father's usual drinking buddies grabs the mic next. "My friends, it's not good to drink individually, much better to do so as a collective." He raises his vodka glass. "To the power of the collective."

"Sounds like a commie slogan," I mutter as I down my next shot.

"Comrades," the next person says. "Let us have as much grief as there are drops in our glasses."

Cheers. We drink to that.

The next toast is, "Let there be people in your life whom you'd want to toast, not those who make you want to get drunk!"

Another shot.

Then another.

I begin to lose count of both toasts and shots—all I see is that Dragomir is somehow keeping up.

Impressive.

"Can someone tell me a Vovochka joke?" Fanny asks when the toasts are finally over. "I really like them, and Vlad ran out."

I lean toward Dragomir and whisper in his ear, "Vovochka is the Russian equivalent of Little Johnny."

"I know," he says. "I even know some of those jokes."

Does this man never cease to impress?

"I'll go first," Alex says and refills everyone's shot glasses. "'Parents having a fight again?' Grandmother asks Vovochka. 'Yeah,' he replies. 'When Mom came back from vacation, she brought back something called *gonorrhea*. First, she gifted it to Dad, then to Uncle Sergey, then the neighbor from across the street. Now they're all yelling and fighting, but I'm not sure if it's because she didn't bring enough, or because she didn't divide it up fairly.'"

Fanny blushes and laughs, as does everyone else.

We take a shot again.

"I've got one," Dragomir says, and my parents exchange an

impressed glance. "Grandmother asks Vovochka why he's crying. 'Mom told Dad he's an ass, and he called her a cow in reply.' Grandmother pats him on the head. 'So what?' He cries harder. 'What animal does that make *me*?'"

Chuckles all around and another shot.

I know I shouldn't, but I can't help myself. "I know one too. But it's dirty."

"Just go for it," Mother says magnanimously.

Everyone's eyes are on me now, so I say, "Math teacher says, 'Vovochka, I will give you 300 rubles. If you give 50 to Vera, 50 to Dasha, and 50 to Elena, what do you get?' Vovochka's eyes gleam excitedly. 'An orgy?'"

More laughter and vodka follow.

"I've got one," Mother says. "'Mom, give me Dad's photo,' Vovochka asks. 'Why?' she replies. 'Because the teacher wants to see the idiot who did my homework.'"

A shot later, Father also tells one: "When six-year-old Vovochka comes back from school, his father asks, 'What did you think of the new teacher?' Vovochka rubs his chin. 'I liked her a lot. Too bad we have such a huge age difference.'"

Yet another round of shots.

The waiters come before anyone can tell any more jokes. They're carrying dessert. Specifically, the cake that's my dog's namesake: Napoleon.

Score. Now it's socially acceptable to leave.

Operation "Dragomir's Place" is back on.

# TWENTY-THREE

I STAND up to make our excuses, but Boris speaks up from the stage. "It's game time, ladies and gents."

Mother claps her hands, waves at Boris, and points at me and Dragomir.

Boris grins. "Looks like we have our first volunteers."

There goes our escape.

Everyone claps as Dragomir and I make our way to the now-cleared dance floor.

Handing me a glow-in-the-dark garter, Boris explains the game to us.

It's the Russian version of what Americans sometimes do at weddings: I'm to put the garter on my leg, and Dragomir's job is to remove it.

Yep.

Vodka is an important prerequisite to this game.

Before either of us can chicken out, the female dancers surround me, so I have the privacy to put the garter under my dress.

Sticking my leg into the stretchy fabric, I grin wickedly and hike up the garter as far as it will go. No reason to make Dragomir's job *too* easy.

The dancers guide me to sit in a chair.

Boris puts a blindfold on Dragomir. Nice touch. The host then leads Dragomir over to my chair and helps him get on all fours.

Yum. When we finally get to his place, I think I'll want to recreate this whole scenario. Having him taste me blindfolded might be hot.

Dragomir feels around blindly at first but soon discovers my ankle.

Oh my. Heat shoots up my leg from his touch. Then his fingers slide up—and up and up, until he's way up there, under my skirt.

I love this game.

I want to play it for hours.

Everyone around us cheers and hoots, reminding me that this is a public place, so none of my fantasies are about to come true.

Dragomir's fingers brush the inside of my thigh. Then, maybe on purpose, he misses the garter and ends up grasping my thong.

Okay. A little higher and to the left and—

Nope. He realizes his mistake and finally clutches the garter.

"No. Get it with your teeth!"

Did my *mother* just scream that?

"With your teeth," everyone chants. "Teeth, teeth!"

Grinning, Dragomir dives under my skirt.

I gulp in a breath.

His mouth is almost where I dreamed for it to be. I can feel his warm breath through my rapidly melting thong.

Did a soft moan just escape my lips?

To my huge disappointment, Dragomir moves away from my aching clit and grabs the stupid garter with his teeth.

He pulls.

The garter rips on my thigh.

Emerging from under my skirt, Dragomir stands up.

At the sight of the garter in his teeth, the spectators cheer wildly.

He takes off the blindfold and kisses my cheek.

The cheering is so deafening my head is starting to spin.

Letting out a shaky breath, I return to the table on unsteady legs.

"Bye, guys," Alex says, standing up. "I have a big day tomorrow, so I'm going to bolt."

Aha! Dessert has been served, and now Alex is leaving. That means it's completely and totally acceptable to proceed with Operation Dragomir's Place—which is good because I'm as close to bursting from horniness as a woman can get.

"Everyone," I say. "Dragomir and I also have to go."

Vlad kisses my cheeks, and Fanny smiles brightly and waves goodbye.

Mother walks over and gives me a bear hug.

Wait, what?

She hasn't done that in years.

Before I can recover, I get an even bigger surprise. Father not only gives me a hug but also says, "It was so nice to see you."

It must be *The Day After Tomorrow*-level chilly in hell.

Then my parental units' behavior becomes more fathomable.

Mother hugs Dragomir hard enough for him to feel some parts of her that he shouldn't, then slobbers on his cheeks, Winnie style.

As soon as she's done, Father gives my date a similar treatment.

I'm in such a daze as we finally escape that my steps are uneven.

When we pass by Boris, I rummage in my purse for cash, find a hundred bucks, and slip it into his pudgy hand. "Pick Vlad and his date for the next game," I whisper. "Make it the garter again."

Boris nods.

I dart my brother a snickering glance. I'm convinced that my place in his life is to push him to have more fun. And for today, that mission is accomplished. I just hope it's not physically possible to die from blushing. Otherwise, when Fanny goes through what I did on that chair, she just might expire on the spot.

Hey, they might name that type of death after her: the Fanny Pack syndrome. Poor girl. I still can't believe her parents named her Fanny when their last name is Pack.

Maybe mine *aren't* the worst.

"Your parents are sweethearts," Dragomir says as we clear the dance floor.

Is he psychic?

I hiccup. Sweethearts in front of him, maybe. "Mother would sell her soul to the devil for a grandkid as gorgeous as you."

Wait. Did I just say that out loud?

Crap. Like most guys, he's probably going to run at the mention of kids—and I can't have him run. I want to have my way with him.

To my shock, he just smirks. "Excuses, excuses. You're going to lose our bet. My parents are just as obsessed with grandchildren, but yours are still angels compared to them."

Grr. I keep losing competitions. Couldn't drink him under the table. Didn't beat him in *Beat Saber*—unless a black eye counts. And now I couldn't even prove that my parents are worse than his— though I guess in this case, I didn't try all that hard.

As we exit the restaurant, I feel a strange, unpleasant sensation in my stomach. If I didn't know how meticulous Mother is about fresh food ingredients, I'd guess I'd eaten something bad.

Dragomir waves his phone at me. "Fyodor tells me he's stuck in traffic. He thinks he could be here in ten minutes."

"Nah, let's just go now." I point at a cab that's already waiting by the sidewalk.

Dragomir agrees and we dive into it. He rattles out his address, pulls out a wad of cash, and hands the guy half of it. "Get us there quick, and you'll get the other half," he promises.

The cabbie nods solemnly and floors the gas.

As the car jerks forward, I feel a small bout of car sickness coming on, but I don't say anything. Getting to Dragomir's place swiftly is worth the discomfort.

Besides, I know just the thing to keep my mind occupied.

Pouncing on Dragomir, I kiss him. Hard.

His return kiss is scorching.

The cab and the world fall away. All that's left are those sensual lips and the strong, warm, lightly callused hands roaming my body.

After what feels like a minute of bliss, the car lurches to a screeching stop.

We're there already?

Time sure flies when you're on the verge of an orgasm.

Dragomir hands the rest of his cash to the driver and leads me into a swanky skyscraper. On the elevator ride, we kiss again—but it lasts only an eyeblink before we have to get out.

"Welcome to my place," he says as we step into a giant penthouse. Before I can so much as look around, a bear-like creature attacks— and slobbers all over my face. Again.

Yuck. Winnie's doggy breath is potent today. It makes me gag.

I must get cleaned up ASAP. Not only is my stomach rebelling at the smell, but Dragomir won't want to kiss me like this.

Done with me, the bear cockblocker slobbers on her master.

He takes out his wet wipes and offers one to me, but I shake my head. "Can I use a sink?"

With Winnie on our heels, he leads me through a living room where every shelf is covered with trophies.

Hmm. Each golden statue holds something vaguely phallic in its hand. Can you get a trophy in masturbation?

Nah, doubt it. If you could, I'd have Olympic gold by now.

"I'm into fencing," he says, following my gaze.

Fencing. Of course. That makes more sense.

"Hey now," I say, doing my best not to get too much dog drool into my mouth as I speak. "You cheated."

He quirks an eyebrow as we step into the kitchen.

"You had an edge in *Beat Saber* because you're good with a sword. Or rapier or whatever," I say as I step to the sink to wash off doggie cooties. My foundation and blush are already toast, but I do my best not to wash off my mascara. If I look like a raccoon, Winnie just might try to eat me.

She's already eyeing me with what could easily be hunger.

As I finish washing my face, he holds out a towel for me.

"Since when is being good at something considered cheating?" he asks as I dry myself.

"It just seems unsportsmanlike for a professional to play a novice like that. You're basically a *Beat Saber* hustler."

With a grin, he leans over the sink and also splashes some water on his face.

I use the opportunity to look around the kitchen for any pictures of a wife or girlfriend. Thankfully, there are none. However, there is a photo of him dressed in full fencing regalia.

Oh, boy.

I hadn't realized this before, but those protective outfits are tight. And what's worse, they look suspiciously like turtlenecks.

As soon as I make the connection, my ovaries kick into high gear. I clear my suddenly dry throat. "I need you to keep Winnie busy for the next few hours."

He straightens and dries his face, his eyes darkening as his gaze falls to my lips. "On it," he says huskily.

Reaching into the cupboard, he takes out what looks like a T-rex femur. He hands it to Winnie, crooning something in Ruskovian, and she begins to gnaw on the bone.

He nods at the kitchen exit.

I tiptoe past Winnie into the living room, and he follows.

Alone at last.

Moving with predatory grace, he closes the distance between us and kisses me once again.

The room feels like it's spinning.

Before I know it, I'm ripping off his clothes, and he's peeling off mine.

Finally.

This. Is. Happening.

Without breaking the kiss, he lifts me up. A moment later, my naked back is on the couch, and his eyes are roaming over my exposed skin.

Hey, unfair. He's still got his pants on—but his muscular torso is making up for that sin for now.

As I take in that gleaming, lightly tanned skin sprinkled with masculine dark hair, my mouth waters.

He leans over me. "Are you okay with this?" His voice is rough, his gaze filled with so much heat I shiver.

"Oh, yes. More than okay."

His face suddenly tightens. "We have to be careful. Don't want to follow in our dogs' footsteps."

I moisten my lips. "I'm on the pill."

His expression turns ravenous. "I'm clean."

"Me too," I say, and kiss him before he can waste more time on trivialities.

We dance the Lambada with our tongues.

He bites my lower lip.

I unzip his pants and snake my hand inside.

Everest is silky smooth to the touch, and hard like... well, a mountain.

Dragomir kisses my neck, then gives it a little nibble.

My skin pebbles all over.

His tongue journeys down my collar bone and over to my right nipple.

As I gasp, my hand tightens over Everest, and I begin to stroke up and down.

He groans with pleasure but pulls Everest away as he proceeds to lick his way down to my navel, traveling lower and lower until he's exactly where I want him.

Where I need him.

"Lie back," he commands hoarsely.

I'm all too happy to comply. Here and now, I will find out if he's the one.

When his warm breath touches my clit, I know without a shadow of a doubt that he is.

This is going to be amazing. Better than chocolate and puppies.

He gives my yearning clit the tiniest of licks.

I moan in pleasure.

He flattens his tongue and makes another contact.

Pleasure begins to coil in my core as another moan is wrenched from my lips.

His licks turn into kisses.

My hands fist in his hair. At this rate, I might scalp the poor man.

His kisses morph back into licks.

Letting go of his hair, I come with a cry. The pleasure is so intense that my toes curl spasmodically, and every muscle in my body twitches and shakes.

It's official. My three-year stretch of toy-only orgasms is over.

He looks up at me with pure male satisfaction, his eyes like molten gold.

Heart rate slowing a smidge, I wriggle out from under him. "Now you lie back."

He takes my place.

The room around us spins like a rollercoaster.

Odd. Must be the orgasm afterglow.

Steadying my hands, I rid Dragomir of his stupid pants, then free Everest from the briefs.

*Fuuuuuck.* Despite Xenia's warning about Ruskovians being well-endowed, and despite having felt it with my hands, I didn't expect Everest to be this huge... or this beautiful.

It calls to me in the way the namesake mountain must call to thrill-seekers the world over. I get why they risk their lives for that climb. Climbing *this* Everest is now on my bucket list—and climb it I will, if it's the last thing I do.

But first, let's see if it can fit into my mouth. It might be tricky, but I've never shied away from a challenge.

I start with a lollipop lick.

Dragomir groans, and Everest twitches under my tongue, urging me on.

Here we go.

Opening wide, I let in as much as I can.

Wait a second. I don't usually have a strong gag reflex, but something isn't right.

Something activates.

Uh-oh.

It's as though all the prior little issues—the maybe-bad food, the rocky car ride, the dog breath, and the room spinning—decide to come to the surface as one.

Oh my vodka gods. I was in denial about losing yet another contest to Dragomir.

*The drinking one.*

Dizzily, I extricate myself from Everest and rise up on wobbly legs.

Yep. I'm wasted. And what's worse, the contents of my stomach are rising.

"What's wrong?" Dragomir's face is tight with concern.

"Bathroom," I gasp. "Bathroom! Where is the bathroom?"

He leaps to his feet, but I'm too preoccupied to admire his glorious nakedness.

"Here." He hurries down a hallway and pushes open a door before facing me. "Are you okay?"

I can't answer, as that would require opening my mouth.

Instead, I save all my strength, all my focus on making it to the promised land that is that bathroom.

I do my best to sprint.

Since the vodka has long since decreased the energy consumption of my cerebellum to a snail crawl, my sprint ends with me bumping into the wall. Hard.

No. No. No.

The smack almost makes me cry out and thus open my mouth.

But I don't. Like a hero.

I must finish my epic quest to that bathroom. The stakes couldn't be any higher.

Utilizing every ounce of my willpower, I walk as fast and straight as is possible under the circumstances. If, besides masturbation, they gave out Olympic gold for walking under heavy influence, it would be in my pocket after this.

Skillfully not walking into Dragomir or the door he's still holding, I dive into the bathroom, drop to my knees, and violently pray to the vodka gods at the makeshift porcelain altar.

Strong hands hold back my hair, and soothing words are murmured above me.

I'm so embarrassed that if I could fall through the tiles into another apartment, I would.

This isn't only a prayer, it's a food offering as well—and I sure hope the vodka gods like boiled beets, potatoes, carrots, onions, sauerkraut, peas, and pickles.

Well, everyone knows they like their pickles, but I'm less sure about the rest.

Looking into the altar is a huge mistake.

Another prayer spews from my mouth, Exorcist style.

Then another.

At some point, I run out of spiritual fervor. Shaking, I flush and back away from the altar.

Unable to meet Dragomir's gaze, I wash my face, then grab the bottle of Listerine from the sink and chug it. Next, I take the tube of toothpaste, squirt some into my mouth, swirl it around, and swallow.

"You can never tell any Russians about this." My words come out slurred even to my ears. "They'll revoke my membership."

He gently envelops me in a bathrobe. "Let's get you dressed."

I let him lead me to the living room, where he helps me put on my clothes.

Winnie is here, and like Dragomir, she looks at me worriedly.

"I'm fine," I lie, but my words are even more slurred now.

"Why don't you lie down," he says.

"I want—" I hiccup. "Want to go home. Need a nap."

He frowns. "Wouldn't it be better if you stayed?"

I violently shake my head and feel another prayer coming on. "I'm going to take a cab."

"You are not."

This sounds like a statement of fact, so I don't argue, letting him lead me downstairs and into the already-waiting limo/RV.

"Lie down," he orders as soon as we get inside.

I do, grateful to be off my shaking legs, and he sits next to me and strokes my hair.

"That's nice," I mumble as my lids drift shut.

"Good. Relax."

I do as he says, and a moment later, I'm out.

# TWENTY-FOUR

I WAKE up in my bed and wish I didn't.

Never. Drinking. Again.

My headache has a migraine, and the taste in my mouth is against the Geneva convention.

How did I get here?

Did last night happen, or was it a cruel nightmare?

Given the smell of vodka in the air, it happened. I must've fallen asleep in the RV. But then what?

Did Dragomir bridal-carry me home?

That actually sounds kind of nice. I hope that's what happened, and not, say, that he and Fyodor carried me together by my arms and legs like a sack of fermented potatoes.

I peek under the covers.

No clothes.

Interesting. He also undressed me?

If so, no big deal. He saw me naked at his place anyway. It's also possible I undressed myself, but can't remember due to alcohol-induced amnesia.

Hmm. If I undressed myself, maybe I had my way with Dragomir as well?

But no. I'm pretty sure I'd remember that momentous of an occasion. Also, given Everest's girth, I'd feel some soreness, and I don't. Almost the opposite. There's a gnawing emptiness in my girly bits that probably won't go away *until* I get Everest in there—assuming that's possible after my faux pas last night.

With a groan, I sit up and slide my feet into the slippers someone left by the bed.

Boner rushes into the room, his tail wagging too fast for my addled brain to process.

"*Ma chérie*, you smell like the butt of a dog who ate fermented escargot in vodka sauce. *Délicieux*."

I stumble to my feet.

Hmm. My motor control seems to be back. That's a start.

When I reach the living room, the couch catches my attention. The pillows are not where my cleaning lady usually leaves them.

Did Dragomir sleep here?

It's possible. If our roles were reversed, I'd stay to make sure he didn't choke on his own prayer.

"Dragomir?"

No answer, but when I stumble into the kitchen, my theory is confirmed.

A pot of oatmeal is sitting on the stove, a glass of some strange liquid is sitting on the table, and my coffee pot is loaded and ready to go.

There's also a note on the table:

*Off to work. In the cup is a Ruskovian hangover cure. Drink it, and you'll be good as new.*

I down the miracle cure. It tastes like Pedialyte with pickle juice, milk, and cherry coke. Not sure how effective this is as a hangover cure, but if someone made me drink this every time, it would be a much better deterrent from drinking than a hangover alone.

By the time I'm done forcing oatmeal into my stomach, I remember what it's like to be human again.

Pouring myself a cup of coffee, I text Dragomir:

*Thanks for the breakfast. And bringing me home.*

His reply is instant:

*My pleasure. Do you have a second for a videocall?*

Leaving my coffee on the table, I sprint into the bathroom, apply makeup, and examine my face.

I'm not looking my best, but not my worst either.

*Sure,* I reply and plop back into the kitchen chair.

A videocall from Dragomir shows up right away.

I accept.

Behind him must be his office—and it's the size of some people's apartments, with several computer monitors occupying a gleaming white desk and a wall of bookcases displaying everything from economics textbooks to fencing trophies.

Piercing hazel eyes scan my face. "The *barabul'ka* must've worked. You're looking better already."

"*Barabul'ka?*" In Russian, that word means "striped red mullet." Which, despite sounding like the haircut of a ginger stripper from the eighties, is a type of fish, also known as a goatfish.

"*Barabul'ka* is the name of the cure," he says.

Was it actually fish broth then, or raw fish blended? On second thought, I don't think I want to know.

"Thanks again." I take a gulp of my coffee. "And sorry about last night."

He stretches back in his throne-like office chair. "Don't mention it."

I quirk an eyebrow. "Can't believe you're not rubbing in your victory. Wish I had that self-control."

His eyes gleam. "Bragging about out-drinking you would be like an opera singer boasting about clearing her throat."

Was that a dig? If so, I'll let it stand. "You have to let me do something for you as a thank-you for taking such good care of me."

I run my tongue over my lips in case my meaning isn't clear.

Mission accomplished. His gaze turns hungry and his body tenses, like he's about to pounce. "What did you have in mind?"

"How about you come over tonight?" I imbue the question with as much lasciviousness as I can. "I'll make you... dinner. I hope you come."

His voice roughens. "I will be there."

"Good," I say, then blow him an air kiss and hang up.

It's finally happening—and no vodka can stop us this time.

Giddy with excitement, I gulp down the rest of my coffee and rush into the bedroom to set things up for tonight. Clean sheets—check. Romantic music ready to go—check. Sex toys? Will skip for now.

I even set up some LED candles around the bed.

Now I need to go through with my pretext and cook us dinner.

What should I make? No clue, but I do know whom to ask. True, she cooks for dogs now, but she was a human chef before that.

I dial Xenia and bring her up to speed on my recent adventures, then tell her about my culinary dilemma.

"I know just the thing," she says enthusiastically. "Here are the ingredients you should incorporate into all the courses: artichokes, asparagus, avocado, coconut, dates, bananas, eggs, mango, mushrooms, okra, pistachios, sesame seeds, parsley, and celery. For the dessert, just mix walnuts with honey."

Is that four courses if you count dessert? I'm beginning to see why Boy Toy looks so jolly.

"Hon, that's a big list," I say. "Also, what dish can bananas and okra possibly share?"

"Who said they have to be the same dish? These ingredients are known aphrodisiacs from around the globe. For example, the French believe that artichokes warm the genitals."

"So do some STDs."

"Warm, not burn," she says, and I can hear her rolling her eyes through the phone. "Being Russian, you should know how potent walnuts with honey can be. Take one spoonful half an hour after dinner, and have him do the same."

Should I crush some Viagra into that dessert while I'm at it?

"Okay, Dr. Xenia. Now if you hook me up with some recipes to make out of all those things, I'll be golden."

She promises to do so and comes through in an hour.

I order my groceries online, and while I wait for the delivery, I walk Boner and work on some designs. When the groceries arrive, I begin cooking, even though it's too early for dinner.

If I end up with just two courses of edible food by the end of this, I'll consider the effort a success.

I'm in the middle of making a salsa with mango, avocado, and parsley when Dragomir texts me:

*Can I videocall you right now?*

I agree and rush out of the kitchen to make myself presentable. I barely make it, as he calls me just a minute later.

The moment his face pops up on my screen, I notice his grim expression and my heart sinks.

"I'm so sorry, but I have to bail on our dinner," he says tightly. "My brother has been in an accident."

# TWENTY-FIVE

"OH, NO! WHAT HAPPENED?"

He puts on a wireless headset. "Let me switch to phone mode so I can pack."

Pack?

He proceeds to tell me that one of his brothers is a huge adrenaline junkie who surfs in the most dangerous waters, snowboards the steepest cliffs, and so on. This time, he was base-jumping off the highest skyscraper in Moscow. Something went wrong and he hit his head, at which point he was helicoptered to Ruskovia by their family.

"He's in a coma." Dragomir's voice is filled with so much pain I wish I could reach through the electromagnetic signals to give him a hug. "I'm flying to Ruskovia tonight."

Tonight? I got so caught up in his story I momentarily forgot about our plans.

I rush into the kitchen and turn off the food before a fire starts.

"What about Winnie?" I ask. "Are you leaving her with Fyodor?"

"No. He's coming with me, and so is she."

"How? I mean, won't the airline have a fit?"

Did he convince them she's a service bear?

"I'm flying on a private jet," he says. "I'll do my best to make her comfortable—though, granted, she really dislikes flying."

"If you want, you can leave her with me," I hear myself saying.

"Thank you, but I couldn't possibly impose on you like that."

He doesn't sound completely certain, so I persist. "Is it even safe to fly in her condition?" I have no idea why I'm trying to persuade him to leave Winnie with me. I mean, a bear in my small apartment? Really?

Maybe I just want him to have a reason to keep in touch... a.k.a. retain a hostage.

"Stress isn't ideal during pregnancy," he admits. "But still, I can't ask you to do this."

"You're not asking. I'm volunteering."

He's silent for a moment. "You don't know what this would mean."

I'm pretty sure I do—and shoveling bear shit is probably part of it.

"If we do this, you have to let me pay for all her food," he says. "She's a big girl, and the expenses of feeding her might—"

"That's fine," I say, fighting the urge to comment on the understatement in the "big girl" comment. I can afford her food, no problem, but if it makes him feel better to provide it, I won't argue.

"I'll also pay a portion of your rent since—"

"Now you're talking crazy. Just bring a bag of food or whatever she needs. If I run out, I'll get more and invoice you when you get back."

"Thank you," he says with feeling. "You don't know how much this means to me."

Great. Now I feel guilty for my nice gesture's ulterior motive.

"When will you bring her here?" I ask.

"In an hour?"

I walk into my closet and look for a bag or a backpack that I haven't decorated with my penis art. "Works for me."

"See you soon," he says and hangs up.

Pocketing my phone, I grab an undecorated JanSport backpack and stuff it with a few choice toys from the teledildonics line Fanny and Vlad tested for me. These toys are meant for use by a man and would allow me and Dragomir to get intimate remotely—assuming I give him the backpack, which I'm not sure I should.

On the one hand, we'd be able to make each other come despite the sudden separation. It obviously won't be as fun as what we would've done tonight, but better than nothing. On the other hand, what if he somehow figures out my company makes these toys?

Then again, how would that happen? As Vlad said, the way Belka is set up makes it impossible to know I own it.

Maybe I'll make the decision when he arrives.

For now, I leave the backpack near the front door and pack some of the stuff I made for dinner in a to-go box for his plane ride.

I spend the next hour reading my email. Apparently, butt plugs in the shape of Woody Harrelson are trending. Does he have a new movie out or something? Well, at least it's not Liam Neeson. I don't know how I would've delivered that bit of news to Xenia.

My doorbell rings.

Boner sprints over there so fast he nearly skids headfirst into the door.

When I open it, the sight of Dragomir in a tight sweater and dark jeans makes my stomach flutter—but then a bear assaults my face with a bucket of saliva, putting a damper on my overactive libido.

"Stop it, Winnie." Dragomir drags her off me. "You're going to be staying with Bella, so you need to behave like a good dog."

He hands me a wet wipe.

"It's okay," I say after I'm drool free. "She *is* a good dog."

Oblivious to us, Winnie licks Boner next.

"*Bonjour, ma petite.* Your tongue is like the perfect strip of bacon, your drool like a heavenly bone marrow."

"*Zdrastvuyte*, Napoleon Carlovich. You're my favorite kind of dog muffin—stud. You make my puppy-filled ovaries swoon, and my ten nipples hard with yearning."

Hmm. This mental ventriloquism session has escalated quickly. There might be a bit of projection in there too.

"Winnie's things are in here," Dragomir says, wheeling in a huge suitcase.

I blink at the suitcase as he steps outside again and wheels in one more.

Two suitcases? For a dog?

When *I* go on vacation, I only take one—and smaller than either of those.

Misunderstanding my expression, Dragomir opens the suitcases and shows me that one is filled with dog toys, while the other contains a blanket, a bed, and bowls of appropriate sizes, along with some other items meant to keep a bear happy.

I arch my eyebrows. "Is that all of it?"

"Of course not," Dragomir says. He goes out again and drags in a bag of dog food that could easily fit a person my size inside of it—without them having to do any contortions.

Before I can comment on it, he carries the bag into the kitchen, fills up a giant bowl with its contents, and pours water into another equally sized bowl.

As though starved for years, Winnie attacks the chow.

And hey, she might be eating for ten, maybe even fifteen.

"You might want to feed Boner too," Dragomir says. "We don't want them getting jealous of each other."

Agreeing, I fill up Boner's bowls—which look comically small in comparison to Winnie's. As soon as Boner starts munching, Dragomir and I sneak away. We take Winnie's suitcases into the living room and spread her stuff around so that, to quote Dragomir, "she feels at home."

When he's done with the last of the toys, sadness flickers in his eyes—like he's missing Winnie already.

"She'll be okay," I say. "I'll make sure of it."

He steps closer to me, his expression shifting to something far more intense. "I'm officially in your debt."

My gaze cuts toward the bedroom, where everything is set for an epic encounter. "We'll have to figure out how you'll make it up to me."

He removes the distance between us in one step. "I have to run."

"Of course." I stare up at him, my heart pounding in my chest as he lays his hands on my shoulders and dips his head.

I rise on my tiptoes.

The kiss is less hungry than our prior ones. Instead, it's filled with tenderness—and it seems to make a promise.

A promise of more to come.

He reluctantly pulls away. "I'm sorry. I have to go."

"Of course. Go be with your brother." Did my voice just crack?

Nodding solemnly, he heads for the door.

Remembering the items I've prepped, I run after him. "Take this." I hand him the to-go box. "This was going to be our dinner tonight."

His eyes take on a warm glow. "Thank you. I'll get in touch as soon as I land and take stock of the situation."

Emboldened, I thrust the backpack with sex toys into his hands as well. "Take this too. But don't open it until you have a moment of privacy."

"Okay." He kisses me again—this time gently on the forehead— and steps out.

I close the door with a sigh. On autopilot, my feet carry me over to the living room where I plop on the couch, hold my knees to my chest, and put on *Frozen* for the thousandth time.

At some point, Winnie and Boner waltz into the living room.

Winnie grabs a rubber doughnut toy the size of a truck tire and cozies up next to me, taking up the rest of the couch. Boner joins us on my lap, and by the time the credits roll, I'm feeling better.

Since I'm not sure if Dragomir walked Winnie before bringing her over, I take both doggies for a walk—and though I usually wouldn't, I bring my phone with me, in case he calls from the plane.

When we enter the park, a familiar king poodle is walking toward us. I remember it because of the lion haircut. This dog was an asshole to Boner the other day.

Yep.

His memory not as sharp as mine, Boner tries to be friendly with the poodle again.

The poodle shows teeth and growls.

Despite being three times bigger, Winnie hides behind me with a whine.

"Pom-Pom, you're not being a nice lady," the poodle's owner says to her charge after I give them both a glare.

Boner's reaction today is nearly identical to the last time. Halting in his tracks, he looks at me with a befuddled look that seems to say, "*Ma chérie,* I thought that I—the stud—was *irrésistible* to bitches."

I pull him back before Pom-Pom can pounce. The snarling creature clearly has rabies.

When the poodle is out of sight, we resume walking, and since I have my phone, I call Xenia and tell her about my day.

"Hmm," she says when I'm done.

"Hmm what?"

"You'll call me a cynical Russian again."

"I'll call you worse if you don't spill it."

"Fine," she huffs. "How do we know there's a hurt brother in Ruskovia? What if he's going to visit his perfectly healthy wife or girlfriend?"

I squeeze the dog leashes in my hand.

She's talking about a Marco scenario, and I can't believe it didn't occur to me first.

"That doesn't make sense," I say, not sure whom I'm trying to convince. "He had the chance to sleep with me. Isn't that what cheaters want? If we'd done the deed and *then* he had to go, that would be a different story."

"Maybe he's a rare guy with a sense of conscience," she says, sounding less certain now. "When the cheating got close, he felt guilty and jumped on the plane to be with his significant other."

"And left his dog with me? Doesn't fully track."

At least I hope it doesn't. I wish I were as sure as I'm pretending to be.

Xenia sighs. "Maybe I *am* just being cynical. Still, if I were you, I'd keep my eyes and ears peeled when I speak with him."

My stomach feels cold and tight. "Can we talk about something else? What's it like being engaged?"

Xenia is happy to tell me all about her recent conversations with the people in her life and how all the Russians were surprised that a "woman her age" has found someone.

By the time we're done talking, I'm home.

Unleashing the dogs, I walk in and busy myself with VR suit design, then some emails from the marketing department—anything to keep my mind from jumping back to the specter that Xenia has raised.

The problem is, those sneaky thoughts ambush me when I finally get into bed. The sexy setup in this room is a huge Dragomir reminder.

The cold tension in my stomach returns with a vengeance, and as I toss and turn, I realize something.

I wasn't careful.

Somehow, I let my guard down and allowed Dragomir to slither in and wrap himself around my heart. Not that I'm in love with him —it's way too soon for that—but I definitely feel *something*.

Fuck. I'm such an idiot.

Was Xenia right? Could he have picked up on my budding crush, felt guilty about it, and decided to flee before things progressed further? Maybe he's one of those people who think sex means nothing, but if there are feelings involved, that's real cheating.

Any way you slice it, I'm glad he's giving me the space to think it over. It's a bad idea to feel anything beyond lust for him. Recused or not, he's still a potential investor in the project of my dreams, and like he said, business and emotions shouldn't mix. Sex and business aren't a great combo either, but at least that's more excusable.

The man was wearing a turtleneck the first time we met, for fuck's sake.

So is Xenia right? Or is she just being paranoid because she knows I tend to attract assholes? Does it even matter? Even if Dragomir is single, he's clearly hiding something about his past.

That should be a deal breaker in and of itself.

Maybe now that I've realized this, I can sleep.

Nope. Not happening, at least not without some aid.

Getting up, I trudge to the kitchen, nearly tripping over Winnie on the way. She's cuddled around Boner, who seems to be in seventh heaven.

When I finally reach the fridge, I gulp down a glass of milk in the hope that a food coma might help me drift off.

It doesn't work. Instead of sleep, I get heartburn.

Fine. I grab a sex toy at random, get back to bed, and attempt to orgasm myself to exhaustion. Unfortunately, my treacherous mind visualizes naked Dragomir every time I climax—without fail. Stupid mind.

It's not until the toy's low battery indicator starts blinking that I manage to drift off.

# TWENTY-SIX

AS I EAT my oatmeal the next morning, I watch my dog doing something peculiar. If I had to guess, I'd say he wants to hump Winnie. He's got that look I know well, the one he wears right before he attacks his sex toy, Remy. However, due to their size difference, he can't even come close to mounting the bear.

He just looks at her butt longingly and whines.

On her end, Winnie either doesn't understand what he wants or pretends not to.

"You've already knocked her up," I remind him.

"*Ma chérie*, what does that have to do with *sexe* time?"

"Touché." I resume eating.

As breakfast goes on, my theory is confirmed. Instead of eating the kibble I've set out for him, Boner stalks Winnie.

Ignoring him, she munches on her food.

With a huge effort, he jumps onto the kitchen chair. That puts him at almost the right height, except the chair is two feet away from the bear's butt, and she doesn't look willing to back into it.

Boner glances down, then at his goal, eyes calculating.

"Don't do it," I say. "You'll break your neck."

Ignoring me, he leaps—but overshoots and lands on Winnie's back.

She doesn't even stop eating.

He looks down, then at me.

"*Ma chérie*, help. *S'il vous plaît.*"

I grab him and set him down on the floor.

If he wants any other kind of help, it's not happening.

He trudges over to his bowl to drown his sorrows in food. Afterward, he humps Remy, but—and I might be imagining it—his usual enthusiasm is lacking.

I glance at my phone.

Nothing from Dragomir.

Wait, why am I even checking?

I dive into work and manage not to think of him too much for the rest of the day. At night, however, I can't fall asleep. It bothers me that there was no call or text from him.

He should've landed by now, I think.

WHEN I WAKE up after another troubled sleep, there's still nothing.

Is this it? Have I been ghosted?

No, that's not logical. I have his dog. But then why is he not calling or texting me?

Finally, a videocall from Dragomir shows up on my phone after lunch, ripping me away from a dildo design.

My finger slides to accept, and I quickly angle the phone to prevent him from seeing what I'm working on.

Familiar hazel eyes peer at me from the screen. Gorgeous eyes, despite how tired and sad they seem.

"Hi," he says, taking me in. "Sorry I didn't get a chance to get in touch earlier."

I look behind him. He seems to be in a living room with a large, expensive-looking rug on a wall behind him—which makes wall rugs another small way Ruskovia is similar to Russia.

"How is your brother?" I ask as my mind frantically tries to figure out what to do with my Xenia-inspired suspicions.

He looks pained. "He's in a coma. The doctors don't know when he'll wake up."

Shit.

He sounds so sincere.

"Where is he?" I ask.

"Here, at the hospital," Dragomir says.

Hospital? The background doesn't look like a hospital.

Wow. If he *is* lying, that's some very bad karma. But how can I tell?

He frowns, peering at me.

Is something of my doubts showing on my face?

"What's your brother's name?" I blurt.

Not very subtle, but hey. If he's making this up, he'll stumble and I'll catch it. Or if he gives me a name, I can pass it along to Vlad to help with his snooping—a win-win.

His frown deepens. "Is something wrong?"

Yeah, that wasn't such a good idea on my part.

"You're at the hospital now?" I ask, deciding to just go for it. "Right now?"

His eyes narrow. "That's what I said a moment ago."

"Then how come it looks like a living room?"

Has someone turned up the thermostat in my apartment? I'm starting to sweat like a pig at a Bikram yoga practice.

He looks at the fuzzy rug behind him, then turns back to face the camera. "It's a private hospital. Why not make the patients comfortable?"

"I guess..."

His kissable lips flatten. "Are you trying to say I'm not in a hospital, even though I'm telling you I am?"

I swallow the sudden lump in my throat. "A rug doesn't seem very hygienic."

If I could rewind time, I'd start this conversation over from scratch and take a different tack.

His gaze hardens. "Are you saying I'm misleading you?"

My stomach twists into knots, and the words spill from my lips of their own accord. "Look, I don't know much about you. When you left so suddenly, I started to wonder if—"

"Enough." He reaches for the phone and turns the camera to pan it around the room.

At first, my living room impression intensifies. I spot a large TV, plush furniture, and an ornate coffee table that belongs in a hospital even less than a rug does. But then a bed comes into view, and my chest tightens painfully at the sight.

It's a hospital bed, albeit the fanciest I've ever seen. Surrounding the bed are stands with what must be intravenous fluids and nutrients, a ventilator machine, a monitor displaying blood pressure and heart rate, and other dread-inducing medical equipment.

My stomach feels cold and hard, like the Siberian tundra.

All this equipment is attached to an unconscious Dragomir.

I gasp in a panicked breath and remind myself it can't be Dragomir. I just saw him a second ago. This dead ringer for him is his brother.

Oh God. His *brother*.

I'm such an asshole. I doubted him at one of the worst moments of his life. If one of my brothers—

No. Can't even finish that thought.

With a jerky motion, the phone pans back to Dragomir's face.

I feel an irrational moment of relief to have proof that it isn't Dragomir in that bed—but my relief is short-lived.

There can be no mistaking the scowl on his face. He's as disappointed in me as I am.

His voice is low and hard. "Satisfied now?"

"I'm so sorry. I shouldn't have—"

"Indeed," he says. "Now if you'll excuse me…"

He hangs up.

I gape at the black screen of my phone for a while.

At some point later, I pinch myself. Hard.

Nope. Not a bad dream. Unfortunately.

So… is this it? Is whatever was happening between us over?

I feel like dog poo—which reminds me of my furry charges.

Ignoring the heaviness in my chest, I make a sandwich, put leashes on the dogs, and go to the park.

"YOU RUSSKIES SURE LIKE THEM BEARS," John mutters as he takes in Winnie in all her fluffy hugeness.

I shrug and launch into a new story about why he needs to do me the favor of taking the sandwich off my hands.

Looking at me strangely, John takes the food. "Are you okay?" he asks gruffly.

How bad do I look that he's skipped his usual commie insults?

"I'm fine, thank you for asking."

"Well." He takes a bite of the sandwich and swallows it without chewing. "Thanks."

Thanks?

Wow.

Maybe I should play the lottery to get the funds I need for my venture. Between this, the hug from Mother, and that "nice to see you" from Father, I might just hit the jackpot.

"Bye, John," I mumble as I head back home.

On my way back, the lottery thoughts lead me down a chain of ruminations I wanted to avoid.

How badly have I messed things up with Dragomir? Besides never getting his body, have I also doomed my chances of getting the funding for my venture?

I guess time will tell.

A videocall is blasting on my phone when I enter my apartment.

Dogs in tow, I rush in.

As I grab the phone, I will it to be him, calling me back.

Seeing the name on the screen, I plop on the couch in relief.

The universe must've heard me.

It's Dragomir.

HEART HAMMERING, I pick up.

He looks tired but no less scrumptious.

I rein in my excitement. Most likely, he's about to make the arrangements for Winnie or something like that.

"I'm sorry I hung up earlier," he says.

Unleashing the dogs, I blink at him.

"A doctor came into the room," he continues. "I hope you understand."

He didn't hang up on me out of anger? Is the man angling for sainthood?

"I'm the one who's sorry," I blurt. "You're dealing with a tragedy. Obviously, you have no room in your life for my paranoia."

He sighs. "You did have a point. We don't know each other that well, and I realize that's partially my fault. My past here in Ruskovia is... well, I don't enjoy talking about it."

"It's not like we're officially together to justify any paranoia on my part," I say, then wish I hadn't because he stiffens at something in that statement.

Catching himself, he visibly chases away the tension and brings the phone a little closer to his face. "Tell me something... Is there more to your mistrust? Has someone hurt you?"

I swallow through the sudden thickness in my throat. "The last man I dated. He was married, and I didn't know that for the entire year that we were dating."

Dragomir's eyes widen, then narrow dangerously as a vein begins pulsing on his forehead. "He lied to you about it?"

I nod, feeling the hot burn of shame on my cheeks. To this day, I feel like such an idiot. "He was an investment banker at Goldman Sachs, a VP in their mergers & acquisitions department, so he worked crazy hours—or so he said. On my end, I was fresh out of college and busy starting my own career." Or rather, my own sex toy company, but I'm not ready to delve into that topic with Dragomir yet. "We only saw each other once, twice a week at most," I continue, doing my best to keep the bitterness out of my voice, "and almost never on the weekends. He'd always claim he had some urgent client meeting he needed to prepare for, and I'm sure his wife thought that the random weekday evenings and nights he spent with me were just the typical all-nighters at the office."

Dragomir barks something angrily in Ruskovian. It must be a curse word that my ex rightfully deserves, but it happens to sound a lot like something benign in Russian: *crapulence*—the sick feeling you get after drinking or eating too much.

Confirming my suspicion, he mutters "fucker" under his breath in English before looking back into the camera. "I swear on my brother's life that I do not have another woman," he says gravely. "Does that help?"

Another woman? Does that make me *the* woman in his life?

It must. I don't think he'd swear on his brother's life if he were lying. Not ever, but especially not under the circumstances.

"How is he? Did the doctor say anything?" I ask, glad to leave the topic of my ex.

Dragomir's expression darkens. "He explained that the coma was medically induced. The hope is that it will protect his brain from further swelling."

My chest fills with a squeezing ache. "I'm so sorry. I don't even know what to say."

"I can't blame you. I don't know what to say on the subject either." His eyes seem more brown than hazel in this light. "The worst part about this is that I'm so furious with Tigger. What kind of a brother does that make me?"

The brother's name is Tigger? Sounds more like a nickname, but I file it away anyway before giving Dragomir a reassuring smile. "A human one. If my brothers had even thought about base-jumping from a skyscraper, let alone done it, I'd be livid. And if they'd hurt themselves doing it, I'd probably finish them off myself."

The barest hint of a smile touches his eyes. "I can easily imagine that."

"So can they, I bet—which is why there won't be any Chortskys base-jumping any time soon."

Dragomir nods, then says quietly, "Tigger was always a daredevil, even when we were kids. Whenever any mischief happened in the household, our parents would interrogate him first." His gaze turns distant. "There was this one time when he stole a World War II grenade from a museum and tossed it into a bonfire that he started next to Mother's favorite gazebo. I don't know how he managed to survive, but the gazebo and half the gardens didn't. Our parents hired him a personal nanny after that incident, but he drove her to quit— and five nannies after that."

Wow. And my parents complain about *my* brothers being troublemakers as kids.

"Brothers can be trouble," I say. "When I was six, mine took me with them to Coney Island. I was tall for my age, so they let me ride the Cyclone—a rickety, extremely scary rollercoaster. When we went swimming after, I was so dizzy I nearly drowned and needed mouth-to-mouth from a lifeguard."

He frowns, as if worried about my childhood self, then shakes his head disapprovingly. "At least they seem protective of you *now*."

"They were always protective of me. It's just that when that incident happened, they were too young to make good decisions—which basically means their protectiveness manifested itself in beating up any bullies who dared pull my pigtails."

"I still say you had it easy with just two brothers to worry about. Imagine nine."

"Wait." I look at him for any sign that he's joking. "All your siblings are male?"

"That they are. It's a source of great pride for Father to have sired so many sons." This last bit is said with distaste.

I whistle. "That's got to be a statistical anomaly. Your poor mother. How did she handle so much testosterone under one roof?"

He rolls his eyes. "Mother never got her hands dirty—that's what the servants were for."

Servants? I recall his mention of his mother's gazebo and the gardens. His family sounds more than merely well off. Just goes to show how true the whole "money doesn't buy happiness" cliché is. He looks distinctly unhappy reminiscing about it all.

"A nanny might've been better than my mom's mothering," I say, unsure if that's going to sound consoling or not.

He scoffs. "Your parents are angels compared to mine."

That competition again? Does he never let up? "They just acted nice around you. They're no angels."

His eyes tighten. "Mine have officially disinherited me. Tigger too. Have yours done that to any of their children?"

I shift uncomfortably in my seat. "No."

"Could they?"

I shrug. "They disapprove of the choices I've made and have let me know it. I'm not sure if they plan to make their displeasure *that* official, though."

A smirk appears on his lips. "So you admit defeat for a change."

"I admit no such thing. Until and unless I meet your allegedly hellish parents, I will not believe they're as bad as you claim."

Then again, do I really want to meet them anymore? Maybe it's better to just give him this one.

The smirk disappears. "They *are* as bad as I claim."

I wish he were here so I could hug him and take at least some of his pain away. "What did you do to piss them off?"

"I wanted to be independent." I've never heard someone channel so much bitterness into five words before. "After college, I handled their investments, but when I made enough capital to strike out on my own, I did just that, and they disapproved."

"That's it?"

Even his sigh sounds bitter. "They like nothing more than getting their way."

So they disapprove of him for basically starting a business. We have that in common—though I'm not going to mention it because I'm not ready for the sex toy company conversation.

"What about Tigger?" I ask. "What's their problem with him? His adventures?"

Dragomir's nostrils flare. "They call it his 'unbecoming behavior.' I suspect that when he comes out of the coma, their first words will be 'we told you so.'"

Hmm. Maybe his parents *are* worse than mine.

He yawns, reminding me of how tired he looked when he called.

"When was the last time you slept?" The question comes out more demanding than I intended.

"Back in New York," he says, suppressing another yawn.

"You should go to bed. You're sleep-deprived and jet-lagged. If Tigger were to wake up, you'd be useless to him in this state."

His faint smile returns. "You're wise beyond your years. Have I told you that?"

"You didn't have to. Now go."

"Thank you," he says and stares at me with a strangely intent expression.

I swallow audibly. Why do I suddenly feel like a fly who got stuck in amber?

"Call me when you wake up?" I manage to say.

"It's a date," he says and hangs up.

I get up from the couch and stumble over to my computer.

Woody butt plugs are still trending.

Alrighty then.

For a while, I busy myself with designing a clit suction device.

If the goal was to forget Dragomir, I'm not sure how much success I can claim. Now that I'm done, I realize the design looks suspiciously like his lips.

Xenia calls me, so I fill her in on everything.

"Sounds like he really doesn't have a side piece," she says when I'm done. "I'm sorry I got you so paranoid."

"You don't need to apologize. I have my own head on my shoulders." And my own baggage predisposing me to distrust men.

We chat some more, then she asks me to keep her posted on Tigger's recovery and hangs up.

I check on my fluffy companions and catch Boner on the kitchen chair again. I think he's waiting for Winnie to come drink so he can try to hump her from the proper height.

"I'd hump Remy if I were you," I tell him.

"*Ma chérie*, how can you compare my baby *maman* to mere *maîtresse?*"

I make myself a turkey sandwich while keeping an eye on him. As expected, Winnie comes to drink but positions her butt so Boner can't even hope to make the jump.

Clever bear.

Looking dejected, Boner jumps off the chair.

Aww. If it weren't for Remy, I'd say my dog is living in a version of male hell—a sexy female in front of him but always just outside his reach. Then again, theirs is the sexual setup of many marriages, so maybe calling it hell is an exaggeration.

Taking the sandwich to the living room, I turn on Netflix and browse through the offerings. Hmm. Should I watch something with Woody Harrelson—in honor of our bestselling product?

I wonder if he's worn a turtleneck in any of his films.

As soon as my movie is chosen, I start to bite into my sandwich, but my teeth click in empty air.

I gape at my sandwich-less hand.

What the hell? Can you get memory gaps from being too horny?

A whiff of dog breath clues me in, and I look behind me.

Yep.

Eyes completely guileless and muzzle covered in crumbs, Winnie is chewing on what appear to be the remnants of my sandwich.

How did she get it so stealthily? If I could teach her to do that with jewelry, we could be world-renowned thieves.

"Bitchy move, stealing my food," I say sternly. "Besides, haven't you already eaten a tub of dog food today?"

"Tsk, tsk, Bella Borisovna. Appetite shaming a pregnant female?"

I head to the kitchen, stick another piece of turkey between two slices of toasted bread, and give the doggies some food of their own, so they're also occupied with eating—a surefire way to keep my next sandwich safe.

After the movie and a shower, I put on my PJs and finally get to bed—but not to sleep. First, I want to relieve my pent-up urges with the help of a vibrator from our teledildonics line. The fantasy I have in mind is that Dragomir is operating it remotely, controlling my orgasms from Ruskovia.

I get the brand-new vibrator out of the box and prepare to link it with my phone.

Insanely pink, this toy is made out of a special material that I recently invented. It feels squishy and reminiscent of *kholodetz*—

though no pig snout, pig ears, chicken feet, or beef tails were involved in the making of this vibrator.

In fact, no animals are ever harmed in the making of Belka toys. We don't test anything on animals... unless Vlad and Fanny count.

Unlocking my phone, I search for the Belka app Vlad wrote, one with controls for the toy.

Suddenly, a videocall shows up on my screen.

My heart leaps into my throat.

Have I already fallen asleep and am dreaming?

Once again, it's Dragomir.

# TWENTY-EIGHT

POSITIONING myself so Dragomir can't see the sex toy on my bed, I accept the call.

Behind him is a posh bedroom that must be a penthouse in some hotel. He's sitting in a chair dressed in nothing but a robe, which allows me to salivate at the sight of the firm groove between his pectoral muscles.

His hazel eyes are beyond red and irritated—the eyes of a prisoner undergoing the enhanced interrogation technique that is sleep deprivation. Yet when he sees me, his lips curve in a smile that makes me feel as if I've swallowed sunshine.

"Hi, *squirrelchik*," he says. "You miss me yet?"

My answering grin is goofy. "Did you just call me a squirrel chick?"

He takes on a professorial tone. "The Russian diminutive for Bella is Belochka, which is also the word for a squirrel. Besides the suffix 'chka,' another way to make a diminutive, especially in Ruskovian, is 'chik.' But since you're pretty much an American, I switched it to English and got *squirrelchik*."

I playfully roll my eyes. "Did you just mansplain my pet name to me?"

"Sorry," he says ruefully. "I should've realized you'd understand how I came up with that. You're smarter than I am. And obviously better at Russian."

"And don't you forget it. But more importantly, don't you think the moniker makes me sound a little squirrelly?"

His smile widens. "I can call you *kiska*."

"That's pussy. You know that, right?"

His left eyebrow rises. "It means *little kitty*."

"Female kitty," I say. "Trust me, I'd rather be the squirrel chick—assuming that, in exchange, I can give you a pet name as well."

He cocks his head. "That would depend."

"*Drakonchik*," I say. Parroting his earlier professorial tone, I explain, "Dragomir sounds close enough to 'dragon,' and the diminutive version of that, in Russian, is *drakonchik*."

He frowns. "It also sounds like Dr. A. Konchik. Doesn't *konchik* mean the tip of a penis in Russian?"

"No," I say, doing my best to keep a straight face. "It's a generic word for tip, like that of a pencil, pen, and so forth. But if you prefer, I *can* call you Dr. Tip."

"No, thanks, *drakonchik* is fine."

"Then it's a deal. Now tell me why you're not asleep."

He shrugs, the weariness returning to his face. "I tried. Couldn't."

"That sucks. I hate it when that happens."

A smirk appears on his lips. "It's not *all* bad."

My breathing speeds up. I think I know where this is going.

"When I tired of lying in bed, I ended up looking for something to do, so I opened the backpack you gave me." He turns the camera to show me the sex toys sprawled all over his bed.

Yep. As I thought. But could this actually—

"So, squirrelchik." His smirk turns downright wicked. "Care to explain this?"

# TWENTY-NINE

DOES he think he can rattle me with the sight of sex toys? Me, the woman who's designed all of them? Or—dare I hope—is my earlier fantasy about to become reality?

I take in a deep breath. "Those are teledildonics toys. 'Tele' is Greek for 'far,' and the dildo part is self-explanatory." I dart a look at the crotch region of his robe. Though it might be my wishful thinking, I think I spot a glimpse of Everest there, tenting the white cloth.

Dragomir's gaze turns a brighter shade of amber, the earlier weariness gone without a trace. "You want to use one of those on me?"

I raise an eyebrow salaciously. "Yes, but you don't get to have all the fun." Turning the camera, I show him the pink vibrator on my bed. "This is a toy that works under the same principle as the ones you have. With the right app, you can do to me what I plan to do to you."

He brings the phone closer to his face. Based on his expression, I half expect him to bite off a chunk of the screen.

"Okay, then," he growls. "Strip."

Wow. It's *on*. Donkey Kong kind of on.

I take off my tank top, exposing my breasts.

His eyes widen.

Turning my back to him, I stick my butt out and slowly push down my pajama shorts.

His phone nearly falls out of his hand.

I turn around and, as seductively as I can, remove my panties.

I've never done this before, stripping in front of a camera. Who knew it would get me so hot? My nipples are hard, and my clit is throbbing—and the best is yet to come.

"Fuck." Dragomir's grunt sounds pained. "You're perfect."

I teasingly move the camera closer to my face, temporarily hiding my body. "Now it's your turn."

He secures his phone on a nightstand, steps away so I can see his whole body, and drops the robe.

My mind—and more private parts—are officially blown.

Again.

The light in his room highlights every groove in his powerful, gorgeously defined muscles, making me want to lick the screen, touch myself, and maybe fly to Ruskovia.

Yeah, definitely the latter. Teleporting would be even better. The man is ovary dynamite—and Everest is particularly tantalizing. It juts out mountainously at the phone camera, stealing the spotlight with ease.

Does Dragomir have some smart zoom feature on his phone that makes it look even bigger? Or was it that big when it was going into my mouth the other day? How did I not dislocate my jaw?

"Now what?" he asks raggedly.

"Put that on." Finger trembling with anticipation, I point at the extra-large cock ring on his bed. "I'll be controlling the vibration."

As he turns to pick up the toy, I get a view of his tight glutes and muscled thighs—and my arousal spikes another notch.

Someone should build me a statue for the noble sacrifice of letting him be the first to come.

He turns back, cock ring in hand.

I gape as he slides it over Everest.

It's official.

This is the most sexually charged encounter of my life.

The snug ring makes Everest bulge, veins popping up all over.

Would he mind if I started playing with myself?

No. More fun to focus on him first.

Still, resisting the urge is hard. There's something about jewelry and other small accessories that makes nudity even more pronounced.

Clearing my throat, I launch the Belka app on my phone and quickly walk Dragomir through the process of having my phone be in control of his ring.

Once all is set, I click the prerequisite button on my end, and Everest begins to vibrate—as though affected by an earthquake.

Dragomir's face goes taut, and his mercurial eyes darken with heat.

I up the speed of the vibration a little bit.

Impossibly, Everest looks even more huge and engorged.

Smiling mischievously, I crank the speed to seventy percent.

A dark flush paints his high cheekbones.

Eighty percent.

He groans, his hands balling into fists.

I wait a few moments, then crank up the ring to full power.

Dragomir groans louder, and Everest erupts.

Holy volcanoes. I think I should've nicknamed that thing Vesuvius instead of Everest.

Cum shoots out in a torrent, landing everywhere, including on the phone's camera—which gives his room a washed-out look.

Damn. Maybe we should have used the sleeve? That way, the eruption would've been contained.

I stop the vibration.

Dragomir slides the ring off, then grabs a few tissues and cleans up the mess. Repositioning the camera, he fixes me with a hungry stare. "Your turn."

Finally.

We quickly link my vibrator to the app on his end, then I slide back on the bed.

"Ready?" he growls.

I touch the vibrator to my clit. "Yes."

Eyes roaming over me, he starts the vibration.

Fuuuuuck. It feels amazing—a hundred times better because he's in control. Masturbation has this in common with tickling—doing it to yourself is substantially different from having someone do it to you.

With a look of purely male satisfaction, he ups the intensity.

A moan escapes my lips.

Though my vision is blurry, I see Everest rise again—which turns me on impossibly more.

"That's it, squirrelchik," he breathes. "Come for me."

I'm about to oblige him—but then his eyes narrow at something behind me, and he shouts in Ruskovian.

My budding orgasm recedes.

What the hell?

Two things happen at the same time.

My nose detects the smell of doggie breath, and Winnie steals the vibrator from my hands with the same ninja skill she'd used on my sandwich.

"Hey!" I shout. "Give that back."

Tail wagging, the bear bolts out of the room.

"Make sure she doesn't swallow that!" I hear Dragomir yell as I leap up in pursuit.

Right. This is the second time she's gotten ahold of a toy covered in my lady juices—and the third toy overall.

I sprint after her.

She vaults over my coffee table with ease, and wags her tail at me, eyes as guileless as usual.

"This is not a game," I warn sternly as I give chase.

She flees, and if her mouth weren't occupied—and more importantly, if dogs could speak—I bet she'd say, "If it's not a game, why is it so fun, Bella Borisovna?"

Since I'm human, and hopefully smarter, I use strategy and eventually corner her in the kitchen.

Boner looks at us, head cocked.

Ugh. I'd better keep the toys hidden going forward. He no doubt wants to play this game now too.

With great effort, I extract the vibrator from Winnie's drooling maw.

She looks longingly at the pink object.

"I'll make you a pink toy that's dog appropriate," I tell her. "But not this."

Boner whines.

"I'll make one for you too."

Winnie still looks sad, so I bribe her with a bacon-flavored cookie, which cheers her up.

Tossing the chewed-up vibrator into the garbage, I wash my hands, return to the bedroom, lock the door, and reassure Dragomir that she didn't swallow the toy.

"You want to keep going?" he asks.

Does the bear shit in the woods—or steal sex toys?

"Oh, yes."

His answering smile does something indecent to my insides. "Do you have another teledildonics toy?"

I do, but I'm not sure if I should admit it. I don't know how many toys it would take before he starts to suspect I make them myself. Also, now that I'm staring at his nakedness, I want to get myself off ASAP—not hunt down a box, open it, set it up with the app, et cetera.

Pasting on a naughty grin, I slowly slide my hand down my stomach. "How about something more low-tech?"

Everest twitches approvingly. "Yes, squirrelchik." Dragomir's voice lowers an octave. "Make yourself come for me."

"And I want you to do the same for me," I murmur, moving my fingers up and down my aching clit.

He fists Everest.

The orgasm that I was denied earlier returns in a heartbeat—and pleasure explodes through my nerve endings with all the intensity of a nuclear blast.

I moan his name.

He grunts in pleasure.

When my breathing evens out, I catch him looking at me with a peculiar intensity. Like he's lost in a desert and I'm a lime-cucumber Gatorade.

"I think I need a shower," I say, my voice slightly hoarse.

He blinks, and the look fades, replaced by another indecently sexy smile. "Of course. I could use one as well. Sleep well tonight, squirrelchik."

"You too."

I wait for him to hang up, but he doesn't. He just looks at me, and I catch a hint of that disconcerting intensity in his eyes again—that strange longing that both buoys and unsettles me.

"Go ahead. Hang up," I say.

His lips quirk. "You hang up."

"No, you."

"You first."

Okay, it's official. I *am* back in high school.

Grinning, I wave at the camera and hang up.

# THIRTY

AS I FINISH breakfast the next morning, Winnie walks up to me and makes a strange whining sound.

Wait a second.

I've heard that before.

Leaping to my feet, I leash both dogs and zoom outside.

As soon as we're out of the building, I look around to make sure there aren't frail-looking old people around. I don't want them to get heart attacks.

The coast is clear, so I look at Winnie and say, "Kraken."

THPPTPHTPHPHHPH.

I launch into a sprint, both dogs in tow, hoping to outrun the smell, but the fart coming out of Winnie's butt keeps on going and going.

When we stop at a red light, Boner shoots Winnie what must be an impressed look. I bet he'd sell his soul to be able to pass even ten percent of that much gas.

At least the wind blowing in my face takes the majority of the fumes away. Even so, it feels like we're walking through a horrific graveyard where sick eggs and cabbage come to die.

"Thanks for the warning," I tell Winnie when we've traveled far enough away from the stench. "If you'd done that in the apartment, I'd have to move—and I'd lose my security deposit for sure."

Winnie doesn't hear me. Her attention is on something to the side.

I follow her gaze and freeze.

It's a black cat about to cross our path, and there's no one nearby to break the curse, so I'll have to turn back like an idiot.

As usual, Boner pretends the cat doesn't exist—which is fair. This cat to him is what a lion would be to me. Then again, if a lion turned up in Central Park, I'm not sure I'd act like he didn't exist.

Spotting Winnie, the cat arches its back and hisses.

Whimpering, Winnie rushes to hide behind me.

The cat stops hissing, turns back, and runs for its life—no doubt thinking, *That bear bitch is acting crazy. Safer to stay away.*

Whew. Bad juju averted, we walk on—that is, until I see Pom-Pom, our enemy poodle, running at me all by herself.

Crap. The owner must've dropped the leash, and the beast is now roaming free.

Stupid black cat must've brought this on, after all.

Winnie is behind me before I can even blink.

Oblivious to his past interactions with the evil poodle, Boner wags his tail.

Pom-Pom snarls and speeds up in our direction.

My heart drums frantically as I pull Boner back. I don't know what to do. Even if I pick him up, we could be in trouble. Despite their goofy appearance, king poodles are big dogs, able to hurt not just Boner but me as well.

Boner must finally realize the danger. He tucks his tail between his legs and whines, loudly.

Encouraged, Pom-Pom lunges toward us.

I scoop up Boner and prepare to fight for our lives.

The curly-haired beast is almost within biting distance.

Suddenly, a blood-chilling growl vibrates the air.

It's what a hellhound would sound like if you really, really pissed it off.

At first, I think the horrific sound is coming out of Pom-Pom.

But no.

Pom-Pom halts in her tracks, eyes widening.

I do a double take.

Winnie is no longer hiding behind me. She's put herself between us and the attacking dog, and as hard as it is to believe, the growling is coming out of her maw.

Actually, given that whole "rid Ruskovia of wolves" bit, maybe it's *not* so hard to believe. Winnie's whole demeanor has changed from cute and cuddly to crap-your-pants feral. In this, she's a lot like a bear too—they look cute, but can be deadly scary if you get on their bad side.

And that's what *this* is.

Winnie has just gone mama bear on this poodle's shaved ass, protecting me and Boner.

"Step any closer, and I let go of her leash," I tell Pom-Pom triumphantly.

The poodle isn't suicidally stupid. Turning on her heel, she tucks her tail between her legs and sprints away—right into the arms of her panting owner.

Exhaling in relief, I set Boner down on the ground.

Back to looking like a sweetheart, Winnie licks Boner's face and resumes walking like nothing has happened.

---

BACK HOME, I'm disappointed not to find any messages from Dragomir on my phone. There is, however, a missed call from my mother—which is worrying. She almost never calls me, preferring to send family event invites as Facebook messages.

Has something happened?

I remember the black cat, and my breath speeds up. Swiftly, I call her back.

"Hi, honey," she says, picking up. "How are you?"

*Honey? How are you?*

Who is this, and what has she done with my real mother?

"I'm fine, Mom," I say cautiously. "Is something wrong?"

"Of course not. I just realized I haven't spoken to you in a while."

Understatement much?

"I'm good," I say. "How are you?"

"Great, great. How's Dragomir? How are things between you two?"

Ah. Things click into place. This call is an investment in the "hold a cute grandchild" project.

"Dragomir isn't so good," I say and tell her about Tigger's accident.

"That's horrible," she says with genuine feeling. "Tell him and his parents that I wish Tigger a speedy recovery."

"Sure." And I will—if I ever meet his parents.

"You know," she says, "I have a great remedy that they should try."

Oh, boy. Mother's remedies can be out there, even for Russians. And for some reason, they're very urine-oriented. I once had to pee on her leg when she got a rash, and there was that time when Alex got the stomach flu and she managed to convince him to *drink* urine— but at least it was *his* urine that time.

"I'm sure the doctors know what they're doing," I say.

If I tell Dragomir to pee on his brother, I don't think he'd get it. He might even think I'm into golden showers, which I'm not.

"What's the harm in trying my poultice?" Mother asks.

"Depends on the poultice..."

If it's raw lamb meat, like her acne remedy, he could get E. coli poisoning or worse.

"Have a nineteen-year-old virgin girl chew up a pound of cabbage, two onions, five cloves of garlic, and a stalk of parsley. Warm the poultice to body temperature and cover as much of Tigger's skin as possible for a few hours."

Virgin? How would that help, medicinally? Do hymens help girls produce some magic enzymes in their saliva? Also, why does this remedy sound like a recipe for a human dumpling—sans flour?

Hey, at least the virgin doesn't need to pee on anyone. That's a first.

"I'll pass this on to Dragomir," I lie. "Thanks."

"You're welcome. Now go and call him, so they can get a head start. It can be hard to find virgins these days."

Was that a dig at me for losing my virginity at eighteen, or a complaint about the morals of millennials?

"Sure," I say. "Thanks, Mom. Bye."

I hang up but don't call Dragomir. He might be sleeping off his jet lag. Instead, I check my email.

Interesting. Alex tells me we have a meeting with Marco and his people next week—I was wondering if he'd left for Ruskovia with Dragomir.

I make a note of the meeting on my calendar and throw myself into suit design, only stopping to feed the dogs and myself.

When my brain begins to hurt from the work, I get up and prepare the bedroom in case Dragomir calls me again.

Instead of a vibrator, I unbox a clit suction gizmo and lay it on the bed. Next, I put on my sexiest bra and panties, and slip into a cute dress.

Just as I'm about to go watch some Netflix to kill the time, my phone rings.

Can it be?

I grab the phone.

Yes!

A videocall from Dragomir.

# THIRTY-ONE

HE'S in that penthouse-like bedroom again, looking much better rested—and proportionally more delicious.

"Hi, squirrelchik."

"Hi, drakonchik," I reply with a grin. "How did you sleep?"

He returns my smile. "Very well. Thanks for tucking me in."

"It was my pleasure. Literally. How is your brother?"

The smile disappears. "Same. The doctors are of no help. He might come out of the coma today, tomorrow, or in a few weeks—they really don't know."

"That sucks." I sit on my bed. "Let me know if I can do anything to help." Besides sparing him Mother's remedy.

He also sits on his bed. "You're doing it already. Speaking with you gets my mind off things."

I feel so fluttery it's a marvel I don't float to the ceiling. "In that case, call me any time, day or night, whenever you want to talk."

"I might just take you up on that. Especially since I'm still on New York time."

"Isn't the time difference huge?" I ask.

He nods. "Ten hours."

"You should probably start getting used to local time. It's not good for your circadian rhythm to sleep during the day and walk around at night, like a vampire."

He sighs. "I guess I can be superstitious myself. I can't help but feel that if I shift to the Ruskovian time zone, it'll be like accepting that Tigger isn't going to recover any time soon—and thus bring it about."

Not for the first time, I wish I could reach out and hug him through the internet. Once my VR suit is complete, hugging at a distance will definitely be one of the applications. As is, I have to try some other means of cheering him up.

"Tell me something about Tigger," I say softly. "Some pleasant memory."

Dragomir's mouth curves slightly. "Well, for a start, he was almost always the striker on our football team. He scored more goals than I could count."

Goals? Aren't they called touchdowns?

I raise an eyebrow. "You sure you mean football?"

"Ah. Sorry. I meant soccer, of course. My father's dream was to have enough sons for a soccer team. He got his wish: with the exception of the goalie who was a cousin, my brothers and I made up the team. For a while anyway."

He proceeds to tell me about their athletic adventures, and it seems to lift his spirits—especially when he talks about the time they managed to defeat a semi-professional team from Russia.

As I listen, I again get the sense that his family is enormously wealthy. The soccer field in the stories was "theirs," their coach sounds professional, and that team for the critical game was flown in from Russia.

"What about you?" he asks. "Did you and your brothers play sports?"

I shake my head. "The closest we got was playing hockey on the Xbox. In general, we played a lot of competitive video games, anything from fighting to racing. I think that's how Alex got his passion for game design."

He smiles. "Is that how you learned to be so competitive?"

I grin. "Doubt it. I beat them effortlessly in pretty much every game." I wiggle my nimble fingers. "I have above-average hand-eye coordination and outstanding reaction time."

His smile widens. "Don't forget your above-average, super-amazing humility. I doubt anyone can compete with that."

"Well, yeah. And here you thought I was just the sexiest woman you've ever met. I'm not—I'm also the most humble."

Heat glimmers in his eyes. "I probably shouldn't encourage you, but you really *are* the sexiest."

I bat my eyelashes at him. "Right back at you—and I'm not sure you realize it, but you've just opened a Pandora's box."

He cocks his head. "You want to know about the women I've dated?"

"I've told you about my ex. It's only fair."

He must agree because he says, "Not much to tell on my end. There weren't that many women in my life, and none of those relationships were serious—with the exception of my last one." His face darkens. "She worked at my parents' fund, and when I lost my inheritance, I lost her too." He clears his throat. "It's for the best, really. She was clearly interested in the wrong things."

Yeah—and her loss is my huge gain.

He brings his phone closer to his face. "Now you have to tell me something personal. It's only fair."

"*Frozen*," I blurt after racking my brain for something to share besides the fact that I own a sex toy company. "It's my favorite movie."

He takes this a lot more seriously than I would've if our roles were reversed.

"I can easily believe that," he says. "It's a story about rebellion and self-actualization, isn't it?"

I pretend to be shocked. "You've never seen *Frozen*?"

He looks genuinely chastened. "I've heard the song. Does that count?"

"No, it doesn't," I say with mock grumpiness. "You now have a homework assignment. You have to watch it."

He nods—either still taking me at face value or acting at Oscar levels. "Consider it on my to-do list."

"You'll thank me later," I say. "What about you? What's your favorite movie?"

He rubs his chin. "It's hard to pick a favorite, but one I rewatch the most is *The Princess Bride*."

"Inconceivable!" I say with a grin. "Actually, it's very easy to conceive. It's got all that fencing, not to mention Robin Wright as Buttercup. She's one of my favorite actresses."

He raises his eyebrows. "She is?"

"Have you seen her as General Antiope in *Wonder Woman*? Or Claire Underwood in *House of Cards*?"

"I have and she's great. But she's not the reason I like that movie—and neither is fencing. I like the messages in it."

I frown. "It's got messages?"

"Yeah, sure. Such as 'life's not fair.'"

I nod. There is that.

"More importantly"—he gives me a meaningful look—"it teaches that good things happen to those who wait."

I blink at him.

Is he talking about his lack of serious relationships? Am I the good thing that's happened to him after he's patiently waited? If so, I think he's just compared the act of meeting me to Inigo Montoya getting bloody revenge on his father's killer—yet I still feel warm and fuzzy.

Since I don't feel comfortable asking him to clarify, I instead inquire about what kind of music he likes.

Turns out, we have a similar taste in music. We even bond over our love of Russian rock bands that Americans have never heard of—like Nautilus Pompilius. We also both dislike Russian pop except for a few select bands, like t.A.T.u.

When we finish talking about music, we move on to books, and here, too, our tastes have a lot of similarities—the exceptions being the engineering books that I read for work versus fencing and investing books on his end.

As we keep talking, I get the feeling that he wants to know every little detail about my life. It makes me feel increasingly guilty that I'm not telling him about my company. Then again, he still gets cagey when the conversation veers in the direction of his past in Ruskovia, so I guess that makes us somewhat even, especially if he *is* hiding something there—something that I no longer think is another woman.

After we talk for what feels like hours, I steer the conversation to sexy times. Flipping my hair over my shoulder, I ask, "Are you ambidextrous?"

"Sadly, no," he says. "Why?"

I waggle my eyebrows lasciviously. "I want to be accurate when I imagine you touching me."

He sits up. "I will first touch you with my left hand. Then—when you tell me it was the most mind-blowing experience of your life—I'll finally admit I'm *not* left-handed."

I grin at his favorite movie reference and turn the camera to show him the clit suction device I've prepared on my bed. "Would you like a repeat of our teledildonics adventure?"

He turns his own camera to show me the toys on *his* bed, ready to go. "As you wish."

"Oh, I wish." I walk to the bedroom door and lock it this time. "And I get to go first."

# THIRTY-TWO

WE STRIP as though our clothes were on fire.

His fingers dance on his phone screen as he sets up the clit suction to be under his app's control.

I sprawl on the bed and ready the device.

"You're amazing," he says, his voice awed.

My eyes roam over every groove of his muscles before settling on Everest. "You're not so bad yourself."

His eyes gleam. "Ready?"

I bring the gizmo to my clit. "Yes."

He reaches for the controls on his phone. "Close your eyes and picture me sucking on you."

Great idea. I do as he says, but before I can let my imagination go wild, the suction begins.

Fuck. Fuck.

The image of his soft lips sucking on my clit is all too easy to bring to mind thanks to how well-designed the toy is.

The intensity of the suction increases. I picture him puckering those lips and inhaling deeply, as though he wants to give my clit a hickey.

An intense orgasm starts to unfurl in my core—and that's before the vibration begins.

Wow.

The vibration is harder to picture him doing—unless I convince myself he's a cat shifter and that is his purr.

The orgasm doesn't care how realistic my fantasy is, though. It explodes through my nerve endings, making my toes spasm and wrenching a moan from my lips.

"Good girl," he murmurs hoarsely.

Attempting to catch my breath, I open my eyes—and do a double take at the sight of my lady parts. The suction was so strong it drew more than the usual amount of blood to my clit, engorging it to almost the size of a tiny penis.

I've never played with this toy in a well-lit room before, so this is good to know. It might also be a good thing that Dragomir isn't here to see me up close. I imagine some guys might get eeked out if their woman were to sprout a penis.

Then again, I doubt Dragomir would be one of those guys. If nothing else, compared to Everest, some actual penises might look like clits.

I lick my lips. "Your turn."

He examines the toys on his end. "Do you have a preference?"

"The sleeve." I point at the gizmo that looks like a pocket made out of a squid.

He takes the thing, lubes it up, and stares at me with visible eagerness as we sync it with my app.

"This time you're going to close your eyes," I say. "Put yourself inside that, and picture being in my pussy."

Something no one knows is that I designed that particular toy based on my own vagina. It's the exact dimensions in terms of depth, width, and elasticity. I also did my best to get the texture just right. It took countless hours of fingering myself and toy prototypes—but I'm always willing to make sacrifices on behalf of womankind.

Of course, I can't tell Dragomir any of this without revealing my secret.

Speaking of secrets, I hope Vlad never finds out this particular factoid. While helping Fanny test my teledildonics line, he stuck his penis into a sleeve just like this one.

Yeah, I'm not going to think about that.

Eyes closed, Dragomir slides Everest into the sleeve. I watch closely—if the toy tears, I might have a big problem down the line.

Nope.

It's a snug fit.

My vaginal walls squeeze in jealousy.

"How does it feel?" I ask huskily.

Dragomir's face contracts in ecstasy. "Squirrelchik..." His voice is a soft growl. "Your pussy feels amazing."

It better.

I initiate the patented back-and-forth motion of the sleeve.

He stiffens.

Reveling in my power, I up the intensity.

He groans.

Why, oh why didn't I make the sleeve see-through? I want to see every detail. Oh, well. I add a little vibration to the up-and-down motions.

He exhales, loudly.

It's my turn to stiffen.

Did I just hear a knock? Is it the dogs?

Nah. Boner doesn't know that particular trick—and I doubt Winnie does either.

Probably my imagination.

Forgetting all about it, I raise the intensity all the way.

The buzzing is super loud now, but I think I hear a female voice speaking Ruskovian.

What the hell? Does he have a radio on?

I should really say something, but I can't take my eyes off Everest—which engorges impossibly more.

Remarkably, the sleeve accommodates it.

Whew. If I had any subconscious concerns about Everest fitting inside me, they're gone now—replaced with a yearning for him to return and try this very thing with the sleeve's inspiration.

Dragomir's neck cords, his fists tighten, and with a grunt, he comes into the sleeve.

When he opens his eyes, they look wild.

"That was fucking fantastic," he rasps, his breath ragged.

Suddenly, there's a screech of a door opening.

Eyes widening, Dragomir looks away from the camera.

There's a loud feminine gasp.

Turning around, Dragomir yells something in Ruskovian.

There's a squeal that sounds like the Russian word for "sorry," followed by the sound of a door slamming shut.

I peer into the camera. "Do I need to be jealous?"

He turns back, his face edged with a hint of color. "No, sorry. That was just the maid. No doubt wanted to clean the room."

"Crap. That must've been the knock I heard. I thought it was just my imagination."

He grimaces. "She's supposed to wait until guests hang a 'please clean' sign on the door."

"She probably thought you were out," I say. "You really should start locking those doors—the hotel might now have a harassment suit on their hands."

"This isn't a hotel," he says. "I'm staying with my parents."

Huh. More evidence of his family's wealth. Their guestroom looks like a penthouse, and they have a maid who's supposed to adhere to signs put out by guests.

As I ponder all that, Dragomir removes himself from the sleeve and locks the door.

"Where were we?" he asks, returning to the bed.

I grin mischievously. "We were about to switch the video to our laptops, so we can use our phones to make each other come at the same time."

He likes that idea, and we do what I suggested.

A couple of times.

Finally, we're both completely worn out. Panting, I lie there, my bones so jellified I can barely hold the phone straight.

"How was it for you?" he asks over a yawn.

"Reminds me of the sixty-nine position." I mirror his yawn. "It's difficult to work app controls when you're screaming in ecstasy."

His gaze sweeps over my body with rekindled hunger. "I'm sure it will get easier with practice."

"Definitely," I say, and even though some part of me wants more, my clit is begging for mercy. Reluctantly, I suggest, "How about tomorrow?"

He gladly agrees, and we return to the "you hang up" dance from the other day, until I eventually relent and do so.

In the dream-filled sleep that follows, I find myself in his arms, having dozens of orgasms nonstop.

# THIRTY-THREE

OVER THE NEXT FEW DAYS, videocalls with Dragomir become a routine. Outside of video, if I want to talk, I call or text him—and he always gets back to me within five minutes or less. It's actually eerie how good he is with responding, better than anyone else I know. I like to think it's because I'm a priority in his life. Of course, it's possible he's just one of those people who see their phone as an extension of themselves, but the fact that he doesn't take it to walk Winnie makes me doubt that.

Either way, each time we speak, we learn more about each other, and every night, we use my teledildonics toys to make each other come.

If I had any doubts that the world needs the VR suit I'm working on, they're gone now. If the suit already existed, this time apart would be that much more bearable—and what's true for us would also be true for soldiers overseas, fishermen on long-term expeditions, patients under quarantine, and so on.

Still, given the current levels of technology, our relationship is as blissful as a long-distance one can be, except for the fly in the ointment: the fact that his brother still hasn't come out of his coma.

"The doctors say the swelling in his brain is going down," Dragomir tells me one evening, "but they're still not certain when he's going to regain consciousness."

And though he doesn't say it, I can hear the unspoken "if" in his words.

---

THE FOLLOWING week is our meeting with Dragomir's company.

"We had some technical questions for you today," Marco says to kick it off.

He's looking at Alex as though I don't exist, so I pointedly say, "I'll be sure to answer any questions you may have to the best of my ability."

"It has to do with VR sickness," Marco says, still looking at Alex. "How is your system going to prevent it?"

Alex looks at me.

I tip my head in thanks to him. "First things first. Let's define the problem."

Everyone's attention finally swings toward me.

Marco clears his throat. "VR sickness is an illness that people get when using virtual reality. Right?"

I inwardly sigh. By recusing himself, Dragomir has left a person in charge who clearly knows nothing about VR.

"That's not really the common definition of that phenomenon," Alex says before I get a chance to reply—and it's just as well.

Out of the two of us, he's more diplomatic.

Marco glances at the tech guy in glasses—Eugenius, if I recall correctly.

"VR sickness isn't a medical condition," Eugenius says. "If you stop using VR, the symptoms go away."

Marco frowns, making me wonder if he's bringing this up to have an excuse not to give us the funding.

"If I may," I say, my voice laced with honey. "I took a course on VR back in school, so I can easily define the problem. As well as explain how we will overcome it."

Marco looks like I've peed in his soup.

"Going back to the definition," I continue. "VR sickness is a set of symptoms some people experience when using VR, symptoms that are similar to that of motion sickness. In fact, the two conditions have a lot in common because in both cases, the underlying cause is the person's brain receiving conflicting messages about motion and the body's position in space."

Everyone nods, and Marco grudgingly waves for me to go on.

"First and foremost, current VR hardware and software as a whole have already made huge progress combating this problem. The number of spatial degrees when tracking the user's body has gone up, latency has been reduced, and graphics performance is better across the board." I look around to make sure I haven't lost anyone. It seems like I haven't yet, but might unless I get less technical. "Having said all that, I should point out that our product will actually have a huge advantage when it comes to VR sickness, because we will have the body suit. When wearing the suit, the person's brain is more likely to be tricked into thinking that VR is happening for real—therefore removing the key underlying cause of the symptoms."

From here, I launch into a laundry list of software tricks we plan to use to minimize this problem further, and then I give the floor to Alex to reassure everyone that he can make said tricks a software reality.

What I don't mention is that we have an extra reason why VR sickness is not a major concern for us. Moving around inside VR is the biggest trigger for the malaise, and our users will be having sex—a more stationary endeavor compared to activities such as sword fighting, dirt bike racing, and other game staples.

"Thank you," Marco says, but he doesn't look like he means it. "How about eye strain? Isn't it another issue with VR?"

He's totally fishing for problems. "Our product will cause less eye strain than our competition's, and here's why."

Tired of Marco's shit, I give them a boring-ass lecture on vergence-accommodation conflict—the key reason for eye strain—and then I go into industry-wide solutions before mentioning a few things that will be unique to us.

The funny thing is, because of the planned sex content, eye strain is another non-issue for us—but I can't play *that* card.

Clearly regretting his question, Marco nonetheless tries to throw me a few more curveballs, but I just bat them all away until he reluctantly concludes the meeting.

---

"YOU'RE GOOD," Alex tells me in Russian as we get tea in the coffee shop where Dragomir and I had our first date.

"Did you get the feeling he was trying to sabotage us?" I ask.

He nods. "But you stopped him. That's what counts."

"Stopped him this time. I'm worried about what he might pull next."

Alex pats my shoulder. "In you, Marco has bitten off more than he can chew. I'm sure of it."

We grab a table, and the conversation pivots to more personal matters—specifically, my brother's love life. Apparently, ever since meeting Dragomir, Mother has been on Alex's case for being her only child who's still single. That leads Alex to probe for the latest on me and Dragomir, so I fill him in on our long-distance relationship.

"Are you done snooping on him then?" Alex asks after hearing all about how wonderful things are between us.

I blow on my tea as I ponder this. For some reason, I haven't thought about this recently. "I don't believe he has another woman," I say finally. "But I do think he's hiding something. I just haven't had a chance to dig deeper into his past."

"Smart girl," Alex says. "Trust but verify."

---

WHEN I GET HOME, a package is waiting for me.

It's a gift from Dragomir—a snowman outfit for a dog Boner's size.

And not just *any* snowman.

It's Olaf, from *Frozen*.

Chuckling, I put the outfit on my poor dog.

"*Ma chérie*, you know those *histoires morbides* of dogs eating their departed owners? Something tells me said owners made those dogs wear outfits like this—and that the humans didn't die of causes *naturelles*, if you catch my drift."

Winnie looks Boner over with a confused expression.

"Napoleon Carlovich, you know I think the world of your studness, but I'm sorry to say, you're not stud enough to pull off that outfit."

I strip the outfit off Boner before he can rip it into shreds.

Next time I'm Elsa for Halloween, I'm bribing him with bacon to wear this for a few dozen pictures.

# THIRTY-FOUR

FOR THE NEXT week and a half, Dragomir and I continue our evening video sessions. Then one day, he calls me in the afternoon.

I pick up immediately. "Is everything okay?"

"Tigger is out of the coma." Dragomir's voice brims with excitement.

Heart fluttering, I sit down. "Tell me everything."

He proceeds to explain how it happened. Apparently, Tigger opened his eyes a few hours ago and recognized Dragomir, the person who happened to be at his side at the time.

"He's very lucid, all things considered," Dragomir continues. "He'll need some physical therapy and the like, but the doctors are now extremely optimistic."

Is it selfish that I want to ask him when he'll be returning to the US?

Yes, very—which is why I don't. Instead, I tell him the truth: how happy I am for him and his family. From the stories he's told me about Tigger as a kid, I feel like I already know the daredevil.

"Thank you," Dragomir says. "I'll go be with him now. Just wanted to share this news with you."

He hangs up, and I get back to work, where my joy translates into a particularly creative solution for the VR suit's nipple-squeezing problem.

---

ON OUR VIDEOCALL THAT EVENING, Dragomir gives me another update on his brother. Apparently, Tigger plans to tackle his physical therapy with the same zest he approaches his dangerous stunts, which bodes well for his recovery.

The updates I get in the following days are each more heartwarming than the next. Tigger's rehabilitation progresses like a dream, and in no time at all, he and Dragomir are taking walks in their family's gardens.

A few days after the walks start, Dragomir videocalls me outside the usual time again.

I eagerly pick up. "Hi!"

His hazel eyes are bright. "Guess what?"

"What?" I ask, but I think I know.

"Tigger has been eager to return to New York, and as of today, the doctor has approved it."

A weight that has been sitting on my shoulders all these weeks seems to lift.

I'm going to see Dragomir again. Touch him for real instead of in my fantasies. Do all the dirty things to him that I've planned.

"How long is the flight?" I ask, not even trying to hide my excitement.

"I'll be there in two days," he says, then frowns. "Having almost lost Tigger, our parents have decided to accompany us to New York, and they need some time to get ready."

Two days.

Forty-eight hours.

Two-thousand eight-hundred and eighty minutes.

Have I been this psyched ever in my life?

"My first destination upon arrival is your place," he says.

My heart leaps, but I make my face playfully stern. "Your first destination is my bedroom."

His eyes gleam pure gold. "As you wish."

"And no left-handed business. Bring your A-game. I want your dominant hand and cock from the start."

His face goes taut, his voice dropping to a low growl. "Oh, squirrelchik, you don't have to worry about that. I've wanted you since the moment I laid eyes on you, and my desire has only grown stronger over the past two months."

I stare at him. Can a surge of lust rob someone of speech? All I can do in reply is fan myself, like a Victorian lady.

"I'd better run," he says hoarsely. "See you soon."

He hangs up, and I just sit there, reeling. I, too, have wanted him since that first meeting. The time between then and now has been like one torturously long foreplay session.

The idea that we will finally consummate whatever's going on between us makes me shiver with excitement.

# THIRTY-FIVE

AS I WAIT for Dragomir's return, I don't masturbate—even though I really, really want to. I don't want any soreness down there until Everest is in the picture. Instead, I channel the pent-up sexual energy into work, creating a slew of giant dildos in a not-so-subtle tip of the hat to the object of my desire.

I also prep for the big event itself. I shave hair from any place on my body where I find it displeasing, and nicely groom the rest. I turn the bedroom into a tantric shrine with mood-setting candles and music, and—though this might be going a tad overboard—I do yoga poses meant to make my body extra limber.

When a call from Dragomir finally appears on my phone screen, I'm like a hormonal bomb ready to blow—pun intended.

I slide my finger to accept. "Hi!"

"Hey. I'm at the JFK airport, and I have news."

That news better be that he's on his way to my place. "What's up?"

"You know how you wanted to meet my parents?"

I frown. "I wanted to prove mine are worse than yours, sure. Why?"

Even as I ask, I have a sinking feeling about this.

"Well, I told my brother about you, and he wants to meet you—and when our parents heard that, they asked to be included."

"Uh-huh," I say warily. "And when is this meeting supposed to take place?"

"Tigger doesn't like airplane food," he says apologetically. "Neither do our parents."

I curse myself for holding off on masturbating. "It's today, isn't it?"

"Are you free in a couple of hours?"

"Well, yeah." I've blocked out my work calendar for the rest of today, and if I'd bothered to put in a reason, it would've said 'to fuck Dragomir's brains out.'

"It's probably for the best," he says unconvincingly. "It's only fair that you meet them before we take things between us any further." He clears his throat. "You might just change your mind about me afterward."

"Why would I? Even if your parents are the reincarnations of Stalin and Hitler, what does that have to do with you?"

He exhales audibly. "In that case, could you bring Winnie with you? My brother and parents have brought Winnie's siblings with them. I'm sure she'll appreciate being reunited with her family for an evening."

I look at the nearby bear, who's oblivious to our conversation. "Their dogs are her relatives?"

"Well, yeah," he says. "The dogs of everyone in my family are from the same bloodline. Haven't I mentioned that before?"

"No. You just said Winnie was of the purest misha bloodline."

"Ah, right. My bad. If it's too much trouble, I could—"

"I'll bring her," I say, though a part of me is wondering if he wants me to bring the dog so he can break up with me without leaving me a hostage.

But no. Who asks you to meet their parents *before* a break-up? If anything, he might want Winnie back because he still thinks his family will scare me away.

"I'll text you the time and the place," he says. "Thank you for being so understanding."

Understanding, my foot. I'm so horny I'm about to rub myself against the kitchen table.

"I'll see you," I say and hang up before we get into the "you hang up first" loop.

Then I run into my walk-in closet and frantically search for an outfit that might impress evil incarnate, also known as his parents.

# THIRTY-SIX

WHEN WINNIE and I exit the cab, Dragomir is standing by the entrance of The Doro—the most expensive restaurant in the city. His thick, dark hair is windswept, his stubble is a little longer than usual, and his tall, muscular frame is clad in a casual yet elegant outfit of dark jeans and an ivory turtleneck.

*A turtleneck.*

Hormones help me. I might just attack him on the table in front of his family.

Before I can blink, Winnie pulls on the leash with all the power of a hungry bear—and I nearly trip as she drags me over to her master, whose face she licks like an ice cream cone.

I watch jealously. It must be nice to be a dog and have that behavior be socially acceptable. I, too, want to lick his face—and the rest of him—but unlike Winnie, I have to wait.

"Come here," Dragomir says to me once he's freed himself and cleaned his face.

Grinning, I go in for a hug. It quickly turns into a kiss that takes my breath away and ratchets up my horniness to moose levels.

"They're already inside," he murmurs, reluctantly extricating himself from my clutches. "You ready?"

I nod.

He puts his hand on the small of my back as he leads me into the posh restaurant.

Is it wrong that I want to lick that hand?

Once inside, I look around and whistle under my breath. With all the paintings and statues on display, the high-ceilinged marble hallway we walk through reminds me of the Metropolitan Museum of Art.

As if to heighten the MET association, a pair of burly doormen greet us in the most outrageous uniforms I've ever seen: capes and bicorns of the Carabinieri, but with the garish colors and pantaloons of the Vatican Guard.

Interesting. This restaurant's reviews didn't mention these uniforms, but I have to admit, they add to the ambiance. Goofy outfits aside, these dudes look like they can double as bouncers should someone try to run away from this place's notoriously astronomical bills.

As one, the doormen/bouncers nod politely at us and open the large doors that lead into the dining hall.

My breath catches.

In the entire restaurant, only two tables are set. At one table are three people—most likely Tigger and the parents. At the other table, one slightly lower to the ground, are two ginormous dogs eating out of big bowls.

"A canine table?" I whisper as Winnie's tail turns into a helicopter rotor at the sight.

Dragomir shrugs. "My family tends to pamper their dogs."

If his treatment of Winnie is an example of this, "pamper" might be an understatement.

Fascinated, I examine everyone.

The dogs at the table make Winnie seem like a normal bear in comparison. One has a distinctly snooty posture despite sporting a funny haircut that makes it look like a throw pillow made out of a grizzly, while the other resembles a panda, thanks to its black and white spots. And, for some unfathomable reason, it's wearing goggles.

The humans are just as interesting. Dragomir's mother is a pale, round-cheeked beauty who reminds me of the women portrayed by the Renaissance painters—an impression possibly influenced by the ambience of the restaurant. Both of the men at the table look eerily like Dragomir, though the father has a mustache and wears a grouchy, sourpuss expression, while Tigger's eyes gleam with all the mischief Dragomir has attributed to him.

Hand still residing on the small of my back, Dragomir leads me to the human table.

They all stand to greet us.

"Everyone, allow me to introduce Bella," Dragomir says. "Bella, this is my mother, Bronislawa; my father, Stanislaus; and my brother, Anatolio."

I desperately repeat all the names in my head to make sure I remember them. Like other Ruskovian words, the names are vaguely but not quite Russian. Vampires from Russian fiction might have such names.

The brother's grin is contagious. "Nice to meet you, Bella. Please call me Tigger. Everyone else does." Like Dragomir, he speaks American English without an accent.

The mother darts Tigger a disapproving glare. "So informal," she says with a mixture of British and Slavic accents. "This country is a bad influence on manners. Next thing you know, we will all be holding our knives in the left hand!"

Oh, no. Knives in the left hand? The universe would surely implode.

Bronislawa examines me from head to foot, frowns, then extends her hand limpidly, as though she expects me to kiss it—Godfather (or is it Pope?) style.

I awkwardly fist bump her instead.

She looks at me like I've licked her face.

Tigger turns his chuckle into a cough, and Dragomir's eyes crinkle in the corners.

Bronislawa pulls her fisted hand away.

The father—Stanislaus—says nothing throughout, just stands there, scowling.

Dragomir says something to him in Ruskovian. The father looks at me, almost imperceptibly inclines his head, says something in Ruskovian with cold politeness, and sits back down.

The only words I make out are "Bella" and "pozor," the latter meaning "disgrace" or "dishonor" in Russian. Hopefully, it means something else in Ruskovian. In Prague, signs that say "pozor" actually mean "warning"—not that such a word choice works better in a phrase like "Nice to meet you, Bella."

Judging by Dragomir's glare, his Daddy-O might've indeed said something mean to me.

Oh well, it doesn't count if I don't know what that something is. Thus far, my parents are still worse. No one here has complained about nonexistent grandchildren, nor shamed me for my passion in life.

"Our father doesn't speak English," Tigger whispers to me conspiratorially, and I get the feeling he means "doesn't deign to speak English."

"Why don't you take Winnifred to her kin and then join us," Bronislawa says imperiously.

I follow Dragomir as he leads Winnie to the doggie table. She gets more excited the closer we get, and when we're a few feet away, the panda dog with goggles turns Winnie's way, barks, and wags its tail.

"That's Caradog," Dragomir says as they exchange face licks and butt sniffs. "He's Winnie's brother and Tigger's best friend."

"I could've guessed," I say. "But what's with the goggles? Does he go skydiving too?"

Dragomir shrugs. "Might be to improve eyesight or to protect sensitive eyes. We'll have to ask my brother."

Done with Caradog, Winnie turns to the snooty, throw-pillow-looking bear.

The creature pretends Winnie isn't there.

"That's Gruffydd, my parents' dog," Dragomir says with an eye roll. "He's Caradog and Winnie's father."

Fortunately, Winnie has a thick hide and recovers from Gruffydd's snub quickly—and hopefully without any daddy issues. She simply gives Caradog's butt a parting sniff and takes her place at the table, where something yummy-smelling is already waiting in a bowl.

My mouth salivates, and this time, not only from the sight of Dragomir. If what passes for dog food at this place smells so amazing, the human food is bound to be divine.

We return to the human table and take a seat next to Tigger.

"I hope you don't mind, I ordered the big cheese plate," Tigger says, rubbing his hands together.

As though waiting for that announcement, a person wearing the same funky outfit as the bouncers shows up from the kitchen, a huge wooden board in his hands.

It turns out to be the cheese plate in question—and it's the biggest such plate I've ever seen, with cheeses of every color, smell, and consistency, from soft to rock hard.

Stupid turtleneck. The thought of something "rock hard" break my concentration and speed up my breathing.

No. Got to fight it. Don't want his parents thinking I'm some nympho.

Mumbling something that might be grace in Ruskovian, Stanislaus reaches for a moldy-looking, blue-colored morsel that smells like an army of unwashed feet. As he grabs it, I see his face in profile, and something about it seems vaguely familiar, though I can't figure out why.

Bronislawa goes next, daintily plating herself some of the five different soft cheeses.

I wait for Tigger and Dragomir to go next, but Dragomir pushes the plate toward me.

"Bronislawa," I say, doing my best to sound like the angel that I'm not. "Is there a cheese you'd recommend?"

There. Olive branch.

"My name is pronounced Bronislawa," she says, which to me sounds just like what I said.

"Bro-nis-la-wa," I carefully enunciate.

"No. It's Bro-nis-la-wa." Again, she says it exactly as I did.

You know what? She can shove that olive branch. "Thanks for correcting me. Is there a cheese you think I should try?"

She points at a yellow, sickly looking slice at the edge of the plate. "How about plain American?" What she seems to leave unsaid is, "Like you."

I'm about to correct her about my Americanness when I feel Dragomir squeeze my knee under the table.

Is he nuts? Between his turtleneck and that squeeze, I lose my ability to think for a moment.

When the hormonal surge recedes, I recall that Ruskovians don't like Russians, which is what I was about to out myself as.

Fake-smiling at Bronislawa, I grab the American cheese and give it a taste.

Wow. It's so good I moan in pleasure. While it's recognizable as American cheese of the type someone might melt onto a burger, it's the tastiest example of its kind and therefore amazingly good.

It's like the Platonic form of American cheese—what every other slice of this substance aims for but never achieves.

Bronislawa whispers something to Stanislaus in Ruskovian, and I recognize one word: *shlyuha.*

In Russian, that means *slut.*

Was that a reference to my moan? What are the odds that word happens to mean *saint* in Ruskovian?

Given Dragomir and Tigger's frowns, not very high.

I do something pretty childish. I feign a sneeze that contains two words: *sama shlyuha.*

In Russian, it means *you're the slut.*

Bronislawa's eyes widen—the Ruskovian and Russian must be close enough for her to understand what my sneeze sounded like. Dragomir and Tigger appear to be suppressing smiles, while the father is as stone-faced as ever. Before anyone can say anything, Tigger animatedly grabs a sample of each cheese, and Dragomir goes straight for a purple substance that I assume is also some form of fermented mammalian baby feed.

"Ready for the next course?" Tigger asks, quickly demolishing his portion. "Culinary adventures are the only type I'm allowed to have right now."

As soon as everyone nods, he claps his hands and another funnily dressed dude runs out of the kitchen, carrying a giant tray. On it are five steaks with mashed potatoes and assorted vegetables—a pretty basic offering for a place this fancy.

I wait for everyone to start eating before I carve myself a piece of the meat and stick it into my mouth.

By the Michelin star.

A foodgasm explodes through my taste buds.

I have no idea what animal I just tasted, but it's deliciously soft, perfectly juicy, and heavenly earthy.

I revel in pleasure until I spot Bronislawa staring at me with disapproval again.

What?

Did I moan again?

No. It's worse than that.

I'm holding my knife in my left hand.

It's official.

I'm a filthy barbarian.

# THIRTY-SEVEN

I SWITCH my utensils from one hand to the other, and in the hopes of covering my faux pas, I ask, "What kind of meat is this?"

"Fawn," Tigger says.

"Venison," Bronislawa says at the same time.

I wait for someone to show that they're kidding, but they do not.

Great. I've just enjoyed eating Bambi.

Avoiding the meat from that point on, I try the mash and the veggies—which, unsurprisingly, also turn out to be the best I've ever had.

"Do you not like the meat, dear?" Bronislawa asks me.

"No, Bambi is delicious," I say. "I'm just not very hungry."

She cocks her head. "Are you sure that's it?"

"What else can it be?"

She shrugs. "Just wondering if you're watching what you eat."

I nearly choke on a Brussels sprout. "Excuse me?"

Is she saying I'm fat?

She wrinkles her nose. "You seem like a model or an actress. Don't they always watch what they eat?"

Given the distasteful way she says the words *model* and *actress*, she might as well have said *bimbo* and *whore*.

On the plus side, she didn't call me fat.

"Bella is an entrepreneur," Dragomir says pointedly, his tone noticeably cooler. "An MIT graduate, in fact. In case you're unaware, that's the most elite technical university in the world, with a seven-percent acceptance rate."

I almost want to thank Bronislawa for being a bitch. I never thought having a guy defend me like this would be such a huge turn-on. Dragomir has just earned himself all kinds of sexual favors.

Wait, who am I kidding? Between how horny I already was and his turtleneck, I'll be turning whatever tricks he wants in the bedroom, no defending required.

"Tigger," I say, deciding to change the topic before I spontaneously combust, "do you know of any fun New York adventures—ideally those that don't involve risking life and limb?"

"Flying air balloon," Tigger says without hesitation. "You can jump off with a parachute attached to the basket. That way, you don't even need to know how to use one."

He proceeds with more ideas along those lines, and I pretend to be interested, though I'd never in a million years do any of it. I like my skull not fractured, thank you very much.

To pass the time, I stealthily run my hand up Dragomir's thigh under the cover of his napkin, then higher and higher until I feel Everest yearning to Hulk out of his pants.

Dragomir's jaw flexes, but he keeps eating his Bambi steak and does his best not to show anything to his family.

Impressive.

Eventually, I take pity on us both and pull my hand away.

A loud bark comes from the doggie table. We all turn and see another bouncer-dude run out of the kitchen, carrying another tray.

That's a new definition of pampered.

On a whim, I throw my voice close to where Winnie's maw is, making it gruff and heavily accented:

"Pace yourself, Caradog Gruffyddovich. Eating kitten stew too quickly can cause heartburn."

Tigger and Dragomir laugh, but the parents look at me like I've sprouted a nipple on my forehead.

I eat in silence from then on, and when everyone's Bambi but mine is devoured, my phone vibrates.

It's a text from Dragomir:

*Do you admit it now?*

I make sure no one can see me reply and type out:

*Admit what?*

When Dragomir sneaks a peek at his phone, he rolls his eyes.

*Do I win the worst parents contest?*

I think about it for half a second, then reply with a resounding *no*.

At almost the same time, Bronislawa leans toward her still-scowling husband and rattles out something in Ruskovian, occasionally darting glances my way.

I make out a couple of words and phrases that have meanings in Russian besides the aforementioned *pozor*, including "rebellion," "just a phase," and "can do better."

Dragomir must overhear because his expression turns livid and he leaps to his feet.

"I've given up dessert," he says coldly. "We'd better go."

Tigger gives his parents a disappointed once-over, then stands up too. "The doctors told me not to overindulge, so I have to run as well."

Bronislawa gives both sons a disapproving glare. "If you must."

"A pleasure, as always," Dragomir says, his voice dripping with sarcasm.

We get Winnie and her panda-like brother and head out.

As we get to the fancy doors that lead out of the dining hall, Winnie makes the now-familiar whining sound.

Dragomir doesn't seem to have heard it.

I sneak a glance over my shoulder. Both Bronislawa and Stanislaus are giving me the stink eye.

Fine. That was their last chance to avoid my revenge, and they blew it.

Pretending to drop my purse, I kneel to pick it up, take in a deep breath, and whisper at Winnie, "Unleash the Kraken."

THPPTPHTPHPHHPH.

Dragomir's eyes widen as he gapes at Winnie's fart-generating butt.

With a doggy grin, Caradog rips an even louder flatus—and I didn't think it could get any louder than Winnie's.

Dragomir's determined expression reminds me of firefighters heading out to combat a blaze. He firmly grabs me and Tigger by the elbows and drags us out, along with the still-farting dogs.

Even though I'm holding my breath as we rush out of the hall, the foulness somehow manages to penetrate my senses, and it's so bad I start to regret what I've done.

To my shock, instead of running for their lives, the bouncers/doormen pull out gas masks from somewhere—maybe their pantaloons—put them on, and rush inside.

In the distance, I hear Bronislawa and Stanislaus making gagging sounds and Gruffydd howling—or also farting. It's hard to tell which.

By the time we get outside, the dogs have thankfully run out of gas.

Holding a handkerchief against his nose, Dragomir hails his limo-RV. It must've been circling the block all this time.

With a screech of tires, the vehicle halts and we leap in.

"Fyodor, punch it," Tigger shouts.

As the RV launches forward, everyone finally resumes normal breathing—except the dogs. They've been enjoying the aroma the whole time.

Once we catch our breaths, Tigger begins to chuckle. "Can you imagine the look on Mother's face?"

Dragomir's eyes crinkle, and all three of us burst out laughing.

"Where are we headed?" I eventually ask.

"A bar?" Tigger suggests.

"No," Dragomir says sternly. "You're still healing, so we're going to drop you off at your hotel."

He doesn't say it, but I'm sure the next stop is one of our places. At least it better be.

Tigger throws out a bunch of alternatives to heading home, but Dragomir shoots them all down.

Turns out, Tigger's hotel is just a couple of blocks away from my apartment. "I recommended it to him," Dragomir explains after we drop Tigger off. "I stayed there recently because my place was getting fumigated. It was actually when we first met."

Ah. That explains why I only ran into him that one time at the park.

The RV comes to a full stop next to my building.

My heart begins to hammer wildly in my chest. "Will you come up... for some tea?"

The look Dragomir gives me seems to say, "Does a bear have weaponized flatulence?"

I bite my lip. "Let's go then."

Ruffling Winnie's fur, he tells her, "Fyodor will take you home. I'll see you tomorrow."

Tomorrow? He's planning to spend the night with me? My heartbeat is at panic attack levels as we exit and sprint to my apartment.

Boner gives us a disappointed look as we enter. "*Ma chérie*, where is *ma petite*?"

"One second," I tell Dragomir and shepherd Boner to the kitchen, where I give him a bowl of his favorite food to distract him from his missing crush.

Once Boner is happily munching, I dash back, grab Dragomir by the hand, drag him into my bedroom, and lock the door.

Ignoring the room's romantic décor, Dragomir looks at me with a hunger that matches my own.

For a few moments, we engage in a stare-off, gunslinger style. Then both of us pounce.

Our lips meet in a deep, ravishing kiss, and caterpillars turn into horny butterflies in my belly. The room spins around us as if we were in a NASA training machine.

We rip off each other's clothes without breaking the kiss, and I'm vaguely aware that I might've torn his turtleneck.

Whatever. I'll get him dozens of replacements.

With a growl that sounds like "you're so fucked, squirrelchik," Dragomir picks me up in a bridal carry, then lays me out on the bed and pauses to run his heated gaze over my naked body.

Dizzy with anticipation, I visually devour him as well—every coiled muscle, every mouthwatering angle, and last but definitely not least, the mountainous glory of Everest.

When his gaze finally returns to my face, his eyes are the darkest I've ever seen them. Muscles flexing with panther-like grace, he joins me on the bed.

Finally.

Here. We. Go.

# THIRTY-EIGHT

HE KISSES MY NECK. Or rather, sucks on it.

I scrape my nails over his back.

He moves the kiss over to my left nipple and nibbles on it until I moan in pleasure.

I can feel his satisfied smile on my nipple. Then his tongue traverses down my breast, past my bellybutton, and down to my eagerly awaiting clit.

After all the tension, the pleasure this causes is indescribable. Compared to his tongue, my clit suction device sucks ass.

My eyes roll back.

If tongues could take IQ tests, I'm sure Dragomir's would fall in the two-hundred range, along with other geniuses—it's that deviously clever.

Is he teasing me?

Fuck that.

I fist his hair to keep him steady and buck against his tongue.

Score!

The orgasm crashes into my every nerve cell, and I cry out his name.

When he looks up, there's a smug expression on his face.

He *was* teasing me. Evil.

Growling low in my throat, I pull him into a deep kiss, tasting myself on his lips as I begin to stroke Everest with my hands.

Stroke it softly, that is. Two can play the teasing game.

He stiffens—in every sense of the word.

Echoing his earlier movements, I slide my tongue down to his neck, move lower to his right nipple, oh-so-teasingly circle the areola, then give his nipple a light nibble.

Both Everest and the nipple harden, and I continue my journey farther down, over his washboard abs and down the landing strip until I reach his balls.

With an evil grin, I give them a catlike lick.

The balls tighten with excitement.

There we go. I give Everest a slow lollypop lick and get rewarded by a twitch that would've sent a rockslide downhill had this been a real mountain.

His hands grip my hair, and his breath turns ragged. "I want you so fucking bad."

I scan Everest, my own breath unsteady from excitement. The last time I took this whole thing into my mouth didn't go so well. But I want to do it again anyway. Surely, it was the alcohol in my system that got me in trouble, not my gag reflex.

Still, in part to tease, in part as a precaution, I take him in carefully, slowly, the silky-smooth skin hard and hot on my tongue.

Did it just get even bigger and harder? Is there blood left for the rest of Dragomir's body to function?

He groans, and I proceed giddily. Having played with Everest remotely for weeks, I've learned exactly what makes it tick, and I use that carnal knowledge now, driving Dragomir to grunt my name in pleasure.

The problem with teasing when you're as horny as I am is you're torturing yourself as much as your victim.

When the pulsing ache in my core grows unbearable, I look up into his amber eyes. "I want you inside me."

He moves like a whirlwind. Before I can take another breath, he has me on my knees.

That's some serious manhandling skill.

He licks my opening from behind, his tongue extending a couple of inches into my crack.

Wow.

So dirty. So hot.

"You ready, squirrelchik?"

I can only whimper.

He ever-so-gently presses Everest into me.

Holy mountain climb.

As ready as I am, there's a moment when the stretching is uncomfortable. Thankfully, it passes quickly, replaced with bliss.

He grabs my ass cheeks possessively, pulling them apart.

Okay, this is getting hotter by the second.

Panting, I look over my shoulder.

His eyes burn with need and his naked body is utterly glorious—reminiscent of a Greek god's statue.

The first thrusts are slow and gentle.

I back into him, eager for harder rhythm and sharper sensations.

His callused hands squeeze my ass cheeks, and his thrusts grow hungrier, more urgent.

I ball my fists in the sheets.

He speeds up more.

My moans of pleasure turn into screams as the tension in my core builds to a crescendo.

Crying out his name, I come. At the same time, he thrusts even deeper, and I feel his release in a warm burst inside me as he groans out his pleasure.

Releasing my ass, he hugs me from behind.

I collapse onto the bed. He reluctantly lets go of me, and I use what little strength I have left to roll over and look up at him.

He sprawls next to me, holding himself up on his elbow. Though he's still breathing unevenly, there's a tender expression on his gorgeously chiseled face.

"That was unbelievable," I murmur, suddenly feeling uncharacteristically shy.

He sweeps a stray lock of hair off my forehead. "*You're* unbelievable."

Flushing, I poke a bead of sweat that's gliding down his flexed deltoid muscle. "You're staying the night, right?"

What I really want to ask is, "Will you stay forever? Do you think this thing between us—whatever it is—can work?"

His gaze softens. "If you'll have me, I'll stay tonight... and tomorrow night, and the night after that."

Wow. Are we on the same wavelength? I want to probe further, but I'm afraid to. In the afterglow of sex, men say all kinds of things they don't mean.

With effort, I gather my scattered wits. "I think I need a shower." The words come out more seductive than I meant.

His eyes grow hooded. "I'll take you."

Matching actions to words, he gets up, picks me up in a fireman's carry, and strides decisively for the shower.

As I luxuriate in the warmth of the water streaming down on us, Dragomir begins to lather me with soap.

A girl can get used to this.

When I'm nice and sudsy, he rinses me off, then washes my hair —throwing in a moan-inducing head massage that would make the best hair salons proud.

It's official. I want to keep this man as my spa slave.

And sex slave, of course.

With an evil grin, I start to return the favor.

Damn. Lathering his hard muscles with soap gets me hot and

bothered all over again, and judging by Everest's reaction to my ministrations, Dragomir might also be amiable to another go.

"Can you put lotion on my back?" I ask as I towel off. "I get so dry without it."

He looks me over appreciatively. "Now?"

"In the bedroom." I imbue my words with carnal promise, then grab the bottle of lotion with one hand and Everest with the other.

His eyes widen as I gently lead him out that way.

"Always wanted to lead a guy by his dick this literally," I say in a sultry voice. "Didn't have access to an appropriately sized victim until now."

Everest jerks in my hand.

"Glad to be of use," Dragomir growls.

When we reach the bedroom, I let Everest go and leap onto the bed, ass up. "I'm ready."

He clears his throat. "For lotion?"

Turning, I pretend to clutch my nonexistent pearls. "What else?"

He grabs the lotion roughly, and I turn away, my heart rate speeding up.

Instead of attacking me, which is what I half expected, I hear him squeeze the lotion bottle.

Oh my.

Instead of merely moisturizing me, he embarks on an honest-to-goodness erotic massage, starting with my shoulders, moving down my back and legs, and finishing with an orgasmic foot rub.

"Is there going to be a happy ending?" I gasp when he runs out of body parts to give a spa treatment to.

He turns me over.

"First, I need to lotion the front."

Teasing again? I guess I started it.

His attempt at teasing is brutally successful. By the time he finishes massaging the lotion into my breasts, I'm ready to beg for his cock on my knees.

Moving with his signature athletic grace, he puts the lotion away and covers my body with his.

As Everest juts into my belly, I suck in a breath to start that begging, but before I can say a word, he dips his head so his lips brush my ear.

"*Now* you can get that happy ending," he whispers.

Hells yeah.

I grab Everest and all but shove it inside myself, ignoring the initial, near-painful stretch.

Oh, yeah. That feels good.

Dragomir takes over from there, his thrusts slow and sensual.

More teasing?

He looks into my eyes and intertwines his fingers with mine.

Okay. So not teasing.

I like this.

If the last session is best described as a hard fucking, this seems like something else entirely.

The word "lovemaking" comes to mind, but I banish it for now, not ready to evaluate feelings and put labels on things in the middle of such bliss.

He gradually speeds up, and I forget all about tricky terminology as an orgasm twice as strong as the last one bursts through me, forcing me to scream. Again.

I want him to finish too, so I put my Kegel-ball-trained muscles to good use and squeeze Everest for all I'm worth.

Nostrils flaring, Dragomir comes again, then hugs me tight, like he never wants to let me go. I bury my face against his neck, inhaling his warm male scent.

Fuck, this man is everything.

"Another shower?" I whisper after what feels like an hour of heavy-duty oxytocin production.

"I'm not sure we should bother." He cups my left breast, and I feel Everest growing once more—a feat I didn't think was physically possible. "How about you bring over all your toys so we can play?" he continues.

Instantly as horny as an Amish teen who's discovered Pornhub on his Rumspringa, I rush to obey and bring *all* the toys I own.

As I dump them on the bed, I realize the pile is huge.

Suspiciously huge.

Oops.

To my relief, Dragomir doesn't so much as raise an eyebrow—as though he's used to women owning enough toys to stock an adult store.

Should I tell him I made these?

I really, really want to.

Before I can utter a word, Dragomir grabs a vibrator that catches his fancy, presses the "on" button, and touches me with it.

Never mind. I can always come clean when not on the verge of another orgasm.

Or another.

Or another.

After about ten, I stop keeping count. All I know is that the sun is rising when we finally pass out, tangled together in a sweaty heap.

# THIRTY-NINE

"SQUIRRELCHIK, I HAVE TO WORK," a voice says from a far distance.

I reluctantly pry open my heavy eyelids.

Judging by the sun in the room, it's way past my usual wake-up time.

Dragomir is standing by the bed, dressed in a suit.

Hmm. Did Fyodor deliver that for him this morning, or did he wake up a while ago and go shopping in tatters of yesterday's clothes?

"I'm sorry," he says. "I really have to go."

Oh right. That. Even though my brain is not fully functioning, I push down the covers to expose as much of myself as I can. "Are you sure you must go?"

A muscle in his jaw flexes. "I wish I didn't. Thanks to the trip, I'm way behind on some projects. I've already skipped all the nonessential meetings today, but the next batch are mission-critical investments."

Shit. I've completely forgotten that I've slept with a potential investor.

Well, I guess the djinni with two backs is out of the bottle now.

"Fine, go," I say with a mock frown and cover myself up. "You *will* make this up to me when you get back."

"Oh, I will." His eyes are filled with scorching heat. "In the meantime, I've left you some breakfast in the kitchen. You should eat and rest some more. You'll need your strength when I come back to atone for my sins."

With that, he exits the room, leaving me flushed and panting.

After I cool off, I debate falling back asleep, but my stomach rumbles so I go check on that breakfast.

Wow. Dragomir has covered all the bases. On the table are Eggs Benedict, waffles, five types of jam, a carafe of freshly squeezed orange juice, a teapot, and a large coffee.

He really meant that whole "get your strength" business.

Before eating, I fill Boner's bowl and call him over.

The little guy trudges into the room and looks around as if hoping to see something. Not finding whatever it is, he hangs his head and listlessly starts on his chow.

Aww. He must be missing Winnie. I'll ask Dragomir to bring her over soon to cheer him up.

After I stuff my face with enough food to sustain me for the next two nights of nonstop orgasms, I take Boner for a walk.

He's definitely not his usual self. Longingly sniffing every patch of grass Winnie has peed on, he ignores all the other dogs we come across and is ready to go back in a quarter of the usual time.

At home, Boner manages to look miserable as he drinks his water—and that takes acting skills, especially for a perky-eared Chihuahua.

"*Ma chérie*, I can't go on without *ma petite* for much longer. If she doesn't come back, I will throw myself off the fridge."

I take out my phone and text Dragomir:

*Let's have our dogs hang out at your earliest convenience.*

As I wait for a reply, I move the kitchen chair away from the fridge—just in case.

As usual, Dragomir doesn't take long to get back to me.

*I can get Fyodor to walk them together this evening.*

I convey the good news to Boner and tell Dragomir that the joint walk should be great.

Dog's needs met, I let myself yawn. Loudly.

Not sleeping all night is catching up with me.

Well, the beauty of owning your own business—at least a remotely run one like mine—is that you can take a chill day whenever you want.

Today, I want.

I locate a sleeping mask, but before I can turn off my phone, it rings.

It's a call from Vlad.

Since we haven't spoken in forever, I pick up.

"Hey, you," I say with a smile.

"Hey, sis. How're things going?"

"Great. Dragomir is back."

"Ah, finally. When did that happen?"

I fill him in on the recent events. When I get to last night's dinner, he asks me to repeat the names of the brother, the parents, and even the dogs a couple of times—as though he's taking notes.

Clearly, he still plans to snoop on Dragomir as per our earlier plans. I don't clarify this, though. In fact, I pretend to have forgotten all about it. It might be silly, but it helps me deal with the gnawing sense of guilt. I've gotten to know Dragomir, have earned his trust, and therefore should respect his privacy. There's also this: I've come to care about him so much that I'm afraid to learn something sketchy.

No, that's crazy talk. At least the guilt is easy to rationalize away. If Vlad snoops without my prompting him to do so, how is that my fault? I mean, I can stop him, but he likes snooping so much he might do it even if I ask him not to.

There. Making deals with my conscience has never been this easy. I might well be on my way to becoming a sociopath.

"You there?" Vlad asks, pulling me out of my reverie.

"Sorry. What have you been up to?"

"Working too much," he says. "But that's about to change. Fanny and I are going camping."

I move the phone away from my ear and stare at it uncomprehendingly. "Camping? As in tents, ticks, bugs up your ass—all that?"

"I'm not asking you to come with," he says as I bring the phone back to my ear. I can almost hear him roll his eyes on the other end. "It's Fannychka's idea. She's taken a day off and wants an overnight adventure that would let us unplug completely from the day-to-day grind."

I scratch my head. "I think she just wants to be alone in the woods with you, her big strong protector."

"And what's wrong with that?"

"Sorry, enjoy it," I say and save my tirade about how he could accomplish something similar by getting them both earplugs, shutting down his Wi-Fi router, and sticking his phone in the microwave. "How are things going between the two of you? Camping seems like a big step... at least to me."

"Amazing," he says—and given how reluctant my brother normally is to share his feelings, those words blow my mind. That is, until he continues, saying, "I think she's the one. You know?"

For some reason, mercurial hazel eyes flit through my mind. "Yeah. I think I know exactly what you mean."

He clears his throat. I guess he's just realized he's gone over his emotion-sharing quota for the century. "I still have some packing to do for tonight's trip, so I'd better get to it."

"Enjoy. And stay away from bears."

He hangs up with a chuckle.

I smile at the phone. When I asked Vlad to help me with the app for the teledildonic sex toys, the last thing I expected was for him to find his other half in the process.

Feeling warm and contented, I yawn yet again.

Right. Too much sex and too little sleep.

I put on the sleeping mask and pass out as soon as my head touches the pillow.

---

THE STUPID DOORBELL RINGS, waking me from a wet dream that featured Dragomir in a spandex turtleneck, armed with futuristic sex toys that I hope I can recreate when I next sit down to work.

The ringing continues as I put on a robe and walk over to the door, stepping over Boner—who's the most excited I've seen him in years. "Who is it?"

"Fyodor," says a voice that sounds just like Dragomir's butler. "My apologies, I have Lady Winnifred with me, and she's eager to take care of her biological needs."

Lady Winnifred? Has he never witnessed a session of the Kraken?

As if to confirm, Winnie barks, and Boner goes even more berserk with glee. Bear pheromones must be making him cuckoo.

"One sec," I say and rush away to make myself more presentable before returning with Boner's leash.

When the door opens, there's frantic barking, butt sniffing, and snout licking.

"*Ma petite! Destin* has bathed you and brought you to me."

I give the leash to Fyodor. "Thank you."

He nods in his butlery way and departs.

I check my phone.

Yep. Dragomir had given me a heads up about this home invasion. I guess he didn't think I was lazy enough to sleep half the day away.

There's also a text from Fyodor:

*I'm coming over.*

I'll need to teach him to wait before just showing up the next time. I could've been out. Then again, I wouldn't want Boner to miss out on Winnie time on my account, so maybe I'll give Dragomir a copy of my keys... strictly for Fyodor, of course.

A voicemail from Vlad catches my eye next. He called me an hour ago.

*Hey, sis. I finally found out something about Dragomir. Call me back soon. You'll want to hear this.*

Shit.

My hands visibly tremble as I frantically dial Vlad.

I get his voicemail.

I text him to call me *now* and wait a nail-biting minute.

Then another.

Then a half hour.

The doorbell rings. It's Fyodor. He hands me Boner's leash and departs before I can talk to him about the protocol for next time—or ask pointed questions about Dragomir.

Freed from the leash, Boner beelines for his sex toy, Remy, and begins humping away.

Does this mean Winnie didn't give him any? I thought she might —distance makes even dog hearts grow fonder. Then again, for all I know, maybe she did, but he got oversexed and needs to burn the remainder of it off.

Done with Remy, Boner lies down, closes his eyes contentedly, and softly snores.

Still no sign of Vlad.

What the hell?

Then I remember. The stupid camping excursion. He's probably there already—with no phone reception.

Damn it. What is it that he's learned?

I begin pacing as my earlier concerns about Dragomir resurface.

To this day, he acts cagey about certain topics. Is Vlad's discovery related to that? If so, what is it?

Dragomir swore on his brother's life that he didn't have another woman, à la Marco, but what if that was a lie?

He also never gave me an explanation for that private detective guy with the camera. What was that about? And why did Dragomir use gold coins with the veterinarian? Is he from the criminal underworld, after all?

Lots of questions, no answers.

I glare at my phone. Vlad said the camping thing was overnight. Does that mean they will also hike in the forest tomorrow?

Just how long do I have to wait before I learn whatever he's uncovered?

I stop pacing and call Xenia.

"You should just ask him," my friend says when she's fully up to speed.

"Ask Dragomir. Just like that?"

"Yeah. That way you get answers today."

"Maybe..."

"No maybe. Do it."

"Fine," I say with a sigh.

"Good. Now that that's settled, tell me about the sex."

I do, and I can almost visualize her reaching for the vibrator that I got her, but then swearing she'd never.

"How is Boy Toy treating you?" I ask when I realize I've been talking about myself nonstop. "Do you have your own stories to share?"

"You know I don't kiss and tell," Xenia says, much to my annoyance.

"No, I don't," I lie.

"Some things are private," she says defensively.

"I've just told you everything. Ever hear of quid pro quo?"

"You don't mind talking about that stuff. I do."

"You suck."

"I do." She giggles girlishly. "With Boy Toy. Happy now?"

Actually, the image I now have in my mind might ruin Christmas forever, so maybe it's for the best she's decided not to overshare.

My phone chirps, making my heart leap.

"I just got a text from Dragomir," I breathlessly tell her.

"Go check what it says. If he does have another woman, I'll help you kick his ass."

"Deal," I say and hang up.

The text from Dragomir doesn't shed light on anything. It merely says:

*Working late. Please have dinner without me.*

Grr.

I do as he says, then watch *Frozen* to calm myself down.

The doorbell rings.

Pointed questions swirl through my head as I sprint over to open it.

As soon as I lay my eyes on Dragomir, however, the questions die on my lips.

Fuck. Me.

He's wearing a tight black turtleneck.

He must've changed before coming over.

Unless... is this another wet dream?

Stepping in, he pulls me to him and crushes his mouth against mine, devouring me with his lips and tongue as his hands squeeze and knead my ass.

Okay. It's real.

Questions? What questions?

Kissing as if our lives depend on it, we stumble over to my bedroom, leaving our clothes behind like the porn version of Hansel and Gretel—minus the incest.

As soon as we tumble onto the bed, a repeat of last night's sextivities begins—except, unbelievably, it's more intense this time.

By four a.m., I've had enough orgasms to feature in the Guinness Book of World Records, and feel like a squeezed orange that's been run over by a truck.

Okay. Now that the sex is over, I'll ask what I wanted to ask.

I yawn so hard I almost dislocate my jaw.

Maybe we talk after I rest my head in the crook of his shoulder?

Yeah. That's the plan.

I cozy up against him and close my eyes.

---

I WAKE up because of the stupid sun on my face.

Dragomir is nowhere to be found, but there's a note on my vanity:

*Didn't want to wake you again, but had to run. Might be another late night. Enjoy breakfast and gather strength.*

*Dragomir.*

Enjoy breakfast, my foot.

I never confronted him, and now I have to wait until evening?

Actually, by this evening, Vlad had better turn up.

Reining in my frustration with effort, I eat the scrumptious spread Dragomir has laid out with the apparent goal of fattening me up. Then I take Boner out for a walk and try to nap again.

Nope.

The questions prevent me from sleeping, so I channel the anxious energy into my work.

When I get hungry, I make a sandwich, but before I can bite into it, my phone rings.

Could it be?

Yes!

Finally.

It's Vlad calling.

I'm about to learn Dragomir's secret.

# FORTY

"WHO DOES THAT?" I ask Vlad as soon as I hear his voice. "How could you leave me a voicemail like that and disappear from the face of the Earth?"

"Sorry," he says, but doesn't sound like he really means it. "It wasn't the sort of information I wanted to discuss over the phone."

I narrow my eyes. "Oh, no, you don't. You're not making me shlep to your office. In fact, make me wait another second, and I'll make you regret it. Remember my tenth birthday?"

"Chill out. Let's at least jump on a videocall. At least those apps pretend to care about privacy enough to use encryption."

Gritting my teeth, I hang up and switch to video.

"Spill it," I say as soon as I see Vlad's face. "Now."

"Okay, so here's the deal. As I was waiting for Fanny to get ready, I did some digging with the aid of the names you gave me."

I narrow my eyes at him. "And?"

"And hit paydirt."

"And?" My voice spikes in volume.

"And I learned who he really is. *What* he is."

"*What* he is? If you say 'a werewolf,' or make some other joke, I'm going to choke you."

He gets closer to the camera. "The truth might actually sound like a joke, but I assure you, it's not. I'm still adjusting to this, to be honest."

I feel a hollow sensation in the pit of my stomach. "What is he?"

"*Knyaz,*" Vlad says solemnly.

I blink. "Say what?"

"*Velikiy knyaz.*"

I blink faster. "Still don't get it."

Vlad frowns. "It means the same thing in Ruskovian as in Russian. The Grand Prince."

At this point, I'm blinking in Morse Code. "A prince? Like Hans?"

Vlad quirks an eyebrow. "Is that the villain from *Frozen*?"

"Seriously?"

He and Alex make fun of my favorite movie, but there's a time and a place for these things. "How can Dragomir be a prince?"

Vlad shrugs. "You know how Ruskovia has a ruling monarchy?"

I nod. That's one of the few things I knew about that place before I met one of its citizens.

"Dragomir's last name wasn't always Lamian. That's what he changed it to when he moved to America. He was born a Cezaroff." He looks at me for signs of recognition. Not finding any, he adds, "As in, the Cezaroff dynasty. As in, a royal prince."

My brain strains to process this.

A prince.

A royal.

"Is he married?" I ask numbly.

"No," Vlad says. "I think his noble status is the only thing he's hidden from you. Everything else he's told you is true—including the fact that he was disinherited. That's public knowledge."

"Yeah, sure," I say bitterly. "He just understated what was on the line a bit—the ability to rule a freaking country."

"He wasn't really going to rule anyway," Vlad says. "Too many older brothers."

Older brothers. Of course. Things begin to click into place—such as why Stanislaus's profile looked so familiar when we had dinner the other day.

I've seen it once before, on that gold coin Dragomir gave the veterinarian.

And there's more. The initials on his hankie: D. C. It must stand for Dragomir Cezaroff.

Other little things make more sense now too. His perfect English, the stories about his family employing servants and owning gardens, gazebos, soccer fields...

"You okay?" Vlad's tone is gentle.

Oh, right. I'm still on the call.

I shake my head. "I better go and wrap my head around this."

He leans in toward the camera. "Do you want me to come over?"

"No. Thank you. This is something I need to deal with alone."

As much as I could use a brotherly hug, I need to go online and check all this out for myself, because a part of me still hasn't accepted it.

"I'm sorry," Vlad says, and this time, he does sound like he means it.

I give him a weak smile. "Unlike Mother, I never shoot the messenger. Besides, it's not like you found out he's married."

I wish I could be as serene as I'm trying to seem.

"Just let me know if there's anything you need," Vlad says. "I could hack into his—"

"Thank you, but no. Can we talk in a bit?"

"Of course."

"Okay, then, bye."

Rushing to my computer, I search the name *Cezaroff*.

A deluge of results pops up.

The majority are articles in Ruskovian that my browser easily translates. One is about Dragomir Cezaroff winning a fencing contest as a teenager. Countless others are about his troubles with his parents.

More interestingly, there's some stuff in English. Apparently, being royals has put the Cezaroff family on the radar of gossip magazines in the US and abroad. While not as popular as their British equivalents, these princes are still interesting enough to obsess about.

I scan the English stuff and find nothing about Dragomir—perhaps because of his disinherited status?

They do love his other siblings, though. Tigger—under his full name of Anatolio Cezaroff—is a particular staple. There are write-ups about his crazy adventures, coverage of his recent accident (with clickbait titles like "Will he die?"), and speculations about the women he's been seen with.

In fact, the most recent article puts him in The Doro on the very night of our dinner there. The writer claimed that his next stunt would be a feat of overeating.

Wait a second.

I recognize the picture of the person who wrote this article.

It's the camera guy, the one I thought was a private detective. Now I see what he was after. He was hoping Dragomir would either do something newsworthy or lead him to a story about his more news-worthy relatives.

More things fall into place.

That strange design made out of diamonds on Dragomir's Patek Philippe watch is the Cezaroff family crest, and the Ruskovian writing on it is the family motto: "In tradition, strength."

The funnily dressed people I mistook for bouncers/doormen at the restaurant were actually the royal guard—which might explain why they had gas masks ready to go.

Even the dogs are famous. The misha breed was originally

created for the royal family centuries ago. To this day, every Cezaroff gets the purest-blood misha puppy in existence. In fact, the royal family is famous for always having one around—a bit like the Starks with their direwolfs on *Game of Thrones*. Dragomir didn't lie when he said he didn't name Winnie. Only the king—or tzar—has the naming privileges, and Dragomir's snobby father would obviously use a fancy name.

The more I learn, the stupider I feel for not figuring it all out on my own. I also get progressively angrier.

Leaping to my feet, I pace the apartment.

We've known each other for two months, yet he's hidden something of this magnitude from me. I told him how much it hurt me when the last man I dated lied by omission, yet he proceeded to do the same.

How could he?

This entire time, I didn't even know his real name.

And to think I almost fell for the guy. Or did fall—which might be why this hurts so much.

I stop pacing and ball my hands into fists.

This is what I get for being stupid enough to trust. I should've known better.

Dragomir was attracted to me—that's a red flag right there. I always attract asshats, yet I thought this time might be different. Einstein was right when he said that "the definition of insanity is doing the same thing over and over and expecting different results."

Well, my insanity ends now.

Or soon.

I still have to face him.

I spin around.

Yeah, that's a great idea. I'm going to march to his work and give him a piece of my mind. Why the fuck not? He deserves my wrath.

Feeling a modicum better, I rush into my closet and put on the sexiest outfit I own—a killer black dress. I top it with a short biker jacket and slip on a pair of high-heeled boots.

Let him see what he's about to lose.

Next, I smear on makeup, war-paint style.

As I stride for the door, Boner steps into my path and whines pitifully.

Great. The poor dude misses Winnie already.

I feel a surge of guilt that really shouldn't be mine to bear. Given what I'm about to do, Boner is going to lose access to Winnie—but it's not my fault.

Hopefully, Boner will move on.

Hopefully, both of us can.

Still, driven by the guilt, I grab Boner's leash.

Seeing this, he perks up a little, as I knew he would. A leash outside the usual walk time means adventure, and he loves those.

WITH BONER on my lap in the cab, I fume all the way to Dragomir's office. As I enter the lobby of the building, Boner has to run to keep up with my furious strides.

Stepping into the elevator, I glare at the buttons.

It's just occurred to me that I don't know where Dragomir actually is. The only area I've been to here is the conference room where Alex and I pitched Project Morpheus.

Deciding to start my search there, I take the elevator to that floor and sprint over to the room.

No Dragomir. However, Marco is there, with the whole team from our meetings.

Fine.

If I have to beat Dragomir's location out of Marco, so be it.

Taking in a deep breath, I barge in.

MARCO'S GREETING IS A SNEER. "Bella. What a coincidence. We were just talking about you."

Confused, I halt within strangling distance of him. "I'm not here for you."

His mouth flattens. "You would be if you knew the topic of our discussion."

I pinch the bridge of my nose. "What are you going on about? I don't have time for—"

"I was just telling everyone your secret," Marco says, rudely cutting me off.

My secret?

Is this about me sleeping with his boss? If so, that's not going to be a—

"You own a company named Belka," Marco announces, and I freeze in place. "A company that makes filth." He steps so close to me I can smell stale coffee on his breath. "So you see, we can't in good conscience invest in a project that has *you* as its member."

As I reel from this, there's a low growl at my feet. Like me, Boner dislikes Marco's tone.

"Where is Dragomir?" I demand.

"Why?" Marco asks. "He recused himself. Our decision is final. You don't need to bother him with more lies."

"Lies?" I bare my teeth. "You'd know, wouldn't you?"

Everyone in the room seems to be on the edge of their seats. It's not every day you can witness a show like this in a corporate setting.

Marco looks indignant. "What is that supposed to mean?"

I pin him with a dagger-like stare. "Does your Ruskovian woman know about the American one? How about vice versa?"

Marco whitens, and the people around us begin to whisper among themselves, some of them frowning.

"She's lying," Marco says, not very convincingly.

"I'd be happy to email the proof to everyone in the room." I pull out my phone and wave it in the air.

I'm bluffing, of course. I have no idea if Vlad has proof, or if I even care to ruin Marco's life to that degree.

Marco tries to snatch at my phone, but I yank it back and give everyone a speaking look.

Judging by the expressions all around us, no one believes Marco anymore.

The growling from below is replaced with a strange sound.

Marco glances down and begins to curse in Ruskovian.

I follow his gaze, and my eyes widen.

It's Boner. He's hiked up his leg as high as he can and is relieving himself on Marco's foot.

Good boy. That's what assholes deserve.

Marco's expression turns livid, and I see his leg pull back—presumably to kick my dog.

My hand jerks forward instinctively, and next thing I know, I have Marco's soft, shriveled balls in my grasp.

Yuck.

"Kick him and you'll sing falsetto," I snarl.

Marco looks ready to kick *me* now, so I prepare to squeeze for all I'm worth.

"Leave them alone," Eugenius says. He's pointing his phone at Marco, no doubt recording a video.

Reddening, Marco mutters obscenities under his breath but pointedly stills his leg.

I pull Boner away, mouth "thanks" at Eugenius, and let go of the grossness in my hand, making a mental note to Purell my palm until it's raw.

"You better leave," Eugenius says to me.

Yep. Marco has sixty pounds on me and might decide to risk violence despite the presence of his colleagues.

I walk out, keeping my back straight, and ponder what to do as I get into the elevator.

The post-adrenaline crash is hitting me hard, and I don't feel ready to face Dragomir anymore. Nor do I really need to. If Marco knows about the sex toys, Dragomir must too. Add to that my unseemly behavior just now, and I'm certain it's over.

Sprinting out of the cursed building, I hail a cab.

Midway to my house, my phone rings.

It's Dragomir.

For a second, I'm tempted to pick up, but what would be the point?

It's over. A confrontation would just prolong the pain.

I let the call go to voicemail.

Unable to help myself, I listen to it a few seconds later. His message is short: *We should talk.*

My reply text is equally terse and to the point: *No, thanks, Your Royal Highness.*

He calls again, and I let it go to voicemail.

He texts next: *Call me.*

I don't. Instead, I ignore another call, then turn off my phone.

For the rest of the way home, I pet Boner to calm myself down, and when I step into my apartment, I beeline straight for the living room.

With the way I'm feeling right now, I have to take out the big guns: *Frozen.*

Sadly, I'm still feeling shitty when the credits roll. Worse even— and I didn't expect that. I thought it would be like when I broke up with my married ex. It hurt, sure, but I also felt liberated once I pulled off that Band-Aid.

Not this time. This time, it feels like the Band-Aid I've tried to pull off is sandpaper that some evil genius has crazy-glued to my heart.

Why am I feeling this way?

Is it because Dragomir has wormed his way deeper into my heart than my ex ever had? Or—and this is unsettling—is it because his lie is less malevolent and therefore doesn't warrant my reaction?

My stomach feels icy as I ponder that further.

Could it be I'm not feeling liberated because a part of me knows that I'm not so blameless myself? After all, Dragomir isn't the only one who's omitted information. I haven't told him about my sex toy business, and an argument could be made that my lie is more selfish— in the beginning, I hid the truth so I could get his fund to invest in my venture.

Leaping to my feet, I begin pacing my apartment, memories of our long-distance phone conversations kaleidoscoping through my mind—along with all the different ways he's brought me to orgasm.

When I nearly trample Boner, I sit down and take out my phone.

Time to be honest with myself.

I still want Dragomir, lies or not.

The question is: does he still want me? When he called before, was it so he could break up with me, or did he want to apologize about concealing his true identity?

If it's the latter, I think I might need to forgive him.

In fact, I might've forgiven him if I'd succeeded in storming into his office—assuming Dragomir had said the right things.

My pulse racing, I turn my phone back on.

It's the moment of truth.

I call Dragomir back.

The call goes to voicemail.

My heart feels like it's shrinking.

Is he retaliating for my not picking up?

I wait five minutes, staring at the phone the entire time.

He doesn't get back to me.

My heart shrivels further. He's always gotten back to me within five minutes before.

Maybe he's in a meeting? Or walking Winnie sans phone, as per his custom?

Just in case, I call again and leave a voicemail: *Call me.*

Five minutes later, I also text the same message.

Maybe he has the world's richest man in his office? Or is negotiating some billion-dollar deal?

A nail-biting hour passes without any reply.

The meeting and dog-walk excuses seem more pathetic with every passing minute.

Two hours later, I have to admit it.

I fucked things up, and there may be no going back.

# FORTY-TWO

I WANT TO CRY, but I fight the urge. Boner is sensitive to my mood, and the poor thing is already suffering from bear withdrawal.

Grabbing my laptop, I dive into work instead.

Nope. I'm so distracted with uselessly checking my phone every two seconds that I can't design the most basic of butt plugs.

I take Boner for a walk instead of pointlessly pacing the apartment, but since I bring my phone with me, it's an hour of wallowing in self-pity and incessant phone checking.

When Boner is done with all his bathroom needs, I take us home, but instead of entering my building, I stop, filled with sudden determination.

The walk has cleared my head enough to make a decision.

If Dragomir won't answer my calls, I'm going to confront him face to face. If he wants to end things, he'll have to do it in person. Not that I will accept rejection meekly—I plan to fight for us if I have to.

Hailing a cab, I direct it to Dragomir's offices again.

When we get there, I grab Boner under my arm and rush to the same meeting room in case luck is with me and Dragomir is there.

He isn't.

The people from earlier are, though. Thankfully, Marco isn't among them.

Setting Boner on the floor, I prepare to enter, but Eugenius spots me and steps out into the hallway.

"You've already heard?" He sounds impressed.

My eyebrows squish together. "Heard what?"

"The funding," he says, looking slightly confused. "It's just been approved."

I rub my eyebrows. "But Marco—"

"Was fired," Eugenius says with distaste. "He was the driving force for that initial rejection. The rest of us actually felt safer investing in your venture when we found out it wasn't just your brother who could run a successful business."

I should be ecstatic about this, but I'm not. Not if this money has cost me the man I care about.

"Where is Dragomir?" I barely resist the urge to shake the information out of Eugenius.

"He left right after he let Marco go," Eugenius says.

"So where is he?" I demand.

Frowning, Eugenius adjusts his glasses. "Is everything okay?"

Does he want me to shake him? "I just need to talk to him. Please. It's important."

The guy shifts from foot to foot. "The boss doesn't explain his comings and goings to us. It seemed to be a private matter, something urgent."

Urgent private matter.

Do I dare hope? Could he have gone to my place to have the same conversation I came here for?

"Thank you, Eugenius. I'm looking forward to working with you guys."

Ignoring the blush on his face, I rush back, and when I jump into the cab, I check my phone.

Nothing.

Ugh. Why did I think Dragomir would go to my place without calling? Of course he wouldn't do that.

For all I know, the funding was his parting gift.

Still, though I've done my best to ready myself for the disappointment, my chest tightens painfully when I get to my place and don't see Dragomir at or near the building. The pain grows to Everest levels when I get to my door.

He's not here.

I wasn't the urgent personal matter, after all.

How conceited of me to think that I was. Not only are his parents in town, but his brother is still in recovery.

Oh, shit.

What if something's happened to him?

*That* sort of emergency could explain the radio silence.

Grabbing a very confused Boner, I run out of my building again—this time heading to Tigger's hotel, which fortunately happens to be nearby.

"I'm here to see Anatolio Cezaroff," I pant at the hotel clerk.

He peers at me down the length of his nose. "Mr. Cezaroff wasn't expecting visitors."

I exhale in relief. "So he's okay? He was recently injured, and his brother Dragomir is missing, so I thought that maybe something—"

"Let me see if I can get him on the phone," the clerk says snootily. "What is your name?"

"Tell him I'm Bella—Dragomir's Bella."

At least I hope that last bit is or will be true.

The guy dials a number with his pinky and waits a few seconds. "Hello. There's a lady here who says she's Dragomir's Bella."

He waits a couple of seconds, then quickly describes what I look like.

"He said he's coming down," he informs me after hanging up.

"He also said that if you're not Bella but some crazy stalker, he'll press charges."

A stalker? Is that a joke, or something Tigger actually has to deal with? More importantly, if Tigger isn't the emergency, where is Dragomir and why is he ignoring my calls?

Could he have moved on to another woman so quickly?

No. He's not like that.

Prince or not, I know him. I know what his core is like.

An unthinkable option occurs to me, and a jolt of adrenaline spikes my heartbeat.

What if Dragomir is in some kind of trouble?

What if he's been hit by a car? Or his RV has gotten into an accident?

My mind has clearly been primed by worrying about Tigger, but now that it's gone to that dark place, I can't get rid of the paralyzing fear.

Wait. No. I'm being stupid. Tigger wouldn't be chilling in his hotel if Dragomir were hurt.

Unless... he doesn't know.

I all but bite my nails until Tigger steps out of the elevator.

Spotting me, he grins—not something he'd do if Dragomir was in trouble.

"Do you know where he is?" I blurt, all but tackling him by the elevator doors.

His grin widens. "You mean Dragomir?"

"Obviously."

"He didn't tell you?"

I bite my lip. "I might've told him not to call me earlier, so..."

"Oh." Tigger's grin disappears. "What happened?"

"Never mind that. Where is he?"

Tigger frowns. "With Dr. Delomalov, of course."

At first, the word *doctor* sends my anxiety through the stratosphere, but then the full name registers. That's the—

"You really have no clue?" Tigger darts a glance at Boner. "I thought of all people, you'd expect this." He grins again. "'Commoner impregnates royal'—that's what all the Ruskovian papers will say once they find out."

"Dr. Delomalov is the veterinarian, right?" I say breathlessly.

"That he is."

"Winnie's gone into labor?"

"Bingo."

My breath whooshes out in relief.

This explains everything.

Dr. Delomalov's office has no cell reception, so if Dragomir has been there for the past few hours, he doesn't even know that I'm ready to talk.

"I need to get to that office," I tell Tigger urgently. I turn to the clerk. "Can you get me a taxi?"

"How about *I* give you a lift?" Tigger suggests. "I rented a Lamborghini and still haven't gotten a chance to test it out."

"Sure. Whatever gets me there fastest."

"I'll tell the valet to get the car out for you," the clerk says.

We step outside, and a few minutes later, a black Lamborghini pulls up—the latest model with all the bells and whistles.

The valet opens the car door for me, and I scramble inside.

Hmm. The seatbelts look like those in a race car. I'm not a huge fan of going fast—is it too late to mention that?

Warily strapping in, I open the window for Boner and check my phone.

Still nothing.

Tigger gets behind the wheel, looking unsettlingly excited.

"You've driven this thing before, right?" I ask.

"Does it matter? Brace yourself."

"Wait. I don't like the sound of—"

Turning the wheel sharply to the right, Tigger floors the gas.

With a smell of burning rubber, the Lamborghini tears forward at

Mach 1 speed—or whatever pace the supersonic jets fly at. Gravity flattens me into my seat, and Boner whines as I squeeze him against my chest. The wind through the open window is like a hurricane, so I release my death grip on Boner long enough to press the button to close it.

"Dude," I say when the wind tunnel effect is gone. "When I said 'whatever gets me there fastest,' I meant *alive*."

In the time it takes me to say those words, we clear four blocks.

"Don't worry," Tigger says, zooming through a yellow light. "Live a little."

Living is the goal.

Boner looks on the verge of throwing up. "*Ma chérie*, I've changed my mind about suicide. Can you get this insane *humain* to slow down?"

"Is there a complication with Winnie's delivery?" I ask Tigger in the hope that he'll slow down if forced to talk.

Nope. He doesn't slow so much as a mile per hour. "I don't think so. Dragomir just wanted to be safe."

Wanting to be safe is clearly a concept Tigger doesn't get.

I don't ask anything else—we have a higher chance of survival if he focuses on the driving.

The rest of the ride is like a scene from *The Fast and the Furious* and will be the source of my future nightmares. The only good thing I can say about it is that it's over quickly.

Very quickly.

"Go," Tigger says when we come to a tire-burning stop. "I'll park and come up."

Knees wobbly, I make my way to the vet's office, shell-shocked Boner under my arm.

When I step inside, Dragomir is sitting there.

He looks so worried you'd think it was his wife giving birth, not his dog. But at the sight of me, he leaps to his feet.

"Hi," I say uncertainly.

His hazel eyes gleam. "Hi."

I inhale a big breath. I'll need all the air to say what I want to say. It's now or never.

BEFORE I CAN GET a single word out, the door opens and Dr. Delomalov rushes out.

"Joyous occasions, truly," he says with a wide grin. "The bitch done. Birthed fifty-teen pups. Want to envision them?"

"Of course," Dragomir says eagerly.

"Me too," I say.

What I really want is to talk to Dragomir, but I'm not sure he'll be able to focus on my words until he makes sure Winnie is okay.

And, of course, I *am* mega curious about the puppies. I'm not dead inside.

We follow the doctor down the hallway and into a room where Winnie is lying on a big dog bed. She looks tired but happy—and she's surrounded by her new family.

The puppies have their eyes closed and look vaguely like koala bears, both in terms of looks and coloring—and each is at least five times the size of their father.

If the dogs' genders had been reversed, this pregnancy would've been impossible.

I set Boner on the floor, clutching his leash.

My heart is filled with enough joy to power a Tesla for a trip to Disney World. Some of the pups are already nursing, and Winnie is licking one youngster who isn't. Spotting Dragomir, she wags her tail, and when her gaze falls on Boner, the wagging turns into outright windmilling.

Yipping excitedly, Boner pulls on the leash.

"Can I let him near them?" I ask.

"Yes, but carefully," Dragomir says.

Well, yeah. We wouldn't want Winnie to go into mama bear mode. That shit is scary.

Preparing to pull Boner back if necessary, I let him approach the newborns.

Winnie eyes him intently.

Boner sniffs one of the pups, licks it almost reverently, then steps back and gives me the most confused look.

"*Ma chérie*, how are they bigger than *moi*? Please say I'm such a stud I broke the laws of *physique*."

We all ooh and ahh over the pups for a while. Then Tigger joins us and begs Dragomir to give him one.

"They're going to live with me until Winnie is ready to part with them," Dragomir says sternly. "I'm not going to take babies away from their mother—not even for you."

Tigger rolls his eyes. "I didn't mean now."

Dragomir rubs his chin. "You'll have to bring Caradog so I can be sure he's going to be nice to the pup. I also want to check that his shots are up to date."

Tigger exhales in exasperation. "Obviously."

"In that case, maybe," Dragomir says. "Depends on your behavior."

Tigger switches to Ruskovian for his reply, and the two brothers start to bicker—but it sounds more like good-natured ribbing than a fight.

I tug on Dragomir's sleeve.

He gives me an apologetic look. "Sorry about that."

"No worries. Can we talk?"

Dragomir nods, and Tigger arches an eyebrow.

"In private?" I look at Tigger pointedly.

"Dr. Delomalov," Dragomir says. "Is there a place Bella and I can get some privacy?"

"Come," the veterinarian says and opens the door.

I thrust Boner's leash into Tigger's hands and follow the doctor, swaying my hips for Dragomir as a way to butter him up before our chat.

When we reach a big wooden door, the doctor opens it and we step into a cramped office.

As soon as the doctor leaves, Dragomir locks the door.

I find the action insanely hot—and reassuring.

A man doesn't lock himself in with a woman he plans to scorn.

Hopefully.

Gathering my courage, I launch into my spiel. "I'm sorry. It was shitty of me not to take your calls." And I mean it. Thinking that he'd done the same to me really sucked.

Jaw tight, Dragomir closes the distance between us. "No. I'm the one who's sorry." His voice is low and earnest. "I wanted to tell you about my heritage so many times, but I kept putting it off."

"Why?" The question isn't bitter. I'm genuinely curious.

He grabs my hand and squeezes it tight. "Because it's always ruined things in my life. I didn't want to lose you over it. Ironic, right? I almost did lose you—because I hid it from you."

My breathing picks up at his warm touch, but I ignore it—I have to speak coherently for the next part. "I take it you know about my sex toy company?"

He smiles. "I've known since the day after you gave me your name."

I gape at him. "You have?"

"Since we're coming clean, I might as well tell you. I have access to the Ruskovian equivalent of the CIA. I wanted to learn more about you—so I did. I hope you can forgive me for that invasion of privacy."

"Well, as far as the invasion of privacy goes, I've done the same to you," I admit sheepishly. "How about we call it even, then? On the snooping and the omitting of information."

He brings my hand to his lips and kisses the back of my knuckles. "I wholeheartedly agree."

I do my best to focus on something other than the tingles radiating down to my core. "Wait. So if you've known about my business all along, how did Marco find out about it just now?"

"My parents, I'm sure. They undoubtedly used the same service to look into you after our dinner."

I sigh. "Doesn't sound like they liked me."

"Take it as a compliment."

Relieved, I smile. "So they don't decide whom you date?"

"Hells no."

"Good. And just to double check—the person you're with doesn't have to be royal, like you?"

He shakes his head. "That's what my parents would want, but not me. In fact, if they liked you, I'd be worried."

My smile becomes a grin. "I bet I could make them like me if I got to know them better."

He grins back. "And I bet yours will still like me more than mine will ever like you."

I bristle. "That's not fair. Mine already love you more than they do me. They're not fans of my business—something I never got the chance to tell you."

His smile vanishes. "Ignore what anyone thinks. Your toys are amazing. You have serious talent and should be proud of it." Framing my face with his palms, he says solemnly, "I want you to always be yourself, and don't ever apologize for it."

Wait a sec. That sounds like a takeaway from *Frozen*. Does that mean he's watched it?

Before I realize what the fuck I'm saying, the words fly out of their own accord.

"I love you."

His face goes taut, his hazel gaze turning a golden shade of amber. "I love you too. Squirrelchik..." His deep voice is husky. "You're a person worth melting for."

Oh. My. God.

It's official. He's watched *Frozen*.

My overfull heart feels like it's pulling an Olaf.

Rising on tiptoes, I throw my arms around his neck and drag him down for a kiss. One that I hope is the best of his life. The kind that will make him think of the ending of *his* favorite movie—specifically, the moment where Grandpa says, "Since the invention of the kiss, there have been five kisses rated the most passionate, the most pure. This one left them all behind. The end."

Except our kiss isn't pure. It isn't PG, like *The Princess Bride*.

Maybe not even PG-13.

Then Everest rises and Dragomir takes over, clearing the doctor's cluttered desk with one swipe of his muscular arm—and the rating of our movie quickly escalates to triple X.

# EPILOGUE

## DRAGOMIR

LOOKING LIKE A FIERCE VALKYRIE, Bella swings her red lightsaber at my head.

I parry her attack with my blue lightsaber, and sparks fly at the intersection of our blades. Before she recovers, I riposte, my blade scoring a hit into her shoulder.

She growls and exposes her breasts.

Fuck. Those breasts. Perky, perfectly pliant, with those oh-so-suckable nipples, they—

No. Must not look there.

She's using her feminine wiles as a form of psychological warfare. Effective psychological warfare at that—I've lost count of how many unwelcome erections I've gotten during our matches.

Well, two can play mind games.

"Ninety-nine hits now, squirrelchik," I say tauntingly. "One more, and you have to yield."

Nostrils flaring, Bella swipes at my midsection.

I parry effortlessly. "You're letting your anger drive you again." I know full well this will actually fuel the anger more, which is the point. "Make your mind calm, like water in a well."

Rolling her gorgeous blue eyes, she performs a decent feint.

If I didn't have as much fencing experience—or if more of her were exposed—she might've gotten me. As is, I parry again but don't yet deliver the finishing blow.

Like a cat, I like to play with my beautiful prey. I find this leads to all the benefits of makeup sex without actually fighting.

Well, unless you count what we're currently doing as that.

She performs another extremely effective attack, especially for a beginner.

Fuck. I might be getting cocky. That swipe could've gotten me—which would mean I'd have to exclusively wear turtlenecks for a month, including tight and scratchy ones.

Then again, if *I* win, she'll have to walk the puppies—or the Chort Pack as we've been calling them, in part as a tip of the hat to Bella's family name, but more so because the word *chort* means *demon* in both Russian and Ruskovian. Walking the Chort Pack is a fate anyone would want to avoid, as it's quite similar to herding the proverbial cats... if the cats were on catnip laced with amphetamines.

Bella makes the rest of her clothes disappear.

Fucking fuck.

All the blood rushes away from my brain.

I want to lick every curve, trace my tongue over that delectable stomach all the way down to—

She attacks so furiously her lightsaber whooshes an inch from my ear.

Fine. If she's going to play dirty, so be it.

Casting the same magic spell as she did, I make my own clothes evaporate.

Her eyes widen. My squirrelchik denies it, but she finds the sight of me naked distracting as well.

Still, she attacks competently—but I'm ready.

Executing a flawless *passata sotto*, I drop beneath her lightsaber.

My free hand is now on the ground to provide me with support and balance, and my eyes get an exquisite view of her pretty pink pussy.

Must stay focused for another moment.

Before Bella realizes what's about to hit her, I straighten my sword arm and make the final stab.

She curses like a Russian sailor.

With my squirrelchik, competitive is a vast understatement.

I jump to my feet. "What did you say?"

"I yield," she grumbles. "Happy now?"

"Thank you. Now if—"

Before I can finish my thought, she makes our lightsabers disappear and replaces the room with an open sky.

Ah. I know what she wants.

Grabbing her, I take flight like Superman with his Lois Lane, except I'm soon buried deep inside her.

Clouds float around us as she moans in pleasure.

When we both come, we hover in the sky, holding each other.

"Ready to get out?" she murmurs, stroking my face.

I kiss her fingers one by one, then take off my VR goggles.

Across the bedroom of my private plane, she also takes off her headgear and climbs out of her VR suit.

I take off my suit as well. What we've just tested is the early prototype that came out of Project Morpheus, and if everyone enjoys it as much as I do, it will be a huge success.

"Remember, don't look out the windows," I tell her. "It'll ruin the surprise."

She nods, her full lips in a slight pout.

"Oh, come on. We're landing in a few minutes. You can see Ruskovia from up high when we fly back to the States."

"I guess…"

Despite the orgasm I've just given her, she's still a little sore about losing, but it'll make her eventual win that much sweeter. With the current rules—a hundred hits for me versus one for her—and the progress she's making, that win is inevitable.

I'd better shop for some turtlenecks.

I dress first, then wait until she does so as well. My eyes mourn her luscious nakedness disappearing from sight, but my brain is glad.

She's so beautiful I can't think around her as is.

Once she slips on the engagement ring I've given her, I unlock the bedroom door, and as usual, the Chort Pack rush into the room like a horde of Tasmanian devils.

Boner and Winnie follow them, beaming with parental pride.

Now bigger than an average bulldog, the adorable pups begin destroying anything and everything they can get their paws on, but I just stare contentedly, a goofy grin on my face.

"Fu," Bella says when Mephistopheles—the pup we plan to house with Tigger—tries to chew on Bella's stilettos.

Mephistopheles stops.

The demon spawn revere Bella—or at least she's the only person who can get them to behave, if only for a couple of seconds.

"Beginning descent," the pilot announces on the intercom.

Bella and I strap ourselves in on the luxurious bed, and the furry family surrounds us with all their love and warmth.

When we land, I wait for Bella to put on the heavy clothing that will shield her from the Ruskovian cold, then hand her a blindfold.

She reluctantly covers her eyes. "The surprise better be worth it."

"I hope it is," I say, then clasp her shoulders and carefully guide her off the plane.

"You can see it now," I say, positioning her just so.

She rips off her blindfold and gapes at the structure in front of us.

I half expect her to quote her favorite movie and say, "I never knew winter could be so beautiful," but she seems to be struck mute.

I must say, even *I'm* impressed, and I was the one who commissioned this to be built in the first place.

A replica of the ice palace from *Frozen* stands one hundred feet tall, glimmering majestically in the light.

"Wow," she breathes, then spins around to face me. "Is that...?"

"Yes, it's for you."

"Do you think we could—"

"Hold the wedding here? Yes."

And as she throws her arms around me, beaming with joy, I imagine our life together in the years to come: Bella in my arms, challenging me in and out of bed... our children riding on Winnie's back... the countless other surprises I will create for her.

It's a glorious future—and to think, it all began when a Chihuahua molested my dog.

# HARD BYTE

# ONE

"THE DEVIL IS about to turn my life's work into porn." I give my twin a pleading look. "You have to teach me how to pick locks."

Gia blinks at me. "What in Houdini's balls are you talking about?"

"Lock picking. Teach me."

She shakes her head as if to clear it, then opens the door wider. "Come inside and explain."

"Fine." Respecting my sister's germaphobia, I bypass hugs and kisses as I gingerly step into the brownstone she shares with her million roommates. She leads me to her room, and as we walk, I fight the temptation to fix the myriad messes all around.

"Sit." She points at a chair in the corner, next to a mannequin.

Is she nuts? That chair is four-legged, the worst kind. I prefer office chairs, as they usually have five legs, or barstools, since they tend to have one or three. How would she like it if I asked her to lick a subway pole?

A mischievous grin quirks her dark-lipsticked mouth. "My bad. Not a prime number of legs. What was I thinking? Your brain could've melted."

Hiding my eye roll, I walk past a deck of cards and other magician's paraphernalia strewn all over the nearby surfaces, not stopping until I'm next to a legless beanbag chair. "You mind?"

Shrugging, Gia takes a deck of cards out of her pocket and hands it to me by the tips of her fingers. "Would you feel more at ease if I gave you this deck to organize?"

Plopping into the chair, I narrow my eyes at the deck. "Fifty-two?"

With a sigh, she tosses one of the cards on a nearby desk—as if it weren't a mess already. "Fifty-one now."

"Fifty-one isn't a prime."

She peers at the deck. "It's not?"

"Three times seventeen is fifty-one. How did you pass fourth grade?"

"We probably had you pretend to be me to ace the math test." She drops four more cards on the desk. "Is forty-seven better?"

"Thank you." I take the cards carefully—God forbid I touch her hygienic majesty with my cooties. "What did you want me to explain before you teach me?"

"Start with the life's work part." She sits on the improperly legged abomination. "I didn't realize you had one. Is it the virtual pet stuff you're always showing me?"

"Kind of." I begin sorting the cards in the obvious logical manner: number cards that are primes first, followed by the rest. "I didn't get a chance to tell you before, but I've been working with the pediatric wing of the NYU Langone hospital. If they hear I'm involved with porn—"

"Back up. Working with them how?"

"I've been beta testing my VR pet project as a type of therapy for children in long-term care." I look up from my sorting and into a face identical to the one I see in the mirror every day: oval-shaped with sharp cheekbones, a strong nose, and wide blue eyes. Of course, unlike my entertainer sibling, my hair is its natural strawberry blond hue, while she's turned hers darker than a black hole. I also don't wear that much makeup. Her smoky eyes would make a raccoon fall in lust, and her foundation is pale enough for a vampire geisha. "The idea is to reduce the kids' pain and anxiety," I continue as she nods approvingly.

"That's not bad for your life's work. So how does the devil's porn fit in?"

I glance at the mess all around me. "Do you mind?"

Gia heaves a sigh. "If it gets you talking faster, be my guest."

As I get up and begin tidying, I calm enough to articulate my thoughts. "I haven't told you this either, but my company got into financial trouble a while back and Morpheus Group bought us."

She wrinkles her nose. "Never heard of them."

I pick up a top hat of the kind a magician's rabbit might leap out of—not that Gia would ever risk touching something happy to eat its own feces. "I hadn't either until they acquired us. I think it was formed right before the takeover." I put the hat next to Gia's headband, mentally designating the spot as *headgear*. "At first, they asked for specs from our VR headset and gloves and disappeared, leaving us to do our thing as though nothing had changed. But we've just learned that they're planning to integrate the headset and gloves with a special suit they've created, one meant to make your whole body feel things inside VR."

She looks intrigued. "Feel things as in... sex things?"

"That's what the rumors around the office say." I pick up what looks like a fake thumb and put it on a shelf next to her gloves, designating the spot as *pertaining to appendages*.

"Hmm." She scratches her chin. "Sex in VR. No germs. No touching. No complications. Can I get one of those suits?"

"You should get a real man," I say, and instantly regret it—the last thing I want is to sound like Mom.

Gia arches her dark eyebrows and mimics the British accent I had to rid myself of after my study abroad. "As they would say in your beloved England, that's the pot calling the kettle black."

She's right. I'm no expert when it comes to men or sex—my one and only real relationship was with a guy who later came out as gay.

My face must change because she says, "Sorry, Holly. Didn't mean to venture there. Next thing you know, I'll go full Octomom and tell you how much you should yearn for 'a sexual union.'"

I cringe. I hate the nickname she uses for our mom. Forgetting respect for one's elders, it's simply not accurate. Mom gave birth to the two of us, followed by our sextuplet sisters. An accurate moniker would be either Bimom (or is it Dumom?) or Sexamom—though, granted, none of those sound great either. Of course, if I'm honest, the main reason I don't like the *octo-* prefix is that it's a reminder of us being eight sisters, as opposed to some normal amount, like seven, five, or eleven.

"—you need some good old-fashioned lovin'," Gia is saying in her best imitation of Mom's contralto when I tune back in to her jabbering.

Grinning, I do my own impersonation of our embarrassing parental unit. "Orgasms alleviate stress, help with insomnia, ease pain, make you live longer, stimulate your brain, keep you looking younger... Oh, and can bring about world peace."

Did she notice I put seven items on that list?

Gia shudders. "Don't forget how helpful orgasms are when one is trying to get a pig preggers."

Ugh, yeah. Even though I'm not as squeamish as Gia, I've also been traumatized by Mom's humblebragging stories about her husbandry skills. One time, Mom said she brought Petunia—a piggie who was like a pet to us growing up—to orgasm during an artificial insemination session. Yeah. Not the image you want to pop into your head when you see bacon.

Realizing we've gotten way off topic, I pin my sister with an intent stare. "So can you teach me what I need or not?"

She drums her black-painted nails on her thigh. "You still haven't explained the whole devil thing."

Ah. That. I pick up a book on card cheating and stick it into a random empty spot on her bookshelf—if I try to sort her library by year of publication, she'll get upset again and refuse to help me. "According to yet more rumors around the office," I say, "the new owners are brother and sister. Apparently, their last name is Chortsky."

"Apparently? They haven't introduced themselves?"

I pick up a glossy magician's cup and put it next to an empty coffee mug on the desk. "Nope. I've been working via email with a guy named Robert Jellyheim. Anyway, when I searched online for people named Chortsky, I found a Vlad Chortsky who owns a software company and an Alex Chortsky who owns a video game studio. No mention of a sister, no pictures of either men, no social media presence. The only useful thing I learned is that the word *chort*—the root of their family name—means *the devil* or *demon* in Russian."

"Ah," Gia says. "So 'the Devil' is just your nickname for whoever happens to be the elusive owner of Morpheus Group. How does that lead to lock picking? You want to take a crack at your chastity belt?"

My heartbeat speeds up at the thought of the lock picking, and I tidy faster to calm myself down. "There's an office on my floor where the integrated VR suits got delivered yesterday." I pick up three metal linking rings and put them on the coffee table next to her keychain. "It's locked. I want to get into that office and see if the rumors are true."

She frowns. "Why?"

"So I can do something about it... if I have to."

Her frown deepens. "Do what?"

I take a flash drive out of my pocket. "The rumor mill claims the owners are meeting with some big-shot venture capital firm in a few days to demo the work they've done. They must need a new round of funding. My hope is that if a computer virus ruins this demo, it will stall the porn project and I'll be able to finalize my arrangement with the hospital before the Devil finds another source of money."

"So you're going to be breaking and entering to commit corporate sabotage?"

I squeeze the USB stick in my palm. "Hardly. I work there."

"But you're planning on releasing a virus. Isn't that a crime?"

I pocket the USB. "I borrowed some tools from Dad. If caught, I can claim I was testing our security."

Our father is a penetration tester—which isn't what it sounds like. He simulates cyberattacks on willing companies to identify their systems' weaknesses and strengths.

Gia studies me with a worried expression. "You're a sucky liar."

"I plan to disable the cameras in the office. No one will ever know what happened."

She jumps to her feet. "I don't know. Maybe I shouldn't encourage this madness."

"If you don't help, I'm going in with a crowbar."

She gives me a once-over. "That's a bluff. You hate violence."

I put on a determined expression. "I can hurt a bloody door if I have to."

She chews on her lip, then sighs. "This will cost you."

Yes! If she's bargaining, this is going to happen.

"What do you want?" I ask, belatedly reining in my oh-so-easy-to-exploit enthusiasm.

She sits back down. "You will stop going Marie Kondo on my stuff."

"Done." I reluctantly drop her phallic-shaped magic wand back onto the mess of objects on the desk. It's not like I know how to categorize it anyway—apart from putting it next to some dildo.

"And you'll owe me two favors in the future, no questions asked."

I almost reach for the wand again but stop myself in time. "Do you also want the keys to my place? Or maybe a blank check?"

She shrugs. "If our roles were reversed, you'd ask for even more."

That's so not true, but arguing would be fruitless. "How about you tell me what the favors are, so I can see if it's worth it?"

"No deal. How about we split the difference? One favor I will ask for now, one at a later date."

Damn, she's good at poker faces. "What's the 'now' favor?"

"Have you already had your lunch with our parents?"

I grit my teeth. "Yes." It's clear what she wants. Our folks are in town, and naturally, they won't leave until they give a painful lecture to both of their eldest daughters on the dangers of spinsterhood.

"You will dress as me and take my place at the lunch," Gia says, confirming my suspicions. "And you will *not* pass on any sex tips you're likely to acquire."

Bollocks. I was hoping she'd use me in a magic trick—having a twin is pretty helpful when you want to display teleportation powers and the like.

"When is the lunch?" I ask.

Looking too gleeful for my liking, she gives me the details.

The time is smack in the middle of my mid-day flossing, but as much as I hate breaks in my schedule, I don't object. Gia won't be sympathetic.

"What's the other favor?" I ask, dreading it already.

She smirks. "Nice try. I'll tell you that when I know myself."

"Fine. You've got yourself a deal—assuming you actually *can* teach me how to pick a lock."

She stands up. "Can the sextuplets drive even Gandhi to violence?"

Oh yes, they can. Abhorrence of violence is why I limit my exposure to the litter of evil. I love them dearly, of course, but combined, they're too much for my psyche. I part envy, part pity Gia for cavorting with them outside of family holidays. I'm nowhere near that brave.

Getting up, she rummages in a drawer and takes out a pair of gloves, a leather case, and a collection of locks.

"Put these on." She hands me the gloves.

I put them on with an eye roll. "There. Now I won't leave germs on your precious equipment."

She thrusts the leather case into my hands. "I'm giving you gloves so you learn how to pick a lock while wearing them. Or do you want to leave your prints all over the crime scene?"

I unzip the case and stare at the tools inside.

If I can pass the dreaded Advanced Artificial Intelligence course at Cambridge, I can do this.

Hopefully.

"First, let me tell you how a pin tumbler lock works," Gia says, gesturing at a lock made of glass where the pins and other bits are exposed.

She proceeds to open the lock both with a key and with her tools, making it look easy.

"Now this is a tension wrench." She hands me a metal thingy and tells me what to do with it. Then she gives me a pick and explains how to use that.

"Sounds reasonable," I say when the lecture is blissfully over. "Let me try."

Her grin is evil. "Go ahead."

I'm famous for my meticulousness when it comes to following directions of any kind, so, like a robot, I execute Gia's instructions to the letter. Yet my attempt fails, much to my twin's delight.

Grr. Picking a lock seems to be more of an art than a science.

Two hours and dozens of snide comments from Gia later, I improve, though I'm not yet confident enough to proceed with the heist.

Finally, Gia says, "I think you've got it. At least there's not much more I can teach you. Go home and play with the locks on your own."

"Okay." I hide the tools of my newly acquired trade. "I'll call if I have any questions."

To my surprise, she actually puts away the locks we were using instead of tossing them onto the still-cluttered desk. "Think about canceling the whole thing, will you? Don't be tempted by the minimalism of prison life."

"I will," I lie as we step out of her room.

"And text me updates." She leads me past the messy living room to the front door. "Also call me if you need me to post bail."

"Cheers," I say—only to realize my mistake when Gia's grin widens to Joker levels.

"'Tis my pleasure, guv'nor," she deadpans with a thick Cockney accent. "Don't forget about luncheon with Mama and Papa."

"I won't," I grumble.

"Jolly good." She waves her hand in a queenly fashion. "Ta-dah."

"Thank you and goodbye," I enunciate with a perfect American accent.

She locks the door, and I hear her chuckling behind it.

I can't believe that of all my siblings, *she* is the lesser evil.

Getting home, I practice lock picking deep into the night, and when I fall asleep, I dream about it.

By Monday morning, I feel as ready as I ever will.

It's time.

I will get to work, wait for everyone to leave, and proceed with Operation Break-In.

# TWO

LIKE THE BLOODY watched pot that never boils, my coworkers refuse to leave for the day.

I bet they're not even working.

In hindsight, this was a flaw in my plan. Since I'm the Chief Technology Officer here, lots of people want to show off how hard they work by staying late—especially in light of the takeover.

As if summoned by the thought of the takeover, an email from Robert Jellyheim, my equivalent from Morpheus Group, hits my inbox.

Crap. Are they somehow on to me?

But no. He's letting me know that they plan to ramp up the integration soon, and that I'll meet him and the upper management face to face shortly.

This must be why the suits got delivered. I have to say, the Devil is pretty confident about getting this round of funding.

Well, we'll see about that—assuming my stupid teammates ever leave, that is.

My stomach rumbles, giving me an idea. Maybe they'll finally leave if they think I'm gone for the day? And if anyone views the cameras later, they'll see me come back with food—perfectly natural.

Grabbing my stuff, I stomp toward the lift—I mean, elevator.

Wait. What if my coworkers don't notice?

Oh, I know. I stop by a few desks and make them more orderly, killing two birds with one stone. By the time I add an extra pen to a cup that contained only four, I'm certain I've been noticed.

Excellent. I head for the elevator, and when I get inside, I press all the buttons for the floors with prime numbers, a luxury I allow myself when I ride alone.

My daily lunch are the nineteen pieces of ravioli I bring from home, but whenever I need to have dinner at work, I always go to the same Japanese place—Miso Hungry. My order with them is always the same as well: miso soup with forty-seven cubes of tofu and seventeen pieces of scallion, and three avocado rolls with one piece held back in order to make the total a proper prime of twenty-three.

After all, one of the things that separates humans from animals is our desire for order and predictability, or at least that's what I say to Gia when she teases me about my idyllic, clockwork-like life.

"To go?" the hostess asks as soon as she spots me.

I nod. "Yep, takeout."

As she rushes to the sushi bar to give the chef my order, I scan the almost empty restaurant—and am stunned to see a man scanning *me* with his piercing, cerulean-blue eyes.

And what a man.

Perfectly symmetrical face.

Silky-looking jet-black hair.

Broad, athletic shoulders.

The cheekbones of an angel and the most kissable lips I've ever seen.

The only thing that keeps him from perfection is the scruffy stubble on his face and the disarray of the black locks on his head.

I fight the urge to sprint over to him, slick back that unruly hair, and steal a sushi knife from the chef to shave that gorgeous face.

Yeah, okay. I must admit I have something of a fetish for clean-shaven guys. When I first saw pictures of Henry Cavill as Superman, all neat and proper, I wanted to touch myself. But I was *not* a happy camper when he took on his role as the scruffy, mustachioed villain in *Mission: Impossible – Fallout*. The $25 million DC Films spent on the CGI removal of his mustache during the filming of *Justice League* was money well spent if you ask me. I can't wait for a day when technology will allow me to delete mustaches from all the faces on my screens.

Bugger. I'm still gawking at him—a situation made that much worse by the fact that he's not alone at his table. With him is a woman as gorgeous as he is. And unlike her scruffy yet sexy beau, she's extremely put-together, with impeccable makeup and perfectly styled black hair.

As I tear my gaze away, I catch the bastard smirking.

What a cad. What a rake.

The hostess comes back with my takeout, and I spot the stranger whispering something to his beautiful date.

The woman gives me a once-over and starts to stand up.

Crap. Is she going to confront me for ogling her man?

I loathe violence of any kind, but particularly one that could involve me. Frantically snatching my order from the hostess, I thrust some cash into her hands and bolt out of Miso Hungry.

My heart rate is still through the roof when I return to the office. I guess getting turned on by gorgeous strangers isn't a good prelude to a proper heist.

At least there's good news here. As I hoped, the floor is finally empty. I bet the frauds scattered like quail as soon as the elevator doors slid shut behind me.

Putting aside the food—I've lost my appetite at the thought of what I'm about to do—I pretend to write some code before launching the camera-killing script I've prepared.

Is this really happening?

Do I have the ovaries to do this?

I square my shoulders.

It *is* happening. I refuse to chicken out.

Ignoring the tightness in my stomach, I get up and hurry to my destination.

When I get to the door, I glance at the hopefully disabled camera.

It's now or never.

# THREE

I JIGGLE the door handle in case someone's unlocked it.

Nope.

I get my tools and start picking.

Blimey. It's not yielding.

Is this lock different from the ones I practiced on? Or is it my trembling hands?

I take in a deep breath and count to seven.

Hands steadier, I pick the lock again until something inside it clicks.

Finally.

Entering, I examine the large office. On the desk are a high-end monitor and an ergonomic keyboard, next to the desk is a top-of-the-line executive office chair (five-legged, as is proper), and in the corner is a small leather couch.

Is this the Devil's future lair? Or the She-Devil's?

Ignoring that issue for now, I examine the suits.

Split into pink "female" and larger blue "male" models, these are clearly prototypes. Some even have parts attached with duct tape. There are also instruction sheets hanging from them, along with a label that states "Sterile."

I'm no Gia about such things, but even I feel grateful about the sterile bit—the suit is going on my body, after all. I also feel a pang of guilt. Once I put one on, it will no longer be sterile, which sucks for the next woman who'll try it on.

Maybe I can leave a note after I'm done?

First things first. I grab the instructions sheet from the pink suit that looks closest to my size.

"Adjust Velcro straps to fit your body" is the first step.

I'm blessed with prime numbers when it comes to my girth and height, so thanks to the labeled straps, this step is a breeze.

"Undress" is the second instruction.

Hmm. Maybe this suit should buy me dinner first?

I walk over to lock the door. Do cleaning people have keys to this office? Hopefully not. Either way, they're not due for a couple more hours—I looked it up when planning this heist.

Stripping in the workplace feels extremely awkward, but since instructions command it, I do it, leaving my clothes neatly folded on the back of the office chair.

"Lie down or sit as you put on the suit," the next instruction advises. "Start with legs, then body, then gloves. The headset is last."

I sit on the couch, the leather icy on my naked bottom, and wriggle into the suit according to the instructions. Then I adjust everything to make sure it's snug.

The headset turns on, and a virtual reality dashboard appears in the air in front of me. The user interface is similar to the one my team had designed for this exact headset, but with obvious tweaks—must be the work of Robert Jellyheim and his team.

There's only a single app icon—"Demo"—in the dashboard at the moment.

Raising my gloved hand, I jab a finger at it.

The suit comes to life and squeezes my body tight, creating the sensation of a hug. At the same time, I find myself in a white room with two orbs hanging in the air, and two lines of text hovering above them: "Design partner" and "Use defaults."

"Design partner" sounds like something a porn app would say, so I click that.

Two more orbs show up with the next choice: "Male" or "Female."

Chances of this being porn rise.

I opt for male, since that's what I'm attracted to, and the white room fills up with disembodied male heads.

Huh. Okay. Books on user interface design don't cover how to avoid making your software creepy—an oversight, clearly. Unless you're making a game about ghosts, disembodied heads are a bad idea.

With a wave of my hand, I summon each head to me so I can take a closer look at the faces.

Very nice. Though not as realistic as in real life, these are the best that current technology allows—Morpheus Group must work with some talented artists.

After some deliberation, I choose a head with a symmetrical face sporting dreamy blue eyes and chiseled features.

"Change chin?" the interface asks me next.

I do so, making it stronger.

"Add facial hair?"

Hell no.

"Change cheekbones?" is the next choice.

I make them sharper, more defined.

"Change eye color?"

I go for a darker shade of blue—cerulean, to be exact.

Next, I swap the short blond hair for black and silky—neatly slicked back, as I like.

Now a disembodied but very attractive head hovers in the air.

Is it wrong that I'm now more turned on than creeped out?

Wait a second.

The head I've designed looks suspiciously like the one attached to the scorching hot stranger at Miso Hungry. This version is just clean-shaven and lacks a body.

Thanks, subconscious. Now I feel like a total perv.

"Upper body type" is the next choice.

The creepy feeling comes back as the hottie's head flies to the side, and a bunch of headless and legless torsos appear.

Since I'm not sure if I should continue recreating the guy from the restaurant—and because I haven't seen him naked—I go for a muscular, broad-shouldered torso with washboard abs. Because why not?

Once chosen, the torso attaches to the head.

I study the legless apparition. Is it weird that I already want to have my way with him? Is it even a *him* without the lower body?

Swallowing audibly, I touch the virtual pecs.

Damn. The glove makes the touch feel real—which should be no surprise as I was part of the team that made this technology possible. Yet I am surprised. When working on the gloves, my priority was to make petting a fluffy, cuddly creature feel as realistic as possible, so sex and the accompanying human skin sensations were the last thing on my mind.

More torso choices follow. I leave his biceps and other muscles as they are and opt out of nipple piercings and tats.

When the next choice shows up, I blink at it for a couple seconds.

If I had any doubts left, they're gone now.

This *is* going to lead to porn.

The space around me is covered with cocks.

Big. Small. Hard. Flaccid. Fat. Thin. Veiny. Smooth. Straight. Crooked. Deep purple. Pale pink. Green and blue? Someone had clearly taken a perverse pleasure in creating as much variety as humanly possible. Speaking of human, some of the choices don't seem to be of my species—not unless there are guys out there hung like unicorns.

This reminds me of the famous scene from *The Matrix* when Neo asked for "Guns. Lots of guns." Only this is penises. Wait, is that the plural, or is it just penis, like glasses and deer? No. That doesn't sound right. Maybe it's peni, as in fungi? No, that only applies to Latin-based words that end with -us, which penis doesn't—it just sounds like it does. It might be penes—but that sounds too much like the plural for penne pasta. I'll have to check all this when I have access to the internet again.

Oblivious to proper nomenclature, the shlongs dance around me, some happily, some downright threateningly—all clearly eager to be chosen.

I close my eyes. It's hard to concentrate like this... very hard.

I should quit now. These disembodied dicks are my proof, after all.

Hard proof.

Yet for some reason, I can't bring myself to end this VR session. I'm sure it has nothing to do with the epic dry spell I've been experiencing. Or that I've designed a replica of the hot stranger from Miso Horny... I mean, Miso Hungry.

No. Nothing so improper.

I work with VR, so this is purely a professional curiosity.

Yeah, that's it. This is about my job.

I open my eyes and gesticulate at the cocks. It's a stiff competition —there are so many, it takes me ten minutes to finally settle on one: a (hopefully) human one, extra-large and not too veiny.

Does the inspiration for this design have a cock like this? No clue, and I'm unlikely to ever find out... or put it in me... or lick it... or suck it.

The cock perches in its rightful place below the torso, and the place fills up with enough balls to generate a small nation's worth of testosterone.

Does anyone really care about testicles enough to need this much variety?

Eager to see the next phase of this demo, I grab a pair of balls at random, then chose legs equally fast.

This is when the next choice fills up the room: butts.

Lots of butts.

Round-shaped. Heart-shaped. Square-shaped. V-shaped. Muscular and not. With buttholes and, for some reason, without. With dimples and without. The choices aren't as exhaustive as they were with the cocks but close.

I choose the first tight tush I see and wonder if there's going to be more choices—like livers or tonsils.

But no. Everything finally attaches, and my freshly designed virtual boyfriend starts dancing—channeling *Magic Mike.*

Damn. My ovaries high-five each other as I shamelessly ogle the digital perfection. There might even be drool pooling in the corner of my mouth—and other types of wetness in my private places.

Whoever designed this is an evil genius, especially given how little time has passed since the takeover. If they had to sell their soul to the Devil, I'd say it might've been worth it. Or did the Wicked One do this personally? It would be in character for the Tempter to create the ultimate weapon of sexual sin.

I'm distracted from my pseudo-theological musings by a speech bubble that pops up above the head of the no-longer-dancing-but-no-less-mouthwatering digital specimen.

"Do you want me to give you a taste of what the suit can do?" it asks. "Yes or no."

I choose "yes," and the guy teleports over to me, getting so close that his jutting erection presses against my belly.

Wow. The suit creates a sensation of pressure that's eerily accurate.

"Continue?" another thought bubble asks.

My finger is unsteady as I choose "yes."

My digital partner cups my breast with his hand.

I gasp. The touch feels luxuriously real—even accounting for the hormones wrecking my brain's ability to have rational observations.

Another "Continue?" later, he lightly squeezes my nipple.

Double wow. The squeeze is realistic enough to send a fresh surge of need down under.

Un-bloody-believable.

"Continue?" the evil thought bubble asks.

My "yes" is reluctant, and as I spot him reaching for my lady bits, I instinctively catch his wrist—which proves just how realistic this all seems.

Hmm. His wrist feels real in my hand, but the action itself was wonky. There seems to be some work required to integrate the gloves with the suit.

Yet another air bubble appears above his head. "Do you want to sample the cunnilingus phase? Yes or no."

"Are you kidding me?" I ask out loud.

The bubble doesn't go away—there's obviously no voice recognition in the suit (unlike in my VR pet project).

How far am I willing to take my curiosity? I'm on the verge of choosing "no," but then I wonder how they fake *that* sensation.

Yeah. More professional curiosity. Obviously. This has nothing to do with how much I want those lips down there. Or with the fact that I've never actually had a man go down on me. Yeah, nothing at all.

Gulping in air, I again pick "yes."

The guy winks out of existence for a moment, then reappears in the cunnilingus position, his face opposite my crotch and his cerulean eyes gazing up into mine.

I lean back on the couch.

His tongue takes the first lick.

Oh. My. Fucking. Golly.

This is exactly how I've always pictured this would feel. His tongue is warm and pliant and beyond amazing. If there were a

Nobel Prize for the most perverted invention, the Evil One would get it, hands down.

Another lick.

And another.

Then he latches on to my clit and starts sucking.

My toes curl.

Holy HR policies. I'm about to come in my workplace.

I grab his head but can't bring myself to pull it away. If anything, I have to fight the urge to press him harder against my crotch.

Suddenly, maddeningly, everything stops.

Noooo! I was an inch away from the big O.

A new bloody choice appears in the air.

"Do you want to sample the penetration phase? Yes or no."

Yes.

No.

I'm ready for it, but getting penetrated right here and now isn't—

There's a sound of a lock turning.

Shit.

My heart jolts into the stratosphere, and my insides turn into a sorbet.

Someone's about to catch me.

# FOUR

LEAPING TO MY FEET, I claw at the headset.

Bugger. The gloves make it hard to get a good grip, so I attempt to violently shake them off me, only to trip on something.

Flapping my arms as though I'm trying to learn to fly, I grab on to the first thing in my path—which seems to be the office chair.

Fuck me. The thing has wheels, which predictably roll, and my fall continues—with more arm flapping and sounds of suit Velcro coming undone.

Bam!

My wrist smashes into something hard. Judging by the thud against the floor and the sound of plastic shattering, I must've just destroyed that nice monitor.

Strong hands grab me before I nosedive farther.

Not expecting it, I go into freakout mode—grabbing what feels like a keyboard and preparing to swing it.

The hands immediately let go of me.

"I was only trying to help," says a deep, velvety voice with a Russian accent.

That's true, so I don't smash the keyboard into the speaker's face. Instead, I let go of my weapon—and cringe as I hear it smash into bits.

"Why don't you allow me to take that headset off you?" the voice asks.

"Cheers," I blurt, and before I can correct it to "thanks," the headset is carefully removed from my head.

Now that I can see again, I gape at my savior.

And gape.

And gape some more.

Did I fall asleep during that demo, or is this still virtual reality?

In front of me is the very guy who was just eating me out in VR—the hottie from Miso Hungry.

# FIVE

"YOU OKAY?" the hot stranger asks, cerulean eyes peering into my very soul.

"Uh-huh." Face burning, I take off the first glove with my teeth, then use the freed hand to take off the other glove. On autopilot, I start working on the rest of the suit—until I remember that I'm completely naked underneath.

"Do you want a minute?" he asks, pointedly keeping his eyes on my face and not lower—as though he's avoiding something.

I look down.

Oh bloody hell.

My right nipple is showing.

I completely forgot about that ripping Velcro sound from earlier.

"Turn, please!" I squeak, spinning on my heels so fast it's a wonder I don't destroy what little is left alive in this office.

"Done," he says.

I peek over my shoulder. His back is to me. The tush inside his jeans is reminiscent of the one I chose for him in VR.

Wait. What am I doing?

Returning to proper priorities, I peel off the suit and tiptoe over the broken monitor and keyboard pieces as I pick up my scattered clothes off the floor.

My hands shake as I pull them on, my skin alternately too hot and too cold.

Bloody hell, bloody hell, bloody hell.

This is bad. So, so bad.

It's not until I'm fully dressed that I'm able to fully process what happened—and as I do, I want to sink through the floor. Maybe all the way to the lobby.

My cheeks feel like the surface of the sun as I mumble, "You can look back now."

"All right." He turns back and gives me an intent once-over. "So, who are you?"

The words escape in a rush. "Holly Hyman, at your service."

Bugger. Why did I just say that?

He frowns, an expression that bizarrely makes his face look sexier. "The CTO?"

"Guilty as charged." Ugh. Why did I just say *that*? In desperation, I try to smooth over my blunder. "And you are?"

"Alex." He extends his large, masculine hand. "Alex Chortsky."

My jaw hits the floor.

Chortsky.

As in the owner of Morpheus Group.

The Devil himself.

# SIX

NO WONDER he boasts the cheekbones of an angel. This is the original fallen angel.

I want to run, but he's blocking my way.

Wait. All is not lost. He doesn't know why I'm here. Maybe there's a way out of this?

Looking confused, the Devil lowers his hand.

Damn it. How could I leave him hanging like that? It's mega rude.

Before I can apologize, he looks down at the floor and grimaces at the sight of the shattered keyboard. "I had just installed rubber O-Rings under all the keys," he says mournfully. "Took me an hour."

A fresh surge of guilt washes over me. I use those things myself; they make mechanical keyboards—the best kind—less loud. I'm about to offer to buy him a new keyboard and install the rings myself when he narrows his eyes at something on the floor.

Oh, no.

He bends down and picks up a flash drive.

*The* flash drive—the one with the virus on it. It must've fallen out of my pocket when my clothes took that tumble.

"Is this yours?" His narrowed eyes home in on my face—yet even the threat in that cerulean gaze doesn't lessen its devastating impact on my hormones.

"No. I mean, yes." I extend my visibly shaky hand. "Can I have that back?"

Sensual lips flattening, the Devil jerks the flash drive out of my reach. "What exactly are you doing in my office?"

I fight two conflicting urges: to run away screaming or fight him for the flash drive. I go for something in the middle. "I, um... that is, Robert told me we're going to ramp up the integration soon." So far true. "I wanted to check out the suit as part of that." That *could* be true.

His grim expression is unchanged. "How did you open the door? I locked it myself last night."

He's been coming here at night? Why didn't the rumor mill warn me of this? Oh, duh. Because they don't work late on days when I don't.

"The door was open." Fuck. I don't sound convincing even to myself. Stupid, stupid, stupid. Why didn't I ask Gia to teach me to lie better?

He puts the flash drive in his pocket with the finality of a prison sentence. "Why are you here so late?"

"I—I had a lot on my plate. Just got around to it."

His eyes are like slits now. "You didn't even touch your dinner."

Crap. He saw me buy that. "I got curious and lost my appetite." God. A five-year-old could've come up with a better lie.

He takes out his phone and makes a few clicks. Whatever he sees, he must not like because his jaw sets as he pins me with that cerulean laser stare. "You wouldn't know why the security cameras aren't working, would you?"

I just stand there, gulping in air. It's official—I've lost my ability to speak.

"Is this corporate espionage?" His words are clipped.

Still rendered mute, I shake my head.

He glares down at me. "Then what is it?"

I don't answer. I can't. My heart is pounding so hard I feel sick.

His gorgeous lips flatten again. "If you come clean, the consequences will be less severe."

"I... I was just..." My throat is too dry to get the words out.

"You just what? Remember, I can find out for myself." He pats the pocket with the flash drive.

I feel like I'm about to barf from panic. "I—I wanted to... I wanted to stop the porn." Oh, bugger. Why did I just say that? That sounds bad. I should've—

He folds his arms over his chest. "What do you mean by 'stop the porn?'"

I swallow my racing heart back into my chest. In for a penny, in for a pound. "My life's work is at risk. Children and porn don't mix."

"Children?" He looks at me as though I've sprouted a unicorn penis on my head. "You think we're making kiddie porn?"

"What? No!" Wait, maybe I should've said yes. Too late now. I scramble for a reasonable explanation but can only come up with the truth. "I've been working on VR pet therapy."

From there, I launch into the full story, stammering my way through my good intentions—that I want to make children more comfortable at the hospital.

As I go on, the Devil's features are unreadable—he could give Gia's poker face a run for its money. I have no idea if he believes me or not. I hope he does. As the Father of Lies, he should be a truth serum and polygraph machine combined.

"So," I say tentatively when I'm done. "Am I fired?"

He runs a hand through his unruly locks, and I fight the urge to tie him up and tame that hair. That action wouldn't help my case in the least.

"We'll discuss your employment status after the investor meeting tomorrow," he finally says.

Hope blooms in my chest. I'm not outright fired. That's amazing. I'd fire me if our roles were reversed. Then again, he's probably just postponing the inevitable. Given the state of his office, he might want witnesses around when he does sack me—along with working cameras and security guards.

"There's something I want you to keep in mind," he says, his expression still indecipherable. "Morpheus Group is as important to my sister as that VR pet therapy is to you, and her work is *not* porn. She wants to bring sexual experiences to people who, for various reasons, aren't able to have them, including patients in hospitals, husbands and wives torn apart by distance, soldiers, deep-sea fishermen, oil rig workers... Her ideals are just as high as yours." A frightening look replaces the expressionless mask. "I won't let you or anyone else destroy my sister's dream."

My head spins. The rumors mentioned a sister, but I didn't realize she was the driving force behind Morpheus Group. I'm even more screwed than I thought. Even if he doesn't fire me, *she* certainly will.

"I need to know that we have an understanding," he demands in a hard tone.

I nod on autopilot.

Having seven sisters, I've always wondered what it might be like to have a brother. Seems that instead of teasing you mercilessly, they actually protect you from threats. Must be nice for the She-Devil.

The frightening expression disappears from the face of the Prince of Darkness, and the much more preferable poker face is back on. "I want you to say that you understand."

I gulp. "Affirmative. I love—I mean, I really need this job."

"That you do. It's not just your project on the line, either. You'd lose a fortune in stock options too."

Well, someone is confident in the future of this company. Or is he confident in his sister? In any case, he's most likely right. To keep me from going over to Google, our old owner gave me a bunch of stock options. If the company does well, I'll be rolling in loot—assuming I keep working here, which isn't looking likely.

"I promise this will never happen again," I say and cringe. Obviously, *this* won't happen again. Even if I were insane enough to try sabotage again, I wouldn't destroy his office, or almost have an orgasm on his couch, or—

The door to the office suddenly opens, and a gorgeous woman steps inside, her gaze bouncing around in confusion.

I blink at her.

That's his companion from Miso Hungry.

Has he brought his date to work?

"What's going on?" she asks.

Does she mean, "What are you doing with my boyfriend/husband/master?"

Her eyes land on the discarded suit and brighten. "Were you just testing that?"

Wait a second. Is she—

"She was," the Devil—or I should say, the Deceiver—says before I can even think of replying. "The rest of the mess was just an accident."

Well, that second part is true.

The woman appears transformed. If earlier she seemed a little cold in her perfection, now she reminds me of a little girl introduced to her pony for the first time. "Tell me how it went."

The Devil's features soften. "I think introductions are in order. Bella, this is Holly, the CTO whose profile you were so impressed with." His gaze turns to me, a silent threat lurking in the cerulean depths. "Holly, this is my sister, Bella, the head of Morpheus Group."

As I started to suspect, she's the Devil's sister.

Not surprising, really—she *is* wearing Prada.

What is surprising is her lack of a Russian accent, but I guess if she's younger than her brother, she could've been just a child when they immigrated.

A huge wave of relief washes over me as I process all the implications.

She's his *sister*.

They weren't on a date.

They must've just been grabbing dinner before coming here.

Wait. Have I gone completely bonkers? Why should I care that the King of Darkness isn't dating her?

"Holly!" Grinning, Bella advances deeper into the room, the remnants of the monitor and keyboard crunching under her stilettos as she extends her hand. "So nice to finally meet you."

I shake the hand instead of leaving her hanging, like I did with her brother. My shake is limp, though, and my palm is sweaty.

She was impressed with my profile. Why? Is it possible that, like Santa, She-Devils have a "naughty" list?

The Devil clears his throat. "Holly is so eager for the upcoming integration project that she's taken initiative on testing the suit."

Bella's handshake turns even more enthusiastic.

"Thank you so much," she says and finally lets me go. "What did you think?"

I'm still stunned. Why is the Ruler of Darkness covering for me? Telling her that I was testing and not sabotaging?

Maybe he doesn't want to worry her? It's possible, given how protective he seems. Or, since this is her life's work, he might be worried that the truth will cause her to attack and kill me, which could lead to pesky legal troubles or calls to Russian mob connections. Because, naturally, all Russians have connections to the mob.

"Oh, no," Bella says, examining my no-doubt-sourpuss face. "You didn't like it?"

Crap. I need to stop thinking and begin reacting. Bella looks like I kicked her sick puppy, and when I sneak a glance at the Devil, his dark expression is saying, "Fix this or else."

"Not at all," I blurt. "It was actually brilliant."

If she believes that, I'll go into acting.

Nope. She doesn't look convinced, so I search for something true. "I was very impressed with how realistic things looked. And all the choices." There we go. Countless cocks *are* choices. And I was impressed with the facial realism.

She tilts her head. "You're not telling me something."

Bugger. "The integration," I say in a flash of inspiration. "When I tried touching something during the demo, the gloves and the suit didn't seem as in tune as they should be."

She nods solemnly and gives her brother a pointed look. "Told you."

A hint of a smile touches his eyes. "I never argued about that. Integration *is* going to be a big priority going forward."

"So." Bella's attention comes back to me. "How far did you get?"

I blink. This really *is* her life's work—I can tell from her unwavering enthusiasm. She can probably talk about this for hours to anyone who'll listen, a bit like new parents bragging about their spawn or me with my VR pet project. I guess it makes some devilish sense. This invention is going to bring a whole lot of lust to the world —and that's one of the seven deadly sins.

Bella must tire of waiting for me to answer because she grabs a glove, puts it on, and presses the headset to her face.

"Ah," she says after a few gestures. "You'd just finished the cunnilingus phase."

I turn redder than the Queen's Guard uniform.

Did the Devil just smirk?

Without removing the headset from her face, Bella asks, "What did you think? Wasn't it realistic?"

"I... err... think so?"

Grr. Now he's definitely smirking. Wanker.

"You think so?" Bella sounds concerned.

I redden further. "I... don't have a basis for comparison." Oh God, why did I just admit that?

She removes the headset from her face and looks at me with such concern you'd think I just told her I've never been out in the sun or tasted tea. Turning to her brother, she asks, "Did you know about this?"

He shakes his head, his smirk even smirkier.

She looks back at me. "But you liked it, right? I worked very hard on the textures and the—"

"I loved it!" The sentence comes out in a squeak.

"Whew." She swipes her hand dramatically over her face. "You had me worried there for a moment. You didn't get to penetration, though, right?"

Why can't the floor swallow me and put me out of my misery?

I manage a headshake.

"But you've experienced *that* before?" She looks horrified at the very idea of me being a virgin, and I want to die. Maybe by spontaneous combustion. Or the HR shooting all of us.

To say that this is a sensitive topic for me would be a massive understatement. I've had sex, of course, but my devirginizer turned out to be gay—and on top of that, as a kid, I was always teased with the not-so-creative nickname of Holy Hymen.

"Sorry. I didn't mean to pry," Bella says, catching on to my distress.

I will my burning cheeks to cool. "It's okay. I've had coitus before, so no worries."

There. I should get some kind of a medal.

"Thank goodness." She presses the headset back to her face. "Still, without having experienced oral sex, you're not the ideal test subject. A pity."

Does that statement require a response?

"Sis, Holly was actually just about to leave," the Devil says. "She's had a long workday and—"

"Eeww!" Bella rips the headset from her face. "The guy you made looks just like Alex. *Naked.*"

Seriously, where's that spontaneous combustion?

The Devil's cerulean gaze swings to me, and I could swear there's a glimmer of fire in it. Then he turns to his sister. "'Eeww?' Really?"

She rolls her eyes. "Did you want me to drool? As you've said, we're not the Lannisters or the Borgias."

Is the Evil One lost for words?

Bella grins sheepishly at me. "You could've warned me."

"I'm sorry," I mutter. "I didn't think."

"No sweat." She grabs the bulky part of the suit where my vagina would be if I were still wearing it. "I bet you're wondering how penetration is supposed to work."

I shake my head, but she either doesn't notice or doesn't care. "Obviously, it's not practical to fit a variety of dildos in the suit, so I was forced to use hydraulics and—"

"Sis." The Devil's tone is more forceful. "Holly hasn't even had the chance to eat her dinner."

"Oh." She looks at me guiltily. "Poor thing. Sorry. We'll talk more later. Eat your dinner and go home."

"Thanks! I'll eat on the way." I zoom out of that office as though the devils were chasing me—and for all I know, they might be about to do just that.

All I want is to get out of here and regroup—assuming that's even possible.

Since I'm running, I fish out my earbuds from my pocket, jam them into my ears, and put on my trusty running music: the *Downton Abbey* soundtrack. Reaching my desk, I grab my takeout, not because I still want it, but because I said I'd eat on the way.

So far, so good. I'm almost out of here. Just a minute until freedom.

Dashing for the elevator, I channel all my pent-up frustration and unburned adrenaline into my leg muscles.

Almost there.

Almost.

Yes.

I'm by the elevator. Jamming my finger at the button, I all but bite my nails in anticipation.

After a century-long wait, the elevator doors crawl open.

Finally.

I'm about to step in when a hand grabs my shoulder.

Fuck.

Didn't make it.

I spin around to face the Devil.

# SEVEN

ONLY IT'S THE SHE-DEVIL, and she's smiling—not something I expected to see before plunging into the burning fires of hell.

I dig an earbud out of my ear. I probably look as wild-eyed as I feel.

"I wanted you to have this." Bella hands me a backpack with hand-drawn genitalia on it.

Ookay.

I snatch the backpack, clutch it to my chest, and blink at her. Something heavy is inside the bag. Could it be the heart or liver of the last person who tried to sabotage her work?

She looks at me expectantly.

"Thank you?" I mutter.

"It's the suit." She waggles her eyebrows lasciviously. "The one you tried. Figured you'd want to finish the demo."

I redden again—my cheeks are now primed for it.

Then I notice that the Devil himself is within earshot, smirking. If I were Hulk strong, I'd throw this penis-inscribed backpack at the wanker's head. Alas, I'm not—plus that sort of thing will get me fired for sure.

"Well, have a safe trip home," Bella says.

"Thanks. Bye." I back into the elevator and press the button for the lobby.

As the doors close, I see the Devil's evil smirk grow into an infuriating grin.

My food tastes like sandpaper as I eat it on autopilot in the cab, and even when I get home and start my seven-step evening routine, my mind refuses to stop spinning.

Am I going to lose my job?

Whatever the answer is, my life's work is still in dire jeopardy.

As I meticulously floss my thirty-one teeth (by luck, I had to get one of my wisdom teeth removed a few years back), I ponder if there's a way to save my project.

Maybe I can call an emergency meeting with the administration at NYU Langone tomorrow and try to convince them to move from beta testing to officially adopting the VR pet therapy. Once there's a contract and data on how useful the therapy is, they'll be less likely to pull out when they learn that the company they've made a deal with is known for its adult content. The Devil might not deem it porn, but they surely will.

Worth a shot. I fire up my laptop and request the meeting.

Now I need two miracles. Or is it called something else when the Devil is involved?

My phone pings. It's a text from Gia:

*Do you need me to bail you out of jail?*

Har bloody har.

*No need,* I text back. *I changed my mind about the B & E.*

I rarely lie to my twin, but I can't bring myself to talk about what happened just yet.

*I knew you'd chicken out,* she replies. *You still owe me.*

I sigh. *Fine. Speaking of that, tell parents to meet "you" at Miso Hungry—a place by my office.*

After she promises she will, I turn off my phone.

According to my schedule, it's time to go to sleep. The problem is, there's no way I'll sleep in this state—I feel like I've just downed a barrel of cocaine-laced espresso.

Time for the big guns.

I turn on my TV and play the series premiere of *Downton Abbey*.

Nope. Still can't sleep. Seems like even bigger guns are needed.

I put on the episode of Rose's wedding, mainly because it contains one of my favorite Violet quotes of all time: "Love may not conquer all, but it can conquer a lot."

When it's over, I try sleeping again.

Not a wink.

I go to my ultimate sleep tool: Jane Austen's *Pride and Prejudice*. Still no luck.

Okay, how about *Emma?*

Nope. If anything, all these romantic stories make it worse, as a pair of cerulean eyes keep popping into my mind.

I switch tactics and go for a cup of chamomile tea. It doesn't remind me of the Devil, thankfully, but it doesn't help either—and I don't dare brew anything caffeinated.

A crazy idea pops into my head. An orgasm might help me get drowsy, so what if I put on the suit Bella gave me?

No. I mustn't.

But I want to.

Curse you, Devil and your sister. This must be how Jesus felt when he was tempted in the wilderness.

But hold on a second. There's a VR activity that might calm me—though, granted, not as much as a virtual shag.

My own VR pet therapy.

Yeah, that's it.

Gearing up, I launch the necessary app and come face to furry nose with Euclid—the VR pet customized for me.

"Holly," Euclid sing-songs. "I mished you."

Brilliant. My nerves are soothed already. I can't help but grin at him.

Euclid can be made to look like a preset of things I figured kids would find cute: a piglet, a koala bear cub, a baby otter, a baby panda, a baby hedgehog, a kitten, or a lemur. Of course, he doesn't look like any of those exactly, since that's no fun. He's an anthropomorphized version of an animal, and with as much influence from the Teletubbies as I could get away with without being sued.

In my case, Euclid resembles a hybrid between an otter and the Laa-Laa Teletubby. Oh, and he's currently purple, like Tinky-Winky, but that just indicates he's happy. The color of his fur is how he emotes—or pretends to. He is, after all, an AI.

"Hi, sweet one," I say. "Are you hungry?"

"Ravenoush." He does a dance that is part Teletubby, part Ellen DeGeneres, with a dash of Barney the Dinosaur thrown in.

I extend my gloved hand, and a pair of digital snacks show up on my palm. Here, again, I've made them look like the Tubby Custard and Tubby Toast that the Teletubbies like to eat, but different enough to hopefully never get a cease-and-desist letter.

Euclid goes for the toast, a star-shaped chocolate cookie with a winking face on it. Of course, the shape of the toast, like everything else, is customizable. I like the star (really, a pentagram) because it has a prime number of points—not because I'm a witch or a Satan worshiper... Bugger, there I go again, reminding myself of the person who got me into this state in the first place.

"Tell me shomething intereshting," Euclid sing-songs after he gobbles down the snack.

"Well, did you know that your namesake proved that the list of prime numbers is infinite?" I ask. "He did it over two thousand years ago, and without internet."

Euclid's fur turns yellow, and he giggles. "You can be sho shilly."

Nodding, I pet his fur. This is what heaven must feel like. This part of the experience is what the gloves were designed for, not feeling the hardness of cocks.

Euclid turns pink. "Letsh play fetch."

With a classic throw gesture, I make a deep purple stick appear in my hand. As I toss the stick, I can't help flashing back to the recent penis selection process—my design of this object happens to look eerily like one of the more exotic choices.

Note to self: keep Bella away from this app. I don't think Euclid's programming can handle what she'd do with the stick.

After he brings back the stick, we play other games for a while, until I'm certain that I'm feeling much better and ready to sleep.

"I'm going to go take a nap," I tell Euclid.

His fur turns an array of colors before settling on a light teal. "Shee you later. I wove you."

"I love you too." I hug him tight, then take off the headset and gloves.

Now I'm ready.

I grab my sleeping buddy, a plush Transformer that I love not because I'm a fan of that super-violent franchise, but due to his name: Optimus *Prime*.

Hugging Optimus, I drift into sleep... only to dream of cerulean eyes and evil grins.

# EIGHT

HALF AN HOUR into the dreaded investment meeting, I realize I'm keeping meticulous meeting minutes in my notepad.

That's crazy. Who documents something they want to fail? My only excuse is that I've been trying to avoid looking at the Devil, and focusing on my notepad is a decent enough distraction.

In addition to me and my team, the room is occupied by a man named Dragomir Lamian, Dragomir's people, and the Chortsky siblings—and it doesn't take long for all my hopes to be dashed.

Given the looks that pass between Dragomir and Bella, he's in her pocket already. That is, if I put things delicately. And hey, good for her. The guy is model-hot and clean-shaven... unlike a certain someone who didn't even bother to make himself presentable for an important meeting.

What's maddening, though, is that I find the Devil more attractive than this clean-shaven stranger. Grr. What's wrong with me?

As if sensing my stare, the Wicked One turns my way, and I feel highjacked by his gaze. I can almost picture the voice of David Attenborough speaking down from the heavens: "And thus, the human mating ritual begins. The female of the species starts ovulating as the male—"

No. Must fight it.

I begin counting my eyeblinks the way I did as a kid.

Nope, not distracting enough. I then also count Bella's—staring into her eyes seems safe enough.

In ten minutes, the counts are 223 (prime) for me and 227 (also prime) for her, so I stop while I'm ahead and surreptitiously check my phone under the table.

Finally, some good news. The folks at NYU Langone are willing to see me at three p.m. I put a reminder in my calendar—though it's hard to imagine I'll need it, given how important this is.

So, all isn't lost yet. If I still have my job when the Devil talks to me after this meeting, I could well succeed in convincing them to expedite the timeline.

"Thank you, everyone," Dragomir says, and I tune in to see if he'll deny them money despite being wrapped around Bella's elegant finger. "And congratulations," he continues. "The next round of funding is officially approved."

So much for that hope.

Everyone stands up, but I remain seated and so does the Devil— seems like he hasn't forgotten about our upcoming chat.

Except Bella isn't leaving either. Grinning, she walks up to me. "Hey, Holly. We're going for a walk in the park with our dogs. Would you like to come?"

She's inviting me to go walk dogs?

Did I hear that right?

"I need to talk to your brother," I say cautiously and dart him a glance.

He looks like he's hiding another evil smirk, but I can't be sure.

"Alex is coming with me." She looks at him. "Can you and Holly have your talk on our walk?"

"It's kind of private," he says. "I was planning on taking care of it first, then joining you."

She pouts. "Can you do it after?"

He heaves a sigh. "Fine."

"Great." She beams at me. "How about you ride with me and Dragomir, and we'll meet Alex and Beelzebub there."

Did she just say *Beelzebub*? Is she in on my private joke?

I don't have a chance to dwell on it because Bella drags me out of the room by my elbow.

"So," she says when we're in the elevator. "Did you use the suit after you got home?"

Reddening, I glance at the Devil, then at Dragomir. "Didn't get the chance."

She looks extremely disappointed for a moment, but then her eyes brighten. "Okay, then tell me about your first demo."

I redden more.

The Devil clears his throat. "No talking shop on dog walks, remember?"

Has the Ruler of Darkness just saved me again? Or is he buttering me up for something even worse—like getting dunked in tar and rubbed in feathers?

Bella's disappointed expression comes back, times five. "The dogs aren't even here yet. Can we at least talk about nipple stimulation? I worked very hard to—"

Dragomir puts a hand on Bella's shoulder. "*Squirrelchik*, didn't you have a bunch of questions about Holly's experience at Cambridge?"

They're on touching terms? And he has a pet name for her? The chances of that funding failure had been less than nil.

"You're right." Bella smiles at me. "You studied computer science, like Alex, right?"

I nod—though I'm not sure if I like being bundled into a category with him, no matter what it is.

She covers the hand that's still on her shoulder and gives it a little squeeze. "What was the ratio of women to men in your classes?"

Finally on safer grounds, I answer her question, and she shares similar stats from MIT, her alma mater.

She turns to her brother. "How about you? Do you recall how many women took computer science courses at Polytechnic University?"

He runs a hand through his unruly hair, making me want to comb it back, maybe violently. "I don't know the official stats, but there were definitely too few women."

I feel conflicted about this. On the one hand, I want more women in my field, but on the other hand, I like the idea of there not being females around him, no matter the environment.

He belongs on a deserted island with me. In handcuffs. There'd be barber utensils there too. And not much clothing—

Blimey. Did I seriously just think all that? I'm clearly off my rocker.

The elevator doors open, and Bella peppers me with more questions about Cambridge as we make our way through the lobby. I reply to her on autopilot, wishing I could fall back and ask the Devil point blank, "Am I keeping the job? Yes or no."

Alas, as soon as we get outside, he jumps into a nearby cab, and I watch it disappear in traffic with longing.

That is, with relief.

Yeah.

Definitely relief.

"That's us." Bella points at a giant car that looks like an RV that's eaten thirteen limousines.

The door of the strange vehicle opens and a ladder descends. A man wearing a tuxedo jacket with tailcoats appears in the doorway and greets us primly in a British-accented voice, "Please, come inside."

Oh my golly.

I'm going to die of jealousy.

This is clearly a butler, à la Carson from *Downton Abbey*. I'd give my right ovary to have one.

"Thanks, Fyodor," Dragomir says and gestures for us to go first.

A proper gentleman. Good for Bella.

We climb inside, and I look around, dumbfounded.

"Doesn't it look bigger inside than outside?" Bella whispers conspiratorially. "Like the TARDIS from *Doctor Who*."

It is big—huge even—and messy, despite there being a butler on staff.

Okay, I have to withdraw my earlier comparison. Real Carson wouldn't stand for this. I have to work very hard to restrain myself from turning into a tidying whirlwind.

"Ready to meet the doggies?" Bella asks as Dragomir and Fyodor join us, and before I can formulate a reply, the hounds of hell descend upon us.

# NINE

THE SHAGGY BEAST who leads the charge is big. We're talking proportional to the size of this RV kind of big.

It's basically a pony—a well-fed pony.

Getting on its haunches, it puts its front paws on Dragomir's shoulders and goes right for his face. I half expect Dragomir to lose his nose at the very least, but the monstrous creature simply slobbers on the poor man.

If this happened to my twin, she'd expire on the spot.

As the beastie does the same to Bella, I examine the second dog—a tiny Chihuahua that instantly makes me crave a burrito.

"Winnie, no," Bella says sternly as the sasquatch-like canine tries to lick *my* face.

Winnie? As in, the Pooh?

Wait a sec. I'd assumed this was a dog, but maybe it's a type of bear? Whatever its species, Winnie doesn't look happy about this licking restriction but settles for sniffing my crotch. And sniffing. And sniffing for the longest seven seconds in crotch-sniffing history, until eventually Dragomir drags it away, muttering, "Bad girl."

Me or Winnie? If the latter, then Winnie is female. I would've guessed differently, given all that crotch sniffing. Also, if that breed/species has sexual dimorphism, how big do the males get? Elephant size?

"Holly, this is Napoleon Bonaparte," Bella says, picking up the Chihuahua. "Or Boner for short."

Boner. Why does this make me think of her brother all of a sudden? Worse yet, that reminds me of my precarious job situation, making my stomach tighten with anxiety.

Since I have a chance at authentic pet therapy right here, I smooth my hand over Boner's short fur.

The cute little bugger closes his eyes in bliss.

"He likes you," Bella says. "And he's a good judge of character."

I grin, absurdly pleased.

My relationship with animals is a complex one. Growing up on a farm, I was surrounded by them—and I don't just mean my sisters. Now that I'm grown, I still love everything furry, but only in theory. Put another way, I love pets when they live with someone else, but for myself, I can't imagine owning one due to the chaos and mess it would create. I suspect most people feel the same way about baby monkeys.

Wanting to play with animals without the mess was part of the reason I came up with my VR pet project, in fact. It provides all the good parts of pet ownership and none of the bad.

"Would you care for a spot of tea?" Fyodor asks poshly.

Dragomir and Bella reply in the affirmative and turn my way.

"Don't mind if I do," I say, beaming at not-quite-Carson. He's really redeemed himself with that "spot of tea" bit.

We sit on a nearby couch while the tea and biscuits get served.

Bugger. Note to self: never say "biscuits" in lieu of "cookies" in front of Gia. For that matter, never say "bugger" either.

As we have our tea, Winnie lies down on the floor and Boner sniffs her butt, making me chuckle.

Noticing this, Bella demonstrates a dubious skill—ventriloquism.

Only she voices the dogs instead of a traditional nightmarish wooden doll.

"Winnie, *ma petite.*" She throws her voice to sound as if it's coming from the Chihuahua's maw and speaks with a strong French accent instead of the Hispanic I would've expected. "How I adore your *postérieure.* It has a certain *je ne sais quoi* that makes me feel like I have rabies."

Noticing the sniffing, Winnie leaps to her feet and jumps onto a nearby treadmill.

Yes. A treadmill. In a car.

Bella throws her voice at the giant creature, giving it a thick Russian accent. "Napoleon Carlovich, I am scandalized. Can't you keep your nose—and other appendages—away from my orifices for at least an hour? We're in new company. Know you no shame?"

I blow on my tea. "Was this your talent at a beauty pageant?"

Bella grins. "I've never done one of those, but it's sweet of you to imply that I could've."

Huh, okay. Isn't vanity supposed to be the Devil's favorite sin?

"How did you learn it then?" I ask. "You throw your voice very well."

"My parents own a restaurant," she says, wrinkling her nose. "I performed there... for a time."

Before I can question her further, the RV comes to a full stop.

"You first," Bella tells me when Fyodor opens the doors for us.

As soon as we exit, I come face to gorgeous face with the Devil. His cerulean eyes meet mine, sucking all the air from my lungs, and it takes all my willpower to tear my gaze away from that hypnotic stare and turn my attention to the dog at his side.

A dog that could just as easily be a koala bear the size of a German shepherd.

I blink at it, thoroughly distracted by its ginormous cuteness. There's something clumsy in the way it stands, making me think it might be a puppy.

Must be the aforementioned Beelzebub.

Seeing me, Beelzebub starts wagging his tail and gets on his haunches.

Oh, no. He's going for my face.

Not willing to be slobbered on, I turn away.

A paw claws at my top anyway.

Laughing, I push the puppy away, and as I do, I feel the material shifting, followed by a cool sensation on my left nipple.

A cool sensation that's unmistakably air.

# TEN

OH, bugger.

My heart rate jacks up, my face flaming violently as I frantically tug my shirt back in place.

I've just managed another nip-slip in front of the Devil—and since it was the right one last time, he's now seen the pair.

To his credit, the Devil doesn't stare as he pulls Beelzebub away, though there's a definite hint of a smirk on his face.

But why not stare? Is my nipple unattractive or something? I've used electrolysis on that one errant hair that sprouted out of there, so it should be gone. Unless it's back?

Under the pretext of continuing to fix my attire, I sneak a frantic peek down my shirt and bra.

Nope. All good there. Whew.

The Devil says something in Russian to the unrepentant, tail-waggling demon.

Whatever he said doesn't stick.

As soon as Beelzebub spots Bella, Dragomir, and their furry charges, he goes berserk, licking the faces of the humans before switching to licking the snouts of the dogs, then sniffing dog butts for dessert.

Hey, at least he didn't sniff the butts of the humans—or their crotches.

"Do you want to hold Boner's leash?" Bella asks me magnanimously.

"No, thank you," I say quickly. As is appropriate for the Tempter, Bella has an uncanny ability to place inappropriate images into my brain. Case in point: I'm picturing the Devil with a huge erection, a cock-ring with a leash attached, and me holding—

"How about Beelzebub?" the Devil asks, wrestling me away from my naughty thoughts. "Do you want to walk *him*?"

Beelzebub wags his tail spasmodically, and I bet if Bella were to voice his thoughts, he'd be shouting, "Please, please, please. Pick me. Pick me. Pick me."

"I'm good," I say, ignoring the overeager puppy. "I'll just walk on my own if you don't mind."

Beelzebub's tail sags and his ears droop. I feel a little pang of guilt. Maybe I should've said yes.

But no. That way lies getting my own puppy, and then domestic Armageddon will surely follow.

We begin the walk, and I remember how much I love Central Park—though apparently not as much as the dogs do. They look like they're having the time of their lives as they sniff every previously urinated-on nook and cranny.

"Has my sister told you why she wanted to buy your company?" the Devil asks.

I shake my head.

Bella pulls Boner away right as he tries to eat an innocent snail. "Women are typically more susceptible to VR sickness," she says. "But Holly's headset is the exception to that unfortunate rule."

Even though it's not fair to call it *my* headset, I stand straighter. "It was important to us that women and children could use the gear.

That's why the headset is adjustable, especially the interpupillary distance and—"

"Folks, you know the rules: no shop talk on a dog walk," Dragomir says.

Bella looks at him sheepishly. "Oops."

I fight the urge to say it's not her or my fault. Her brother started it.

A squirrel crosses the road, and Beelzebub looks like he'd sell his grandmother to catch it. In contrast, Winnie doesn't pay the furry creature any attention, while Boner has clearly seen it but is pretending that the rodent doesn't exist.

I notice that Bella and Dragomir have gotten a little bit ahead of me and the Devil, as if giving us privacy on purpose.

Huh. Weird. Is that because Alex said he and I needed to talk?

As if reading my thoughts, she peeks at us over her shoulder with a sly smile.

Wait a sec.

Is she playing matchmaker? Is that why she's invited me here—to act out her own personal *Emma* fantasy?

If so, she's certifiable. Her brother and I are like oil and water. Then again, didn't I read something about MIT researchers developing an emulsions preparation process that allows oil and water to mix and stay that way? And Bella did go to MIT, so—

No. No way. Besides, even if she fancies me now, once she learns I tried to sabotage her dream, she'll hate my guts—an idea I find quite discomforting.

Well, whatever her motives, I should take advantage of the situation and ask about my job.

Yes, that's exactly what I should do—only I'm having trouble launching into it. Maybe I'll make some small talk first to build up to it.

"Is Bella your only sibling?" There. Better than bringing up the weather—which is nice and sunny, by the way.

Since Beelzebub is taking a leak, the Devil stops and I do the same. "We have a brother too," he replies. "His name is Vlad."

Aha. So every Chortsky I came across during my research is related. Makes sense.

"How about you?" the Fallen Angel asks as we resume the walk. "Are you an only child?"

I wish... unless, is that question a diss?

"I have seven sisters." Did I just sound braggy?

His eyebrow shoots up—yet another bizarrely attractive expression on him. "Seven?"

"Yeah. Me and my twin, plus the sextuplets—everyone monozygotic."

A second eyebrow joins the first. "Monozygotic as in identical?"

Why are those eyebrows so sodding attractive?

"Indeed. My twin and I look the same, as does the litter of evil."

His satyr-like grin is as seductive as the eyebrows. "The litter of evil sounds like what we call Beelzebub and his siblings: the Chort Pack. You see, my last name means—"

"Of the devil," I blurt.

He stops, though I'm not sure if it's to focus on me or to allow Beelzebub to pee on a tempting-looking oak trunk. "You speak Russian?"

"Sadly, no. There were just rumors about you guys at the office, so I looked up your name."

"I see." Beelzebub pulls on the leash, so the Devil resumes walking. "Sextuplets are exceptionally rare, right?"

"That they are. The chances are astronomically small for a regular pregnancy, but more likely when using assisted reproduction technology, which is what my parents did."

"Ah. And are all of you close?"

"Only me and my twin. I mainly interact with the others at family events. They're a bit much for me. Too chaotic and messy—especially when together in the same space."

The Wicked One chuckles. "I bet. There were only three of us growing up, and it was pretty crazy some days. Hard to imagine eight."

Grr. I hate the reminder that there are eight of us. Why couldn't the Hymans be like the Chortskys and have a nice prime number of kids? Especially three.

Three would be so much better than eight.

Can't say that to him, though, so I opt for something safer. "You and Bella get along well enough. Are you also close with Vlad?"

He pulls on Beelzebub's leash to prevent him from molesting a yorkie. "Vlad's my best friend."

"Tidy." I smile. "Same for my twin and me."

He cocks his head. "I know you went to school at Cambridge, but did you also live in England before or after that?"

"Why?" I ask, sounding defensive.

"Certain words you choose," he says. "Like tidy."

This again. "It was just the four years. Turns out, I absorb languages and dialects like a sponge. I even had a British accent when I got back, but after merciless teasing, I managed to drop it."

He grins. "Maybe if you hang out with me enough, you'll learn Russian. And get a Russian accent."

Cheeky bastard. Does he want me to be tempted by the idea of hanging out with him? Of course he does. He wouldn't be the Tempter otherwise.

No more dilly-dallying.

I take in a breath and expel the words in a rush. "Can we talk about my employment status? If I need to update my CV, I should—"

He locks eyes with me. "No shop talk on dog walks."

"But—"

"Rules are rules," he says sternly. "Once we're done here, we can set up—"

The alarm on my phone goes off.

What the bloody hell?

When I check it, I want to smack myself.

The NYU Langone meeting is in a half hour, which is barely enough time for me to get there.

I look up from the phone to see the Devil frowning.

"Is everything okay?" he asks.

"I'm fine. But I do have to skedaddle."

The frown morphs into a confused expression. "You do?"

"I'm sorry." Louder, I belt out, "Bye, Bella. Bye, Dragomir!"

Bella turns around and hurries toward me.

Crap. I shouldn't have said goodbye. Now I'm getting delayed.

"Did I hear you say you're leaving?" she says, reaching me.

"Yep. Got to run."

Bella gives her brother a narrow-eyed stare. "What did you do?"

"No one did anything." My voice jumps an octave. "I have a prior commitment, that's all. When I agreed to join you guys, it slipped my mind."

"Oh." Bella takes out her phone. "Before you go, please give me your contact info."

I'm so going to be late. Then again, I find the idea that Bella wants to get in touch a little exhilarating. Reminds me of being in middle school, when I wanted the prettiest girl in class to befriend me.

Could Bella become my first friend with whom I don't share one hundred percent of my DNA?

Wait, what am I saying? Once she learns what I tried to do, she won't want to be friends. Quite the opposite: she'll fire me—if her brother doesn't beat her to it.

Not showing any of this on my face, I put my number into her phone and hand it back.

Just as I prepare to sprint away, the Devil hands me *his* phone. "In case I need to reach you for work."

Hmm. Do I want him to call me? I'm not sure, but denying him my number would be a pointless gesture. He's now my boss, so he can get access to it from the HR records if he wishes.

"Well, actually, I wanted Holly's number for personal reasons," Bella says to him and sticks her tongue out, causing Dragomir to give her a heated side-eye. With a warm smile at me, she says, "I'll text you so you have my number as well."

I feel a pang of sadness knowing a close friendship with Bella can never happen. Side note: what's the female equivalent of bromance? Is it homance, as in *hos before bros*? No, sounds offensive. A quick internet search reveals the term: womance.

Realizing I'm delaying myself, I quickly enter my info and thrust the Devil's phone back into his hands.

The Wicked One's fingers brush against mine, and a surge of seductive energy shoots down my arm, zips around my heart, and electrocutes a few butterflies in my belly before settling sinfully in my core.

Blimey. Did his cerulean eyes widen?

Nah. All I see on his face is a smirk. "Thanks," he says, his accent sounding particularly delicious. "I'll text you too."

His "too" makes me think of "two," one of my favorite primes. "Cheerio," I blurt. Bugger. The British accent I thought I'd gotten rid of is back with a vengeance. "I really have to run."

"Bye," Bella says.

"*Do svidaniya*," says the Ruler of Darkness, the smirk still on his gorgeous face.

"It was nice to meet you," Dragomir adds.

"Au revoir, *chèrie*," says Boner. "I look forward to sniffing you again in the future."

With a queenly wave, I dash for the park exit, where I leap into the first available cab and bribe the driver to punch it.

Once on the way, I look up "*do svidaniya*."

*Svidaniye* means "meeting" or "date", and the phrase is used as an optimistic farewell with the meaning of "until the next meeting."

*"Do svidaniya,"* I say out loud.

Becoming animated, the driver catches my gaze in the mirror and rattles out a torrent of Russian words.

"Sorry, I don't speak Russian," I say.

"Oh, I'm sorry. You said *do svidaniya* like a true Russian. Forgive my confusion," the driver says, his accent much thicker than the Devil's.

So it has begun. Before I know it, I will have a Russian accent as prominent as this guy's and will say *do svidaniya* instead of *bye.*

Hey, that might work better with Gia than *cheerio.*

I look up other Russian greetings in case they come in handy. There are many, but the easiest to say is probably *privet,* which is an informal hello.

A text chimes.

It's the Devil.

I store his number as first name Lucifer, last name Satan.

Bella's text comes soon after.

It might be a double standard, but I enter her into my contacts with her real name.

For the rest of the ride, I count the seconds my mind wastes picturing a certain pair of cerulean eyes. At a hundred and thirty-seven, I halt the count, as I don't want even more proof of how mental I am.

When we stop next to NYU Langone, I'm already seven minutes late—and the fact that it's a prime number is little consolation.

Grabbing a hundred-dollar bill and a single, I throw them at the driver and dash out of the car with a shout of "keep the change."

Time to pull off a miracle.

# ELEVEN

ON THE WAY to my destination, I do accomplish a small miracle: I don't knock anyone over during my mad sprint.

Once I get to the meeting room, however, I find it empty.

Bloody hell. Did they leave already?

I sit down to catch my breath.

The door opens and Dr. Piper walks in.

"Sorry to keep you waiting," he says. "The others will arrive shortly."

Hurrah!

Instead of being late, fate has made me look early. Fingers crossed this continues.

We make small talk as we wait for the rest of the administrative staff to arrive. Once they're all in, Dr. Piper gives me a fatherly smile and says, "It's a good thing you reached out. We were talking about your project at the morning scrum."

I smile nervously. "Good things, I hope."

"Absolutely," he says. "We've been talking to the children who are part of the beta test, as well as their parents. The feedback has all been positive. We should discuss the next steps."

Wow. Maybe I won't even need to convince them?

"That sounds great," I say with feeling. "I'd love to talk next steps."

"Glad to hear it," Dr. Piper says. "We've started our due diligence and have involved an external consultant to assist us with the aspects of this technology we're not familiar with." He chuckles. "Which is most of it."

Reasonable. They can't just rely exclusively on my say-so all the time.

"Talking with this consultant, we got an idea for the next step, one that the parents and the children also liked," he continues.

Why do I have a feeling I'm not going to like what he's about to say?

"What idea?" I ask.

"First, I just want to say that a VR pet is a very effective use for this technology, the best even."

My heartbeat speeds up. "Why does it sound like there's a but coming?"

"No buts. Only the truth. You only have the one app, the pet. It's limiting. Kids like video games. The consultant suggested we expand the list of apps."

I gape at him. What he's talking about is a classic in project management. It's called scope creep—except this isn't even a creep, it's a bloody elephant stampede.

I clear my throat. "Pet therapy is a real therapy. Games aren't."

"The consultant sent us an article about this very topic. VR games have been shown to reduce pain."

Who is this evil consultant? I fight the urge to swear and point out that I already knew about those studies—they were the starting point for my work. In fact, said studies were how I convinced these very people to give my project a chance.

Taking in a calming breath, I speak evenly as I lay out the truth of the matter. "I'm working with limited resources. The pet app is the result of many months of work. Adding more apps is—"

"I'm sorry to interrupt, but we have a solution to this problem already," he says.

"You do?" I fan myself with my shirt, but carefully, so as not to have another nip-slip.

"There's a company that makes games for the tablets the kids currently play with. This company has recently branched out into VR as well. We can introduce you to them, and you can work out a way to put their games onto your platform. Much less work, right?"

Except we needed to be all squared away *today*, and this is the opposite of that.

"It all depends," I say cautiously. "What's the name of the company?"

"1000 Devils," he says. "Ever hear of them?"

I lose my ability to speak and just sit there, holding in a scream.

When I researched the Chortsky name, what little I learned about the two brothers was from the websites of the companies they own.

One of which was a game studio called 1000 Devils.

A game studio owned by none other than Alexander (Alex) Chortsky, the Devil himself.

# TWELVE

HOW HAVE I gotten so screwed so fast? What were the chances they'd want me to work with that company out of so many others?

Well, 1000 Devils *is* famous for their kid-focused content, and it's local to NYC, so it's not completely out of the blue.

Unless...

No. Can't be.

But what if? Could the Devil be the Evil Consultant? I mean he's the Evil One, so this—

"Are you okay, dear?" Dr. Piper looks at me with a worried expression.

How long have I just been sitting here, mind imploding?

"I'm fine," I lie. "This is something I need to process." For a year.

"Fair enough," Dr. Piper says. "How about we adjourn the meeting for now? Offline, I'll introduce you to Robert Jellyheim—my contact at 1000 Devils."

Robert Jellyheim. If I had any hope that there's a different game studio called 1000 Devils, that hope is now caput. Robert is my contact at Morpheus Group—a company I can't mention here at all, because porn.

The Devil must be using the staff from his gaming company to help his sister.

I'm so, so screwed.

Everyone leaves the meeting room except Dr. Piper.

"Are you *sure* you're feeling okay?" he asks.

"Fine." I leap to my feet.

"It's just that"—he readjusts his bowtie—"if you *are* sick, I don't think you should visit Jacob and the others."

"I'm not sick, I promise," I say.

Also, he's a genius. Visiting Jacob might help brighten this otherwise rubbish day.

We say our goodbyes, and I navigate to the pediatric long-term care wing.

Bugger. Bobze the clown is here, entertaining Jacob and the others. Even though I don't have proper coulrophobia, and even though Bobze doesn't look like he's escaped from Stephen King's basement, I prefer to stay away. Bobze is the epitome of messiness: every color of the rainbow in his wild wig, disproportionate shoes, and, adding insult to injury, he always carries not one, or two, or three, or five, but exactly *four* balloons.

Realizing I'm famished, I sneak out to the cafeteria and get my hospital usual: seven apples and a pack of twenty-three almonds.

I gobble down the fruit and the nuts, then check on Jacob.

Whew.

No more clown.

Preparing to channel my inner Mary Poppins, I walk up to Jacob. His nose is in a tablet, so I cough to steal his attention.

Looking up, he rewards me with a heartwarming boyish grin. "Hi, Aunt Holly."

Jacob and I are not really blood relations—he's the grandchild of one of my parents' friends. He landed in this hospital after an accident where he broke a number of his bones. With his legs in casts, boredom and pain (in that order) are big issues for him, making him a perfect candidate for my VR pet therapy.

"Hi, kiddo." I muss his hair. "How's Master Chief?"

Master Chief is what he calls his version of Euclid. It also happens to be the name of a character in *Halo*, a video game that Jacob once coerced me to play. Sadly, I could only tolerate the uber-violence for seventeen seconds before I had to bail—and he called me lame, perhaps rightfully so.

Jacob's grin widens. "He grew a few inches and learned a few new words."

No doubt curse words, but I'll leave that for Jacob's parents to worry about.

He tells me about the games he and his VR friend have played, and I gently probe how he'd feel about VR games outside pet therapy. Not surprisingly, he's brimming with enthusiasm for such a scenario, especially if they're to be games of the shooting variety.

Bollocks. I hate to admit it, but adding more games might be a good idea. Too bad it will ruin everything by giving Dr. Piper's team time to learn about the porn connection.

Then again, how much time would it take to port existing games onto a new platform?

"Aunt Holly, are you okay?" Jacob asks.

"Sorry." I smile at him, banishing all errant thoughts from my head—the kid deserves my full attention.

When Jacob and I run out of things to talk about, I combine his clean socks into three pairs, fold the blanket next to his bed into a neat triangle, and chat with a few of the other kids nearby while tidying up their areas as well.

As I exit the hospital, there's a grin on my face. I think I could've been a teacher in another life. Whenever I talk to my pint-sized beta team, I end up feeling supercalifragilisticexpialidocious.

In the cab heading home, I check my phone. No texts or calls from the Devil. Sigh. On some level, I was wondering if he'd set up a meeting to sack me... or text me a dick pic.

I guess the ball is in my court on that—the meeting, I mean, not the nudie pic.

Once home, I follow my routine, but in the background, my mind tries to figure out a way to extract myself from the current kerfuffle.

Just as I'm all set to go to bed, an insane idea congeals out of a horde of equally bad ones.

It's a classic, really. Faust went through it. Brendan Fraser did it in *Bedazzled*. Keanu Reeves also, in *Constantine*, and something like it in *The Devil's Advocate*. Cher, Michelle Pfeiffer, and Susan Sarandon did it in *The Witches of Eastwick*. *Ghost Rider* and *Spawn* did it in the movie and the comics. Katy Perry and Oprah might've done it in real life.

What if I make a deal with the Devil?

# THIRTEEN

NEEDLESS TO SAY, sleeping on that idea becomes an impossibility. By morning, I'm beyond knackered and require three cups of strongly brewed tea to stay semi-coherent.

On the way to work, I text the Devil what might be famous last words: *Do you have time for a chat?*

The reply is instant: *7:30 p.m.?*

*Great*, I text. *Where?*

This time, he takes a few seconds to get back to me: *How about my office? You remember—it's the place you decimated.*

*See you there*, is what I say back, even though my fingers are itching to type out something a lot ruder.

Plan for the meeting: figure out a way not to get fired. Also on the to-do list: no making moony eyes at the Devil, no drooling, and no fantasies of grooming him. Must resist his masculine wiles at all costs.

I'm the first in the office, but I'm brimming with too much nervous energy to actually do anything useful. One thing leads to another, and I catch myself moving a few desks that look out of alignment, as well as adding/removing pens and other minutia on people's workspaces so that they have nice, prime totals.

The elevator door opens, halting my endeavors.

It's Alison, the manager of the quality assurance team.

"Hiya." I smile at the older woman. "How are you?"

"Hi, Holly," she says. "Did you get my email about a bug my team found with Euclid?"

Skipping the pleasantries—I like that about Alison. "Sorry, no. Haven't had a chance to check my email yet."

"Everything crashes if you feed him four toasts and toss the fetch stick six times right after that. I had a few people replicate this issue on multiple devices."

Four and six. Nasty, non-prime numbers. Of course they crash the bloody app. "I'll look into it, thanks."

She scurries to her desk as I unlock my workstation and jump into Euclid's code.

By the afternoon, I've fixed Alison's discovery and let her know about it.

"I'll have someone retest," she says. Lowering her voice, she adds, "I heard a new rumor, by the way."

I lean in. She's as good at uncovering juicy gossip as she is at detecting software bugs.

"The Chorstkys are moving in," she says. "Maybe even tomorrow."

Yep. That sounds about right—but I don't tell her that. Nor do I mention the very real possibility that I won't be here tomorrow to witness the Devil's invasion. It all hinges on our upcoming conversation.

"Let me know if you hear anything else about the Chortskys," I whisper. "And if you find any other ways to crash poor Euclid."

She promises that she will, and I retrace my steps to my desk—where, unfortunately, Buckley is waiting to speak to me.

I'm not Buckley's biggest fan. He likes to clear his throat a lot—and usually an even number of times.

"Hi, boss," he says and clears his throat twice. "Got a minute?"

This man is an enigma. I got promoted to CTO over him, so I figured he'd hate my guts afterward. Imagine my surprise when he asked me out instead. Of course, I had to refuse, mostly because I don't think office romances are proper, but there was a shallow reason too: I find his asymmetrical body and face aesthetically displeasing.

"I can talk," I say. "What's up?"

He clears his throat twice more. "I was just wondering if you've heard from the new management."

I shrug noncommittally. "Why?"

He scratches his perpetual stubble—a grooming choice that didn't help his chances when he asked me out. "I was wondering if the merger means there will be opportunities for us to move within the bigger organization. Not that I don't like working for you, but—"

"Say no more." I smile at him. "I'll write to my equivalent on the other side and see what they have for you."

"Thanks, Holly," he says and clears his throat just once—a miracle. "I really appreciate this."

As soon as he leaves, I write an email to Robert Jellyheim in which I wax ecstatic about Buckley. If he gets the move he wants, I might just never hear his throat-clearing again.

Since I'm on an email kick, I take a stab at the million messages awaiting my attention. By the time my inbox is empty, it's already past normal working hours.

Just like yesterday, people aren't leaving, no doubt waiting me out again.

Fine. I can use the same leaving trick again. I should eat before the big meeting anyway. And for the record, my going to Miso Hungry has nothing to do with the hope of seeing the Devil there, like the last time.

Nothing at all.

Nope.

I even out a few more desks and move some pens around to get prime totals on my way out too, both because I want to and to get attention. Then I rush to the restaurant.

"To go?" the hostess asks as soon as she spots me.

"Takeout," I say and glance around.

No Devil, no Bella.

Ugh. What's with the wave of disappointment crashing into me? They must not be as much creatures of routine as I am.

Oh, well. Not everybody's perfect.

Food in hand, I return to the empty office and eat my miso soup with forty-seven cubes of tofu and seventeen pieces of scallion. Then I consume the twenty-three avocado roll pieces. Sadly, in my current state, I could just as easily chew on the paper bag the sushi came in as far as tasting any of it goes.

At a quarter past seven, the elevator doors open and the Chortsky siblings step out.

Bella looks even more like she's just come off a runway, and the Devil is somehow even scruffier than usual—so much for those grooming fantasies I was hoping to avoid. *Or keeping my heart rate even and my libido in check.*

"Hi." Bella waves her delicate hand at me in a suspiciously beauty-pageant-like way for someone who's allegedly never partici-pated in one.

I wave back. "Lovely to see you again."

"*Privet,*" the Devil says.

"That means hi," Bella translates.

"Ahoy," I say back to the Devil.

Wait, ahoy? Last I checked, today isn't International Talk Like a Pirate Day. Bloody adrenaline is really messing with my head.

Acting as though ahoy is a normal reply to a Russian hello, the siblings go into their offices.

The next eleven minutes drag on for a year.

Finally, it's time.

Getting up, I head to the Wicked One's office.

Pirates are still on my mind, it seems, because I can't help feeling like I'm about to walk the plank. His door creaks—like the plank—and once I open it, I half expect to see the mess I created yesterday.

Nope. Someone's cleaned it up.

Good. I won't be having my nose rubbed in my sins, like a puppy. Then again, he hasn't replaced the broken keyboard and monitor—and is instead working on a laptop, which must be a lot less comfortable.

Here goes nothing.

I step into the Devil's lair.

# FOURTEEN

THE PRINCE of Darkness closes his laptop. "Please, sit."

Since the couch is the only place available, I plop there—and do my best not to think about the things a virtual version of him was doing to me last night on this very surface.

The Tempter's cerulean eyes scan me carefully, as though he plans to create a 3D model of me for VR.

Did my eyelashes just bat at him prettily?

Afraid so.

Does that count as moony eyes?

Close enough.

Bugger. Nothing is going as planned.

At least I'm not drooling. Or am I? Would it look weird if I checked?

"Since you might get a reminder about a more important meeting at any second, I'll get to the point," he says. "You're not fired."

"Pardon?"

Wait. What am I doing?

He said I'm not fired.

I heard him just fine—I just didn't expect it.

Also, is it hot in here?

I feel equal parts dizzy and euphoric.

"I said you get to keep your job," he enunciates. "Under certain conditions, of course."

Ah. Here we go. Knowing there's a catch makes me feel better. Otherwise, things would be too good to be true.

"What are the conditions?" I ask.

Is he about to make an indecent proposal?

More importantly, is that something I'm hoping for?

"There are two." He drums his long, masculine fingers on the desk. Is it wrong that I can picture them stroking me? "You're going to help with the integration project," he says, wrenching my mind away from delicious massages. "The issues you mentioned, where the headset and gloves don't work as they should with the suit, will become your top priority."

"Fair enough," I say and mean it. "What's the second thing?"

"Right." He frowns. "This should go without saying, but I will spell it out for you. There will be no more monkey wrenches into my sister's work. If you so much as introduce a bug into the integration code, you're done. If cameras malfunction at any of our offices, that will be it. If a virus infects any of our computers, or critical employees for that matter, you're a goner. If there's—"

"I get the picture," I say. "We have an accord."

"It appears we do." He opens his laptop. "*Do svidaniya.*"

Channeling Buckley, I clear my throat. Not getting fired is just the first item on my agenda, but I'm not sure how to proceed.

"We can discuss the details of the integration project tomorrow, after my sister and I officially move in to these offices," he says, clearly misunderstanding my hesitation to leave.

Here goes nothing. "There's something else I wanted to discuss with you."

"Oh?" He pins me with that intense cerulean stare. "Work or personal?"

My skin feels overly warm and tingly. "Work. Strictly professional. Not personal in the slightest."

I force myself to shut up, as methinks I sound like that lady that doth protest too much.

He frowns. "So, work."

Did I catch disappointment flitting across his features? Nah. Must be my overactive ovaries playing mind games.

"1000 Devils has a contract with NYU Langone hospital," I say.

His eyes widen. "I thought you didn't do corporate espionage. How do you know that?"

I remind him that his company website publicly lists him as the owner, and I tell him about my meeting at the hospital and why Dr. Piper informed me about the contract.

"So you want my help getting some games onto the headset?" he asks when I'm done explaining.

"Yes. I figure you'd make even more money from NYU Langone this way. So win-win."

He scratches that cursed stubble on his chin—activating my grooming fantasies once again. "I'm not sure they would pay more. I bet they'd just include VR as a platform in the existing contract—they don't make a distinction between tablets, consoles, or phones at the moment, so this is like that."

My heart feels like a witch doctor has just shrunk it. "So you won't help me?"

A satyr-like smirk illuminates his gorgeous features. "I didn't say that. I think I might help you... for a price."

Here we go.

I can practically envision myself pricking a finger and signing a contract that asks for my firstborn.

My insides start quivering, and not just my ovaries anymore. "What do you want?"

"Two more things," he says, his voice low and deep. "Not work-related this time."

I knew it. The Devil is demanding a deal—one cannot hide one's nature.

"What are they?" I'm impressed with myself. My voice is steady, and the British accent hasn't reappeared.

"Bella is going crazy wanting to know what you thought of the suit," he says. "I want you to give her a full report. It'll make her happy."

I gape at him. On the one hand, this is not completely unrelated to work, but on the other, it's bonkers.

"I'm not qualified for that," I say, realizing I'm grabbing at straws. "I'm not QA."

"Oh, don't worry," he says. "Bella has a form and everything. Also, she can put you in touch with Fanny—she's got experience in these things."

There's someone named Fanny involved? Poor woman. In England, that means vagina—though here in the US, it means butt, so also not a great association.

Bugger. Now the Devil is making me think about vaginas and butts.

"What else?" I ask noncommittally.

His eyes gleam. "It's my father's birthday tomorrow. I want you to come with me to the celebration."

My breathing quickens. "Like... a date?"

The smirk is back. "Not a real date. A pretend date. My mother has been trying to set me up with random women, and I want it to stop."

That twat. How dare she try to set him up with some harlot? Why I—

Wow. That escalated quickly. For all I know, his mother might be a lovely lady.

"Not a date." I taste the words and find them lacking.

Shouldn't I be relieved he didn't ask for that firstborn—or to father said firstborn? Also, why is it so easy to picture this hypothetical devil spawn? It would no doubt have his cerulean eyes, my oval-shaped face, his—

"So," the Devil says, ripping me out of my hormone-induced delirium. "Have you ever been to a Russian party before?"

I shake my head.

"A Russian restaurant?"

Another shake.

"You're in for a treat, then. There will be amazing food and a show." He looks me up and down. "Just bear in mind, the dress code is pretty formal, so you might want to wear something nice."

Is he saying I'm not wearing something nice *now*? Wanker. Also, he's wearing a hoodie. Pot calling the kettle black much?

"Fine," I grit through my teeth. "I accept your terms."

"Great. I'll text you the details."

Turning angrily on my heel, I head for the door.

With a speed worthy of his supernatural nature, the Devil leaps to his feet and gets the door for me.

Seems that convincing the world he doesn't exist isn't the only trick the Devil tries to pull. He also wants me to think he's a gentleman.

Bugger. Now if I want to leave this place, I'll either have to pass close to him or rudely ask him to move, which I don't want to do.

I take a step forward.

A faint aroma of a yummy tea enters my nostrils, making my mouth water. Oolong, keemun, maybe lapsang souchong, along with something ineffably male.

Another step.

Our gazes fuse.

There's a tumult in my belly—my treacherous ovaries are no doubt trying to choke each other to death.

The closer I get, the more hypnotized I become by his gaze.

Maybe I should back away—or be rude after all?

That would be wise, but I don't do either. Like a doomed star trapped by the gravity of a black hole, I'm drawn to him—which must be why I close the distance.

*Leave, Holly.*

My feet feel welded to the ground.

*Don't do it, Holly.*

I rise on tiptoes.

His head dips toward me.

No. No, no, no. Can't do this. Shouldn't do this. If we actually kiss, my ovaries will explode and—

"Oh, sorry," Bella's voice says from just a few feet away. "I'll come back in—"

I don't hear what she says next. Finally tearing my gaze away from the Devil's, I bolt for the elevator.

Thank heavens the doors open instantly—I might've gone for the fire exit staircase otherwise.

As I ride down and sprint for the cab, my mind is blank, my heart racing madly. It's not until I get home and change my soaked knickers that I finally shake off the shock brought on by that brush with the Devil.

I follow my usual evening routine like a robot, but that leaves room in my brain for errant thoughts. Thoughts like: was he going to kiss me, or did I imagine it? And if he did want to snog, does that mean our fake date isn't so fake?

No. Can't be. I'm sure he doesn't want me like that.

More importantly, even if he did, it can't happen.

After the disaster with my ex, I'm not ready to date. Might never be—though if I were, it wouldn't be the bloody Devil.

There's nothing messier than mixing work and love life, even when a relationship would be deemed appropriate by HR—say, when the two people are in different departments. In this case, though, he's pretty much my boss, so it's definitely against corporate policy. And let's not forget that he's evil—might in fact be the Evil Consultant himself. Worse still, he's untidy.

Speaking of that, why am I even attracted to him?

It's a mystery of Bermuda triangle proportions.

When my routine is complete, I go to bed, but even with the weight of all that recent insomnia pressing against the backs of my eyes, I lie there for an hour before admitting I'm unable to sleep yet again.

Fine. I might as well do something useful instead of tossing and turning for hours.

Getting up, I open my closet to pick out an outfit for the upcoming birthday.

The problem is, my usual philosophy about clothing is going to bite me in the ass. To limit the time wasted on decisions, I wear the same thing every day: one of seven identical white button-up shirts (each with five buttons in the front) and one of seven pairs of identical black pants. Since I was wearing this exact combo when the Devil said to "wear something nice," it implies my usual work outfit won't do. Nor will my home clothes suffice. They're also identical, with the t-shirts and yoga pants optimized for comfort, not "niceness."

Sigh.

I look at the "outlier" section of the closet.

There are three identical dresses left over from when I went out on dates with my ex.

I hope they fit the Devil's "nice" criterium.

I wriggle into one.

Grr. I can't breathe and my boobs look on the verge of bursting out. Seems I've gained some weight.

Bloody hell. I can't have nip-slip number three—especially since I will be in front of the Devil's whole family.

Ugh. This means shopping.

I hate shopping, mostly because if there was such a thing as fashion intelligence, my IQ in it would be something abysmal, like thirty-one.

Oh, well. At least I'm otherwise intelligent enough to know to ask for help.

Getting my phone out, I text *Hi* to my twin. Despite her Criss Angel-inspired, rock-star-meets-vampire appearance, her fashion intelligence is at least three standard deviations higher than my own.

She instantly replies: *You're not asleep? Isn't going to bed at eleven sacred?*

Of course. She doesn't know about my insomnia since I lied to her about the B & E.

Might as well come clean.

*Can you do a video call?* I ask.

Turns out she can, so I call her and tell her everything, including my lack of appropriate outfit.

When I'm done speaking, she has that mischievous expression on her face that I and the sextuplets learned to dread in our childhood—the one you see before you learn that she hid a dozen alarm clocks in your room, or duct-taped an air horn under your chair, or replaced the cream in your favorite doughnut with mayo.

"Before we talk about shopping," she says, "I have to tell you, I strongly disagree with you."

I audibly sigh. "What do you disagree with?"

"This restaurant outing totally sounds like a date."

I bring the phone closer to my face so she can clearly see my disapproving frown. "No. It's not."

She also brings the phone to her face, so all I see is a giant blue eye. "Is too."

"Is not."

From here, the sophistication of our argumentative techniques regresses all the way down to:

"Yuh-huh."

"Nuh-uh."

The giant eye rolls, then she pulls the phone away from her face. "Agree to disagree?"

I also pull the phone away. "If that's what it takes to get you to help."

"Oh, I was going to shop with you regardless," she says. "I've seen your closet. This is long overdue."

I narrow my eyes at her. "We're only getting what's needed."

Her grin is downright devious now. "Exactly. How about I meet you at your place at nine? We're going to Madison Avenue. You can afford it."

"Tidy," I say without thinking.

"Toodles," she replies hoity-toitily and hangs up.

Bugger. Forgot to warn her there's no way in hell I'm wearing something slutty for the party—which will be her first instinct, no doubt.

As I put my phone on its charger, I realize a slight problem with our plan.

Being the CTO, I've never needed to explain my comings or goings to anyone at the office, but things are different now. Tomorrow is the day when the Devil and Bella are moving into our offices, and they'll surely wonder where I am.

The solution is simple. I type out a text to the Devil:

*Will not be in the office tomorrow. Have to prepare for the birthday. If you have a problem with this, I'd be delighted to call the whole thing off.*

There. Maybe shopping can now be avoided?

His reply is instant:

*See you at the party.*

Oh, well. It was too much to hope he'd just call it off. Not that I really want him to do that anyway. Not if my sister is right and there's even a sliver of a chance this thing *is* a date.

Which it isn't.

No way.

And I don't want it to be.

I head to bed, but sleep is again as elusive as an oiled eel.

It doesn't take me long to pinpoint the main culprit. It's the Devil's second demand: sharing my suit experience with Bella. There are so many problems with that, I don't know which is the worst. To start, when I do things, I like to do them properly—and in this case, I lack the QA experience to do the task justice.

I sit up. The problem is pretty solvable. Alison has a training manual for new QA employees.

Firing up my laptop, I look for the manual and hit paydirt quickly.

I start reading.

Fascinating. This is exactly what I needed.

When I'm done, I have a new respect for Alison and her team, but sadly, I'm no closer to sleep—even though some folks would find the reading material I've just finished sleep-inducing.

A part of me is tempted yet again by the suit. An orgasm might help me sleep, and without sleep, the party ordeal might be that much harder.

No. I'm not going to give in to my base desires, or use the suit as a sleeping aid.

But wait. Why are my legs taking me to the genitalia-decorated backpack?

And why am I taking the damned suit out?

When I lay the suit out on my bed, I readily come up with the reason: I will use it for Bella's report. Yeah, that's it. I didn't finish the demo the last time and thus can't give Bella a complete picture. Speaking of completeness, unlike cunnilingus, coitus *is* something I have done in real life, so I can answer any pesky "did it feel real?" questions.

Yeah, that's it. I'm not doing this because I'm randy, but because the completionist in me demands it.

Jolly good. That's my story, and I'm sticking with it. After all, using the suit with the QA manual in mind will allow me to pay attention to all the little things I might've missed before—like girth, length, and hardness of certain things.

When it comes to the schlong of the VR Devil, it's all in the details.

Once I shimmy into the suit, I go through the same selection criteria as before—with a small difference.

I give the VR Devil a much, much bigger cock.

THE NAKED DEVIL simulacra starts dancing, like the last time.

Gulping down drool, I desperately try to look at this as a QA person would.

Nope. I'm now picturing poor Alison having a heart attack, and looking at him this closely makes my distracting arousal worse.

Maybe this wasn't such a great idea.

"Do you want me to give you a taste of what the suit can do?" the demo asks me once more. "Yes or no."

A "yes" teleports the VR Devil next to me, his bigger cock making it hard to stand next to him.

Hard indeed.

How did Bella give the suit such a variety of phalluses without a bunch of hidden dildos?

I'd better not ask her that. She will never shut up about it if I do. Plus, like with Gia's magic, some things are more fun when they retain their mystery.

Also, is it actually phalluses or phalli, given that phallus is Latin-based and has that -us ending? Must check—along with the plural for penis, another important item on my to-do list.

"Continue?" the demo asks.

When I agree, he cups my breast again.

QA manual? Report for Bella? What is that nonsense? I certainly don't recall anymore.

After a prompt, he squeezes my nipple again.

I'd bet my life this is what it would feel like if the real Devil did it —which he never would.

Another prompt.

He touches my clit—and I nearly come on the spot.

"Do you want to sample the cunnilingus phase? Yes or no."

Gee, I don't know. Yes, sodding please.

The sensation of a wet tongue down under is so real I again dimly wonder how Bella accomplished it.

He licks me once, twice, thrice.

I'm getting close.

He sucks on my clit.

My toes curl.

Almost there.

*Please finish. I've been good, I promise.*

Nope.

Bugger. It all stops, just like the last bloody time.

Also, I've totally forgotten all about QA.

"Do you want to sample the penetration phase? Yes or no."

I think about this for all of a second. I've never felt this empty before. Never been so ready to receive—

The whole VR world goes red, and a big box appears in the air, "Please charge batteries."

Noooo.

This is what hell must be like—access to a big cock that loses its charge at the worst possible time.

Peeling the suit off me, I locate its charging port.

Whew. Regular USB port.

Feeling a little jealous of the USB hole that gets plugged instead of me, I leave the suit attached to my laptop to charge, then sprawl on my bed and debate if I should wait and resume testing today or finish myself off manually and deal with this another time.

My lids grow heavy, so I close my eyes—I don't need them open to make this decision.

As if it were waiting for this opportunity all this time, sleep pounces and knocks me right out.

# SIXTEEN

I WAKE up to the sound of the bloody alarm.

In my dream, the Devil—the real one, not the VR imitation—was just about to finally make me come.

Woe is me. If I didn't know any better, I'd theorize this to be the work of the Wicked One—he's building up my horniness past teenage-boy levels and into the territory where I just might sell my soul for an orgasm.

Wait.

My deal with the Devil. The party.

Gia is going to be downstairs at nine, so I need to get my butt out of bed and start my seven-step morning routine.

---

"SO, I have a magic effect I wanted to try out on you," Gia says as we walk into a ritzy department store.

Great universe. Shopping wasn't bad enough; now I have to deal with this too? As children, our siblings and I sat through our share of

Gia's beginner magic, with me getting the brunt of it. If I had a dollar for every card I've picked in my life, I'd own this whole store.

"It's a good one," Gia says, no doubt picking up on my hesitation. "And short."

Short? I guess not all is lost. "Go ahead."

"Can I help you?" says a snooty-looking saleswoman before Gia can continue.

"She needs a new outfit," Gia says, nodding my way.

The lady looks me up and down with a look that seems to say, "Boy, do we have our work cut out for us."

"Before we shop, maybe you can participate in a little experiment my sister and I were just about to undertake," Gia says, her stage persona in full force.

The lady looks at her suspiciously, but that doesn't deter my twin in the slightest.

"When I say so," Gia says, "you will think of a two-digit odd number. A number so odd, in fact, that both digits are odd. Okay?"

The lady's nod is more reluctant than my own, but not by much. I also wonder if Gia is blind to the irony of asking us to think of an odd number while acting so odd?

Unless that's part of the trick?

"I have one in mind," I say, since I know how to handle my twin better than the salesperson does.

"I do too," the lady says with all the enthusiasm of someone who's entered *The Twilight Zone*.

With a flash of fire and smoke, a notepad and a pen appear in my sister's hand.

Wow. Gia has gotten much better since the last time she showed me stuff. I have no clue how she just did that.

The saleswoman clutches her chest, no doubt worried the fire alarms are about to blare.

Gia writes something on the pad. "I've just committed myself."

I'm glad to hear that. She's certainly acting like someone who needs to be committed.

She thrusts the pad into the hands of the stunned saleswoman. "On the count of three, you will say your numbers out loud."

She counts to three.

"37," I say at the same time as the helper lady says the exact same thing.

Double wow.

"Check the pad," Gia says.

Yep. On the pad is 37.

Not only did I and a perfect stranger think of the same number, but Gia also knew what it would be ahead of time.

How? She could've guessed I'd say 37—it's a permutable prime because you can make 73 out of it, which is also prime, and I like that sort of thing. Then again, nothing stopped me from choosing 13. It's a twin prime to 11 because they are two apart, and it fits her "both numbers odd" criteria.

The real question is, why did this lady say the same thing? And how did Gia know she would?

"Is it subliminal messaging?" the lady asks.

Rookie mistake. Gia will never admit how she did what she did—not even to someone with identical DNA.

My twin smiles with an air of mystery. "Can you keep a secret?"

The lady nods.

"So can I," Gia says triumphantly.

If I had a dollar for every time I've heard this joke, I'd also own this store.

The lady rubs her temples. "I have a headache. Did you do that?"

"No, but put your hand out." Gia waves her gloved hands over the lady's extended palm and a white pill appears there.

The lady stares at the pill.

"It's Tylenol," my sister says.

"Thanks," the lady says but doesn't put it into her mouth—and I can't blame her in the slightest. "Are you ready to shop now?"

Gia says we are, and before I can argue to the contrary, I find myself shepherded into a fitting room with a strappy black cocktail dress designed for a femme fatale in a James Bond film.

Taking off my clothes and bra, I shimmy into the dress and look in the mirror. "I don't like it."

"Who cares?" Gia asks. "Come out so I can see."

I step out of the fitting room.

The helper lady nods approvingly, and Gia examines me like a butcher about to make a prime cut.

"Too conservative," she concludes, making it sound like a bad thing.

"I'll get something else," the lady says, scurrying away.

I look back into the mirror, then at my twin. "My problem was the opposite. It doesn't look proper."

She rolls her eyes, walks into the fitting room, and gingerly lifts up my perfectly functional beige bra with her gloved hands. "Is this your idea of proper?"

I shrug.

"I assume you have granny panties to match this atrocity?" she asks.

I put my hands on my hips. "Oh, pish posh. Who cares about my underwear? No one is going to see it."

She snorts. "Not with that attitude he won't."

I flush, the thought of the Devil seeing me in *any* underwear making me uncomfortably warm inside.

"How about you grab a dress you like?" my sister says, suddenly sounding conciliatory. "I'll go find some normal underwear for you."

Leaving her to it, I locate something appropriate.

By the time I return, she's waiting for me, hiding something behind her back. "That is something a sadist would ask her bridesmaids to wear," she says, wrinkling her nose at my choice.

Ignoring her, I go into the fitting room and try the dress on.

Outside, I hear her saying something to the salesperson, but I can't make it out.

The dress looks okay, I think. Reminds me of what I wanted to wear to the prom before my siblings talked me out of it.

"I think this is it," I say.

"Show us," my sister says imperiously.

I come out.

The salesperson's eyes widen, and she struggles to keep a professional expression. On her end, my sister just laughs in my face, like a maniac. "This might work as a Halloween outfit," she says when she catches her breath. "You can be Cinderella... before she got the ball makeover."

I huff indignantly. "This isn't a maid outfit."

"Go back and take it off," Gia says. "We'll hand you things to try."

I return to the changing room and strip.

"Start with this." Gia tosses in two lacy atrocities. "You're not going in granny panties."

I hold the items between my thumb and index finger, far away from my body in case they bite. "This is stupid. I'm not here for new underwear."

"Just try it," she says.

To shut her up, I put on her selections.

The so-called panties make me understand why they call these "butt floss," and the bra pushes my boobs just a few inches shy of my chin.

"What do you think?" Gia asks.

"I look like a French courtesan circa the Middle Ages."

"Which is good, right?" she asks.

I readjust my squished boobs. "It's not proper, but I don't care as much because it will be invisible."

"Great." She tosses in a dress. "Even if no one sees the new undies, you'll feel sexy wearing them."

Does feeling sexy have a lot in common with feeling scratchy? Maybe. Knowing men, they just might find it hot if they saw you readjusting your knickers.

With a sigh, I put on her chosen dress and gape at all the exposed skin. "This will not do."

"Show me," Gia says.

I shake my head. "A streetwalker would hesitate to wear this."

Gia knocks on the door. "Come out."

"No."

"You'll have to, eventually."

No, I won't. I'm just going to change back into—

Wait.

Where are my clothes?

"I hid them all," Gia says before I can ask. "If you want to come out of there dressed, you'll have to do it in that dress."

With a growl, I step out of the dressing booth.

The salesperson and Gia exchange knowing glances.

"You look hot, sis," Gia says, and the lady nods enthusiastically.

I look in a mirror again and frown. "My cervix is showing."

Ignoring me, Gia asks the salesperson for a pair of high heels.

"You're wasting your time," I say when the lady is gone. "I'm not wearing this."

"You are," Gia says.

"Am not."

In déjà vu, we go back and forth until we get to:

"Yuh-huh."

"Nuh-uh."

"You forgot something important," Gia says.

My stomach turns cold at the wicked expression on her face. Surely, she's not going to—

"Yeah, that's right, you owe me one," she says, confirming my fears.

"But—"

"I'm calling in my favor," Gia says ceremonially. "I want you to look hot for your date. That means this dress, professional makeup, this lingerie, high heels of my choosing, and last but not least, a Brazilian wax."

# SEVENTEEN

IF HER MAGIC career never takes off, Gia can always give law a shot. No matter how hard I try to argue that heels plus lingerie plus dress plus makeup plus wax is five favors, she expertly contends that "looking hot" is just one.

Handing me a shoebox, she makes a summation of her case. "Teaching you lock picking required talking, gesturing, breathing, and much more, but I didn't consider those subparts separate favors. You should be grateful I'm using up my favor for something as selfless as making *you* look good for *your* date."

"Yeah, you're a saint," I say and open the box. "These are fuck-me pumps."

"Show us."

With a sigh, I clickety-clack out of the fitting room and twirl for my tormentors.

"Perfect," Gia says. "Now let's pay and go get you made up."

The makeup artist is so slow with her task she makes a slug seem zippy by comparison.

When it's done, I look like a proper strumpet, with a touch of trollop thrown in—which, of course, means Gia loves it.

After this metaphorical torture is over, we sprint across the street to a salon where a much more literal torture of hot wax awaits.

"The aesthetician will be right with you," says a smiling older woman.

I do a little research on my phone, then look up. "Is she licensed?"

I don't ask for the gender—if it's a man, I'm going to revolt.

"Of course," the lady says, smile faltering.

"When was the last time she got her physical?" I ask.

"Ah, there she is," the now-frowning lady says and gestures at who I presume is the aesthetician.

Tall and broad-shouldered, the woman looks more like a wrestler than a beautician, but hey, at least she should pass any physical with flying colors.

"Good luck," Gia whispers to me. Louder, she says, "She wants a Brazilian."

"No problem," the aesthetician booms in a masculine voice with a thick Russian accent.

Great. The last thing I need is an accent that reminds me of the Devil.

As she leads me to the torture room, I ask her all the standard questions I'd ask my surgeon, like if she drank the night before (no), and if she got enough sleep (yes).

"Do not be twitchy," she booms after my fifth question in that vein. "I take good care of you."

I know she wants to be reassuring, but it actually comes off menacing.

"In here," she says.

I step into a sterile-looking room with a big table in the middle.

"Strip," the aesthetician orders.

Fighting the urge to whimper, "Yes, mistress," I take my clothes off and follow directions until I end up on my back, legs spread, ready for further indignities.

"Nice bush," the mistress says, looking over my pubes approvingly. "Make job easier."

"Thanks?" I mutter. Who knew never trimming myself down there would come in handy?

Muscles flexing, the mistress treats the area with cleaning products and who knows what else while I lie there and remind myself that this is a licensed professional, and that I've survived a gynecologist's office with my sanity mostly intact.

When she applies the first batch of hot wax, I realize my teeth are clenched so tightly I just might need a dentist's visit after this—and wouldn't that put a shit cherry on top of this crap cake.

"Relax," the mistress growls after she attaches the first strip to my skin a few inches below my navel.

Relax? That is what all the doctors say before they do something—

Aargh! The sound emitting from my mouth is as shrill and desperate as that of the proverbial stuck pig would be in this situation —though if anyone waxes pigs before sticking them, PETA should get on it, posthaste.

The door opens and the receptionist lady rushes in, along with Gia and a couple of women I haven't seen.

"Are you okay?" my twin asks.

I redden. Could this be any worse? I guess they could've brought some random men with them. Or my dad. Or the Devil himself.

"She okay," my mistress tells them. "First time always hard."

"No, I'm not okay," I gasp. Giving my twin a narrowed-eye stare, I grit out, "I'll get you for this."

"Oh, you'll thank me once it's all over and you feel like a sex goddess," Gia says and herds all the spectators out of the room.

"Not bloody likely," I yell, but by then the door is closed.

"No worry. I make it better," the mistress says and applies another strip.

How?

She rips. I yelp in pain—but not as loudly.

She bends her head until it's inches away from my crotch and blows gently on the booboo.

Oh, this is what she meant?

Hmm. It does feel better—but at the same time, I really don't feel comfortable with how close her lips are to my clit, or the sensations my clit experiences from that airflow.

"Ready?" she asks.

I nod, resigned.

She rips again, then blows on the smarting flesh.

To stay sane, I count the number of rips and think of England.

After I survive a few more rounds, my tormentor says, "Now more sensitive area. Take a deep breath."

Wait a bloody sec—

Aargh! The pain is so intense I inadvertently squeeze my legs shut, no doubt giving the mistress a flashback to her wrestling career.

"Now look what you do," she says when my legs come apart again. "You glue your vagine shut."

She's right, and the process to undo the damage is probably the most humiliating thing I've ever experienced—including everything that's just preceded it.

"Try again?" the mistress asks when my mistake is finally undone.

I take in a deep breath. "Do it."

She does.

I yelp in pain and swear vengeance on Gia—but my legs stay apart this time.

My yelp is less loud the next round, and even less the one after that. I wonder if I'll reach subspace—a state of mind I read about in the context of BDSM. As the process continues, the subspace never materializes, so I desperately count the rips as I mentally draft a letter to whoever puts together the United Nations Convention against Torture—they clearly missed a technique.

After a century of pain, the aesthetician stops.

Dare I have hope? Is it finally over?

"Get on all fours," she orders.

I furrow my eyebrows. "Pardon me?"

"Doggy style," she says with a deadpan expression. "I finish Brazilian."

Oh, well. In for a penny of indignities, in for a pound of humiliation. I get into the required position, and hot wax is smeared around my bumhole for my troubles.

Can this get any worse?

Yep, sure can.

Though the pain of the rip is less severe, her subsequent blowing on the spot is as close as I've ever come to someone blowing smoke up my butt—sans the smoke.

On rip sixteen, she says she's done.

Sixteen? Not a prime. It's going to drive me mad.

No.

Must let go.

Can't.

Bugger. Am I really going to do this now?

Seems like I am.

Looking over my shoulder as I would at a lover mounting me, I ask, "Can you do one more strip?"

She stares at me like the hair she's just waxed has sprouted from my eyeballs. "Why?"

"Please?" I sound like I'm begging, which no doubt cements her "kinkiest client ever" impression of me for good. "I'll give you an extra tip."

With a slow headshake that clearly means "the shit I do to make money", she applies a little bit more wax to my bumhole, then rips— but without blowing this time.

That's fair. I guess now she thinks things have gotten weird.

Whatever. I got my seventeen rips, so I can leave.

In hindsight, counting wasn't the best idea.

I swiftly dress and pay, then walk out of the place while pointedly ignoring Gia's attempts to chat me up.

"Let me buy you lunch," Gia says after a few minutes of silent treatment. "You seem hangry."

She must feel very guilty indeed if she's willing to part with cash—her magic career doesn't pay all that well.

Let's see if I can call her bluff. "How about Nemo and Chips?" I ask, picking a restaurant near my place that I order from on the days I feel particularly thin and/or nostalgic for the UK. A place I happen to know she hates.

"That fish and chips shop?" Gia asks with an eye roll.

"At least it's clean enough for you," I say. "A-rating all the way."

She scoffs. "Yeah, like no one's ever gotten food poisoning from fish. But sure, why not? Brits are famous for their delicious cuisine."

Despite the grumbling, she hails a cab and takes us there—a sign of just how guilty she must feel after my banshee shrieks.

When we get a table at the place, I sip my tea and she guzzles her bottled water while giving me unsolicited advice for my upcoming "date"—advice I studiously ignore.

The food arrives. As I bite into my fried Nemo, I frown.

It tastes different than usual.

I hate it when that happens. If a dish has a name, it has to be consistent forever—that's why I always go to the same restaurants.

"What's wrong now?" Gia asks.

I explain.

"Please don't make a big deal out of this," she says. "Pretty please?"

I put my fork down. "Would *you* not make a big deal of it if they spit germs into your food?"

She sighs. "That's exactly what they'll do the next time if you make a scene."

"I'm not going to make a scene." I wave the waiter over.

Gia cringes.

"The fried Nemo was different than usual," I announce. "And I don't mean just the normal variation you can have in pollock."

"Different?" The waiter doesn't seem as concerned as a professional should be.

I explain that I've had the dish countless times, so I'd know better than anyone.

The waiter gets the manager, who offers to make the meal free.

"No," I say. "I want the recipe restored."

The manager gets the chef, who claims the dish is the same.

I challenge him to bring out the ingredients, which he reluctantly does. Then I proceed to taste it all, until I find the culprit: a different brand of beer in the batter.

"That's an impressive palate," the chef says. "I'll be sure to get the old beer going forward."

Whew. Order in the universe is restored.

Since Gia was a trooper through this ordeal, I pay for the meal after all, then magnanimously lie to her face that I had a great time today.

She grins. "Sure, let's pretend you did. Good luck on your not-a-date."

"Thanks," I say, matching her snarky tone.

"Don't mention it." She leans in and lowers her voice to a conspiratorial whisper. "Whatever you do, don't complain about the food like you just did. That's a sure way to turn a date into not-a-date."

"I won't," I say, and it's true.

How could I? I've never eaten at the place where the party is happening, so I don't have a baseline for what the food ought to taste like.

WHEN I GET HOME, I check my email. Seems that Buckley has impressed Robert and quickly too; they're having a chat today. Great. The throat-clearing might cease even sooner than I hoped.

There's an email from Alison too, filling me in on the Chortskys' move into the office. Apparently, both gave a speech and everything. She says they promised I'd lead the most important project—suit integration.

Speaking of the latter, an email from Robert gives me a link to the source control with the code I'll need to review. I don't look at said code just yet. I'm not in the state of mind to focus with everything that's happened already, not to mention my anxiety over what is about to happen in a few hours.

Since the Devil is proceeding with his part of our arrangement, I email Dr. Piper and tell him that I'll be able to get 1000 Devils on board. To make sure that actually is the truth, I email the Wicked One and ask him when he wants to meet to talk about the games.

Once my inbox is clean, I can't help but begin to worry.

What will the Devil's family be like? How sure am I that this isn't a date? What if his father doesn't like the gift I picked out—a tiny can of caviar that put me way over my usual birthday gift budget?

Also, what if Bella asks about the suit tonight—a query I now have an obligation to respond to?

Would she bring that up at her father's birthday?

She seems like the kind of person who might.

I level a speculative glance at the suit. It's charged now, so in theory, I could go through that last step of the demo now. It might even be wise. I've got so much pent-up sexual energy in me I might flirt with the Devil tonight... or worse.

If I use that suit now, it would be like that scene from *There's Something About Mary*, where Ben Stiller jerks off as a way to seem less twitchy on the date.

But no. That didn't work out so well for Ben Stiller—the last thing I want is for the Devil to end up with my pussy juices as hair gel. I'm sure I can control myself, and in any case, my post-wax skin is tender down there, so getting rubbed by the suit material isn't what it needs.

So, no sex with the virtual Devil for me... for now. If Bella brings it up, I'll ask her about the testing documents the Devil mentioned. That should delay things until I see her next.

Yeah, that's it. Now the question is: where are those details the Devil promised me? Where is the place and what time is the event?

Dare I hope he doesn't provide them? I obviously can't go if I don't know where to go. But in that case, did I go through all the ordeals with Gia for nothing? Also, why does it seem like I might get upset if—

My phone dings.

Wow. The phrase is "speak of the devil," but thinking of him works just as well.

*What's your address?*

Since he can look it up in HR records anyway, I text it to him.

*I'll pick you up at seven.*

I have no words—via text or otherwise. In fact, I'm so flummoxed I visit Euclid in VR, but even that doesn't lower my blood pressure. It takes two episodes of *Downton Abbey* and several chapters of *Emma* to calm me down enough to put on my new clothes and double-check that the makeup still looks tidy.

It does. I'm all set to go.

I just hope I don't die of awkwardness by the time the night is through.

# EIGHTEEN

AS I STEP out of my building, my waxed privates are still on fire, and I feel almost naked in my new dress.

If this is what sex goddesses feel like, it's a marvel they don't commit suicide in droves.

I'm a couple of minutes early for the pickup, so I pace the sidewalk, my new shoes making it sound like I'm tapdancing. My heart rate is through the roof again, and not just because I'm about to see the Devil.

Okay, fine, mainly for that reason.

"Holly?" a deep, sexy, Russian-accented voice says, and I nearly jump out of my skin—an act that would be made easier by how much of it is exposed by the bloody dress.

I turn on my heel and gasp.

It's the Devil, but he looks different.

Better.

Tidy.

Dressed up.

Groomed.

To say he cleans up nice wouldn't do it justice. We're talking drool pooling in my mouth, heat gathering in recently waxed places, and a standing ovation from my ovaries.

His hoodie and jeans have been replaced with a perfectly tailored suit. The stubble is gone. Even the unruly hair is tamed—though not as much as I would've liked. There's some product in there, but all he must've done is run his fingers through those dark locks instead of combing them back, as would've been ideal.

Still, combined, the look robs me of coherent thought.

His cerulean eyes gleam as he gives me an equally thorough once-over. "You look amazing."

"No, you do," I blurt, and an English proverb pops into my head: "When flatterers meet, the devil goes to dinner."

His wicked smirk is back. "Thanks." He gestures to the sidewalk. "This way."

A limo is waiting for us. He gets the door, which makes him somehow look even more dashing.

Must. Stop. Ogling. My. New. Boss.

Doing my best not to flash him any lady bits, I climb into the car, and he follows.

Will he sit next to me?

*Please sit next to me.*

*I mean, don't sit next to me.*

He sits across from me.

Good. Why am I disappointed? Also, can he see under my dress from there?

Just in case, I cross my legs.

His eyes suddenly look hungry.

Bugger. Did I accidentally pull a Sharon Stone from *Basic Instinct?*

No. Impossible. I'm wearing knickers.

"Do you want something to drink?" he asks, his voice low and smooth.

I do feel parched, but I'm not sure I can handle alcohol at the moment. Or ever around him. "Is there any tea?"

What am I saying? Of course not. This isn't the UK.

And yet, he grins and opens a cupboard on the side.

Wow. It's tea porn in there. There's every variety I can think of, from black to white to matcha.

I blink. Nope. The tea isn't an illusion. "Why does this limo have so much tea?"

He pulls out a box with Russian writing on it. "Because it's my ride, and I love tea."

"You love tea?" Maybe the fact that he has his own limo should be more of a surprise, but it's not.

His grin widens. "Why can't I love tea?"

"I love tea," I say dumbly.

He winks. Winks! "Now we have this in common."

A shrug is all the reply I can manage.

"What kind do you prefer?" he asks.

"Um, Earl Grey."

He shakes the box he took out earlier. "What about Russian Caravan tea?"

"I've never had the pleasure."

He opens the box and takes a sniff. "Want to try?"

Why was that so seductive—the question *and* the sniff?

"What's in it?" I ask unsteadily.

"It's a blend of oolong, keemun, and lapsang souchong," he says, and now I'm wondering if he's trying to tempt me on purpose.

I mean, a prime number of ingredients listed in that sexy voice of his?

"It's very aromatic," he continues. "Sweet. Malty. Smoky."

Is there such a thing as a nosegasm?

"What do you say?" He shakes the tea box again.

"I want." Great reply. Then again, it's better than "shag me."

He chuckles and reaches into the bar to pull out an ornately decorated metal contraption that reminds me of a funeral urn.

Weird. Does he want to drink a cuppa for his departed grandmother who happens to be inside that thing?

"This is a samovar," he says as he putters with it. "Russians traditionally use these for tea."

Ah. I think I've heard of a samovar. Never thought I'd see it in real life... especially in a limo.

A minute later, he's handing me a teacup on a proper saucer.

As the handover commences, his fingers brush against mine again, sending pleasurable energy through my nerve endings and rendering me capable of nothing more than blowing on the bloody tea.

Then he starts blowing on his, and I watch his puckered lips in fascination. Why do they look so beautiful that way? So kissable? So... lickable?

Eventually, I recover my wits and tire of blowing... the tea.

Taking a dainty sip, I have an honest-to-goodness teagasm.

There might even be a moan.

Those kissable lips curve. "Better than Earl Grey?"

I eagerly bob my head. "I didn't think that was possible. Where can I get this?"

"Online or in Brighton Beach. That's our destination, by the way."

Ah. It's also known as Little Odessa—a part of Brooklyn famous for the high population of Russian-speaking immigrants. Not surprising that his father would want to have his birthday there.

"I think I'll get some and make this tea part of my daily ritual," I say.

"Here." He hands me the box. "Use that for now."

"Thanks." I reverently accept the gift and hide it in my purse.

"Don't mention it. It's just tea."

"Amazing tea," I say.

He smiles widely. "How was your day?"

"Jolly good," I lie. "How was the move into the new offices?"

He runs his hand through his hair, ruining what little orderliness it had. Seriously, would I get arrested if I attacked him with a comb? "All fine," he says. "I finally got a new keyboard and monitor."

Bugger. I almost forgot about the damage I wrought.

"Do you have any biscuits—I mean, tea cookies?" I ask, desperate to change the subject.

"I do, but I don't think you want to ruin your appetite," he says. "My parents have pulled out all the stops with the menu tonight."

"They found a restaurant that lets them change the menu?"

Because that sounds great to me. The problem with restaurants is that you can't get the same thing in all of them.

"Better," he says. "They own the restaurant."

Huh. That didn't come up when I researched the Chortsky name.

"Does it serve Russian cuisine?" I ask.

"Naturally."

"What's it called?"

"The Hut. Heard of it?"

I shake my head.

"It's an abbreviation for The Hut on Hen's Legs—a reference to a Russian fairy tale in which a child-eating witch by the name of Baba Yaga lives in such a dwelling."

A child-eating witch? I'm not Gia, but that doesn't sound very hygienic... or ethically acceptable.

"There." He points out the window. "That's the place."

As if in confirmation, the limo stops.

Fascinated, I study the restaurant. There's a wooden staircase that leads to the entrance, and around it stand two decorative hen "legs," as per the longer title.

"I hope they serve chicken inside," I say. "Otherwise, Americans might be confused."

He exits and holds the door for me. "Chicken, among many,

many other delicious things."

The stairs are rickety, but the door he holds for me is solid.

Inside, the place is downright posh, with lots of marble, fancy tablecloths, and covered chairs—a nice touch since it makes it hard to count the number of legs. Music with a strong beat is blasting loudly enough to vibrate my internal organs, and a pudgy mustachioed man is rapping in Russian on a central stage.

Right. The Devil mentioned food and a show, so a stage makes sense.

The folks inside the restaurant seem to enjoy the song, so I launch the translation app on my phone to get some idea of what the lyrics are.

*Boys are the drug poop*
*At school gave in box*
*Narcotics suck kvass*

Hmm. A lot must've been lost in translation there. What's *kvass?* Not that it would help me understand the lyrics.

Turns out kvass is a fermented drink. If anything, that makes the lyrics less comprehensible. All I can tell is that the song is vaguely anti-drugs, so that's good, I suppose.

Looking up from my phone, I see the Devil grinning as he notices what I'm doing.

"That's a pretty bad translation," he says, peering at my phone screen. "What it should've said is: 'Drugs are the shit I gave at school in a matchbox. Kvass is better than drugs.'"

"That doesn't make sense either. Why would you put feces in a matchbox?"

"It's something we did back in Russia. Stool samples."

Gia would die if she knew. "Why?"

He shrugs. "Maybe to test for parasites?"

Seriously? There goes my appetite.

He leads me to a table in the back just as the music quiets down.

I recognize some people at the table right away: Bella and

Dragomir, sitting side by side, clearly as a couple. The rest I don't know, though I can guess. The bespectacled man who looks like the Devil's brooding twin must be the brother, Vlad. The two older people must be the parents. Also guessable is the man who looks like Dragomir's more cheerful copy—must be *his* brother.

The main enigmas are the two women: a pale, cherubic-faced one who's looking adoringly at Vlad, and a striking blonde who's giving me the stink eye for some reason.

"Hope we're not late," the Devil says.

The maybe-parents get to their feet, and everyone else follows their example.

"You're not late, Sashen'ka," codename-mother says with a Russian accent that's molasses thick. "And you really brought a date."

The blond woman's stink eye turns stinkier.

Hold on. The Devil mentioned his mother setting him up. Is this blonde a backup date, in case I didn't show up?

I resist the urge to hiss at her—I've got first impressions to make, after all.

"Everyone, this is Holly," my fake date says. "Holly, this is my brother, Vlad, and that's Fanny." He gestures at his poker-faced doppelgänger and his pretty, round-cheeked date.

The brother nods coolly, but Fanny smiles brightly as she waves.

Wait. So she's the expert tester the Devil mentioned earlier? She looks way too sweet and innocent to have experience with porn-related testing.

"You know Bella and Dragomir," the Prince of Darkness continues. "And this is his brother, Anatolio."

Smiling, Anatolio comes up to me, bows, then grabs my hand and gives it a kiss faster than I can blink.

A strange sound emanates from beside me.

I blink.

Did the Devil just *growl?*

"It's Tigger," Anatolio says. "That's what my friends call me."

Tigger? Does he like to bounce a lot and have a stuffed bear for a friend?

The Devil pointedly steps between me and Tigger before continuing the introductions. "This is Snezhana." He gestures at the blonde. "She works in a store next door, though I'm not sure what she's doing here." He glances disapprovingly at codename-mother.

The blonde also looks at codename-mother—in her case, with a confused expression.

"I can explain," codename-mother says, not meeting either of their gazes. "I heard that Anatolio—I mean, Tigger—is single, so I invited Snezhana in case they might... get along."

"That's odd," Bella says. "We only told you that Tigger was coming today."

The look the older woman gives her maybe-daughter could melt lead.

Tigger frowns at Snezhana, whose expression makes it clear that this is the first time she's heard of the setup with him.

My earlier guess must've been right. She was originally invited here for the Devil.

Twat.

With a barely perceptible headshake, the Ruler of Darkness says, "Last but not least, this is my mother, Natasha, and the birthday boy himself, Boris."

Boris and Natasha? Huh. They even look like the cartoon characters by the same name.

I catch Fanny grinning—I bet she's thinking the same exact thing.

Before I know what hits me, the mother is hugging me and kissing me on each cheek.

Well, that's a bit too friendly.

As soon as Natasha is done with the smooching, I receive the same treatment from the patriarch—that is, until the Devil clears his throat. Aggressively, I might add.

On my end, I can feel Boris and Natasha's saliva on my cheeks, and I make a mental note to tell Gia that she can never date a Russian. She wouldn't survive such a greeting.

When Boris finally disconnects from me, I dig into my purse, take out the jar with caviar, and thrust it into his hands. "I wish you many happy returns."

He looks at the jar, then at me. Exchanging an impressed glance with Natasha, he booms, "Thanks, Holly. Thank you very much."

He pronounces my name almost like "holy," and like his wife, he sounds just like the cartoon character who shares his name.

"Sit, everyone," he says. "Drinking must commence."

The Devil catches my gaze and pulls out a chair. "Sit here."

Who knew the Evil One would bring chivalry back from the dead?

I sit.

He takes the chair next to me.

I smell that yummy scent of his—and recognize that it is, in part, that heavenly tea he gave me.

A tea cologne? I may come on the spot.

Snezhana ends up across the table from us, next to Tigger, but neither of them seems interested in each other. Tigger checks out other women in the room like a total rake, while she ogles my fake date.

A very popular UK word that starts with a "c" is on the tip of my tongue.

Natasha looks at Vlad. "I get the first toast. Pour, please."

Vlad grabs a giant bottle of vodka and starts filling the shot glasses in front of everyone's plates.

"Watch how much you pour for the non-Russians," Snezhana says. Her voice turns out to be smoky and melodious, her accent annoyingly sexy. "Can't expect them to keep up."

Tigger's lips quirk. "This non-Russian can drink anyone under the table."

"I meant Americans," Snezhana says, looking right at me.

Boris grins at Tigger. "That sounds like a challenge I'll gladly accept."

"Bring it on, birthday boy," Tigger says good-naturedly.

Boris waves at the passing waiter and says something in Russian.

"Don't," Natasha growls.

"It's my birthday," Boris snaps.

"Fine," she says sharply. "But don't complain to me tomorrow."

The waiter comes back with two glasses the size of flower vases.

"Pour one for me and one for my soon-to-be-drunk friend," Boris says.

With a disapproving look, Vlad pours the two vases to the brim.

"You sure about this?" Dragomir asks his brother.

With a cocky smile, Tigger takes a pickle from a nearby assortment and places it on his plate.

As Vlad continues with the vodka distribution, the Devil leans toward me and whispers, "When he gets to you, tell him to stop before your glass is full."

"Why?" I whisper back.

"It's the custom to drink until you can see the bottom of the shot glass, and since it's my dad's birthday, he'll want everyone to do that. However, no custom says your glass needs to start off full."

Interesting. Now that he's said it, I notice that Fanny is already aware of these peculiarities—her shot glass is only a quarter full.

When Vlad gets to me, he pours slowly while looking at me, clearly expecting me to stop him early. Unfortunately, Snezhana is also watching, and her superior expression makes the contrarian in me allow Vlad to fill my glass to the brim.

According to a DNA ancestry test, I'm a mix of English, Scottish, Cornish, and Irish. Some of these ethnicities are as famous for their drinking prowess as the Russians—so there.

Eyeing my shot glass disapprovingly, the Devil puts a pickle on my plate.

Is this symbolic of the pickle of a situation I'm in? No, it must be another custom—Snezhana and everyone else get a pickle also.

"I will make my toast now," Natasha says as soon as Vlad is done with his vodka duties. "I dedicate this poem to my beloved husband and soon-to-be proud grandfather." She looks very pointedly at me.

Blimey. Does she know something I don't? Is the Antichrist supposed to come about via immaculate conception?

Done making me uncomfortable, Natasha looks at Fanny next—I guess as another source of a soon-to-be grandchild.

Fanny's cheeks pinken with a mighty blush.

Skipping Snezhana, Natasha levels an even pointier stare at Bella. Then she returns her gaze to her husband—which is why she misses Bella's eye roll.

"My poem is in my mother tongue," Natasha continues. "So, I hope those of you who don't speak it, bear with me."

Snezhana looks triumphant.

Seriously?

I launch the translation app on my phone—I can use modern technology to follow along.

Hopefully.

Natasha begins her poem, and the app tries to keep up.

*My support.*

Okay, good start.

*My master.*

Hmm. Hopefully a mistranslation.

*My soulmate.*

Cute.

*My protector.*

How many of these "my" bits will this poem have?

*My defender.*

Okay, we get it, lady. He's a lot of things.

*Ever faithful.*

Hey, at least the list of "my" is over.

*Ever eager.*

TMI?

*Ever ready to please.*

More TMI?

*No woman has been as grateful as I to obediently serve at the side of a man.*

Is this another mistranslation, or has feminism not reached Russia yet?

The poem goes on in the same vein, so I quit following the translation and just wait for it to be over—which takes what feels like another hour.

"Now for our American friends," Natasha says when she's finally done. "A shorter toast."

Another one? I'll believe the brevity when I hear it.

"What is the difference between a faithful and an unfaithful husband?" Natasha asks.

Everyone stays politely quiet.

"Huge," Natasha says. "The faithful sometimes feel remorse."

As one, we all politely chuckle.

"So," Natasha says. "Let us drink so that remorse does not torment this faithful husband."

I'm confused. Does she want him to be a sociopath?

Everyone grabs their shot glasses/vases, and I do as well.

Until now, I've only imbibed wine, beer, and cocktails, and rarely at that. I don't like the loss of control that alcohol and drugs bring with them, so I've never really indulged in either.

Well, at least this will be a new experience.

Natasha sniffs her pickle, downs her shot, and eats the condiment with great enthusiasm.

Looking at me challengingly, Snezhana gulps her vodka down without any pickle-sniffing or eating—which must be the more hard-core way.

Tigger and Boris down their gallons of vodka as though it were water.

Okay. How bad can it be?

Sniffing the briny pickle for shits and giggles, I down my vodka.

Holy bollocks of fire!

The magma travels down my esophagus and explodes in a mushroom cloud in my stomach, filling it with unwelcome warmth.

Is this the expected result?

If so, why would anyone do this to themselves?

Desperate to ease the pain, I devour the pickle.

Nope.

Though salty, the pickle isn't an ice slushy, which is what's needed at this juncture.

Is that the look of schadenfreude on Snezhana's face?

Schooling my features, I say as evenly as I can manage, "That was nice."

Boris smacks the Devil on the back approvingly. "That one's a keeper."

Snezhana narrows her eyes and stands up. "The time between the first drink and the second ought to be short."

Natasha frowns at her, but Boris grins excitedly. "Indeed," he says. "Out of the mouths of babes."

"How about we eat something more substantial than a pickle first?" Natasha says.

"After the second one," Boris says. "Traditions must be followed."

Natasha gives Snezhana a glare that seems to say, "That's the last time I invite *you*," and I feel a little schadenfreude myself.

This time, Tigger pours the vodka, and because Snezhana stares challengingly at me again, I let him fill my shot glass to the brim.

Bella stands up. "My toast. To Dad: May you have health above all and happiness."

Are Russians allowed to make a toast that short?

Seems so. Everyone starts downing their shots.

Okay. I guess I have to do this again.

I sniff the pickle and knock back the vodka.

# NINETEEN

SURPRISINGLY, this shot burns only a fraction as much as the prior one.

Is this why the break between the first and second had to be short?

"You should pace yourself," the Devil whispers in my ear, his warm breath sending goosebumps down my arm. "Say 'stop' sooner the next round."

Excuse me? Is he telling me what to do? He's not the boss of me. At least not in this restaurant.

"Here." He grabs a bowl of something that looks like potato salad and deposits some on my plate. "Eat something."

Since everyone else is digging into the food also, I taste the offering.

Yum. Unlike regular potato salad, a dish I don't care for, this has meat, green peas, and (of course) chopped pickles, which might be why it's so good.

"What's this called?" I ask.

"Oliver salad," Natasha says with a smile. "You like?"

"It's amazing," I say, in part because I mean it and in part because they own this restaurant and have "pulled out all the stops with the menu."

As we eat, the music comes back on. The new song reminds me of the opera the blue alien was singing in *The Fifth Element*, right before things turned too violent for me to watch, except the pudgy singer's testicles seem to be in the way of him hitting the high notes.

Dragomir pours the next round of shots, and I stare defiantly at the Devil as my glass is filled to the brim again.

The third shot goes down even smoother.

They might make an alcoholic out of me yet.

The waiters bring out a hot dish of small dumplings.

"That's *pelmeni*," Natasha explains. "It's a simple food, but my pookie loves it."

The Devil puts some pelmeni on my plate and adds a dash of what he calls *smetana,* which turns out to be sour cream.

The combo is so good I moan in pleasure, which causes the Devil to eye me with a strangely intent expression.

Swallowing the deliciousness, I gush compliments to the chef.

"I have to agree with my husband," Natasha says to the Devil with a grin. "This one *is* a keeper."

"You have to teach me how to make these," I say earnestly. "I'll eat it instead of ravioli."

Natasha is beaming with enthusiasm as she tells me how to make the dish. Then she turns to the rest of the table. "While we're talking restaurant-related things," she says, "your father and I have an announcement to make."

She waits until every one of the Chortsky offspring gives her their full attention.

"We've decided to leave The Hut to the first of you who gives us a grandchild."

With that, Fanny, Bella, and I receive a new round of pointed stares that seem to say, "Are you ovulating yet?"

Snezhana looks on the verge of Hulking out from jealousy. It makes me wonder if it's not my fake date that she wants but this restaurant. She does work next door, after all, and at least according to Hannibal Lecter, we covet what we see every day.

Bella groans. "Mom, please. You know we all have successful businesses of our own, right?"

The Devil and his brother nod, and Vlad says, "When you're ready, we want you to sell this place and enjoy the money yourselves. You've earned it."

"In any case, we're not going to engage in a fuck race for your sake," Bella says, not bothering to lower her voice.

Fanny's cheeks turn crimson.

"Sorry you have to witness this," the Devil whispers into my ear.

He thinks this is bad? He should spend some time with *my* family.

"Such language!" Natasha appears on the verge of throttling her daughter. "You're going to upset your father. On his birthday."

Actually, Boris doesn't seem interested in anything but the vodka bottle—he keeps eyeing it like it's a naked woman dancing.

The Devil seems to pick up on this. Grabbing the bottle, he states that he'll pour the next round and fills Tigger and Boris's vases again.

Damn. Didn't I read somewhere that a liter of spirits could kill you?

"To the brim for me," Snezhana says huskily when he gets to her shot glass. "I can handle... all of it."

Is it the vodka that's making me want to scalp the blonde?

No wonder there are so many brawls in bars.

When the Wicked One gets to me, he only pours me a drop—as though I've told him to stop.

Snezhana looks at my measly vodka level with triumph.

Oh, yeah?

"Thanks, sweetheart," I tell my fake date and pat his upper arm—only to feel my breath catch at the hard, sinewy muscle under the layers of cloth.

Damn. The Devil is built.

He gives a slight start at my familiarity but recovers quickly and plays along. "No problem, *kroshka*."

Whatever that word means, the result is a double whammy. Natasha looks clam-happy, while Snezhana gulps down her vodka without waiting for the toast.

I lock eyes with her, take the Devil's fully filled shot glass, and knock it back.

"Holly," he exclaims.

Everyone turns his way.

"It's not the custom to drink before the toast," he says lamely.

Ha. So stealing someone's vodka is okay?

"I'll fix this." Boris grabs the vodka bottle and refills the two shot glasses in front of me, then hands one to his son.

I notice he didn't give Snezhana any, but I don't want to be a snitch.

Putting the vodka down, Boris declares, "I'll make the next toast. Sorry, it will be in Russian."

I ready the app, and while I'm at it, I check the meaning of *kroshka*.

Breadcrumb?

Okay, fine. Then I'm calling him *breadcrust*—or Crusty for short.

Boris starts speaking.

*A wife is the most wonderful invention since the discovery of the wheel.*

Great. Is this another poem?

*A wife is a man's best friend.*

Isn't that a dog?

*A wife is—*

The next part sounds like slurred speech, which might be why the app translates:

*—how much is a kilo of kielbasa if you bite off a screwdriver from a locomotive?*

I don't follow the rest. I'm suddenly feeling very nice, all warm, relaxed, and eager to party on.

"To my wife," Boris concludes and downs his gallon of vodka.

Tigger looks a bit more apprehensive as he downs his.

I knock back my shot on autopilot—and there's zero burn this time. Has someone switched out vodka for water?

The music starts up again. This time, the singer butchers a familiar song: "Hips Don't Lie" by Shakira.

Doing my best not to think too much about the pudgy dude's hips, I devour the remaining pelmeni as everyone focuses on the countless other delicacies that keep coming to the table.

"Will there be more pelmeni?" I ask the Devil when my plate is sadly empty.

Grinning, he calls over a waiter and tells him something in Russian.

"Why don't you try something else, dear?" Natasha asks me. "There's so much other food."

I hiccup. "When I find something I like, I tend to stick to it."

Natasha glances at her son with a grin. "Admirable attitude when it comes to men, but I'm not sure it's transferable to food."

"It is," I assure her. "We make countless decisions every day. Why add to that stress with unnecessary food choices?"

Before Natasha can argue, Tigger picks up the vodka bottle. "My turn."

Is it me or is his hand a bit unsteady?

"I think the ladies have had enough," the Devil says sternly.

"That's sexist," I say.

His cerulean eyes narrow. "It's biology."

"Well, I want one more," I say stubbornly, and it's true. According to my mental count, I've had four.

I can't end on a four. Five is much better.

Bugger. How many pelmeni did I eat? Also, is that the plural of—

"I want one too." Bella winks at me. "I know we look dainty and frail and all, but we can handle ourselves without a man's supervision."

I've got to hand it to Dragomir. He nods approvingly at her words.

"I wasn't being sexist," the Wicked One mutters. "Not on purpose, anyway."

"I'll have a little more too," Fanny chimes in. "Also, I volunteer for the toast."

Natasha nods approvingly, and Snezhana says something incomprehensible... maybe in Russian.

"Your wish is my commando," Tigger says. "I mean, commander. I mean, command."

Dragomir shakes his head at his obviously buzzed brother but says nothing.

Once everyone has their shots, Fanny stands up, her cheeks red. "I wanted to salute our hosts, Natasha and Boris. Thank you for creating such wonderful children." She looks adoringly at Vlad. "And thank you for being so welcoming. Amen."

Wait, that sounded more like she said Grace.

"I'll drink to that," Boris slurs and swallows another vase worth of vodka.

Ignoring the Devil's disapproving stare, I finish my fifth shot.

Ah, smooth. Prime vodka is the best.

"Ladies and gentlemen," says the pudgy singer from the stage. "It's showtime."

Right. There was mention of a show.

The lights dim, and semi-naked burlesque dancers take the stage.

What happens next reminds me of Cirque du Soleil, only rated R. The dancers perform impressive acrobatics, but the miracle is that their tiny outfits stay on. No doubt glue is involved.

To his credit, the Devil looks completely uninterested in all the flesh on display. Same is true of Dragomir and Vlad.

Boris, on the other hand, is drooling, while his drinking buddy/nemesis Tigger is clapping with equal enthusiasm.

When the show is over, the singer returns to the stage.

"We start our dancing program with a White Dance," he announces.

Bella winks at me. "That means the ladies invite the gentlemen."

A vaguely familiar melody blasts out of the speakers.

Bella executes a dramatic bow before Dragomir, and Fanny shyly asks Vlad if she could have this dance.

The men accept, and the two couples head to the dance floor.

Do *I* want to dance? I've been known to say that dancing is an excuse for public cuddling and dry humping, but it looks really appealing right now.

Natasha is inviting Boris. Some random girl from another table is inviting Tigger. Snezhana's eyes are like the laser sights of the Terminator's gun as they zero in on my fake date.

Yeah, no. That's not happening.

I leap to my feet.

Wow. Is the room a little wobbly?

No matter. Curtsying in front of the Devil, I shout, "Wanna dance?"

"It would be an honor." The Ruler of Darkness rises gracefully to his feet.

Snezhana halts in her tracks.

Yeah, she better.

On the stage, the pudgy singer belts out in broken English, *Holy water cannot help you now.*

It probably can't. After all, isn't what I'm about to do a colloquialism for ill-advised behavior?

I'm going to dance with the Devil.

# TWENTY

THE EVIL One takes my hand.

Golly.

The heat of vodka has nothing on this. My palm feels like it's been branded.

He leads me to the middle of the dance floor and assumes a ball-room stance.

I join him.

He pulls me against his powerful body.

Until now, I hadn't realized just how tall and broad-shouldered he is.

It's intoxicating.

We start to sway to the music.

The aroma of tea mixed with something deliciously masculine makes my head spin as cerulean eyes pin me like a butterfly. And speaking of those little flying bastards, they're having an orgy in my stomach and need to stop it.

To break the hypnotic pull of his gaze, I burrow closer and hide my head in the crook of his neck.

Oh my.

There's a hardness in his pants, and it's the size of the proverbial flashlight.

A massive flashlight.

The Devil is happy to see me, that's for damn sure.

Did I underestimate his manhood in VR?

Maybe. What's worse is my lady boner is just as ready.

Before I realize what I'm doing, I lick his neck.

Lick. His. Neck.

Not good.

Not proper.

I totally should've masturbated before coming here. The urge to lick him again—or worse—is strong.

His entire body stiffens, and the skin on his neck breaks out in goosepimples.

I pull away, only to get caught in his gaze again, the blue depths now dark and heated.

I no longer have any doubt what the Devil's favorite sin is.

I audibly gulp.

The heat flaring between us is as scorching as the fires of hell.

On the stage, the pudgy singer belts out, "Seven devils all around me…"

Seriously, universe? I recognize these lyrics. It's from my playlist of songs that have prime numbers in their titles—"Seven Devils" by Florence + the Machine. Sure enough, if I count Bella's and Vlad's significant others as part of the Chortsky clan, there are indeed seven of them. All around me.

I meet my devil's eyes again.

If the Tempter means to seduce me, consider me succumbed to his charms.

I dampen my lips.

Pupils dilating, he bends his head.

I rise on tiptoes.

Our lips are a millimeter apart.

"Borichka!" Natasha screams in panic.

What the bloody—

Boris crashes between us.

The Devil and I spring apart, and Boris grabs onto me as he falls to his knees, his face burrowing into my crotch.

"Dad, what the hell?" my maybe-not-so-fake date exclaims, grabbing for his father.

Boris doesn't respond. He's channeling Winnie, the bear dog—the smell of my crotch must've driven him into a stupor.

"Does this mean I win?" Tigger asks, his speech slightly slurred.

His brother gives him the stink eye before helping the Devil drag Boris off me.

"Why don't we girls go powder our noses?" Natasha says, her voice overly bright. "Let the men help the birthday boy to the table."

Yeah. Great idea. I have a feeling Boris might put on a show any second—maybe even a recreation of that scene from *The Exorcist*. And if that happens, there might be a chain reaction across the restaurant—a horrid visual.

Fanny and Bella must be on the same wavelength because they join us in the stampede for the loo.

The place turns out to be fancy, with a bathroom attendant and everything. She's broad-shouldered and vaguely reminds me of the mistress from the salon, but I don't fret because I have no pubes left.

Getting into the stall to drain my lady lizard, I'm shocked by how pleasant the endeavor turns out to be.

I must've needed to go badly. That, or this is an effect of vodka no one ever talks about.

Exiting the stall, I wash my hands and accept a towel from the mistress clone.

Okay. Time to face the Devil again.

I turn toward the door and find Snezhana blocking my way.

Damn. She's a blond ninja, this one.

"You and Alex will never work." Every word coming out of her mouth is slurred. "He needs to be with someone of his own kind. Like me."

I scoff. "I didn't realize Alex was a bitch."

Where did that come from? I'd expect it from Gia or my other sisters, but not me. Alcohol clearly agrees with me.

Slight problem: Snezhana doesn't like my retort.

Nostrils flaring to the point where her nose hairs show, she takes a step toward me.

"I think it would be best if you left," Bella says coldly from my right.

"Yeah," Fanny says in a softer tone from my left. "And just so you know, Holly and Alex make the cutest couple."

Snezhana doesn't seem to care about their words, or the fact that she's outnumbered.

She takes another menacing step my way.

Oh, well.

I've never been in a fight in my life, abhorring violence as I do, but I guess today is the day for a lot of firsts.

Balling my hands into fists, I jut out my chin. "Bring it on."

# TWENTY-ONE

THE BUFF BATHROOM mistress steps in Snezhana's path. "No one is bringing on anything in my bathroom."

"Stay out of this," Snezhana growls.

"Bella already told you to leave," the toilet mistress booms. "Scram."

Snezhana lunges at her. Before I can blink, the mistress has her upside down in a wrestling grip.

Snezhana is literally kicking and screaming as the bigger woman carries her out.

"Wow," Fanny says, her blue eyes huge. "That got intense."

"Some people are bad drunks," Bella says philosophically. "I'm sure she'll be petrified at her behavior once she sleeps it off."

I grin at them both. "Thanks for having my back."

"Of course," Bella says. "What are friends for?"

She called me a friend. Bugger. I'm not too drunk to forget about my transgressions against Bella's dream. Once she learns about them, she won't think of me as a friend. In fact, she'll ask the toilet mistress to toss me out as well.

There's a sound of a flush. The farthest bathroom stall opens and Natasha steps out, frowning. "I heard a commotion."

Bella talks to her in rapid-fire Russian, and as she goes on, Natasha's frown deepens.

"I'll have words with Snezhana's mother," Natasha says decisively when Bella is finished.

"You do that," Bella says. "Better yet, you shouldn't have invited her in the first place."

Natasha starts washing her hands, her movements jerky and clearly impaired. "I can't believe the girl had a chance to be with Tigger and blew it so badly. I love my son to death, don't get me wrong, but that boy—"

"Mother, I think you might've had enough to drink," Bella says. "You're married, remember?"

Natasha sniffs. "Married doesn't mean dead."

"I disagree," I find myself saying. "Not with the married means dead part, but the other thing. Your son is superior to Tigger in every way."

Why did I just say that?

Bella grins at me. "I'd say you may have also had enough vodka for today."

I bob my head. "Probably. I don't think I can handle two more shots in any case, and six would surely kill me."

"Six?" Fanny asks, looking confused.

"If I had one more, that would be six," I say. "Needs to be seven. Or eleven."

"Right, the 7-Eleven." Fanny nods solemnly, but there's a hint of a smile dancing in her eyes. "In solidarity, I'll stop drinking too."

"Same here," Bella says.

"No more vodka for me either," Natasha declares. "I'm going to be too busy dancing with Tigger now that his date is gone."

With that pact in place, we return to the table, where we find Boris with his head next to his plate, loudly snoring. Tigger—who clearly won the drinking contest—is surrounded by two women from another table. The trio of the Devil, Vlad, and Dragomir are speaking animatedly in Russian.

Blimey.

If a plain chap looks good with vodka goggles on, the Devil is downright beautiful, as befits the brightest and most powerful of all the angels.

Would he mind if I sat on his lap instead of my chair?

"Back to your husbands," Natasha barks at Tigger's entourage, and they scram. Natasha then bats her eyelashes at the younger man and says huskily, "How about a dance?"

Tigger rises, albeit a bit unsteadily, and leads her to the dance floor.

"How about we go keep an eye on them?" Bella asks Dragomir. "I don't want your brother as my stepfather."

Dragomir grins, and they head over to the dance floor, with Fanny and Vlad on their tails.

Should I dance with the Devil again?

"Here," he says, pulling out a chair for me again.

Spoilsport. No dancing and now I have to sit on my own bloody chair? Next thing I know, he'll ask me to join a nunnery.

Sighing, I plop into the chair a little too quickly, and the restaurant spins around me.

"I got you more pelmeni," he says. "Eat. Food slows down alcohol absorption."

"That takes the cake." I grab a fork—the thing is heavy for some reason. "The Devil is worried I might be sloshed."

Wait, did I say that out loud?

Yep.

He quirks an eyebrow. "The Devil?"

I hiccup. "That's what I call you. Well, also Crusty—but that one's so recent I haven't used it yet."

He shakes his head. "As much as I don't like the sound of 'Crusty,' I just might prefer it to 'the Devil.'"

"Seriously?" I attempt to spear a dumpling, but the bugger slithers away—must be all that butter and sour cream.

He grabs my fork, expertly nails the morsel for me, and hands the utensil back, our fingers brushing orgasmically in the process. "Back in Russia, kids would tease us with variations on that theme because of our last name," he says. "So it's something of a sore spot. At least 'Crusty' is original."

I blink at him owlishly. "But you named your dog Beelzebub."

He shrugs. "That name isn't known in Russia, and it's okay to call your dog something you wouldn't want to be called yourself. Besides, I don't want the assholes from my past to have any power over me— that's why I named my company 1000 Devils."

"Ah. The Devil is your Holy Hymen." I bring the fork to my mouth and close my eyes, enjoying the flavor explosion that is the pelmeni.

When I open my eyes, he's eyeing me with confusion. "Holy hymen? Didn't you say you've had 'coitus'?"

Flushing, I swallow the pelmeni. Why did I open my big mouth?

"Not that it's any of your business, but no, I'm not a virgin," I say in a low voice. "Holy Hymen is what the kids called me back in the day. On account of me being Holly and having the last name of Hyman."

"Ah. So you do understand." His face hardens, his cerulean eyes tightening dangerously. "Give me the names of the assholes who insulted you."

I have to blink at him again. Is he serious? "Um, I don't remember them now. In any case, I'm sorry—I didn't mean to press on your sore spot. You're Crusty going forward. Or however you say 'crusty' in Russian."

The dangerous look in his eyes fades, replaced by a bemused expression. "How did you arrive at 'crusty?'"

"You called me breadcrumb, so I decided you should be bread-crust—or Crusty."

A wicked grin curves his lips. "You know, in Russian, crusty is synonymous with hard."

Hard? My breath hitches as heat streaks down my spine. "Why did you call me breadcrumb?"

"*Kroshka* also means *little one*," he says. "I'm sorry if it sounds like I was infantilizing you. That wasn't the idea."

"I... see." I look him up and down. "How do you say 'huge one' in Russian?"

His grin widens. "How about you just call me Alex?"

"Alex." I taste the word.

"Or Sasha. That's another diminutive of Alexander, which is my full name."

"No." I trace a finger along his strong chin. It's a little scruffy already. "I like Alex."

His gaze darkens as he catches my hand in his strong grip. "Is that so?"

I dampen my lips. "I like Alex a lot."

He looks hungry—and not for the pelmeni.

Before I can think better of it, I wrap my other hand around the back of his head and pull it toward me.

His whole body stiffens, and his head doesn't budge.

Insulted, I release him and draw back—and then I see why he's so still.

Dragomir and Bella are coming back from the dance floor, along with Tigger, Natasha, Vlad, and Fanny.

I guess the Devil—I mean, Alex—isn't into PDA.

"No dessert?" Natasha asks no one in particular as she sinks into her chair.

Alex's cerulean eyes are trained on my face, the expression in them hotly intent. "Not yet."

Natasha waves over a waiter and gives an order.

A cornucopia of desserts is soon brought out, along with tea—the same wonderful kind I tried in the limo.

As I put the last lump of sugar in my cup, they bring a plate of pelmeni and set it between all the cakes, candy, and fruit.

"Is that for me?" I ask Natasha.

She nods. "I had the chef make it. This type is called *vareniki*. Try it."

I get one and taste it.

Yum. It's not filled with meat, like regular pelmeni. Instead, the stuffing is sweet cherry, and I can totally see it as dessert.

"Does anyone know any new Vovochka jokes?" Fanny asks shyly.

"That's a boy who's the butt of many Russian jokes," Alex whispers in my ear, making my neck tingle. "As a bonus, it also happens to be the diminutive form of my brother's name."

"I know one," Natasha says. "Vovochka comes home with an F in math. 'Why?' his father demands. 'She asked me what's 2 times 3, so I said 6.' 'That's right,' the father says. 'Then she asked me what's 3 times 2?' 'What the fuck is the difference?' the father asks. Vovochka sighs. 'That's exactly what I said.'"

Chuckles all around.

"I have one too," Bella says and darts a glance at her sleeping father. "The mother is trying on a fur coat. Vovochka says, 'Mom, don't you understand, that coat is the result of the suffering of a poor, unfortunate animal.' She looks at her son sternly. 'How dare you speak of your father like that?'"

More chuckles.

Vlad goes next. "'Why is the flounder flat?' the zoology teacher asks. 'She had relations with the whale,' Vovochka says. 'Out,' the teacher says. 'Now let's continue. Who knows why the crawfish has such big eyes?' From the door, Vovochka says, 'Because he saw the whole thing.'"

When the jokes run out, everyone enjoys dessert for a while. I wonder if alcohol gives you munchies, the way cannabis does. I'm enjoying my vareniki a little too much. Like 137 sit-ups too much.

As I reach for more tea, I feel someone loom over me and look up.

It's Tigger.

With a courtly bow, he hiccups and says, "May I have this dance, milady?"

Alex's teacup smashes into the table with a bang. "No, you can't." The words come out in a growl.

"Hey," I say indignantly. "Why are you speaking for me? What if I want to dance with him?"

I don't, but still. Who does he think he is?

"Dude, relax," Tigger says to Alex. "It's just a dance."

Alex launches to his feet and steps between Tigger and me. "She's here with me."

I leap to my feet as well. "I'm still here. Why are you talking as though I'm not?"

"I know she's with you," Tigger says. "I just—"

Dragomir barks something angrily at his brother, but I don't catch the words.

Still ignored, I debate stomping my foot in frustration but decide against it.

Tigger raises his hands. "Chill, people." He looks at Alex. "Sorry, man. Didn't mean any disrespect. Plenty of dance partners at other tables." He hiccups and winks at me. "Alas, milady, a dance is not in the cards. If you had an equally attractive sister, maybe I'd dance with her."

I push Alex out of my way. "As a matter of fact, I do. How about I give you her number, so you can—"

"Hey." Bella gently pulls on my elbow. "Mind going to the bathroom with me?"

I let her lead me away, and when we're out of everyone's earshot, I say, "I was just going to give Tigger my twin's number, so that—"

"I suggest you sober up first," Bella says. "Then, if you still think that's a good idea, you can ask your twin if she wants to be set up."

That's a good point. The men aren't the only ones who've let vodka mess up their thinking. It might be impacting me a little bit too. Gia would be pissed if I pimped her out without her permission, the way Natasha seems to do with her kids.

I shudder. When Gia gets pissed, her pranks get mean—like the time she rubbed half the objects in our middle school with hot pepper powder.

"Now," Bella says with a grin. "Tell me about the suit."

Ah. Of course. It's been seconds since I've been made to feel off-kilter. Speaking of, is my walking off-kilter? I seem to be bumping into people a lot.

Bella is still looking at me expectantly, so I say, "Not much new to tell. The batteries died before I could experience the last phase. I read some QA manuals, so I can document it better if—"

"I was hoping you'd say that." She pulls out a stack of papers from her purse. "Fill this out when you're ready."

I glance at the first page.

There are questions like, "Was orgasm achieved?" and "How many times?" But nothing about, "Do you have the lady equivalent of blue balls?"—which is where I am.

What would you call that condition? Blue ovaries? Blue clit?

"Fanny's helped me with that document," Bella says as she opens the door to the loo. "And I'd really appreciate your help as well."

I read more of the questions as I use the facilities and then wait for Bella by the door.

"Can you give us a moment?" Bella says to the bathroom attendant.

With a huff, the bathroom mistress leaves.

"So," Bella says with a mischievous grin. "I have a gift for you." She digs into her purse and pulls out a giant dildo.

I nearly drop the testing document.

Does vodka cause hallucinations?

Nope. My new boss is really standing there with a dildo.

A gift. For me.

As if to add to the surrealness, Bella clicks a button on the side of the silicon shlong, and it hums to life and begins to vibrate with all the enthusiasm of a jackhammer.

"Enjoy." Turning the vibration off, Bella thrusts the dildo into my hands.

I gape at it. Besides being enormous, it's blue with chrome swirls and a red mushroom top—which combine to remind me of Optimus Prime from *Transfomers*.

Bella frowns. "You don't like it?"

"I'm just a little stunned," I say, my tongue feeling strangely heavy in my mouth.

"I made it myself," Bella says. "Not sure if Alex mentioned it, but I own a sex toy company called Belka."

Huh. That would've been a fun conversation between Alex and me:

*"Did you know my sister makes fake cocks?"*

*"Why, no, I didn't. Tell me more. Spare no detail."*

Hey, at least this explains Bella's interest in the VR suit—it's the logical next step for a sex toy company owner.

"Thank you." I stash Optimus deep in my purse. "It's very thoughtful."

It must've been the right thing to say because Bella beams with pride as she prances back to the table, which has been cleared of everything but tea and coffee.

Spotting me, Alex leaps to his feet and pulls out my chair.

I know I'm supposed to be upset with him, but it's difficult when he's being so gentlemanly.

Vlad stands up. "We're going to head out."

Smiling at me, Fanny follows his example. "It was great to meet you."

I fight the urge to ask her if she also got a dildo from Bella, or if I'm special. "Nice to meet you both."

Bella glances at her still-snoring father. "I think Dragomir and I should head out as well."

Dragomir nods and rises to his feet. "Great to see you again, Holly. Sorry about my brother." He glares at the dance floor, where Tigger is sandwiched between Natasha and some random middle-aged woman from another table.

"It's okay. All he did is ask me to dance." I look at Alex pointedly. "I took it as a compliment."

Is that a growl from Alex?

"I'll see you at work." Bella kisses me on the cheek. "Bye."

"*Do svidaniya,*" I say without a second of hesitation.

"See?" Alex says with a devilish smirk. "You're already saying goodbye in Russian. How long before you acquire our accent?"

I can't help but grin.

His expression turns serious. "Are you ready to leave, or do you want to finish your tea?"

My heartbeat speeds up. I hadn't given much thought to how this night might end, but now all sorts of X-rated scenarios are performing the Kama Sutra in my brain.

"I'm ready," I say breathlessly.

"Great." He extends his hand to me. "Let's go."

Pulse quickening further, I clasp his palm.

It's big, warm, and callused, and I never want to give it back.

"Bye, Dad," Alex says to the sleeping Boris. "Bye, Mom!" he yells toward the dance floor.

Natasha waves, and we head out, hand in hand.

The walk to the limo happens as if in a dream.

He holds the door for me again, and I slide inside. He joins me and, unlike before, sits next to me.

Blimey.

Is this about to turn into a real—and really hot—date?

# TWENTY-TWO

NOW THAT HE'S inches away, I drink him in with my eyes.

The man is the visual equivalent of crystal meth for the ovaries.

"Have I told you how amazing you look tonight?" he murmurs, his eyes greedily scanning me back.

Heat rushes over my skin as I slide closer, emboldened both by the alcohol and by the obvious hunger in that cerulean gaze. "The subject might've come up."

His voice turns husky. "You also smell delicious."

"Not as delicious as you." I lean in and shamelessly breathe in the yummy tea aroma that's been driving me insane all night.

He cups my chin and stares into my eyes.

Losing the fight with my self-control, I reach out to tame his unruly hair—which turns out to be deliciously smooth and silky, cool at the tips and warm closer to his scalp.

His breath hitches at my touch, his eyes darkening, and he retaliates by tucking an errant tuft of my hair behind my left ear.

The heat inside me intensifies, and the limo begins spinning.

Like two magnets, we're pulled to each other by a force greater than ourselves.

Our lips fuse.

Time seems to stop.

The kiss is good. Scary good. I'm drunk on all the sensations it wrenches out of me. He tastes like that delicious tea, his lips soft and warm, gentle yet merciless in demanding a response—a response that makes me feel completely out of control.

The limo is spinning like a NASA training module now, and an inferno is raging in my core. A touch of a feather applied at the right place would probably make me come.

This has to be some kind of vodka side effect. No mere kiss can feel like this.

Panting, I slide my hands down his back.

His muscular, broad, impossibly strong back.

He pulls away.

What the hell?

My ovaries are so far on the blue spectrum they just might turn violet and then green.

The limo stops.

Ah. We've arrived.

I glance out the window.

Indeed. My place.

Heart pounding, I turn back to face him. "Come up with me."

He tucks another strand of hair behind my ear, his touch sending another bolt of heat down to my core. "I can't." His voice is hoarse, his tone deeply regretful.

"You can't?" I look uncomprehendingly at the bulge in his pants.

He sighs. "I want you to issue this invitation when you don't have pure vodka in your veins."

"I'm not drunk." Bugger. The words have come out slurred.

His gaze turns sympathetic. "How about I help you get inside?"

Aha. Loophole. All isn't lost.

He exits the car without any sign of inebriation.

I climb out after him, my treacherous body feeling weirdly heavy and clumsy.

He steadies me by the elbow as I step out.

Hmm. My knees feel wobbly. Must be all the bloody hormones stirred up by the bloody kiss.

He gently tugs on my elbow. "Let's go."

I enjoy the feel of his strong hand supporting me as he leads me to my door. Unlocking it, I smile as seductively as I can. "Let me make you some tea?"

There. Who can refuse the lure of a good cup of tea?

The look on his face is that of a parched man who's crossed the desert. "I'm not thirsty."

I grind my teeth. "Fine. Don't need you anyway."

He quirks an eyebrow.

"I have the suit, remember? There's always virtual Alex."

His lips flatten. "Virtual Alex?"

"Yeah, that's right. That bloke is a lot more accommodating than the real thing."

His eyes narrow. "You should just go to bed."

I lift my chin. "What? Jealous of a little competition?"

"That suit is my company's property," he says flatly. "I'd like it back. Now. Right away."

With a growl, I stumble inside and almost trip over my pentagram-shaped coffee table before he catches me.

So *now* he comes in? Wanker.

I pull out of his grasp and dash to the bedroom. Hands shaking from anger, I pack the suit into the penis-decorated backpack and throw it at him.

He adroitly catches the projectile and gives me an annoying smirk. "Thank you." He puts the backpack on his back. "Rest now."

Grr. Why is that commanding tone turning me on?

Time to get serious. I plop onto the bed in a hopefully seductive pose. Of course, I may also look like a drunk lump. "Last chance to join me," I slur—again, hopefully seductively.

His nostrils flare. "I need to borrow your door key."

"My key?" Sexy pose forgotten, I jerk upright. "Why?"

"So I can lock the door on my way out," he says, enunciating each word as though I've suddenly lost forty-seven IQ points.

"I can lock my own door, thank you very much."

He shakes his head. "You might trip on that witchy table again."

"Not witchy. I just like five-pointed furniture."

"I'll leave the key in your mailbox," he says. "Does it lock?"

I nod jerkily.

He extends his hand. "Be a good girl now."

Ugh. I scramble off the bed, dig through my purse, and slap the key onto his palm.

"Good. Now sleep tight." With one last heated once-over, he turns on his heel and leaves without shutting the bedroom door.

Fine. I don't need him and his real sodding cock. Or the suit.

I have his sister's dildo.

Actually, I should think of it as my dildo now. Or as Optimus Prime.

I almost yell the bit about the dildo after him but contain myself at the last moment.

What if he goes all caveman jelly and steals the dildo?

Can't have that. Blue ovaries must be appeased.

I'm going to lie here and wait until I hear him lock the front door before pouncing on the dildo.

I wait.

Is he gone?

Better wait a few extra minutes. I can't have him catch me with my pants down again.

I yawn.

Maybe it won't hurt to close my eyes for just a second?

The moment my upper and lower lashes meet, sleep hits me like a bomb and I pass out.

# TWENTY-THREE


IS THAT BIG BLOODY BEN?

The sound has to be at least 127 decibels—loud enough to cause permanent damage to my ears.

Oh. It's my alarm clock.

I slap the snooze button before my eardrums explode.

What the hell? I'm nauseated, and my headache is sporting a migraine.

Bugger. I know what this is.

Hangover.

But that implies inebriation.

Oh, no. It's all coming back to me—especially the part where I came on to Alex at the end of the night.

What was I thinking? Talk about making a mess.

With great effort, I sit up, realizing dimly that I'm fully dressed.

The room spins around me. A fly passes by, sounding like a buzzsaw.

How drunk was I that I feel this awful? Are those things directly proportional?

By the time I get to my feet, the headache worsens.

Hey, at least I seem to be walking straight.

I go through the motions of my morning routine until I find myself in the kitchen.

Hmm. There's a Gatorade in my fridge.

I didn't buy that.

Did Alex get it for me?

Unsure if I should be upset that he let himself in or pleased that he was concerned about my electrolytes, I chug the drink until my stomach is about to burst.

There. Now if I take a barrel of Tylenol, I might be able to go to work.

———

I TAKE a cab because public transportation would probably make my brain explode today.

A few blocks from home, my phone begins to vibrate.

"Hello?"

"Hey, sis," Gia shrieks. "How was the date?"

"Ugh." I move the phone a few inches away from my ringing ear. "Lower your voice."

"What are you talking about?" she shouts even louder. "I'm practically whispering."

I tell her about what happened, and with each word that leaves my mouth, greater mortification and horror set in.

I kissed Alex... then threw myself at him, like a hussy.

I pretty much sexually harassed my boss.

"So," Gia says when I'm done with the whole awful story. "What are you going to do now?"

"No clue. Somehow salvage my career?"

"I meant about him. Are the two of you dating now?"

"Not bloody likely. We still work together."

And that's just the tip of the messy iceberg. In any case, who says he'd want to date me? After all, he refused my advances after that kiss. If it had been as hot for him as it was for me, he wouldn't have.

"Fine. I won't push this," Gia says with a dramatic sigh.

Has hell relocated to Antarctica?

"Great, thanks."

"I just hope you're not too hungover for the lunch you owe me."

I bring the phone back to my ear, certain I misheard her. "What lunch?"

"With our parental units," she says, and I can almost hear the eye roll. "Crystal and Harry Hyman. Chicken sexer and penetration tester. Remember them? The reasons we're so messed up?"

If we *are* messed up, it would be thanks to our siblings as much as our parents, but I don't say that, opting for a horrified, "Is that today?"

"You know it is," Gia says. "And no, you don't get out of it by playing the hangover card."

"Fine," I grumble. "I wish the headache was a pain in my ass instead—it would help me pretend to be you."

"That makes no sense. Unless you're talking about anal. No, not even in that case."

"Good. Making no sense should also help me pass for you."

"If you want them to believe you're me, don't attempt to make jokes, especially like that," she says. "And avoid the Britishisms. Also, a friend of mine is going to bring you a bag with supplies."

"Supplies?" I feel an absurd pang of jealousy at the mention of a friend. Despite our identical genes and upbringings, and even with all her studious germ avoidance, Gia has a much better social life than I do... in that, she has one.

She snorts, happily oblivious to my thoughts. "Were you going to show up in the same outfit you wear to work?"

I glance down. Yep. I have my usual on—as it should be. "I didn't even think about that. I guess I'm more like you today than I realized."

"Har har. The bag will have some clothes, a wig, and makeup."

I feel my headache intensifying. "Great. I'm looking forward to looking like Morticia Addams... if she'd joined a motorcycle club."

"I'd watch that," Gia says. "Also, show them magic. Do that thirty-seven thing I showed you the other day."

"Sounds good." I know she wants me to ask how she can be sure our parents will think of thirty-seven when I do the trick, so I resist the temptation. "What about Tigger?"

"That's Bella's boyfriend's brother?" she asks.

"Right. Do you want to be set up with him?"

"Of course not," she says. "He sounds like a manwhore, and that's the last thing I need."

The urge to argue is strong, but I decide to be a nice sister and resist it. After all, she's mainly skipping lunch with our parents so she won't be pressured into dating.

"Fair enough," I say. "Let me know if you change your mind."

"I won't," she says firmly. "Anyway, I'd better go."

"Do svidaniya."

"Well, that's new," she says, and with a bye, she hangs up.

# TWENTY-FOUR

I STEP out of the elevator on my office floor and cringe at the racket my coworkers are creating. Holding my ears, I sprint for my desk before anyone asks me something stupid, like, "How are you?"

As I run, I notice something weird. There are extra chairs next to the desks of the developers.

What's that about?

Launching my email, I grimace at the sight of my inbox. You skip one day, and the stupid thing overflows.

I start by checking if I have anything from Alex. If I'm fired, I will at least be spared the rest of the inbox, not to mention the abominable cacophony of my coworkers.

The first email is about the games for the hospital. Alex suggests we meet with Dr. Piper and his people, so he can make sure everyone is on the same page. I'd be happy about this if it weren't for the fact that this email arrived yesterday—hours before my improper behavior.

As if to add to my job-related anxiety, the next item from Alex is a lot more sinister.

A meeting request.

Location: his office.

Agenda: blank.

Time: an hour from now.

Bugger.

Should I even bother with the rest of the inbox?

I think I will. I need something to do if I don't want to go crazy for the next hour.

First things first, though. If I keep my job, I want the meeting with Dr. Piper to happen ASAP, so I email him about it—the window before he associates my work with porn is closing fast. Then I check if I have anything from Bella; after all, she's also my boss, and according to Alex, this is more her company than his.

There's just one email from her, also from yesterday. Apparently, Bella and Alex have decided to implement something called pair programming—a technique that's proven highly effective at 1000 Devils. She says if I have good arguments against it, I should talk to her right away, and that if some developers prefer to work alone, exceptions can be made.

This must be what the extra chairs are for.

Though I have some idea of what pair programming is, I read up on it some more.

Also known as pairing, it is as the name suggests: two programmers sit side by side and work together. The driver types the code, while the other person, the navigator, reviews the code as they go. Naturally, the roles are frequently switched.

Why have I never tried this? According to research, code quality goes up when you do this, and it leads to everyone on the team sharing knowledge better.

Jolly good. If I'm not fired, I'll be curious to see how this pairing thing works out.

Someone clears his throat. Twice. "Hi, Holly."

Rubbing my throbbing temples, I look up.

I should've guessed by the throat clearing.

It's Buckley.

"Hi," I say. "What's up?"

He clears his throat twice more. "I just wanted to say goodbye."

"Oh?"

A single clearing of the throat. Thank God. "I got the move I wanted already. The new management are fast."

"Ah." I do my best not to look *too* pleased. "Congratulations."

He clears his throat twice more. "Today is my last day."

He's at seven throat clearings now. How do I get him to leave things at that?

"Great," I say. "I wish you the best."

I wave goodbye.

Nope. He clears his throat twice, as though he's intentionally trying to drive me mad. "We should stay in touch."

"Sure," I say. "Will do."

Not bloody likely.

Giving me an unprofessionally lingering look that I definitely won't miss, he clears his throat yet again and leaves.

I pretend that it doesn't bother me that his throat clearing total is ten.

Not bothered at all.

Nope.

I'm as Zen as eleven Hindu cows. As cool as seven cucumbers.

Okay, fine. I need something more absorbing and stimulating than checking email, and I know just the thing—the code Robert emailed me the other day. If I keep my job, I'll be working on suit integration, so I might as well have a look.

I didn't think my headache could worsen, but here we are. The code itself is good, elegant even, but it's not tidy.

I frantically make sure all the lines are indented by four spaces, and then I fix spelling errors in the comments until I get a reminder about the upcoming meeting with Alex.

Bugger. Almost forgot. Forget fun, time *really* flies when you're cleaning up.

Before I get up from my desk, I type out the command to submit the cleaned-up code into the shared repository; otherwise, if my computer dies, my work will get lost. I do this carefully because I once gave the whole team a heart attack when I messed up this step and made it look like a year of hard work had disappeared. Fortunately, I had all the code they thought we'd lost stored locally on my computer, so I redid the code submission and everyone stopped freaking out.

Is it my imminent meeting with Alex, or is the term "code submission" vaguely BDSMy? Also, is BDSMy a word?

Grr. Why am I pondering linguistics? Alex and my fate await.

As I rise to my feet, the pain in my head sharpens to a throbbing.

Well, there's no helping it.

I speed-walk to the office I broke into and knock.

"Come in," Alex says, his sexy accent in full force.

I take a deep breath and step inside.

# TWENTY-FIVE

AT A GLANCE, I see that he indeed got himself a new monitor, a keyboard, and even an extra chair. What really commands my attention, though, is the man himself.

Though I doubt he shaved this morning, he's not as scruffy as usual thanks to the grooming from the prior day, and even his hair is less of a mess—all enhancing the scrumptiousness I should ignore.

Would getting fired by someone this hot hurt a little extra?

Hard to say.

Speaking of hard, he totally was last night. Throbbing hard, like my headache.

Ugh. Shoot me now.

"Hello," I say when I realize I've been standing there mutely for far too long.

His expression is unreadable, which makes him look like his brother, Vlad. My palms grow sweaty, my stomach tightening into a knot.

"*Privet*," he says.

An informal hello? Maybe that's a good sign?

"I—I think I know why I'm here," I stammer.

He lifts his right eyebrow the smallest fraction of a millimeter. "You do?"

I bob my head. "I'm sorry about last night."

A crease shows up on his forehead. "You are?"

"I behaved unprofessionally." I cast a yearning glance at his guest chair. I'm not sure if it's the hangover or this encounter so far, but my legs feel like jellified rubber.

"Sit." He makes it sounds like an order.

I gladly obey. "As I started saying, I'm sorry about my unbecoming behavior. It won't happen again."

His expression grows even harder to decipher. "It won't?"

"I promise. Please let me keep my job. I—"

"You think I asked you here to fire you?"

Now his face is easy to read. The angry expression states that if he didn't think I should be fired before, he's considering it now.

I swallow hard. "You didn't fill in the agenda on the meeting request."

His cerulean gaze darkens. "So you assumed you're getting fired? Is your opinion of me that low, or are you trying to be as pessimistic as a stereotypical Russian?"

Whew. I guess he's not firing me. My sigh of relief is audible. "What did you want to talk about then?"

"Suit integration." He turns his screen my way, and I see the code I just tidied.

"Oh."

A hint of that wicked smirk appears on his face. "Specifically, I wanted to talk about how we're going to work on the code."

"We?"

He's not about to say what I think he is, is he? That would be unthinkable. Like letting a bear into a honey storage facility. Like—

The smirk is clearly there now. "I want the two of us to pair."

# TWENTY-SIX

HE MEANS pairing as in the programming technique, but images of us copulating invade my brain and refuse to leave. Or more accurately, they never really left, but now they're at the forefront.

He turns the screen back toward himself. "Pull your chair closer."

Wait. Now?

We're pairing now?

He looks at me expectantly.

I guess that's that. We're pairing.

Binary gods help me.

I drag my chair over until I'm close enough to detect his yummy scent.

"You just submitted some code," he says, turning his focus to the screen. "Let me sync so we're looking at the latest."

Is it normal to notice how sexy his fingers are as they type out those commands? I picture them dancing around my body instead of on the lucky keyboard keys, and my breathing quickens. The way he just pressed that C key—

"You've made some files look nicer," he mutters, his attention still fixed on the screen. "It's easier to understand what's going on. Thank you."

Damn it. Why does that praise flash me back to last night's kiss?

"No problem," I manage.

"Do you want to drive or navigate?"

"I want to drive," I say quickly. Thankfully, I don't add "you crazy in bed."

Bugger, my thoughts are an inch away from becoming an article in *Cosmo*.

He scoots his chair away, and I slide in behind the keyboard.

"How about we work on that issue you mentioned to my sister?" he says.

"Sure. Can you help me navigate to the relevant file?"

He tells me where to go, and we review things together. Unfortunately, his proximity and the hangover make it extremely difficult to concentrate.

If this pairing is to go on, I'll need to aggressively hydrate... and masturbate.

Once we open the file, I scan for any low-hanging fruit when it comes to smoothing out the issues I saw. I find something and he agrees the change would help, so we work on it as I battle the urge to kiss him again.

Who knew coding could be so sexually frustrating?

"We'll need to test this," he says when I declare that I'm done with the change.

I nearly fall off my chair.

Test. As in use that suit?

I spotted the initial problem while canoodling with the replica of him in VR, so that's how I imagine the testing he's talking about. Except this time, I'd have to strip in front of him and—

My phone rings.

Ignoring it, I close the file.

The stupid thing rings again.

"You should take that," he says. "I have another meeting soon anyway. We'll pick this up in the afternoon."

So the X-rated testing is going to happen in the afternoon.

Jolly good. I'm so calm now.

The phone rings again. Stammering something incomprehensible, I finally accept the damn call.

It's security from downstairs. Someone's left a package, and I need to pick it up.

"See you later," Alex says when I explain that I have to go.

"Do svidaniya," I say on my way out.

"Do *skorovo* svidaniya," he says with a grin.

In the elevator, I pull out my phone and learn that *skorovo* means *imminent*.

Yep.

More pairing and testing is imminent—assuming I survive this lunch with my parents.

# TWENTY-SEVEN

PACKAGE IN TOW, I return to my floor.

I have to kill some time before lunch, so I decide to fill out as much of Bella's questionnaire as I can.

Damn.

Some of those questions are X-rated, to say the least. I hope no one stops by my desk—or questions why I'm blushing so profusely.

Questionnaire complete, I decide it's time to prep for lunch, so I sneak into the loo to try on whatever is in Gia's package.

No, not loo. Bathroom.

Must watch my Britishisms at that lunch.

In the box is my vampire makeover: a black wig, a bottle of foundation a shade too pale, a pair of biker boots, a dark lipstick, and an outfit consisting of black jeans, a black long-sleeved top, and a leather vest with metal studs on it. There are also fancy black gloves that will serve double duty, making it seem like I'm worried about germs while also covering the lack of black nail polish on my hands.

By the time I'm done putting it all on, I look enough like my twin that my own mother would not be able to tell us apart—which is the goal.

Hiding my own stuff in the now-empty box, I prepare to head out, only Bella walks in and does a double take.

"Wow. I've heard of Casual Fridays, but never of Goth Thursdays."

I grimace. "It's a long story."

She grins. "Let me guess. Your hangover is as bad as mine, so you've decided to look the way you feel."

"That's not a bad guess," I say, smiling back.

Her grin turns wicked. "So did you and Alex pair?"

Blushing through the foundation, I nod. Then, since I'm flustered anyway, I pull out her naughty form and thrust it into her hands. "That's as much as I'll ever be able to fill out. Alex took away the suit."

She chuckles. "Not surprised. Even as a kid, Alex never liked sharing his toys."

Am I the toy here, or is it the suit? Or maybe she's talking about virtual Alex?

"I've got a thing." I glance at the door.

"Me too." She heads for one of the stalls. "Bye."

I sneak a look at my phone and sprint back to my desk, ignoring my coworkers' startled glances. Dropping the box with my normal stuff by my chair, I hurry to the elevator.

Wait a sec.

Did I just see Alex in the corner of my vision? Hopefully not—I don't want to explain my look to him most of all.

To my relief, the elevator arrives quickly, and from there, the trip to Miso Hungry is uneventful.

My parents are waiting at a corner table when I step inside.

They don't see me yet, which is good.

I walk over to the hostess.

She doesn't seem to recognize me.

Sweet.

"Hi," I say. "I know I look different today, but I'm the customer who asks for forty-seven cubes of tofu in her miso soup."

"Ah," she says a bit too loudly. "That is a nice look for you."

"Thanks. I'll be sitting there." I point at my folks. "When I order miso soup and rolls later, can you make them the way I usually get them?"

She nods.

Great. Maybe I'll pull this off.

I approach the table. "Hi, Mom. Hi, Dad."

When he was young, Dad looked like Bob Dylan—or so Mom says. Nowadays, he looks more like a hobo, with a wild beard and a creepy silver ponytail that sticks out of a beanie that hides his bald spot. A well-fed hobo—his belly looks like Mom's right before the sextuplets aliened their way out of her. In contrast to Dad, and despite growing eight human beings inside her, Mom's stomach is flat, her hair is shiny, and her skin is smooth. She looks like she could be my older sister, which makes me optimistic about aging gracefully.

Note to self: must not give Dad grief about his eating habits, as that is something Gia wouldn't do.

Or would she?

Mom leaps to her feet and folds her hands together, yoga style. "Namaste, sunshine."

Sunshine? Is that sarcasm? I look like a creature of the night that sunshine kills.

"Thing 2." Dad's smile is goofy as he pats my shoulder.

Score. He called me Thing 2. The deception is working thus far. I'm actually Thing 1 on account of being the oldest, though that simply means I beat Gia by a few seconds in our race out of Mom's vagina. The sextuplets are Things 3 through 8, so I'm very lucky. I'm not Thing 4, or Thing 6, or—shudder—a very nonprime Thing 8.

"I'm sensing tension," Dad says. "Are you uncentered? Care for a shoulder rub?"

"We eat first," Mom says in the motherly tone she perfected while dealing with eight growing monsters—I mean, girls.

With a slight pout and a sigh, Dad plops back into his chair. He's a huge people pleaser, so denying him the chance to give a shoulder rub is like taking s'mores away from a starving hippie with the worst case of the munchies in cannabis history.

Mom sits, so I take the remaining chair, which happens to face the door.

"How are things going?" I ask, eager to keep the conversation as far away from my person as possible. "Did you do anything interesting while in town?"

"Things couldn't be better." Mom opens her menu. "Last night, we saw a burlesque performance. Afterward, your father turned into a beast."

And so it begins. I bet if I were to take a drink each time Mom says something that makes me want to poke my ears out, my current hangover would seem like a tickle.

"How are things in Thing 2's land?" Dad asks. "Still following your dream?"

"Yeah," I say. "Magic is great."

If they buy this, the rest of the lunch will be a breeze. Though I always try to be supportive of Gia, I can't help but see her magic more as a hobby than something a grownup does to pay bills on time.

Dad nods approvingly. "I so much admire what you're doing."

I carefully lift an eyebrow—the heavy layer of foundation on my forehead feels like it might peel off at any second.

"Manifesting your dreams," he clarifies. "I still haven't quit my day job."

"Your day job lets us travel like this," Mom says reassuringly. "Plus, as a penetration—"

"Mom." I glance worriedly at the hostess. "Please don't make penetration-related jokes, I implore you."

Dad tugs on his beard. "It just sucks working for *the man*."

The waitress comes over, and we order. As soon as she departs, I offer to show my parents a magic trick, since Gia would've done so by now.

To my deep annoyance, they think of the number thirty-seven when prompted—Gia manages to do magic without being at the scene.

"That was great." Dad pours the three of us little platters of soy sauce. "Reminds me of that video I sent you the other day."

Interesting. He sends Gia videos of magic tricks? The last thing he sent me was a theoretical computer science treatise on NP-hardness (where N and P stand for Non-deterministic Polynomial-time and not, say, Naked Penis.)

"Yeah, great video," I say. "Thanks."

To prevent more magic talk, I stuff a piece of avocado roll into my mouth and pretend that it's bigger than it is.

Mom picks up a piece of sushi with her chopsticks. "I'm sorry to move the conversation away from magic, but there was something I wanted to talk to you about."

I tense but try to hide it. The last thing I want is a shoulder rub from Dad. "What's up?"

"We're worried about your sister," Mom says.

Rolling eyes is Gia's bread and butter, so I give in to the urge. "Which one?"

"Your twinsie," Mom says. "Obviously."

Bugger. They're worried about *me?* I mean, the real me? Also, what's with that "obviously?" If you pick a sextuplet at random, she's bound to be more of a concern than I am. Unless Mom means "obviously, Holly's troubles are a conversation to have with *Gia.*"

Yeah. I'm sticking with that.

I fake Gia's mischievous grin. "What has my Posh Spice clone done now?"

Did that sound like Gia?

Both parents frown.

Great. Now they're upset with me for mocking my own self.

"She seems off," Mom says.

"Not living," Dad says. "Merely existing."

I narrow my eyes at him. "What did you smoke today?"

He waves a dismissive hand. "Ever since Beau came out, she—"

I miss what he says next because I'm caught off-guard by my ex's name and the accompanying tightening in my chest.

I do my best not to show anything on my face. I have to act as Gia would. Actually, she'd scowl, so I do that. She hates Beau on my behalf. To cheer me up, she admitted that she'd broken into his house after our breakup and added laxatives to everything in his fridge.

"I think she's fine." I dip a piece of avocado roll into the soy sauce. "Apart from needing a better wardrobe, of course."

There. It's like I was born for this role.

"She hasn't dated anyone since Beau," Mom says. "You know how important orgasms are, and I don't think she's getting them."

I grit my teeth. Does she think Beau was giving me orgasms? "My own sex life isn't exactly flourishing. How can I help her?"

Crap. Both are looking at me funny. Not good.

"I mean, I obviously play with myself," I add, figuring Gia can talk like this in front of Dad without feeling suicidal. "I'm pretty sure Holly does too. Just a prime number of times per day."

Boom. Where is my Oscar?

Mom sits up straighter. "You really think so?"

You'd think I'd told her that her daughter discovered a cure for cancer instead of a dildo.

"Totes," I say. "I'm more worried she'll get carpal tunnel from all that masturbation."

"That's a relief," Mom says. "Of course, the real goal is getting a human being to deliver those orgasms."

I'm Gia. Gia should be embarrassed, not me.

"Because love is lovely," Dad adds.

"Right. Holly and I will get right on that," I say with Gia's signature sarcasm. "Real human. Got it."

"Let me know if I can help in any way," Mom says with an earnest expression that makes me doubt my sarcasm skills. "I have decades of experience with the most toe-curling, mind-boggling, tantric sex in the universe. If you need any advice, I'm always here for you."

"*We* are," Dad corrects her.

Why didn't I order Fugu—the Japanese dish made out of the deadly puffer fish? The sweet release from tetrodotoxin might be preferable to this conversation.

"Thanks, guys," I force myself to say.

Dad scratches his beard. "If you put out loving energy into the world, the karmic balance will always be in your favor."

Did the waitress sneak him a fortune cookie?

If I weren't pretending to be Gia, I'd remind them that this isn't just about orgasms for them. I suspect they want a son-in-law, and a grandson if they're really lucky. Their desire for a male child is widely known. It's why they underwent that fertility treatment all those years ago—the one that yielded them six more daughters instead.

That's what made Dad believe in karma. He's convinced he must've been a serial killer in a prior life.

"So, we have some news," Mom says.

*Please don't say you're starting a sex commune. Or a nudist colony. Or opening your marriage.*

"We're staying in town for an extra few weeks," she says.

Whew. "That's great, Mom. You should see *Mary Poppins* on Broadway."

Mom and Dad exchange glances.

Bugger. Gia would've recommended a magic show. Or a mentalism show—like there's a difference.

Well, the nanny is out of the bag now. If I backpedal, it will look even more suspicious, so I just stick a piece of food into my mouth and chew.

The restaurant door jingles.

I glance at the newcomer, and my heart leaps into my throat.

It's none other than Alex Chortsky, my maybe-fake date and definitely-not-fake boss.

# TWENTY-EIGHT



I SWIFTLY LOOK AWAY.

Maybe he didn't see me? Or saw me but didn't recognize me in my Gia guise?

The chance is there but low if he saw me like this in the office.

My phone dings.

I check it instinctively.

It's a text from Lucifer Satan: *Is that you?*

I'm an idiot. I just looked at my phone, confirming his suspicions.

I throw a panicked glance toward him.

Yep. He's coming this way.

There are so many problems with this, but Gia's deception is the biggest—and that, unlike my dignity, is something I can still protect.

Grinning like a loon, I wave at him. "Alex! It's me, Gia. Over here."

With a frown, he picks up his pace.

Parents turn. Dad scratches his beard while Mom begins to drool.

"Gia?" Alex says, clearly confused.

"I know." The loonie grin is approaching Joker levels. "I'm

usually much paler, but you know how it is. I was in the sun for a whole five minutes today."

Everyone chuckles nervously.

"Mom, Dad," I say. "This is Alex."

They look at me expectantly.

Right. At this point, one usually explains the relationship between one's self and the person they're introducing.

What do I say?

Then it hits me. I can do Gia a huge favor—and get back at Alex for parading me in front of his parents the other day.

"Alex is my boyfriend," I say nonchalantly. "I asked him to join us. Surprise!"

Alex blinks but seems to go along with it. At least he doesn't refute my claim as he drags a chair from another table to ours.

My parents gape at him with shell-shocked expressions.

Wow. Do they consider Gia completely undatable?

"Alex, this is Crystal and Harry Hyman, my parents."

Alex shakes Dad's hand, then kisses Mom on the cheek in the Russian style.

She looks like she might lay an egg. Breathlessly, she stammers out, "How did the two of you meet?"

"Alex works with my twin," I say. "Obviously, *she* couldn't date him; his name doesn't have a prime number of letters."

In reality, I *can* live with the letter count in "Alex" because I really like the way it sounds. Also, I can appease myself with the knowledge that his parents call him Sasha, which *is* five letters long.

Alex sits down. "Yeah. Dating Holly would not be appropriate, would it?"

Mom doesn't seem to be listening. Judging by the looks she directs toward "my boyfriend," it will be her turn to be a beast tonight.

"You seem tense," Dad says to Alex.

Alex shrugs. "It's not every day I meet the parents of a woman

I'm dating. Plus, there's an important project I'm working on with Holly, so…"

"Say no more." Dad leaps to his feet. "This will recharge your energy for the week."

Before I can shout something like SOS, Dad's hairy fingers are digging into Alex's shoulders.

I'm Gia. Gia should be mortified, not me.

Dad's massage is so vigorous his ponytail comes within an inch of hitting Alex in the face. Also, Dad is making odd grunting sounds. What is that? Is he so out of shape that even squeezing his fingers is difficult for him? Or is he trying to create a vibration effect for Alex, like a fancy massage chair or a cat?

Mom looks on jealously, but probably not because Dad is getting handsy with someone who's not her. I think she wants to be touching Alex herself… and maybe not just his shoulders.

To his credit, Alex's face doesn't show what he must be really thinking. There's only a hint of a smile dancing in his cerulean eyes.

"Sir," the waitress says to Dad with exaggerated politeness. "Could you not do that in here?"

Is she being homophobic? Unclear, but she does get results. Dad slaps Alex on the back, then plops back into his chair, muttering something about the dumb bondage of societal norms.

"What would you like?" the waitress asks Alex in a tone that makes me think she shooed my dad away to get rid of competition.

"For Holly's father to never, ever touch me again" is what I expect Alex to say, but he simply asks for a sushi lunch special.

"Your accent," Mom says huskily. "Where are you from?"

With a delectable smile, Alex explains that he was born in Murmansk, a city in the northwestern part of Russia.

Mom and Dad pepper him with questions about his hometown, and I learn that it was the last city founded by the Russian Empire. And that it's cold even for Russia, with bitter winters and short, cool summers.

"When would you recommend someone to visit it?" Mom asks, her eyes still annoyingly moony.

"I wouldn't recommend visiting at all," Alex says. "But if you really want to, I'd say always visit Russia in the summer. And check out Moscow before you bother with Murmansk."

"Is your whole family here?" Mom asks.

He nods, then tells them about his parents and siblings. "My grandparents stayed behind," he says in conclusion. "That was before video conferencing, so I missed them a lot." He looks wistful. "They're gone now."

I feel the urge to kiss the sadness off his face. Bugger. What's wrong with me? He's not *really* my boyfriend. Seeing him vulnerable isn't supposed to give me the feels.

"I'm sure they feel your love wherever they are," Dad says to Alex reassuringly. "Love transcends time and space."

To his credit, Alex doesn't roll his eyes. Instead, he asks, "What about your parents?"

"Florida," Mom and Dad say at the same time.

Alex smiles. "That's pretty much the opposite of Russia."

Before anyone can say anything else, the waitress comes back with Alex's food, and he attacks it with gusto—Dad's massage must've stimulated his appetite.

"What do you think of Gia's magic?" Mom asks when Alex slows down his sushi devouring to match everyone's pace.

He gives me a questioning glance. "She's... amazing."

"He's being kind," I say. "In reality, whenever I perform for him, he begs me to tell him how I did it. Not knowing drives him crazy."

Mom and Dad exchange another look.

Bugger. Did that not sound like Gia?

"What's it like to work with Holly?" Mom asks, her blue eyes shifting between me and Alex.

"She's brilliant," Alex answers with a sexy grin. "My sister and I are lucky to have her working with us."

Aww. I'm sure he's just playing along, but it's still nice to hear.

Dad beams with pride. "I like to think she went into the computer science field because of what I do for a living."

Alex picks up a piece of tuna. "Which is?"

Ugh. Dad was clearly angling for Alex to ask that question.

"I'm a penetration tester," Dad says with the usual relish. "But it's not as dirty as—"

"Oh, I know what penetration testing is," Alex says, not batting an eye. "And this makes sense. Holly did show me some tools of your trade recently."

Thanks, Dad. Let's remind my boss about my attempted sabotage.

"Right," Dad says eagerly. "She borrowed some of my stuff. Glad it was useful."

"Is it strange to date one twin while working with the other?" Mom asks.

Hmm. I don't like this line of questioning one bit.

Alex shrugs. "They're so different it doesn't matter."

Mom looks at me unblinkingly. "And Holly's idiot synchronies don't bother you?"

"It's idiosyncrasies," I say sternly. "And Holly doesn't have any."

"She doesn't?" Mom's eyes narrow. "What about the prime mania?"

"You made that up," I say.

"Prime mania?" Alex asks, intrigued.

"My sister just likes prime numbers, that's all," I say. "Anyone mathematically inclined will have favorite numbers."

Alex nods. "I'm partial to the Fibonacci sequence. There are actually primes in that sequence, like 2, 3, 5, 13, 89, 233."

Can I ask him to marry me right here and now?

"Fine," Mom says. "If you claim her number obsession is normal, surely wearing and eating the same thing isn't."

Am I ready for matricide?

I take in a calming breath. "She just wants to organize her life so as to limit the number of mundane decisions each day. That way, she can focus on what's bloody important."

Mom's eyes narrow further.

Bugger. Have I just betrayed myself?

"I think Holly is smart to do what she does," Alex says, and I want to kiss him—more than usual, that is. "Didn't Albert Einstein always wear the same thing for the same reason?"

Moving like a cobra, Mom grips my wig and yanks it off with a triumphant expression.

Bloody hell.

"Hello, *Holly*," Mom says with a stern emphasis on my name. "Care to explain?"

# TWENTY-NINE

BUGGER.

Gia is going to kill me.

Dad looks betrayed. "Thing 1?"

I pick up my untouched water glass and gulp down half of it under everyone's penetrating gazes. "I'm sorry. I owed Gia a favor."

Mom shakes the wig over her sushi. "That doesn't explain this at all."

My skin burns with heat—and not the nice, Alex-related kind. "Gia thought you'd drill her about her nonexistent love life, but apparently, today is Worry About Holly Day. Which sounds like a holiday. The worst holiday ever. If I—"

Alex puts a reassuring hand on my elbow, unleashing a hive of horny bees in my stomach.

Dad tugs on his ponytail. "Sorry about that, kiddo. It comes from a loving place."

Mom looks at Alex's hand on my elbow. "So, which of our daughters are you dating?"

Before I can say none, he says, "Holly."

My hand is trembling as I pull out of his hold, grab my glass, and greedily gulp down the rest of the water, crunching on the ice as I go.

I know Alex is lying, but the bees in my stomach are lactating honey nevertheless.

Or is it pooping honey?

Peeing?

No, I vaguely recall David Attenborough saying something about regurgitation of nectar, so I guess it's more like puking.

I put the glass back down.

Isn't it weird that we all eat honey and never question its insect origins? Spider webs might taste like cotton candy, but I'd never know because that seems like a gross thing to eat. Yet bee vomit is great with tea.

Actually, spiders aren't insects. They're Araneae, though that doesn't make their—

I realize everyone is looking at me expectantly.

"Can you repeat the question?" I ask sheepishly.

Mom's frown finally softens. "I didn't ask anything. I was just saying you two make a very cute couple."

Blimey. The bees are getting buzzy again.

"Thank you," Alex says. "My parents said the same thing."

And now the bees are puking enough honey to survive a long, cold, Russian winter.

Mom's smile is mischievous—this is who Gia inherited hers from. "You've met his parents? Things must be serious indeed."

Golly. We have met each other's parents—and I always thought that if a guy ever met mine, that would be the end of the relationship.

Wait. What am I even saying? Alex and I don't have a relationship. He needs me for a work project, which must be the only reason he's not running away screaming. Still, he's being a good sport about this whole thing, I have to give him that.

"We should head back." I glance at Alex. "Coding awaits." And we'd better escape quickly because it's just a matter of time—seconds, probably—before Mom inquires about our sex life and begins dishing out shagging advice.

"Before you go…" Mom bats her eyelashes at Alex. "You wouldn't happen to have a brother, would you?"

Alex grins. "As a matter of fact, I do."

I suppress a groan. "You're married, Mom, remember?"

Mom chuckles while Dad looks zero jealous, making me wonder if they've opened up their marriage after all.

"It's not for me, dear," Mom says with mirth in her voice. "I wanted to circle back to Gia."

Ah. Pimping out my twin. What else is new?

Alex pulls out his wallet. "In that case, I'm sorry. My brother is already taken."

Yep. Given the way Vlad was looking at Fanny—her face, not her fanny, though I'm sure he looks at it too—he's all settled.

I rummage in my purse for my own wallet and realize I never took out Bella's dildo.

I mean, *my* dildo.

"Gia is too picky," I say as I carefully bring out the wallet without sending the dildo flying into Mom's face. "I offered to set her up with Alex's sister's boyfriend's brother, but she refused."

"Why?" Mom asks.

I toss forty-one dollars on the table. "Said he was a manwhore."

"Oh, please." Mom directs a worshipful look at Dad. "Your father was a player in his day, but I—"

"We really don't want to hear that," I say, tugging on Alex's sleeve.

I'd bet a thousand quid the rest of Mom's sentence was going to be "tamed him with my pussy."

"It was a pleasure to meet you, Crystal," Alex says and gives her another peck on the cheek. "And you, Harry." He shakes Dad's hand.

Though she's never worn pearls in her life, Mom clutches the place where they would be as she gasps, "The pleasure was all mine."

Dad clears his throat.

"I mean ours," Mom amends hastily.

Right. Like we could forget the pleasure Dad took in touching my pretend date.

"Bye," both parents say in unison.

"Do svidaniya," Alex and I say, also in unison, before rushing out of the restaurant.

———

"THANKS," I mumble weakly as we get into the elevator in our building.

"What for?" he asks, his lips curving in that devilish way of his.

"For pretending to be my boyfriend."

His smirk grows more wicked. "Pretending?"

The doors open, and he gestures for me to come out.

I do so on unsteady legs, so shell-shocked I can't think straight.

Of course he was bloody pretending. He can't be my boyfriend without my being aware of it.

Right?

# THIRTY

"READY FOR OUR TESTING?" he asks, following me out of the elevator.

With effort, I pull together my scattered wits. "I need to call my sister first. It's best she hears about the lunch disaster from me."

He nods. "Come to my office when you're ready."

In a daze, I watch him stride away. Then I step into the first empty conference room and dial Gia.

"Hey," she says. "How was your lunch as me? Did you feel much, much hotter?"

"I'm sorry," I say, and explain what happened.

Gia sighs. "I should've known." To my relief, she doesn't sound overly pissed. "You're a shitty liar."

"Sorry again."

"You know what this means, right?"

"What?" I can already tell I won't like it.

"You still owe me. And this time, I think I'll use you in one of my upcoming illusions—unless even just standing on a stage without talking is too much deception for you to handle?"

"I'll help you with your bloody illusion. I said I was sorry."

"Fine. I'm going to call our parents and grovel."

"Good luck," I tell her and hang up.

"What's with the outfit?" Alison asks when I exit the conference room.

Bugger. Forgot about my Gia guise.

"Long story," I answer and rush to my desk to grab the box with the change of clothing.

De-vampirefied, I head over to Alex's office, my heart pounding and my legs wobbly once again.

When I step inside, a suit my size is sprawled on the couch. Next to it is a bigger suit that must be for him.

What the hell? We're testing at the same time?

I picture him creating a replica of me in VR, and every inch of me catches fire.

Alex looks away from his screen. "Ready?"

I gulp.

I suppose there's no help for it.

My face feeling like fresh lava, I reach for the buttons of my shirt with trembling fingers.

He frowns. "What are you doing?"

I blink at him. "Last time I used the suit, the instructions said to do so nude."

His eyes darken and rake over my body, as if he's picturing me exactly that way. When his gaze returns to my face, spots of color burn on the edges of his high cheekbones. "We're not going to be testing the features that require that." His voice is tinged with hoarseness. "I'm keeping my clothes on, and I suggest you do the same."

Oh. Okay then. I don't know whether to be mortified or relieved. There may be some disappointment mixed in too.

He walks up to the bigger suit.

"Hold on," I blurt. "You're doing it at the same time?"

"Why not?" he asks, his eyes gleaming.

The man is a bloody enigma.

Not asking any more questions, I get inside the suit.

Like before, there's a single app in there, labeled Demo.

Bollocks. Even with clothes on, seeing naked Alex—assuming that's who I want to assemble—will be awkward with him here. Not to mention, I'm already jealous of whatever VR woman he'll create for himself.

No helping it.

I launch the Demo.

I find myself in a white room again, and at first, it seems like the demo has skipped right to the cock selection.

Except these shimmering, multicolor phallic objects aren't penises, or peni, or penes—I still haven't looked up the proper plural. They aren't dildoes either, though I guess anything can be a dildo if you're brave enough.

They're swords.

Laser swords that remind me of lightsabers from *Star Wars*, and metal swords of various kinds, everything from broadswords to katanas. The variety is not quite as exhaustive as with the cocks, but close.

Is this a demo of some weird fetish?

I choose a blue laser sword because it seems like the least sharp one. Even though I doubt I can be penetrated with it while my clothes are on—or that penetration is even part of what's about to happen—it's still better to be safe than sorry.

The sword feels good in my hand, and when I slice from side to side, the shimmering blade hums.

Neat.

Suddenly, Alex appears in front of me.

Not the real one, but a close approximation—and, sadly, dressed in a tunic and a black cloak.

"Good choice," he says and salutes me with a red laser sword.

"Are you real?" I ask.

"Yep."

"How?" I look down and see I'm wearing an outfit identical to his.

"This is a multiplayer demo. I had my team at 1000 Devils prepare it. This is a small portion of a game we put out on another VR platform, but Robert's people have adapted it to the full suit."

"Wow." I wave the sword in a wide arc. "This will make the testing so much less awkward."

"That's the point," he says. "Want to spar a little?"

Without answering, I stab him.

Or try to.

He parries my attack and slashes at my leg—which the suit turns into a slightly unpleasant pressure on my thigh.

He throws down his sword. "Now tell me, did our code change help with the issue you saw?"

"Let's see." I let go of my sword as well. "Come over and try to grab my shoulder while I catch your wrist. That should approximate the wonky part of your sister's demo."

I'm glad my VR face doesn't show my real-world emotions. The previous demo's Alex tried to grab something a lot more private than my shoulder.

He saunters over and reaches for me.

I grab his wrist and hold, enjoying the solid feel.

How in the world am I turned on by this?

Why is my real-world heart racing from touching his avatar?

"Better?" he asks.

"Very nice," I murmur.

"So the fix helped?"

Oh. Right. Work stuff.

I let go of his wrist and step back. "Yeah. A little better. Lots of work still to do." I reach out and touch his chest, doing my best not to hyperventilate at the warm sensation. "Slight timing issues abound."

He nods. "How about we fix more of them?"

"Sure." I reluctantly drop my hand. "Though I think there are so many, we might want to write them up and delegate a bunch to my team."

"Of course." He reaches for his head and disappears.

I reluctantly take off my headset as well, then wriggle out of the suit.

"Ready to pair again?" he asks.

I pull up a chair to his desk. "Can I drive?"

He lets me, and I spend some time describing the issues that need fixing and assigning a bunch of tasks to the appropriate developers.

The exciting—and terrifying—thing is that Alex insists "we" keep a bunch to work on "ourselves."

"Don't you have some responsibilities at 1000 Devils?" I ask.

He shrugs. "Bella needs me. We have to get the suits ready for production."

I turn from the monitor to meet his very distracting cerulean eyes. "So who will be porting the games for the hospital project?"

"My people at 1000 Devils. There's actually a dedicated team for that."

A peculiarly warm sensation unfurls in my chest.

Must be hope about the VR pet therapy. It can't be joy at the prospect of working side by side with Alex for the foreseeable future. Because that wouldn't do. Not at all.

"That reminds me," he says. "I wanted to see your VR pet therapy for myself."

Would it look unprofessional if I jumped up and down with glee?

I love showing off my work to anyone even remotely curious, but the idea of Alex seeing it tickles me on a different level. I wonder if this is what a single mom might feel when a guy she's been dating finally meets her child for the first time. Except, of course, Euclid isn't a real child, and Alex and I aren't dating.

"I'll be right back," I say and hurry out of his office to get a headset and gloves from my desk, the ones with my Euclid setup.

"Mind if I stream what you'll be doing to your monitor?" I ask Alex when I'm back.

He doesn't mind, so I set it up.

"Ready?" I ask.

Alex puts on the gear, and I walk him through which app to launch.

"Wow," he says when the purple otter-meets-Teletubby creature shows up in front of him. "Aren't you a cute one."

"Hi, Holly," Euclid sing-songs. "I mished you."

I smile. Just seeing my little VR pet on Alex's monitor gives me a jolt of joy.

"He thinks I'm you," Alex says with a grin.

With the headset on, he can't see me staring at his lips, so I allow myself to enjoy that sexy smile.

On the screen, Euclid's fur turns a mix of colors that indicates confusion. "What are you talking about? You can be so shilly."

I walk over and rise on tiptoe to whisper into Alex's ear. "Of course he thinks you're me. It's not like there's a camera inside the headset."

How did I resist the urge to lick that ear?

"You're right," Alex says.

"I'm always right." Euclid turns a proud brown shade. "That means you really are shilly."

Wow. Very good response. The cool thing about AI is that it can sometimes surprise you.

Grin widening, Alex bends down and fluffs Euclid's fur until it's a happy purple again. "You're right, little one. I can be very silly indeed."

Hey now. Was that a dig? After all, Euclid thinks he's talking to me.

"I'm ravenoush," Euclid says and does his hungry dance.

"What do I do?" Alex mouths.

I again enjoy whispering the instructions into his ear. Also breathing in his scent.

I'm not being creepy. Not at all.

Looking almost giddy, Alex extends his hand to get the digital snacks to appear on his palm. Then he feeds Euclid each and every one with an enthusiasm that rivals mine.

Bugger. My ovaries are aching as I watch Alex do all this, and they go into overdrive when the two start to play fetch and I see the joy on his face.

If this little test is anything to go by, Alex would make a great daddy to some lucky little human.

Perhaps a little human that I make for him?

Wait. What? I've never had these kinds of thoughts about a man before. It's way creepier than sniffing him, if we're being honest.

"I'd better go," Alex tells Euclid reluctantly. "I have a friend waiting for me."

Euclid's fur turns several shades of gray before settling on a light teal. "Shee you later. I wove you."

Alex hugs him. "Love you too, bud."

Okay. I'm officially a puddle of swoon.

Alex looks reluctant as he removes the headset.

I hide improper feelings as quickly as I can.

"Amazing job," he says when he can see me again. "He's the next best thing to mainlining oxytocin."

I feel all floaty all of a sudden, like I've just mainlined oxytocin myself. "Little known fact," I say without thinking. "Oxytocin can produce more frequent and more powerful orgasms in women. Most people think it's just for fostering feelings of bonding, but it does so much more."

Blimey. Why did I just rattle out all of that? I need to get myself off, and soon. Orgasms are too much on my mind, so much so I'm talking about them with my boss like the creep I'm turning into.

Or my mom.

Alex chuckles. "Don't tell Bella. Knowing her, she'll start wondering how to incorporate Euclid into the pleasure functions of the suit."

All the blood leaves my face. With everything going on, I've almost forgotten about the porn-shaped sword of Damocles hanging over my VR pet project.

He frowns. "I'm kidding. She wouldn't actually do that."

"It's not that," I say. "I'm just worried NYU Langone will not work out." There. It's actually the truth... just not the whole truth.

He walks over and tucks a stray strand of hair behind my ear. "We're going to kill at that meeting tomorrow. I promise."

I fight the tsunami of oxytocin to raise a questioning eyebrow. "Tomorrow?"

"Well, yeah. Weren't you copied on the invite from Dr. Piper?"

"No." I grab the headset and gloves. "I'll be right back."

I sprint to my desk, stash the gear, and check my inbox.

Sure enough, there's an invite for a meeting at NYU Langone tomorrow morning.

The jittery excitement I feel as I dash back clears away whatever remained of my hangover.

"Want me to walk you through my strategy for the meeting?" Alex asks as I come in.

"Yes. Please."

He puts up a presentation on his screen and explains that someone on Robert's team prepared it for him.

Note to self: learn to delegate better. I totally would've done the presentation myself by staying late, and then I would've felt like rubbish the next day.

Alex walks me through the presentation, which includes the games they plan to pitch for phase one—all kid-appropriate and the furthest thing from porn.

"When can all this be ported to the suit?" I ask. It's the closest I can come to, "Do you think this can be finished before they somehow find out about the porn connection?"

Alex closes the presentation. "Robert is comfortable with a pretty aggressive timeline."

If I didn't already want to kiss him (again), I'd want to kiss him now.

But no.

Professional and proper is my new motto.

"So," Alex says. "What are your plans for the rest of today?"

"I'm game for us to pair," I say.

Bugger. That didn't sound either professional or proper.

"Great." He takes his seat. "Can I drive?"

We begin to program together, and I lose track of time. Whenever he explains the logic behind his code changes, I feel myself getting deeper into trouble. If my inappropriate attraction to him was mostly physical at the start, I'm now just as drawn in by the way his mind works—and that's not good. That way dwell feelings that I'm not ready to have for anyone, let alone my boss.

When we switch and I get to drive, things aren't that much better. Alex has a dangerous habit of telling me how clever he thinks I am. There's only so much praise I can take before I strip off my clothes and beg him to ravage me on the couch.

Or on the desk.

Maybe right in this chair?

"I'm starving," Alex says, pulling me out of my licentious thoughts.

I glance at the clock in the corner of his screen.

It's eight. Way past my usual dinner time.

As if to confirm that, my treacherous stomach rumbles like a bloody motorcycle.

"That's it." He jumps to his feet. "The least I can do is buy you dinner."

Dinner?

All I can do is flap my eyelashes at him in shock.

"Let's go." He holds the door for me.

Mind spinning, I step out of the office onto the now-empty floor.

Bella pops her head out of her office. "Hey, guys."

"*Privet*," I say. "We're going to dinner. Want to join us?"

Boom. Inviting a guy's sister makes the dinner not a date.

"Thanks, but I already ate." She winks at me. "You two go on ahead."

Bollocks. She's playing Emma again.

I guess this is happening.

As he herds me to the elevator, Alex asks what food I'm in the mood for.

"Sushi," I say without thinking.

Ugh. Could I be any more boring and predictable? To make this worse, my parents flat out told him I eat the same thing all the time.

"I'm so glad you suggested it," he says, sounding earnest. "I want their chicken teriyaki."

Whew. It's going to be stressful enough resisting the temptation to turn this clearly professional dinner into a date.

We walk into Miso Hungry.

The usual hostess isn't here, which is reasonable. It is late.

"Welcome back," says the waitress from earlier, her gaze glued to Alex's face. "Your usual table?"

He nods, but when we sit down, he whispers, "I don't think I've been here often enough to get a usual table."

Well, this *is* the table where he sat with Bella when I saw them, and I guess anything related to Alex is burned into this waitress's memory.

Twat.

She comes back, and when I ask for my usual, she makes a confused face.

I'd bet anything she knows it. She just wants me to say it out loud in front of my not-a-date.

"Three avocado rolls with one piece held back," I grit out. "A miso soup with forty-seven cubes of tofu and seventeen pieces of scallion."

I expect Alex to smirk, but his face is completely unaffected—like he hears people order prime numbers of food items all the time.

"How many pieces is the teriyaki cut into?" he asks with apparent seriousness when it's his turn.

"Eight?" The waitress's smile is a little too chummy for my liking.

"Please tell the chef to make that seven," he says, again completely deadpan.

She raises an eyebrow. "Your order comes with a soup. Do you also want—"

"Yes," he says. "Same number of tofu cubes and scallion for me, please."

This is it. I'm going to propose to him and get fired.

*No. Get it together, Holly.*

I excuse myself to go to the bathroom, and when I get there, I stare into the mirror, chanting a single mantra:

*Do not fall for him.*

*Do. Not. Fall. For. Him.*

# THIRTY-ONE

WHEN I RETURN from the bathroom, Alex pulls out a chair for me —a gentlemanly gesture that wreaks havoc on my determination to keep things professional between us.

The waitress comes back with a little pot of green tea.

He pours a cup for me first, then one for himself.

Seriously, he needs to do something rude and soon. Else I'm not holding myself accountable for any creepazoid behavior.

Like dry-humping him right on this table.

"What gave you the idea for VR pet therapy?" he asks.

I blow on my tea—and pretend I don't see him staring hungrily at my puckered lips. "As hard as it is to believe, I grew up on a farm, surrounded by animals—and I don't mean just my sisters."

He chuckles.

"It was insane," I continue. "Untidy, chaotic... Yet after I left, I realized that a part of me missed the animal companionship—and hanging out with my twin sister didn't help that go away."

He laughs.

"What I like about VR in general is how everything in it can go away when you take off the headset, leaving no messes behind. When

I thought of a VR pet, I hoped it would tap into that need for companionship, but would let me keep my living space ordered. And it's worked out exactly as I hoped."

He nods. "What about the hospital? Why did you decide to partner with them?"

I take a sip of the tea. "I had my appendix taken out when I was ten. It was the worst time of my life, and the only thing that made it semi-bearable was my dad's Game Boy. VR is a bit like that Game Boy, but much, much more effective as a distraction—and studies prove it."

Alex looks intrigued. "What games did you play?"

"At that time?" I strain my memory. "One with Mario and one with Kirby."

He looks disappointed. "Any falling block puzzle games?"

"Not then, but I've played *Dr. Mario* since. Why?"

"I was hoping you'd say *Tetris*," he says. "I might be slightly obsessed with that game."

The waitress comes back with our soups and lingers next to Alex a few seconds too long.

"Your *Tetris* obsession is somewhat logical," I say when she finally leaves. "You own a video game company, so you're clearly into games —and *Tetris* was created in Russia, your country of birth."

He picks up his spoon. "You know a lot about it considering you've never played."

I blow on the soup, mostly to see if he stares at my lips again—and he does. "I have played it, just on the PC."

"Ah, good. Did you know *Tetris* can improve spatial reasoning and help with anxiety?"

Huh. He sounds like my mom when she touts the benefits of orgasms.

"Surely *Dr. Mario* has the same advantages?" I ask.

"Doubt it." He grins. "What's your favorite tetrimino?"

I wrinkle my nose. "I don't like the very idea of tetriminos. Sorry."

There's a hopefully joking look of outrage on his face. "Why?"

"They're all four squares," I say apologetically. "If I'd designed that game, I would've made them pentominos."

He rubs the stubble on his chin. "You don't think five square shapes would've made the game too difficult?"

I shrug. "Difficult could mean more fun."

He seems to seriously consider this, then shakes his head. "I just can't picture that version of the game becoming as popular as the original."

I swallow a spoonful of soup after making sure there's a prime number of tofu and scallion pieces in it. "What's *your* favorite tetrimino?"

"The T-block, hands down." He makes a T in the air with his index fingers, conjuring up inappropriate images of one of those fingers going into me instead. "The T can bridge gaps, square up edges, and set up places you can put Z- or S-blocks."

"Interesting." What's really interesting is that I somehow find his explanation erotic.

"Yeah," he says animatedly. "You can also stick a T into otherwise impossible holes with a T-Spin maneuver."

Okay, now I feel less like a weirdo for getting turned on. I mean, sticking things into holes?

I clear my suddenly parched throat. "I thought the I-block is what everyone prefers. It's long and straight and helps you clear four lines at once."

Is this flirting? I did just talk about something long and straight. Add in hard, and I might as well be talking about his cock.

"I'll agree that the I-block is better than J and L," he says. "But it has nothing on the T."

"I'll take your word for it."

He smiles. "If you had to choose a tetrimino, which would you go for?"

"A square. It's symmetrical, nice and tidy."

He nods approvingly. "Dependable choice, especially early in the game."

The waitress brings out the main course, and he pours soy sauce for me when she leaves.

"How did you get into *Tetris*?" I ask before sticking the first avocado roll piece into my mouth.

"When I was a kid back in Russia, we didn't have a computer at home, but there was a business nearby that rented computer time by the hour. I think my love of games and coding goes back to that time and those games—of which my favorite was *Tetris*." He smiles. "I guess now it's nostalgic. Reminds me of Russia and all that."

Since he's brought it up, I pepper him with questions about growing up in Russia, which was still the Soviet Union when he was a child. The stories he tells me about Perestroika and the wild corruption of the nineties are equally chilling and fascinating, and the more he talks, the more I feel like I understand him—which is terrible for my goal of not falling for him.

"What about you?" he asks. "What was it like growing up with so many sisters?"

Of course. Many people ask this out of the same kind of curiosity that makes them slow down at a scene of a car accident.

"For someone who likes order as much as I do, it was unadulterated hell," I say honestly. "Going to college abroad felt like getting out of jail."

"The college being Cambridge, right? You didn't do a year or two in an American school first?"

"Nope. It was the UK from the start. As you can tell by my occasional verbal slips, I loved it there."

"And yet you came back here." He looks at me with so much interest I feel equal parts giddy and unsettled.

"Not surprisingly, I wanted to work in VR," I say, averting my gaze to hide from the naked intensity in his. "The best job I found happened to be in New York, so I took it. My whole family is in this country as well, so that was a variable too."

He covers my hand with his. "I know it's selfish, but I'm glad you took the job."

Wow. His skin is touching my skin, and the warmth of it destroys what passes for my resolve in a heartbeat.

If we weren't in a public place, I'd jump him.

"I'm glad too." I stop avoiding his gaze and get lost in the cerulean depths.

"Will you be having dessert?" the waitress asks, wrenching me out of my trance-like state.

"No." I reluctantly pull my hand free.

"Just the check please," Alex says.

She glares at me and stomps away.

Oblivious to her anger and the cause of it, Alex asks, "Have you been back to the UK since you finished college?"

"Unfortunately, no. But I have watched every non-violent movie and TV show set there, from all the entries in Masterpiece Theater to *The Office.*"

He cocks his head. "What's your favorite?"

"*Downton Abbey*, of course."

"I haven't seen it." He rubs his stubble again. Is that why he doesn't shave, to have something to touch? I'm going to have stubble in a place he can touch soon—

"—is it any good?"

The question acts like a cold shower. "Is *Downton* bloody *Abbey* any good?"

Was my voice a tad too shrill there?

He raises his hands palms out. "Hey, I didn't mean any offense. I just thought it was about a bunch of rich people having tea in a fancy castle."

"That's like saying *The Lord of the Rings* is just a bunch of social rejects on a hike."

He chuckles. "I guess I'll have to see it now."

And afterward marry me.

No. I seriously need to stop this.

"Here you go." The waitress slaps the bill on the table.

As I dive into my purse for my wallet, I see Alex reach into his pocket with a frown.

"What?" The question carries a good dose of challenge in it.

"I thought it was clear the dinner would be on me," he says, plunking down his credit card.

I match his frown with one of my own. "I can pay for myself, thank you very much."

"I don't doubt it. But when you work late and your company feeds you, that's on their dime." He pushes the credit card toward me, and I see that it's his business one, not personal.

"Fine." I'm about to put my purse back, but it slips out of my hands.

Bloody hell.

The open bag hits the floor—and, of course, the dildo rolls right out of it.

I suppress a horrified yelp.

*Please don't let him see.*

*Please, for the love of virtual reality, don't let him see.*

I lean down to get the purse, my eyes following the path of the escaping dildo.

Wait. What's this shadow over it?

Bugger.

It's the waitress.

She's heading back to our table.

"Wait!" I shout at her, but it's too late.

She steps on the dildo, trips, and flails her arms in desperation.

I leap to my feet to catch her, and in the corner of my eye, I see Alex do the same.

Only we're too late.

She faceplants.

We rush over to check if she's okay.

By some miracle, she is—which is good, but it doesn't answer the next question that becomes rather urgent for me.

Where the bloody hell is my dildo?

# THIRTY-TWO

ALEX GETS the sushi chef to take care of the poor waitress, then signs the bill and drags me out.

I leave reluctantly. The dildo was a gift from Bella, but more importantly, I'd like to be able to come back to Miso Hungry one day, and I won't be able to if they find that dildo.

A limo is waiting for us.

I'm so flummoxed I let Alex shepherd me into it without so much as a, "Where are we going?"

Just as I recover enough wits to ask the question, Alex pulls something from his pocket and hands it to me. "I believe this is yours."

Of course.

It's Optimus Prime, the dildo.

It didn't disappear. Alex found it and hid it—as though that would minimize my shame.

For a second, I'm surprised I don't sink through the floor of the limo and get run over by the cars behind us.

It would be a relief if it happened.

"Thanks," I stammer and violently thrust the dildo into my purse.

"Bella's gift, right?"

Face on fire, I nod.

He grins. "She gifts stuff like that to everyone. For what it's worth, it means she likes you."

She likes me because he didn't tell her what I tried to do—else she would've shoved that dildo up my bum.

"Do you mind if I ask you for a favor?" he asks, his expression suddenly serious.

Is the favor sexual?

Cheeks flushing even hotter, I realize we're sitting next to each other exactly the way we did when we kissed.

My breathing quickens in anticipation, and I instinctively dampen my lips. "What did you have in mind?"

"At the meeting with the hospital tomorrow, don't let Dr. Piper and the others know that I'm part of Morpheus Group."

His words are like an ice compress to the face. My flaming blush recedes. "They don't know?"

He shakes his head. "Bella is both the official and the de facto head of the venture. I was originally there to help her secure funding, and now I'm just supporting her."

"So you *are* worried they'll associate 1000 Devils with porn. Didn't you say it *wasn't* porn?"

And if he's worried, I was justified to be worried as well.

He rubs the back of his neck. "It's not that. I don't think Dr. Piper would care about 'porn,' as you call it. But he is a very thrifty administrator, and would make an argument for incorporating your VR pet project into our existing contract. To him, I'm 1000 Devils, so if I'm also Morpheus Group, he'll see an opportunity to save money."

"So this is about money?"

"Exactly."

I massage my temples. "Isn't that playing loosey-goosey with your contract?"

"Not really. Even if he pays extra for your project for the

remainder of our current contract, he can pounce when it gets renegotiated."

"So you don't think he'd care about what the suit will be used for?"

Alex shrugs. "I can't be sure, of course, but it's a moot point anyway because I don't see how he'd find out. The suit isn't out yet, and won't be until your VR pet trial is well underway. If the trial is a success, we can talk to Bella about spinning off your project as a separate venture, so there should never be an issue."

I feel floaty, like I've taken off a thirty-pound weight vest I've been wearing all day.

If what he's saying is true, my worries were groundless. I didn't need to break into his office and attempt that sabotage. I didn't need to owe my evil twin. I didn't need to jeopardize my relationship with Alex and Bella—not that I knew there was a relationship to be had at the time I broke in.

Alex must read some of my thoughts on my face. "I'm sorry. I should've reassured you when we spoke after your break-in. I was upset then, and there wasn't a good time later."

"You're apologizing to me?" I grab his hand. "I'm the one who is sorry. I should've talked to you guys instead of acting so rashly."

He squeezes my palm, his fingers warm and strong around mine. "Water under the bridge."

Uh-oh.

My eyes lock on his lips, and a familiar magnetic pull draws me toward him.

He leans toward me as well, his lips about to fuse with mine.

The limo stops a little too jerkily, yanking me out of the sexual trance.

Blinking, I draw back.

"Your place." He nods toward the window, answering the question I never got the chance to ask.

"Jolly good," I mumble.

His eyes glint. "Do you want to stay with me a little longer?"

I swallow hard. "I do. But I shouldn't."

His face turns solemn. "I understand."

Why is he being so bloody professional and accommodating? If he pushed even a little bit, I'd kiss him and not look back. More than kiss him, in fact.

I reluctantly grab my purse. "I guess I'll go?"

"If that's what you want." He comes out of the limo and holds the door for me.

I get out clumsily and stand there, unsure how to say goodbye under the circumstances.

Would a kiss on the cheek be inappropriate?

"See you tomorrow at the hospital," he says with a wave.

Unsure of what I'm doing, I snatch his hand from the air and give it an awkward shake.

Great job. Maybe I should curtsy or kiss his ring while I'm at it?

The corners of his eyes crinkle—he's obviously trying not to laugh at my expense.

Mumbling "do svidaniya," I beeline for my building. A part of me is grateful he didn't push. This is how things should be between us. Professional.

I just wish being a saint didn't feel so crummy.

---

ONCE HOME, I run through my usual routine on autopilot, my mind already on tomorrow's meeting—except I'm more worried about seeing Alex again than the fate of my project.

Ugh. What is wrong with me?

Getting into bed, I decide to finally do something about my raging hormones. If I don't sleep tonight, I will jeopardize tomorrow, and that can't happen.

So, the big question is: dildo or au naturel?

Before I decide, I check my lady parts to make sure the irritation from the waxing is gone.

Yep. I'm smooth.

In fact, I really like this look. It's like a clean-shaven guy versus a scruffy one. I think I'll keep everything neat and tidy like this going forward. I can't believe I didn't think of it before—I might need to thank Gia, after all.

In any case, the best part is that the lady wank is *on*. And I might as well use Optimus Prime, for novelty and all that. Also, since Alex touched the dildo today, by dodgy transitive property, it'll be as if *he'll* be touching my bits.

And just like that, I'm as ready as can be.

I wash and sterilize the dildo—because restaurant cooties—and turn it on.

Wow. The vibration is strong. Twice the power of my toothbrush, and that thing packs major hertz.

Deciding to touch it to my clit before attempting any penetration, I bring it into position.

Blimey.

I come in a fraction of a millisecond.

Things must've been pent up in there.

Should I go on?

No. Feeling sleepy now, must take advantage.

Turning off the dildo, I hug it to my chest, the way I do with the plush toy of Optimus Prime.

Sleep comes instantly, but I dream of cerulean eyes and inappropriate behavior all night long.

# THIRTY-THREE

I'M all nerves as I step into the meeting room at the hospital the next day.

Wow.

Alex is clean-shaven again and is wearing a suit—just like the day we kissed.

Focus. VR pet project. Not here to lust.

I manage to sit my horny ass down and reply to the preliminary niceties.

When the talk of weather and such is done, Alex starts his presentation—and I want to kick myself for not masturbating a lot more the day prior. I'm as randy as I've ever been, and that's not a state I want to be in during such an important meeting.

"This is great," Dr. Piper says when Alex is done. "I'm glad we went down this path. Now VR therapy will be even more comprehensive."

I want to jump up and down. My dream took a little detour, but it seems to be back on track.

The rest of the meeting is spent on Q&A. When we adjourn, Dr. Piper asks Alex to stay back to discuss 1000 Devils' business.

As I exit the room, Alex sneaks a wink at me—which is like an injection of aphrodisiac right into my clit.

This is ridiculous. And the worst part is that I have no idea if I should wait for him. We didn't come together, which implies I shouldn't. We're also pretending not to work at the same company—another reason I shouldn't.

But it's a friendly thing to do, isn't it? Or is that my hormones talking?

Whatever. Since I'm here, I might as well visit Jacob.

I buy a candy bar for Jacob and a tea for myself, then make my way to the pediatric long-term care wing.

To my relief, no clowns lurk in my path. However, when I get to Jacob's room, he has a VR headset on—must be using VR pet therapy as we speak.

I should leave him to it.

Just as I start to turn, he takes his headset off, spots me, and shines that boyish grin at me. "Hi, Aunt Holly."

"Hi, kiddo." I hand him the candy. "Were you just playing with Master Chief?"

"Did you say Master Chief?" says a familiar Russian-accented voice from behind me.

I turn.

Yep.

It's Alex.

"How did you—"

"Dr. Piper told me where to find you," Alex says. "And who is this?"

"Jacob, this is Alex," I say to the boy.

"Hi, Jacob," Alex says in the friendly tone he used with Euclid the other day. "It looks like you're as big a fan of *Halo* as I am."

Jacob's eyes light up. "*Halo* rules."

With matching grins, the two start an animated discussion about some gibberish. I recognize only a few words, like *grunts*, *jackals*, and *plasma beams.*

As they talk, I tidy up around Jacob's bed, bundling his clean socks into three pairs yet again and folding the blanket next to his bed for what feels like the one hundred and thirty-seventh time—as cute as kids are, they wreak havoc everywhere they go.

When everything is to my satisfaction, I settle into a chair to watch the two of them, and as I do, the feeling I got when Alex interacted with Euclid comes back with a vengeance.

He *would* make a good dad. An awesome dad.

Blimey. My ovaries are going to turn into a tuna melt.

"Do you want to see clips of me playing?" Jacob raises the tablet.

Alex eagerly agrees, and a minute later, a vicious shootout is on the screen. I sip my tea and force myself to follow along despite the violence.

Jacob is good—or at least, he stays alive for an entire five minutes of an apocalyptic firefight. Then some guy in a blue spacesuit kills him with a plasma sword.

As Jacob's character lies there vanquished, the asshole who killed him starts squatting up and down over his head.

Alex frowns. "Is he—"

"Yeah," Jacob says. "He's teabagging me."

I choke on my tea. "He's what?"

"It's also called corpse-humping," Alex says. "It's a kind of victory dance meant to insult and aggravate the person you just killed."

I roll my eyes. "Boys."

"You know who that is?" Alex asks Jacob, frowning at the screen.

"Yeah. We go to school together."

Alex's frown turns threatening. "How about you and me team up one of these days? I promise I'll make that guy regret his unsporting behavior."

Huh. I can suddenly picture Alex as an enforcer for the Russian mob.

"For teabagging my friend, you die," he'd say with a thicker accent and swing a bat at the poor guy's knee.

Jacob is thrilled at this opportunity to team up, and they exchange the prerequisite info.

"Do you play anything else?" Alex asks once they run out of *Halo* stuff to talk about.

Jacob eagerly rattles out a list of games he likes, but Alex looks a bit put out by the end—maybe because *Tetris* is not on the list?

"What about *Tetris*?" Alex asks, confirming my suspicions.

Jacob shakes his head. "Old."

"What about *War of Sword*? That's new."

"Yeah," Jacob says. "I've been meaning to try that one. Is it any good?"

Alex nods. "*Tetris* is my boredom-killing game, but if I'm stressed, I like to turn off my phone and just quest in *War of Sword* for hours."

"Okay then." Jacob searches the name of the game on the tablet. "Maybe I'll try it."

Maybe I will as well. I'm curious.

A nurse shows up with a tray of food.

"Ah, lunch," Jacob says eagerly.

We watch him eat and talk about everything under the sun—but especially his VR pet, which turns out to have grown a little more.

He might be feeding his friend a bit too much, but in VR, pet obesity has no harmful side effects.

"We'd better go," I say when Jacob finishes his lunch and appears eager to get back to his games.

"It was nice to meet you." Alex extends his hand to the boy.

Jacob shakes it solemnly. "You too."

"Bye," we all say in unison.

When we step outside, Alex looks at me with an unreadable expression.

"What?" I ask.

He nods at the limo that's just pulled up to the curb. "Would you join me for lunch?"

Are those bees in my stomach or am I simply peckish? "Sure!"

Oops, may have sounded too eager there.

He opens the door for me. "I know a place that specializes in pelmeni."

"Sounds great," I say and climb inside.

To my disappointment, Alex sits across from me this time.

No, wait, he's right to do that. It's the proper way, even if the seating arrangements are the only proper things on this ride—my thoughts are anything but.

"Tea?" Alex asks.

Since it's my favorite kind, I say "yes, please" and get treated to samovar-brewed heaven in a cup once again.

"So how did you and Jacob meet?" Alex asks, sipping his tea.

A smile splits my face. "His grandparents know my parents, and they brought him to my parents' farm while I was visiting. When I came across him, he was petting Spock, my favorite Kirk's dik-dik."

It's Alex's turn to choke on his beverage. "What was he petting?"

"Kirk's dik-dik," I say, grinning. "Dik-diks are these tiny antelopes. My parents rescued Spock and his family from a bankrupt zoo."

I take out my phone and locate Spock.

"See?" I show him my screen with a cute creature that's about a foot tall despite being fully grown. Like other dik-diks, Spock has pretty eyes and sharp little horns on his head.

Alex leans within kissing distance of me and peers at the screen. "Adorable. Is this a male or a female?"

"That's Spock. He's a male. Unlike some of the other critters on the farm, dik-diks are pretty docile." I meet his cerulean gaze. "They're famous for mating for life."

That last bit charges the air between us until it feels like every tiny hair on my body stands on end.

Is he about to kiss me?

*Please kiss me.*

Wait, no. What am I thinking? Propriety must be maintained.

"You realize what we're looking at there," I blurt. "Right?"

"What?" he murmurs, his gaze on my lips.

"A dik-dik pic," I say and thank Gia for coming up with that particular pearl a few years back.

That startles him into a laugh. Eyes crinkling, he says, "Oh, yeah. And this one looks horny."

I groan. That's another one of Gia's.

The limo stops.

Whew. Kiss avoided.

I should be happy, but I'm not. I'm disappointed.

But I shouldn't be.

We exit in front of a building with a drawing of a giant pelmeni outside. It's called Pelmennaya, which Alex translates as "the place you get pelmeni."

How creative.

Once we're seated, Alex orders for both of us—twenty-three pieces for me and thirty-one for him.

"Do you want to stop by 1000 Devils after this?" he asks. "You've been talking to Robert over email, but it might be nice for the two of you to meet face to face."

"Sure," I say.

Does he want to show me his life's work? Because I want to see it, and for all the wrong reasons.

Bugger.

I can't believe I need to remind myself of this again.

Whatever this lunch feels like, it is *not* a date.

# THIRTY-FOUR

THE PROBLEM IS, just reminding myself that it's not a date doesn't make the feeling go away, and Alex doesn't help matters. Whenever I try to steer the conversation toward work, he pulls out random bits of Russian wisdom, such as, "Talking business is not good for one's digestion."

So, we talk about each other instead, and each new tidbit I learn about him is like an extra knot added to a rope wrapping around my heart.

"I hope this place delivers," I say when I'm done gobbling down my portion of the pelmeni.

"They do," he says and gives me a piece from his plate. "That's just one, so still prime, right?"

I eat the piece. "Yes. Thank you."

He scratches his clean-shaven chin—an evil move that's clearly meant to direct my attention there. "I've been wondering... Do you like prime rib?"

"Not every day, but yeah. Dad used to make a great one on the farm."

"What about prime-time TV?"

I see where he's going with this, so I smile and nod.

He grins. "Do you use Amazon Prime?"

"Yep, I subscribed to it as soon as the program was introduced."

He takes out his wallet. "How deep does this love of primes go?"

I shrug. "I prefer the UK government to the US one because I think *Prime Minister* sounds much better than *President*. Does that answer your question?"

"It does—and makes me wonder: do you use a prime broker?"

I shake my head with a grin.

"Ever see the movie *Prime Cut* or play Nintendo's *Metroid Prime*?"

"Neither."

"Do you own a Prius Prime?"

"I don't have a car."

"Ever take out a subprime mortgage?"

"No."

He scratches that sexy chin. "Are you interested in primeval history?"

I chuckle. "Now you're pushing it."

His grin broadens. "How about the primaries?"

"Nope."

"Privates? As in soldiers, of course."

"Nope. I'm not especially keen on soldiers, though some private parts might strike my fancy."

*Ugh, stop flirting, Holly.*

He laughs. "What about primates?"

I lick my lips. "I like some apes, sure, but not because of primes."

*Seriously, stop flirting—or whatever that was.*

He pins me with an almost predatory stare. "I'm sure primates like you too."

Is he saying that—

The waitress comes with the check, and he insists on covering it again.

"Ready?" he asks when we get into the limo.

"For what?

He smirks. "For the 1000 Devils offices, of course."

---

A TRAFFIC-FILLED RIDE LATER, we step out of the elevator in front of a plaque that proudly states, "1000 Devils."

The contrast with my company's offices and these is stark. There are bright colors all over, and I hear laughter in the distance—like in a petting zoo.

"We have some fun traditions here," Alex says and leads me into a walk-in closet to the side. "Let's gear up."

I blink, looking around.

Instead of clothes, there are nerf guns.

Lots of nerf guns.

Hey, given my recent experiences, these could've been cocks or dildos.

"Take this one." Alex hands me a sturdy-looking gun. "It's good for a beginner."

I accept the gun and watch him pick out a rifle.

"What do I do?" I ask when we step out of the armory.

A dark smile dances on his lips. "Shoot anything that moves."

With that, he shouts something like *hoorah* and rushes forward.

I sprint after him. I guess when in Rome, you have to act like Jacob's peer.

The first bullet—or dart—whooshes by my ear two seconds later.

Wow.

Do these hurt?

I sidestep the next projectile and shoot back at the attacker, a forty-something, red-headed bloke with a belly reminiscent of Dad's.

*Bam.*

The guy is grunting and rubbing his left eye.

Oops.

A new attacker leaps out of the corner.

Alex lunges in front of me and takes the projectile in the chest. Had that been a bullet, chivalry would've been the cause of my boss's untimely demise.

Since nobody's shooting at me for the moment, I get a millisecond to take in the office space—and hate it with all my tidiness-loving passion. The desks stand in a haphazard manner. Nerf gun ammo is everywhere. And what's worse, there are four chairs next to many of the desks.

The net effect is overwhelming, and that's before armed people leap at me from every direction. My guess is, someone took the whole 1000 Devils branding a tad too far and gave this place the feel of a satanic ritual.

The next attacker joins the fray, a lady about Alison's age.

I shoot her with dart two and three.

Double oops. One of my darts hits her groin, another her right boob.

More attackers join in.

A cloud of darts is flying my way.

I duck behind the nearest desk.

A throat clears above me once, twice.

Wait. I know that sound.

I look up.

Yep. I'm face to crotch with Buckley.

In the heat of battle, I didn't even notice him there.

"Hi." As I leap to my feet, I catch a glimpse of the code on his monitor. It looks misaligned, and I have to fight the urge to push him out of his chair and tidy it up, and then do the same with the anarchy that is his desk.

Buckley clears his throat twice more. "Hi, boss." With a goofy grin, he smacks himself on the forehead and clears his throat two more times. "Sorry. Force of habit. I guess you're not my boss anymore."

"Right. Sorry. No time to talk," I rattle out and rush into the gunfire.

That proves it. I'd rather be shot at than listen to Buckley's throat clearing.

Another enemy dart whooshes by my ear.

I respond with dart number four and shoot the next person with the fifth.

On the next shot, my gun makes a weird clicking sound.

Must be out of ammo.

Hey, at least it was on the fifth shot and not fourth or sixth.

I drop the gun and raise my hands, hoping that will make the assault stop.

Nope.

A shower of darts flies at me.

I cringe.

There's a blur of movement, and Alex is suddenly in front of me, taking the projectiles in the back.

Wow.

My heart is hammering as if I were in a real firefight—and Alex's proximity isn't helping matters.

He's so close I can smell his tea scent and feel the warmth coming off his big body.

He looks down.

I look up.

Slowly, he bends his head and—

"That's enough shooting," someone says nearby, and Alex jerks away.

I turn to face the messiest man I've ever seen in my life.

His Hawaiian shirt is wrinkled, his hair is disheveled, and his glasses are warped—as though he microwaved them by mistake.

"Robert," Alex says with a grin. "This is Holly. I believe you've spoken over email."

As Robert walks by Buckley's desk, he accidentally knocks over a pen holder.

"Sorry," Robert says and bends to pick up the pens.

"It's okay." Buckley clears his throat a few times. "I got this, boss."

As Robert shakes my hand, I make sure Buckley actually picks up the mess—not that it would help this place become magically ordered.

Alex must sense some of my discombobulation. He insists we talk to Robert in a meeting room and chooses one that's blissfully tidy—no doubt a place where they hold meetings with clients and the like.

As we settle around the table, Alex gives Robert an overview of the conversation at the hospital and a list of games in the scope of the project.

"What about *War of Sword*?" Robert asks. "It would be a good fit for the target hardware."

Alex sighs. "Too violent for the target demographic. Maybe in a later phase."

"Wait," I say. "*War of Sword*—the game you like so much—is one of yours?"

Robert nods so vigorously his warped glasses nearly fall off his nose. "It's Alex's baby."

"More of a passion project," Alex says. "The idea was to make a game for myself and see what happens."

"Yeah," Robert says with a measure of pride in his voice. "Financial success is what happened."

"Tidy," I say. "Now I really want to see it."

Robert and Alex exchange excited looks.

"We have a room for that," Alex says. "Want to see it?"

"Of course," I say, though now I'm not so sure.

The room better not be as much of a mess as the rest of the floor.

Leaving Robert, Alex and I head over there, and when we enter the room, I blow out a relieved breath. It's empty, the only furniture being a dresser-like thing in the corner.

Alex walks up to the dresser and pulls out a pair of VR headsets. "Are you okay using gear made by your competition?"

I nod. "I have that brand of headset at home. It's one of the few besides ours that fit my head."

He hands me the equipment, and I put it on.

"Are all these games made by you guys?" I ask as I take in the cluttered dashboard.

"Yep," Alex says. "The icon with the sword is what you want."

I start the game and let Alex walk me through character creation.

Minutes later, I'm an elf female with facial features not so different from my own, just cartoony. As my weapons, I choose a bow with arrows, plus a thin, one-handed sword.

When I start the game, I show up in a medieval village, and Alex tells me to go into the inn and grab a chair.

"This is a multiplayer game," he says as I comply. "I'm about to join you."

Excited, I look at the inn entrance. A minute later, he walks in.

His avatar is a minotaur, horns, hoofed feet, and all. More importantly, it's a shirtless, muscular minotaur—with a face that looks eerily like Alex's.

Bugger. Now I'm turned on by a half-human, half-cow. Next thing you know, I'll have a fetish for lactating men.

"Hi," the minotaur says, and his voice comes at me twice—from the headset speakers and from real Alex.

"You look horny," I say and wince. He made the same joke about the dik-dik just hours ago.

He's kind enough to chuckle before handing me a ball of yarn.

"With that in your inventory, you'll be able to find me no matter where I am in this world."

As I put the yarn into my travel bag, I realize a horrific fact I hadn't noticed until now.

It's my elfin hands.

They only have four fingers each.

Why? Bloody hell, why?

It's not like elves are known for their non-prime number of fingers. Quite the opposite—they're supposed to be long lived, which a four-fingered elf would not be on account of being suicidal.

"I'm going to join a friend in battle," Alex says. "Shake that yarn to follow me."

"Sure," I say uncertainly.

Usually, I'd be anti-battle, but maybe this will work out in my favor—someone just might chop off a finger on each of my hands in the upcoming fight.

A girl can hope.

Alex disappears. I take the yarn out and give it a shake.

*Whoosh.*

The inn around me is gone... and is replaced with a scene from hell.

# THIRTY-FIVE

THE FOREST MEADOW is littered with body parts, the gore made that much worse by the fact that all the hands and feet have four fingers and toes.

I shudder. It's not just the elves that are thusly cursed, it turns out.

With a cacophony of sounds, a menagerie of creatures is tearing each other apart. Despite the cartoony looks, the violence feels vicious and brutal, too much so for me.

Something leaps out from behind a tree. I yank my sword from its scabbard and behead what turns out to be a fellow elf.

So, this is an elf-eat-elf world.

Far in the distance, Alex is ripping into someone with his minotaur horns.

Bugger. My gag reflex cannot take a second more of this.

I remove the headset and try to even out my ragged breathing.

Alex pulls off his headset as well and looks at me worriedly. "You okay?"

"Yeah," I lie. "Just a little bit of VR sickness. It will pass."

He hurries over to the dresser and brings back a bottle of water and a pill. "Take this."

"What is it?" I ask.

"Dramamine."

"No, thank you. I'll just drink the water." I take the bottle and chug it greedily until the images of four-fingered limbs are but a distant memory.

"Feeling better?" he asks.

I nod.

"Want to take the rest of the day off?"

I shake my head.

"How about we head back to work?" he suggests.

"Great idea," I say, and that is what we do.

---

"DO YOU WANT TO PAIR?" he asks when we step out of the elevator back at our offices.

I glance at my desk. "Let me check my email first, then I'll pop in."

"Deal." He heads over to his office.

When I finish with my inbox, I don't feel ready to face Alex just yet, so I move some of the misaligned desks and remove objects from them to make sure there's a prime total.

"Want to organize my office?" Bella asks as she catches me putting Alison's stapler into a drawer.

I try to hide my eagerness. "Can I? Right now?"

"Maybe another time." She grins. "I'm pretty sure my brother is waiting for you."

Gulp. She's right.

"See you later," I say bravely and head over to Alex's office.

If he's annoyed at having waited, he doesn't show it.

"Will you drive?" is all he asks, and when I say yes, he lets me. A few hours later, he takes the reins.

Just like the prior day, pair coding with Alex is a type of sensual torture. I lose track of time, and he again drags me to Miso Hungry at eight p.m.

In déjà vu meets wet dream, this dinner not-date feels just like a real date would—and I have to constantly remind myself not to do or say anything inappropriate to my boss.

The temptation is huge.

Heroically, I resist it, and he gives me a limo lift once more, where it's a miracle we don't kiss again.

At home, I take out all my sexual frustration on Optimus Prime—until its batteries die.

Then and only then, I fall asleep.

---

THE NEXT FEW days follow the same formula: I get to work, check my messages, and pair code with Alex until lunch. He then insists on taking me to Pelmennaya. Afterward, we work together some more and have dinner at Miso Hungry.

Each day I get a lift home and each day we almost kiss—but don't. And each day Optimus Prime has to pick up the pieces.

"The suit integration is progressing so well," Bella says to me one morning as I'm checking emails at my desk. "You guys are amazing." She proceeds to tell me how she's tested the suit in every blush-inducing detail.

"Anyway," she says when her TMI avalanche is over. "Alex is no doubt pining for your company."

Before I can respond, she sashays away, so I rejoin Alex and the whole coding-lunch-coding-dinner-limo-wanking cycle happens once again.

And then again. And again.

# THIRTY-SIX

AS THE WEEKS PASS, I get to know Bella better, and I learn just how brilliant she is. On her end, she's treating me more and more like a friend, which propels my girl crush on her into ready-to-stalk territory.

I dread the day she learns of my original intent to harm her dream product.

In fact, I pray she never will.

The worst part, however, is that each passing day chips away at my resolve to stay strictly professional with Alex, especially since on each limo ride, he seems on the verge of kissing me but doesn't.

It's getting to the point where I'm not sure if I'm grateful for his restraint or pissed off.

---

"I NEED A FAVOR," Alex says as I'm about to exit the limo the following Friday evening.

Wow. Is this it? Are we about to throw the bloody propriety out the window?

I'm ready. Or am I?

Bugger. Must answer.

"What's up?" I ask, failing to sound casual.

"You know what, never mind," he says. "It's not appropriate."

Yes. Yes. Yes. Seems he finally has the decency to make an indecent proposal.

I lean forward. "Please. What did you want to ask me?"

He sighs and rubs his forehead. "Okay, so this Sunday morning, my parents' restaurant will be closed for repainting, and Bella wants to stage an intervention for my father about his drinking."

Bloody hell. That's not what I thought he'd say at all. In a heartbeat, I go from wanting to hump him to feeling terrible for him. "Has it gotten that bad?"

He frowns. "He never used to pass out the way he did at his birthday, but Mom says it's happened twice since."

I want to reach out and give him a reassuring hug but manage to resist—I've gotten pretty good at controlling my urges lately.

"Do you want me there with you?" As horrible as the idea of this event sounds, if he needs me, I'll be there.

"No. Dad's going to be upset as is. If someone who isn't family turns up, he'll just storm out."

"I see," I say and instantly feel guilty for the relief washing over me. "Then what's my role in it?"

"My usual pet sitter will be away for the weekend," he says.

I blink at him, not sure what that has to do with anything.

He pinches the bridge of his nose. "It's too short of a notice to look for someone else, but I want someone there with Beelzebub."

My eyes widen. "You want me to babysit your dog?"

Images of nip-slips or worse flit through my mind—his puppy deserves that demonic moniker.

"You know what, never mind," he says. "Now that I hear it out loud, I realize how weird it is for me to ask you this."

Not weird if he sees me as a friend or more—but I don't say that. Instead, with a will of its own, my mouth replies, "I'll be glad to help. You just caught me by surprise, that's all."

He looks at me so intently my stomach flutters. "You sure?"

"Quite sure." I wish I were as confident as I sound.

"Great." He flashes me a grin that makes me feel like my upcoming torture is worth it. "You'll have to let me do something for you as thanks."

The X-rated images from my evenings with Optimus Prime are suddenly at the forefront of my mind. "Like what?"

He hesitates for a second. "How about I make you dinner?"

*He* will cook dinner for *me*? The proverb states that the way to a man's heart is through his stomach, but I might not be immune to the reversal of that—which makes this a bad idea. "You don't need to do that."

"I insist. Besides, it might be good if you came the day before, so I could show you where all his stuff is. This way, we can sleep in on Sunday morning—I know I'll need the extra zzzs."

So a dinner Saturday night? A dinner he'll prepare himself? Why does that feel so much more date-y than all the non-dates we've had?

"What time?" is all I trust myself to ask.

"When do you usually eat dinner?"

"7:09," I blurt.

He smiles. "Of course. That's a prime time to eat. 7:09 it is—though maybe come a bit earlier so we can start at that exact moment."

"Spiffy," I say, a little lightheaded. "How about I come over at 6:31?"

"Perfect. I'll have the limo waiting for you at 6:13."

I hope I don't feel as I do now tomorrow, or else I won't be able to eat.

"I'll see you tomorrow," I say and scramble out of the limo before I do something I'll regret—like asking if he wants to come up or giving him a pentagram-shaped love bite on his neck.

Or both at the same time.

# THIRTY-SEVEN

I BARELY SLEEP THAT NIGHT, so I spend most of Saturday re-watching *Downton Abbey*, rereading *Pride and Prejudice,* and interacting with Euclid.

None of it calms me down.

No matter how many times I remind myself that tonight's dinner isn't a date, my blood pressure refuses to normalize. I feel off-kilter, unable to focus on my usual routine. I even skip lunch, which might turn out to be a good thing if Alex's cooking is subpar—hunger being the best spice and all that.

Maybe I'll calm down if I research what's customary when visiting a Russian home?

Nope.

Knowing that you should take your shoes off and not shake hands over a doorway isn't that helpful.

Then again, I do see a useful tip about bringing a gift—something I almost forgot about. Apparently, a box of candy is traditional.

Hmm. I don't have a box, but I do have a stash of individually wrapped Fry's Turkish Delight that I ordered from the UK. Hopefully, the key is the candy part, not the box part. I put nineteen of them into my purse.

When it's closer to prime time, I groom my lady bits, taking care of all the fine hair that's reappeared since the wax—not because I'm planning on Alex seeing my bits but because that puppy might rip my knickers off instead of my bra this time. If that happens—and if Alex happens to look—I want to make sure things look tidy down there.

Another question occurs to me: what does one wear to a dinner her boss is cooking?

After a long deliberation, I decide I can't go wrong with the outfit Gia forced me to get for the birthday party. Also makeup wouldn't hurt. And nice shoes. And for consistency's sake, I make my hair look nice as well.

When my phone alarm rings at 5:57, I examine myself in the mirror and nod approvingly.

I'm as ready for this not-a-date as I can be.

THE BURLY LIMO driver opens the door for me when I approach.

"Thanks," I say.

"No problem," he replies with a heavy Russian accent.

A tea is waiting for me inside the car—a nice touch.

I catch the guy texting something to someone—probably letting Alex know he's picked me up. Then he closes the partition between us, and I'm left hoping he doesn't text more as he drives.

By the time we stop next to Alex's building, I feel so jittery it would take a week of *Downton Abbey* to calm me down.

The chauffeur opens the limo door for me.

The skyscraper in front of us is sleek and shiny. The guy leads me into the lobby and waves at the security guard before escorting me into an elevator. Without a single word, he presses the button for the 107th floor before turning to leave.

"Do svidanyia," I say.

Finally, a smile from the taciturn man. "Do svidaniya."

The doors close.

I hold my breath all the way until the doors open right into an apartment where Alex is already waiting. At that point, the breath escapes in a loud gasp—and not because the place is a posh penthouse that must've cost millions.

Like me, Alex got dressed up and is wearing a suit similar to the one he wore at the restaurant, only even more stylish. Bespoke, perhaps?

There's even a tie. A tie!

I force my mouth to close before any drool leaks out.

He's also clean-shaven again, like he was at his father's birthday. Yet even *that* isn't the reason I have to fight the urge to rip off that suit and shag his brains out right here and now.

The problem is his hairdo.

The black locks are neatly slicked back—exactly the way I've always fantasized about.

He's the very epitome of tidy.

Knickers-dropping, nipples-hardening, mouth-watering kind of tidy.

Bloody estrogen hell.

How am I supposed to act all proper now?

# THIRTY-EIGHT

"YOU LOOK AMAZING," we both say in unison.

He grins. "Ivan told me you dressed up. You really didn't have to." I can almost hear the unsaid, "But I'm glad you did."

So that's what that text was about? I guess I have the driver to thank for prompting Alex to clean up as nicely as he has.

Suddenly, a loud bark echoes in the large hallway, followed by the clickety-clack of puppy claws on hardwood floors and then the sound of something crashing.

The koala-bear-meets-dog creature rushes at me, his tail wagging so quickly you can barely see it move.

With a Russian curse, Alex leaps for his pet, but Beelzebub dodges him and jumps on me, rising on his haunches so we come face to maw.

Instinctively, my right hand covers my crotch and my left covers the top of my dress.

No more wardrobe malfunctions at his paws, thank you very much.

Since the puppy can't make me expose my nipples or clit, he

settles for doing to me what I've been dying to do to his master—licking my face like I'm covered in peanut butter.

If Bella were here, she'd probably give the eager puppy a voice-over that would say something like, "You're yum. So yum. Want to play? Want to chase flies? I'm Beelzebub—that's the Lord of the Flies, you know. Do flies like bacon? Do you want some bacon? I live for bacon. Is your name Kevin?"

"Bad boy," Alex says sternly, pulling Beelzebub away. "We don't lick guests."

We? Alex can lick me, no problem. Hell, I'll take a dog licking again if that's a prerequisite.

"Sorry about that. You can wash your face in there." Alex gestures at a door down the hall.

I start to take off my shoes as per the Russian etiquette, but Alex says that I don't have to. When I insist, he hands me a pair of slippers. "These are Bella's, but she won't mind if you use them."

I'm glad I insisted. Taking shoes off is clearly important enough that Bella keeps slippers here.

Properly slippered, I hurry over to the loo, wash up, and reapply my makeup.

When I come back out, Alex is alone.

"I put a treat inside a special toy," he explains. "He'll be trying to dig it out for a while, so we can enjoy the peace for now."

I look around.

The hallway is littered with dog toys of every kind.

The urge to tidy is strong, but I fight it and look at the walls for help.

Surprise surprise. Everything is covered with posters featuring *Tetris Payout, Super Tetris, Tetris Plus, Tetris 4D, Tetris League*—the list goes on and on.

"I didn't realize there were so many versions of the game," I say as I look from one to the next.

Alex beams with pride. "Come, let me show you something."

He leads me into a large room that can only be called a man cave —though there's a serious presence of said man's best friend as well, in the form of half-chewed bones and toys.

Must not tidy. It would be as crazy as kissing his neck.

"See that?" Alex points at the wall next to a giant TV.

Wow. Every single video game console I've ever heard of is attached to that TV, and inside most of them is a *Tetris* game, some from the posters I just saw and some not.

I guess this collection makes sense—video games *are* his passion.

His phone beeps.

"It's 7:01," he says. "Let's head to the kitchen so we can start dinner on time."

As I follow him from room to room, I realize just how huge this penthouse really is—especially for New York City.

Game developers clearly make bank.

The kitchen turns out to be the only tidy room in the house. There are flowers and candles on the table—all very date-y if you ask me.

He pulls out a chair for me, and as I take a seat, I look at the two plates in front of me.

One contains twenty-three pieces of avocado roll, while the other holds the same number of pelmeni.

Tearing my eyes away from the feast, I look up at him in wonder. "You made this?"

"Well, yeah." He sits across from me next to a similar spread. "I wasn't sure which food you prefer on weekends, so I went with both."

"Good call," I say, salivating like one of Pavlov's dogs. "I think I'll go wild and have both."

He grins. "I think I'll do the same. Crazy town."

I attack the pelmeni first.

Yum. Usually, I don't like variation in recipes, but this batch is different in a good way.

I tell that to Alex.

"I added a secret ingredient to the recipe from my parents' restaurant," he says.

"A secret ingredient?" I taste the avocado roll—and it also tastes better than usual, but more subtly so. "Is there one in the roll as well?"

"Yep. And I guess now I have to tell you what it is," he says with mock reluctance.

I match his tone. "It's only the polite thing to do."

"Fine. I figured since we're having Japanese and Russian, why not fuse the two—so I put a touch of ginger into the pelmeni and a little bit of sour cream into the rice in the rolls."

"Ah." I taste another piece of each. "That *is* what you did. You clearly have a backup career as a chef. I'm not usually a fan of dishes tasting different. I hate it actually. But I love these."

He covers my hand with his and smiles. "I guess I have the magic touch."

Oh, yeah. The magic of his touch shoots zings of awareness throughout my whole body and makes my breath catch in my throat.

"Sorry." He pulls his hand away.

"It's okay," I choke out, and it takes all my willpower not to add something like, "I really, really, *really* enjoyed that."

"I'm glad you like it," he says.

The touch? No, he means dinner. Bollocks, that neat hair is making it difficult to think.

"I do like the food," I say when I've unscrambled my brain. "But now there's a problem: I won't be able to eat the regular versions of these dishes going forward."

Just like if any other man touched me the way Alex just did, it would also feel inadequate.

Bugger.

I'm ruined for other chefs *and* men.

He pulls out his phone and types out a message. "I just sent you the exact recipe for the pelmeni, and I can talk to the folks at Miso Hungry about the rolls."

"Thank you," I say and stuff my mouth before I can say something improper, like, "Can I repay your kindness with my body?"

"You're welcome." His gaze is warm on my face. "I have to admit, I enjoyed making this for you."

My heartbeat quickens. "Have you cooked for other women before?"

*Good going. As subtle as a bull in a china shop.*

His eyes gleam a rich, dark blue. "Only the ones I've dated."

"Oh." So I'm the first one he's doing this for without dating? To be honest, I don't like the idea that he's dated anyone, but obviously he must have. Figuring I might as well keep going with the inappropriately personal questions, I ask as casually as I can, "And how many was that?"

He bites his lip in concentration.

Crikes. Is the number astronomical? It could be. A guy like this must have women falling at his feet.

Those twats.

He's still thinking?

Why, oh why did I even ask this? Why ask something you might hate the answer to?

"Six," he finally says.

Oh.

Well, six is not bad. I mean, it's a terrible number in and of itself, but as far as former exes go, it's nice and low, which is good. Also, this means that if I somehow became his girlfriend—a pleasant fantasy— I'd be his seventh.

As in, a prime girlfriend.

I like the sound of that.

Or is a prime girlfriend another term for wife? If it's not, it should be.

"There were some dates and such outside those six," he continues. "But only those relationships got to the cooking stage—and all but one didn't go much further than that. That last one lasted a couple of years but then petered out."

"Why?" I ask. What I mean is: *Why would any sane, warm-blooded woman let you escape her clutches?*

He shrugs. "She didn't like me being into video games."

I gape at him.

No. Not a joke.

"But that's your passion," I say, a bit too vehemently for propriety. In a calmer tone, I add, "You're brilliant at it."

"Thank you." He leans forward, his gaze intent on my face. "I guess she just wasn't the one."

My pulse is pounding in my ears. "I guess not."

It might not be a kind thought, but I'm super glad she wasn't the one—whoever she was. I don't care if it's selfish, but if I can't have my boss, nobody should.

"What about you?" he asks.

Bugger. I guess I started this. "I haven't cooked for anyone."

I stuff my face again in the hopes he'll leave it alone.

Nope.

He tsk-tsks. "You know what I meant."

The food tastes bland now. Taking a deep breath, I tell him about the clusterfuck that was my relationship with Beau.

As I speak, something about the sympathy and understanding in his eyes makes me share more than I ever have with anyone.

"I was a late bloomer, so I didn't date much in high school or college. I just didn't click with a lot of guys, you know? So when I met Beau a couple of years after graduation, I was so relieved I ignored a lot of the red flags. All of them, really. We dated for months before we so much as French-kissed, but all I cared about was that he was a mathematician who also liked routine." I grimace, still mad at myself. "I didn't know he was gay, obviously, so I just didn't feel wanted. First, he treated my hymen as if it were actually holy. Then, once we'd finally done the deed, he didn't want to do it again for ages—nor do things like go down on me or even kiss me much. We eventually broke up, and when he came out the following year, it was a relief, because it explained so much. Still, I haven't been in a dating mood since."

Alex's jaw flexes. "That fucker. I can't believe I'm mad at a guy for *not* wanting to do things to you, yet here we are. Not to steal lines from Rhett Butler, but 'you should be kissed and often, and by someone who knows how.'"

I grab my glass with water and chug it. This is beginning to feel even more like a date than the time he kissed me.

Well, since I was the one who bollixed professionalism with my tale of woe, I should be the one to fix it.

But how? Ask for more food? I'm kind of stuffed, and he looks to be done. Maybe I should talk about something gross—like snot, or squares of even numbers?

Since nothing comes to mind, I ask for something that's interesting but not in a sexual way. "Can you show me your *Tetris* skills?"

He grins. "I'd love to, but how about I show you all the dog stuff first?"

Duh. That's way less sexy than *Tetris*. Why didn't I think of that?

We finish up what's on our plates, and I take a raincheck on his offer of tea—a testament to how truly stuffed I am. He seems to be just as full, as he accepts my gift of candy without eating any.

I then help him tidy up the kitchen—an activity that turns out to be way too erotic for my comfort. Seeing him dry the plates I washed is a definite turn-on.

When we're done, he shows me where the dog food and bowls are, then leads me out of the kitchen while explaining more doggy stuff, including when to walk the furry beast.

"Speaking of Beelzebub," he whispers as we enter what looks to be his home office.

The sleeping pup is curled on the carpet around some ball—must be the toy with the treat inside.

Aww. Beelzebub is clearly dreaming about chasing something—his paws are moving in the air and he makes little barking sounds.

Okay, so puppies may be unpredictable and messy, but they sure are adorable... especially when they're asleep.

"Come," Alex whispers. "I owe you a *Tetris* demonstration."

We tiptoe into the man cave and close the door so as not to wake up the puppy.

Alex fires up his Xbox.

His version of the game is called *Tetris Effect: Connected*, and it's a work of audiovisual art that's more of a full-fledged psychedelic experience than a block puzzle game.

Aesthetics of the game aside, watching Alex play is a trip in itself.

This is what Mozart must've looked like at the piano in his prime.

I was so, so wrong when I thought this would be a safe, nonsexual experience. It's the opposite. This is even hotter than watching Alex code.

Every time he clears four lines at once—which is called a tetris—the game shows a celebratory animation of fireworks. It makes me picture him entering me the same way the I-block enters the hole that is its destination, and the fireworks that will result from that.

Bugger.

Between the tidy look, the dinner, and this, I should get a medal for not attacking him. A pink star for suppressing libido under extreme temptation.

Maybe I can sneak to the bathroom and rub out a quick one?

"Check that out," Alex says, bursting my wank-bubble. "Jacob says he's playing that guy who deserves a comeuppance. Should I switch to *Halo*?"

"Sure," I say.

A moment later, there are armed people in colorful spacesuits on the screen.

"There," Jacob's voice says from the speaker, and his character shoots at a guy in the distance holding a big rifle.

Alex's character rushes for his prey, somehow dodging all the bullets, then pistol-whips him in the face.

"Wow," Jacob says excitedly. "That was awesome."

And it was. I'm even hornier now. This must be tapping into whatever cavewomen used to feel when their men would protect the tribe—or fight other cavemen for them.

All I know is I want to jump his bones, but I can't. Not while Jacob can hear—not to mention all the usual reasons.

To stay sane, I grab a box with dog toys and pick up a chewed-up duck from the floor to drop in it.

Alex looks up from the game. "Are you cleaning up?"

"Is it okay if I do?"

He grins. "Be my guest."

Jolly good. I channel my sexual frustration into the cleanup.

When all the dog toys are in the box, I sort Alex's haphazard video game collection by console, genre, and year of publication.

Oh yeah, this is nice. Too nice, in fact.

Cleaning up always puts me in a good mood, which in this context is having an aphrodisiac effect.

Bugger.

I should head home or else.

"Wow, thanks," Alex says, and I realize he's turned off the game and is staring at my handiwork in awe. "I've been meaning to do that forever—but I doubt I would've used such a clever system."

I'm a volcano of lust that's about to explode.

He means what he said, I can see it—which makes him the rarest of unicorns: a person who welcomes my tidying efforts instead of finding them annoying.

Well, that does it.

While I coded with him all these weeks, I stood strong.

When he dressed up and slicked back his hair, I managed to keep my knickers on.

As I watched him play *Tetris*, I was already on the verge of giving in—and he didn't help matters by vanquishing that bully in *Halo*—but I withstood the temptation.

His liking my tidying is what pushes me over the edge.

If I don't kiss him now, I'll forever regret it.

Closing the distance between us, I grab his tie and pull his mouth to mine.

# THIRTY-NINE

OUR LIPS CLASH.

Holy primes.

Who knew snogging could be this blinding? I wondered if maybe the last kiss seemed so amazeballs because of the alcohol I had coursing through my system, but no. If anything, this time is better—and the bar was already sky high.

Our tongues dance.

The room seems to spin, this time without the help of vodka.

He lightly bites my lower lip.

My nipples are so hard they hurt, and the heat in my core is reaching 1373 degrees.

He pulls me closer, and I feel his erection against my belly—which makes me want to rip off his pants so I can see it, taste it, and shove it deep inside me.

After what feels like an hour of make-out bliss, he pulls away and cradles my face in his big hands. "You sure about this?"

"Your bedroom," I gasp. "Now."

He replies with an affirmative growl, then sweeps me up in a bridal carry and strides out of the room.

"I'm on the pill and clean," I whisper. There, if the word *bedroom* didn't clue him in as to my intentions, that bit should make things crystal clear, shouldn't it?

"Me too," he says raggedly. "I mean clean, not on the pill."

My blood turns lava hot, my knickers drenched. This is real. It's happening. His reply means, "Why yes, Holly, I will shag your brains out, thank you very much."

Approaching a closed door, he kicks it open and strides inside, then gently deposits me onto the bed.

As I frantically peel my clothes off, I take in my surroundings with relief. The bedroom is even tidier than the kitchen—and that pushes my already-insane arousal into frightening territory.

Do I need to worry? I've heard of people laughing to death, so can you get so randy as to hurt yourself?

That question is put to the test in the next few moments. Alex rakes his cerulean gaze over my body and growls, "You're gorgeous."

I can't speak as I watch him strip off his suit and shirt.

Bliiiiimey. This is like staring at the sun. The delicious muscles I chose for VR Alex pale in comparison to the real thing. I guess my imagination—and digital technology—were not ready for this level of male perfection.

He steps out of his pants.

Here, too, the powerful muscles exposed to my gaze leave the VR version in the dust.

And then he takes off his boxers.

There's an ache in my jaw that makes me realize my mouth is open to the width of a python about to swallow her prey.

Speaking of pythons, Alex's cock is bigger than any available as choices in that VR selection. I think it would feel more at home in the other app—the one with all those swords.

Why am I not scared?

His erection dwarfs Optimus Prime—which means that honorable title should be transferred over.

Yep. Henceforth, *that* is Optimus Prime.

Or just Prime for short—the only short thing about it.

Alex approaches the bed. "I'm going to taste you." The hunger in his gaze underscores the roughly spoken words.

I swallow hard. "Taste me?"

Muscles flexing, he climbs over me and slides his callused palm down my thigh. "I want to make you burn as you never have before."

No words. Speechless.

He drags his tongue up my calf.

I barely hold back a moan.

His tongue continues the trip over my knee and up my thigh until he finds the apex between my legs.

The moan escapes my throat now.

This isn't fair. He can't just start this sexcapade with my deepest, wildest fantasy.

His tongue goes flat against my clit.

Balling the sheets in my hands, I come with a choked cry.

He looks up with a wicked smile, then goes back down and licks me once, twice, thrice—and another orgasm energizes my every nerve ending.

Whew. I'm glad I came on lick number three and not four.

He doesn't stop, though, and I can feel that sensual smile of his against my sex.

Another lick. Two. Three. Four.

His is a bloody clever tongue.

Before giving me lick number five, he teasingly abandons the clit in favor of my folds—which I don't include in my count.

Gritting my teeth, I buck against him, desperate for a release. He gets the hint and returns to the clit for a lick number five—but I'm not there yet.

Lick six.

Closer but still no cigar, which is fine. I don't want to come on a non-prime.

Okay. Now a lot is riding on this next lick. If I don't come then, I'll have to survive the next four licks until we get to the eleventh.

He must know what I need because he makes lick seven slow and languid.

Yes! Finally. My toes curl and my moan sounds closer to a scream.

Before he can resume his ministrations, I wriggle out from underneath him.

He looks up, a question in his eyes.

"My turn for a taste," I pant. "Lie back."

He does.

I kiss and lick his face the way I've always dreamed of doing, then press small, teasing kisses to his neck before gliding my tongue over the hills of his pecs and down the washboard ridges of his abs until I'm at the base of Prime.

Looking up to meet his ravenous gaze, I ice-cream lick up the whole hard, massive length.

Like a tomcat enjoying a stroking, he closes his eyes in pleasure.

Is that a bead of pre-cum at the tip?

Curious, I lick it off. It's yummy—and a prelude to what it would be like if he came in my mouth, which is another fantasy of mine.

In response to my attention, Prime grows impossibly harder.

I wrap my lips around the head and let it slide deeper into my mouth.

It's like silk over steel.

"Fuck," Alex groans.

Encouraged, I swirl my tongue around the head—three times clockwise, then three times counterclockwise.

He grabs my shoulders, his strong fingers digging into my flesh.

I do seven clockwise swirls as he squeezes my shoulders almost to the point of pain, and then I do seven swirls in the other direction.

Breathing hard, he pulls me away. "I want to be inside you," he rasps, his accent the thickest it's ever been.

"Me too," I gasp. "I mean, you inside me, not me inside you."

With a hint of that devilish smirk, he recaptures my mouth in a kiss, and without our lips unlocking, he arranges me on my back.

My heart hammers in my ribcage, my senses utterly consumed by him, by his scent, his feel, his warmth. It's like I'm surfing through an ocean storm on the wave of our kiss, his body over mine the only harbor from the sensual upheaval, his lips the only anchor keeping me safe.

He enters me, and I feel like bursting into fireworks, the way the game did earlier, when he'd make a tetris with a long, hard I-block.

His first thrust is too gentle, so I grab his steel-hard glutes and pull him into me.

His pupils dilate, and the second thrust is faster and deeper.

My body curves and bends, molding against his.

"That's it," he growls, and the third thrust is better still. The fourth is pretty good also, considering the number.

On the fifth thrust, I moan in pleasure. An orgasm is coiling in my core, but it's far away, which is frightening because what if it falls on the wrong count?

I moan on thirteen, and nineteen, and by thrust twenty-three, he's pistoning into me—yet I want it even faster, so I squeeze his muscled ass and pull him deeper.

Yes. Fuck, yes. Moans escape my lips at twenty-nine and thirty-one, and as though through some kismet, he grunts something along the lines "you feel so fucking good" at thirty-seven.

At forty-one, the thrusts turn punishingly hard and are almost too fast to count—and I love every one of them.

By fifty-three, I'm counting the sound of flesh slapping against flesh instead of the thrusts themselves because everything is a blur of pleasure with no discernable start or end.

Eighty-three. I'm close, but I can't come yet. Nor at the non-prime eighty-four, eighty-five, eighty-six, eighty-seven, or eighty-eight.

Here is eighty-nine and it's a prime, but I'm not there yet, though I'm so close I can taste it.

Can I hold off until ninety-seven?

Slap, slap, slap, slap, slap, slap, slap, slap.

My nails dig into his buttocks on ninety-seven as I come undone with a scream.

A satisfied, purely male smile curves his lips as he keeps thrusting.

And thrusting.

Counting is harder now.

Was that one hundred and forty-nine?

Another orgasm starts to build, this one of tsunami strength.

By one hundred and ninety-seven, I don't care if I come on a prime or not. I just want the sweet release.

By two hundred and twenty-three, my throat is hoarse from screaming in pleasure.

Three hundred and seven. I'm *so* fucking close.

"Me too," he grunts.

Fuck. Did I say that out loud?

Doesn't matter.

We're at three-hundred and seventeen, and the black of his pupils nearly overtake the cerulean—and I'm about to explode.

Must hold off just a little bit.

Just a few more.

The release builds and builds.

And then, at three hundred and thirty-one, a prime, Alex grunts in pleasure, his eyes closing as Optimus Prime jerks inside me.

Fuck, yeah. My own orgasm storm makes landfall. All my muscles contract as one as I scream in ecstasy.

Dimly, I'm aware that Alex is hugging and kissing me, but I'm still riding the pleasure wave—one infinitely more intense than all my dildo sessions combined.

By the time I've recovered enough to think again, he's cleaning me with a warm, wet towel.

"That's nice," I mutter, then yawn.

He moves me until we're in a spooning position, with me as the small spoon.

As I lie there, surrounded by his warmth, I feel incredibly content—and in that hazy land between wakefulness and sleep, a thought comes to me.

Whatever this is between us might actually work. He's not the Devil I thought he was when we first met. I like him. Really like him. Way more than I ever did Beau.

The biggest obstacle is our joint workplace. But maybe no one will judge me for sleeping with the boss. Maybe being with him won't be as big of a mess as I feared, and maybe I'll be able to deal with the messy aspects of his life.

On that pleasant thought, I sail away into the land of dreams.

# FORTY

I WAKE up from a wet tongue licking my face.

Memories of last night rush in.

Is this Alex's way of initiating more?

If so, yes, please.

Hmm. His tongue feels long. I don't remember it being that long last night. Only his cock was extraordinarily long. And thick and—

I open my eyes.

Golden eyes stare at me from a koala-like face.

Eeew.

The tongue doesn't belong to Alex.

With a doggy grin, Beelzebub gives my face one more lick.

"Shoo!" I push him away with a giggle.

If you got to first base with a puppy, would it be more pedophilia or bestiality?

His insane enthusiasm undiminished by my rejection, Beelzebub simply switches his licking attentions to Alex's face—and who can blame him.

"Holly?" Alex murmurs sleepily.

"Nope."

He opens his eyes, chuckles, and pushes the puppy away while telling him that waking us like that is a "bad dog thing to do."

"Hi," I say when he's done with his lecture.

Even with dog drool on his face, Alex looks delicious. He grins at me. "Hi, yourself."

"What time is it?" I glance at the sun pouring through the window.

"Fuck. Time." Alex leaps to his feet, gloriously naked.

Grabbing his phone, he barks a few words in Russian.

"I'm running late," he explains at my questioning look. "Forgot to set an alarm. Here." He hands me a robe five sizes too big and begins to dress.

When his glorious nakedness is sadly covered, I slip on the robe and, at his prompting, follow him to the bathroom. Beelzebub scrambles after us and starts slurping water from the toilet bowl.

"No!" Alex says sternly and closes the lid. "That's a bad dog thing to do also."

Beelzebub gives him a contrite look, tail wagging apologetically.

Ooh. I like bossy Alex. Maybe we could play puppy and owner one of these days?

Alex hands me a still-sealed toothbrush that has a dentist ad on it, and then we perform our morning routines side by side, the domesticity of it all tugging at something in my chest.

Meanwhile, the pup is over his contrition. He's running circles around us, sneaking between our legs like a cat, and in general acting like he might've overdosed on cocaine and amphetamines.

"I've got to run." Alex pulls out his phone. "What do you like for breakfast?"

"Oat porridge."

He makes a few swipes and clicks. "One should arrive in a bit." He grins at Beelzebub, who's just jumped into the bathtub and is attempting to chew on shampoo. Shooing him away from the bottle, he glances at me. "You mind taking him for a walk?"

I give the little devil a dubious look but bravely say, "No problem. After that, can I use your computer? I was going to bring my laptop to catch up on some work, but as you might recall, I didn't get to go home last night."

His grin is directed at me now. "You remember that it's Sunday, right?"

I shrug. "Some folks on my team said they'll be working this weekend, so I feel obligated to do the same—solidarity and all that."

"Suit yourself." He leads me to his office, where he gives me access as a guest user. "You can remotely log into your work computer. That way, you'll have everything set up the way you like it."

"Go to your thing," I say with a smile. "I'll figure things out."

Alex doesn't seem to want to leave. He leashes Beelzebub—even though I could've done it—and sets up a snack inside the toy, explaining that I should use it when I want a break from my furry charge.

"You're late," I say with mock chastisement.

"Give me a kiss, and I'll go."

I'm happy to oblige. This goodbye kiss is as hot as the one from last night—and suddenly, I don't want him to leave. And if his longing stare is anything to go by, he'd rather stay and shag me as well.

Are we both turning into sex fiends like my parents?

"I'll see you later," he says reluctantly.

"Later," I say, trying not to drool as I watch him walk to the elevator.

Beelzebub cocks his head and whines as the doors slide closed behind his master.

I pat his big, fluffy head. "I know how you feel, bud. Now let me get dressed so I can take you out for a walk."

# FORTY-ONE

IT'S OFFICIAL.

The best way to fall head over heels for a puppy is to take one on a walk.

Fueled by seemingly endless energy, Beelzebub sniffs every inch of our way to the park and barks at things I didn't realize anyone would want to bark at, like blooming dandelion flowers and an empty cardboard box.

Once we get to the area in the park where he can be unleashed, he runs full speed at some mirage only he can see, then jumps at whatever he's imagining. Afterward, he locates a stick and brings it to me with clear intent: "Let's play fetch."

I toss the stick until my arm is tired, but he doesn't seem remotely out of breath.

Well, no help for it. I leash him again, and we resume walking until he finally does his business on a nearby lawn, at which point I learn that when it comes to collecting dog poo in a bag—Gia's worst nightmare—it's not as gross as one would imagine, though this could be a "love is blind" situation at this point.

When we get home, Beelzebub runs after me through the apartment like a duckling imprinted on his mama, even when I need to use the bathroom.

It's so cute I forget to be annoyed.

Still, as soon as I come out, I set up his food and water in the hopes that a food coma will calm him down a bit, and he enthusiastically digs in.

As I watch him eat, the door buzzer goes off.

It's a delivery person with my porridge.

Finally. I was about to try dog food myself.

Pouring the plain porridge into a bowl, I get comfy in the kitchen and devour my meal while browsing the news on my phone. It's not until I'm done with my food that I realize something's off.

Beelzebub is no longer in the kitchen with me.

With a sinking feeling, I go seek the little beast.

Bloody hell.

All the toys I'd collected neatly into the basket are all over the floor again.

I grab the box and begin putting them away—that is, until Beelzebub jumps on me and causes me to drop the box. Barking excitedly, he begins tossing the toys throughout the apartment once more.

Maybe I should simply let this mess be.

I can do that.

Sometimes.

I mean, I do survive Gia's place with my sanity intact.

I hold out for a solid thirty seconds. Then, driven by an irresistible compulsion, I collect the toys again.

Beelzebub immediately recreates the mess. He must see this as a fun game.

I'm beginning to feel overwhelmed, and unlike with Euclid, I can't just take off a VR headset when I tire of dealing with this kind of pet.

Then I recall the hidden treat toy Alex set up.

Aha.

I'm able to clean up the mess once again, and Beelzebub couldn't care less. All his attention is on the treat-hiding toy.

Jolly good. Maybe I could do a little work while I'm at it.

I go into Alex's office, and as I log in, my thoughts drift to the events of last night. Immediately, questions such as, "What did it mean?" and "What would my coworkers think if they found out?" sprout their unwelcome heads.

Maybe Beelzebub did me a favor when he kept me chasing after him.

Deciding to distract myself with work, I remotely log into my office computer and work on Euclid's code—something I haven't gotten a chance to do in a while. When I'm done, I open my inbox so I can ask Alison to test my work, but an email from her is already waiting there, a message she sent last Friday.

The subject is ominous: "I heard a rumor about you."

I open the email and my stomach freezes.

According to Alison, the whispers at the watercooler are all about one thing: Alex and I are sleeping together.

I stare at the screen blankly, then reply with:

*Who started this rubbish rumor?*

After I click send, it really hits me.

How could someone from the office know? Is there a spy cam in Alex's bedroom?

No, that's ridiculous. And even if there were, Alison's email is from Friday, *before* we slept together.

Someone lied when they started this rumor, but now it's not a lie.

I grasp my suddenly aching head.

What was I thinking last night?

I wasn't. I just unleashed my hormones. We both did, and now my work life is becoming as big of a mess as this apartment—and it's too much for me to handle.

My phone rings.

It's Alex.

Does he know already? Is he about to say how much he regrets what we did?

Taking in a deep breath, I pick up. *"Privet."*

*"Privet."* There's a smile in his voice. "Just wanted to see how the day is going so far, and give you an update."

So he doesn't know.

Do I tell him?

No. He's got his father to worry about.

"The day went well, and Beelzebub is doing great," I say. "How did the intervention go?"

He sighs. "As well as such a thing can. Dad offered us a compromise. He'll drink beer instead of vodka."

I gape at my phone. Has stress robbed me of ability to understand, or is this alleged compromise totally wonky?

"Last I checked, beer has alcohol," I say cautiously. "Isn't that what you wanted him to give up?"

"Yes, but this is a step in the right direction. If he sticks to beer, he won't have enough room in his stomach to reach the blood alcohol levels of vodka."

"I guess..."

"It's a decent result, trust me. Dad's generation of Russians scoff at things like the twelve-step program."

Okay, do I tell him about the rumor now?

"All right," he says before I can work up the courage. "I'm heading back. See you."

He hangs up before I can say anything.

Fine. It's fate.

I hurry back to my inbox to see if Alison replied.

Nope, and why would she? It's still Sunday.

Just as I'm about to exit the email dashboard, an email from Alison arrives after all.

*I was hoping you'd be on this weekend,* it starts. Only instead of naming names, Alison proceeds to say that she'll have to carefully ask around to find out who started the rumor.

Bugger. What's really telling is that she doesn't ask me if the rumor is true. Does that mean she doesn't believe it, or that she thinks I *am* sleeping with our boss?

Sleeping with the bloody boss.

How did I become such a messy, improper cliché?

I pace the room, then sort all of Alex's pens in order of length.

When I run out of physical messes to fix, I look for some more code to work on—and settle on an easy bug from the integration queue list.

As soon as I start, I realize I miss having Alex at my side.

Seriously? Has our pair programming ruined my ability to code independently?

What a bloody disaster.

Before long, I find myself unable to concentrate on fixing the bug, so I type out a command to reverse any changes I just made.

Wait, did I type that in correctly?

Before I can check, my phone rings.

It's Dr. Piper.

I grab my phone. "Hello!"

"Hi," Dr. Piper says, and he doesn't sound like his usual cheerful self. "I fear I have some bad news."

# FORTY-TWO

MY HEARTBEAT SHOOTS UP to one hundred and thirty-seven beats per minute. "Did something happen to Jacob?"

"Sorry, no. Not that kind of bad news."

I exhale loudly. "Thank goodness. What did you mean then?"

He sighs. "Do you remember that consultant I mentioned?"

I almost ask, "The evil one?" but go with a simple "yes" instead.

With everything that's been going on, I'd actually forgotten all about the Evil Consultant.

"Well, he emailed me," Dr. Piper says. "He told me what kind of products Morpheus Group is about to launch."

What?

Oh, no.

No. No. No.

How did the Evil Consultant even find out about the porn? And why bloody tell them?

This doesn't fall into a consultant's purview.

Dr. Piper sighs again. "I was hoping you'd say it was a bunch of lies."

I shake my head, then realize he can't see me. "I can't deny it," I say reluctantly.

A louder sigh. "I'm sorry, dear, but this is a problem then. I mean, not for me personally, but for the rest of my team. They'll want to cut ties when I tell them tomorrow—and I have to tell them. I'm sorry."

I stupidly shake my head at the phone yet again.

"I'm going to give the folks at 1000 Devils a heads up," he says. "Again, sorry about this, but my hands are tied."

"I understand," I manage to squeeze out and hang up.

Tears prickle at the backs of my eyes, and the walls of the office feel like they're pressing in on me.

This is bad. So, so bad. What am I going to do? How do I fix this enormous mess? How do I—

There's the sound of the elevator doors sliding open, followed by enthusiastic barking.

I stagger out of the room toward the commotion, nearly tripping over the dog toys twice.

Beelzebub must've taken a break from the treat to make a mess again—creating a metaphor for my bloody life.

"Bad dog," Alex is saying sternly when I reach them.

Beelzebub's ears are drooping.

I follow Alex's gaze.

Of course. My fuck-me pumps have been ripped into tiny shreds —just like my dreams.

"I'm so sorry," Alex says, looking over at me. "You can wear my sister's slippers when you go home. And I'll get you new shoes."

My hands ball at my sides. "I don't bloody care about the bloody shoes."

He winces. "You've spoken to Dr. Piper, haven't you?"

So Alex is the "folks at 1000 Devils" that Dr. Piper said he'd get in touch with.

I nod, not trusting myself to speak.

"It's a fucked-up situation," Alex says, scrubbing his hand over his face.

I feel the urge to get out of here before I scream or do something else to make him think I'm insane—or scare the poor puppy.

I head toward the door, but Alex blocks my way.

"Where are you going?"

"Home." I try to squeeze past him, but he's like a concrete wall.

"There's something else I wanted to talk to you about," he says as I take a step back, and I could swear there's a look of disappointment on his face.

He dares to be upset with me?

I narrow my eyes at him. "What is it? Did you also lose your contract with the hospital over the stuff you claim isn't porn?"

He sighs. "Morpheus Group is a different company from 1000 Devils. We talked about this."

Yeah. I remember. It was when he said what just happened wouldn't happen.

My anger is intensifying by the second.

I get that life can be unfair, but this is ridiculous. He sleeps with me, but only *my* reputation is in tatters. We both get caught working on porn, but only *my* project is sacked.

He frowns. "I saw the emails from the people writing code today."

My jaw drops. "You want to talk shop in the middle of all this? Is suit integration the only thing you care about?"

His face is stormy now, reminding me of the day he caught me breaking and entering into his office. "I told you it's important to Bella, remember? You said you wouldn't sabotage it again. Remember that part?"

I back away at the anger in *his* voice. "What are you talking about?"

He advances on me. "Look, I get this was a stressful day for you, but that doesn't mean you can—"

"Stressful?" My emotions boil out of control, all the pent-up stress and frustration releasing at the same time. I know I'm shouting, but I don't care. "Stressful doesn't cut it. This is the worst day of my life!"

"And I sympathize, but—"

"Are you going to get out of my bloody way?" I sound so hysterical at this point that Beelzebub whines—which is exactly what I wanted to avoid.

Jaw hardening, Alex moves out of the way. "Go, if you must."

I rush into the elevator and stab my finger at every prime-numbered floor. As the elevator shoots down, I yell my lungs out between each of the stops.

Ignoring Alex's limo, I grab a cab.

The ride home passes in a haze of tumultuous emotions, and once I get there, I put on *Downton Abbey* and cry until I pass out on the couch.

# FORTY-THREE

I WAKE up with a stiff back and pounding head. Pushing up to a sitting position, I rub my gritty eyes, and as the world comes into focus, the events of Sunday morning rush back. My stomach knots, a vise squeezing my chest as I recall everything.

I lost the hospital contract I've worked so hard for.

My VR pet project is as good as dead.

And, to add the cream cheese on top of this cucumber shit sandwich, all my coworkers know I've been sleeping with the boss.

Speaking of which, why was Alex acting so weirdly last night?

I'm the one who should've been upset, not him.

Also, what was that bit about some email? Why was he talking about sabotage?

I jump to my feet and look for my phone, but to no avail.

Bugger. Now that I think about it, I might've left it on the table in Alex's office.

I open my laptop to check the time.

Wow. It's Monday morning. No wonder my back is stiff—I slept all night on a tiny couch.

Okay, back to the email mystery.

I remotely log into my work computer and look in my inbox for messages from Sunday.

Bloody hell. People are panicking because a year of work seems to be missing from the code repository.

Did I do that again?

I frantically pull up the window where I tried to undo my coding efforts from yesterday, and sure enough, I really messed up that command. I even felt like I might've and was going to double-check, but the call from Dr. Piper distracted me.

No wonder my coworkers are freaking out.

The good news is I know how to fix it, since I made this kind of mistake once before.

It takes me a few minutes, but everything is copacetic once I'm done.

Whew.

I reply to one of the panic emails and explain that the issue is now fixed. As I click "send," I notice Alex's name in the address field and recall his accusation.

Oh, fuck.

Now I understand why he looked disappointed.

He must've thought the bad news from Dr. Piper had driven me to mess up the code on purpose—and I didn't deny it or explain what really happened.

I fire off an email asking him if we can talk, then rush to the bathroom to wash my face and brush my teeth.

When I'm done with my morning routine, I check if Alex replied.

Nope.

I eat my oat porridge and check again.

Nada.

It's official.

Alex hates me now. For all I know, he's blocked my email address so I go right into spam—or maybe I've been fired, and my emails no longer reach anyone in the company.

I set my empty bowl into the sink with such force it shatters.

My heart hammers sickly, and the knot in my stomach grows until the oats threaten to come up.

I screwed up.

Alex and I might be over.

If I were rational, I'd be happy about this fact. Assuming I still have a job, us being over means we go back to the employer and employee relationship, which is the proper arrangement. The one that's less messy. The one where people can't talk about me shagging the boss behind my back.

I should be glad, but instead, my heart resembles that poor, shattered bowl.

My interactions with Alex play out in my mind's view. The pair coding... us dancing at his dad's birthday... the kiss... Sunday's orgasms... All the time we've spent together has etched Alex into my heart, and knowing that I've lost him is making me realize that fact—or more like, admit it.

Desperate, I check my email once more.

There are thank-you messages from the developers confirming that the code is back, so I'm still in the company email system.

Nothing from Alex, though.

My chest squeezes even tighter, the tears threatening to flood my eyes again, but I beat them back and square my shoulders.

Fuck moping around and crying.

I refuse to let our relationship unravel.

I need to fix this—and if Alex wants to bloody ignore me, he'll have to do it to my bloody face.

Throwing on my clothes, I grab Gia's lockpicks on a hunch and hurry to the office.

It's time my devil and I had some words.

IN MY RUSH TO get to Alex's office, I nearly knock over Alison.

"Hey," she says. "I'm getting to the bottom of the source of the rumor. Just give me a few more hours."

"Cheers," I pant. "Email me what you know. I don't have my phone today."

She nods, and I resume my sprint—only to find Alex's office locked when I get there.

I knock.

He doesn't open.

Is he ignoring me?

Wait, no, that doesn't make sense. This could be someone else knocking.

Unless he can see me through a security camera?

The idea infuriates me. Then again, I must've suspected this could happen on some level, since I did bring those lockpicks.

I look around.

No one is paying attention to me, but it's still insane that I'm about to do this in broad daylight.

Well, if Alex is watching, he can stop me by opening the door.

I knock for the last time.

Silence.

I make short work of the lock with the lockpicks.

Heart in my throat, I push open the door.

Empty.

Where the bloody hell is he?

Then again, if he's not at work, maybe he's not ignoring my emails after all. Maybe he's simply taken a day off.

Shutting the door, I rush to Bella's office.

She's not there either.

I hurry to my desk and check my email for any messages from either of the Chortsky siblings.

Nothing.

Since Alex is incommunicado, I write to Bella:

*Wanted to chat. Don't have my phone. Can we Skype? My user-name is PalindromicPrime1035301.*

I wait for a few minutes, but Bella doesn't reply or video conference me.

Fine. Since I know where Alex lives, I'll just pay him a visit.

---

RUNNING INTO ALEX'S BUILDING, I smash into the chest of a security guard.

"Can I help you?" he growls, steadying me when I stumble back.

Bugger. He's not the one I saw on Sunday, so I must look like a complete stranger to him.

"I'm here to visit Alex Chortsky," I say breathlessly, stepping back. "On the 107th floor."

The guard walks over to his desk and checks something in his computer as I reflect on how fortuitous it is that Alex lives on a prime-numbered floor.

If that's not a sign that he belongs with me, I don't know what is.

"Sorry," the guard says, not sounding the least bit apologetic. "Mr. Chortsky left."

Damn it. "When?"

He looks up from the screen. "It doesn't say, but it must've been after I started my shift."

Is this true, or is it an excuse Alex gave in case I showed up?

Then again, the guard didn't even ask my name.

I could be Bella. No, he probably knows Bella.

I dart a glance at the elevator.

Would the guard tackle me if I just went for it?

Even if he did, I think I could make it.

I make a mad dash.

The guard isn't chasing me. At least I can't hear him doing so.

Panting, I reach my destination and frantically jab at the button.

Nothing seems to happen for a year.

"You need the card for the elevator to open," the guard says from his seat in an exasperated tone. "I take it you don't have one?"

Cursing under my breath, I turn to face him. "Can't you press something on your end to let me in?"

"Sure I can. But I most definitely won't."

Why, that bloody... I stop that line of thinking, as you catch more annoying flies with honey. Returning to the front desk, I make puppy eyes at the guy. "Please. Alex said I can visit even if he's not there."

"Can I see your ID?" The guard extends his hand.

When I give it to him, he types something into his computer and shakes his head. "You're not on the guest list."

"He didn't get the chance to put me there," I say.

The guard's expression hardens. "Look, lady, you're lucky I'm not calling the cops. And I'm only doing you that courtesy on the off chance you really *do* know Mr. Chortsky."

"I swear I do."

"Then have him put you on the list, or come back with him, or have him give you his card."

I hate it when people use proper logic against me.

With a huff, I turn on my heel and step outside to get a cab.

There's one more place Alex could be.

A place I'm not keen on visiting again, if I'm honest.

A place that reminds me of a circle of hell, which is fitting because it's called 1000 Devils.

Then again, Alex is worth it.

I rattle out the address to the driver and mentally prepare for the trial to come.

A bloody Nerf gun assault.

# FORTY-FOUR

WHEN THE SECURITY guard in *this* building asks me whom I've come to see, I give Robert Jellyheim's name instead of Alex's.

They call Robert, and he tells them to let me in. A quick elevator ride later, I step onto the 1000 Devils' floor and dive into the armory closet.

It's time for the big guns, literally.

I search for the biggest weapon and end up choosing a shotgun-looking thing.

Feeling like a badass, I fish out my earbuds, jam them into my ears, and launch the *Downton Abbey* soundtrack on full blast.

Yeah. The bodies are about to hit the floor.

I sprint out, and as soon as my foes spot me, a dart flies at my face.

I sidestep it.

*Boom.*

At least that's the sound I assume my shotgun makes when I unload it, sending a cloud of darts flying at the forty-something red-headed bloke I recall from the last gunfight.

That'll show him.

A new attacker jumps up from her desk.

I unleash another cloud of darts at her chest.

How do these people work here? The desks are still haphazard, gun ammo is caking the floor, and the worst part is that no one has fixed the "four chairs next to some desks" situation.

A lady I previously shot in the crotch and boob joins the fray, looking eager for revenge.

I squeeze the trigger of my shotgun.

Nothing happens.

Why?

Oh, right. I should've known. Shotguns aren't exactly known for large ammo capacity.

The lady shoots.

I dodge her dart.

More attackers join in.

A swarm of darts is about to turn me into an orange porcupine.

I duck behind a familiar desk.

A throat clears above me once, twice.

Yep. I made this exact mistake the last time too.

I look up.

Indeed. I'm face to crotch with Buckley once again.

It's the second bloody time I haven't noticed him in the heat of the battle.

"Sorry about that." As I take out the earbuds from my ears and stand up, I catch a glimpse of his monitor—he's reading an email.

The "To" field looks familiar, but before I can fully process it, Buckley minimizes the window.

"Hello," he says, then clears his throat three times.

Wait. That email. Was it—

A dart smashes into my temple, and another one hits me in the bum.

Huh. These don't hurt as much as I feared. Or at all, really.

"That's enough shooting, guys," Robert calls from his desk nearby.

I turn to face him.

He's no less messy than the last time I saw him.

"Thanks for letting me in," I say, wiping the sweat from my brow. "I'm actually here for Alex."

Robert frowns. "He isn't here today."

Did Alex tell him to say that?

No. They wouldn't let me up here if that were so.

I walk up to his desk. "Do you know where he is?"

Robert shakes his head.

Damn it. "Can I use your computer to check my email?" I ask, beginning to feel defeated.

"Sure, but please make it quick."

He gives me access, and I remotely log into my work machine and check my emails.

Nothing from Alex still, but there is a reply from Bella:

*Hey, hon. Just tried to conference with you, but you didn't pick up.*

Bugger. I want to videocall her back, but this is Robert's computer, and I'm supposed to make it quick.

I'm about to sign out when I see an email from Alison.

Another moment shouldn't hurt.

I click on it.

Alison says she's triangulated the origin of the rumor and has a name for me.

I read the name, rub my eyes, and read it again.

Yep.

Still Buckley.

Then it hits me.

The "To" in the message I just saw on his screen—I'm pretty sure it was Dr. Piper's email. Or if not, definitely someone with an @nyu-langone.org address.

But why would he email them? Unless...

I storm over to Buckley's desk.

"You're the Evil Consultant?" The question comes out much louder than I planned.

Buckley clears his throat. "What?"

"No more games," I growl. "You spread lies about me at the office, *and* you torpedoed my project?"

His next two throat clears sound angry. "What lies?"

"That I slept with Alex," I hiss under my breath.

He rolls his eyes. "And you didn't? I saw how he looked at you when you were here the last time. 'Sexual harassment' was practically written on his forehead."

I'm the most anti-violent person I know, yet I have to fight the urge to punch him. Hard.

"Why would you do something like this to me?" I ask instead, though I already suspect the answer.

"Why?" He clears his throat twice more. "Office romances aren't proper," he says with a British accent that I think is supposed to be a parody of my speech. "I guess that's only when it doesn't help your career, right?"

Twat. He *is* mad about my rejection of his advances.

Since I'm too busy seething in anger to reply, he clears his throat four more bloody times—as though he knows how painful that is for me to hear. "*I* should have been the CTO," he says, his tone dripping with bitterness. "Not you."

So it's not just the rejection. He *is* sour that I got promoted to CTO over him.

"That project at the hospital was extremely important," I say. "Not just to me, to little kids too."

He shrugs, a nasty expression on his face. "You're not my boss anymore, so there isn't much you can do about it."

"No," Robert says. "But *I* can."

Blinking, Buckley turns to face his new boss—who I now realize must've been there through the whole exchange.

Buckley looks like he's just choked on a throat clear. "I didn't do anything wrong."

Robert crosses his arms over his chest. "Didn't you just admit to making libelous claims about the owner of this very company?"

Buckley's next set of throat clears sounds frightened. "You can't fire me over something like that."

Robert's eyes narrow. "Oh, I can. I could fire you even if you weren't on the probationary period. But since you are, it won't even require that much paperwork."

Buckley glares at me. "I hope you're happy."

"Ignore him," Robert says.

I give Buckley a look designed to shrivel his manhood for at least a year. "Oh, don't worry. He doesn't exist as far as I'm concerned."

Turning, I hurry back to the elevator.

***

AS SOON AS I'm home, I grab my laptop and video conference Bella.

The dial music rings and rings.

"Please pick up," I say to the empty screen.

The app keeps ringing. Just as I'm about to hang up, Bella's face shows up and grins at me. "Hi, Holly. Sorry, I'm all over the place today. My other company is dealing with an emergency: Woody Harrelson is suing us for using his likeness for our line of butt plugs."

"Hi," I say breathlessly. "Do you know where Alex is?"

As though in reply, a bark sounds in the background.

It's a strangely familiar bark, one that makes my chest ache.

"Beelzebub," Bella says sternly.

Wait, why is he there?

The puppy barks again.

Bella glares at someone outside the camera—presumably, the

adorable koala-dog hybrid. "I bet this is why Alex wants you in doggy school."

Doggy school?

"Where is Alex?" I ask again.

She looks back at the camera. "He didn't tell me. Just dropped off the little demon and asked about the school where Boner learned to be so well-mannered." She frowns. "Now that you mention it, he did seem very stressed. Is everything okay?"

"Bloody hell," I mutter. "I looked for him at our offices, at his home, and then even at 1000 Devils. Where is he?"

Her frown deepens. "What happened?"

What can I say? There's no way to explain everything without coming clean about the sabotage—and if I do, I'll lose her, just as I've lost Alex.

But I can't *not* tell her. She has the right to know.

"It's a long story," I say, and taking a deep breath, I launch into it, starting at the beginning.

To my shock, when I get to the part about sabotage, she just sits there calmly, looking almost bored.

"You're not upset?" I ask her when I finish.

She cocks her head. "About which part? If it were up to me to decide who my brother sleeps with, I would choose you, hands down."

I lean closer to the screen. "But I almost sabotaged your venture."

She shakes her head. "Alex told me about your break-in the day we went for that dog walk. He also told me why you did it, and that made me like you even more. In my experience, driven people are rare."

I tap the screen so it zooms in on her face. "So you knew?"

She nods.

I suck in a giddy breath. "And you still want to be friends?"

She grins. "Hells yeah. And before you ask—I'll be your friend even if my brother ends up being stupid enough to let you slip through his fingers."

That brings me right back to earth. I draw back from the screen. "So you really have no idea where he is?"

She shakes her head. "Let me text him."

I watch her do it and wait. And wait.

"Hmm. Let me try calling." After a minute, she mouths "voicemail" to me and rattles out something in Russian. Then she hangs up and says, "Why don't you chillax for now? When I hear from him, I'll let you know."

"Thank you. Just please tell him that the code mess from Sunday wasn't another sabotage. It was an honest mistake that I've already fixed."

"Will do."

"Okay," I say dejectedly. "Talk to you later."

"Yep, and we'll arrange a brunch then too."

I nod and hang up.

Even the prospect of brunch with Bella can't cheer me up right now.

Getting to my feet, I begin to pace.

An hour passes.

Then two.

No more videocalls from Bella.

Did Alex not call or text her back? Or maybe he did but asked her not to tell me?

Could it be that he doesn't believe the mistake story? Or is he just pissed that I stormed out of his apartment the way I did?

More importantly, where is he?

A completely unsubstantiated idea sneaks into my brain—and makes my knees go weak.

What if Alex got hurt on the way to work?

He *has* been missing for a while.

But no. Surely, his family would be notified—and Bella would tell me if that were the case.

Wait. Something Bella said earlier triggers a memory.

He seemed stressed, she said. And I remember Alex telling Jacob that when he's stressed, he turns off his phone and plays *War of Sword*... for hours.

I exhale a relieved breath.

Can the answer be that simple?

If not for that unpleasant encounter with the security guard, I'd rush back to Alex's apartment and demand to go up again. As is, I grab a VR headset.

As I download *War of Sword*, I do my best to banish the memories from the last time I played this game. Between the violence and the four-fingered limbs, this will be as fun as getting punched in the stomach... four or six times.

Still, since this is the fastest way to banish the specter of Alex in an accident, this is what I will do.

Yeah.

Brimming with determination, I click the game icon.

Four-fingered creatures, I will be your doom.

# FORTY-FIVE

APPEARING IN THE MEDIEVAL VILLAGE, I do my best to ignore my elfin hands with their abominable finger count.

If Alex is playing, I should be able to reach him the way I did the last time.

Taking out the special yarn he gave me for this purpose, I give it a shake.

*Whoosh.*

I show up in a dank underground hall littered with body parts.

Unsheathing my sword, I scan the battle raging all around me and fight my gag reflex.

All manner of creatures are fighting to the death here, and the violence once again feels nauseatingly real.

Still, I will not quit this time. Not until I find what I came for.

Tightening my grip on my sword, I look for Alex's avatar amid the chaos.

With a sudden battle cry, a dwarf jumps at me, holding an ax bigger than his head is in his lets-not-count-how-many-fingered hands.

I sidestep the ax swing and behead the dwarf, fighting the urge to vomit at the digital gore.

Then my heart leaps with joy.

There's a minotaur with Alex's features a few feet away.

He's not in the hospital or someplace worse. As I hoped, he's simply playing his game to destress.

I wonder if I'm the cause of that stress—and where he is in the real world. Was he home when I came by his building but chose to avoid me? Or did he not even realize I was there?

Before I can think up more questions, I spot an orc rushing at the minotaur at full speed.

Bugger. Alex is currently fighting a female elf. He's going to get slaughtered.

Well, not if I have anything to say about it.

Drawing my bow, I send an arrow into the orc's head.

*Squelch.*

The arrow pierces the orc's eye, killing him instantly.

At the same time, Alex pierces the elf with his right horn.

Hmm. Do I need to be jealous?

"Holly?" Alex says, spotting my avatar.

I grin in the real world. *"Privet."* Here, I switch the bow for the sword and disembowel a pink goblin mid-leap.

"Behind you!" Alex yells.

I duck as I turn, and a cyclops's spear misses my shoulder by half an inch.

I swing my sword in a wide arc, cleaving the cyclops in half.

Turning around, I see Alex fighting his way to me.

Great idea. Fighting like a berserker, I kill a golem with my sword and shoot an ogre with my arrows while Alex uses his horns and trident to decimate a group of gnomes and leprechauns.

Soon enough, we're fighting back to back.

"No fair," booms a bigfoot-looking fella. "Collaboration isn't allowed in a free-for-all."

Alex silences him with his trident.

"He was right," hisses a hydra, but I cut her snake body in half.

If only winning arguments were so easy in the real world.

We keep fighting until only the two of us are left.

"What are you doing here?" Alex asks.

I turn to face him, my real-world heart pitter-pattering in my chest. "I didn't sabotage the code. It was a mistake, and I fixed it."

The horned avatar's face doesn't change—the game lacks that technology.

Before I can launch into further explanations, the minotaur speaks. "I know that. I saw your email when I got home a couple of hours ago. Replied to it too. Then I called you, but you didn't answer."

A huge weight lifts off my neck. He came home a couple of hours ago? That means he didn't ignore me when I came to his building.

And he replied? Bugger. I was so busy waiting for Bella to video-call me, I forgot to check my work email.

"Sorry I didn't take your call," I say. "I think I left my phone in your home office."

"Oh. I didn't hear it ring—must be on vibrate."

I realize I might look confrontational with my sword out and proud, so I drop it. "I'm sorry I ran out on you. I was overwhelmed with the bad news."

He tosses his trident away also. "No. *I'm* sorry. I shouldn't have suspected you'd intentionally mess up the code. In my defense, I didn't at first, but when I saw how you were acting, I—"

I hold up my four-fingered hand. "Don't worry about that. I'm just so glad you're okay."

He cocks his head, a gesture that looks wonky due to his horns. "Why wouldn't I be okay?"

Not caring that I sound like a crazy stalker, I tell him how I couldn't reach him and that I looked for him at both of his offices and his home.

He shakes his horns. "Sorry about that. I only checked Morpheus Group emails when I got home from the hospital."

"The hospital?" Worry tightens my chest again. "Are you okay?"

"Oh, it wasn't a medical visit. I met with Dr. Piper."

My jaw is gaping open in the real world, but I guess he can't see that in VR. "Why?"

"I saved your VR pet project," he says.

"What?" My heart is racing anew. "How?"

He scratches his head, his hand unrealistically going back and forth through his left horn. "Remember the conversation we had the day before we met with the folks at the hospital?"

"The one when you asked me not to mention you were part of Morpheus Group?"

Bugger. That came out bitter.

"That one," he says. "I reassured you, but later that day, I spoke to Bella about it, and we decided to take a precautionary step in case I was wrong—and I'm glad we did."

I readjust my headset. "Bella didn't mention any of this when we spoke."

The minotaur shrugs. "Maybe the subject didn't come up?"

I resist the urge to shake the information out of him. "So what was the precaution?"

"We started a new limited liability company. Due to all the red tape, the registration only went through this weekend—and just in time. The new company is called Pet VR LLC, and you'll be the CEO while Bella is just the silent investor—and through Dragomir's company, just in case. This way, there should be no porn association, ever."

I'm on the verge of tackling him in joy, but I don't yet. If I've misunderstood something, I'll be crushed. "But Dr. Piper already knows about the porn."

The minotaur's head bobs. "That's why I went to talk to him first thing this morning, before he told the others. I convinced him to keep it between us. As far as they're concerned, they've had a change of vendor, that's all."

I want to believe this so badly. "And he agreed, just like that?"

The minotaur shrugs his broad, hairy shoulders. "I did have to promise him some favorable terms for when the 1000 Devils contract is renegotiated. He's a practical man, and he doesn't really care what Morpheus Group does—only his colleagues would have."

I walk up to the minotaur and try to kiss him, but the game doesn't support such a thing, so my intention is translated into a head butt.

"I don't know how to thank you," I say, cringing at the sight of blood pouring from the wound I just inflicted.

"Meet me face to face," Alex says, his voice roughening. "I'll think of a way you can thank me then."

My pulse leaps and my ovaries perform a series of cartwheels. "Yes, please. My place?"

"On my way," he says and disappears.

Brimming with excitement, I take off the VR gear.

There's so much to process.

My project is saved, and Alex wasn't ignoring me today. He was busy helping me—even though he thought I sabotaged his company for the second time.

I can't believe I even jokingly called him the Devil.

He's more like a guardian angel and a saint rolled into one.

Rushing into the bedroom, I set up some candles while the implications of what's happened continue to race through my brain.

Alex is not my boss anymore. Not with the way the new venture is set up.

That means I'm free to date him—and date him I shall.

Actually, I think I would've done that even if he'd remained my boss, mess or no mess. In general, I think I'm more comfortable with chaos as of late. I managed to stay in that violent game until the end, I survived the Nerf massacre, and I even held my own with Beelzebub.

Speaking of which, Bella mentioned Alex inquiring about doggy school for the pup. Is that to make *my* life easier?

Knowing his thoughtfulness, probably.

I smooth out all the creases in the pillows, fold the blanket into a pentagram, and am counting the candles around the bed to make sure there are nineteen when I hear the video conferencing tune in the distance.

And there's Bella, grinning at me. "Alex just called."

"I know," I say. "He told me everything."

Her grin turns lascivious. "Let me guess. You guys are about to consummate the new venture."

"When a lady plans to kiss, she doesn't tell."

She laughs. "I'm pretty sure that's not the expression."

My doorbell rings.

"Sorry, I have to run."

She waggles her eyebrows. "Good luck."

I disconnect and hurry to the door.

It's Alex—and he looks so, so much more delicious without the cow parts.

Once again dressed in a bespoke suit, he's slicked his hair back and is clean-shaven. I'm suspecting he's figured out that it's the quickest way to get me randy, and he's ruthlessly using it to full advantage.

Without saying a word, he sweeps me up into a hungry kiss, and I feel like the ground has dissolved under my feet.

We stumble toward my bedroom, lips locked and hands eagerly roaming each other's bodies as our clothes fall off as if by magic. He deepens the kiss, and the next thing I know, it's seven orgasms later— six for me and one for him.

Combined, a perfect prime.

"THANK YOU FOR COMING," I say as I'm lying blissed out in his arms hours later.

"No." He smiles tenderly. "Thank *you*."

I cozy up closer to him. "I've decided to tell you something."

He lifts up onto one elbow and tucks a strand of hair behind my ear, his touch sending a pleasurable shiver down my spine even after all the orgasms. "Me too."

"What?"

His smile turns devilish. "Ladies first."

Fine.

I take in a deep breath to quell the bees fluttering about in my stomach. "I think we fit together really well. Like L and J Tetris blocks."

He chuckles. "Wouldn't that make us two squares?"

"Exactly. Nice and tidy."

He squints at me. "You're more of a T-block."

As in his favorite? The bees in my stomach throw a wild orgy.

"Back to my point," I say, drawing upon all of my courage. "Ever since I learned that a heart has four chambers, I thought it was my least favorite organ—but I don't think that anymore, thanks to you."

He sits up all the way. "As a wise woman said in an awesome show, 'I'm not a romantic, but even I concede that the heart does not exist solely for the purpose of pumping blood.'"

Did he just quote Violet from *Downton Abbey*?

He must've watched it. For me.

Suddenly, what I want to say crystalizes perfectly in my mind.

I sit up also and clasp his hand with both of my palms. "I love you," I say with utmost sincerity. "I love you with all four chambers of my heart."

A slow, wickedly sensual smile blooms across his face. "I love you too, kroshka. With all five vital organs in my body."

Cradling my face between his palms, he kisses me again, and we tumble back onto the mattress in a tangle of limbs, our hearts racing in sync as the kiss leads to so many more orgasms I lose count.

Hopefully twenty-three.

As I lie in his arms afterward, I feel like I've reached Heaven— and all I had to do to get there was make a deal with my very own, personal, lovable Devil.

# EPILOGUE

## ALEX

"WE'RE ALMOST THERE," the limo driver whispers to me.

I change into my livery and slick back my hair with a tea-scented pomade I got for this occasion.

My sweet kroshka is going to love this, but to everyone else, I look like a butler—which I guess works, all things considered.

The limo stops, and I tap her shoulder. "We're here. You can take that off."

She turns, and her soft, full breast brushes against my hand.

Fuck me.

My dick—or Optimus Prime to close friends and family—instantly gets diamond hard, as it does whenever I touch her.

"*Do svidaniya,* Euclid," she says, and I can picture her cute little friend replying in Russian. The VR pet venture has been such a success that she's about to launch it in my motherland—a wonderful thing because many of the Soviet-era hospitals there are drearier than anything imaginable in the US.

As a result of this—and of dating me, of course—her Russian is rapidly improving. Also, as I predicted, her Britishisms are giving way to Russianisms, which isn't a word but should be.

As soon as she removes the VR headset, her intelligent blue eyes zoom in on mine. "Can I finally see the *yobaniy* surprise?" Then her eyes widen at my outfit. "I love it. Now take it off."

"The outfit isn't the whole surprise," I say with mock exasperation.

She levels a meaningful glance at the bulge in my pants. "I'd say."

I laugh. "He's not the surprise either. Not yet anyway."

She folds her lips in the most kissable pout ever. "Well, he and you in that outfit had better be somewhere on the agenda."

"Definitely. But after the real surprise." Someone, give me a medal for restraint.

"Fine." She squints at the blackout windows of the limo. "Reveal whatever it is already."

I readjust Prime, then slide out of the car and hold the door for her.

As soon as she comes out and sees our surroundings, she clutches her chest and greedily drinks it all in, speechless.

My smile is devious. I had to ask her illusionist twin to help me with planning and misdirection, so I could arrange this surprise. I even bribed the limo driver into breaking the speed limit in order to make the trip duration short—and it would be fair to say that I suggested bringing Bella and Dragomir on this UK trip as part of that same plan. All they like to do is explore London—which is why my kroshka was expecting to see something like Hyde Park or Hampstead Heath right now.

But no. Bella and Dragomir aren't here. It's only us... and a huge group of butlers, maids, and groundskeepers.

"Is that what I think it is?" she finally says.

"Indeed, Lady Hyman," I say in my best British accent. "Highclere Castle, at your service."

The smile she beams at me is as radiant as her bright blue eyes. Reverently, she whispers, "This is the real Downton Abbey."

I nod, keeping my expression as impassive as her favorite butler would.

"What about them?" She gestures at the sharply dressed people waiting for us.

"Actors I hired," I say. "A few are even from the show."

She squeals like a kid, and I tell her what else we have planned for today. Dragomir used his connections to get us a royal treatment that includes multiple tea services, a stay in the best rooms, and—especially for Holly—the chance to tidy any room she wants while wearing a maid's uniform.

She looks around again, as though not believing her eyes. "This is the best surprise ever."

"There's more," I say and ceremoniously hand her a thick package, custom made in the shape of a pentagram. "This is the last surprise of the day, I promise."

There's confusion on her face as she fumbles with it—the problem with that shape is knowing which side is up or down.

I'm slightly nervous about this next bit, so I remind myself of all the reasons why it should work out just fine. She's grown to love Beelzebub as much as I do, and the furry traitor probably loves her more than he does me. More to the point, he's finished his doggy school education, so he doesn't make as many messes as he did when she first met him—and I've been following his example by keeping my place neat and organized... with prime numbers whenever possible, of course.

Oh, and it goes without saying that we love each other, and she's been spending most of her time at my place without complaint. Still, I can't take her for granted. For all I know, she might not be interested in my proposal.

"What is this?" She holds a metal key in one of her delicate hands and a plastic card in the other.

Must not think about those hands on Prime—makes it hard to walk. I mean, *difficult* to walk.

She looks at me expectantly.

I point at the metal key. "That's for the door to our room in the Castle. And *that*"—I point at the plastic card—"is the second surprise." I wait a moment to build up the drama—another tip from her twin. "That's a key to my apartment. Your permanent key."

Her eyes widen.

I give her my best butlery bow, then ask in the most formal manner possible, "Lady Hyman, would you do me the honor of moving in with me?"

With a squeal, she tackle-hugs me—a great sign, as is the passionate, Prime-engorging kiss that follows.

"Yes," she says when we finally pull apart. "It would be my pleasure to move in with you, Lord Chortsky."

It would be unseemly to pump my fist in the air in this outfit, so I settle for another kiss.

Now that this is out of the way, I'm much more hopeful about the success of my next proposal. The challenge there will be to somehow top today's surprise.

Maybe I'll discover a new prime number for her?

Or buy some prime real estate and build a replica of this castle?

No, that's not good enough. But I'll figure it out when the time comes. For now, all I need to know is that she's my future—and that means the future will be everything I want.

# SNEAK PEAKS

Thank you for following the stories of Vlad, Bella, and Alex! As always, your reviews are greatly appreciated.

Can't get enough of this lovably geeky, raunchy universe? Order your copy of *Royally Tricked*, a feel-good royal romance featuring Gia, Holly's twin sister from *Hard Byte*, and daredevil Tigger from *Hard Ware*!

Also, check out *Femme Fatale-ish*, a fun-filled addition to the Hyman sister saga involving Blue, a spy-in-the-making, her top secret mission, and a suspicious (and sexy) Hot Poker Club member.

Visit www.mishabell.com to sign-up for our newsletter so you can receive updates on new releases featuring your favorite quirky characters!

Misha Bell is a collaboration between husband-and-wife writing team, Dima Zales and Anna Zaires. When they're not making you bust a gut as Misha, Dima writes sci-fi and fantasy, and Anna writes dark and contemporary romance.

Turn the page to read previews of *Royally Tricked* and Anna Zaires' *Wall Street Titan.*

# EXCERPT FROM ROYALLY TRICKED

## BY MISHA BELL

A daredevil prince wants to pay me mega-bucks to train him to hold his breath underwater for ten minutes? Sign me up.

Except I'm a magician, not a stunt consultant. My record-beating dive without air was a trick. Of course, I can't tell that to my client, the royally hot Anatolio Cezaroff, a.k.a. Tigger. Not if I want to be able to pay my rent.

Also, I'm not exactly comfortable around germs. All germs, including those lurking on uber-attractive men. So falling for my gorgeous client is out of the question, and I fully intend to keep my distance.

That is, until he offers to train *me* in bed.

---

"Holly?" an unfamiliar male voice says from the street.

I glance at the newcomer, and suddenly, it's my turn to gape.

I didn't realize this kind of masculine perfection existed outside of Hollywood.

Chiseled features. A Roman nose. Vaguely feline hazel eyes that zero in on my face predatorily, making me feel like an about-to-be-devoured gazelle.

I swallow the overabundance of saliva in my mouth with a loud gulp.

The stranger's broad-shouldered, muscular torso is clad in a tight white t-shirt, and despite the raggedy jeans riding low on his narrow hips, there's something regal about him—an impression supported by the strange design on his belt buckle. It resembles a crest that a medieval knight might put on his shield.

I've been told I compare people to celebrities too much, but it's hard to do with this guy. Maybe if the love between Jake Gyllenhaal and Heath Ledger in *Brokeback Mountain* had borne fruit?

Nah, he's even better-looking than that.

Realizing that I'm staring at his face too intently for it to be considered polite, I drop my gaze lower and notice that he's holding two leather straps in his fists. Leashes, presumably.

Half expecting to see willing sex slaves on the other end of those leashes, I instead find two weird dogs.

At least I think the creatures are dogs.

One sports black-and-white spots that make it look like a panda. Actually, given the creature's ginormous size, I can't rule out the possibility that it *is* a bear. And, if looking like an endangered ursine species wasn't odd enough, the beast is wearing goggles.

Is it because of bad vision, or is the panda about to go snow-boarding?

The second creature is eyewear-free and reminds me of a koala, just much bigger and with a lolling canine tongue.

I force my gaze back to their ridiculously handsome owner. "Hey," is all I can manage. My overactive hormones seem to have robbed me of the ability to speak.

The stranger narrows those hazel eyes. "You *are* Holly, right?"

*This is your chance,* my inner magician pipes up. *Trick the hot stranger. Fool his pants off.*

Banishing lust with a heroic effort of will, I inwardly rub my hands together, à la evil villain. Until I adopted my current pale-skinned, raven-haired stage persona, I was mistaken for my identical twin on a regular basis, even by people closest to us. Our oval-shaped faces are exactly the same, right down to sharp cheekbones and a strong nose. I was literally born for this particular deception.

Adding the slightest touch of poshness to my voice, I say, "Who else would I bloody be?"

There. If he knows that Holly has a twin named Gia (as in, me), he'll voice that guess now and I'll stand down.

Maybe.

I bet I can bluff him out even if he does know I exist.

He stares at me intently. "You've changed your hair."

"*Addams Family* cosplay," I say in my best Morticia Addams voice. It's not my most convincing lie, but the guy looks like he's about to buy it anyway. Then I see a problem. Waldo, who's blinking in confusion, is about to speak. I kick his leg under the table and cheerfully ask the stranger, "Have you met Waldo?"

I'm hoping the hottie will extend his hand and introduce himself, thus letting me learn his name.

My evil ploy is thwarted by the panda. It pulls on the hottie's pant leg with its teeth. Seeing this, the koala does the same on the other side, except its movements are clumsy, puppy-like, leaving a hole in the pants.

If this is how the dogs get his attention, no wonder he wears something so raggedy. Also, yuck. I hope he washes that dog saliva off his pants ASAP.

"One second, guys," the stranger says to his furry friends in a warm, paternal tone that tugs at something in my chest. "Can't you see I'm talking to Holly?"

Score! He believes I'm Holly.

Looking up from the dogs, the stranger gives Waldo a once-over. Does he also think my friend looks like Willem Dafoe, only when he played Aquaman's mentor, not the Green Goblin from *Spider-Man?*

Before I can ask, the stranger's gaze returns to me. "That's not your boyfriend."

I blink. He knows Holly's boyfriend? Where does my sister find all these hunks? This one is even hotter than her Alex.

"Indeed," I say, channeling her again. "This bloke is just a *friend* friend."

The stranger's wicked smirk is like a flick on my clit. "I don't think men and women can be just friends."

They so can. My sisters and I have been friends with one particular guy forever, and he's never made a move on any one of us. Granted, he's gay, but still.

Waldo stands up, all wounded dignity. "Look, chum, I'm allergic to dogs, so if you don't mind…"

"Chum?" The stranger's feline eyes are mocking as they capture mine. "See? He doesn't like me horning in on his territory."

The heat that flashes through my body is no longer lust. The nerve on this guy. "I'm nobody's territory." And certainly not Waldo's. He's never made a move on me either, not in the entire eighteen months we've known each other.

Waldo's face reddens, and he tightens his grip on the knife that he never gave back.

Seriously? Can testosterone make you *that* stupid?

"She's right, chum," Waldo says in his most menacing voice, which, if we're honest, sounds a bit like he's doing a Cookie Monster impersonation. "You'd better skedaddle."

The stranger curls his upper lip at him. If he's aware of that knife, he doesn't show it. Another testosterone-poisoning victim, no doubt.

"Skedaddle?" He looks back at me. "Where did you find this Waldo?"

Okay, that's it. I'm the only one allowed to make "Where's Waldo?" jokes at my friend's expense.

The hot stranger has just crossed a line.

I push my chair back and rise to my full five-foot-five height. "How about 'get the fuck out of here?' Is that a better choice of words for you?"

This is when the panda growls at Waldo—a threatening sound one wouldn't expect to come out of such a cute, if overlarge, dog. It reminds me of this news report about a man who tried to hug a panda at the zoo, only to end up in the hospital after the frightened bear mauled him.

Paling, Waldo sets the knife on the table. There are clearly at least ten brain cells inside that thick skull of his.

The stranger pats the bespectacled beast's head and murmurs something soothing in a language that sounds Eastern European.

Huh. He didn't have any accent when he spoke to me, but English must be his second language. Otherwise, he wouldn't address his dogs in that foreign tongue.

Crap. With our luck, the hottie is some Russian mobster.

"Sit down," I hiss at Waldo, and to my relief, he does as I say.

Make that twenty brain cells.

The stranger's beautiful eyes roam over my face before narrowing again. "You're not Holly. She's nice." A touch of that wicked smirk returns to his lips, and his voice deepens. "Whereas *you* are naughty."

That does it. No more Mrs. Nice Magician.

I slowly saunter over to him.

Although... maybe this isn't such a good idea.

Now that I'm closer, I realize just how tall he is. And wide-shouldered. The giant dogs threw off my perspective, creating a visual illusion that their owner was normal-sized. He's not. Worse yet, he smells divine, like ocean surf and something ineffably male.

A trick under these conditions will test all of my abilities.

Hold on. Will the dogs get mad that I'm so close?

As if reading my mind, the stranger gives them a stern command, and they sheepishly fall behind him.

Was that command intended to make *me* want to behave like a good, obedient bitch? Because I kind of want to.

No, screw that. I'm sticking with my plan, which requires me to get within pickpocketing distance.

"Do you want to see just how naughty I can be?" I ask in the sultriest voice I can muster.

Is it normal for human eyes to go all slitty like that, as if he were a lion?

"How naughty is that, *myodik?*" the stranger murmurs.

Did he just say "me dick?" Nah. It was something in whatever language he used with the dogs. Still, his dick is now firmly on my mind, which doesn't help the hormonal overload situation.

Forcing away the X-rated images, I purposefully lick my lips. "I'll steal your wallet. Or your watch. Your choice."

The supposed choice is misdirection, obviously. My real target is neither of those things, but he doesn't need to know that.

His nostrils flare as his gaze drops to my lips. "Is it stealing if you warn me?"

If it were possible for me to forget my concerns about germs and consider placing my lips on someone else's, I'd do that now. It's the strongest such urge I've ever felt.

"What's the matter?" I say breathlessly. "Chicken?"

He pats the right pocket of his jeans. "How about you steal my wallet?"

I take in a steadying breath. "Thanks for showing me where it is."

Before he can reply, I delve into that pocket. I need major misdirection for what I'm really trying to steal.

By Houdini's eyebrows, is that what I think it is?

Yup. There's no mistaking it. As I brush my gloved fingers over the wallet, I feel something else behind the fabric of the pants.

Something big and very hard.

Well. Someone is overly happy to be pickpocketed.

Maybe he *was* saying "me dick" before?

I do my best to hold his gaze and not clear my suddenly dry throat. "Can you feel me stealing it?"

As I speak, I work on unclasping the fancy buckle—his belt being my real target.

His lids lower to half-mast, and his voice deepens further. "Your nimble fingers are exactly where I want them."

Crap. Between my gloves and his ridiculous sex appeal, I'm having trouble with the clasp.

But no. I can't get caught. That would be like revealing a magic secret—the biggest taboo I can think of.

"These fingers?" I ask huskily and gently stroke his hardness through the layers of fabric, using the misdirection this slutty move creates to pull harder on the clasp with my other hand, finally opening it.

I'd like to see David Blaine do *that*.

The stranger's low, guttural groan is animalistic and makes my nipples so hard they feel on the verge of turning inside out. He now looks like a lion about to pounce.

Gulping, I yank my hand out of his pocket and try to give him a sneaky smile. It comes out faltering instead. "I changed my mind. I'll steal your watch."

I grab his wrist and give it a tight squeeze while pulling out the belt with my other hand.

Yes! Got it. Hiding the belt behind my back, I pout at the watch. "On second thought, I think I'll let you keep your possessions."

He looks triumphant, probably convinced that his sex appeal has defeated my pickpocketing skills. Since it almost did, I can't really fault him for thinking it.

I carefully back away. "Oh, by the way, did you lose this?"

I show him my prize.

Eyes wide, he shifts his gaze back and forth between my hand and his pants.

"How?" he asks.

The question is music to my ears.

"Extremely well," I say, but I can't manage my usual bluster.

He extends his hand to get the belt back. "You're a dangerous woman."

Two things happen simultaneously as I step toward him to return the belt.

The panda tries to get his attention again by pulling on his left pant leg. Not wanting to be outdone, the koala does the same thing on the right side—only this time, there's no belt holding the pants up, and they slide down.

All the way down.

Fuck. Me.

Visit www.mishabell.com to order your copy of *Royally Tricked*!

# EXCERPT FROM WALL STREET TITAN

## BY ANNA ZAIRES

**A billionaire who wants a perfect wife...**

At thirty-five, Marcus Carelli has it all: wealth, power, and the kind of looks that leave women breathless. A self-made billionaire, he heads one of the largest hedge funds on Wall Street and can take down major corporations with a single word. The only thing he's missing? A wife who'd be as big of an achievement as the billions in his bank account.

**A cat lady who needs a date...**

Twenty-six-year-old bookstore clerk Emma Walsh has it on good authority that she's a cat lady. She doesn't necessarily agree with that assessment, but it's hard to argue with the facts. Raggedy clothes covered with cat hair? Check. Last professional haircut? Over a year ago. Oh, and three cats in a tiny Brooklyn studio? Yep, she's got those.

And yes, fine, she hasn't had a date since... well, she can't recall. But that part is fixable. Isn't that what the dating sites are for?

## A case of mistaken identity...

One high-end matchmaker, one dating app, one mix-up that changes everything... Opposites may attract, but can this last?

---

I'm all but bouncing with excitement as I approach Sweet Rush Café, where I'm supposed to meet Mark for dinner. This is the craziest thing I've done in a while. Between my evening shift at the bookstore and his class schedule, we haven't had a chance to do more than exchange a few text messages, so all I have to go on are those couple of blurry pictures. Still, I have a good feeling about this.

I feel like Mark and I might really connect.

I'm a few minutes early, so I stop by the door and take a moment to brush cat hair off my woolen coat. The coat is beige, which is better than black, but white hair is visible on anything that's not pure white. I figure Mark won't mind too much—he knows how much Persians shed—but I still want to look presentable for our first date. It took me about an hour, but I got my curls to semi-behave, and I'm even wearing a little makeup—something that happens with the frequency of a tsunami in a lake.

Taking a deep breath, I enter the café and look around to see if Mark might already be there.

The place is small and cozy, with booth-style seats arranged in a semicircle around a coffee bar. The smell of roasted coffee beans and baked goods is mouthwatering, making my stomach rumble with hunger. I was planning to stick to coffee only, but I decide to get a croissant too; my budget should stretch to that.

Only a few of the booths are occupied, likely because it's a Tuesday. I scan them, looking for anyone who could be Mark, and notice a man sitting by himself at the farthest table. He's facing away from me, so all I can see is the back of his head, but his hair is short and dark brown.

It could be him.

Gathering my courage, I approach the booth. "Excuse me," I say. "Are you Mark?"

The man turns to face me, and my pulse shoots into the stratosphere.

The person in front of me is nothing like the pictures on the app. His hair is brown, and his eyes are blue, but that's the only similarity. There's nothing rounded and shy about the man's hard features. From the steely jaw to the hawk-like nose, his face is boldly masculine, stamped with a self-assurance that borders on arrogance. A hint of five o'clock shadow darkens his lean cheeks, making his high cheekbones stand out even more, and his eyebrows are thick dark slashes above his piercingly pale eyes. Even sitting behind the table, he looks tall and powerfully built. His shoulders are a mile wide in his sharply tailored suit, and his hands are twice the size of my own.

There's no way this is Mark from the app, unless he's put in some serious gym time since those pictures were taken. Is it possible? Could a person change so much? He didn't indicate his height in the profile, but I'd assumed the omission meant he was vertically challenged, like me.

The man I'm looking at is not challenged in any way, and he's certainly not wearing glasses.

"I'm... I'm Emma," I stutter as the man continues staring at me, his face hard and inscrutable. I'm almost certain I have the wrong guy, but I still force myself to ask, "Are you Mark, by any chance?"

"I prefer to be called Marcus," he shocks me by answering. His voice is a deep masculine rumble that tugs at something primitively female inside me. My heart beats even faster, and my palms begin to sweat as he rises to his feet and says bluntly, "You're not what I expected."

"Me?" *What the hell?* A surge of anger crowds out all other emotions as I gape at the rude giant in front of me. The asshole is so tall I have to crane my neck to look up at him. "What about you? You look nothing like your pictures!"

"I guess we've both been misled," he says, his jaw tight. Before I can respond, he gestures toward the booth. "You might as well sit down and have a meal with me, Emmeline. I didn't come all the way here for nothing."

"It's *Emma*," I correct, fuming. "And no, thank you. I'll just be on my way."

His nostrils flare, and he steps to the right to block my path. "Sit down, *Emma*." He makes my name sound like an insult. "I'll have a talk with Victoria, but for now, I don't see why we can't share a meal like two civilized adults."

The tips of my ears burn with fury, but I slide into the booth rather than make a scene. My grandmother instilled politeness in me from an early age, and even as an adult living on my own, I find it hard to go against her teachings.

She wouldn't approve of me kneeing this jerk in the balls and telling him to fuck off.

"Thank you," he says, sliding into the seat across from me. His eyes glint icy blue as he picks up the menu. "That wasn't so hard, was it?"

"I don't know, *Marcus*," I say, putting special emphasis on the formal name. "I've only been around you for two minutes, and I'm already feeling homicidal." I deliver the insult with a ladylike, Grandma-approved smile, and dumping my purse in the corner of my booth seat, I pick up the menu without bothering to take off my coat.

The sooner we eat, the sooner I can get out of here.

A deep chuckle startles me into looking up. To my shock, the jerk is grinning, his teeth flashing white in his lightly bronzed face. No freckles for him, I note with jealousy; his skin is perfectly even-toned, without so much as an extra mole on his cheek. He's not classically handsome—his features are too bold to be described that way

—but he's shockingly good-looking, in a potent, purely masculine way.

To my dismay, a curl of heat licks at my core, making my inner muscles clench.

*No.* No way. This asshole is *not* turning me on. I can barely stand to sit across the table from him.

Gritting my teeth, I look down at my menu, noting with relief that the prices in this place are actually reasonable. I always insist on paying for my own food on dates, and now that I've met Mark—excuse me, *Marcus*—I wouldn't put it past him to drag me to some ritzy place where a glass of tap water costs more than a shot of Patrón. How could I have been so wrong about the guy? Clearly, he'd lied about working in a bookstore and being a student. To what end, I don't know, but everything about the man in front of me screams wealth and power. His pinstriped suit hugs his broad-shouldered frame like it was tailor-made for him, his blue shirt is crisply starched, and I'm pretty sure his subtly checkered tie is some designer brand that makes Chanel seem like a Walmart label.

As all of these details register, a new suspicion occurs to me. Could someone be playing a joke on me? Kendall, perhaps? Or Janie? They both know my taste in guys. Maybe one of them decided to lure me on a date this way—though why they'd set me up with *him*, and he'd agree to it, is a huge mystery.

Frowning, I look up from the menu and study the man in front of me. He's stopped grinning and is perusing the menu, his forehead creased in a frown that makes him look older than the twenty-seven years listed on his profile.

That part must've also been a lie.

My anger intensifies. "So, *Marcus*, why did you write to me?" Dropping the menu on the table, I glare at him. "Do you even own cats?"

He looks up, his frown deepening. "Cats? No, of course not."

The derision in his tone makes me want to forget all about

Grandma's disapproval and slap him straight across his lean, hard face. "Is this some kind of a prank for you? Who put you up to this?"

"Excuse me?" His thick eyebrows rise in an arrogant arch.

"Oh, stop playing innocent. You lied in your message to me, and you have the gall to say *I'm* not what you expected?" I can practically feel the steam coming out of my ears. "*You* messaged *me*, and I was entirely truthful on my profile. How old are you? Thirty-two? Thirty-three?"

"I'm thirty-five," he says slowly, his frown returning. "Emma, what are you talking—"

"That's it." Grabbing my purse by one strap, I slide out of the booth and jump to my feet. Grandma's teachings or not, I'm not going to have a meal with a jerk who's admitted to deceiving me. I have no idea what would make a guy like that want to toy with me, but I'm not going to be the butt of some joke.

"Enjoy your meal," I snarl, spinning around, and stride to the exit before he can block my way again.

I'm in such a rush to leave I almost knock over a tall, slender brunette approaching the café and the short, pudgy guy following her.

---

Visit www.annazaires.com to order your copy of
*Wall Street Titan*!

# ABOUT THE AUTHOR

We love writing humor (often the inappropriate kind), happy endings (both kinds), and characters quirky enough to be called oddballs (because... balls).